EVOKE

REFRACTORS VOLUME I

BRANDON EPPS

MILAN EPPS

REFRACTORS VOLUME I: EVOKE

Second edition. November 21, 2021.

Original Publication February 5, 2019.

Written by Brandon Epps and Milan Epps.

ISBN: 9781386097563 (ebook)

ISBN: 9780578421971 (Paperback)

Published by Unified Future Media

For inquiries, visit our website at

www.thebrothersepps.com

CONTENTS

The Kingdom of Aruria

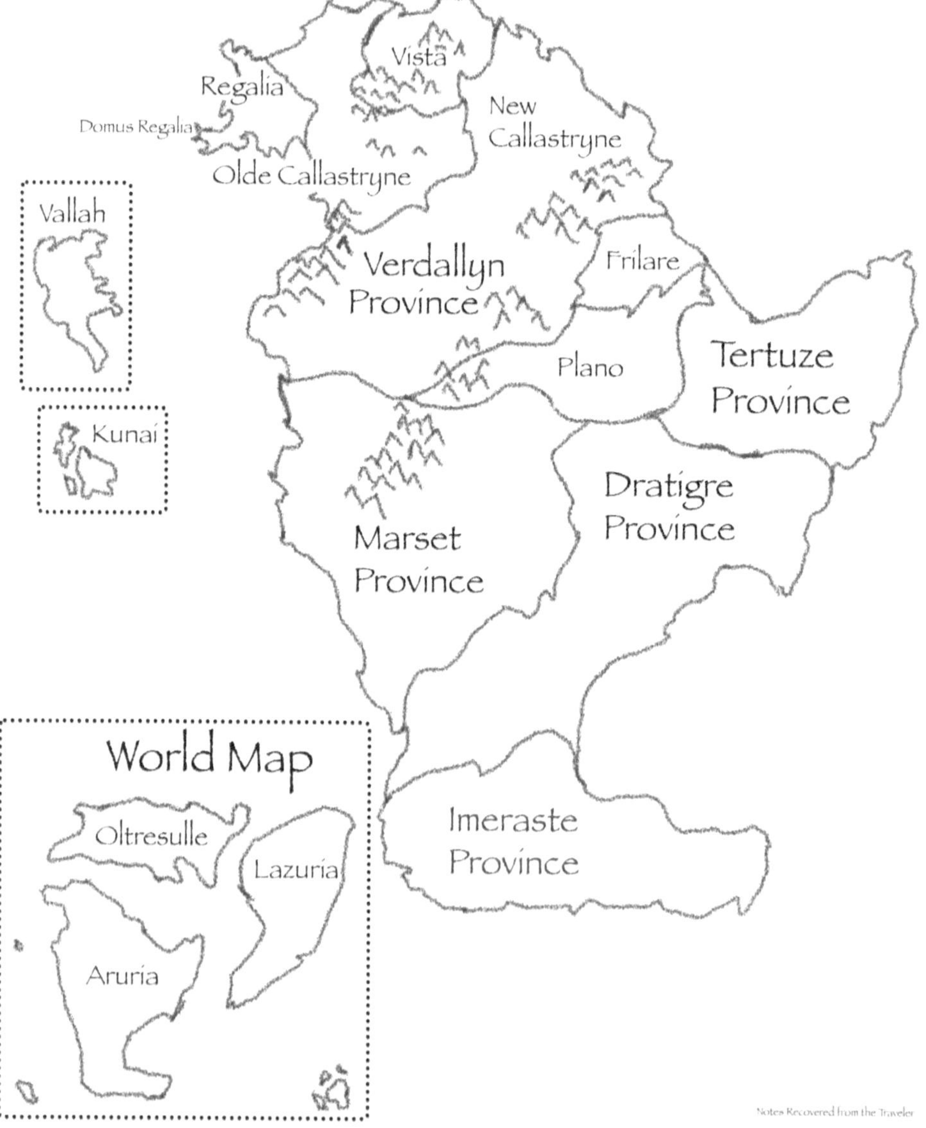

Orbis Time

Pocket Watch
Earth Chonometer

Hours
8:40
Minutes

Timechain
Orbis Chronometer

Segments
15.75
Hashes

Conversions

50 Seconds
50 Beats
1 Hash

100 Hashes
1 Segment
1.39 Hours

20 Segments
1 Day

10 Days
1 Dec
1.65 Weeks

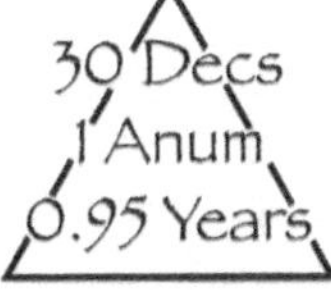

PART ONE | STRANGERS

[ELEMENT 1]
THE BOOK OF SEREC

[1]

FATAL DECISION

The sickly green sky loomed overhead; a reminder of how far we'd come; how much we'd lost. Saldarian Flats sat at the far end of New Callastryne; which made reaching it by terrarail an utter slog. The azure glow of Aio—our larger moon—beamed along the edges of the clouds, as the sun retreated behind the mountains. I navigated the cluster of condemned buildings and barred windows, trying to ignore the shifty-eyes targeting me from every direction. Busted street lumens littered the road replaced by several trash bin fires that filled the air with a noxious stench. I glanced at my timechain; 18.75. Half the night on the ground and the smell was the worst threat I detected. As I made one final pass, something moved erratically in my peripheral.

A shadow flailed across an alley wall. I jogged over to investigate. But all I found was an empty corridor.

"Must've been my imagin—"

"No—!"

The cry pinged sharply in my right ear, then cut off as suddenly as it started. I raced down the alley and peeked around the corner.

The sight was enough to churn the bile in my stomach. A sloppy blob of a man was pinned over a woman. She kicked and shrieked as he tore at her dress like a starved predator ripping into prey. Her resistance earned her a hard smack to the face.

"Keep it up, and I'll knock your teeth down your windpipe," he spat.

The woman fell silent. Her petite frame trembling in an attempt to stifle her breaths. But I could hear it all the same. The plea for help that accompanied every inhale; resonating deep in my chest. I wish I could say this was an uncommon scene in Aruria. But, for as long as I could remember, the weak have been victimized under the inattentive eye of the Department of Peace; our national law enforcement organization. That's where I entered the equation.

A flame ignited within me, setting my body on autopilot. My fists clenched, and my legs propelled me forward.

"Hey, you disgusting creep! Let her go before I bash your face into the pavement!" My voice was more forceful than I expected.

The fat man twisted around with wild eyes that gave me a once-over as I advanced. "You're gonna regret sticking your nose in other people's business, you little punk."

I charged him, preparing to introduce my foot to his teeth. But, just as I twisted my weight behind my attack, something blurred, and I was suddenly tumbling backward. He was quicker than expected. Too quick to ignore the obvious.

I sprang to my feet. His dark sunken eyes trained on me, filling my veins with ice at the realization. I was facing off with another Gifted. My mind raced as much as my heart. But I tuned out my nerves and started toward him again.

"Don't be stupid," he grumbled. "Mind your business, or I'll take it out on her."

His words nearly stole my nerve. But, if I didn't act, it just meant he could do what he'd planned from the start with no resistance. No threats he made against her could be any worse. Still, I couldn't exactly take him on with her trapped under him.

Scanning the area, I spotted a loose metal pipe between some trash bins. I felt his eyes on me as I moved to pick up the pipe. My shaky hands revealed the anxiety my face fought to hide. Tapping the pipe on my heel brought reassurance. Sturdy enough.

I removed one of the trash lids, nearly gagging at the odor of rotting who-knows-what. Better than nothing. Maybe. With tools in hand, I turned and met eyes with Aruria's fattest predator. But I wasn't about to give him the time to determine my next move.

I rushed him, my elbow high as I reached across my body and launched the metal disc toward his face. He effortlessly leaned to one side, and the lid shot clear past him.

His expression intensified, and his arm became a blur again. I lunged at him, swinging the pipe from my shoulder like a peace enforcement baton. His arm moved up just in time to deny me my target. Just in time to complete my plan. The hard thwack rang in the alley, from the trash lid curving around and catching him in the back of the neck. He nearly toppled over. It was the perfect setup to distract him long enough for me to strike him clean across the face with the pipe, sending a hollow ping echoing deep in my ears as he lumbered to one side and collapsed.

I rolled him away so the woman could get up. "You okay?" I asked. She lifted her head, and my breath caught as her large autumn eyes snapped onto mine. A cold prickle crept down my spine. *She's stunning.* Thankfully, the lapse between my thoughts and my words kept the situation from turning awkward.

"It's you," she whispered with wide eyes. There was a subtle edge to her voice that felt as sobering as it was serene. "I've finally found you."

Before I could respond, she took my hand, and the world fell silent. Energy pulsed from her hand into mine surging through me. A blinding flash followed, engulfing everything around us in darkness. I found myself floating in cold, deafening nothingness. Separate from the world... separate from myself. *Am I dead?*

Another blinding light provided my answer. Bathed in radiance, the woman reappeared. Her golden skin gleamed. Her hair sparkled a blooming scarlet. Her eyes shined a luminous, winter blue. She looked like the woman I'd just saved in the alley. And yet, I somehow knew I was looking at an entirely different person.

"Your path leads only to ruin. Intervention is required." Her frigid, almost robotic voice resonated deep in my chest. It was like she was speaking directly to my soul. Her words infected my consciousness with awe, until I could hardly speak. "Fate is an illusion, experienced by the ignorant."

I tried to question her. But my tongue felt heavy; my mouth, disconnected from my brain.

"What if I told you this life is one of many—infinitely branching—on an endless river of time and space?" Each idea was an invasion of my mind and body —becoming a seamless piece of me. "This world is full of beauty—a beauty that must be preserved."

A rich array of images flashed before me: a child playing, waves washing over the beach, a blooming flower, a vibrant sunset, Aio and Karon glimmering in the night sky. Each one pulled at me, compelled me. "A war rages in the shadows, as a great malevolence toils to bring it to light. I offer you the power to take arms against this force and break free of fate. Should you accept this power, you will embark on a journey unlike any other. Outside of time. Outside observation. Outside reality itself. Mathematica, mens, animus, aether, tempus, materia, vis — all will bend to your will. You need only accept this mantle and begin your journey."

I could hardly breathe. Much less make sense of her words. And yet, in that moment, clarity shined through. "Y—yes! I accept," I said, taking her hand.

"So, let it continue," her voice boomed, as the world around me crumbled into darkness. When the darkness lifted, I was at the edge of the alley. Alone.

I checked my timechain and nearly collapsed. 18.75?! How is that possible?! The answer was simple: it wasn't possible. If it was quarter til 19.00, that meant that somehow, I hadn't yet stumbled upon... "No—!" a woman shrieked. "Stop!"

I turned to find the fat man backing the woman into the alley. The attack hadn't happened yet. And this time, I would ensure it didn't. I peeked around the wall. The hefty man had his back to me, fully engaged in forcing the shrieking woman down, as she fought with all she had to escape. The pipe was right where I remembered it. I grabbed it and crept up behind big rapey, my heart throbbing in my ears. With a grip so tight, I thought the metal would crumble in my hands, I raised the pipe high...and swung.

I was so determined not to screw it up, I nearly screwed it up, tripping over a crack. A grunt hissed through my teeth, and the man turned just in time to catch the pipe with his face. His eyes went dead, as he collapsed like a sack of rice.

I turned to the woman. Her eyes were back to their vibrant autumn hue. "You okay?" I asked.

"Yeah," she sighed, reaching for my hand. I hesitated.

"Can you help me up please?"

"S-sure."

I braced myself and took her hand, a little surprised when the woman only pulled herself back to her feet and brushed the dirt off her clothes. She offered a curious glance. "Everything okay?"

"Huh? Y-yeah. You?"

"Thanks to you." She smiled. "My hero."

A wide smile painted my face, as the word sunk in. "Hero." It sounded even better coming from her. But the moment was short-lived. A weak groan escaped the man. "You should go," I prompted.

"What about you?"

"I'll keep him busy. Call the PEDs." Not that calling them would do much good. But getting her out of danger would at least free me up to make sure my new friend didn't escape to find more victims.

She nodded and hurried off. "Be careful," she yelled over her shoulder.

The groan intensified. He was already back on his feet, blood trickling from the open gash on the side of his face.

"Appalling how disrespectful kids today are. Inserting themselves into affairs that don't concern them." Malice overtook his eyes. "Guess I'll have to show you the dark reality of trying to be a hero." He settled into a wide stance, closed his eyes, and sucked air into his flared nostrils. In mere moments, the bleeding had subsided, and his skin was knitting itself back together.

He has more than one ability?! It was the first thought to cross my mind, as he charged me. The second, more critical thought was that I probably should've run when I had the chance.

I narrowly dodged and made a show of cracking my neck to hide the trembling in my jaw. "Watch it, big guy. Or maybe I should call you Fat Felo."

"What in *Hadal* are you blathering about?"

I don't know why I'd said it. But at a glance, the guy was a saggy ball, turned human, turned assailant. A fat guy who commits felonies. Fat Felo.

His cruel eyes locked onto me as he inhaled; holding for a moment. Then, with a sinister smile, his image blurred, then disappeared. I tensed, guarding my face just in time for something to plow into my forearms with enough force to nearly fracture them. Fat Felo stood in front of me with a toothy grin.

Pain seized my focus. Then another blur. Fat Felo was gone again. Panic gripped me; my eyes darting through the empty whirling wind around me. By the time I heard something, I was knocked into the air by something akin to a battering ram; jerking my head forward, while my body pulled in the opposite direction.

My turbulent flight was brought to a sudden end by the hard embrace of a lumen pole. I slid to the ground, huffing as a thick, warm liquid trickled down my face and collected at my chin. Sharp pain ricocheted down my spine and ignited my limbs. I blinked hard, waiting for the ground to steady out. It didn't. I closed my eyes and desperately took hold of my shallow breaths.

"You take hits pretty well. Let's see how good you do when I throw some weight into it."

His rushing deep breath was haunting. But, as my wits returned, it became instructional. Using the pole as support, I forced myself to stand in time for the thump of approaching feet to trigger my reflexes. I involuntarily dipped right, just in time for his fist to catch the lumen pole. I seized the opportunity to retreat across the alley and get to my feet. Fat Felo yanked his arm from the pole. A hollow screech echoed as it bent past ninety degrees, the lumen halfheartedly flickering. He turned and smiled, probably noting how petrified I looked.

This monster of a man was more than I could've hoped to handle. And were it not for the fact that I'd actually saved someone, I'd have regretted ever stepping foot into that alley. Another breath, and he disappeared again. But his power was finally starting to make sense. Fat Felo only had to focus his breathing for his face to heal so perfectly that it looked like I'd never hit him. The super speed and strength were also connected to his breathing somehow. Was it possible for me to pull something like that off? *If I had that kind of power, I cou—*

My head jerked left, and the rest of my body followed. Everything tilted to one side as the ground embraced me with open arms. Blood ran across my cheek, rolling into a crimson pool. A stinging radiated from the right side of my face; my ears ringing so loud, my eardrums felt like they would burst.

I squeezed my eyes shut and slowed my breathing—my sole focus filling my lungs with air, and controlling the release. The pain radiating from my chest and face gnawed at my concentration, but I persisted; even as Fat Felo closed in on me.

Slower. Deeper. Control it.

I needed it to work or I wouldn't stand a chance. I drew in one more breath, and something finally clicked. Suddenly, the echo of mad laughter abruptly cut through the ringing. Something was happening. The dizziness drained from my head my body went from throbbing to buzzing with energy.

I opened my eyes to a world in vivid slow-motion. The air sparkled around me like near-microscopic stars. *What is this feeling? And why am I suddenly so...light?*

"How are you standing?" he asked darkly, as I straightened.

I shrugged. "Maybe you hit like a girl. Is that why you pick on them?"

His face went red—a vein bulging from his forehead, as his nostrils flared.

Another enhancement. But this time, I was ready. I closed my eyes and visualized every muscle vibrating with energy. As I exhaled, a warm tingle enveloped me like a thick coat. My body went heavy. But this feeling was different. This feeling was…powerful.

Fat Felo let out a war cry and stampeded toward me. Four strides put me in striking range, where I leaped at him. I pulled as far back as my shoulder could manage, then hammered down, crunching my knuckles into Fat Felo's jaw. A crack drowned out all other sounds and his head jolted back so hard, his body couldn't help but follow. Fat Felo teetered back like a massive tree uprooting from its base until finally, he crumpled to the ground with a loud thump.

"Doesn't feel so good, does it?" I taunted. He took a beat before rolling over and pressing onto all fours; the struggle to control his breathing almost palpable. He was trying to heal. But I had other plans for him.

I took another step, and fire shot up through my legs. The air thinned, and everything began to blur. I squeezed my eyelids shut; forcing shaky breaths. But my knees buckled, and I hit the ground.

Laughter was close in tow, and I forced my eyes open to find Fat Felo back on his feet. His prodigious girth eclipsing the street lumens.

"Pushed too hard," he said, his voice thick with nauseating satisfaction. A sharp pinch from Fat Felo dug into the back of my neck, yanking me to my feet, and my arms locked in a painful shrug.

"Amazing how similar people are to animals," he mused. "Even some of the pressure points. Since you decided to interrupt my fun, how 'bout I show you what I mean?"

Declining his offer was a no-brainer. But I could barely move my arms. Fat Felo cackled sadistically. "It's more fun when they put up a fight. Thrill of the kill." He smacked his palm against my temple, and the ringing returned. Darkness crept into my field of view as my body began shutting down. I had to do something—anything before it was too late.

Desperately, I lifted my leg and jammed my foot down behind me. My heel caught Fat Felo's kneecap, and his leg buckled, forcing him to release my neck. The pressure subsided, as I hit the ground like a puppet. If the rest of my body wasn't feeling so numb, I probably would've felt it everywhere else on the impact.

Somehow, I managed to get back on my feet. Without hesitation, I drew back my leg and drove my foot into his face like my life depended on it. His head jerked back with a bit of resistance, so I kicked harder the second time, losing my balance and falling onto his wide, pudgy back. The stench of his sweat unapologetically invaded my nostrils. But I was too tired to be grossed out. PED sirens blaring in the distance registered over the ringing in my ears. My cue to exit.

"They actually came," I chuckled to myself.

[2]

GOOD INTENTIONS

I was 12 when I finally woke up. All the fear, sorrow, shame and regret
flooding back like a hungry swarm threatening to devour my frail psyche.
All that stood between me and the crushing weight of my past transgressions—past failures—was my conviction to see this arduous mission through.
-The Travler

"19.99: As good a time as any for breaking and entering," I told myself,
easing the back window shut. I paused, peering into the darkness. Every
hum and creak in the house was deafening. And it had my nerves firing,
all while the night replayed in my head like a glitched recording. Fat Felo, the
woman, and whatever happened when she took my hand. It was a lot to process.
But until I reached my room, it only served as a distraction.

I crept forward, legs trembling; eyes hovering in front of me until my bedroom
door glided into view. Four long strides could put me there. But the pins shooting
up my feet would make it nearly impossible to get past Hachi's razor-sharp senses.
At least the Royal Army was good for something. With my back against the wall, I
carefully slid past Hachi's door and found my own. A slow twist of the door knob
and I was in.

I sunk into the carpet, gasping for air. My heartbeat gonged in my eardrums
as I crawled to my bathroom. Leaning into the wall, I wrestled my clothes off and
nearly lost my balance tapping the light switches. The buzzing light, the shower

vent, and the deep ringing in my ears were competing for my attention. None obtained it.

Icicles shot up my legs with each step along the frozen blocks of bathroom tile. I paused at the mirror, which clued me in on how much of a beating I'd actually taken. I blinked hard at the battered face looking back at me. Whatever power I used to heal before, had long since abandoned me. All that remained was the dirt and dried blood smearing my face; accompanied by deep red bruising and a busted lip. *No way I'm sleeping this off. But a shower won't hurt.*

I turned the handle and waited as water vapor billowed around the ceiling light. My skin tingled as the water made contact. But I was too tired to tell if the sensation was more of a dull sting or a lackluster soothing. Verdallyn's autumn nights were unexpectedly cold after sunset. A fact I'd only realized while shivering outside on my way home. With the dirt and blood flowing down the drain, I slipped into a soft set of clothes, and burrowed under my thick stack of blankets. I hardly remember closing my eyes, before the world fell silent.

I awoke to bright bars of lemon-lime sunlight flooding my bedroom. I rolled over and stared at my blurry ceiling fan; a large blue 'X' against a sea of white. Creatively speaking, it wasn't much to look at. Hachi's strict rules restricted much of my life. Though it affected only me, I still had to get his approval on my setup before starting. But it was also a reminder that Hachi could be reasoned with, under the right circumstances. Unfortunately, I strongly doubted that he'd find any part of my situation reasonable.

The hum of my *processor* drew my eyes toward the swaying trees in the back-yard, and I opened the window to let in a breeze. The sweet scent of honey and buttery bread danced in the air and my stomach went ballistic; suddenly aware of the void.

According to my *Power Clash Comics timeboard*, it was 6.05. The earliest I'd been up in a while. Hachi would be halfway to work at the *Bureau*, which gave me time to focus on my appearance after resolving my hunger issue. As I rolled out of bed, memories of the previous night grasped at my attention.

Did I really copy that fat guy's powers? And what about that woman with the autumn—or blue eyes? What on Orbis was she talking about? Fate is an illusion. What does that even mean? Too many questions to process without adequate brain fuel. So, I decided not to think about any of it until after breakfast.

I opened my door, and the savory aroma hit me like cool water on a scorching afternoon. Macha rolls for breakfast seemed unusual. But the lake forming in my mouth meant my stomach had no qualms with it. The smell grew stronger as I entered the kitchen. The oven light was on, a dish of cheesy macha rolls bubbling inside.

It wasn't like Hachi to leave in such a hurry that he forgot to turn off an appliance that could put the whole house in flames. And he'd never let me hear the end of it if the tables were turned. I reached for the off button, when the door suddenly opened and Hachi stepped in. I froze, mouth agape.

"You've been in night clothes all da—" He paused, incredulous eyes scanning me. "What happened to your face!?"

"Nothing, I... umm." My mind blanked so quickly, I couldn't even come up with a bad excuse.

"You what?" His tone was stern. Scary stern. "Why is your face covered in bruises?"

"I umm..." Now the sign was clear in my head: *Back in twenty, but don't wait up.*

"Were you fighting again?"

My brain was so not ready for the scenario that only the truth seemed logical. A terrible sign. "Yeah, but I..."

"Yeah, but what?! You felt like my rules became invalid once you turned seventeen? Or perhaps you felt like I wouldn't find out?"

"No," I said. "I didn't 'feel' anything."

"Well, you had to be feeling something, because you certainly weren't thinking."

Biting back a response made my jaw so tight the muscles in my neck started twitching. Hachi studied me, irritation bubbling in his eyes like the macha rolls in the oven. "What happened?"

"Nothing happened."

"What...happened?"

I forced a deep breath through flared nostrils to relieve the tension in my face. "A woman was being attacked." I shrugged. "I jumped in and helped."

"You—" His eyes trailed into his classic 'how stupid can you be' look. "You 'jumped in?'" He was nodding his head as he repeated my words; confirming to himself exactly how ridiculous it all sounded out loud.

"Whatever," I muttered.

Hachi's head jerked up. But I didn't wait for his eyes to find mine before retreating to my room.

"You have ten hashes to change and find your way back to the table," The boom in Hachi's voice echoed through my chest. "NaRyn will be here any moment."

"Yes, sir!" I nearly yelled back, before slamming the door behind me.

I glanced at my Power Clash timeboard again; 16.14! *Thanks, Serec! Way to pay attention.*

I thrusted my palms against the bathroom sink; my arms trembling as dry heat swirled around my face. If not for NaRyn I would've skipped dinner altogether. But I wasn't about to hold NaRyn up on her studies. Royal Verdallyn Academy—Aruria's top university prep school—was borderline sadistic with their curriculum. She was probably drowning in schoolwork, and I'd be just as angry at myself as I was at Hachi if I let our issues weigh her down.

If nothing else, changing afforded me time to cool off a little. I paused at my door. *Keep the peace — for NaRyn.* I closed my eyes, took a deep breath, and opened the door.

The moment I stepped out, I was tackled.

"Rec Rec!" NaRyn bubbled. Her slender arms squeezed my torso with an unexpectedly strong grip that might as well have been sandpaper against open skin. I winced as she took her time releasing me.

"Not so tight, Ryn Ryn," I groaned.

"What do you mea—" Her eyes widened. "Ohmygosh! What happened to your face?"

"Your cousin," Hachi interjected, "thought it wise to play peace enforcer for an evening. Now that we—and the rest of Aruria—understand how manly he can be, let's have dinner."

Dinner with NaRyn only happened every few decs. So, as usual, Hachi filled the table with enough food for her to take back to her dorm. Steamed plant greens, fresh bread, and Hachi's signature triple-cheese macha rolls. It all looked as good as it smelled. And the sooner I could focus on eating, the sooner I could tune out Hachi's infamous small talk.

"So," Hachi started, "how are your studies, NaRyn?"

"I thought I'd be more stressed," NaRyn said. "Finals are approaching fast, and my interview for King Martinel University is coming up. But for some reason, I'm really excited."

"You should be. With your work ethic and responsibility, you'll be a great candidate for KMU."

Hachi threw a quick glance in my direction. If my mouth wasn't full of food, I might've reminded him that NaRyn was the non-male seated to my right.

"Principal Matta also tells me you're in the running for the King Elite Youth Scholars top ten?" NaRyn's smile widened. "If I'm not mistaken, a near-perfect career grade average is a prerequisite."

"It is," NaRyn answered. Then she looked over at me. "But, I'm only at a 99.75%."

"No need for modesty," Hachi said. "I'm very proud of you. You've got your cousin's average beat by 12.86%."

I stabbed some steamed greens, and my fork clanked against the plate. "Sorry," I said without looking up. "I got distracted from all the non-eating at the dinner table."

"You shouldn't be so averse to talking," Hachi replied. "If you employed a bit more of it perhaps you wouldn't experience so many situations escalating to fisticuffs."

"There's a theory."

"These macha rolls are delicious," NaRyn said with forced enthusiasm.

"Here's another theory," Hachi said. "The Department of Peace hired peace enforcers to quell the city's squabbles. Not you."

I forced a smile. "And yet they're never around when you need them."

"They're so cheesy, and I love the spices," NaRyn continued.

"Exactly what authorization were you given to act on their behalf?" Hachi asked.

My eyes snapped up from my plate to meet his. "How much authorization do I need when crime is at a record high? Or would you rather I just ignore it when I see a woman in danger like any other coward on the street?"

"How about calling for help? They can't see everything that happens in Callastryne, and you've already had a close call with detention. Or have you forgotten how many favors I had to call in to reduce your five-anum confinement to 60 days of house arrest?"

"If only I could. But it's not like you'll ever let me live it down!" I yelled.

"Because I need you to understand that I can't bail you out of every mess you get yourself into! You're not helping people; you're looking for trouble. And if you're even suspected of using your powers, there isn't a thing I can do to get you out of that kind of trouble." His intensity matched mine.

The longer I stared into his wild eyes, the hotter my face got; until I could've warmed what was left of the macha rolls on my plate. I pressed my teeth tightly together, hoping to temporarily sever the connection between my brain and mouth before I ended up saying something I regretted.

I usually looked forward to NaRyn's visits. But thanks to Hachi's small talk escalating into a shouting match, all I wanted was to go back to my quiet non-meddling room.

"Even the plant greens complement the bread well," NaRyn said with a forced smile. "You want to try some, Serec?"

"No," I said. "I just want to live my life without spoon-fed opinions on how I can do better."

"Then do better," Hachi said flatly.

"Please don't argue," NaRyn pleaded. This was the closest thing to a family dinner any of us were going to get. Considering how stressful school life often was for her, she probably needed it more than Hachi or I did.

Hachi laced his fingers and rested his chin against his thumbs. "We're not arguing. Because this discussion just ended."

We could at least agree on that much. I pushed away from the dinner table and hurried off to my room. I plopped into my squoosh bag and shut my eyes. Despite the bag being just a cheap piece of novelty furniture, letting myself sink into it always seemed to sink my problems right along with it. My mind tuned everything out so quickly, I almost didn't hear the knocking on my door.

"Rec Rec? May I come in?"

"Is your uncle with you?" I called back.

"No."

I paused for a breath. "It's open."

With the clank of the knob, the door smoothed over the carpet, and NaRyn stepped in, eyes glued to the floor.

"You want the squoosh bag?" I asked.

"I'm fine," NaRyn sighed.

I slid onto the floor cross-legged. "Go ahead."

She sat on the bag. "Uncle Hachi wanted me to remind you to wash your plate."

"You offered to clean it again, didn't you?"

"I'm a guest."

"No, you're family. And I can handle my own mess."

"I just wanted to buy you some time to cool off."

I snorted and shook my head. I'd never known anyone sweeter than NaRyn. We were always close growing up. But things between us drastically changed when I lost my parents, and moved to Callastryne with Hachi. I was in a dark place. And she was my light. She's always been that way. Which made me feel even worse for allowing Hachi to get under my skin during dinner.

"Thanks, Ryn. But you've got plenty on your plate already. No pun intended."

"How'd you get into a fight anyway?"

Before I could answer, Hachi's voice penetrated the door. "Goodnight, NaRyn."

"Goodnight Uncle Hachi! Thank you for dinner!"

"I'm glad you could join us. Did you tell Serec to wash his plate?"

I rolled my eyes. "She told me."

There was a pause before his door clicked shut signaling the 'all clear.' I hopped to my feet.

"I need some fresh air. Wanna come?"

Aio hung lazily in the sky as we hiked up the steep hill.

"Remember back in intermediate school?" I asked. "When I fought those kids for picking on you?"

"How could I forget when they were twice my size?" NaRyn said with a soft chuckle. "And replace 'fought' with pummeled."

A grin pressed into my mouth even as I had to squint through the walls of chilled wind, whistling against my face. I looked up, noticing the thick clouds dampening Aio's soothing blue light.

"You know how I feel about unfair fights."

NaRyn sighed. "Yeah. But you know how Uncle Hachi feels about you fighting at all."

My grin faded. "He wasn't there. There isn't always time to get help. Sometimes you have to be the help."

NaRyn got quiet; her eyes trailing the sidewalk. "If you get caught using your powers, then what? The punishment is pretty severe."

I shrugged. "It's not like anyone can tell when I use it anyway."

That much was true. Mostly. Despite the utility of adaptive muscle memory, it would've taken a trained eye to detect it. My newer ability of mimicking other powers, however, might have been a little harder to hide.

"Serec, I'm serious!"

"Be smooth Ryn, I'll be careful."

NaRyn sighed. "Is it any easier for you to control it?"

"Hit or miss. Simple moves are a cinch to copy. Advanced moves are still usually a miss. Weird as it may sound though, I think that might've changed recently."

"Changed how?"

"I think I copied a healing ability during my fight last night."

NaRyn studied me for a moment. "Then, what's up with your face? Or am I looking at the healed version?"

"So funny. Too bad telling jokes doesn't improve your ranking for the KEYS 100. But I'll bet if I could copy something smooth like gravity, I'd have all of Royal Verdallyn Academy eating out of my hands too."

NaRyn nudged me. "Don't be so frostie, Rec Rec. I'm more popular than you were because I'm smoother than you. That's all there is to it."

"You're still a nerd."

The highest point in Callastryne, the cozy half-park, half-landmark known as Olde Hill, sat on the southwest edge of town. Entirely contained within Olde Callastryne, and complete with trees, a track, and a few benches.

For NaRyn and me, it was a great place to think — mostly because it was usually empty. But there was one other thing. An inspiring, peaceful view, overlooking most of New Callastryne from the far edge of Olde Hill, where our favorite koa tree, Brain grew.

Coming up with the name was easy enough for NaRyn and me. It was exceptionally large, with thick, abnormally-curving branches that looked the way a child might doodle a brain. Perched on the edge of the hill, Brain stood watch over all of Callastryne for generations. And every time we sat under Brain, our thoughts just flowed effortlessly.

I sat in the grass and leaned back against Brain. NaRyn followed pulling her knees to her chest.

"It looks so eerie tonight," NaRyn said.

"When doesn't a green sky look eerie at night?" Leftover sarcasm polluted my words. I'd have to work on that.

"So, what changed?"

"With the sky?"

"With Uncle Hachi's rules. You haven't broken them in anums. And I've never seen you guys argue like that. I can only imagine how that would have gone if he knew about the other four times."

I looked out at the twinkling city lights and wondered if they ever changed color or arrangement while the world was too busy to notice. "He also caught me like two decs ago. The conversation was pretty similar, since he refuses to ever see my side on anything. After my time in the Royal Army and the six decs of house arrest it earned me, I've spent a lot of time reflecting—ya know? What kind of impact I'm making on the world with the gifts I've been given."

"Like Uncle Amani used to say?" NaRyn asked. I nodded, and she responded with a smile before wistfully returning her attention to the sky. The waning glow reflected softly over her light brown eyes. "How can you be certain you're doing what your parents would have wanted?"

I shrugged. "It just feels right I guess." It wasn't much of an answer. But it was true for me.

"Even if it means ignoring Uncle Hachi's rules? The public isn't too fond of people like us, and he's just trying to protect you."

Leave it to NaRyn to be the voice of reason. It's my favorite quality of her's that I absolutely hate.

"You're probably right. But keeping in line all this time hasn't made life easier for anyone but me. I have to try something new. Even if there's a risk. Even if Hachi doesn't approve."

"So, is your plan to just jump into the deep end and see what happens?"

I chuckled. "When you put it that way, it sounds pretty half-baked. I guess I just want to do what peace enforcers do, without all the rules and bureaucracy. Despite how Hachi feels about it, I say there can be honor and merit in vigilantism."

NaRyn raised an eyebrow. Most girls her age weren't so analytical. Of course, most girls hadn't endured what she had in her fifteen anums of life. "It may not be the best plan, but I don't hate it."

I sighed. "Sounds like that's the best I'm gonna get as far as support."

"For now. But seriously, I'm proud that you're trying to continue in your parents' legacy." She frowned. "Sometimes I wonder if that should've been the case for me too. But it's not like we spent that much time figuring that kind of stuff out."

"You've got time. Just keep living. If I can do it, then you definitely can."

"Think so?"

"You're smarter than me, more personable, more talented, and your crazy-good grade average ranks you in the top twenty of the KEYS 100. Are you seriously asking or do you just like being reminded how amazing you are?"

NaRyn shrugged, her face colored with smug. "Little from column A, little from column B."

I rolled my eyes. "Anyway, I'm crazy-proud of you, and I know uncle Vyctor and aunt Mara would back me on that if they were still here. Besides, you should be focused on what you want for yourself at this point."

"Sounds ideal. But what if I'm not sure what I want after Royal Verdallyn? KMU sounds great, but I've also been toying with the idea of joining the Bureau of National Peace, like mom and dad. I'd be helping people, and the fact that Uncle Hachi's the Director would help with the application process."

"I imagine so. Which department are you considering? Intelligence?"

"Occult Division."

Even though I tried, it was hard to imagine someone like NaRyn as a BNP agent, especially in the Occult Division—a unit that specializes in altercations with Gifted. Physically, she was more than capable; especially with her powers.

But she'd always been too reserved and way too non-violent for something like that.

"Wouldn't you have to fight against other Gifted?"

"Only if I fail to apprehend them peacefully."

"Are you expecting every criminal to come along quietly?"

NaRyn scrunched her face and shrugged. "I said I'm toying with the idea, didn't I?"

There was a hint of frustration in her voice that felt all too familiar. From the outside listening in, it was enough to pinch at my stomach.

"Sorry," I said. "I'm just...giving you a hard time. Honestly, I'd be more worried if you didn't at least have some ideas floating around."

"Why's that?"

"I'd hate to see that much brain power go to waste." I gestured toward her head. "You could probably fuel a machine with that thing."

She nudged me. "Quiet you," she said with a chuckle. "Thanks, Rec Rec."

I wrapped an arm around her shoulder and squeezed. "Welcome, Ryn Ryn."

"Ready to head back?" I asked.

"Actually, can we sit here a little while longer?"

"Sure," I said, and leaned onto Brain's trunk. "But don't you need to get ready for class?"

NaRyn snorted. "I need as much peace from school life as humanly possible. This anum has been a huge dose of stressful, and—per usual—that stupid attention hog, Mina, goes out of her way to outdo me in everything."

"Isn't that what prep school is all about? Drama, rivals, and a bunch of other crap that only matters until you graduate. And then, before you know it, school's done, and you'll never see her again."

"I can only hope," NaRyn scoffed, then paused. "I wonder how she did it."

"Mina?"

"Blissful Martinel. She also ranked thirteenth in the KEYS 100 during her eleventh anum. But by the end of her final anum, she was number one."

I had a few theories as to whether or not Aruria's beloved princess earned the top ranking, on merit alone. But the last thing NaRyn needed was someone to deflate her dreams when there was so much ahead of her.

"Two anums is a long time," I said. "If she can do it, I'm sure you can too."

"If nothing else, fighting seems to be improving your encouragement skills."

"See? That's the kind of stuff Hachi needs to hear."

We shared a chuckle and looked out at the twinkling city lights. A smooth breeze roused the grass and leaves around us, carrying a crisp scent that relaxed me more than anything. At least, until my timechain beeped. I fished it out of my pocket and frowned as soon as Hachi's face appeared on the tiny screen. I sighed inwardly as he began with, "You forgot to clean your plate. But that's not why I linked. Come to my study when you get home. There's a matter we need to discuss."

[3]

ULTIMATUM

This world is distinctly different from others I've encountered. I find time particularly irksome. Seconds and what they call beats measure the same time but that's where the similarity ends. The hash, analogous to a minute is fifty beats versus sixty seconds. The segment, similar to an hour is one hundred hashes. At least they still have days here, though the day is twenty segments as opposed to twenty-four hours. There are no weeks or months, just decs; a ten day period that when multiplied by thirty make up an anum; the equivalent to a year. I suppose this is yet another adjustment I'll need to make.

    -The Traveler

Hachi's study was equal parts library and military history museum. The antique weapons, military uniforms, and even suit of armor predating the Martinel dynasty were a stark contrast to the books on philosophy, strategy, and politics lining the shelves. But it summed up the legendary career of Royal Army General Hachinatus "the Hatchet" Arenyu rather well. And although Hachi was understandably proud of his accomplishments, I always respected how humble he was about the whole thing. He'd bled for our kingdom and risen to its highest military rank, but most would never know he was even in the military. Unless they entered this room.

"You wanted to see me?" I asked, the gently crackling fireplace becoming me. Hachi was sitting in one of two armchairs that looked even more inviting than the fire. He gestured to the empty chair.

"I'm going to be very direct with you and I only ask you do the same."

"Fair enough."

His eyes found mine. "We never finished our conversation and the more I think about it, the more I must know what possessed you to risk your safety and freedom playing peace enforcer."

I should have known. Hachi never was one for unfinished business. Unfortunately, my time with NaRyn had afforded me no good excuses.

My eyes lowered. "I... well, I..."

"Speak up, Serec."

I knew he wouldn't understand if I told him everything that happened. But my brain was too sluggish to determine which details to leave out without him finding holes in my story. "Like I said before, a woman was being attacked. So, I—"

"Took it upon yourself to police the situation, despite my warning." He interrupted.

"She would've gotten assaulted if I didn't step in."

"You should've helped by calling the Peace Enforcement Department."

"There wasn't time."

"How would you know if you didn't even try?"

"You weren't even there," I said more forcefully than I meant to. "Would you have just sat back and waited for PEDs to show?"

"This isn't about me, Serec. It's about you disobeying my rules and breaking the law."

"I'm not some stupid little kid who needs rules. I'm seventeen—old enough to do what I want with my life. I can start a career, go into detention, or rescue someone from a predator if I want to."

Hachi's jaw tightened, and his eyes twitched as he glared with the intensity of a silent storm. I'd gotten myself into quite the mess. But it was too late to back down.

"It sounds to me," he said, "like you feel ready to live by your own rules. Am I hearing you correctly?"

His tone was flat. Another sign that a storm was brewing inside him. I needed to choose my words wisely, or all Hadal would break open. "The Department of Peace is struggling in Verdallyn—especially New Callastryne. And the Bureau hasn't been able to bridge every gap the PEDs have missed."

Hachi tilted his head. "And you don't find it presumptuous to think you—a boy with seventeen anums and no formal training—can single-handedly bridge that gap?"

"I never said I could do it alone. But just because someone can't do everything, doesn't mean no one should do anything."

I might've imagined it, but the sharpness in Hachi's eyes seemed to briefly soften. "Serec, do you remember the first thing I told you when we moved here?"

I tried to remember. But, tired as I was, recalling memories from seven segments ago felt nearly impossible, much less seven anums. I shrugged.

"'Do your best to blend in,'" Hachi said. "This was supposed to be a second chance. 'A clean slate', remember?'"

An image of my parents flashed through my head. And with it, memories of my last day in Frilare. The worst day of my life.

"Yeah," I sighed.

"We've been fortunate, living so peacefully for all these anums. But that can change for you, NaRyn, and me in an instant, if your attempts at vigilantism bring unwanted attention."

"I wouldn't have needed a second chance if the world wasn't so quick to turn a blind eye to people in need. My parents would still be here."

Hachi's mouth pressed into a tight line, and an ache formed in the base of my throat as the look in his eyes turned glassy. My comment was unfair, hurtful even. And it affected him more than I'd expected. I'd always focused so intently on how I'd lost a dad and mom. Sometimes, I forgot that meant Hachi lost a brother and a close friend.

"I'm not asking, Serec," he finally said, keen edge returning to his eyes.

"Uncle Hachi, I'm of age."

"Then act like it! You want to live your life your way, then do it under your own roof. I promised Amani and Arianna that I would keep you safe. And as long as you're under my care, I intend to keep my promise." Hachi leaned in closer. "So, allow me to be as clear as quartz here. You can either stay here and abide by my rules or you can do as you please, while fending for yourself. Because the next time I catch you fighting, your bags had better be packed. Have I made myself clear?"

For as long as I'd known Hachi, there was never an instance where his words could be taken at anything less than face value. So, the gravity in his ultimatum was almost as intense as the news that I'd never see my parents again. Ironically, Hachi was on the sending end of those words as well. The muscles in my face tightened, as fire pricked at the back of my eyes. I turned away, blinking to keep tears from forming. "As quartz," I said.

The conversation left me burdened with emptiness. By the time I was in bed, Hachi's ultimatum was the only thing floating through my head. I read once that being a hero was often a thankless job. And it still sounded better than my situation.

[4]

REUNION AND ACQUAINTANCE

In my experience, monarchies cannot coexist with advanced civilizations that have largely democratic governments. Yet here we are in the kingdom of Aruria; a nation comprised mostly of elected officials with an autocrat at its head. While I have noticed obscure mumblings of dissent, mainstream sentiment seems to support this system. Peace simplifies my mission considerably, but I can't help but wonder just how stable that peace is.

-The Traveler

My day started the same way the night before had ended: Stuck on Hachi's ultimatum. I couldn't just stop helping people. But as much as I hated to admit it, I'd barely made it out of Saldarian Flats alive. I couldn't control my new powers like Fat Felo could. And if my luck ever ran out, things could get bad, quick.

I stepped out of my room to find Hachi checking himself in the entryway mirror. "You're up early," he noted. That the understatement of the anum. At 6.03, the sun had barely rolled out of bed.

"It's too hot to sleep. And I'm sure you'd complain if I ran the heat dampeners too long." Olde Callastryne — and most of Verdallyn province had been suffering from an unexpected autumn heatwave. Which I'd had to endure while I worked on feeling like my brand-new old self.

"Just sleep without covers." He said, smoothing his uniform to a creased perfection. In Hachi's mind, every problem had a solution so simple most people couldn't see it.

"Don't you think it's a little hot to wear your Army uniform?" I redirected.

"Not when it's a special invite from the Monarch."

"How special can it be if he invites you to every event he has?"

"Today is the thirtieth anniversary of the Monarch's coronation. I would think that counts as fairly special."

"Monarch's Day?" I sucked my teeth. "So much for hitting the comic bars."

"Why are comics your primary focus when you still don't have a job?"

"Because I have an interview next dec."

That caught him off guard. A small win but, still a win. "I should look your credential sheet over. Make sure you've avoided unnecessary mistakes."

"Are you gonna be in Regalia all day?" I asked, eager to deviate from the topic.

"Most of the day. I may stop by the Bureau to check in on—"

"Really, Uncle Hachi? It's a royal holiday. Even national security threats recognize Monarch's Day."

Hachi paused at the door. "Possibly. We'll see how things go. See you tonight." That was the best I was going to get out of a man whose generation had been hardened by fear and conflict. If we were talking about nightlife, I could understand his sentiments. But during the day, life in modern-day Aruria was relatively peaceful.

Of course, keeping fear at the forefront of everyone's attention proved advantageous to people like Nel Laurelli. Even on Monarch's Day, it was hardly a surprise seeing the political reporter and commentator's face plastered on the vid screen in the den.

Nel Laurelli, was notorious not only for bashing the Crown, but also for his shamelessly persistent promotion of political reform. If you needed a daily dose of negativity, Nel Laurelli was happy to provide it. His current report on Saldarian Flats, aside from being incredibly coincidental, served as a prime example.

"Saldarian Flats remains one of the most dangerous districts in New Callastryne," he preached. "Crime rates have nearly tripled in recent anums, and statistics have shown an undeniable link to the spread of both the plague and consumption. I've also received reports of Rho criminal activity spiking in impoverished districts just like this one. All the signs are clear and still the Department of Peace has yet to devise a plan to address these issues. It's more than a little obvious to me that they understand just as well as the residents of this forsaken district that some places are beyond saving."

There was little to like about the Nel Laurellis of this world. Focusing the public eye on the worst of times, went a long way to kill the hopes of the masses. Although we actually agreed on this issue, I couldn't appreciate hearing his bleak truth after what I'd experienced firsthand.

Still, his mention of the plagued and consumed pointed to a greater issue that had to be more complex than the Department of Peace was equipped to handle. With the arrival of the viridescent sky came Plaga Viridi and Malachite's Consumption; two prominent disorders that had become a significant challenge for the medical and law enforcement communities.

In the six anums following the sky's sudden and unexplained shift from blue to green, many people had become stricken with either of these ailments. Plaga Viridi was an autoimmune disorder that caused symptoms ranging from muscle weakness to full paralysis. Malachite's Consumption, however, was far more sinister. Affecting the part of the brain governing self-control and reason, the consumption lowered the inhibitions of its victims. This caused them to exhibit more aggressive behavior leading to outbursts of anger and even acts of violence. It wouldn't surprise me to hear that Fat Felo had been consumed though a part of me suspected that pervert had been a bloated tub of sadism long before the sky changed.

The thought of that night and what might've happened to that woman was plenty reason to change the vid stream. I stood in front of the vid screen sensor and motioned a finger flick. The stream shifted to one of those tawdry this-changed-my-life-forever ads for a martial arts academy in New Callastryne. "...because in these times, learning the fundamentals of self-defense could save your life. In honor of our noble Monarch, your first dec is our gift to you. So, come on in today!"

"Seriously?! Ulti-smooth!" A dec of watching martial arts masters in action would be great training for my eyes. It was low-risk, and I could avoid all the bruising I'd taken from real fights. And all for the amazing price of free!

The *Crossroads Martial Arts Academy* sat a few blocks into New Callastryne, about fifteen hashes by terrarail. I went into my bathroom to try and somehow mitigate the bruising on my face. But, to my surprise, the face staring back showed almost no signs of the punching bag treatment I'd received less than two days ago.

But even as I marveled at how one problem had literally solved itself, I wondered why the rest of my body hardly felt any better. *Is there a limit to how much I can speed my healing?* This was the first power I'd copied. Maybe I'd done it wrong. Maybe the ability had worn off. That would've sucked, considering all I had to go through to get it. I had to make sure I still had it.

I sat in a comfortable position and closed my eyes. I visualized myself healing and held the image; breathing deep and slow through my nose. But even after several breaths, the aching persisted. *Something's off.*

"Am I doing it wrong?" I pushed to my feet, and suddenly, the air went thin. Heat radiated from every pore until my face and neck were beaded with sweat. I struggled to open my eyes, as the air caught in my throat.

I rolled onto my back, my lungs begging for oxygen, as the room went hazy. I tried to focus only on breathing. But each strained breath felt like it might be my last.

My throat tightened, pressure on my eyes intensifying like they were in a vice grip. My vision dimmed and I lay paralyzed as everything blurred out of focus. Suddenly, my throat opened and air flooded my lungs so violently, it was like fire scraping my throat. I curled up in a hard fit of coughing.

By the time my breathing had calmed enough for my body to reach a reasonable temperature, I was drenched in sweat and confusion. I cautiously pushed to my feet and ran the shower as cold as I could bear.

Hungry and thirsty from my bout with suffocation, I diverted to the closest soho shop in New Callastryne. Sohos were by far my favorite drink; especially on a hot day. Made from blending soho juice and frozen fruits that had been ground into an icy powder, the drink provided a burst of cool sweetness along with restorative nutrients.

The line to the soho shop stretched out the door, compliments of the autumn heatwave.

A woman behind me sighed. "Can you believe this? I bet, they're only holding us out here to increase soho sales," she remarked. Her voice sounded familiar, but I fought the urge to look back. "A reply wouldn't hurt, you know."

I turned. "Sorry," I said. "I didn't know if you were..." I trailed off. Golden skin. Vibrant red hair. Wintery blue — no warm autumn eyes. "You." I nearly yelled.

"Who else would I be?" The pep in her voice was a stark clash to her sarcasm.

"From the other day." She nodded, her lips curling into a soft smile. "I didn't expect to see you— or...um..." She lifted her thin eyebrows and tilted her head. "I mean, are you okay?"

Her smile widened. "Thanks to you, I'm great," she said with a wink that made my cheeks go warm. "I'm Anne." The woman with eyes of blue ice flashed through my head. "And you are?" she prompted, and I realized she was holding her hand out.

I blinked the thought away. "Sorry," I said, gripping her wrist. "I'm Serec."

Seeing her in the daylight, it was safe to assume she was nearly twice my age. But that didn't detract from how pretty she was.

"You from around here?" I asked.

"I live nearby. You?"

"Olde Callastryne."

Her eyes twinkled. "You must not be a fan of *Soho Time* if you came all this way."

"Actually, I am. But this is just a detour. The martial arts academies in Olde Callastryne are fatally expensive, so my search for affordable instruction brought me here."

"Martial arts?" She grinned. "Looking to pummel more criminals."

"That depends on the criminals."

"Aren't you a little young to be so cynical?"

I snorted. "You sound like my uncle."

"Your uncle must be a wise man."

"He has his moments."

"May I take your order?" the cashier called once we'd finally reached the counter. Her voice was distant, as if the life had been sucked out of her.

"Oh," I said, examining the menu. I'd gotten so caught up in our conversation, I hadn't even considered what to order.

"You like candor fruit?" Anne asked.

"Sure. Why?"

She slapped her hand on the counter revealing a data ring. "Two large Soho Truths, please," she said as her ring projected an image of a digital credit chip.

"No. I can't let you—"

"It's the least I can do to say thanks." She smiled, and warmth bubbled up in my chest.

"I suppose you'll be heading off to the academy now," Anne said between sips as we walked out.

"Yeah. But we should..." Frozen at Anne's sidelong gaze.

"We should?" Anne said, turning to face me.

Blue eyes. Just like...

"We should?" she repeated slower. *Is she...?*

She snapped, and I flinched. "Are you alright?"

In the beat it took to refocus, the season in her irises had shifted back to autumn.

"Serec?"

"Yeah? I mean, we umm...we should...do this again."

Anne frowned and chuckled. "Okay. Brain freeze?"

"What? Oh, yeah!" I blurted. "Brain freeze."

"I hope so. You're too young for senior moments."

I laughed nervously.

"Sorry," Anne said, pulling out her timechain. It was much sleeker than mine; a Locket Omnia model. Newest version. I knew whatever she did for a living, it paid well. She opened it and looked at the screen. "This is Dr. Kartnia. Yes. I'm on my way." She closed it. "It would seem we both have somewhere to be. But I'm glad I was able to thank you in person, Serec."

"Yeah. Same here."

"Until we next meet." She hugged me, and the aroma of serenity blooms filled me with a nostalgic warmth that reminded me what it was like to feel safe and loved. Not too different from the feeling I got when my mom used to wrap her arms around me and squeeze tight. For those few beats, everything felt right in the world.

Before I could collect my thoughts, Anne released me and hurried off; disappearing into the sea of people. I waved goodbye, wondering if I would ever see her again in so grossly overcrowded a city. The Regalia Metropolitan Area consisted of Olde Callastryne, where I lived; New Callastryne, the largest region; Vista, mostly populated by the ultra-rich; and Regalia, our nation's capital. Collectively, the densest population of Arurian citizens lived between these four regions. I was more likely to be struck by lightning than to coincidentally cross paths with her again. But, in that moment, I made hope a guest in my mind.

I entered the academy to find only three people inside. And one of them was off in the corner, sweeping the floor. Probably a custodian. The other two were older men—one with grey hair and the other completely bald. They moved fluidly, sparring with the kind of focus I'd seen in some of the martial arts vids I'd watched as a kid.

"Are you requiring assistance, patron?" I jumped and looked over my shoulder. The custodian was standing behind me, still holding his broom. Seeing him up close, he looked to be about my age.

"I'm good, thanks."

"Did I startle you?" he asked flatly.

"Yeah, you kinda did."

"That wasn't my intention." He said it so matter-of-factly.

"Don't worry about it." He nodded, maintaining his uncomfortably close distance as he stared blankly. "You're not from around here, are you?"

"I'm a citizen of Aruria." He sounded almost defensive.

"Okay. Congratulations. So, I'm looking for someone who can sign me up for classes here. Do you know who I need to talk to?"

He nodded, but didn't move.

I nodded back and forced a smile. "Like, right now?"

He nodded again. "Follow me please." Instead of taking me to an office or desk, he led me over to the two men sparring...while they were still sparring. "Here they are."

"Great," I said. "I guess I can take it from here."

He nodded, still watching me and not leaving. The distant look in his uncanny grey eyes was starting to creep me out.

"You know, it's not polite to stare."

"Do you find it to be impolite?"

"Not just me," I said with a forced smile.

His eyes lowered momentarily. *Did I hurt his feelings?* His face was so stoic it was hard to tell.

"Shawin," the bald man said. "How many times have I told you not to..." He trailed off when he noticed me. "May I help you?"

"Uh, yeah. I saw your ad on the vid stream and was hoping to sign up for classes."

"Were you interested in our eight dec or twenty dec program?"

"Oh, I just wanted the one free dec that you are offering for Monarch's Day."

The men glanced at each other before their mouths curled into a grin. "I believe you've suffered a misunderstanding young man. Our ad states that there is no charge for your *first* dec. However, you still must sign up and pay in advance for one of our programs."

I should have known. Smooth wording to get people in the door only to crush their dreams and siphon their union accounts.

"Seriously?!" I said. "I can't afford that."

"Then, I suppose we're done here," the man said, turning his back to me.

"But—" I couldn't even come up with a good argument. It was my fault for assuming that anyone in the most materialistic place in Aruria would be that charitable. I let out a heavy sigh and walked out.

"Do you think it's wise to abandon your goal so easily?" a voice called from behind me. It was the custodian, Shawin.

"That a problem?" I asked.

"Not if your intention was to waste time and leave empty handed."

The words: "Can you just get to the point and leave me alone?" almost escaped my mouth. But, I decided: "I don't have the credits to pay for a program here," was the better response.

"Perhaps you should seek a different instructor."

Oh, really? I hadn't thought of that. My frustration had piqued and my patience was on the brink of collapse. "Look, guy."

"Shawin."

I sighed. "Shawin. I can't afford to pay a different instructor."

"What if you paid with food?"

"What kind of instructor would take food as payment?"

"I would."

I paused. *Is this guy for real?* "You know martial arts?" He nodded. "And you would teach me martial arts in exchange for food?"

"That's what I was implying. Sorry if I wasn't clear."

I paused again. "Why?"

"Because I didn't mean to confuse you with my lack of clarity. I guess everything is subjective in—"

"No. Why would you teach for food?"

"The pay here isn't great, which leaves few credits for food. Also, I can't cook."

"What if you don't like what I bring you?"

"I'm not picky. I'm sure it's better than anything I can make."

"You any good?"

"I've never lost a fight. And you're better off learning efficient technique from me than you are learning the sloppy technique they use." he nodded toward the academy.

Sloppy technique? "If you're so much better than them, why were you sweeping the floor?"

He half-frowned. "Because it was dirty." He extended his hand. His eyes held a curious warmth that shined through his otherwise apathetic face "Do we have a deal?" Maybe I should've given it more thought, but I had nothing to lose minus a few credits on lunch.

I gripped his wrist. "When do we start?"

"In one dec, if that works for you. I have a vid I'd like you to watch to familiarize yourself with the basics first. Never got your name, by the way."

"Serec."

He nodded. "Good name. I'll see you next dec, Serec."

[5]

SLOW IS SMOOTH

As I headed back to *Crossroads*, a stiffness nagged at my shoulder reminiscent of Royal Verdallyn Academy's swim team tryouts. I hated how that dull ache lingered until my body could adjust to intense daily exercise. The instructional vids on the data stick Shawin had given me weren't too hard to follow. They featured the men I saw sparring at *Crossroads*, back when their hair was less gray and still covered their heads. And despite the low budget look of them, the vids were thorough enough to both teach the basics and leave me pretty wiped after each session.

Shawin spotted me the moment I entered Crossroads. "How are you, Serec?" The glint in his eyes was hard to miss.

"Smooth. You?"

"I'm well. What's for lunch today?"

"Aren't we right to the point?"

"Should we not be?"

I started to point out the etiquette of small talk—and rhetorical questions for that matter. But, to be honest, I wasn't feeling too chatty myself. So, I shrugged instead. "I have a place in mind."

Shawin led the way, turning the first corner, then heading straight for the next few blocks. There was something unusual about him. He had a listless quality that made his company not unlike that of a mannequin or a machine without conversational programming.

"So, how long have you worked at Crossroads?" I finally asked.

"Nine decs."

"How was the hiring process?"

"The application and interview took a day. But I was searching for almost three decs before learning that they were hiring."

"Which site did you use?"

"Eyesight."

Alright, smart guy. "I mean, which net site did you use?"

"Net site?"

"Yeah, net site."

"What's that?" *Is he serious?* "And why are you frowning at me?"

"Haven't you ever been on the arnet?"

"Ar...nat?"

"Is this a joke or something?"

Shawin's face remained blank. "About...?"

I paused and cocked my head to one side. "Where did you say you were from?"

"Aruria."

"Have you ever heard of a processor?"

"I use a processor at work sometimes. That's the...net site, right?"

I shook my head. "You've gotta be close to my age. How do you not know what the arnet is?"

"What's your age?"

"Seventeen."

"I'm sixteen. Perhaps, your additional anum—"

"I've known about the arnet most of my life!"

He paused. "I see. So, if you have knowledge of the net site, why don't you have a job?"

"I lost my job."

"Why?"

"I punched my platoon leader in the face."

Shawin paused again. "Did he deserve it?" It was a reasonable question that no one had ever bothered to ask. Maybe that's why I couldn't help grinning. "Did my question amuse you?"

"It kinda did. And yeah, he totally deserved it."

Shawin led me through a wooden gate and into the backyard of a beige, cube-shaped, two-story house. The mostly concrete yard was unremarkable, save for a large red-leaved fleeting tree, surrounded by pink rocks.

"You into landscaping?" I asked.

"My landlords are," Shawin said. "They live on the top floor."

"Must be nice, living on your own. Sometimes I can't even eat without my uncle suggesting a better way to do it."

"You must have lively dinner conversations."

"Not lately."

"That's unfortunate. I really enjoyed dinner conversations with my family."

"Where are they?"

Shawin smiled wistfully. "Too far away to drop in for a meal. But that's where you come in. Now, show me what you've learned."

Shawin leaned against the tree and watched as I went through the moves I'd seen in the instructional vids.

"You have impressive memory, to recall so many movements after one dec," Shawin remarked.

I shrugged to downplay the pride welling in my chest.

"Our next step will be correcting your form. Then, we can expand on the basics."

I frowned. "Correcting? I did everything exactly like in the vid."

"Yes, but the masters at Crossroads have poor form. So, I have my work cut out for me." His tone was annoyingly chipper.

I frowned. "Right. So, the vids were a waste of time then?" The words came out sharper than intended, but Shawin seems unfazed.

"Correcting your form is easier and faster than teaching you from scratch. The vids saved me time with covering the basics. So, once your form is correct, I can expand on it."

The tightness in my jaw eased slightly. "So, what am I about to learn?"

"It's a fighting style called Yenta-Gin."

"That's the style with perfect defense, right?"

"There's no such thing as perfect defense. Yenta-Gin simply reduces openings, and uses an attacker's momentum against him."

"Very smooth. How long does it take to master stuff like that?"

"That is highly dependent on you. Yenta-Gin is very different from other martial arts. Slow, deliberate movement and perception are vital. In other words, the more you learn to slow down, the faster you progress."

"Uh huh. So, like, in days, what are we talking?"

His lips pressed into a thin line. "We have a saying back home: 'slow is smooth.' All good things come in time. And rushing only distracts from your ultimate goal."

I almost wanted to clarify that my ultimate goal was to learn as quickly as possible, but I resisted.

We focused on breathing and defensive movements specifically, avoiding oncoming attacks. But the multi-step maneuvers were making avoiding practically impossible.

"You think we can just skip to the attacks?" I finally asked. "I'm not much of a dodger."

Shawin looked at me thoughtfully. "Is punching your opponent on your way to the ground more important to you than avoiding the ground altogether?"

"If I hit harder than my opponent, I'll never see the ground."

"You assume hitting harder gives you an advantage."

"Doesn't it?"

Shawin studied me with stoic eyes. "Which requires more energy: a fist that can break stone or a finger that can stop a heart?"

"The fist for sure."

"Which attack would end a fight faster?" I started to answer, but paused as his question sunk in. "We fight the same way we train. And impatience is the worst trait to have in a fight. But, if it's that important to you, we can skip everything required to use Yenta-Gin effectively, and I'll just teach you to break things."

I looked down, feeling like a child who'd just been reprimanded. "No, sorry. Let's just...get back to dodging."

"How about I show you one offensive maneuver in good faith?"

"Like, right now?"

"Sure. It's a simple technique for disabling an attacker at close range."

Shawin grabbed a handful of rocks and placed them in my hand. "This technique works best when the person's hands are full because the nerves and muscles bulge more." He gripped my wrist with one hand. "Watch closely. I doubt you'll want to see this a second time."

What's that supposed to mean? I found out soon enough, when he successively jabbed two fingers into three different points under my forearm, keeping constant pressure on the last spot. My hand jerked open as a burning numbness raced up my arm. The burning intensified as I attempted to abandon the rocks and pull away. But his grip was much stronger than I'd expected.

"Okay," I said through gritted teeth, cringing until my eyes nearly closed.

"Watch," Shawin said, easing his grip. "If your finger placement is right, it won't take much pressure to disable an attacker." My jaw clenched as I studied Shawin's finger placement, anxious to commit the image to memory before I lost all feeling in my arm. I nodded, and Shawin released my arm. Shawin was right about one thing. I did *not* want to see that move a second time. I was happy to spend the next segment on defensive exercises before we quit and ordered lunch.

Shawin led me down a small, empty hallway that ended at his bathroom. To my right was one other room. But it was practically empty, save for a bed roll and four neatly folded piles of clothes.

"How long have you lived here?" I asked.

"Just over twelve decs."

"It's emptier than I expected."

"I only have what I need. Plus, I'm still paying my landlords back for letting me live here rent free while I was searching for a job. So, credits are tight."

By the time I cleaned up and made it to the table, the food was already laid out. Shawin was sitting on a box, leaving the only chair for me.

"Hope you don't mind, but I started without you." He said, mouth half-stuffed.

I shrugged and grabbed two pumil wraps. The first bite was the best. An explosion of plant green and cheese flavors covered in a mild sauce that practically begged you to keep eating it.

"How long did it take you to get smooth with that dodging maneuver?" I managed between bites.

"Not long. With enough practice, it becomes second nature."

That should've put my mind at ease. But it only reminded me of my issues with my powers.

"Are you going to finish that?" Shawin asked, eyeing my remaining pumil wrap.

"I guess you can have—"

By the time the words reached his ears, he'd already confiscated what remained on my plate. Watching him devour the food made me wonder if the lessons at Crossroads would have been cheaper.

The next couple decs were more of the same. My days were divided between training with Shawin's and job hunting on the arnet. Unfortunately, the latter turned out to be a monumental waste of time. Despite filling out over a hundred applications ranging from PED patrolman to nightclub security guard to deliveryman, only three employers even bothered letting me know they weren't interested. It was a sad reminder that you can make a valiant effort, but when a dishonorable discharge comes up in your background check, you become about as desirable as dry dirt.

Shawin was waiting under the fleeting tree when I walked up. At least, I think he was waiting. The way he stared into space sometimes, he could've just been watching leaves grow.

"Hey Serec," Shawin said, holding out a closed fist.

"Hey." I looked down at his fist, then back at his expectant face. *Maybe he wants to see what I can do after two decs of practice.*

I stepped right, and leaned forward, dipping under his fist. His arm followed, and I twisted right to avoid it. I dipped back, careful not to touch his arm. He kept up perfectly with every movement I made. The more I dodged, the faster his arm followed, until I could swear his hand was beating me to where I was going.

I needed to hold my focus with smooth nerves. But I ended up trying to predict his next move, which only made me more tense. I unconsciously tried to use my power to gain the advantage. But a sharp, stabbing pain in my eyes, stopped me cold.

"You okay?" Shawin asked after a beat.

"Yeah. I just...didn't know what to do next."

"What were you trying to do?"

"Avoid your arm."

"Why?"

I frowned. "Because you were testing me."

"I was trying to bump fists with you, before starting today's session. It's an act of acknowledgment between warriors in Yenta-Gin."

"Why didn't you say something before?"

"When you began darting around, I grew curious about your intentions."

I wondered if Shawin had that kind of offbeat humor my brain couldn't hope to latch on to. "What province did you say you were from again?"

"I didn't." He raised his fist again. I sighed and bumped it. "Anyway, since your form is improving faster than expected, today would be a good day to try dynamic meditation; which is performed while moving."

He said it like the chances of running face-first into a wall weren't extremely high. And Shawin's constant reminders weren't enough to stop instinct from compelling my hands in front of me every few steps.

"It works better if you walk normally," he said.

"Maybe if my body didn't feel so off, I would."

"You feel off because you're fighting it."

"I'm fighting to keep my face from hitting a wall, which is inevitable when you walk around with your eyes closed."

"Yenta-Gin is all about perception. It requires calm flow with every movement. Trying to force anything will only make things harder for you."

"How am I supposed to fix that before I flatten my face?"

"Exactly my point. Your only concern is how quickly you can fix the problem. But remember, slow is smooth. Ignore your impatience and find the cause. You must train slower to learn faster."

The more I thought about it, the less sense his advice made. "Sorry," I said, "but I still haven't figured out what that's supposed to mean."

Shawin sighed.

"Let's try some sparring. Maybe then you'll better understand what I'm saying."

"But you haven't taught me how to attack."

"Something tells me you've thrown a punch before."

I may have had my share of fights. But, even with my powers, I wasn't sure I could do much against Shawin. I hesitated.

"You look worried," Shawin began. "But don't be. I intend to hold back."

So much for the vote of confidence. I got into a stance.

I didn't know what I was expecting. But the moment Shawin dipped out of sight, I'd totally lost him. And before I could find him, his hand was under my arm, fist pressing into my ribs.

"Don't freeze up, just because I've caught you. You need to move, or you'll leave yourself open for more." I nodded, and Shawin stepped back. "Let's try again."

We tried three more times, but every attempt ended the same.

Shawin kept me completely off track, zipping around and knocking me off balance repeatedly. Worst of all, my eyes couldn't catch any of it until it was too late.

Maybe one try won't hurt. I fixed my eyes on Shawin and concentrated. He dipped low again, but this time I tracked him like a homing missile. Two half-steps forward and Shawin appeared, reaching for my arm again. I moved my hand to block it. But before my hand found his, a horrible pain stung the back of my eyes, and they shut on reflex.

I flailed and stumbled back, shaking my head in a panic. When I opened my eyes, Shawin was watching curiously.

"You okay?"

I cleared my throat. "Yeah, of course."

Shawin leaned in, close. Like, violating-my-personal-space close. He squinted up at me; his grey eyes shifting back and forth between mine.

"What?" I said, leaning away.

"How long have your eyes been bothering you?"

"Not long," I lied. "I didn't get much sleep last night. That's all." Without a word, Shawin kept examining and my stomach grew tight. "But it's nothing. I'm sure I'll be fine by tomorrow."

"No," Shawin said in a half-whisper. "You won't. Your eyes are suffering from overexertion, which should be expected, considering your lack of control over your powers," Shawin grinned.

My face went numb. "How long have you known?" I probed.

"I've had my suspicions since day one."

"Are you gonna report me?"

"To whom?"

"The PEDs," Shawin's thick eyebrows furrowed. "The Peace Enforcement Department," I added.

"There's no lack of peace requiring enforcement," he said. Judging by his tone, he probably wasn't playing dumb. So, I took a risk at stating the obvious.

"Using your powers is illegal."

"Seems you've avoided using your powers for quite some time, which is disappointing in its own right."

"What's that supposed to mean?"

"Your ability could have accelerated this process, and yet you've decided against using it." A larger smile crept onto Shawin's face. "Not an ideal situation for you, but it does allow me additional free meals."

I smirked the realization setting in. "Your power is in your eyes too, isn't it?"

"It is."

"You gonna tell me what it is?"

"Certainly. I'm a precognitor. pre-cog for short. We see what happens before it happens."

"Like a psychic?"

"Psychics are said to experience visions surrounding someone's life by attuning themselves to that person's fate. They can usually see far into the future. But I've never personally used such an ability."

I nodded. "So, does your foresight let you see what you're going to figure out in the future or something?"

Shawin shook his head. "A pre-cog sees what will happen mere moments before it happens. In my case, I can only see what will happen to me. It's a pitifully *selfish* ability." His tone was sharp.

"But that doesn't make you a selfish person. I mean, you're helping me right now. That counts for something, right?"

Shawin took a breath and looked away. "We should refocus on your training. I haven't earned my lunch yet."

"Okay," I said, not wanting to press the issue.

"Can you tell me how your ability works?"

"It's referred to as adaptive muscle memory, but I call it mimicry. Basically, it allows me to copy whatever I see. It's mostly useful for mimicking fighting moves, but recently, I've been able to copy other abilities too. I definitely haven't figured out the nuances of that part though. My body nearly shut down a few decs ago just trying to use one ability."

"How long have you known about your powers?" Shawin asked.

"Since I was small. But my uncle wasn't keen on the idea of me using my powers."

"So, you haven't used your ability since you were a child?"

"Pretty much. The past few decs, I've been trying to get a better grasp of it, but it's not working out as I'd hoped."

"That explains your symptoms of overuse. My guess is that you've temporarily burned out your nervous system."

"How do I *unburn* it?"

"Give it time. It could take a couple decs, but it'll heal eventually."

I cleared my throat. "Okay, so I know we keep rushing things. But isn't there some faster way than eventually?"

"Maybe."

"Why maybe?"

"I'm not a doctor. So, I can't be certain my technique will solve your problem."

I thought for a beat. "Does it hurt to try though?"

Shawin paused to consider my question. "I suppose not." He rubbed his hands together, then held his palms close to my face. "Keep your eyes open."

He didn't hold them there for long, but an oddly soothing warmth radiated from his hands. A light tingling spread throughout my entire face until he pulled them away.

"How do your eyes feel?" he asked.

I blinked a couple times and looked around. "The pain's gone. Did you fix my nervous system?"

"I promoted a gentle healing to speed up your recovery. But you'll still need to take it slow until you've completely healed."

"How will I know if I'm burning out my nervous system?"

"Basic sense, really. Listen to your body. Allow your brain the necessary time to adjust to your ability."

His words were reassuring. Still, I could've done without the 'basic sense' remark.

"I suggest you practice that healing ability you mentioned earlier, focusing specifically on your nervous system. Instead of trying to force it, visualize the energy running throughout your body. Once you have a clear image in your mind, strengthen that flow of energy. This will give your body the gentle nudge it needs." I nodded, still a bit hazy on his instructions.

"You sure you're not a doctor?"

"Positive. I'm just showing you a couple of things, someone taught me." Shawin's tone suddenly became flat and lifeless. Well, flatter than normal.

"You say it like it's a bad thing."

"It's not. It's just that it reminded me..." Shawin cleared his throat and folded his arms.

"Hey man. You okay?"

"We're friends, right Serec?"

"What else could we be after all this time?"

His eyes trailed to the ground. "And friends shouldn't keep secrets from each other, should they?"

That kind of depends a lot on the secret. It's one thing to secretly be a mogul living a pauper's life. It's an entirely different thing to be a serial killer who targets his closest friends. Not that Shawin struck me as either. But his tone wasn't too encouraging. "I — guess not."

"There's something very important, I'm hoping you can help me with while there's still time. But, as my friend, I need your word that you'll keep it a secret."

[6]

INTENTION

Oppression is an interesting phenomenon. Those in power maintain their hold by dividing the oppressed. In the case of Orbis, those individuals possessing special abilities must hide themselves from the populace under threat of persecution. Entire communities live on the fringes of society to maintain a peaceful existence. Yet conflict still finds them; not from the dominant human population, but something far more sinister.

-The Traveler

"Okay," I said. "Shoot."

"Shoot what?"

"It means tell me."

"I don't see how shooting and telling are connected."

I sighed. "Can you just tell me the secret?"

Shawin took a breath. "I'm looking for my uncle. I haven't seen him in a long time, but he comes from the same place as me."

"Aruria?"

"Not exactly. Although I am considered a citizen of Aruria, I was actually born on the island of Vallah."

My breath caught. "Seriously?! Isn't that like where secret Gifted tribes live or something?"

"Something like that."

"So, you're from one of the tribes?"

Shawin nodded.

"That is so smooth! I can't believe I know someone from a Gifted tribe. In my geography classes, they claimed Vallah was uninhabited, but I figured they were lying." I snorted. "They probably just didn't know."

"As far as mainlanders know, the island *is* uninhabited. And it's crucial that you help maintain the integrity of this secret."

With a broad smile, I placed my right fist over my heart. A gesture that served as an affirmation of fidelity and the Arurian military salute. "You have my word, man. So... your uncle is here too?"

Shawin nodded. "And I need to speak to him before my Journey of Intention ends."

"What's that?"

"It's a rite of passage that will determine my path in life."

"That's pretty deep."

"At the end of my uncle's Journey of Intention, he chose to remain on the mainland, and I haven't seen him since. I came to New Callastryne hoping to ask why, before making my own decision."

"You can't ask after your decision?"

He shook his head. "The decision includes where I will live for the rest of my life. And once the choice is made, it's final."

"Is that why your uncle hasn't returned?"

"I believe so. He's not forbidden from visiting. But to maintain his decision and prevent outsiders from discovering us, he's probably keeping his distance."

"Wild." I leaned close. "Can you tell me anything else about your tribe?" Shawin hesitated. "It's fine if you don't want to."

"We're called the Wolfhounds." I froze; wide-eyed and mouth agape. "Did you say Wolfhounds!?" I asked in an excited whisper. Shawin nodded.

Since I was a kid, I'd been engrossed in the tales of secret clans around the world. Clans with unique fighting styles and mysterious abilities. And no clan was more mysterious and intriguing than the Wolfhounds. I would sometimes fantasize about what it would be like to meet someone from one of the clans, but most of the information surrounding their existence only made them out to be a myth. Several characters from the *Power Clash Comics* franchise hailed from the Wolfhounds. But details about their home and past were always murky. At least now I understood why.

"We are one of many factions of Gifted that live in secrecy," Shawin said. "The rumors are a necessity since our clan has become the target of a very aggressive faction that's been going to great lengths to coerce our allegiance. We've had to take multiple countermeasures to avoid them. So, public knowledge of our existence is practically placing a target on our backs."

"Aren't you taking a huge risk telling me?"

"I trust you. Also, I need your help. The net you mentioned—the one that searches for employment."

"You mean the arnet?"

Shawin nodded. "Can it also locate a person?"

"Possibly. There's no guarantee it would work though."

"All the same, I believe you and your arnet could make greater strides in finding my Uncle Kaz than I have in the last few decs."

I doubted I could be of much help. But I wouldn't be much of a friend if I let him put himself and his clan at risk for nothing.

"I'll start looking today," I assured him. "If he's in Aruria, we're bound to find him."

I wished I were half as confident as I sounded. If Shawin was right about his uncle keeping to the shadows, the arnet would probably be of little to no help.

That night, I had a weird dream. Shawin and Fat Felo were standing in front of me, trying to show me how to use my healing ability. Needless to say, their methods clashed. "Listen to your body," Shawin kept saying. "It's basic sense."

Fat Felo's approach was even more abrasive. So abrasive I wanted to punch him. "Deep breath in, hold it, breath out, and erase the pain. It's simple, stupid." It was annoying trying to make sense of his instructions. But I really wanted to get the hang of it.

Still, at one point, I had my fill of insults and I remember yelling, "You're stupid!" at the top of my lungs. They laughed in unison—which was strange, considering I'd never seen Shawin laugh. But that didn't matter. It was infuriating being the object of their amusement. And that fury quickly became a heat that enveloped my entire body. They fell silent as hot energy surged through me. And just as my pride started to get the better of me, the blue-eyed Anne appeared.

"Access to one power means access to them all." Her words penetrated my mind like they were my own.

"Anne, wait!" I called, springing up in the classic please-don't-go waking position. Then, I realized it was only a dream. Anne's words lingered like a riddle. "Access to one power — access to them all. Does she mean my healing ability?" I was too tired to try healing my nervous system the night before. So, that seemed as good a place to start as any. I sat cross-legged on my bed and closed my eyes, trying to build up a mental picture of my nervous system.

I visualized a wave of energy flowing throughout my body, not sure if I was feeling what I was supposed to. But whatever I felt, it was different from before. This feeling was soothing and cool all over. But the feeling was short-lived; replaced by a geyser of heat, radiating in every direction.

My breaths grew shallow. My heart raced. Fatigue followed as I trembled so much I couldn't hold myself up. Vertigo took hold, before I flopped onto my back, eyes wide. My room looked fuzzy, and sweat rolled down my face as I fought to regain control over my breathing. It may not have been as terrifying as before, but I wasn't feeling especially anxious to try again before meeting up with Shawin.

"Are my eyes still acting up or are you happy that I was in pain this morning?" I asked a smiling Shawin.

"What you're describing sounds normal. Your body might've gone into a temporary shock, but it sounds like you're making great progress in recuperating. I wouldn't be surprised if your recovery time is half of what I originally expected."

"Does that mean it'll take less time to learn what you teach me?"

"As far as technique goes, I can only hope so. I've taken a job as a school groundskeeper, which leaves me nine days to teach you all I can."

I frowned. "You can never just have good news can you?"

"I need the money. But if you're up for it, we can train five segments daily until I start this new job."

Five segments was a lot, even by my standards. And whether I wanted to or not, I knew my body might give out well before my willpower did. Still, I had to try.

"I'm up for it if you are," I said.

The next eight days were some of the most physically demanding days I'd had since my time in the Army. Five segments of training with Shawin, and two more at home, turned napping into the only reasonable way to spend my downtime. And with helping Shawin find his uncle, every night after dinner, I had almost no energy left to search for employment. Especially since neither was seeming to yield any decent results. The fact Shawin was able to find a second job when I couldn't even secure one was even more discouraging.

"Morning Serec," Shawin said through a yawn.

"It's midday."

"Oh. Well, I guess we should..." He stopped to inhale the aroma, which locked his attention onto the large bag in my hand. "Is that nibos?"

"Good nose," I said, holding up the bag. "It's your favorite, right?"

His excited nod was gratifying for more than one reason. There were only two nibos farms in all of Aruria; mainly because the large six-horned beasts were so aggressive that raising them was both dangerous and expensive. My union account had taken a serious hit in ordering it for our final lunch together. A hit made more severe, considering I'd ordered it from *The Blue Leaf*, one of the top restaurants in Verdallyn province. They made flaky steamed cheese and veggie pumil wraps like you wouldn't believe. And all for a price that you didn't want to believe. But again, it was our final lunch. So, I figured it should be a memorable one.

"We should hurry before the food gets cold," Shawin said.

"What are we covering today?"

"Sparring."

"That's it?"

"Unfortunately, I have nothing new to teach you." He smiled.

"Then, why are you smiling?"

"Because, fortunately, I have nothing new to teach you. We've covered plenty. Now, we can put it to the test."

If this test had a score, I might've flunked. Shawin made it look easy dodging most everything I threw at him. And the few attacks that connected somehow still ended with me flopping to the ground.

By the end of the match, two things were undeniably evident. One was that Shawin had been holding back the whole time. The other was that defensive maneuvers could be just as effective as attacking, if you knew what you were doing. And Shawin knew *exactly* what he was doing.

"Perhaps it's good our training has come to an end," Shawin said. "You might've caught up with me in a few more decs."

I wondered if he really meant that, then remembered how straightforward he was. "Thanks for teaching me. I really appreciate it."

"And I appreciated the meals. So, what will you do now?"

"Once I've got a little more control of my accelerated healing, I'll pick up where I left off with patrolling the streets."

"What do you hope to accomplish?"

"As long as there are criminals, there'll be victims. Even if I have a small part to play, I want to save as many people as I can."

Shawin paused. "Do you have someone you wish to improve your world for?"

"I never really thought about it."

Shawin paused again. "I see."

"You look like there's something else you want to ask me."

"Well, there is. When I went to speak with my new employer yesterday, I met this girl on the caelrail."

A wide smile pressed into my face. "Oh, you want advice on girls."

"Aside from my little sister, I'm not very experienced with talking to girls."

"Well, I'm not sure how much help I can be. My uncle's massive list of restrictions made dating tough. Plus, I uhh..." I trailed off as an image rose to the surface of my mind.

"You what?"

"Uhh, nothing," I said, shaking my head. "Just a random memory of someone I used to be really close with."

"Did something happen?"

"I honestly don't know. I haven't seen or spoken to her since I moved away seven anums ago. But anyway, you should just tell this girl what's on your mind."

Shawin nodded thoughtfully. "Then what?"

I shrugged. "That's it. Girls are complicated. But I know they like guys who speak their mind."

Shawin smiled. "Thanks, brother. Don't become scarce. Training or no, we're still friends, right?" Shawin reached out his fist.

I bumped my fist against his. "You know it."

The whole way back home, my mind swam through memories of her face. And the more I thought about her, the worse I felt. We were best friends. And when I moved to Olde Callastryne with Hachi, I'd left without so much as a goodbye. I wouldn't be surprised if she hated me by now, or forgot all about me. I told myself if I ever saw Liza again, I'd do everything in my power to make things right between us.

In the meantime, I couldn't lose sight of my mission. If anything, making the world safer for people like Liza and Anne would make all I'd endure worth it. Shawin's training had given me a huge boost. And if I was smart about preparations, I could be back on patrol within the dec.

[7]

OPPORTUNITY

Boredom struck me on a particularly slow day of my investigation. So I occupied myself with calculating the relationships of this worlds absurd time system. I started by examining the only commonality between the time systems of this world and others: the beat and the second. After some quick math, I determined that a segment is roughly 1.4 hours or 83 minutes long. This makes days here about 28 hours long. Decs replace both weeks and months at ten days. Interestingly enough, an anum, which is 300 days, is about 4% shorter than a standard year when measured in in seconds. That means that the people of this world have longer days but shorter years. What could have caused the planet to rotate slower but have a shorter orbit? It must have something to do with *the Others*.

-The Traveler

The Central District was business as usual, except that it wasn't. Four nights in, I hadn't seen so much as a litterbug. It was starting to look like Hachi was right about the Department of Peace getting things under control. As far as I was concerned, their timing couldn't have been worse.

On one hand, I wouldn't have to worry about being kicked out of the house for fighting anymore. But that meant the only thing left for me to do was live a boring life doing some spirit-crushing job.

I detoured through *Monument Park* to help ease my mind. Aio's pale glow barely penetrated the clouds. And yet, through the park's cluster of bushy trees, it shined like it did before the sky's color changed. Before everything changed.

As the name implied, Monument Park had its fair share of monuments. Mainly national figures, like previous monarchs, generals, and civil rights leaders. But the most significant monument was the one standing before me. A stone representation of a fleeting tree sat in the center of a square garden; a narrow stone path leading to its trunk. I ran my hands over the trunk, painful memories rising to the surface of my mind. Inscribed into the trunk were names; names of Peace Enforcement Department officers and Bureau of National Peace agents who lost their lives that day. The day four Gifted terrorists attacked Hiyama Square, killing and wounding hundreds. Over a hundred Department of Peace officials fought to save innocent lives that day. Among them were Vyctor and Marra Hayden, NaRyn's parents. I never thought I'd be the one consoling someone who'd lost their parents. But I guess my circumstances made me especially qualified.

The night air brushed my brow, and I started to pull back my hood when a female voice grazed my ear. "Heroes aren't defined by what they do in times of peace, but in moments of crisis."

"That's a quote from the monarch, ri—?" Ribbons of unmistakable red hair waved in front of me. "Anne!?"

"You know your quotes… and your stalkers," she remarked playfully. "Of course, I wouldn't be surprised if you were the one following me." We hugged, and the scent of serenity blooms filled my nose so quickly it was like I inhaled a shot of calm.

"I hate to disagree with you," I said, "but this is the second time you've appeared behind me. So, what brings you here tonight?"

"Evening stroll. You?"

"Uh, same." It wasn't exactly a lie considering how quiet things had been.

She looked up at the fleeting tree. "This is my favorite monument in the park. It's a wonderful reminder of the beauty and fragility of life. So many sacrificed themselves to save others. Not at all unlike what you did for me."

Her autumn eyes found mine and my cheeks warmed. Anne was probably one of the kindest people I'd ever met. Just knowing her made two things clear to me. I had to preserve the beauty in this world, and when the time came, whomever I ended up marrying had to be the kind of woman she was.

"Oh, you're um…you're welcome." I cleared my throat, wishing for a redo.

"Spoken like a true hero." The chuckle in her voice ended with a sigh that might as well have been a lumen pointed directly at my face. "I'd best head home before it gets too late. If I get into trouble too often, you may think I'm just trying to get your attention." We shared a laugh, although mine somehow sounded a lot more nervous and awkward than it should've. "Don't stay out too late yourself, okay?"

I nodded, and Anne placed a hand on my cheek. Her light brown skin was so soft—soothing even—I could hardly think to respond, before she turned away; her scarlet hair dancing in the wind like a gentle flame.

Anne had the right idea. The night was nearly over, and my focus was quickly shifting to getting home before it got any chillier. At least, until the scream rang out behind me so suddenly it made the hairs on the back of my neck stand on end.

I ran through the fleeing crowd as it radiated outward from the center of the park. Once I got a clear view of what everyone was running from, my first impulse was to follow right behind them.

A pot-bellied humanoid beast was gripping a young boy between long, stubby fingers. Its dark gray skin was a sharp contrast to the glow in those piercing orange eyes sunken in their sockets. Saliva dripped from its jagged fangs as it twisted around and snarled. If the creature hadn't erupted with a blood-curdling roar, I would've been certain I was hallucinating.

I stood there, breathless and afraid, my brain urging me to run. But, the sanguine hue in the boy's face, drew me toward the conflict.

"Help!" the boy managed, voice raspy.

I had to act fast if I wanted to free him. But the man and woman sprawled on the ground behind him, made my doubts press back. Saving one person from a monster with claws long enough to eviscerate me was a bad gamble at best. Which made saving three people borderline impossible. But, given the situation, I had to try.

"I said I wanted to save people," I thought aloud.

The two on the ground weren't easy to make out, but I assumed they were the boy's parents. I could only pray that—by El's blessing—they were still alive. With a deep, focused breath, I willed my body's flow of energy into a condensed ball around my heart, and held it there until my chest warmed and my skin started tingling so intensely it made my body vibrate.

Without a moment of hesitation, I charged and swung my fist with enough force to punch a hole in a brick wall. But the monster dodged my attack and slashed with its free hand. I barely dipped in time to save my face, before throwing another punch that connected just under the creature's arm. It yelped and tried to reposition itself. But it was too slow to avoid my follow-up attack aimed at the center of its stomach. Its body was like a solid tree trunk, but I wasn't about to let up.

The beast stumbled back, and I lunged forward, preparing to kick it like an enraged nibos when it held the young boy in between us. I tripped over myself, trying to slow my momentum, and the monster used the opening to swat me away with the force of a boulder.

I pushed off the ground, wincing at the shooting pain in my shoulder. For a wild beast, it was surprisingly intelligent.

"That thing's out of your league, Kid," a voice called from behind. "We'll handle it from here."

I glanced back at a tall man with his hands in his pockets as he stood between two women. They were all dressed in sleek, black combat gear, and their eyes were hidden behind what looked like thin rectangular visors. *Are these guys from the Bureau? Those uniforms definitely aren't standard issue.*

"I've got this," I called over my shoulder as I brushed the dirt from my arm. I rushed the creature again, more confident in my strategy. I just needed to keep it on the offensive in order to control the fight.

As soon as I was in range, the creature unleashed a small flurry of attacks. I rolled behind it and jammed an elbow into the center of its back. The creature stumbled forward, and my heart flipped as it nearly toppled over and flattened the boy.

"Careful, Kid!" the guy in the visor shouted. "Don't get the hostage killed!"

Anxiety gripped me as the monster held the boy close to its fangs, reminding me who had the advantage. I was starting to think I should've accepted the visor guy's help when the idea finally hit me. *Slow is smooth.*

I held my hands up and crept toward the monster. The beast tensed, but I avoided sudden movements.

"It's smooth," I said, trying to keep a calm voice. "Everything's...smooth."

The monster growled, shielding itself behind the boy again. I stopped within range of the boy—close enough to see the snot and dried tears covering his face.

Our eyes locked and I nodded to reassure him. Without warning, I lunged forward, grabbing the creature's wrist and jamming two fingers under its forearm in three places, before digging my thumb into the final pressure point.

The monster shrieked and roared, trying to pull away. But I dug my heels into the ground and held firm. The monster's hand jerked open, and the boy dropped to the ground. I released the monster's arm, grabbed the boy, and jumped away in time to narrowly avoid a deadly swipe.

I lowered the boy next to the unconscious man and woman and turned to face the creature again. It snarled, trying to back away while nursing its arm. But I wasn't about to let it find another victim. Then, just as I inched closer, it lunged at me so suddenly I couldn't react in time to stop it. And to be clear as quartz, not reacting probably meant death. Just as I flinched into the least smooth pose before death imaginable, my senses went haywire.

Something shot past me, crashing into the monster with a thunderous flash. Blue sparks fizzled around the beast as it struggled to its feet. Looking over my shoulder, I saw one of the two women was holding an odd-looking bow with blue sparks dripping from it.

With a sharp twist, the monster charged at the woman. But the visor guy thrust his hands forward and a furious wind tore the monster from the ground.

Are they all Gifted?

The monster screeched, and I snapped back to focus. The creature lunged at me again, flailing wildly. I leapt back, narrowly dodging its flurry of attacks. But the berserk beast was coming at me too fast for me to back away forever. At this rate, I'd be the next victim on the news stream.

I can't really explain what happened next. I just knew I couldn't die yet; not while this monster was on the loose. My eyes shut reflexively and I punched out in front of me. A flash of warmth engulfed me. My arm tingled with a pulsating energy that was as foreign yet familiar. When I opened my eyes, the monster stood frozen, mouth agape. Its fangs were so close, I could smell its putrid breath. I jerked away and a dark liquid spilled out from its belly.

Stumbling away, I realized that liquid was blood—the same blood covering my arm. The monster groaned, holding its stomach as it staggered toward the tall row of hedges. After some fight to pull itself up, it made it over with a delayed thud, followed by slow, heavy footsteps.

I started to go after it, but my legs refused.

"Good work, Kid," the man in the visor said; moving closer.

"Oh, uhh...thanks," I said.

He waved me toward him. "What's your name?" he whispered.

"Serec," I whispered back.

"We have work to do," the woman with the bow called, as she and the other woman started in the monster's direction. "Aid the victims."

"Yeah," the man yelled. "I'm on it." He turned back to me. "Serec, huh? That's different. Do me a favor and stay here for a beat, alright Serec?"

I nodded.

The man in the visor knelt in front of the boy and said something I couldn't quite make out. The boy looked up at him and nodded; still half-curled in a ball with fresh tears in his eyes. The man rubbed his hands together and held them over the boy's stomach. After a moment, the boy sat up, wiped his tears, and offered a weak smile. Next, the man placed his hands on the foreheads of the unconscious woman and man. The moment they began to stir a weight lifted from my chest. He said something else to the boy, then walked back over to me.

"Everyone's alright, and the boy should be fine until medics arrive. You should go."

"Hold on," I said. "What was that creature anyway? And on that note, who are you?"

"I'm sure you're flustered," the man replied, "but now's not the time for questions. Everyone's alive, thanks to you. But peace enforcement is close by, so you might wanna get going before you end up in detention."

"But, I don't—"

"You've got real potential. And we may have a use for it. But you're no good to anyone if you're caught at the scene." He hurried past me. "We'll be in touch."

"What do you mean?" I called after him. "You don't have my chainlink."

"Don't need it." With the sweep of his hands, he leapt into the air and zipped out of sight.

Over the next dec, the streets had gone quiet again. I hadn't heard anything from the man in the visor, and my job search had been as fruitless as ever. The lower the number of credits read in my union account, the closer I came to financial desperation. Aruria was undergoing a bit of a technological revolution coupled with an infrastructure revitalization. So, I knew there was an abundance of jobs in both engineering and construction which were about the closest things I could find to manual labor, and about all I was good for. Unfortunately, neither were enough of a manual labor position for me to actually be qualified for hire.

With all the segments I'd been putting into searching for Shawin's uncle, trying to find a job I actually liked and qualified for, and running patrols, life was starting to wear on me. I needed some time to consider my next move without the pressure that came from even being in the same house as Hachi. If I had to be a caged bird, the least I could do was perch near my favorite tree.

I walked into Olde Hill Park feeling like my timing couldn't have been better. It was just after 13.00, which meant the majority of Olde Callastryne's well-to-do retirees were either tuned in to some boring justice stream or taking an afternoon nap. I sat on the grass and leaned against Brain. The bright and peaceful backdrop of the city brought my focus to my sheltered upbringing in Olde Callastryne. The thought made it difficult not to feel some resentment towards Hachi for stifling my progression with my abilities and subjecting me to a monotonous existence "for my own good." But it would be equally unfair not to acknowledge all the sacrifices he made to keep NaRyn and me safe. Fleeting as it was, neither of us could've done a better job than Hachi had.

I laced my fingers and sank against Brain's trunk with a sigh, as the cool breeze blew over my skin. In no time at all, my eyelids grew heavy, and my vision blurred.

"Is this how you kids spend your free time nowadays? Must be nice." The voice was so close, my body jerked up awkwardly. I twisted around to find a tall man in a designer suit and shades, looking down at me.

"Do I know you?" I asked.

"Not yet. But don't act like we've never met."

What's that supposed to mean? I frowned. "When have I seen you?"

"Just the other day." His casual tone only worked to annoy me further.

"I think you've got the wrong guy."

He raised an eyebrow. "Forgot me that fast, huh Kid? Remember Monument Park?" It finally clicked. "Oh, the visor guy, right?"

"Visor guy, huh?" He half-mumbled. "This where you waste all your teenage afternoons?"

"I'm not wasting anything. How'd you find me anyway?"

"What's it matter, so long as I found you?"

"Can you just answer my question without asking another question?"

"Why? That bother you?"

"Not as much as waiting to hear from you in the first place."

"So, waiting also bothers you?"

"Did you just come here to see how I think or something?"

"I came here to offer you a job."

"Doing what?"

"The same kind of thing you did at the park."

I paused. "I don't even know your name."

"And?"

"How do I know your offer is legitimate?"

"How does knowing someone's name make anything legitimate?"

"I don't know. But you look an awful lot like some kinda hitman or something."

"And?"

"Are you?"

"No."

"Then, why are you still hiding your face when no one's around?"

"Aren't you around?"

At this point, I didn't know which was more irritating; his overly casual tone or the fact that he was still answering my questions with more questions.

"You want me in your group, right?"

"Organization," he corrected. "And I'm not certain, since you haven't accepted my offer yet."

"How can I when I'm not sure I can trust you?"

"I'm not asking you to trust me."

"But you expect me to say yes?"

"Not necessarily. But we don't usually ask twice. So, if you would rather not be in consideration, you are free to decline — in which case, this will be the last time we speak."

"I'm not saying no. I'm just...Wait. You just said you don't 'usually' ask twice, right?"

"Glad you're listening."

I decided against arguing further for sake of the more pressing question. "Can this be one of those times you ask twice?"

"Want some time to think it over, huh?" He ran his finger through his short neatly trimmed hair. "Yeah, I guess it's fine if you want to consult your physician or librarian or whatever."

"You don't have to be so sarcastic about it."

"Point taken," he began, turning away. "Man, Ari and Amani must've had their hands full with this one," he sighed.

His words were like an arrow to the chest, sparking a both anger and curiosity. "What did you just say?"

"You have until tomorrow to decide."

"Wait! How do you know my parents?" I demanded, starting after him. But he swung his hand forming a small cyclone around him. I shielded my eyes from the swirling leaves and dust, and by the time the wind had died down, he was gone. With my peace and concentration thoroughly ruined, I headed back home.

The lines of sunlight shined through my window painting the ceiling a yellow-green. *Why'd I even bother asking for more time? I already knew what I'd wanted to say.* I'd lucked into a once-in-a-lifetime offer. But I couldn't help feeling anxious about it.

Of course, for all I knew this "organization" was another army disaster waiting to happen. And if it was, there'd be no Hachi to bail me out this time around. Still, it wasn't like I had much time to think it over. In fact, I had already taken so much time thinking, it was getting dark. "A quick patrol might help me come up with something," I said to myself, getting up to change. "Hopefully."

[8]

GREEN EYES

Fighting alone has its advantages. You have all the decision power. You're both your best and worst member. And the moment you don't like how things are going, you can call it a night.

But being part of a team automatically makes you a democracy. You can be outvoted by the majority or vetoed by the leader. In other words, you're a lot more likely to get forced into situations you'd rather avoid.

So, what was compelling me to blindly join Mr. Sarcasm-in-a-suit's organization? He'd practically made a game of dodging my questions. Even the Army gave me the info I needed before joining the Academy. I shook away my doubts as I took to the rooftops of the Eastern Port District in New Callastryne. The echo of cracking wood pulled my attention, beckoning me to investigate. Imagine my surprise at stumbling upon what looked a lot like a burglary in progress.

There were six men in total. Two smaller men were clearing debris from the back door of the warehouse, while four larger men kept a lookout. I figured the smaller men were the brains of the operation. But, judging from the trouble they were having breaking in, "brains" sounded pretty generous. One signaled a big thief over, who ripped the remainder of the door from its hinges like cardboard and carelessly tossed it aside. The two smaller burglars entered with the door destroyer and one other lookout.

"Two on one sounds like decent odds to me," I said, focusing energy into my legs. I leapt from the rooftop and landed; hitting the ground with a boom. The lookouts noticed and immediately rushed me.

The first guy tried to bowl me over. But I slipped past him and caught the guy behind him with an uppercut to the solar plexus before he could get a good grip on my shirt. The guy doubled over and sank to the ground; accepting defeat.

I spun around and leapt at the first guy. He tried to block as I threw my fist at his chin. My knuckles slammed into his forearm and he yelped in pain. I followed up with a left hook to the jaw that put him down next to his buddy. *Two down, four to go.*

I rushed over to the doorway and put my back against the wall. If anyone was listening, they would've heard the scream. Sure enough, a third lookout rushed out to check on his partners. By the time he'd realized I was behind him, it was already too late.

I stepped into a shadowed corner, until the other three emerged, shocked to find the rest of their team out of commission. Each of them dropped what they were carrying and pulled strange looking firearms from their jackets. Each one resembled a stone claw holding a jewel — likening them more to an artifact than a weapon. My stomach tightened. *What kind of guns are those? More importantly, why wasn't I expecting something like this?*

If Shawin's training had included dodging projectiles, I could've at least been certain my night wouldn't end in a hospital or morgue. I'd have to make due with enhanced speed and hope for the best. I crept closer. But my foot hit something heavy that scraped the ground and clunked over. I froze, certain I'd alerted them. *No, their ears aren't that good.* I took a breath and knelt down to reach for the item; a brick. I grabbed it, aimed, and tossed it.

They all jumped around—weapons pointed—as it clanged against the ground behind them. I shot out from the shadows, both arms extended. Before they could react, I clotheslined the two scrawnier guys so hard they nearly back-flipped before hitting the ground. I spun and started toward the last criminal, but his weapon stopped me in my tracks. The jewel in it glowed a fierce orange.

"I dunno who you think you are, but it's game over for you kid," the big guy said.

A chill slinked down my throat, my mind a swirl of panic. I quickly assessed my options, wondering if my next words would end with a hole or three in my chest. But the devilish grin coloring his face provided confidence that saying nothing wouldn't end any better.

"What's wrong? Afraid to fight like a man?" The words pressed out before my frontal lobe could properly filter them.

He shrugged. "Cleaner this way. I bash your little face in, my hands get bloody."

"You're afraid of blood? Your excuse is as weak as you are." I don't know where the words were coming from, but they'd hit their mark.

The burly man glanced at the others then tucked his weapon away. "By the time I'm done with you, you'll wish I'd ended it quickly."

He charged me, swinging with enough force to take my head off. Ultimately, Shawin's focus on defense worked in my favor as I slipped through his offense. The bonus was that he was sloppily throwing his punches as if brute strength alone could somehow chip away at speed and technique. News flash—it couldn't.

Just as he started to tire himself out, I threw a side kick into his chest to make sure he got the message. He bounced off a concrete wall and fell to the ground. The fight was over in one hit. Or so I thought.

Before I could turn away, he pressed off the ground. I lowered into a stance, preparing to kick harder when the skin on his face and hands suddenly turned rigid and gray. Almost like...stone.

He rocked to his feet and brushed a hand over his chest. "Let's see you try that again." He charged headlong like an enraged beast, his heels booming against the pavement with every step.

I dove out of the way, narrowly avoiding him. He slowed to a stop, turned, and charged again, his arms swinging like sledgehammers attached to meaty shoulders. A rocky fist hammered down, and I twisted away. Stone arms tore through the air with so much weight, it was like the vacuum they created could've sucked me in if I wasn't careful.

The moment he left an opening, I dipped and drove my fist into his side with all I had. Pain sparked from my fist and rocketed through my arm to shoulder. It felt like I'd just punched a brick wall. But in the end, I was still on my feet, and he was back on the ground.

He clutched his side looking surprised. But he wasn't alone. My knuckles had become jagged mountains amongst the thick layer of gray skin, reaching from my fingertips all the way up my elbow.

He stood with a grimace, his eyes darting between me and my arm. I shifted into a defensive stance, which he took as an invitation to swing again. I slipped to one side and connected a kick to the back of his neck. He skidded and tumbled over; the layer of stone crumbling from his body.

Before I could make sure he was actually unconscious, the scrape of footsteps pulled my attention. The rest of his team was back on their feet, trying to escape. I started to give chase, but they broke off in different directions. I turned back, expecting to at least make do with the one I'd put down. Except he wasn't down. He was already on his feet and stumbling back into the warehouse. My frustration took the form of an audible sigh, as I ran in after him.

Maybe he's a heavy breather. The thought crossed my mind as I boosted my hearing. I took a deep breath and listened quietly. Nothing. I lowered myself to the ground, listening for footsteps. After a beat, I made out rapid tapping hitting the pavement. But my excitement only lasted a few beats, before the sound suddenly faded.

But it wasn't just the footsteps. All sound was fading out until I couldn't even hear myself breathe. I felt like the planet was shifting around me until my body went numb, and I collapsed face first. Heat radiated from my chest, pulsing throughout my body. I felt so...empty. *What in Hadal is happening?*

I couldn't have overextended myself. I would've felt it coming. My heart jack-hammered in my chest, like it was trying to break my rib cage.

I racked my brain, hunting for some explanation for my sudden plight. Before I could come up with anything, darkness slithered into view. Confirmation of how dire my situation was. *This can't be how it ends.* Suddenly, clear blue eyes sliced the darkness, and the spinning world ground to a halt. My throat opened up, and my senses returned just in time for me to taste my dinner as it sprayed from my mouth.

Stomach successfully emptied, I pushed myself to my feet and stumbled forward. Voices were coming from just around the corner. I wiped away the sweat beading on my forehead and realized the layer of stone skin on my arm had fallen away. *All my powers must've faded. But why?* I peeked around the corner and found the burglars had regrouped in front of someone in a tattered hooded cloak. They didn't hesitate to pull those unusual weapons on him, taking aim like an execution squad.

What I witnessed next filled me with terror. Flashes of green glowed under the hood as the burglar's firing arms spontaneously separated from their bodies. Before they even realized what had happened, the larger men's torsos split at the waist. Organs fled the bodies as they flopped to the ground.

Oh sh—! My eyes bulged as a shadow of dread engulfed me.

The next thing I knew, the last two burglars were hovering in front of him, eyes wide with fear. He fished through their pockets and pulled out a data stick.

"Third spheres entrusted with this task? Disappointing," the guy in the cloak remarked.

"You will burn for this!" One of the men spat.

"You first."

Without warning, azure flames enveloped the two men. My eyes remained fixed on the horror; wishing I could unsee it all, but too afraid to look away.

The figure tucked the data stick into his cloak. Then things went from terrible to much more terrible when his emerald eyes snapped onto mine with an intensity that made the hair on my neck stand on end. It should've been my cue to run, but my legs weren't taking messages from my brain.

"You're gifted too, huh?" I blurted as the man started in my direction. It wasn't the smoothest thing to say, but I figured it was better than, "Good job murdering those six burglars." Still, my words had no effect. He was one step away from being within attack range — and I was the only one left to attack. With his next step, my breath caught. And by the time I'd realized I still had the option to breathe, I also realized that he was already passed me.

"This isn't a game," he said in a tone so dark, chills rippled through me. "If you get in my way, you will join them."

I whirled around, but no one was there. The emptiness that'd lingered ever since I went all woozy became a flood of energy, heightening my senses so suddenly, my head jerked at the blaring of peace enforcer sirens off in the distance. The sound was getting louder, which was ample reason to call it a night. Of course, Mr. Green-Eyed Bandit's death warning did a number on my nerves. All I could think about on the way home was what I would say to the visor guy when I saw him again.

[9]

THE GUILD

I t's not every day the bags under my eyes have bags of their own. But after a restless night, dreaming of the many ways the Green-Eyed Bandit could end me, I was starting to consider becoming nocturnal to help chase away nightmares. It wouldn't take long to settle into a new rhythm, and my job search might even turn up better options if I was open to the shifts no one else wanted.

The fact that we were on entirely different levels didn't sit well with me for another reason. The gap between us was much larger than the one between Shawin and me. It was the kind of gap that could take anums to bridge. So, why did I feel a twinge of excitement as I entered the kitchen? Speaking of the kitchen, why was mine void of breakfast options? My answer came in the form of a note on the counter:

I'll pick up more groceries after work. Credits for breakfast are in your union account.

Love, Uncle Hachi.

I checked my timechain. Ten aurins had been deposited into my account. Not much. But it would at least get me a monarch-sized soho from *Soho Time*.

The door chimed as I entered the shop. And like clockwork, the tangy, sweet scent of fresh fruit flooded my nose. As I waited for them to finish my order, my mouth was like a dam barely holding back water. I slurped it so fast, a sharp pain filled my forehead. Not that anyone cared. The girl behind the counter made a gesture as if to say I was occupying a necessary space that somehow made her job more difficult.

I headed for the door and I realized she wasn't the only one with eyes on me. To my right, a man in a suit was holding his digipad just below eye level. He offered a nod and waved me over to his table. It took a couple beats to realize it was the guy from the park.

"You're early," I said.

He nodded again. "Have a seat."

"So...?" he said before taking a sip of his soho.

"So...?" I repeated.

"Your answer?"

"A little impatient, don'tcha think? It hasn't even been twenty segments."

"Who said you had twenty segments?" He took another sip.

I gave a deadpan look. But his expression was even more apathetic than anything I could've produced. I sighed at the realization that my effort was wasted. "I want your name first."

"Excuse me?"

"I still don't even know who you are. Far as I know, you belong to some terrorist organization or some crazy cult or something. The least you could do is tell me your name."

He paused, still completely void of expression. "K."

"'Kay' what?"

"Just K."

"Like the letter 'k'?" He nodded. "Is that your real name?"

"Why's that matter? You asked for a name."

"Not *a* name. *Your* name!"

"I go by lots of names. You want me to list them all?"

I leaned onto my elbows. "Sure."

He stared for a beat. "Just call me K." He took another sip.

"You're not too good at rolling out the welcome mat, ya know?"

He sighed. "Look kid, the choice is yours. Don't drag this out for me. We both know you've already made your decision, which has nothing to do with my name."

"Fine," I said, leaning back. "I don't wanna know your name anyway."

"Do we seriously have to go through this every time?" He murmured to himself.

"What?"

"Listen," he refocused. "This isn't like the Army."

"How do you know about the Army?"

"It's our job to know. Makes it easier to avoid the kinds of mistakes that you can't afford many more of in your current position. That said, I'll ask one more time before I walk."

He took another sip.

I hesitated. "What if I don't like how you guys operate?"

"There's no penalty for changing your mind, somewhere down the line." The look in his eyes turned dangerous. "But I'll warn you now. We have a way of doing things. So, if you're with us, you operate how we operate. Understood?"

I nodded.

"Good. Now, you in or out?" He rolled up his digipad and slid the device into his jacket pocket.

The next words out of my mouth would be the most important in my young life. I'd seen what it was like going it alone. And after my run-in with the Green-Eyed Bandit of Death, I wasn't too keen on keeping things as they were. "You promise you guys can make me stronger?"

A small curl creased into the corner of his mouth. "Much stronger."

"Then, I'm in."

He stood up and started for the door. "Excellent. Follow me."

The walk was longer than expected, finally ending at the eight story caelrail station. I didn't ride caelrails often but compared to the more common but slower terrarails, the ride was considerably faster and smoother.

Our stop was the Central District Downtown, which was bustling with too many people to hold much of a conversation. Of course, K seemed to be completely ignoring me the whole ride anyway. So, I endured the awkward silence until we'd reached our stop.

"Didn't wanna talk on the rail in case anyone was listening," K said, just as I started to speak.

"Who would be listening to our conversation?"

"Any number of entities. Secrets can be traded for more secrets or used to remove obstacles. And for many, we're an obstacle."

"So, a bunch of bad guys want to get rid of your organization?"

"It's not always that black and white."

"Why not?"

"There's a time and place for that conversation too. This is neither."

"Is that why you haven't told me your real name?"

"No need for risk, when you don't know what's at stake. By the way, do you have enough sense of direction to know which way we're heading?"

"We're heading north."

"Now you know my real name."

"North?"

"The 'e' at the end is silent."

I paused. "Visor guy sounded better."

"Everyone's a critic."

"You never told me where we're going, by the way."

"Headquarters. The rest of the team is waiting for you, and today is your first day of training."

"That fast, huh?"

"That a problem?"

I shook my head. "Just making an observation."

"Speaking of observations, here's mine: I'm not keen on training you, but the boss is forcing me to as the condition for recruiting you."

"It wasn't up to you?" Northe shrugged.

"Yes and no. The boss usually approves a request before approaching a potential candidate."

In the pause, I remembered that Northe approached me as soon as my fight with the monster was over. It could only mean —.

"I'm not the boss."

On the corner of *Central Avenue,* a massive skyscraper stood between two buildings that collectively made up roughly half its height — The *BNP Administrative and Logistics* building. There was a sheen to the brick red edifice that made it look like it'd been sprinkled with glitter and contrasted with the tinted windows lining up the center in three columns. The automatic glass doors slid open to reveal a large lobby with an elderly security guard sitting behind the security desk to the right.

Northe raised a hand at the guard, and he gave a slow nod, as we passed him and stopped at one of four lifts. Northe pressed the lift call button like five times.

"You in a hurry or something?" I asked.

"Not particularly." The far-right lift door opened, and as I started toward it, Northe held his arm out. "Not that one." He pressed the button again, holding for a count. The far-right lift closed, and beats later the far-left lift opened. "This is us."

As we stepped in, I heard the scuffling of feet. Someone else was rushing towards the lift. I reached for the door as a woman came into view when Northe pulled me by the shoulder and pressed the door close button. The woman's eyes intensified as she ran at the lift. But the door shut before she could reach it.

"This lift isn't for her." There was a hint of aggression in his voice that contrasted his previously casual tone.

"Does this lift ever work for anyone not in your organization?"

"No. And I'm not a fan of employing our current methods for keeping it that way whenever an outsider slips in unwanted." I started to ask what kinds of methods they used when Northe interrupted the thought.

Pressing two buttons per finger — starting from his index and working down to his pinky—Northe chose eight different floors. He held his thumb over the ninth button, releasing after the panel beeped. At a glance, it looked like he was goofing around. But there did seem to be some order to it. He waved and smiled up at the top left corner of the lift.

"What are you—?"

"Might wanna brace yourself," he said.

"Brace myself for whaaaaaaaa!"

The lift plummeted down into what felt like the depths of Hadal. My feet lifted off the ground, and my stomach jumped into my throat. Northe lifted too, but he seemed completely indifferent to it. He reached into his jacket pocket and pulled out a timechain and tapped his ear. "Yup," he answered calmly.

"Heeeey!" I yelled, but he completely ignored me.

"Yeah, I got him...Yeah, that's him screaming...He'll be fine."

The lift ground to a halt, slowing so quickly, I thought somebody had turned on the emergency brakes. I landed on all fours, intense pressure forcing me to the floor.

"See you in a few," Northe finally said, before severing the link. "You alright down there?" he asked.

"Wonderful. Just need a hash." I muttered.

"Sure? This is the easy part."

I ignored him, eventually stumbling to my feet as the wave of dizziness passed. All I could do was hope the lift ride wasn't an everyday thing.

We stepped out of the lift and into what looked like a terrarail station. White lighting flooded the immaculately kept subterranean station which housed a white-on-white terrarail. The terrarail door opened, welcoming me as I reluctantly followed Northe inside, hoping I wasn't about to experience a horizontal version of the lift.

Surprisingly, the ride was smooth and quiet. And despite us being alone, Northe was equally quiet. I still didn't know what to expect when we reached headquarters, and instead of filling me in, Northe pulled out his digipad, quickly becoming engrossed in whatever was flashing across the screen.

"You know, staring a hole into my forehead won't cure your paranoia," Northe said without looking up.

"I'm not paranoid," I said.

"Then relax and enjoy the ride, Kid. This terrarail is as safe as it gets."

"Did you...read my thoughts?"

"Let's just say I've learned to read faces. And yours is what psychiatrists refer to as an open book."

The terrarail coasted to a gentle stop, and the doors opened revealing an identical station. Unfortunately, it put us in front of another lift.

"Are there stairs I can take?" Northe stepped in shaking his head. I swallowed stepping in after him and immediately lodging myself into a corner.

Northe studied me, an eyebrow raised. The doors closed and the lift rose at an astonishingly safe speed.

"Nearly two billion people make up the Orbis population, but only an estimated ten thousand possess the potential for refracting."

"Refracting?"

"Our term for using special abilities. Users are called Refractors; our term for Gifted. And the number may sound high, but of all the supernatural beings here, we're the minority."

"Supernatural beings?"

"Yup. Aengel, daemon, people with superpowers."

"Seriously? Aengel and daemon?"

"Who else would toil against El's will?"

I stopped to consider Northe's question. "People?"

Northe placed a hand on his forehead and chuckled. "Alright. Quick history lesson. The *templum* tells us that aengel and daemon have been around since before Orbis came into existence. What you may not know is that daemon—and even some aengel—have been working in secret for centuries to enslave or altogether eradicate humankind. You'd think those of us with the power to stop them would band together. But people are people, regardless of common ground. So, instead of taking the logical path to survival, Refractors have only emulated the dissension and segregation amongst themselves that initially led to the separation of nations and authority that every person is forced to deal with today." Northe shrugged and shook his head. "Thankfully, someone had the good sense to create an organization to keep the world's 'supernatural entities' in check, before the balance of power could tip so far as to ensure humankind's destruction. We are that organization. Welcome to the International Guild of Investigators of the Supernatural—IGIS for short."

I followed Northe out of the lift and into the most technologically advanced place I'd ever seen. It was like walking through a science future vid. Triangular panels formed a massive transparent dome that surrounded dozens of glass and metal buildings. Sunlight beamed through to paved sidewalks neatly lined with strips of grass.

"Why does this place look so much like a city?" I asked.

"Probably because it is. But you won't find it on any map. Vaticia is home to IGIS headquarters, housing all of our offices and local agents."

"Where did all this come from?" Northe shrugged. "You don't know?"

"It's my policy to only ask questions when especially inconvenienced. Speaking of which, we'd better hurry. The girls are waiting. And they're not half as patient as I am."

If he qualified as patient, I didn't want to think about what that meant for the rest of the team.

We arrived at an inconspicuous white three-story house. "This is the team seven dormitory. D7 for short." He stopped me at the door. "Listen to me very carefully. Do not—I repeat—DO NOT allow the girls to goad you into a fight."

Is he joking? "Why would I fight girls?" The look he gave made me regret asking.

Inside, the house was surprisingly spacious, sporting an ultra-modern array of whites and grays that were so polished you could almost see your reflection. A faint spicy-flowery scent wafted through the air.

"What am I smelling?" I asked.

"Nice, right? It's a blend of oils I threw together to help calm the energy in here."

"Does it work?"

"So, this is the new recruit?" a voice called from behind. It carried a faint accent that I couldn't place.

I turned, to find two women approaching. The taller woman was easily some-where in her late twenties, while the shorter one looked younger than me. But they were both very striking.

"Yes ladies," Northe said. "This is Serec." Northe gestured toward the taller woman. "Serec, this is our team commander, Surket." Up close, she was notice-ably taller than me, which made her tower over the girl. Her sharp features and muscular build, likened her to a world-class athlete.

"You guys were there when that weird creature attacked," I said.

"We were," Surket confirmed, extending her hand. "Nice to finally meet you." Her grip on my wrist was as firm as mine on hers. And the piercing gaze of her violet eyes had an edgy sense of danger that made Northe's warning about fighting her seem like a lot less of a joke. Still, her partially shaved head, long wavy hair, facial piercings, and tribal tattoos pointed to an exotic appeal that I could appreciate.

"Likewise," I said. "I'm excited to be a part of the team."

"Except you're still a recruit," the shorter girl commented matter-of-factly, stepping between Surket and me. "That means you aren't a part of the team yet."

I tilted my head left. "I'm sorry, and you are..."

Northe gave my shoulder a gentle squeeze. "This is our technician, Raven. Anyway, let's go have a look at—"

"I'm the person telling you that you must earn your place on this team," Raven interrupted. There was a condescending edge to her voice that I found masterfully exasperating. "Or did you assume that you could stroll in and be welcomed with open arms?"

"I assumed," I began failing to keep things smooth, "that I was being recruited to fight monsters, not a teenage girl with an attitude problem."

"Calm down you two," Northe said.

"I am calm," I said. "She's the one who's making things tense for no reason."

Raven's eyes narrowed into an icy death glare, as she closed in, bringing her face so close, I could feel her breath. "You will quickly learn that nothing I do is arbitrary. Despite your lack of understanding, I assume you possess the sense to know when you are outmatched."

My jaw tightened. "What's your problem?"

"To be honest, I'm disappointed. I was expecting more from you. But I can now see that I was wrong."

There was any number of things I could've said, but Northe's grip on my shoulder tightened. Remembering his warning, I turned away. At a glance, Surket and Raven were complete opposites. While Surket looked like the captain of a professional sports team, Raven seemed like a petite spoiled prep schooler. As I stared at her over my shoulder, it all started to make sense. As the youngest member of the team, she was probably trying to prove how tough she was. Considering that, I should've taken pity on her. But if in her mind, strength was the key to earning a place on the team, the least I could do was prove I wasn't a pushover.

"Uh, Surket?" Northe said with an expectant look.

Surket shrugged. "Your recruit, your responsibility."

"I got this," I said, facing Raven. "I know what you're trying to do. But, unlike you, I don't need to antagonize strangers to prove how tough I am."

"Unlike me, all you've proven is how quickly you can back down once it's clear you're outmatched. I wonder, was this the reason your Army career was so short-lived?"

I've heard that patience is a virtue. But, sometimes, I'm okay with the fact that it's one of those virtues I may never get under control.

"Actually," I said. "I was court-martialed for breaking the nose of the last person who felt like invading my personal space and provoking me for no good reason. Kind of like you're doing right now."

I was hoping my tone would—in the immortal words of Hachi—make my point as clear as quartz. But for someone so quick to call me dumb, Raven just wasn't getting it. She stepped back and offered a breathy smile, before heading toward a glass door at the far end of the room.

"I'll be in the training room," she called over her shoulder. "I'd be interested in seeing if you can actually demonstrate what happened to that last person you spoke of. But that's a pretty big if, I'm sure."

Before my reasoning could tell me how bad of an idea this was, my legs pulled me away from Northe's guiding hand. "You were gonna show me the training room anyway, right Northe?" I asked.

"Yeah," Northe said after a pause.

I followed her into an open space with dark, padded flooring. The space split into a small area with weights and other workout equipment, and a larger open area that looked like it was made for sparring.

"The rules are simple," she began. "If I put you down, I score a point. If—by some fluke—you manage to knock me down, you earn a point. The first to three points wins."

"Who's keeping score?"

"You can't count to three?"

"I just don't want you trying to cheat in a victory."

Raven gave a smug look. "Fine. I'll scan you in at the HMI."

"The what?"

"Holographic Mapping Interface." She pointed to a large touchscreen in the corner of the room. "It tracks your movement and records the number of times you go horizontal on the mat."

Northe and Surket stepped in as I followed Raven over to the HMI. Northe looked disappointed, but Surket seemed amused.

"Good afternoon, Raven," a robotic female voice said.

"Good afternoon, Anni. Please scan in a new user."

"Confirmed."

"Just follow her instructions," Raven said.

"State your name," Anni instructed.

"Serec."

"Pleased to meet you, Serec. Please place your hand in front of the screen."

I held out my right hand, and the screen turned green. "Scanning complete. Lower your hand and take one step back, please." I followed the instructions. But nothing happened.

"Is it—"

"Let it finish." Raven's cold tone nearly pulled a less than gentleman-like response. But I told myself to save it for sparring.

"Scanning complete," Anni finally said.

Raven led me back to the sparring area. "Let's see if Monument Park was just an anomaly."

Raven assumed a fighting stance, and I followed suit.

"Ready when you are," I said.

But Raven didn't move. I started to repeat myself, when she lunged at me, nearly catching my face with her fist. She maintained momentum, swinging with crazy accuracy and speed. Keeping me on the defensive.

Her persistence was enough to back me into the wall before I knew it. But when she finally switched out from furious punching into a roundhouse kick, I knew I could take the advantage. I raised my arm to block. But the sheer force behind her kick was more than I expected. I cringed at the sharp sting it caused. But she'd have to do better than that to throw me off my game.

In one motion, I rotated my wrist to grip her ankle and lifted her leg. Then, before she could react, I swept my foot behind her supporting leg, knocking her flat on her butt.

"Point—Serec," Anni announced.

I held out a hand. But she swatted it away and lunged again with an elbow. I slipped to one side, grabbed her arm, and pulled it down while pressing my other hand into her leg. Her momentum forced her into a somersault and ended with her back smacking against the mat.

"Point—Serec."

"Do you wanna stop here?" I asked. "Despite your terrible attitude, I'm not too thrilled about beating up a girl."

Raven's scowl faded, and I caught her glance over at Surket, who gave a single nod. *Does this mean the match is over?* Raven gave me an uncharacteristically sweet smirk; something I would have appreciated over the grimace she offered at our introduction. "I'm impressed. I gave two intentional openings and you exploited them without fail."

Intentional? She's gotta be bluffing.

"Do you possess the necessary skill to earn the final point?"

"Guess we'll see," I said, trying to hide my building anxiety.

Suddenly, her aspect completely changed. Her expression. Her fighting stance. Even the look in her eyes. I tried not to make much of it. But there was a building anxiety in my stomach. With palms facing down, and arms at her side, she looked like she was preparing to perform a sophisticated cultural dance.

Before I could fathom a guess at what Raven was preparing to do, she tucked her chin and rushed me again; focusing all of her attacks at my face. It wasn't easy keeping my eyes open through her foreign movements. But the longer I only focused on defending, the more I started to notice a pattern.

Once I had her rhythm, I went for her arm. But she slipped around me and dipped out of sight. I twisted around to find her, and something slammed into the back of my legs; tearing my feet from under me.

"Point—Raven," Anni said as Raven stood over me with a stoic expression.

I jumped to my feet, wanting to rub at the dull throb in the back of my legs. But if I showed any weakness, I knew she'd try and exploit it.

"Good move," I said.

She waved for me to come at her again. "I know."

In that moment, nothing would've been more satisfying than tackling her to the ground and knocking the self-satisfaction right out of her. But I was only one point away. The last thing I needed was to give her an opportunity to catch up with an amateur head-on attack. The techniques Shawin taught me were the surest way to finish the fight.

I crept forward until we were little more than an arm's length apart. I started to make a move when she slipped past me again. I turned, but didn't she her until immediately after her leg jammed even harder into the back of my knees. She clasped her hands over my forehead and yanked—forcing my legs to fold and the back of my head to thud against the mat.

"Point—Raven."

"Would you like to stop here?" she asked. "Despite your gross incompetence, I'm not too thrilled about beating up arrogant little boys."

Heat pulsed through me so quickly that my arm lashed out at her out of pure reflex. She leaned away and jumped to her feet. But I twisted over and leapt at her, taking another swing. In my frustration, I'd forgotten that I didn't actually want to hurt her.

That ended up being the least of my worries though. During my swing, I barely caught any movement from her before my head and feet had somehow switched places. The next thing I knew, my body was folding into itself over the mat. The feeling of prickling needles stretched all the way from my legs up my back.

"Point—Raven. Score limit reached. Raven wins," Anni announced.

By the time I'd realized what'd happened, Raven was walking away.

"You couldn't even last three hashes," she said.

"Rematch." I yelled at the back of her head.

"Don't be a sore loser. Check with Anni if you want to review the fight."

"You afraid? Is that it?" Raven followed Surket out the door without a second glance.

I started to taunt her again, when Northe's hand on my shoulder drew my attention. "Don't worry. You're not the first person to take my warnings too lightly. Anyway, wanna see your room?" He started for the door without waiting for my answer. I peeled my body from the mat, leaving some pride behind as I hurried after him.

Northe led me through the rest of the house; pointing out several interesting gadgets along the way. He ended the tour at the massive vid screen in the den that I had been too preoccupied with Raven to notice before.

"We've got archives of every popular program," Northe said, leaning close. "I'm partial to those prep school dramas. Sure, they're trashy. And some of the plots are kinda stupid. But you know what they say: one man's teen drama is another man's last-ditch pastime."

A chuckle bubbled up from the back of my throat.

"At least your face still works. I thought I'd lost you after you fell into Raven's trap, despite my warning."

"I get it. I should've taken your advice more seriously."

"Yeah, you should've. Now I'm down one segment of gaming tomorrow."

"What do you mean?"

"I wagered with Surket that you'd at least recognize Raven was out of your league before she beat you. Now, I have to start my day helping her with office work tomorrow, instead of playing Call to Arms 3, like I should be. Guess it's my fault for having faith in a newbie." Northe folded his arms and turned away. "Maybe I could just wake up a segment earlier."

"Thanks for the vote of confidence."

He raised an eyebrow. "Raven's been training under Surket for half her life. She may look like a timid teenager, but she's actually a highly lethal operative. Besides, if she lost, Surket would've had her skip dinner for more training."

Hearing that made losing a little easier to stomach. Even if Raven was a snobby brat, I wouldn't want her to starve "Speaking of which, where'd you learn to fight like that?"

"Nowhere really. Just stuff I picked up from watching people."

"That was a lot to pick up just 'watching people.'"

"I've got good eyes."

Northe eyed me for a beat, then shrugged. "Well, here's a little nugget of wisdom for you. Whenever a woman rubs you the wrong way, find a way to handle the problem peacefully."

I nodded; more than a little doubtful it could ever be that simple.

"In fact," Northe continued, "I'm feeling generous. So, here's a second nugget for the price of one: Never ignore the wisdom of your mentor."

"Mentor?"

He pointed at himself and winked. "Or perhaps you enjoy having your ego crushed by angry women."

"You don't have to say it like that."

"Lighten up. You're not the first guy Raven put down."

"Raven beat you? Or maybe Surket?"

Northe snorted. "Of course not. Why would you think that?"

"Well, you just said—"

"Okay, forget that part. Let's just say that every defeat teaches you something about yourself."

"Like what?"

"You'll figure it out sooner or later. Anyway, this is you." Northe pointed to the door behind him. "My room's two doors over, in case you need something."

"Are we the only ones up here?"

"The girls are down the hall—which is pretty wise, considering the old saying." I lifted my eyebrows. "You know? About women being hard to live with?"

"Harder to live without?"

"No. Well, I mean..." Northe sighed. "The first part's the only part that makes any real sense. Anyway, here." Northe handed me a sleek silver bangle.

"That's your Tactical Action Band or TAB. It may look like an ordinary bangle, but it's actually your access to most things in D7, including the team. We use it to communicate, as well as open any electronic lock in here."

"That's pretty smooth. But how often am I gonna sleep here?"

"How much sleep do you need?"

"That's not what I meant."

"We work most days, so it's easier living here. We can make arrangements if you'd like to have a few essentials sent from home." My chest went cold. So much had happened in one day, I'd forgotten all about Hachi. And I couldn't just say I was working for some top-secret organization. "Something wrong?"

"No," I lied. "Everything's smooth."

"Great. Cause dinner's in ten."

"Dinner?"

"Yeah, it comes after lunch. Usually around 16.00 for us."

I didn't realize so much time had passed. Hachi's note said he'd be grocery shopping after work, which left me just over a segment before he'd be home. Hopefully, I could think of something during dinner.

The spread was like nothing I'd seen in-person. The scent of steamed plant greens mingled with the sweet aroma of freshly baked bread in a way that could make a hunger strike worth breaking.

I arrived last to the table. But of the five seats, I made certain to choose the position farthest from Raven and her attitude. Even if something about her seemed oddly familiar, she wasn't exactly the type of girl I'd willingly associate with.

"About time," Raven huffed, as I took a seat.

"What's your hurry?" Northe said. "We can't eat until everyone's here anyway."

"Who else are we waiting for?" I asked.

"The Director," Surket replied. "He wanted to welcome you personally."

"Not that Derek deserves such an honor," Raven said under her breath.

"It's Serec," I corrected.

Raven shrugged. "Close enough."

"She's just trying to get under your skin, Kid," Northe remarked.

"So," I said as if pondering his words, "you're saying that Raven is like a common parasite?"

Surket grinned, but Raven looked unamused.

"I imagine you had plenty of opportunities to come up with insults, while you were kissing the floor earlier," she shot back.

"I did, actually. I can write them down for you, if you like."

A knock at the door interrupted us, and Surket went to answer it.

"Alright children," Northe said, "The Director's here, so play nice."

Raven cut her eyes at me, but I pretended not to notice.

Surket returned with a man in a hat and trench coat. When he pulled the hat away, the blood drained from my face.

"Serec," Surket started, "this is—"

"Uncle Hachi?" I interrupted.

"Uncle Hachi?!" Surket and Raven exclaimed in unison.

Hachi smiled. "Hi Serec. I take it, you've settled in and gotten acquainted with everyone?"

I frowned. "Uh, yeah. Uh..." was all I could manage as he took the seat next to me.

"How long did...I mean, why didn't you—?"

Hachi placed a hand on my shoulder. "Relax. It's late, I'm certain you've had a long day. Plus, I think I've held everyone up for dinner long enough. I promise I'll explain everything soon."

I nodded, still struggling to wrap my mind around what was happening.

"Tonight, I am honored to have my nephew join us for dinner. My hope is that—with the help of each of you—Serec will flourish here and make significant contributions to IGIS and to our cause." Hachi raised his glass high. "Please join me in welcoming Serec to the Guild." Everyone raised their glass, then took a drink. Even Raven.

[10]

DIVARMA

Division has made progress among the people here frustratingly slow. In-fighting has led to so many missed opportunities. Factions war against one another, depleting resources in a futile bid for power. Even those that seek to unify, create distrust through questionable actions. I can only hope that my involvement is not worsening this problem.

-The Traveler

The next morning, I awoke to a note on the closet that read: Wear this. Inside was a sleek black suit with a white dress shirt. Next to it, a stylish belt and a pair of black dress shoes sat on a small shelf. Some small circular insignia was embroidered over the left chest of the coat. The symbol in the circle was made up of thin intersecting rings that resembled a flower. An odd emblem, but it wouldn't even come close to the strangest thing I'd see that day.   I opened my door to upbeat music. After reaching the bottom of the staircase, I realized it was coming from the team office, where Surket was sitting behind a processor, clicking keys at lightning speed.

"You're up late," Surket commented without bothering to look up at me.

"Sorry," I said. "I didn't realize how late it was."

The words lingered momentarily as her eyes remained locked on the screen. "Don't make a habit of it," she finally replied. The tapping of keys cut through the music as it fought to fill the awkward void. "You're looking better."

I laughed nervously. "Yeah. Sorry for not keeping a cooler head yesterday."

She smirked. "I'm sure the experience was humbling. Don't make a habit of that either." I was starting to understand where Raven learned her lack of sympathy. But unlike Raven, Surket's tone held a subtle, reassuring warmth.

"Right. So, what are we doing today?"

"K has your assignment." She turned the music down and spoke into her TAB. "Time to get to work, Peipei." A hash later, Northe strolled in. "Serec's awake. Turn off your kid games and start your assignment."

"Vid games," Northe corrected.

"Don't care, just turn it off."

Northe half-scowled. "Ya know—"

"Stay sharp and keep your wits about you today, Serec," Surket interrupted.

I nodded and followed a newly disinterested Northe out of the office.

"You like vid games?" Northe asked.

"Yeah."

"How 'bout a quick round before we hit the streets?"

"I'd prefer not to make Surket mad."

Northe gave a breathy snort. "When isn't she mad?"

"Can't we wait 'til we get back? My first day with Raven was rough enough."

It only made sense that immediately after my comment, we would pass the training room and find Raven throwing a flurry of attacks into a translucent heavy bag. I stopped just long enough to take her in. Watching her made me unsure of what to appreciate more — her artful technique or the way she artfully fit into pink leggings and a sports top. I never imagined someone could be so alluring while dripping with sweat.

"You love conflict, don't you?" Northe remarked.

"What are you talking about?"

Northe nodded at the training room. I turned my head and nearly jumped out of my skin at the sight of Raven standing right behind me. I didn't realize someone looking up at me could be so intimidating.

"Unless you would like to take the place of that bag, I'd kindly advise you to keep your eyes to yourself."

Surprise only lingered momentarily, before abruptly swirling into exasperation. But Northe's first nugget of wisdom hadn't fallen on deaf ears.

"Sorry," was all I could manage. Raven cut her eyes at me and evaporated into droplets of light, reforming a moment later in front of the heavy bag.

"Did she just—"

"I don't think I've ever seen her hitting the bag that hard," Northe interrupted, patting me on the back. "Guess you bring out the best in people." He nodded for me to follow him, but Surket called just as we reached the den.

"Rima Peipei! I've got the intel on your mission," she said, handing him a digipad.

A wry smile crept onto his face as he tapped the screen. "Another arms dealer? That's three in three decs."

"It is odd. But I'd wager this one's also related to you know who."

Northe frowned. "Wagers only make sense when there's a chance you can win."

"Was helping me organize files really that hard?"

"Helping? I organized. You played with your knife."

"Speaking of games, why is this one still on?" Surket asked, pointing at the vid screen.

"Because I'm two hashes from finally unlocking the best weapon in the game." Surket folded her arms. "We're outta here as soon as I finish this mission."

Surket pointed at the vid screen. A spark crackled from her finger instantly powering everything down. "Mission complete," she said, turning toward the office. "Now start your real mission."

"Two segments of unsaved work," Northe said through gritted teeth. He closed his eyes and breathed deep through his nose. "Let's go, Kid."

Watching Northe and Surket almost felt like a replay of Raven and me, minus the climactic bare-knuckle ending. As the thought sank in, I suddenly understood the significance of Northe's warning about the girls. We left the compound the same way we came in. But knowing what to expect, I could at least mentally prepare for the lift from Hadal.

"What's today's mission about?" I asked.

"There've been recent reports of illegal distribution of stolen technology. So, we're stuck playing peace enforcer." Despite how easy it was to tell Northe was upset about his game possibly being fried, he was taking it a lot better than I would've if my vid game console had been short-circuited.

"I was thinking about what you said yesterday. About bringing some stuff from home."

"And?" Northe prompted.

"I was wondering how long it would take after I made a list."

"Depends on what you want sent over."

"Small stuff. Clothes, decor. Stuff like that."

"By 'small' are we talking gaming console small or…?"

"That was on my list. At least until I saw how Surket treated your console today."

Northe shook his head. "She's had a vendetta against me gaming, since the day I started."

"Any particular reason why?"

Northe shrugged. "Women don't like fun stuff. So, when they see us having fun without them, it flips their whole world upside down. At least, that's my theory. Third nugget for ya: keep your hobbies to yourself."

My stomach tightened as the lift doors opened to reveal the woman from the day before. The one that Northe closed the lift door on. But Northe seemed unaffected. In fact, a small chortle erupted from Northe as soon as he saw her. The woman's cold eyes followed Northe as we walked past her.

"Is it okay for her to take that lift?" I asked.

"Yep."

"But I thought outsiders weren't supposed to use that one."

"Minerva is the lead researcher in the Guild's Science & Technology division. But I've honestly hated her troll guts and nasty little attitude ever since we were in flight school together eight anums back. I guess you could say it's become an ambition of mine to take advantage of every opportunity to throw a fragment or two of revenge her way. I call 'em revenge-ments. Fourth nugget: Sometimes, a little revenge-ment can go a long way."

I didn't know if Northe was being serious or not, but at least he was smiling again. "I wouldn't have thought you were a pilot."

"Of course not," Northe said matter-of-factly. "You just met me." He'd missed the meaning behind my comment, which was probably for the best.

"Where are we going for today's mission?" I asked.

"Port District. Thankfully, it's a short caelrail ride away."

New Callastryne's Port District was where Green Eyes nearly ended me. For all I knew, we were intruding on his territory. And, even with Northe there, I wasn't keen on the intrusion. The caelrail ride was a blur. One hash, I was contemplating if I'd ever be strong enough to take on someone like Green Eyes. And the next hash, we'd reached our stop and—worst case scenario—I would have to find out firsthand what having a team really meant.

"How long have you been with The Guild?" I asked Northe.

Northe thought for a moment. "Roughly twelve anums."

"And Surket?"

"Hmm," he thought aloud. "Has it been nine anums...? Ten. Ten anums."

My next question was an obvious one. "Is she stronger than you?"

"Commanders don't have to be the strongest on the team if that's what you're getting at. They do, however, need excellent leadership skills and the willingness to do what a good leader does of their own volition." Northe's lackadaisical attitude definitely ruled him out of the second part. But I wondered if there was some other reason a twelve-anum veteran could be outranked by a junior agent. The caelrail slowed to a halt, and Northe stepped out onto a busy street lined with shops and food vendors. Northe seamlessly waded through the sea of consumers, while I struggled to keep up. Out of range of all edible smells, the walkways had finally cleared up enough for Northe to brief me on the mission.

"Our target is two blocks ahead," he said. "A repeat offender, suspected of illegal distribution of stolen weaponry."

"We're chasing an arms dealer?"

"An arms dealer with weapons of great interest to the Guild."

"Like lasers or missiles?"

"Not quite. We call them Divinus Arma—Divarma for short. One of the Guild's main purposes is to secure Divarma, which helps us maintain the balance of power between refractors, regular people, and the other supernatural beings running around. Of course, if the aengel had never come into our world, then we wouldn't have so much work on our hands." Everything Northe was saying might as well have been from out of some crazy science fantasy vid or something. It was hard to believe, much less understand.

"I get the danger of refractors and aengel. But what about the...Diva's Mama thing?"

Northe's lips pursed into a thin line. "I'm gonna need you to listen a little closer. Divarma are powerful supernatural weapons that came from the dark world: *Orbis Tenebris*. They can bend various forms of matter and energy, so against your more conventional magnetic or laser weapons, divarma wielders have a devastating advantage."

"And how exactly did these weapons end up here?"

"Aengel have always been drawn to the light of our world. But an event we call the Great Calamity created rifts in space-time that they've exploited to get here. And many of them bring stolen divarma along from Orbis Tenebris. If all that wasn't enough, we suspect a mysterious yet powerful aengel is responsible for turning the sky green six anums ago. Whatever the case, we can't let that kind of power go unchecked." Northe stopped in front of a rundown jewelry store and slipped on a pair of sunglasses and sleek black gloves—hitman gear if I'd ever seen it. "Which brings us here."

The windows were barred in the shoddiest way imaginable, and the wooden 'Ron T. Foster Jewelry' sign behind the window looked like it'd been written by a child. It was kind of odd, naming a jewelry store after something other than a jewel. But the name was the least of this store's problems. I followed Northe inside, pretending to browse the selection of wares until a tall, wiry man with an unusual accent appeared behind the counter. "Were you gentlemen looking for anything in particular?" It definitely wasn't an Aururian dialect. I could barely understand him, but Northe didn't miss a beat.

"I'm looking for a bangle," Northe answered. "Something elegant and stylish."

"But of course," the man replied. He opened the glass case, pulled out a tray of fancy bangles, and handed the first one to Northe. "This is one of our best pieces. It is of top quality and its sleek design is—"

"Ya don't say. You know, I have an eye for quality, and I can tell," Northe began, lowering his glasses, "that this bangle is as fake as the store housing it."

The man blinked hard. Northe leaned in closer. "I'm a little disappointed though. I mean, Ron T Foster is pretty obvious, don't you think? As far as anagrams go, I've seen better from you guys." It would've been nice if Northe clarified what made the anagram so obvious. But I'd have to just go with it. Northe turned and with the flick of his fingers, the window sign flipped over and cracked against the ground. The tall man's face grew feral like a cornered animal. "I'm not in the mood for games," Northe said. *Ironic choice of words.* "Where's the divarma?"

As the man's eyes shifted between us, I prepped my legs with a little extra power. The tension was at a boiling point, and the last thing I wanted was to get burned. "This one's yours, Kid." Before my brain could even process Northe's words, the tray of counterfeit bangles was flying toward my head. The man leapt over the counter and bolted for the door with a metal briefcase in hand.

I moved to block his path, which turned out to be a huge mistake. The man plowed into me, and I unexpectedly played the role of shield as we crashed through the front door and rolled along the ground. Well, more like I rolled, as he pushed away and took off down the road. I jumped to my feet and raced after him. Cool air brushed along my arms and legs; a sign that my uniform was in bad shape.

"Just leave him in one piece," Northe called after me, noting the damage. For such a lanky build, the man was faster than expected. But I managed to close the distance between us. I tackled him to the ground, and he tried to knock me away as we tumbled forward. At least, until a couple hard jabs to his ribcage took the fight out of him, and he wised up enough to curl into a ball.

I pushed to my feet and looked down at my suit. The sleeves were torn and my left pant leg was tattered. The sight alone boiled the blood in my face. But before I could move to hit him again, a gust of wind whistled past and Northe appeared.

With a stoic look, he yanked the man by the collar to his feet. "You don't seem to have a very high tolerance for pain," Northe began. "And yet you do something stupid like run away when I'm already in a bad mood. In the process, you've ruined my colleague's brand-new suit, and now I'm thinking it might not be a bad idea to let him treat you like a punching bag...unless you answer my questions truthfully and promptly." I'd really wished Northe hadn't thrown in that final condition. I bit down, clenching my fists in silent hope that the man was dumb enough to call Northe's bluff. But he just nodded nervously.

"Good," Northe said. "Who do you work for?"

"Y-you don't understand," the man said meekly. "If I talk, he'll—"

"Kid." Northe nodded at me and a smile etched into my face as I started toward the whimpering man.

"Zalier," he blurted. "It's Zalier."

"Zalier, huh?" Northe said, holding up a hand. "Why does that sound familiar...?" He thought for a moment, then smiled breathily. "Right. Anagrams. We're taking Ronald—or whatever his name is—with us."

"With us where?" I asked.

"To pay a visit to an old friend."

Northe turned and started in the opposite direction, which meant it was up to me to bring Ronald along. I sighed, grabbed Ronald's arm, and yanked him behind me.

"You're hurting me," Ronald yelled.

"Get over it," I said picking up the case and following Northe.

After several blocks of actively ignoring Ronald's whimpering, we finally reached the Callastryne Archives—a library containing the most extensive collection I'd ever seen of old books and rare books—all boring enough to put a city to sleep in beats. Public access was usually restricted, but Northe strolled right through the front entrance like it was his home away from home.

A guard blocked our path. "Please present your badge," he instructed sternly.

"We're here for a meeting with the superintendent," Northe replied. "Would you mind calling him for us?"

"I'm sorry sir, but Superintendent Zalier is very busy and has requested not to be disturbed."

Northe grinned. "I'm pretty sure he'll want to make time for me."

"I'm sorry sir, but the superintendent's orders were clear. You'll have to reschedule."

"Lovely," Northe nodded. "RAZIEEEEEL!" He roared so loudly, I cupped my hands over my ears, out of fear my eardrums would burst. "RAZIEL, I KNOW YOU HEAR ME!"

Dust rained from the ceiling as the building trembled. Beats later, a well-dressed man in a long dark robe rushed over to us.

"Just the man I wanted to see," Northe said. "How ya doin' buddy?"

The man frowned at the guard, then forced a diplomatic smile at Northe.

"How may I assist you?"

"We really should discuss this in private." Northe nodded at Ronald, who cowered the moment the man's eyes reached him.

The man sighed. "We can discuss this matter in my office."

We followed the superintendent through a large walkway lined wall-to-wall with shelves of books nearly reaching the ceiling. Sculptures and framed art were arranged throughout the area like a museum. There was even the familiar museum smell of old sterilized paper. Nostalgia reared its head as my mind drifted to days spent in the museum with my friend Liza. For a moment I wondered how she'd feel about me working for a secret organization. But I quickly refocused on Ronald, ensuring he remained between Northe and me until we were inside the superintendent's office. It was a dark room that resembled the wall-to-wall shelving of the rest of the archive, except the warm herbaceous aroma of thyme filled this room. It was safe to assume that Ronald wouldn't try running once we were inside the office.

"You become more brazen every time we meet, K," the superintendent said, closing the door behind us. "I'm certain I've requested that you not use my real name enough for you to remember by now."

"And I've requested that you stop arming your comrades, Raziel." Despite Northe's flat delivery, his tone contained a hint of danger that commanded the attention of the room.

Raziel walked over to a hardwood desk and sat in the large, intricately designed chair behind it. For a moment, I could have sworn I saw massive brown-feathered wings extending from Raziel's back. But upon blinking, I found nothing. The chair creaked as Raziel leaned forward, looking like he was searching for words.

"So, why is he on this side of the divide?" Northe pointed at Ronald.

Raziel's face went flush. "He had a specific purpose."

"Like the ones who almost annihilated a city block a couple decs back?"

"I told you, that was Lailah's doing. The little monster will be the end of us all. Were you aware that she had one of her minions steal one of my artifacts from here last night?"

"You can't be serious," Northe maintained his flat tone seeming more annoyed than concerned.

"Yes, my men reported that the girl escaped by running on the ceiling," he explained.

Ceiling!? No... it's just a coincidence.

"As troubling as that is, it doesn't change the ugly truth standing beside me." Northe motioned to Ronald.

"But, I was planning to—"

"Clearly you've forgotten how this arrangement works," Northe interrupted. "We've allowed you to remain in this world solely because I find you useful. But when your actions create problems for me, I find you a lot less useful. And when I can no longer find a use for you — well, we both know what happens, right?"

Raziel cleared his throat. "Right."

"Good," Northe said, flashing a dangerous smile. "And while we're on the matter of usefulness, you tracking anything on the creatures that have been popping up around town recently?"

"You mean those feral abominations that attack anything that moves?"

"Those would be the ones. I need info—anything you can get on them."

Raziel nodded. "I'll get my people on it."

"You do that." Northe nodded at me, and we started for the door.

"By the way," Raziel called, "I see you recovered a silver briefcase." He eyed my left hand.

Northe pointed to the case. "This case?"

"That would be the one. I'd be happy to take it off your hands. No need to bother yourself with it."

"How's it work?"

Raziel smiled nervously. "Pardon?"

"Razi, Razi. You know I hate when you play dumb with me, right?"

"We've only just acquired it. I've yet to determine its exact nature."

"But you knew it would be of interest to us, didn't you?" Shame covered Raziel's face. "Well, I'm certain we'll figure out the nuts and bolts of it soon enough." Northe turned for the door. "I'll be in touch."

"Who was that guy?" I asked as we exited the archives.

"Remember what I said about the supernatural powers we keep in check? Raziel's one of them."

"He's a refractor too?"

"Refractor?" Northe said, almost in a laugh. "He's not even human."

I paused, wondering how someone could look human without being human. "Then...he's an aengel?"

"You got it." Northe stuffed his gloves back in his coat pocket.

Once we were back on the terrarail, Northe unrolled his digipad and the more he tapped, the more his attention glued to the screen. It didn't take long to realize he was immersed in some game. Somewhere near our stop, he finally thought to ask if I had the briefcase secured. But his eyes never once left the screen. I was starting to understand Surket's frustration with his gaming addiction.

"Ya know, you handled yourself pretty well for your first day."

"I just tried to follow your lead."

"Do too much of that, and we'll both end up dead."

I chuckled hoping he was joking. "So, what are we going to do with this case?"

"Once we drop it at Science & Technology, there's a short debriefing. Then, our day is done, and I can pick up where I left off with Call to Arms—assuming Surket didn't completely fry the hardware this time."

"And that Raziel guy. What did you mean when you said he only gets to stay here if you find him useful?"

"Raziel belongs to a group known as Watchers. Aengel who possess the ability to literally see through the eyes of their targets. Because Watchers are a rare asset for intel collection, I convinced the Director to let him live amongst the general population, as one of our sources. But, occasionally Raziel and a few of his compatriots dabble in illegal trades, and think it's smart to hide them from me."

"Does IGIS make the laws about what aengel can and can't do?"

Northe nodded. "We have to. No other organization's aware of what we're dealing with."

"All this time, I thought Uncle Hachi just sat at his desk, had boring meetings, and signed papers for a living."

"He does. But the role of Director goes a lot deeper than that; even at the BNP."

I looked down at the metal case, wondering how dangerous whatever was inside really was. "So, whatever's in here is illegal?"

"Considering how anxious Raziel was to take it off our hands, I'm guessing that it is."

"A divarma?"

"Probably."

"Can I see it?"

"I wouldn't open the case since the wrong move could set one off. Divarma come in several shapes and sizes, and can react to any number of stimuli."

"Are they really that dangerous?"

"Their destructive force is comparable to a nuclear weapon."

A chill of danger circulated through my chest as I carefully lifted the case to Northe. "Maybe I shouldn't be holding this."

"If it was that volatile, we wouldn't have survived your chase with Ronald."

I didn't know if I should feel reassured or leery of Northe's seemingly mixed messages.

"How often do you go after Divarma?"

"Not often. Surket and Raven do most Divarma missions. I only come along when needed."

I tried to imagine how a Divarma mission with Raven would go. But all I could visualize was us arguing until we inadvertently set one off.

"Speaking of Raven," I began, "what's her problem? I mean, why was she so hostile toward me?"

Northe shrugged. "Raven's life is remarkably complicated, but she's always struck me as a paradox of strong will and equanimity. Maybe she's just being cautious."

"But what about me is making her cautious?"

Northe shrugged again. "For all I know, she's waiting to see something from you, or just testing you or...who knows what."

I don't know why, but something about the idea of Raven testing me really irritated me. What gave her—of all people—the right to test me? A beep came from Northe's TAB. He read its face. "Your uncle wants to see you in Stratcom before we drop off the case."

"Stratcom?"

"IGIS is organized much like the BNP. The Director and every Guild staff member responsible for running things are in the Guild's main command node, Strategic Command, or Stratcom for short. The remaining ninety percent of the Guild, fall into one of five branches. Intelligence is our largest branch, where all information collection and analysis is done. Science & Technology deals with research on all things supernatural. Operational Support consists of logisticians, maintenance personnel, engineers, and everyone else who keeps this machine moving. Clandestine Services is our unit of spies, interrogators, handlers, and undercover agents. And then there's Kinetic Operations—our division. Kinetic Ops is a field branch, just like Clan. But we're the Guild's muscle. So, our combative and ability-adaptive training is the most rigorous."

"That's why you said I'd get good training if I joined you guys."

"Exactly. Make no mistake, though. Even though we have the advantage of raw power, Clan is very competent in the field, and they shouldn't be taken lightly in battle. Still, when you want someone KO'd, you call KO."

"Is that our motto, or did you make that up?"

"You like it?" When his eyes lit up, I pretty much had my answer.

"I'm sure it'll grow on me."

I followed Northe into Strategic Command, a cylindrical building that towered over all others in Vaticia.

"Welcome to seven stories of brains and bosses," Northe said, walking toward the reception desk. Behind the desk was an attractive, dark-haired young woman. "Working late again, Juli?"

"Agent K," the woman said, immediately straightening in her seat. "I'm just waiting for the Director's final appointment to arrive." Her eyes went to me then back to Northe. "Who's your friend?"

"Team Seven's newest member." He placed a hand on my shoulder. "Juli here is the most talented and beautiful assistant to the Director that anyone's ever laid eyes on."

Juli covered her face, giggling like a schoolgirl. "Pleased to meet you," she said, reaching out one hand and fanning her face with the other.

"Nice to meet you as well," I said, gripping her wrist.

"Have you been given a designation yet?"

"Designation?"

"Our term for codenames," Northe clarified, before returning his undivided attention to Juli. "And no, he hasn't yet. Today's his first full day, so we haven't gotten to the formalities just yet."

"In that case," Juli said, "be careful around Agent K. He's a bad influence." Juli winked at Northe.

Northe winked back. "Only when I need to be."

Juli giggled again. "You know, I'm free as soon as the Director's appointment arrives, in case you'd like to join me for tea."

"I'll have to catch you next time, since we're that appointment you were waiting on."

"Oh," Juli said, voice deflating. "Next time then?"

"Next time."

"You can head up now, and I'll let the Director know that you've arrived."

"Thank you, Juli," Northe said, offering a smile before turning for the lift.

"Are you guys dating?" I asked once the lift door closed.

"Juli's a lovely girl, but no. I like the simplicity I've got going right now. Why add a factor to threaten it?"

"You mean a girlfriend?"

Northe shrugged. "A girlfriend anchors you. And I like having the freedom to go wherever the wind takes me."

Interesting choice of words, considering I'd only seen the wind take him to his bedroom, the den, and the dining table.

"If you ask me, Juli seems pretty great. She's nice, and she doesn't strike me as the hormonal, stomp-your-face-into-the-ground-every-time-she-sees-you type."

"We back on Raven? You seem to care a lot about what she thinks of you. Any particular reason why?"

My face went hot. "No," I almost yelled. "I'm just speaking generally. I'm just—"

"I'll keep your secret," Northe said. "But be warned, she isn't the type to accept mediocrity. So, I'd work hard to catch up to her if I were you." It was hard to appreciate Northe's advice when he had such a sly smile on his face.

The lift opened, revealing a pair of wooden double doors. The right door was wide open, and the gold panel on the left door read: "Director" in thick stylish print.

"You good?" Northe asked.

"Yeah." But I didn't feel good. All that stood between me finally getting the answers I might not even have been ready to hear was a single door.

Northe smiled and gave me a pat on the back. "You'll be fine."

Northe knocked twice and led me into a huge, half-empty room surrounded by large windows on the two curved walls, behind a wide wood and glass desk. Hachi was standing in front of one of the windows, hands clasped behind his back

"Have a seat," he said, smiling as he gestured toward two upholstered antique chairs. "You must be filled with questions by now. So, I'll let you get things started."

[11]

SMOOTH IS FAST

These beings, these *Others* are consolidating power. Weapons, people, anything of value is being gathered and organized under the banners of a privileged few. What am I missing here?
   -The Traveler

Out of all the questions floating through my mind, one question burned its way to the tip of my tongue.

"Why am I just now finding out about IGIS?"

"IGIS functions as a clandestine paramilitary organization," Hachi began. "As such, we find ourselves immersed in an unavoidable dilemma. As our power and influence grows, so does our risk of exposure. This would leave us open to investigation and scrutiny, which would ultimately compromise the integrity of our work. If other entities could handle supernatural threats, we'd have no need to exist. Presently, however, we're the world's only defense. Every member undertakes the necessary precautions to lower our risk. Myself included."

The situation sounded a lot like Shawin and the Wolfhounds. Unlike Shawin, however, Hachi wasn't so quick to believe in me. It was frustrating, to say the least.

"But you knew I wanted to help protect people. Why would you forbid me from fighting, when you could've just brought me into IGIS?"

"We both know why I didn't condone you fighting. It should go without saying that bringing you into IGIS wouldn't be my first choice."

"But if I'm here now — something must've changed your mind."

"Yes. You did."

"Me?"

"You forced my hand. Your powers are maturing, thanks in large part to your desire to place yourself in harm's way — despite the risk of prosecution if you're caught by the authorities. I was forced to act in both of our best interests once Agent K made the request to recruit you. As a member of Team Seven, your team can both train you and steer your efforts in the proper direction."

My eyes trailed to the floor. "Steer in the proper direction? Why does it still sound like you don't think I can do anything on my own?"

"Why are you so certain you can?"

I don't know why Hachi's answer caught me so off guard. But it left my mind as blank as my face probably was.

"I believe IGIS is the best place for you at this point," Hachi continued. "But if you disagree, I am willing to welcome you home with open arms. All the same, I assumed that you would at least be interested in hearing what K thought of your performance out in the field today, since that would determine whether or not you would be considered any further for Team Seven."

My attention went to Northe and he offered a passive shrug.

"What happens if K doesn't think I'm good for the team?"

"Same as if you decide against staying. You'll be sent home immediately, and you and I will need to reassess your career path. But, my house rules won't change. If you live under my roof, I will not tolerate fighting."

My ego aside, the idea of leaving IGIS honestly terrified me. And it was enough to form my answer without a second thought. But that still left Northe's take on the matter. I wanted to believe that there was nothing to worry about, but Northe had already admitted that he'd tried to recruit other Refractors before me, and Team Seven was still only three members strong.

"If it turns out that I'm not right for IGIS now, what are my chances of returning when I'm stronger?"

"There's no revolving door policy here, Serec," Hachi said. "Once you're out, you're out."

A swirl of panic flooded my chest as I refocused on Northe expectantly. That was the last thing I wanted to hear.

"Our mission was to look into a jewelry store dealing in illegal arms — specifically divarma. After witnessing Serec single-handedly capture the rogue aengel responsible and confiscate what we believe to be another divarma, I'd say Serec shows a great deal of promise. I stand by my request to initiate him into Team Seven."

As the tension in my chest eased, I realized my lungs had been waiting until Northe gave his report to take in air. Hachi looked me over, noticing all the rips and tears in my uniform.

"Any damages to report, aside from the obvious?"

Northe cleared his throat. "Nothing significant."

Hachi raised an eyebrow, and Northe offered a diplomatic smile. "Serec, assuming you choose to remain here, each member of your team has agreed to take part in molding you into an efficient Kinetic Operator. The choice is yours." If Raven was included in "each member," I could only assume that "agreed" was the Guild's term for "unapologetically forced." Whatever the case, I'd already made up my mind.

"I'm in."

The corners of Hachi's mouth curled slightly. "Excellent. Your official initiation will commence once your training has been completed. In the meantime, you should pour some thought into your designation."

"My codename, right?"

"Correct. Everyone here has one."

"What if I can't think of anything?"

"We'll have a designation prepared in case." For a beat, I thought I caught Northe smirk. But when I glanced at him, his face was as apathetic as ever. "K," Hachi began, "you have the best grasp of Serec's current shortfalls. You'll be responsible for constructing the first four decs of his training regimen, before Surket and Raven each spend an additional two decs with him. Please keep them abreast of his progress." Hachi turned back to me. "Do you have any other questions for me, Serec?"

Questions? I had so many I could list them onto a ten-page report. But the conversation already had so much spinning through my mind I couldn't remember a single one. "No, not right now," I said. Hachi offered a warm, nostalgic smile. The kind of smile that used to instantly ease my angst. The Hachi I once knew offered that smile every time I saw him. But over time, it had dwindled to special occasions. Still, a well of warmth filled my chest, because it was his way of reminding me that everything would work out.

"Take good care of my nephew, K." Northe nodded and slapped a hand on my shoulder.

"Now," Northe said, leading me out of the office, "let's get reacquainted with the training room."

Northe pressed the lift call button. "Next nugget," he began. "And you'll want to take this one seriously: Come up with your own designation. Stratcom is top notch when it comes to battle strategies and tactical warfare. But let's just say that choosing designations falls well out of their field of expertise."

"Gotcha. I'll see what I can come up with before then. Your designation is K. How'd you come up with it?"

Northe gave a breathy chuckle. "That's a long story."

"What? About Surket and Raven?"

"By now, I'm sure you understand how serious we are about maintaining privacy. That also applies to agent identities."

"That's why you didn't tell Juli my name?"

Northe nodded. "In any other situation that would've seemed awkward, but Juli understands the rules as well as anyone. Only a handful of guild members know my real name, since most of us prefer designations. But Surket is a different story."

"Surket isn't her designation?"

Northe shook his head. "It's Bolt. She always said she wanted something both simple and fierce. But ferocity wasn't the kind of feeling she wanted to instill in her friends, so she doesn't respond to it off the field. Raven, on the other hand, always goes by Raven. Almost no one knows her real name."

"You mean, you've been on the same team as her all these anums, and you still don't know her real name?"

"I never said that."

"Oh, Then, what's her name?"

"You don't listen very well, do you? Each agent has to decide who gets to know their real name."

"I get it."

I shouldn't have cared whether or not Raven wanted to tell me her real name. After all, it's not like it would affect our teamwork. And as annoying as she was, I couldn't imagine I would have much reason to ever use it. But I still wanted to know. And no matter how I looked at it, the fact that she didn't want me to know felt painfully personal.

"Don't look so glum. Give her time to come around."

I shrugged. "Yeah, sure."

Northe sighed. "In the meantime, we'll need to drop that briefcase off at Science & Technology before we can head back to D7."

"You sound kinda glum yourself."

"You'll understand why soon."

We walked down the sterile hallway extending the length of the Science & Technology building. It was like walking into a huge lab, except everyone was anxiously scurrying about.

"Why's everyone in such a hurry?"

"Because their lead scientist is a real slave driver. I've considered reporting how poorly she treats her subordinates."

"But...?"

"It wouldn't matter since she's known for getting results fast."

We stopped in front of a thick metal door, and Northe placed his hand on a small screen in front of it. The screen gave two blue flashes then went red. With a frustrated sigh, Northe tapped the screen a few times and tried again, only to get the same result.

"What's wrong?" I asked.

"Usually, the team commander takes samples and contraband to SciTech. But, since I forgot Surket's badge, I have to punch in a bunch of stupid access codes."

"I've got it, K," a short, nervous-looking lab coat called. He scanned his badge against the screen and the door opened, revealing another extended hallway.

"Thanks, Worm," Northe said.

"No problem. Are you here to see the boss?"

"Unfortunately. She around?"

The man tapped his ear. "Can't you tell?"

Angry screeching echoed from further inside.

"Did you just call that guy 'worm?'" I whispered to Northe.

"A prime example of why you don't want someone else choosing your designation."

"Who chose his designation?"

Northe tapped his ear. "You'll see."

The voice grew louder as we followed Worm through the hall and came to another door. Behind it was a large laboratory area. And the source of the angry screeching.

"What part of 'bring me weapons-grade Morrium' did your brain fail to comprehend? Don't bother showing your worthless face around here again until you have it!"

"B-but ma'am," a second voice stuttered, "I don't know—"

"Are you deaf too? Hadal take you from my sight, Maggot!"

A man appeared from behind one of several rolling holoboards and ran past us with a bewildered look on his eyes.

The air suddenly grew tense. Judging by Worm's expression, I was about to learn why.

"Worm!" the angry voice screeched. "Why is your report still not in my inbox?"

"I-I have it right here ma'am."

A woman stormed from behind the holoboards.

"It's about time you..." the woman trailed off the moment she spotted Northe. Her eyes narrowed. "K," she growled

"Minerva," Northe said flatly.

It was the woman Northe closed the lift door on—the target of his revengements.

I felt a chill as Minerva's hard amber eyes fixated on Northe. She was smaller than Raven, and she didn't look half as strong. But something about her seemed dangerous and unnerving, like being stuck in a room with a wild beast.

Minerva snatched the report from Worm. "Here to waste more of my time?"

"If it's a waste of your time, imagine how I feel," Northe replied.

"You sit on your butt, playing vid games all day. You're the epitome of wasted time."

"You should love technology considering your only successful relationship is with a computational device. The epitome of a maladjusted she-troll."

"Anni pulls her weight a lot better than you ever could. And there's no point in associating with severe under-performers. Speaking of which..." Minerva paused just long enough to scan over Worm's report. In beats, her face warped into a mix of irritation and disgust. "This report is awful!" she said, crumpling the paper. She held it out in the palm of her hand and it suddenly exploded into tiny shreds. My eyes went so wide they could've fallen out of their sockets.

"Waste my time with garbage like this again, and your head will be next, Worm."

"I-I'm sorry ma'am."

"Tell me something I don't know. Clean this mess up."

"Right away, ma'am."

I stiffened as Minerva's eyes shifted to me. "What are you looking at?"

"Slow down paper killer," Northe said. "He's with me."

"Then, he can blame you for getting onto my list." If associating with Northe put me on any list of hers, there was no way it could be a good one. Minerva looked me up and down. "Are you Team Seven's new recruit?"

"I am." I hesitantly extended my hand realizing it was shaking a little. "I'm Serec."

The corners of her mouth curled.

"I heard about you." She was thin to the point of looking frail, but her grip on my wrist was surprisingly firm. Her amber eyes contrasted her long dark hair which further contrasted her pale skin. "I'm Kareen—designation: Minerva. I've been anxious to see if the rumors were true—that you can pull a divarma out of thin air."

"Is that how you explain that creepy look on your face?" Northe muttered.

"Shouldn't you be wasting D7's oxygen right now?"

"Once you take this case, you can bet that I'll remove myself from your vicinity as quickly as possible. But I'm only leaving the case."

"What're you babbling about?"

"Don't be coy. Last time I saw that look, Raven was "administratively relocated" to your team for nearly half an anum."

"That must've put a real damper on your deplorably lackadaisical lifestyle."

"The kid is coming back with me."

For a moment, the tension in the air skyrocketed as Northe and Kareen stared each other down with more silent animosity than two mountain ligorns fighting for the alpha role of their pack.

"Worm," Kareen finally said, eyes still burning into Northe "take the case. Anni run a diagnostic."

"Confirmed," Anni replied.

I handed Worm the case.

"Let's go, Kid." Northe turned for the exit. "My report will be in tomorrow," he called over his shoulder.

"Why accomplish today, what you can put off for a dec?" Kareen said in a deceptively pleasant tone.

"She didn't seem all bad," I noted aloud. "Even if it was just with me."

"Don't fool yourself. Minerva's reputation as the Guild's most undesirable person to work with remains unchallenged. But as much as I hate to admit it, there's a brilliant mind under all that cynicism, which makes her a valuable asset to the Guild's scientific and occult pursuits. And that forces us to endure working with her a lot more than we should have to. So, here's your next nugget: develop a thick skin quickly. If Raven can get to you, you'll have quite a time here once you get to know the troll that is Minerva for yourself."

I covered my face in stone and smiled. "How's this?"

"A bit disturbing. But it's a start."

Surket and Raven were gone when we finally returned to D7, which was honestly a bit of a relief. The last thing I needed was a snide comment from Raven about how I couldn't complete the mission without destroying my clothes in the process. "You still up for a late day training session," Northe asked. "Or would you rather start tomorrow? It's fine, either way, since I've got a few things left to knockout anyway."

"I thought all you had to do was train me today."

"Officially, it is. But unofficially, I need to get a jump on that new Call to Arms mission I unlocked before Surket gets back—assuming she didn't fry my console."

"If playing Call to Arms could somehow keep me from losing to Raven, I'd be more than happy to go that route."

"That did happen, didn't it?" Northe said as if the memory was slowly coming back to him.

I frowned, and Northe gave a smug smile. "Alright, alright. Gimme a moment to think about where to start. You need a lot of work, Kid."

"'A lot?!' I've got the hang of my abilities already. Plus, Raven barely won."

Northe looked unimpressed. "Are you asking me or telling me?"

"...Asking."

"Then, like I said, you need a lot of work. Especially if you can't tell that Raven was playing you from the start. Now go change, so we can get this underway."

As I walked up the stairway, the thought struck me that I only had one change of clothes. But, when my door slid open, I almost couldn't believe what was there.

My rug and squoosh bag were in the middle of the floor. So were my posters and *Power Clash* timeboard. I opened the closet and found three brand new uniforms and a complement of casual and workout clothes. Even my clothes from the day before were washed and folded neatly at the foot of my bed. "They don't waste any time do they?" I said to myself, as I changed.

"You said you picked up your fighting ability from watching people, right?" Northe asked as I entered the training room.

"Yeah, why?"

"If you expect to beat Raven, you'll need more work in hand-to-hand combat. So, I'm going to test exactly how much you've learned."

"Okay." I walked into the sparring area with Northe. The moment I was in front of him, he rushed me, going into an offensive that was almost impossible to keep up with. I did all I could to fend off his attacks, but he was too fast. Raven's style resembled an elegant dance, but Northe's movements were even more fluid —more natural. I couldn't read his attacks, and even when I tried to slow him by throwing my own attacks, he slipped right past me maintaining momentum. I was too slow. *But I don't have to be.* I started to take in a breath, when my lungs suddenly locked up. I strained to take in air but, for some reason, I couldn't. Panic ensued as fatigue set in. My eyes darted to Northe. An arm was extended toward me, his fist closed tight. He shook his head.

"No using powers. I can't assess your technique if you're cheating your way into hitting me."

He opened his hand, and a rush of cold air flooded my lungs. I doubled over, coughing and wheezing until my throat burned. "Once you've caught your breath, we'll start again." As much as I hated to admit it, Northe was right. I needed to fight fair if I wanted to learn to beat Raven. Which meant street rules were out. Still, if I'd learned nothing else from Raven and Northe, one thing was clear: the first to strike gains the advantage. Without warning, I lunged at Northe punching and kicking as fast as I could. But he dipped between everything I threw at him without so much as flinching.

"You're trying really hard to hit me right now." Northe remarked dipping past my fist.

"Shouldn't I be?" I huffed.

"It's definitely a technique. But at this rate, your impatience will only earn you this." Northe shoved his palm straight into my chest. The sheer force made me feel as if my mind had temporarily separated from my body. I crashed into the mats, chest throbbing. "How are you doing this?" I managed, frustrated. "It's like you're not even trying."

Northe offered a hand, pulling me up. "We have a saying back home: Slow is smooth, smooth is fast."

"What's that even mean?" I nearly yelled.

"You'll soon find out. For now, let's get back to it."

We continued our bout for what felt like segments. Eventually, fatigue started working against one of us. And it wasn't Northe. He was probably waiting for me to burn out. And even though that would eventually happen, I had to at least land one hit first. Huffing, I threw a flurry of jab-cross combinations. It was only a matter of time before I caught him off guard. And thankfully, that moment came sooner than expected. Just as I'd pulled back from a jab, Northe started leaning to one side in anticipation of my next attack. At that moment, I switched into a front snap kick that would knock the wind out of him, just like he'd done to me. But my foot never connected. Northe's feet left the ground, and the next thing I knew, we were shoulder to shoulder.

I twisted around with a knife hand strike, but Northe slipped to my other side. I twisted again swinging another knife hand. Northe knocked my arm away and moved in to end the fight. Desperation flooded in; an all too familiar feeling. As I moved to counter, my hand began buzzing with a bright glowing heat. Startled, I pulled back, just as Northe knocked my arm away. And the light disappeared as suddenly as it came.

"That's the same move you used when you fought that monster."

I nodded, staring at my shaking hand in confusion. "Yeah. It felt the same too."

"How'd you do that?" Northe asked.

"I—I don't know." My voice cracked. The last opponent I used that attack on ended up with a hole in their gut. I had to figure out how to control it before I hurt someone.

"Well," Northe said, studying me, "I guess we'll cross that bridge when we get there. In the meantime, I'll bring the girls up to speed on my training plan."

"You've already figured it out?"

Northe nodded. "Each of us will be using our greatest strengths to help you with your greatest weaknesses. Give us eight decs and we'll make you a well-rounded agent and refractor. From that point on, it'll be up to you to determine how far you progress. Deal?"

"Deal."

"Then, get all the rest you can over the next day. Starting tomorrow night, you'll see what it really means to train hard."

My timechain beeped the next morning stirring me out of my hard sleep. It was a burst message from NaRyn. *Guess I know how I'm spending the day.* NaRyn's dorm sat in the sleepy Paxis Hills district; a mostly affluent area that primarily contained neighborhoods and Royal Verdallyn Academy. Given the location, I couldn't think of a safer place in New Callastryne for NaRyn to spend her Academy anums. Unfortunately, it wasn't fully insulated from crime like the gated Olde Callastryne, and several cases of consumed individuals had been reported in the district in recent decs.

"Rec Rec!" NaRyn's eyes lit up as she pulled me into an embrace. I needed a hug; more than she knew. But for some reason hugging her made me feel... anxious. The decs I'd spent training with Shawin left me feeling stronger than ever before. NaRyn's slender build made her seemed almost fragile in my arms; like I would break her if I wasn't careful. Sadly, when our eyes met again, it appeared something had already broken her.

"What's wrong Ryn?" I asked.

"Let's talk in my room," she said, tears welling in her eyes. NaRyn led me through her dorm which was more like an apartment than a traditional dorm room consisting of a kitchen, den, and three bedrooms. The dorm was empty; her friends Shuran and Harra probably out doing teenage girl stuff.

"It's over," NaRyn said pacing as I sat on her bed.

"What's over?"

"Everything! I can't believe I was so stupid. But what was I supposed to do?"

"Ryn," I began, calmly. "It's alright. I'm here. We can figure this out together. But I need to know what happened first."

NaRyn took a deep breath, sitting beside me on the bed. Her hazel eyes had a tinge of red despite her attempt to hold back her tears.

"They know," she finally said. "They know about my powers."

"Who?"

"Practically the entire school. It was an accident but I... couldn't just leave her. That thing would have torn her apart."

"Thing?"

"Beast, monster, whatever you want to call it. All I know is that Shuran was in danger and I used my powers to save her. Now, I've been suspended from school and I am under investigation by the BNP." The dam holding her tears finally broke and they began flooding her cheeks like she'd been holding them back for decs. "Why!? Why am I being punished for helping my friend? It isn't fair."

I put an arm around her, pulling her close. "I know Ryn. And I'm sorry. You're the last person who deserves to go through something like this." For a moment, we sat there, silent. Then the next logical question rose to the surface. "Does Hachi know?"

"Not yet, I don't want to say anything but I know it's only a matter of time before Matta tells him," the resentment contaminating her words worried me more than her tears. Thankfully, that gave me an idea.

"Matta's still the principal?" I began casually. "I know she used to love when I would get in trouble. It gave her an excuse to talk to Hachi. I bet deep down, she's thanking you."

A grin broke through NaRyn's wall of dejection, venting some of the melancholy air in the room.

"I knew I could trust you," she said, smile growing.

"Trust me?"

"The last two days have been tough. School has defined my life for so long. It's what makes me special." She paused for a moment. "I mean, yeah I can lift stuff with my mind and all but there's no place in the world for something like that... for someone like me."

The cloud of gloom began to creep back in as a familiar sentiment worked its way into my mind. NaRyn was expressing the same feelings I'd felt for anums; wanting to belong, but knowing I was an outcast. Recent decs had opened my eyes to a new world; a place where I could be myself. If only she knew about groups like the Wolfhounds and IGIS. If only I could tell her.

"Your powers may make you a bit different, but they don't define you. The fact that you're an amazing student, an awesome friend, and above all, a great person is what makes you special in my eyes."

NaRyn looked at me for a few beats, then burst into laughter startling me out of the moment. "That—was fatally saccharine," she managed, nearly falling off the bed.

"You sure know how to ruin a moment," I said crossing my arms.

"Look at it this way: you've raised my spirits and given me something to ponder. I'd call that a win." She smiled a toothy, carefree smile. The kind that told me despite everything that was happening, she was going to be okay. It was the best I could hope for considering the situation. I'd never been keen on school, but it was NaRyn's life for as long as I could remember. Unfortunately, with her powers now potentially exposed to the entire academy, it wouldn't surprise me if suspension was the first of many problems. Of course, the bigger concern was the monster she mentioned. But I had already formulated a plan to address that issue should it arise a second time.

The fleeting tree stood bare in the center of the rocks. Its exposed branches pointed skyward like a thousand withered fingers reaching for the stars. Though far less inspiring than it was just a few decs ago, it still gave me hope that my plan would work out. Either by accident or intention, NaRyn had begun following the same path I was walking. And though I hated to admit it, luck had often been the only thing separating me from the hospital, detention, or the grave. I refused to hand NaRyn's future to luck. Which is why I turned to the only person I could trust to prepare her for the road ahead.

"Serec, it's been a while brother. How have you been?" Shawin said extending a fist. "Fair to medium" I began, bumping his fist. "It's good to see you again. But unfortunately, I didn't stop by for a simple visit."

NaRyn stepped from behind me, locking eyes with Shawin. When she did, something unexpected happened that made me immediately rethink my decision. Before my eyes, stoic, boring Shawin began to take on a completely different demeanor. Normally, he carried himself like a man of forty anums with a stick somewhere it didn't belong. But in this moment, he began to take on the aspect of a vibrant, hopeful teenager. A grin even started breaking through. But what really unsettled me was that when I looked at NaRyn, she shared his enthusiasm.

"It would seem fate has brought us back together," NaRyn said, in a voice that was almost... enticing.

"For that, I am thankful," Shawin replied, voice soft and smooth.

"Did I miss something here?" I said, disrupting whatever moment they were having.

"NaRyn was the girl I was telling you about. I had no idea you already knew her. It would have made talking to her much easier."

NaRyn giggled, covering her mouth. These were sides of them I'd never seen before and I wasn't exactly thrilled about them. Still, it didn't change the fact that I needed Shawin's help.

"Well, I'm glad you guys already know each other, since I need a huge favor. I'm sure you're super busy with work and all, but I was hoping you could train NaRyn in your spare time."

"Train her?"

"Yeah. She's recently run into some trouble and I was hoping you could teach her some basic defense techniques. I still can't pay you or anything but—"

"I'll do it," Shawin interrupted. Convincing him almost seemed too easy; like he'd been waiting for me to ask the whole time. When I looked to NaRyn to ask if she'd be okay with Shawin training her, the smile that she was failing miserably to suppress gave me my answer. I couldn't help suddenly feeling out of place at that moment. Neither one of them had said or done anything to make me feel unwelcome. I could just sense the energy between them. It was... unfamiliar... exclusive.

"Why so down E?" A voice echoed in my head. *"You look like you've lost something."*

It was so familiar, so comforting, yet so distant. It felt like returning home after a long tiring journey; like sanctuary. *Liza?*

"Rec Rec?" Another voice pulled me out of my head.

"Oh, sorry, I missed that last part," I admitted.

"I was just saying that it would be great if we could grab a soho. Shawin's never had one."

My mind was still a bit foggy. But I could tell it was getting late.

"You guys go ahead, I'm going to head back in."

"You feeling alright brother? I can put together a remedy if you have an ailment," Shawin offered.

"No, I'm fine. Just a bit tired."

They shared a look of concern that I couldn't help but appreciate. These were my friends; the only true friends I had. So much had changed for me in such a short time. But I couldn't share any of it with them. It made me feel really, lonely; like I was a ghost in a room full of people. I could only hope that one day, I could tell them the truth. NaRyn wrapped her arms around me and squeezed.

"I'm here, if you need anything. You can't do it all yourself you know." Her hazel gaze pierced my facade of strength and heat pressed against the back of my eyes.

"She's right," Shawin began reaching out a fist. "We're here to support you. Don't forget that."

I nodded, bumping his fist. The road ahead would be tough. But just knowing that I had people who cared about me, would give me the strength I needed to press on.

[12]

ZERO

I'm beginning to understand why the differences of this world are so stark. Despite the common beginnings, the intervention of the... *Others* is far more prevalent here than any other place I've visited. This meddling has drastically altered all aspects of this reality; including but not limited to time, flora, fauna, and even astronomy. I suspect this event, referred to by many in the shadows as *The Great Calamity* was the culmination of this manipulation. Could this finally be where my journey ends?

    -The Traveler

Four decs of training with Northe made Shawin's training feel like a distant memory. My body had never ached so much for so long. But I couldn't argue with how much stronger or better prepared I felt for Surket by the time we were done. And yet, those feelings melted away when I entered the training room on day one.

"You're nervous," Surket observed with a subtle smirk.

"W-what makes you say that?"

"Your body language. It's practically screaming to the world how anxious you are."

The fact that it was so obvious to her made me even more anxious. I cleared my throat. "Maybe I am. But only because Northe said my toughest days with him wouldn't remotely compare to what you were going to put me through."

Surket shrugged. "I didn't say you shouldn't be nervous." In the pause, Surket's deep violet eyes penetrated every bit of bravado I tried to muster, until nothing but nervous energy circulated through my veins.

"I only have you twenty days, so there won't be time for breaks. We'll begin with something both basic and fundamental to your growth as a refractor. Now, how efficient are you at copying abilities?"

"Pretty good, I guess."

"You don't sound very confident." Something other than an absent-minded shrug would've been nice. But I couldn't think of a response. "So, you can copy anything you see? Or should I be aware of certain limitations before we begin?"

"I still haven't mastered mimicry. So, I can't copy everything I see. I'm not actually sure if I'm supposed to be able to."

"I see," she paused—thoughtful. "I refract electricity. And as an archer, I prefer to mold the energy into concentrated bolts that I can fire from my bow. We will start there."

"I'm not sur—"

"Try," She interrupted, taking her bow from around her shoulder. The bow was unlike any I'd seen before. It appeared to be made from stone with intricate designs carved into the jagged body. There was no string. At least, until her fingers pulled at the space where the string normally was. A thin blue line suddenly appeared forming her bow string. She aimed at a spot on the rubber padding. "It'll take some time to begin perceiving the subtle electrical charges in the air." Her fingers glowed as small blue sparks fizzled into the space around her hand. "Direct the charge into one spot, and..." She released the string and a bright bolt snapped out and crackled against the floor. There was something both beautiful and dangerous about it that reminded me of fireworks.

"How am I supposed to do that?" I asked. "I don't have a bow." Of course, a bow was the least of my problems. The real question was how was I supposed to pull electricity out of thin air?

"Using a bow is advanced work." Surket held out her hand. "I want you to do this." Tiny orbs of light pooled into a wild, crackling ball of energy in her palm. She held her hand there as I tried to follow her example. But feeling for the electrical charges in the air was just as difficult as it sounded.

"How do you know if you're feeling charges in the air?" I asked.

"What are you feeling right now?"

"Nothing."

"Are you trying to feel what's in your body or the air?"

"The air."

"Try your body instead. It's not as effective, but it tends to be easier when you're just starting out."

I gave it a few beats. "Nope."

"Perhaps I should've started with a different question," she said holding her hand out and aiming the ball of energy at my chest. "Do you only learn by what you see? Or can you learn faster if the energy makes physical contact?"

I jumped back. "No, no! I mean, I'm not sure exactly how it works, but I can learn abilities without being hit by them."

She closed her hand dispersing the energy. "A last resort then." Suddenly, she grew stern. "But understand that the longer you take to gain full control of your powers, the more you'll disadvantage yourself. And a team is only as strong as its weakest member."

A lump formed in my throat. *I'm a disadvantage to the team?* If that was true, I could understand Raven's attitude against accepting me.

"Let's start with the abilities you've successfully acquired," Surket continued. "Our focus will be employing your refracting abilities during combat. Assuming K did his part, your endurance and reaction speed should've improved enough for you to make it through this portion of your training." That didn't sound half as encouraging as Surket probably thought it did.

For the next dec, Surket had me practicing refracting while moving. From walking, to running and jumping, to dodging and strafing; I quickly realized that walking was the closest thing I would get to a break. And if I stopped for more than a couple beats to catch my breath, Surket would zap me and yell, "Rima! Team Seven doesn't need an anchor." I began to hate that word; partially because I didn't understand it, but more because it always accompanied a zap. But it turned out to be more encouraging than I thought.

By day ten, I was using two abilities at once. And by day eighteen, my face set a new record for the number of times, it could hit the floor. But, just like with Northe's training, I was improving faster than I ever had before. And that was more than enough to keep me going. Day nineteen, and "rima" was no longer the worst word in whatever dictionary she was using. If fact, it served as a warning, allowing me to dodge incoming sparks. By my final day with Surket, my body had settled into a manageable soreness that seemed like a small price to pay for a newfound strength and unwavering confidence. Then Raven walked in. Bright orange leggings and a black sport top had never looked so appealing...or so dangerous.

"What's she doing here?" I said loud enough for Raven to hear.

"It appears you still have that staring problem," Raven said.

Can she honestly blame me? "Where were you expecting me to look during a sparring match?"

Raven rolled her eyes. *Big mistake.* I hadn't forgotten how both she and Northe used the element of surprise to catch me off guard. I figured the least I could do was show her I was paying attention. I threw the first punch at her stomach. But her reflexes were sharp. She parried my arm and followed up with a swing that probably would've broken my jaw if it connected. She leaned into a second punch, but I leaned back with a perfectly timed kick at her waist. It was anyone's guess how she dodged it. But she folded back just enough to slip under my leg, then knocked my legs from under me, sending me crashing to the ground hard. "Point—Raven." Anni said.

"Too bad your staring problem doesn't help you avoid getting hit," she said. I knew she was trying to throw me off my game. But I could endure it for the chance at showing her what six decs of intense training could do for someone like me. Unfortunately, twelve faceplants later, Northe's message was finally sinking in. My few decs of training between Shawin, him, and even Surket, paled in comparison to Raven's anums as Surket's apprentice.

Surket walked over, as I picked my dignity up off the floor. "You've lost four matches," she began. "What weaknesses have you noted?"

"In her or me?"

"Both."

"I'm too slow." With each word my throat tightened. "But speed probably wouldn't be enough to beat her anyway. She's just too good."

Surket watched as Raven went from a cold stare to folding her arms and turning her back to me. "But what's Raven's weakness? With eyes like yours, it should be obvious."

I shrugged. "It's not. And I don't know how I could've spotted it when she's been training under you for so long."

Surket sighed softly. "Of course not. You've already lost sight of your goal— just like the first time you sparred with her."

"What do you mean 'lost sight?' My only goal is to win."

"Exactly my point. Alter your goals." I stared in confusion. But Surket only cocked her head to one side and lifted an eyebrow. "What else do you think about when you fight?" I tried to remember what else went through my mind when I fought Raven — or anyone for that matter. But all I could come up with was winning. I shrugged again.

"If you learn nothing else from me, learn this: The whims of your emotions will only sway you toward regret and disaster. Keep a cool head if you plan on long-term survival." I looked up at Surket, a light tingling in my throat as I took in her sobering gaze "Some battles aren't fought for the sake of winning. Instead of 'what' consider 'why'," she said, starting for the door. "He's all yours, Raven."

Raven stood there for a beat, her back still to me. "Don't be late tomorrow." Her tone was so frigid, I honestly didn't know how to respond. But I didn't have to. She trailed after Surket, before I could get a word in.

Getting dressed the next morning ended up taking longer than usual. One hash I was standing in front of the mirror, making sure nothing was off about my appearance—only to find things weren't off enough. Next thing I knew, someone was knocking at my door.

"You're eight hashes late." Northe said, opening the door.

"I'm la—"

"As in not on time, yes."

"Hadal!"

"Yeah, it happens."

I scrambled across my room and rushed past him. Raven was leaning against the wall in the training room, arms folded. "I specifically told you not to be late," she said with quiet intensity.

"Sorry, it took me a little longer to get dressed than I expected."

"Then, plan ahead. If you required additional time, why didn't you get up earlier?"

"Like I said, it took longer than expected."

"Making up excuses. Typical of dead weight."

I narrowed my eyes at Raven, and she returned the gesture. The longer our eyes held, the more everything around us drowned out, until I could only hear my heart pounding.

"This is pointless," she finally said, breaking me out of my trance. "You're too arrogant to even follow simple orders. How can someone like you learn to be a soldier—let alone an agent? Hopefully, we can find an advantage in your stubbornness." The urge to retort compelled me. But between showing up late and Raven's attitude, we'd wasted enough time. "Now that you've gotten a taste of physical training and refracting during combat, we will bring it all together. We will strengthen your abilities through mental training and cover basic Operator tactics."

"Operator?"

"Agents in the Kinetic Operations branch are known as Kinetic Operators. Most teams are made up of five to seven Operators—each specializing in a specific field, be it medic, engineer, infiltrator, transport, vanguard, or commander."

"Then why does Team Seven only have four members?"

"For the record, our team remains three strong, until you complete your training." *She can't go five hashes without a smart remark.* "Team Seven benefits from the fact that its Operators are skilled enough to fill multiple roles simultaneously. An Operator that can do so is called a Technician."

"I take it that's you."

"Glad you're paying attention," she smiled, and I wondered if it was intentional.

"So, do you fill all the gaps alone?"

"Technicians are never alone on a team because commanders must first serve as Technicians before being considered for command. Surket and I both specialize as medics, infiltrators, and engineers which actually puts us at an advantage over other teams."

After an explanation that, thankfully, felt more like a conversation than a lecture, I had a better grasp of how small-unit tactics worked, and it became clear just how impressive it was to reach the level of Technician. It made it a little easier to see why she seemed so strong and in control, when she couldn't have been any older than I was.

"Surket tells me you haven't mastered adaptive muscle memory enough to copy everything you see. Is that correct?"

"It's improving, but my power doesn't work perfectly every time just yet."

She nodded thoughtfully. "So, you're saying it's an unreliable ability?"

"No. It just—"

"Doesn't work every time," she interrupted. "That means it's unreliable." I bit back a response. "Perhaps I can help. But, I'll need your consent first."

"Consent for...?"

"Entering your mind."

"Seriously?"

"One of my abilities is telepathy. With a little probing, I may be able to help you determine what's preventing your adaptive memory from working properly."

"'May?'" I repeated.

"'May.' As in not definite. I make a point to skim the surface of your mind, only uncovering what you've permitted me to see."

"What if there's some connection between what I don't want you to see and whatever's keeping my power from working?"

"I'll make certain to avoid it, unless you allow me permission to probe deeper." Something about that unsettled me.

"How can I tell what you're seeing?"

"You can't."

"The more you reveal about this 'probing,' the more it sounds like snooping. And with no way to tell what you saw, it's anyone's guess what you'll find out."

"Listen, we can discuss the ethics of mental probing, or you can simply trust me. Your choice."

"Alright, alright. I'm in. So... how do we do this?"

"All you have to do is stand there, while I scan your mind passively. It won't take long."

I swallowed as Raven took a step closer and looked up into my eyes. Her light brown eyes took on a soft glow as peace overtook her face. It was awkward, staring at her while she stared at me. But I didn't know where else to look. Not that there was anywhere I'd rather look. She was beautiful. With our face's mere breaths apart, and the serenely silent room, it was even more obvious. *If only we'd met under different circumstances—maybe we'd be...* Just then, a wave of panic hit as I recalled Raven's explanation of her powers. *If she can see what's on the surface of my mind, and the main thing on my mind is Raven, does that mean...?*

"Alright. Let's see if..." Raven trailed off. She looked... exhausted. In that moment, something about her seemed strangely familiar. But it was fleeting. "What's wrong?"

"What? N-nothing." I laughed nervously.

Raven frowned. "Do your pupils always dilate when you look at people?"

"No—I mean... What'd you see?"

She paused. "It's difficult to explain. But I want you to try using Northe and Surket's abilities again."

"Okay. But it's honestly easier to copy whatever's right in front of me. Maybe if you used your power, I could try—"

"Let's just focus on Northe's and Surket's abilities for now, okay?"

I held out my hand and visualized energy pulsating at the rate of my heartbeat. Within beats, a tingle moved through my arm and into my palm. Small, translucent sparks buzzed in and out like fireflies. Not a bad start, but I needed to do better. I tensed to force more energy through, until thin lines of electricity shot up from each fingertip, melding into a small orb in the center of my palm.

"It worked," I said, half in disbelief. "Whatever you did, it worked."

"So far," she said. "Try Northe's power."

I blew a steady breath into my other hand, and visualized the air swirling in growing circles. Slowly, the wind picked up speed and force, until it was lapping against my face in rhythmic waves. Exhilaration engulfed me, as a smile etched into my face. "Raven, you're amazing." I froze, and the air in my hand dissipated. The words escaped before my mind could filter them. And now they were out there. Floating awkwardly between us. I wanted to say something—anything.

My eyes darted to the floor and held there for what felt like an eternity. She cleared her throat. "You're welcome," she finally said. "We should continue."

Fortunately, it couldn't have gotten any more awkward than it already had. So, the next nineteen days were a little easier on that front. Unfortunately, training with Raven was almost as hard as training with Surket. It almost made me wish I could go back to Northe. But, by the final day I had more control with mimicry than I thought possible. I was one step closer to achieving my goal.

I walked into the training room to find Raven holding a large metal case, more than half her height. "Northe told me that despite your first mission, you've never actually seen a divarma."

"Yeah," I said. "He said it could be dangerous to open the case it was in."

"Then I'll show you mine." Raven lowered her case to the floor. She held a hand over it and the case evaporated into specs of light.

"You have one?" Excitement drove my voice up an octave higher than expected.

Raven's mouth curved into a confident smile. "I do." She reached into the light and pulled out a thin, black blade. At over half her height from hilt to tip, it almost looked too dangerous for someone Raven's size to be holding. "This is Nightfall. It took me nearly four anums to earn it. The process was arduous—but well worth the effort."

It turned out Raven knew a fair amount more than I could ever think to ask about divarma, which was also a lot more than I could hope to remember. I was almost moved when she saw my brain turning circles and suggested a sparring match to end our training. But by the time I was face-up on the mat, with Raven walking away, I remembered why I wasn't a fan of sparring with her. Still, under her usual attitude, I was starting to see a side of her that wasn't so cold. A more caring side. And as she neared the door, I started to think that if I could find a way to make peace with her, it wouldn't take another few decs before I saw that side of her again.

"Raven," I said, pushing to my feet. She turned and I extended my hand. "I just wanted to thank you for training me. And I'm sorry I got on your bad side when we first met."

She looked down at my hand, then back up at me. "How did you get on my bad side?"

I shrugged. "I don't know. I just—"

"I'd advise against, apologizing when you don't know what you're apologizing for." She turned on her heel and continued toward the door. "Lest you end up making the same mistake and giving another pointless apology." My jaw went tight. Anger burned through me like a wildfire. Peace or no, it was time someone challenged that attitude. But just before I could be that someone, Northe appeared at the door.

"Serec's still breathing. Guess you two made it through the training." Northe sighed after a moment of silence. "Kids these days have no sense of humor."

"Please don't tell me you only came here to tell jokes," Raven said.

"Actually, I came because Surket needs to talk to you."

Raven nodded. "Thanks K," she said placing a hand on Northe's arm as she walked past him.

Northe turned to me. "You aren't looking so good?"

"I don't know what the issue is. I just tried to set things right with Raven for the second time, but I guess she's too high and mighty for apologies."

Northe thought for a moment, then shrugged. "Women do that sometimes."

"Why?"

He snorted. "Like I understand women. Anyway, now's as good a time as any to remind you to think about your designation. Unless, you've actually put some thought into it since we last spoke." I hadn't. My entire focus had been on getting stronger and beating Raven. "I'll take that as a no. If it's too hard, I will have a backup ready."

"What is it?"

"Tell you later. Otherwise, it wouldn't be a backup. It's a good one though." His words didn't inspire confidence. So, I spent what was left of the day brainstorming designations in my room. I was drawing blanks for a while before anything worth considering came to mind. Unfortunately, the energetic knock at my door broke my concentration before I could write the first idea down. It was Northe. Something had him excited. Too excited to even notice the frown on my face.

"Hey," he said. "Time to go."

"Go where?"

"I'd explain, but we're already late."

"Late for wha—"

"Meet me out front in ten hashes. In uniform." I changed as fast as I could but by the time I was out front, Northe was looking impatient.

"Took you long enough," he said.

"You said I had ten—"

"Let's get going." Northe started walking.

For someone who tended to take things slow, Northe was the fastest walker I'd ever seen. I quickly became so focused on keeping up that I paid no attention to where we were headed. And by the time I'd noticed the dimly lit alley, we were in a part of Vaticia I'd never seen. We came up on an inconspicuous park and Northe finally slowed down as we approached what looked like a small shrine. "This is it, Kid. The end of your free trial."

"End of my what?"

"Up until now, the Guild considered your time here 'at-will.' But your training is over, and so is that privilege. I'll ask one final time: Are you absolutely certain you want to be a part of IGIS?"

"I am." I didn't even stop to consider the question.

Northe's expression softened. "Alright then. No turning back." He placed a hand on the shrine and the ground started shaking until something behind me cracked. I spun around, eyes wide at the ground suddenly splitting into stairs leading down to who knows where. I followed close behind Northe as he descended the staircase. It got so dark I could barely make out his bobbing silhouette until faint light off in the distance crept into view. The light turned out to be torches, lining the stone walls. Thankfully, there were enough to light the remainder of the pathway, leading us to a small room. I followed Northe inside and stopped at the realization that we weren't alone.

"Welcome Recruit Arenyu," an unmistakably grizzled voice said from the center of the room. "I am the Kinetic Operations Branch Chief—designation, The Colonel."

"Colonel Cross!?" I exclaimed. "What are you doing here?" Colonel A.J. Cross was a long-time friend of Hachi's who'd served as Hachi's right-hand man in the Army. Ever since I was small, I'd thought of him as a silent giant. The kind that was completely void of anything close to humor. Everything about Cross said that he was born for military service, which was probably why I only saw him on holidays, or when Hachi dragged me to special military events.

"You'd be surprised who you might run into in this organization," Cross retorted. "Small talk aside, we'd best begin. This," he began, "is the Antechamber. The gateway to becoming a fully recognized agent of the Guild. I'm certain K has asked you already, but are you certain a path with IGIS is the path for you?"

"I am."

The Colonel looked to Northe. "K, do you endorse his entry into the Inner Sanctum?"

"I do," Northe replied.

"Then, let's proceed." A door behind the Colonel slid open and we followed him into a short hallway that led to a massive circular chamber. Waterfalls surrounded a circular platform where Surket and Raven stood with Hachi. He held a massive brown tome that looked older than all of us combined.

"Welcome to the Inner Sanctum," Hachi said. "Here we will determine if you possess the potential necessary to join our ranks as an agent of the International Guild of Investigators of the Supernatural."

"So, Raven was right about me not really being a member this whole time?"

Hachi nodded. "You were granted access into Vaticia, but you have yet to be initiated, commissioned, and granted agent status."

"Then, why bother training me?"

"Your training was the means by which you were evaluated. Your team members have noted your progress and potential, and now must voice whether or not they feel you are right for the Guild." I glanced over at Raven. The look in her eyes was calculating. Plenty reason for all the flips my heart kept turning.

"Each team member will now give their assessment and cast their vote as to whether or not you should join our ranks." At least the odds were in my favor. Northe was a given, and Surket and I got along well enough. That only left Raven.

"Keep in mind, this is a team effort," Hachi added. "And because you must work with your entire team, the vote from your team must be unanimous."

Hadal!

"K," the Colonel said, "as Serec's recruitment agent, you have spent the most time with him. Therefore, your assessment will be first."

Northe took a step forward. "The kid shows potential. He learns quickly, works hard, and reminds me of myself at his age. His feelings can get the best of him, but he clearly has a good heart."

"How do you vote?" Hachi asked. As Northe pretended to be deep in thought, it wasn't hard to imagine why Surket gave him so much strife. His timing for jokes was terrible.

He grinned. "It's a yes for me."

"Surket," the Colonel said, "your assessment and vote, please."

"Echoing K's assessment, Serec has proven himself to be a fast learner with tremendous potential. However, he is short-sighted, and his temper causes him to lose sight of his goals, making him a potential liability." My eyes locked onto Surket as my heart flipped around in my stomach. "I do, however, believe that in time, he will correct his shortcomings and prove a valuable asset to the Guild. I vote yes." My throat relaxed and air started flowing into my lungs again. The initiation process was about as mentally taxing as one of Surket's workouts.

"Then," Hachi said, "it comes down to Raven to give the final vote." Raven stepped forward, avoiding eye-contact with me. I would've honestly preferred her scowling. At least then I would've known what she was thinking.

"I have found Serec to be arrogant, quick to anger, immature, and rebellious against authority. He's rash and obsessed with power, which clouds his judgement." Nothing about what Raven said surprised me. If Northe and Surket's assessments were that harsh, there was no way Raven would have anything nice to say. And in the pause that held, my heart slowed to enough of a steady gallop for me to wonder what job options Hachi would throw at me, once I was officially kicked out of IGIS.

"That said," Raven continued, "I am admittedly impressed by his sense of justice, loyalty, and determination. At the start of our training, he allowed me to explore his mind. What I found was a wealth of untapped potential, and a strong desire to help others." Raven's eyes finally found mine. "I vote yes." I stood there, filled with warm tingles and disbelief. *I couldn't have heard her right.*

"Serec," Hachi said, "please step forward." Everything was so surreal, I almost didn't feel myself approaching Hachi. My mind was stuck on making sense of Raven's words. Everyone gathered around, as Hachi read from the giant tome:

SINCE MAN SET FOOT ON ORBIS, NEFARIOUS SUPERNATURAL ENTITIES HAVE THREATENED HIS EXISTENCE. DRIVEN BY JEALOUSY AND GREED THESE OTHERS HAVE THWARTED MANKIND'S EFFORTS TO THRIVE. HOWEVER, THE DIVINE OVERSEERS OF ALL EXISTENCE HAVE BLESSED MANKIND WITH A MEANS OF DEFENSE. A POWER WITH THE POTENTIAL TO REFRACT THE VERY FORCES THAT WOULD FABRICATE OUR SALVATION OR TWIST OUR FATE TOWARD A DOOMED OBLIVION.

Hachi closed the book. "Referencing this tome, we refer to this power as 'refracting.' The Guild has charged itself with doing everything within its capacity to understand these powers, and to ensure they are used for the preservation of life, and the prevention of destruction. You may have proven yourself worthy of joining our ranks, but I urge you not to take this mantle lightly. Remember that you are both an agent of IGIS and divine mandate."

His profound words made the weight I'd convinced myself I was willing to carry exponentially heavier. I took a deep breath. "Yes sir."

Hachi held out the tome. "This is Apocalypsis, the oldest written account of history and our window into the world before. Place your hand on it, and repeat after me." My hand trembled as I placed it over the tome. I took another breath, almost jumping at the pressure against my back. I looked over my shoulder, and there was my team, their hands pressing lightly in support.

"I, Serec Arenyu, do hereby swear to protect the people of Orbis from enemies— both supernatural and mundane. I will only use my divine abilities to defend mankind, and never to harm the innocent. I swear to selflessly answer the call of duty, uphold the laws of IGIS, and guard its secrets at all costs. I take this oath freely and without reservation, in the presence of my peers, the divine, and El the Almighty."

One hand pulled away from my back and Northe appeared in front of me to clip a shiny pin onto my collar.

"Serec Arenyu," Hachi said, "I hereby commission you an agent of the International Guild of Investigators of the Supernatural, under the rank of lieutenant." Hachi smiled proudly. "Please state the name you have chosen for your designation." I froze in terror as my brain went into panic mode. There were so many other things to focus on that I still hadn't come up with anything. "Serec?" Hachi called. *I had decs to think of something. Ugh! Why is this so hard?! Whatever I pick, I'm stuck with!*

"I believe we've let him sweat enough sir," Surket said almost playfully. "Raven, state the designation you've chosen for Serec—as is customary of Team Seven."

I turned with wide eyes. Surket gave an approving nod and looked to Raven. My eyes jumped to Raven, as I wondered if she could be my ray of hope, or the thunderstorm to my reputation. For all I knew, she might've only approved me joining Team Seven to suggest something like Maggot Jr. or Worm Number Two, as a final dig against me. If only I'd thought of —

"Zero," Raven said, taking a step forward.

Zero? What kind of a—?

"It sums up Serec's power quite well, from what I've observed. Adaptive muscle memory is of little substance on its own. But when paired with other abilities, it can become a limitless multiplier."

"Interesting," Hachi said thoughtfully. "Serec, will you accept this designation?"

At first, I wanted to say no. But I wasn't exactly bursting with ideas. Plus, the more I thought about it, the more it made sense. Wanting to become the strongest agent in IGIS meant I had a long road ahead of me. But I had to face facts. I was the weakest agent on my team — possibly in IGIS. By any other definition, I was a zero.

"I do," I affirmed. I thought I caught what looked like a smile from Raven. But as soon as I turned to look at her, her face turned serious.

"Then, it is decided," Hachi said. "Team Seven, I present to you Lieutenant Serec Arenyu—designation: Zero." In that moment, everything felt right. More right than ever before. I had a goal and a place where I finally belonged. That was more than enough reason to do everything I could to become an asset to IGIS. Even if that meant starting from zero. After words of congratulation and encouragement from Hachi and The Colonel, I walked back to D7 with the team—my team. After all the excitement, I was ready for a breather. Instead, I was summoned alongside Raven to meet Surket in her office.

"I trust you've picked up a few new skills, Zero?" Surket asked, as she handed a digipad to Raven.

"Yeah," I answered. "Thanks to Raven."

Surket smiled warmly. "And your designation?" There was a tinge of playful curiosity in her voice.

"I like it. It explains my ability pretty well."

"Good. Raven spent much time mulling over that name." Raven's face took on a rosy hue as she pretended to be too preoccupied with the digipad to hear what Surket was saying. "Anyway, I'm glad the two of you are finally getting along, since we've been tasked with compiling all the information we can on the creatures you saw at Monument Park."

"Creatures?" I said. "I only saw one."

"Then, let me be the first to inform you that there are more. A dec before we found you, Kinetic Ops Team Six disappeared after encountering a pack of them. Under Raven's command, the two of you will collect data on these creatures over the next three decs."

"Why just me and Raven?"

"K and I won't be necessary, as long as you stick to your mission objective of gathering information without engaging them. Unless you have any further questions, I'll leave it to Raven to bring you up to speed."

I started to say something, when Raven pulled me by the arm. "No questions, Commander."

"Then you two are dismissed," Surket said. "Stay sharp and keep your wits about you."

Raven saluted and pulled me out of the office behind her.

"How long have you guys known there were more monsters like at Monument Park?"

"Since, before Monument Park. That's why we were there in the first place. It all started when we recovered this vid, left behind by Team Six."

"Left behind? As in...?"

"As in it's been almost ten decs since they went missing, and we still haven't been able to find them. Team Seven was sent out to search for them, and we ended up having our own encounter with the monsters."

"I still don't see why Surket and Northe can't just come help us wipe them out. I mean, I was able to take one down by myself. And that was before I had any formal training."

"Let me be clear," Raven said sharply. "We lost an entire seven-person team. These creatures are fast, strong, and intelligent. They hunt in packs to overwhelm their prey. The last thing I want is to be surrounded by those things again. Our mission is—and will remain—centered around stealth."

Raven pulled up the vid and sat at the processor with me. There wasn't much to see at first. But then, I heard it. A blood curdling scream and what sounded like a pack of ravenous beasts—or worse—attacking people one by one. I cringed at the shrill howls accompanied by sudden booms and bangs, that had my heart skipping beats the longer I watched. It might as well have been a horror vid. But this was real.

[ELEMENT 2]
THE BOOK OF SA'SHA

[1]

ANNIHILATION

The radiation pressed against my mind, warning me of the impending conflict. I concentrated on the signal, as we sprinted through the dark alleyway. "I've located the divarma," I confirmed. "Follow me!" Flames danced in my lungs as we raced toward our objective. But we were already out of time. "Annihilation engine...ignited," I said between breaths. "...Antimatter field active." A bright light flashed ahead that only my eyes could see. *Gamma radiation. We have to hurry.* The light intensified, until we were so close I had to switch my spectrum of vision back to that of a normal human's. We stopped in a large clearing, surrounded by buildings. Four figures—two in black suits, two in white—loomed over an object up ahead.

That object turned out to be a man on his knees, blindfolded and bound. One of the white suits moved in front of the blindfolded man, holding an axe-shaped divarma. The blade edge glowed an enraged orange that filled the air with wispy white vapor. The white suit raised the divarma over the blindfolded man's head, and my breath caught.

"Divarma, straight ahead!" I yelled.

Surket drew her bow and skidded to a halt. "K, prisoner. Raven, black suits."

Northe and I rrushed ahead, as a bolt of blue electricity shot past us. The bolt exploded against the face of the suit holding the divarma, throwing him into his accomplice. The weapon let out a loud clang as it struck the ground.

I tackled the first black suit and twisted his arm to cuff his wrists together, before he hit the ground. His partner rushed me with a dagger. But I slipped under his blade and delivered a chop to the back of his neck, sending him stumbling past. *Neutralized.*

"We're done here," Surket said.

"Sounds good," Northe said, helping the once blindfolded man to his feet.

"Alright then. Let's—"

"Forget something?" a voice called; though it sounded more like a jumble of sounds. It was the white suit Surket had shot in the face. He gripped the divarma with trembling hands; struggling to stay on his feet. Blood dripped from the charred gory mass that used to be his face. He pointed it at us, smiling darkly with what remained of his mouth as the weapon glowed. My heart leapt into my throat, pounding like a piston. Being on the receiving end of a divarma strike was like staring death in the face. But I wasn't about to give him the opportunity to strike. I clutched Nightfall and threw myself forward, when another bolt zipped past me. The man angled the blunt end of his divarma between him and Surket's bolt, deflecting it. It hit the divarma with a mad crack breaking into a sea of sparks.

Clearly desperate, the man twisted the handle and pulled the divarma apart, revealing a small glowing sphere in the center. The weapon's core. The annihilation engine. The man laughed maniacally as the core slowly expanded, indiscriminately consuming everything it touched. The white suit and his partner were the first to go. And I knew if we didn't act quickly, they wouldn't be the last. This particular energy was from an active divarma, and it was beats from reaching critical mass. Once the core overloaded, Team Seven and the entire Port District would be annihilated in a matter of beats.

"We have to contain the core, bef—" Another bolt shot past, crashing into the core. The bolt encased the core, placing it in stasis.

"On you, Bird," Surket called. I stepped in front of the glowing mass and reached my arms out wide. Slowly, deliberately, I brought my arms together, condensing the core. It was dense. So dense that within moments, my arms began to grow heavy. I concentrated, suppressing the mass slightly on each exhale. But time was working against me. The electrical energy from Surket's bolt was nearly consumed, and by the time my hands were shoulder width apart, the core refused to shrink any further, despite my efforts. Sweat beaded into tiny streams, running down my face as the air grew thin; so thin that the world began to tilt. *Just a little more.* I told myself as a dark haze invaded my periphery.

"We're with you, Bird," Surket said. At least I think it was Surket. The voice was too distant, too muffled to know definitively. A rush of cool air raced from behind me breaking my concentration and nearly acquainting me with the ground. My mind rattled as I tilted forward eyes fixed on the glowing mass. "Rima!" A voice sliced through the haze as a hand gripped my shoulder. "Head in the game, Bird." Surket said. "You're not sitting this one out."

Surket's voice rang out through the darkness, as my senses slowly returned. I took a deep breath and the glowing mass came into focus. I found Northe standing beside me, both arms raised. The sphere was steadily rising, propelled by a vortex of Northe's creation.

"Feel free to jump in whenever." Northe said. "Pressing up this near-critical antimatter core isn't getting any easier." A bolt fired past, shattering against the core.

"We're finishing this," Surket declared. "Time for some fireworks."

"Confirmed," Northe and I said, prepping our next moves. In one elegant motion, Northe dropped his arms, made a fist, and performed an uppercut that transformed the vortex into an upward squall, sending the core above the clouds. I held two fingers against my temple, and inhaled, enhancing my vision to acquire the distant core. The air around me thickened with heat as the world fell silent. With one sharp exhale, I fired a concentrated wave of psionic energy at the sphere. Moments later, a blinding light flashed in the distance, followed by a thunderous boom, and a shockwave that nearly knocked me to the ground.

Alarms wailed and lights flickered but that appeared to be the extent of the damage — thankfully. But I still couldn't help but wonder how different that would have been had Surket and Northe not stepped in. "Still with us, Bird?" Surket asked.

"Yeah, barely," I admitted.

She placed a hand on my shoulder. "Lives were saved today, and you played a vital role in that." She offered a warm smile, and I managed one in return. She always had the right words. "Now get it together. Self-doubt doesn't suit you." Always.

Sirens blared in the distance.

"Peace Enforcers," she said. "It's time we took our leave."

Northe tapped his HOOD earpiece. "K here. We're leaving two reds and a green here for you...Thanks."

"ETA on Clan is two hashes."

Surket gave me a smirk. "I wonder if the little bird can keep up this time." She turned and sprinted off toward a nearby alley.

"Why do you always take a head start?" I yelled, hurrying after her.

"You two are pretty carefree after losing a divarma," Northe said over the HOOD communicator.

All things considered, we were acting rather carefree. But lives were saved. And it was nice to celebrate the victory while we could. Especially since Kareen and the Colonel would give us plenty of reason to lose sight of it during the debriefing.

[2]

ABDUCTION

They are everywhere. Appearing in random places. Contacting me at the worst times. Reminding me that I am theirs and nothing short of death will change that. I sometimes question how I keep it all together with this burden looming over me. A part of me would have rather died than be a tool in their stupid war. But they knew too much. About Me. About Us. So I compromised. My morals. My sense of self. To carry out these missions.

-The Waif

"**W**hat do you mean 'the divarma was lost!?'" Kareen shrieked.

"It was lost." Surket's dismissive tone failed to mask her irritation. "As in, destroyed."

"I gathered that. I'm asking how in Hadal it happened!"

For such a petite woman, Kareen was surprisingly aggressive. Likely the result of her long-standing caffeine addiction and obsession with her work. Still, she was wickedly smart and highly respected among the Guild's senior staff as the foremost authority on the occult science—specifically divarma—earning her the position of Lead Researcher. A true feat, considering she only had twenty-two anums. Although, the frown lines creeping onto her pale face suggested she was closer to thirty. Suffice it to say, Kareen had a reputation for taking her work very seriously. So seriously, in fact, that it had become commonplace seeing her quarrel with anyone she perceived as impeding her research. In this case, Surket.

Unfortunately for Kareen, Surket had similar credentials. Surket was brilliant in her own right and her aptitude for tactical combat made her, arguably, one of IGIS's most skilled Operators—rightfully earning her the rank of major. It was safe to say that Surket was the kind of person who commanded the Guild's collective respect. But Kareen had a way of turning a pacifist hostile. And that same hostility was building in Surket's eyes by the beat. I was one of the select few who actually got along with Kareen. Mostly, because—like Surket—Kareen was my mentor. It was thanks to her that I'd gained control over my technopathic powers. So, it fell to me to diffuse the situation.

"The core overloaded," Surket replied.

Kareen paused as the information turned in her head. "The illustrious Team Seven was incapable of preventing a divarma core overload? Is that what I'm hearing?"

Another intense pause. "What you're hearing—"

"One of the targets exposed the core before we could secure the divarma," I blurted. All eyes focused on me. There was a momentary silence as the tension in the air eased slightly. "Did he manage to escape?" Kareen asked.

"If you consider annihilation a means of escaping." I responded.

Kareen reached into her lab coat and pulled out a handful of sweet chews. "Serves the bastard right," she muttered stuffing the candy into her mouth.

"Cold as ever, I see," Northe finally chimed.

"Can it, oxygen thief." Kareen's tone was especially dangerous with Northe. But he only shrugged and pulled out his digipad. Unlike Surket, Northe was content with remaining as distant as possible. Unless he was forced, he would quietly observe from the sidelines. But even he couldn't resist a verbal jab or two if he was around Kareen long enough. I couldn't blame him though. The three of them had a convoluted history that made putting them in the same room ill-advised. Fortunately, if there was anything Northe was good at, it was tuning out the rest of the world.

"Anyway, I know you've got some good data on the divarma for me Raven." Kareen prompted.

"Of course," I began. "The divarma was relatively weak—Class VIII at best. I only detected around 0.15 grams of antimatter in the core."

Kareen took a slow breath and folded her arms. "That's low. Even for a Class VIII. But if that's what you saw..."

As a complement to my ability to communicate with machinery, my ability to see frequencies outside the visible spectrum allowed me to gauge the mass and energy level of radioactive materials with an exceptionally thin margin of error. So thin, in fact, that after much tinkering and multiple upgrades, even the spectrometer on Anni—her prized AI—couldn't beat my eyes in accuracy.

"Is 0.15 grams significant?" Surket asked.

"No — not particularly..." Kareen trailed lost in thought.

"Then...we're done here."

"Not just yet," Kareen refocused tapping on her TAB. "Ari, sent this strange vid over from Intel. Your official mission to investigate what's in this file should be coming down soon. But I figured you'd like a sneak preview." She swiped against her TAB and our TABs dinged.

"We can wait," Northe called, making his way to the door.

"We'll review it when we get back." Surket said. "Is that all?"

Kareen nodded. "Watch yourselves out there." The concern in her voice was uncharacteristic enough to give me an uneasy chill.

"Ya know," Northe called over his shoulder, "it's not becoming of a witch your age to consider the welfare of others."

"Perhaps I should clarify. Surket and Raven: be careful out there. K: choke on your unfathomable stupidity."

"That wasn't so hard, was it?"

By the time we were back at D7, the sun was peeking over the horizon. Night missions were commonplace for us but I'd never fully adjusted to the varying sleep periods.

"Peipei," Surket called to Northe who was already powering up his console, "if you're not in the office by the time this vid starts, I'm using that game box for target practice."

Northe froze for a moment, then led the way to the office with a sour look. When Northe was determined to do something, few people could shake him out of it. But Surket was undoubtedly one of the few. Surket started the vid. According to the date in the bottom right corner of the screen, the footage was recorded two days ago.

"This is Striker—Kinetic Ops Team Six," said a voice that I immediately recognized as Major Olan Miles, Commander of Kinetic Ops Team Six. "The time is 19.03. We're currently in pursuit of an unknown lifeform, said to have attacked citizens within New Callastryne's Central district." Despite how fast he was running, he managed to maintain normal respiration—a testament to how fit KO team commanders were. The HOOD camera struggled to focus, bouncing with the commander's footsteps.

"What in El's name?" another voice said, and the camera immediately panned to a connecting alleyway where a group of bloody victims lay lifeless. It looked as though they'd been mauled. But what in New Callastryne could've been responsible for something so horrific? Miles slowly approached the bodies, and my stomach turned. I'd seen my share of combat injuries while serving as a medic. But this wasn't combat—it was a slaughter.

"Don't lose focus, Bird." Surket began, sensing my discontent. "We're watching for intelligence. We can't afford to slight this advantage." Surket's tone matched her somber expression. Northe likely felt the same way—his unblinking eyes watching intently. I swallowed and looked to the screen again.

"Total body count is seventeen," Major Miles said solemnly. "Doc, get me a cause of death on these." The camera panned to Doc, Six's team medic. He nodded and performed a cursory examination of each body.

"Each victim has deep lacerations across the neck and torso," Doc said. "My guess would be death by exsanguination."

"Layman's terms, Doc."

"They suffered severe cuts and bled out, sir. The cause is, thus far, unknown."

"Stay alert, team. Whatever attacked these people is likely nearby." As soon as the words left his mouth, something crashed. Miles spun around. "Defensive formation!" The agents clustered into a circle with their backs to each other. The camera panned left, then right, then left again. A shadow zipped across the corner of the screen, faster than Miles could follow.

"What was that?" an agent whispered.

"Contact righ—Aahhh!" An agent yelled and Miles turned just in time to spot his legs, as he was whisked into the darkness. More yelps pulled Miles' attention. He whirled back to find three more agents missing. Aside from Major Miles, only one agent was left. Teresa Althea—designation Willow. She came into IGIS an anum behind me. I'd always wondered how someone as sweet and timid as Teresa ever worked up the courage to join — especially as an operator. And in that moment, I was still wondering. Her eyes were wide with terror, as she shook so much that even amidst the panic and chaos, the camera had no trouble capturing it. My heart ached as I internalized her dread. Especially, since — given the circumstances — I was fairly certain what would happen next.

Save for Striker's quick, shallow breathing, everything had gone deathly silent. Beats passed like hashes as the camera panned quickly, then slowly, then quickly again in all directions. My heart was beating in my eardrums when the camera finally stopped on Teresa. But not for the terrified look on Teresa's face. It was for the pair of orange eyes glowing in the darkness behind her.

"Behind you!" Teresa shrieked. Miles spun just fast enough to catch the blurred form approaching with a vicious snarl. The form was dark gray with jagged fangs and an almost human-like figure. But the way it moved was anything but human. Neither was the shrill scream it let out, before skittering forward and launching itself at Miles. That was the final frame.

Surket and Northe were quiet. But unlike me, they looked to be quiet in thought. I was speechless, frozen in place. Not sure how to process what I'd just witnessed. Not sure I wanted to.

"Don't get too excited you three," a grizzled voice echoed. The Colonel stood in the doorway, as poised as ever. Northe and Surket snapped to attention and Surket saluted. But I stood in place, quietly frozen in both mind and body. "Carry on," the Colonel said. "I take it, the three of you have looked over the recovered footage?"

"We have, sir," Surket replied.

"I've seen some disturbing things in my anums." He folded his arms. "This one fits neatly into that category."

Kinetic Operations branch commander and former Arurian Army Colonel A.J. Cross was — by all definitions — the epitome of a military officer. He helped build the Guild from the ground up, trained the first group of Kinetic Operators, and functions as direct supervisor to the Kinetic Ops team commanders. I could only imagine what someone like the Colonel had seen in all his anums. If he found the footage unsettling, it had to mean trouble.

"Will we be responsible for determining what happened to them, sir?" Surket asked.

"Affirmative. That vid made it clear that I'll need my best team on this. You'll leave after a good day's rest." That last statement pulled my undivided attention. Apparently, it pulled Northe's as well. "That's right, K. This is a night mission so I'd advise prepping for tonight, in lieu of rushing off to your virtual world."

"We won't disappoint, sir," Surket said, giving a second salute. The Colonel returned the salute, and took his leave. "Alright. Take this opportunity to rest up and prep for tonight. We'll meet in the war room at 18.oo to go over the plan for tonight's mission."

Northe gave a half-hearted salute and left the office, not bothering to hide his reservations about the mission. For once, I didn't blame him.

[3]

ENCOUNTER

My father always told me it is better to be a segment early than a hash late; wisdom I've held on to long after losing him. I've come to recognize that for me, the key to being punctual is a proper waking routine which starts with a favorable alarm. For early rising, I've found that nothing is comparable to the melody of a harpsichord. Some may call me "eccentric", but I believe the proper pronunciation is "cultured". I sat up as the harmonious twangs danced from my timechain. *That's enough Phoebe,* I directed my timechain, immediately silencing her. She replied that it was 17.50, a half segment until our mission started. And yes, I'll admit that naming electronic devices is eccentric, but it's difficult not to when we regularly converse. As I was adjusting the last of my gear, Phoebe buzzed. This time with a burst message:

Looking forward to seeing you next dec for the Autumn Gala.
With Love, Alanda.

Alanda had a way about her that always put a smile on my face—something I needed at the moment. But the mission was priority, and I couldn't afford any distractions. In the War Room, Surket and Northe were standing on either side of the Game Board. Kinetic Ops had only recently been issued the holographic displays, as they were relatively new. They were fatally more effective than flat vid screens or digipads for mission planning. So, as soon as they were approved for issue, Surket took full advantage, despite her preference toward lower-tech tools.

"Glad to see you're finally up, Bird." Surket said. All I could offer was a frown.

"Don't let her fool you," Northe said. "Surket and I just got up here too."

"Minor details. Anyway, now that everyone's here, we can go over the mission." She tapped on the board's table-sized display and a three-dimensional holographic model of New Callastryne appeared. She pointed her index finger and the data ring she was wearing interacted with the map, zooming in on a red dot. "Team Six disappeared here, according to Intel," she began. "Their ingress route was Central Avenue, but after encountering one of the creatures in question, they gave chase, which put them near the Central tower drop point before their disappearance."

"I take it we're starting at their drop point and walking." Northe observed.

"We're scouting for clues. Using the same infiltration point would be the wisest option."

"Does it have to be?"

"Let's hear your idea then."

Northe's face froze, examining the map with squinted eyes. "Fine," he conceded with a sigh. "Then what?"

"Then, we address what's been concerning me most about Team Six's mission." She pointed to another dot on the display. "Based on their start point and what should've been their endpoint, Team Six appeared to have detoured, before they were attacked."

"You're suggesting that Team Six was led into a trap," Northe said.

"Why else would any Kinetic Ops team willingly move into an area where freedom of maneuver and egress are restricted?" Surket said it with such certainty, that it could only mean one thing.

"You're implying that these creatures are intelligent," I said.

"Precisely. We must stay vigilant."

"Won't that be unnecessarily difficult at night?" Northe asked.

"Actually, I was wondering the same thing," I began. "Even with my abilities, we could easily miss something during a late-night site exploitation."

"Consider the scenario, Bird," Surket said. "Why else would we be performing a SITEX under cover of night?"

I paused for a breath. "It makes no sense, going at night when the creatures are more likely to..." I trailed off as the ugly truth finally emerged. "We're bait, aren't we?"

Northe sighed. "I was hoping to be the only one to come to that conclusion."

"But why are we focusing on baiting the creatures? Shouldn't our focus be locating Team Six?"

Surket and Northe both had a soft look in their eyes. "Clan already conducted an initial search and came up empty-handed on that front," Surket explained. "Honestly, I'm a bit thankful."

"Thankful?" I repeated.

"If anyone was still there," Northe said, "it would've meant that they hadn't survived the attack. Wherever they are right now, there's at least some chance they're still alive."

"Well said," an immediately recognizable voice called from the doorway. Everyone snapped into position and saluted as the Colonel's combat boots thudded with each step, echoing throughout the room.

"Carry on," the Colonel said. "And forgive the intrusion. I only came to provide clarity on your mission. The focus of your SITEX is both to locate clues about Team Six's assailants, and to increase your chance of getting eyes on said enemy."

"And what if we end up in a similar situation as Team Six?" I asked more aggressively than intended. It was frustrating, to say the least.

"How about a little faith in your commander that that won't happen?"

"Is that the authorization to punch out at the first sign of trouble?" Northe asked.

"It is. If spotted, you are to break contact immediately and return to base." It sounded reasonable enough. But that didn't change the fact that walking into a ligorn's den was essentially asking for more trouble than we might be equipped to handle. And I couldn't see how what we were about to do was any different.

Once we'd reached the Central Tower drop point, we navigated New Callastryne's alleyways, stopping at an inconspicuous brick wall.

"HOODs on," Surket ordered. We uniformly tapped our earpieces. The dark veil of violet light banded from each earpiece, covering our eyes and noses as they converged dead-center. A one-of-a-kind SciTech invention, the *Head-mounted Optical Obscuration Device* or *HOOD* functioned much like a one-way mirror. It concealed our identities while serving as a heads up display while on mission. A benefit to the latest update was that the HOOD did not obscure the face of the wearer to another user which was especially useful to me considering Surket often talked with her eyes.

Surket brought up a hand and a field of electricity crackled around it as she pressed her fist into the wall in front of her. The wall gave two soft beeps and lowered into the ground, revealing a garage door with a fingerprint scanner. Surket placed her thumb on the scanner and the door slid up.

"It's been far too long," Surket said, wistful, as she stepped into the darkness. Moments later—VROOOM! VROOOM! The familiar roar of Artemis, her prized *firecycle* echoed throughout the garage. The roar steadied into a smooth purr.

"If I didn't know better," Northe said, "I'd say her obsession with that firecycle is worse than my vid game habit."

I shook my head. "Nothing is worse than your vid game obsession." I began emphasizing the word "obsession". "And last time I checked, you were quite fond of Boreas as well." I added, referring to Northe's firecycle.

Northe smirked. "Don't get me wrong. I never said I blamed her for obsessing." The head lumen beamed brilliantly as Surket emerged, Artemis' black and violet paint job casting a luminescent sheen under street lumen.

"Don't keep us waiting," she said, as she hovered by.

Using front and rear miniature jet engines to generate downward thrust, firecycles were a marvel of modern engineering. They were also fatally expensive. Thankfully, the Guild took outfitting its agents very seriously. Northe and I entered the garage, loaded up, and pulled behind Surket. Sitting atop our cycles was nothing short of a thrilling experience. And because each was custom built from the ground up, it was safe to call Artemis one of Surket's most prized possessions.

But, as evidenced in the unique designs, we all were attached to our cycles. Unlike Artemis' sporty design, which exuded a mix of fierce and mysterious, Northe's cruiser style firecycle, Boreas, was a minimalist mash of gray and blue. My cycle, on the other hand, was in a completely different class. And like Phoebe, it had a name: Raiden.

Her experimental electric motor and magnetic field generator allowed her to smoothly hover over any surface without making a sound. They also made her the quickest of the three, despite the raw power of Artemis. And her onboard processor allowed me to quickly fine tune performance based on requirements. Design wise, she was considerably flashier by comparison, blending shades of orange, white, and magenta into a fashion-forward swirl of gradient-rich floral patterns. A sight to behold, for anyone fortunate enough to spot her.

The moment we were behind Surket, her engines roared furiously, and she shot off, leaving a cloud of smoke in her wake. I engaged Raiden's motor and quickly closed the gap. But she gladly sped off just as I was passing her, a display of the sheer power her engines generated and another testament to Surket's obsession. Still, we did all we could not to lose the ever-shrinking streak weaving through Central Avenue traffic with reflexes that only Northe could hope to match. Thankfully, we all knew where we were heading, since Surket had all but lost us without so much as a glance over her shoulder. A clear indicator that she was enjoying herself. But she wasn't the only one. Before I knew it, I was zipping between slow moving raedas and screaming in exhilaration, as the crisp night air whipped through my hair and briskly brushed across my face. We turned off and parked a block from the infiltration point.

"Rima," Surket began, "eyes on the eye." She nodded to the security camera, mounted atop a nearby street lumen.

Tapping into cameras was considerably easier than tapping into someone's mind; which made it absurdly easy to learn. But, like mind-reading, it felt a lot like an invasion of privacy. So, I'd long ago resolved only to use it when necessary. I infused my mind into the camera and the other three it was networked to. "Done."

I could see everything the cameras saw behind their night vision filter. But dividing my attention between the cameras' sensor and my eyes, was inconveniently difficult. It was like staring directly ahead, while tracking items in your periphery, making it difficult to walk and requiring me to frequently break and reestablish the link. The walk to Team Six's last known location wasn't a long one. And due to the lack of physical indicators, it seemed like a rather arbitrary point within the alleyway.

"This is the spot. We'll start with an ultraviolet sweep here." Surket instructed activating the UV light on her HOOD. Northe and I followed suit as we started through the alley. I looked along the ground and walls for clues but to my surprise, everything looked clean. Too clean.

"Peace enforcement's clean-up crew must've gone through Hadal scrubbing the area," Northe said.

"Bird, are your eyes picking anything up?" Surket asked.

I shifted my vision into ultraviolet, and looked around. "Nothing out of the ordinary."

Surket pulled out a can of luminol, and sprayed a large space along the ground and the wall next to her. "How about now?"

"Every time you use that, I feel like we're at a crime scene," Northe commented. We might as well have been. Bright blue patches started glowing in every place Surket had sprayed.

"Yeah," I began. "I'm getting something." As that something came into focus, so did the taste of bile at the back of my throat. Despite the world-class cleaning job by the PEDs, the luminol illuminated the remnants of the blood that had been spilled. And it was everywhere. Northe and Surket took out swabs and scrubbed them across the areas I pointed out. I would have helped but I found my mind curling into itself contemplating just how much blood was senselessly spilled; how many innocent people were butchered; how Team Six may have suffered the same fate.

"Rima," Surket pulled me back into reality. "Eyes on our rides."

I shifted focus to the camera aimed at our cycles. "All clear so far."

"Good. Sever the link. I need you to place your full attention on a more meticulous search. K, guard our egress."

"Now we're talkin'," Northe said, heading for the cycles.

"That doesn't mean play games on your digipad."

"Yeah, yeah. I got it."

Scanning the area more closely, I could distinguish peculiar looking splotches next to each blood stain. But they didn't glow the way the blood did. If anything, they contrasted with the blood stains. "Do you have any more luminol? I'm detecting something unusual."

"All out. What do you see?"

I refracted my vision further outside the visible spectrum. Somewhere just above ultraviolet, a set of green splotches came into focus next to the blue splotches of blood. "There's a trail of..." I frowned. "I don't know what that is. But it looks like it leads that way." I pointed to one corner of the alley.

Surket and I followed the trail that stopped at an industrial trash bin. Lodged in one side of it was what looked like a small, pointed beige rock. But as I knelt down to reach for it, that rock appeared to be more like a talon. *What kind of animal did this belong to?* I picked up the talon and placed it in my evidence bag. Suddenly, what sounded like a moan radiated from behind the bin. I froze, trying to pinpoint what and where the sound was exactly. Surket made her "what are you doing" face, and I tapped my ear. She nodded and stood in place. The silence held so long, I starting wondering if I was just being paranoid. But as I shrugged the moan sounded again, and I nearly shrieked.

I whirled to face the trash bin. Someone was behind it. I looked back at Surket, nodding as she prepped her bow. I took a careful step to one side, when the thought crossed my mind that it could have been another victim. Perhaps it was even a member of Team Six. Like Teresa. For all I knew she was hiding this whole time, waiting for us to find her. Hope sparked within me as I braced myself and pulled at one corner of the trash bin.

The bin suddenly jumped forward, and sent me stumbling backward. *That couldn't have been me. I barely pulled the bin.* But the moment I looked up, I wish it had been me. A grotesque humanoid creature with slimy fangs and jagged talons emerged from behind the bin, walking on two digitigrade legs. I stared in disbelief as a suffocating terror seized me. The vid did little justice when it came to accurately capturing the macabre details of the horrid beast. The sound of its phlegmy breaths. The smell of rotting meat escaping its mouth. The inhuman malevolence in its glassy orange eyes. All came together to form a reality far worse than anything I could've imagined.

The creature let out a spine-tingling scream, that peppered my body with fear bumps. It bared its fangs as its narrow orange eyes locked onto mine. A tidal wave of adrenaline held me in place as it washed through me. It was nothing short of a fight-or-flight moment. And my mind chose or. I forced a trembling hand toward Nightfall, praying that I could draw it while I still had a pulse. The creature lunged, and a flash of blue light slammed into its chest. It faltered, screaming in pain.

"Raven, on me!" Surket called, as everything suddenly got unbearably loud. She had a huge bolt pinched between her bowstring and arrow rest. The creature howled and Surket loosed the bolt. It hit its mark with a sizzling crack. The beast convulsed violently, before its legs buckled. Northe darted out from behind the corner. "What's going on? I heard a crash and... Hadal is that thing?" He exclaimed, taking in the creature sprawled along the ground.

"Take a guess," Surket answered.

The creature cried out, struggling to move. I took a step closer, examining the beast but Surket held out her arm. "Any reason why we're not killing it yet?" Northe asked. But Surket only sniffed the air. "We should be killing it, before it finds a way to kill us."

"This thing couldn't have taken Team Six out on its own. Which means it wasn't planning to attack us alone." Her eyes narrowed. "Something smells off here."

"It's probably that thing," Northe retorted, pointing to the monster. "And whatever it was planning, I'm in camp 'kill the damn thing' before it makes another move."

"Look little camper, it's too dangerous."

"We outnumber it three to one!"

"My bolts will keep it down for a while. Right now, we should—"

"We should act like we care more about the safety of the people. Sniffing out alleged traps should come second."

Surket watched Northe for a beat. The muscles in her face subtly tensing. "After all the effort you've put into taking a backseat, you finally want a place at the adults table?" The air grew thick with tension, as they held each other's glare. I'd never seen Northe and Surket argue so fiercely during a mission—or at all, for that matter. It was almost enough to forget there was a monster lying just a short distance away from us. But what had Northe so incensed?

"You may have had a sudden change of heart," Surket finally said, "but it's my call, and I say—" Another terror inducing shriek echoed, and their conversation came to a screeching halt. I traced the shriek back to the roof behind us, and froze at the sight of three figures—monsters. I focused my vision on infrared. The moment I did, my veins ran cold as trepidation gripped me. More were approaching, fast.

"More monsters inbound!" I said with growing anxiety.

"Then, we're punching out!" Surket ordered. The creatures on the roof, drew closer. But instead of giving them time to make their next move, we whirled around and broke into a full sprint down the alley. Howls echoed from close behind, as I ran for what felt like an eternity. But I didn't look back. I poured every bit of focus into filling my lungs with air, as I pumped my legs for all they were worth. Through El's grace, we reached the cycles.

I was the first to reach my cycle. Surprising, considering I'd never once beaten Surket in a race. I activated the motor, and turned to get eyes on Surket and Northe. They weren't far. But the monsters had gotten too close for comfort, causing them to shift focus behind them. They unleashed a myriad of wind and electric attacks to keep the growing mass of creatures at bay. But the mass continued to grow. Continued to draw closer. I had to help before the horde overwhelmed them.

I held my hand to my temple and focused on the center of the horde. *Just don't miss.* With a breath that felt like my last, everything fell silent, darkness enshrouding the world. Three things glowed amidst the shade: Northe, Surket, and the horde. Heat began to condense, swirling around me as I acquired my target. With an ironic sense of calm, I unbridled my power and sent forth a devastating wave of psionic energy. A beat later, and the hoard exploded, sending monsters hurtling in every direction. The threat was neutralized, I'd saved them. Or so I thought.

"Five rounds, Bird," Surket called over the HOOD.

"Excuse me?"

"Five rounds tomorrow in the training room for cheating me out of a good workout," she elaborated.

"But I..."

"We were working up a sweat and we were almost friends again. But you had to jump in." Northe added.

"I-I don't get you guys!" I didn't bother suppressing a pout. Surket and

Northe were far better equipped to handle themselves than I realized. And it made me wonder just how powerful they were. We headed straight to Kareen's lab, only to find that Kareen wasn't there. I don't know why she—or most anyone —would be awake at 2.00 for that matter. But her erratic work times had surprised me before.

"Head back to D7 and get some rest, you two," Surket said, as she logged into the processor next to the drop box. "I'll give you details on the debriefing as soon as I get word."

"Don't have to tell me twice," Northe said, turning away.

"I don't mind waiting while you write up the report," I said.

There was a pause as Surket continued typing. "Not tired?"

"After what just happened? Not really."

"I'm still good, right?" Northe asked.

"Get some sleep, Peipei." Her response was almost robotic. But Northe wasn't bothered by it in the least. He quickly headed toward the exit. Of course, he didn't get far before a spark jumped from Surket's finger and stung the back of his neck.

"Oww!" Northe said with a jump. "What was that for?"

"You're leaving two defenseless ladies to fend for themselves, and you have the nerve to ask that question?"

"Ha!" Northe laughed bitterly. "Alright 22. I'd consider you many things, but defenseless ain't one of them." Surket flicked another spark, catching him in the leg. "Stop proving me right," he yelled as he hurried off. In the quiet pause, Surket watched him go with a look I so rarely saw from her, I could't deduce its meaning. It was—sad. Almost bitter. But it was fleeting, and Surket's eyes quickly found mine.

"22?" I asked, hoping she hadn't noticed me watching her.

"I took down 22 monsters back there—he only managed 20."

I forced myself to suppress the incredulity growing on my face.

"What's on your mind, Bird?" she asked, calmly.

"Nothing important." Surket gave a side-eyed glance. "I was just a little anxious to hear what Kareen would say about the creatures. I was hoping she figured out something that could help us against them."

Surket held my gaze for an uncomfortably long time. More than enough time for my eyes to leave hers in favor of my feet. "It was your first time seeing some-thing like that," she finally said. "Freezing is a natural reaction. And it doesn't make me doubt you in the slightest."

My breath caught. *How does she always know?* I swallowed and looked up at her. She was so patient—so pragmatic about a topic I assigned so much emotion to, that I almost couldn't respond. But I knew I had to say something, or the fire prickling at the back of my eyes would make matters worse. "I could have put you and Northe in danger, freezing like that."

Surket tilted her head to one side. "What would have happened if you hadn't frozen?"

I thought for a moment. "I don't know."

"And you never will. What's passed has passed. No one can be ready for everything. But, you can grow by facing challenges head-on. And learning from missteps. In time, you'll learn to overcome these challenges and finally begin to recognize the potential I've always seen in you. An important step, if you're going to surpass me."

I blinked hard. "Surpass you? How could that even be possible?"

"How couldn't it? It's every master's dream to witness their apprentice surpass them. A final testament to our legacy as teachers. Like my master before me and his master before him, I know that day will come. It'll prove quite the uphill battle for you though, if you waste time focusing on the would'ves and could'ves." She offered a warm wistful smile, and I smiled back. Even if there was doubt—and believe me there was—I at least owed it to her to try and reach the potential she saw in me. She pressed her thumb against the processor screen. It scanned her print and the drop box slid open. She placed the samples inside. "Despite your thoughts otherwise, today proved that you have potential."

"How so?"

"I scored 22. Northe scored 20. You—scored 21"

A few segments were all we had before we were summoned to Kareen's office for a debriefing with her and the Colonel. "You guys notice anything curious about these creatures?" Kareen asked the moment we stepped in.

"You mean aside from the fact that they're rabid and ugly as sin—even compared to you?" Northe asked.

"I'll rephrase the question," Kareen said with a scowl, "for the dullards who speak before they think. Did the creatures seem intelligent to you?"

"I had my suspicions," Surket said.

"I'm asking because the initial analysis came back. There's still room for testing, but an important piece of information has presented itself."

"A viable means of obliterating these abominations?" the Colonel asked.

"Perhaps in time. But I'm speaking more specifically about the similarities these creatures share with humans."

"What similarities could there be?"

"The tests are far from conclusive. But my hypothesis is that whoever's creating these creatures, is splicing human genes into them, to make them clever enough to trap humans. And if my guess is right, this is just the beginning."

[4]

MADS

Something has changes. They seem more cautious, scared even. Could this be connected to the other changes I've seen?
    -The Waif

"These are monsters we're talking about. How can they gain human-like intelligence?" The Colonel's tone was rightfully incredulous. Kareen's assessment that the monsters would eventually reach our level of intelligence took the severity of this problem to new heights.

"How soon can you verify your hypothesis?" Surket asked.

"Not soon enough using the samples you all provided."

"You want us to go out and collect more." Surket deduced.

Kareen turned to the Colonel. "It would greatly improve my chances of arriving at an irrefutable conclusion."

"Hold on a beat there, mad scientist," Northe interjected. "What makes you think we want to go put our lives at risk, just so you can have more materials to tinker around with in your lair?"

"Sounds like you're trying to buy yourself more time to tinker around with those stupid vid games."

"Games can't be stupid if they don't have a brain. You, however—"

"Furthermore," Kareen said, focused on the Colonel, "We still don't know much about these creatures. Every piece of information we can gain on them grants us an advantage."

"You, however—" Northe said louder.

"So long as the necessary precautions are taken," Kareen continued even louder, "Team Seven should be more than capable of handling themselves around these things."

Northe's eyes burned at Kareen like hot coals. But the Colonel held up a hand, before Northe could get another word out. "All valid points," the Colonel began. "But the last thing we want is to be caught with our pants down. So, we'd better make damn sure we do our part to seize the advantage over those creatures, and not the other way around."

"Just give us the target and we'll execute sir," Surket said.

"Already on it," Kareen said. "Using your HOOD cams, I've extrapolated a sound bite of the monster's war cry. Cross-referencing that audio with Team Six's recordings, I can build a database of every type of sound the monsters have produced thus far."

"So what?" Northe started. "We're gonna make a playlist of growls and groans and hope it sounds seductive enough to catch one in heat?"

"Shut Up, you imbecile!" Kareen screamed.

The Colonel got in Northe's face, "This is your warning, K. Cool it, or I'll make certain your vid games end up in tomorrow's scrap heap." Northe and the Colonel held each other's glare for a moment, before Northe finally relented. "Sir," he said, folding his arms and looking away.

"Minerva," the Colonel said, turning back to Kareen, "you were saying?"

"Thank you, sir," Kareen said, smiling smugly at Northe. But he was already hard at work ignoring her. "Using that database and Raven's technopathy, I believe we can track the creatures."

It was not until all eyes went to me that Kareen's words fully registered. "Excuse me?" I said.

"I already made the necessary adjustment to your HOOD cam. Once your mind is connected to the network, we can track the creatures using your technopathy." I hesitated as Kareen motioned me closer. I wasn't particularly excited to hear monsters in my head. But the silent optimism in everyone's eyes propelled me forward. Kareen clipped a tiny device over my index finger and the blue light at its tip illuminated. It was soothing despite the tension in my chest.

"The sound bites will mold into a recognizable frequency. Your mind should be able to create a signature for each sound. Anni will then record that signature and project it as a dot on my game board. Your brain will do this automatically so you just need to relax. Anni, Verdallyn," Kareen commanded. A holographic model of Verdallyn sprouted from her game board in the center of the lab.

"How will the sound bites help us determine their location?" Surket asked.

"Raven will be connected to every surveillance network across the kingdom. Any security device that picks up a similar sound will cross-reference through the database Raven's mind imprints onto Anni. If it's a hit, I'll see it on the game board." Kareen took a draft from her tea mug. "Alright, Q&A is over. Time to make history...again," she said, tapping her TAB." The sound bite played in a continuous loop through the speakers. "Just focus on the sound," she instructed.

I closed my eyes, attempting to internalize the sound without feeling completely unnerved by the horrid wails and snarls. But within beats, the previous night played through my mind in nightmarish detail. My body went rigid as the monster stalked out from behind the trash bin. The way it watched me. The terror in knowing it had every intention of tearing me to bloody shreds. I tried to push the image away, but my mind held fast. The air grew thin, as the creature closed in. Just like before, I was paralyzed. Trembling as I stared death in the face.

Kareen's voice touched my consciousness. But she sounded so distant it was difficult to understand her. "—going—slow it down. Try and break it down in your mind." The growling slowed, and the monster's movements kept in perfect tempo as it crouched low in preparation to pounce. Its palpable bloodlust stained the air, making breathing arduous. My heart pummeled my ribcage, desperate to escape my chest before the monster's claws tore into it. The monster leapt forward with a chilling wail. *Move! Please move!* The words echoed throughout my being as the distance between the monster and me—between life and death—diminished, until...

My eyes burst open as my lungs frantically took in as much air as possible. I felt dizzy and disoriented. Like waking from some terrible nightmare. The recording stopped as Surket approached.

"Something wrong, Bird?" I was almost taken aback at how callous she sounded. But I could understand why. With everyone counting on me—in an otherwise safe setting—there couldn't have been a more foolish time to let my fears get the best of me. I needed to focus. More importantly, I needed to remember it was all in my head.

"It's nothing," I managed. "I just...lost focus. I'm a little tired."

"Sleep won't be an option for any of us, until we're done here."

I nodded. "I'll get it this time," I said loud enough for everyone to hear.

Surket gave my shoulder a gentle squeeze. "Of course you will. You're my apprentice."

"Alright," Kareen said. "Let's try it again."

I got back into place, closing my eyes as the recording resumed. The image of the creature, emerging from behind the trash bin, played in my mind again. But this time, I stood firm. I met its gaze, unflinching, as its growls and roars filled my head. The noise got progressively slower, until I could find the patterns in each sound. The sound broke into smaller pieces, until every bit had become distinct, weaving into its own identifiable signature. Suddenly, the recording ended and the monster faded. A brush across my hand pulled me out of my trance. It was Kareen, removing the device from my finger. "Much smoother than the first run," she said. I forced a smile.

"Analyzing" Anni said. Kareen moved back to her game board.

"Thanks to Raven, we now have an imprint to cross-reference through the Department of Peace's surveillance network. Anni and I will overlay it and fashion an alert system that'll pinpoint monster locations within Aruria—as long as a security device is within audible range. I'm calling it the Monster Audio Detection System—MADS for short."

"How long will it take to get your detection system up and running?" The Colonel asked.

"Pending some minor calibrating, we'll have it ready by the end of the day."

The Colonel nodded and turned to Surket. "Consider yourselves officially on standby. Once we locate more creatures, Team Seven will intercept one and acquire additional samples."

Have we seen all there is to these creatures? Or is the worst yet to come? I wondered, staring at my bedroom ceiling. My racing mind made sleep elusive, despite my exhaustion. Then Surket came to mind again. Specifically, her dream that I would someday surpass her. As things stood, all it would ever be was a dream. I didn't possess half her strength or experience, and fear still crippled me in the field. I couldn't continue to depend on Surket and Northe, lest I become dead weight. I covered my face and sighed into my hands, twisting onto my side. Breathing deeply, quietly in the silence that followed, until my heartbeat steadied. I slowly sank into the bed until—I everything faded.

A quick, sharp knock at the door jolted me out of sleep.

"Come in," I said. The door slid open, and Surket drifted in.

"On your feet, Bird. A monster's attacking Monument Park."

I sprang up. "Monster? Minerva's system found one that fast?"

"Didn't have to. We intercepted a dispatch to peace enforcement."

"But a call to peace enforcement means—"

"We can't afford to waste time."

[5]

SEREC

We raced toward the cacophony of screams, dodging waves of fleeing citizens. The scene was more chaotic than anticipated, making it difficult to mentally prepare for what we were running toward. We closed in on snarling emanating from just beyond a row of hedges. Unfortunately, another—much more human—sound accompanied it.

"Sounds like the creature's attacking a citizen," Surket said. "Civilian safety comes first." We picked up the pace as adrenaline coursed through me.

"Now or never," I said under my breath. But the moment we turned the corner, I froze. Stricken by surprise rather than fear. A young man was engaging the creature, which stood nearly twice his height; considerably larger than the monsters we'd encountered in the alley.

The young man panted heavily, as he rushed headlong toward the beast. It all seemed so surreal. The teen attacked the creature without hesitation, yet it was somehow agile enough to evade the assault and throw attacks of its own. And all while holding... My heart dropped, when I finally noticed it. "The creature has a hostage."

"Which is why we can't rush in aimlessly," Surket said.

The hostage was a small boy, helpless and stiff with terror. The fight—although necessary—was only making matters worse. Especially, since the creature was clever enough to use the boy as a shield while it sought an opening in the young man's defenses. The creature swatted the young man back. He rolled, then slowly pushed to his feet. He was at a clear disadvantage.

"That thing's out of your league, Kid," Northe called. "We'll handle it from here."

The young man looked over his shoulder, and time slowed as I took in his features. A rough, boyish face. Brilliant green eyes. And an unmistakable look of determination. *Serec?* My heart flipped in my chest. My mind a mass of confusion. *It can't be...that's impossible.* But it wasn't. Just a short distance away, the boy I'd once known as my best friend, was battling a monster to save a life. Somehow, the boy who died over seven anums ago was alive and well; bearing nearly the same appearance I'd remembered.

"I've got this," he said, breaking me out of my trance before charging the creature again. Surket and Northe watched quietly as Serec and the monster exchanged blows. But it was obvious there wasn't much he could do, so long as the monster had the boy. More than ever, I wanted to do something—anything that might help. But, seeing Northe and Surket holding their positions, I hesitated. Serec slipped behind the monster and landed a hit to its back that knocked it off balance enough to nearly crush the little boy. But just before it was too late, the monster managed to brace itself with its free hand.

"Careful, Kid!" Northe yelled. "Don't get the hostage killed!"

Northe's voice caught the monster's attention, and a chill slivered down my stomach when its orange eyes met mine. But they didn't linger. Serec was its main concern.

"It's smooth," Serec said, inching closer to the creature. "Everything's...smooth."

Even from afar, I could see he'd grown more handsome over the anums. His athletic physique was visible even through his baggy clothing. And seeing him play hero against a monster of that size, could only mean he'd either grown far more courageous or far more stupid. The monster growled, and shielded itself behind the boy as best as it could as it sidestepped into my view of Serec. I couldn't tell what had happened, but after a moment of silence, the monster suddenly yelped and howled wildly, before dropping the boy.

Before I could piece together what Serec could have possibly done to accomplish such a feat, an electric bolt zipped past, striking the monster and disabling it. Surket's bow sizzled as she lowered it. Enraged, the beast regained its footing and stampeded toward us. I swallowed, reaching for Nightfall as adrenaline flooded my veins. But Northe quickly stepped forward and summoned a squall that knocked the creature on its back. The creature twisted around and charged, yet again, towards Serec.

Erratic slashes and swipes were all the beast could manage. But as time advanced, Serec began to slow, until clean dodges became near misses. Anxiety swirled within me as I watched—silent—hopeful. Then, something unexpected happened. An almost mystical, glowing light radiated from Serec as he threw himself toward the monster and plunged his hand through its stomach, clear to its back. For a moment, everything froze. Then, Serec pulled his hand back, and a pool of dark liquid spilled between him and the creature. The monster made short groans, faltering as it backed away. Then, it scurried toward the hedges and leapt, half of its body clearing the obstacle, before it flopped over with a louder groan. I watched as Northe approached Serec and the boy, wondering if I should follow.

"Rima," Surket prompted. "PEDs are inbound and we still have a SITEX to complete."

Peace Enforcement sirens grew louder by the beat; an omen of the imminent conflict. Surket and I raced around to the spot where the monster had fallen. A trail of black blood painted its escape route. We collected a few vials of the creature's blood and started toward the cycles.

"Time's up, K," Surket said, over the HOOD communicator.

"Calm down, will ya?" Northe began. "I'm right behind you."

But he wasn't right behind us. He was still talking with Serec, and it was anyone's guess what they were discussing. But I'd be lying if I said I wasn't a bit envious. There was so much I wanted to ask him. So much I wanted to say, after seven anums. After all that had happened. But the timing couldn't have been worse.

"He must think I'm joking," Surket began. "Let's give him a reason to be 'right behind' us." Surket sprinted off, before I could respond. "Wait up!" I ran after her, but—as usual—the gap between us quickly grew. In no time, she was on Artemis and igniting the engines. In little more than no time, Northe had dropped out of the sky and landed perfectly onto Boreas.

"Don't get left behind, Raven," he said with an almost childish grin.

"Just go already," I said, kicking a leg over Raiden.

"Looks like you made a new friend back there, K," Surket said over the HOOD communicator.

"He was a little wet behind the ears," Northe began, "but the kid's definitely got potential."

"Are you looking to recruit him?"

"I'm not certain I'm sold on him yet, but I'm also not ruling him out as a potential asset. I mean, that trick with the divarma was nothing to scoff at. Right?"

"Perhaps. But he clearly had no control over that ability."

"So, you aren't at least a little curious about his potential?"

"Time will tell if he has what it takes."

If it meant seeing him again, I hoped time would tell that he did. There were so many unanswered questions. For starters, what really happened seven anums ago? I hadn't seen him, since before I'd stopped going by my second name. And all that time, I thought I knew why. Everything changed since then. But with all that had happened, I wondered if that meant everything had changed between us. My imagination went wild, considering all the possibilities of our reunion.

"Still with us, Bird?" I snapped out of my daze, realizing we'd already arrived at transport storage. "You've been quiet this whole time."

"Sorry," I said. "I'm...still a little tired, I guess."

"Once we've dropped these samples to Minerva, we can get some rest."

Unfortunately, I couldn't keep my mind from drifting to Serec, even when we were back in Kareen's lab. While Northe maintained his usual safe distance,

Surket explained the details of the mission. And all the while, questions about Serec swirled in my head.

"But someone beat us to the objective wielding what looked like a divarma." Surket explained.

"Are you certain?"

"She didn't stutter," Northe chimed.

"Quiet, you buffoon! If there was a divarma, you all owe me an explanation."

"Owe? That how this works now?"

"If you withhold information that could further my research, I'll—"

"He drew the divarma from etheric space," I interjected. "But it remained in light form, even as he drove it through the monster's stomach. So, I wasn't able to analyze it."

"Hmm," Kareen pondered my account. "Whatever it is, it can't be a divarma. I've never, in any of my studies, come across a divarma capable of being pulled from etheric space."

"If it wasn't a divarma, what was it?" Surket asked Kareen.

"Hard to say without seeing it," Kareen answered. "Raven, were you at least able to get a look at the annihilation engine?"

I shook my head. "It disappeared too quickly. But as far as I could tell, it didn't have one."

"Impossible. All divarma have an annihilation engine."

"You said it yourself," Surket rebutted. "This isn't a divarma."

Kareen nodded and sipped her tea. "And now I'm confirming it. Anyway, the Director wanted in on the debriefing so we'd best make our way there." Without a word, Northe led the way to Stratcom. Surket and Kareen started after him, just as Phoebe vibrated. Another burst message from Alanda:

Blissful,

His Royal Highness has called an emergency meeting of the Executive Council in three segments. Your attendance has been requested.

"Three segments?" I thought aloud.

"Everything alright, Bird?"

"I've been summoned to the palace."

"How soon?"

"Three segments."

"Then you should hurry."

"Actually, I was hoping to hear the Director's thoughts on the guy with the strange weapon. You know, in case we encounter him again."

Surket's eyebrows lifted slightly as her eyes met mine. "Are you more interested in the weapon or the guy?"

My face grew hot. "He...I mean, we..." My mind grasped for anything that could be considered a valid reason to bring up Serec. "We don't know anything about that weapon. It presents a serious threat if left unaccounted for."

Surket paused, analyzing me in a way that had my heart beating double time.

"Excellent forethought, Bird. Seems your daydreaming served you well." Sometimes I hated how good Surket was at teasing me.

"This is troubling," the Director said, interlacing his fingers and resting his chin between his thumbs. "We should maintain a close watch over both the young man with the mysterious weapon, and the unknown creatures."

"What would you have us do upon spotting the young man again, sir?" Surket asked.

The Director paused momentarily. "What is your assessment of the young man in question?"

"K is the one who spoke with him, and seems the most interested in recruiting him. I'm not against giving him the assessment, though I do have my reservations."

The Director looked to Northe. "What say you, K?"

"I believe he has the potential to be a great Operator," Northe said matter-of-factly.

The Director nodded. "Then, I will assign you to personally keep a close watch over him, for the time being. Report any interesting developments to me directly."

"Yes sir."

"That is all for now, Team Seven. Fantastic work, as usual."

We saluted the Director and the Colonel in unison, and Kareen bowed respectfully.

We walked out of the office, and I darted off the moment the lift doors closed behind us. "See you guys later," I yelled.

"Stay sharp," Surket yelled back. I needed to reach the palace as quickly as possible. But another thought rested in the back of my mind. The Director was considering recruiting Serec into the Guild. The thought alone, colored a wide smile across my face, as I opened Phoebe to record a burst message to Alanda.

ME: ON MY WAY.

ALANDA: SIR DORIEL AND I SHALL MEET YOU AT THE USUAL LOCATION.

ME: PERFECT! BE THERE SOON!

With less than two segments remaining, the best I could hope for was arriving either right on time or unfashionably late. And I was desperately hoping that I didn't end up unfashionably late!

[6]

THE PRINCESS

While mostly democratic, the heart of the Arurian government is a monarchical system. Divinus Martinel is the central power in the nation. Below him are the heads of five noble houses that rule over each of Aruria's five provinces. This division of power seems to have helped gain and maintain stability among the ruling class. Aside from the nobility, there also seems to be a hierarchy of elected officials that serve as counterpart to the nobles. I will have to investigate further but this system seems a bit... complicated.

-The Traveler

Domus Regalia finally glided into view, as Phoebe informed me that I had 45 hashes remaining; barely enough time to make it to my room. I detoured from Central Avenue into Atnia, a sleepy Regalia suburb situated in the northern edge of the capitol city. The calm whir of Raiden's motors blanketed the quiet street as I cruised toward an unassuming two-story home. It greeted us with an opening garage door, beckoning as we hovered into the darkness. The door closed behind us, denying all light entry; concealing our deception.

"It's lovely to see you again Blissful," a girl's voice echoed in the darkness.

"You as well, Alanda," I replied. A small lumen illuminated the garage revealing a teenage girl dressed in a stylish burgundy robe and bonnet. The Martinel Phoenix took the form of a pin clipping the robe together at the chest signifying the house she served; my house. Her blue eyes twinkled as they met mine. Despite only being apart a few decs, our reunion felt like it was anums in the making. The disarming aroma of lenio flowers danced around us as we embraced.

"I've missed you," I said, squeezing her tightly.

"And I you," she replied squeezing just as tight.

The *Sutherland* purred to life beside us; breaking the moment as we parted. An artifact in our world of fuel cell vehicles, the raeda's sleek chrome on black design and perfectly tuned biofuel engine gave it a classic elegance. It was one of five of its kind remaining, and this one belonged to me. A disinterested Sir Doriel sat in the driver's seat as the vehicle hovered, eyes fixed forward. Despite being an expert in the Royal Sword Art of *Semovet*, his true mastery was in the subtle art of finding the politest way to be rude.

"It's nice to see you as well Sir Doriel," I said.

"Highness," he replied in an even tone. He was always so flat; so emotionless that it made him nearly impossible to read. Per usual, it was taking an immense amount of restraint to avoid reading his mind. But like Alanda, Sir Doriel was assuming an astronomical amount of personal risk by aiding me. I couldn't betray that loyalty by sifting through his thoughts, despite the temptation. Alanda held up a set of clothes and I wasted no time changing. As I slipped out of my riding gear, she folded it and stashed it inside a false wall. The house was uninhabited, serving as the portal between two identities. One given. One chosen.

The final part of my transformation was the most drastic. While my natural eye color was a light brown accompanied by rusty brown hair, Blissful Martinel had striking green eyes and a crown of snowy locks. My powers made this change instantaneous and admittedly underwhelming in comparison to my other abilities. Still, it was critical to keeping my personas separate. The ride between my modest hideout and my far from modest home was short but vital. Alanda and Sir Doriel officially served as my handmaiden and personal guard. Yet their true roles were considerably more important.

"The situation has deteriorated Highness," Sir Doriel briefed. "In response to the uptick in crime involving consumed Gifted, the Department of Peace has drastically increased their efforts in all regions. Our agents have reported a greater presence of BNP Occult division and the PED Special Tactics Unit personnel on the streets. An emergency meeting of the Executive Council has been called in response to the spike in Gifted activity as well as these monster attacks that have occurred recently. Reports indicate that there have been seventeen attacks to date with the majority concentrated in Verdallyn province."

The Executive Council was the most powerful body in Aruria, if not all of Orbis. Comprising the heads of each ruling house in Aruria, the council influenced decisions at the highest level. And I cannot remember the last time a major decision was made by the crown without their input. If the council was being assembled, it could only mean the situation had grown dire.

"Any indications on the objectives of this meeting?" I asked.

"We believe," Alanda began, "that the *Primus* is using this as an opportunity to garner more support for his... objectives. I would be prepared for a fight Blissful."

"Lovely. And here I was concerned that this would be an uneventful night." I said as we passed security and pulled into an inconspicuous parking structure.

In no time, I was upstairs and racing to my quarters, flanked by Alanda and Sir Doriel. As I did, I overheard voices echoing faintly from the grand hall below. The meeting was set to start any moment, and if I wasn't down there, that meant Uncle Charlemagne wasn't either. I could only imagine what they were saying. Uncle hated being tardy. But it was commonplace that he refused to enter an Executive Council meeting without me, if he expected my presence. It was important to him that I absorbed all that I could, before the day arrived. The day when I would assume the throne of Aruria. A thought that made me nauseatingly anxious.

"I informed his Divine Highness that you would meet him in his study at 18.90—twenty hashes from now," Alanda said, as we stepped into my quarters, Sir Doriel closing the door behind us and assuming his post outside.

"Best to hurry then. Should I wear blue or—." Alanda's warm hand grazed my cheek and for the first time, I noticed how focused on me she was.

"I'm glad you're safe," she said, sapphire eyes peering into my soul.

"You're a natural-born worrier," I said, trying to dispel the awkwardly serious energy in the room. "How's your mother, by the way?"

Alanda's expression turned solemn. Well... more solemn. "She has her moments. But lately, she's had a tough time keeping her strength up."

A chill gripped me as I tried to determine something encouraging to say. "Then, we'll have to be strong for her. We have the best doctors in the kingdom searching for the cure."

Alanda nodded and hugged me, both of us taking a moment of silence, before pulling away. Honestly, I was likely saying it for myself as much as for her. Shora, was the closest thing to a mother I had known since I'd arrived at Domus Regalia. It was one of many reasons Alanda often felt far more like a little sister than a personal maidservant. When Shora contracted Plaga Viridi, an autoimmune disease caused by the green skies, it cast a dark shadow over Domus Regalia. *Fidelissima* to the king, Shora's love and leadership could be felt throughout the palace. The number of citizens impacted by Plaga Viridi, better known as the plague, had swelled to noticeable levels since the sky's mysterious transformation six anums prior. Many initially thought the sudden change was some type of biological attack orchestrated by our adversaries Lazuria and Oltresulle. But foreign intelligence reports later revealed that their citizens were actually faring worse than us.

"When this is over," I said, "I'll make certain to visit."

Alanda nodded and took a deep breath. "She'd like that. But for now, let's focus on what you're wearing." Alanda pointed to the dress on my bed. "I trust your weight hasn't fluctuated recently?"

"Well, a lot has happened in the last few decs." I slipped off my clothes and stepped into the dress.

"By 'a lot' are we possibly talking about a boy?" Warmth tingled through my cheeks as Serec came to mind. But they might as well have been glowing with someone like Alanda. "That looks like a yes." She grinned mischievously. "Your timing couldn't be better. His Highness was just questioning the staff on word of any potential suitors for you. Now, I can tell him—"

"Tell him nothing," I interjected. "He should keep his focus on Aruria's future."

"Princess, your love life is the future of Aruria. As his heir, why shouldn't he concern himself with such things?"

"I understand that. It's just...there are more pressing matters than my finding a husband right now."

"Point taken. But, about that boy. Do I know him?"

I sighed. "Not unless you attended Frilare Primary School seven anums ago."

"Primary sweethearts?"

"Not sweethearts! Just good friends, in another life."

"But your eyes scream: 'sweethearts.'"

"Stop looking in my eyes, and help me get ready."

Despite her questions, I would've preferred a lengthy chat with Alanda over a council meeting. And that brings me to the crux of princess' life: every part of it is riddled with obligation. Sure, the Guild has its protocols and responsibilities as well, but at least I'd chosen that life.

I knocked on the door to Uncle's study. "Is that you, Sa'Sha?" he called.

"It is," I answered.

"Enter."

"Please forgive my tardiness," I said. "I know I'm five hashes past the time you'd graciously allotted me."

"No," Uncle said, rising from his chair. "I told Alanda 19.00. And here you are—no less lovely than she promised." I shouldn't have been surprised. Alanda's forward thinking often left me speechless. So, instead of saying anything else, I opted for a hug. He kissed my cheek and gave a wide smile. "Now," he continued, "let us make haste. The council is expecting us, and I doubt they'll be delighted if we keep them waiting." He raised an elbow. "Shall we?" I slipped my arm around his and gave a matching smile. The irritating echo of Aruria's two most nefarious politicians buzzed ever louder, as we neared the Council Chambers.

"Your Excellency, how wonderful to see you," Primus Nicosta said, schmoozing. "I must say, I was growing concerned that a less pressing issue had stolen your attention." Nicosta swiftly glanced at me, then back at Uncle.

"I do implore your forgiveness," Uncle replied. "I make every attempt at punctuality, but the matter could not be helped."

"Of that we are certain, Your Divine Highness," Chancellor Faron said, offering an artificial smile as his eyes shifted to me. "Some things are just beyond one's help."

Dante Nicosta and Sylas Faron were, by far, the most duplicitous politicians I'd ever had the displeasure of meeting. Both highly regarded political scholars, anums before taking office I regarded them more as serpents with dubious intentions. Through admittedly genius maneuvering, they were on their way to becoming the most powerful men in the world. Unfortunately for them, Uncle and I stood firmly in their path. The collective power of the Primus and the Chancellor was second only to the Divine Monarch, or myself in the Monarch's absence. But many had long criticized our system of government, arguing that a modern society warranted a more democratic process. Though we did have a legislative body in the Senate, the crown still held most executive and judicial powers.

"Be that as it may, I am very pleased to have my daughter's assistance today. She only recently returned from her travels."

"So, I see," Faron said. "And where might you have explored this time Blissful? An area filled with untold flora and fashionable textiles?"

It would be too easy to wipe his pompous brain clean. "Actually," I said, "I've taken up studying fauna. I've come to find a particular interest in those of reptilian nature. Their characteristics are surprisingly similar to those of some of the people I've encountered."

Faron's visage of smug presumption betrayed him just long enough for contempt to show through. His eyes snapped back to Uncle. "The council is already inside, Divinus. We shouldn't keep them."

We stepped into the expansive grand chamber and all fell silent, as Aruria's five dukes, their provincial premiers, and several other officials stood in reverence.

"His Divine Highness—Charlemagne Martinel VII, Monarch of Aruria, and Blissful Sa'Sha Martinel, Princess of Aruria and Duchess of Regalia," the royal herald called as Uncle and I each took our place on two large thrones at the front of the round room.

Primus Nicosta slithered behind the podium in front of us. "Good evening, ladies and gentlemen. This council has been convened in response to a newly emerging threat to Aruria's peace and security. By now, I am certain you've heard the rumors of monsters attacking citizens in the dark of night. The urgency with which this meeting has been called, should serve as confirmation that this is no mere rumor. The crisis at hand necessitates swift, deliberate action, and we have, therefore, developed a plan of action to ensure our nation's safety and continued prosperity."

The council blindly clung to Nicosta's every word. But I knew better. People like Nicosta always have ulterior motives. "His Divine Highness," Nicosta continued, gesturing toward Uncle, "is indeed a busy man. Despite being in deep negotiations with *Geringrad* to lift the embargo and restore favorable relations with Lazuria, he's been spearheading the renewed effort to determine the cause of the green skies. Perhaps my assumption is a bit of a leap but, in my humble opinion, I would surmise that our green sky and these savage beasts may bear some connection. I, therefore, propose swift, deliberate action be taken in a way that shan't burden His Divine Highness in his quest to find the answers that Aruria so desperately requires. That brings me to the executive order sitting before each of you."

I scanned over the council, heat building in my throat and expanding outward, as each member quietly perused the document placed at his or her seat. The very same document that Nicosta had conveniently not provided to either Uncle or myself, but would surely implore Uncle for a quick decision on.

"Just what exactly are you proposing, Primus?" I asked, breaking the silence.

Nicosta's attention went to Uncle as though he'd asked the question. "I was just about to get to that, Your Excellency." He walked the official executive order to Uncle. "Here you are, Divinus."

He moved back to his podium, without as much as a glance in my direction. It took great effort, pulling my eyes away from the back of Nicosta's head. It would've been the perfect spot to burn an excruciating hole.

"Based on your proposed course of action, I assume all the necessary pieces are currently in place?" Faron asked.

"You assume correctly, Chancellor," Nicosta said. "Because time is of the essence, I took measures to prepare for swift and—"

"Deliberate action," I finished. "Yes, we heard you the first two times. Would you permit us a moment to finish examining your executive order?"

Nicosta forced a smile that failed to hide the irritation in his eyes. "But of course, Blissful. All his Highness need do is sign this executive order, once you both have finished."

The document was brief, but disconcertingly riddled with archaic and ambiguous wording. Another glance at the council confirmed my suspicions. Puzzled faces and whispers between dukes and their premiers. I was not the only one the document had confused. I leaned over to Uncle and pointed to the second paragraph. "I'm having trouble making complete sense of what is written here in particular. Can you explain it to me?"

"Yes, of course," Uncle said. "Let's see...hmm..."

I watched patiently, eyes innocent, as Uncle struggled to decipher the texts. It was safe to assume that he would've signed off on whatever the document proposed, without a second thought. Another sign that Faron and Nicosta were too deeply enveloped in Uncle's trusting graces. But I held the look, until Uncle finally conceded.

"Primus," he said, "would you care to explain, in greater detail, what this document proposes?"

Nicosta's eyes finally found mine, his expression quickly deflating. "But of course. Simply put, the order would allow the Department of Peace to take action against these abominations the instant they are spotted."

"I must note that what you're proposing is anything but 'simply put' here," I commented.

"Sa'Sha, please," Uncle whispered. Alanda warned me to prepare for a fight. I had to stand my ground.

"I beg your pardon, Blissful?" Nicosta said.

"I find specific concern with the 'shoot on sight' order," I continued.

"And why, pray tell, might that be? Have you found some deep-seated compassion for these heartless beasts?" The room chuckled.

"I can assure you, I have not."

"Then, what do you find particularly distasteful in this order, Blissful?" His tone was almost dark.

"You propose to extend the 'shoot on sight' order to all Department of Peace officers, in regards to anything considered 'non-human.' I am simply curious as to why such a term was chosen."

Primus Nicosta and Chancellor Faron both harbored a strong hatred for Refractors. I'd known of that fact for quite some time, whether or not anyone was aware. But it should've been obvious. In legislative matters, their stance was clearly anti-refractor, no matter how pitifully they hid it amongst legitimate issues. This, however, was the biggest step I'd seen since Judicial Code 7713Q—a law declaring refracting as a punishable offense. As it stood, it was foolish not to assume that refractors were among their personal list of 'non-human' entities.

"I can assure you that you are judging my proposal far too critically. This will not grant DOP officials free rein to mindlessly slaughter animals. That said, I am more than certain that no harm will befall your beloved serenity bloom garden either." The room cackled again. Even I didn't know what was about to come out of my mouth the moment before Uncle's hand grasped mine.

"Really now, Sa'Sha," he whispered, "You should be showing due respect, especially in front of the other houses."

I paused as my jaw tightened. I took a breath to slow the blood simmering in my veins. "Apologies," I whispered. "But do you intend to sign his proposal as is?"

"I should think so. His point has been made clear. More importantly, the longer we deliberate, the longer we place the lives of Arurian citizens at undue risk."

Uncle's concern was admirable, but his response was predictable. Predictable enough for Nicosta to have his solution in writing and a speech to stir both the council and Uncle from the start. Given the situation, Uncle was probably more than willing to push the matter into someone else's hands, certain that an indecisive stance was akin to putting lives at risk and appearing weak before the other houses. But it was out of character for the Primus to employ wording of this nature in an executive order. And his explanation was far too succinct. He had to be hiding something. And the cost of keeping quiet could be the lives of innocent refractors.

I scanned the room one last time. The council was growing impatient. All but one who looked quite amused. Svari Yadin. Matriarch of house Yadin. Duchess of Dratigre. And my loving aunt. *She would relish a verbal bout between Nicosta and me.* Unfortunately for the Primus, Svari's ironic smirk was all I needed to strengthen my resolve.

"Please do excuse my request," I said sternly, "but before the document is signed, would you accommodate me with a more readily comprehensible rewrite of this order?"

"Rewrite?" Nicosta repeated incredulously. "There is no need for such a thing, when an interpreter can be provided for one such as yourself, Blissful."

"It is for that very reason that I must ask for a redrafting of this document. I would prefer not to include additional parties in such a delicate matter, when the document itself can be made to read more clearly."

"With all due respect, we haven't the time for that. Your lack of familiarities with legal vocabulary should not obligate a redrafting for layman's sake. Especially when someone as wise as your father—sitting right beside you—can assist. I should think his Divine Highness would be more than willing to familiarize you with the document at a less pressing time." Nicosta's eyes held on Uncle, dragging him into a spotlight that he couldn't have wanted less. Uncle placed a hand over mine and looked at me with stony eyes that nearly silenced me. Nearly.

"Were the matter so simple, I would do just that," I said. "But, as you yourself stated, this is a delicate issue—demanding swift—and more importantly—deliberate action. When the time comes for my father to bestow the crown upon me, I should hope to reign as eruditely as he does; familiar with every clause and stipulation outlined in the executive documents that I must enforce. And to do that, the laws I enforce must appear as clear and objective as possible, so as to prevent my discretion from becoming compromised by inadequate and subjective interpretation." I held Nicosta's glare, unyielding.

"Blissful," Nicosta protested, "you cannot honestly expect me to—"

"Primus," Uncle interrupted, "I must agree with my daughter on this matter and insist you accommodate her in this way. Your intentions within the document need not change. But I will agree that a less complicated version would more readily allow for objectivity in the matter."

The color drained from Nicosta's tan face. "Divinus, time is—"

"Of the essence, I am aware. I must therefore implore that you waste no time in this endeavor. I suspect the stroke of dawn would allot sufficient time, as your document is rather short."

A silence lingered before Nicosta's next words. "Would her Divine be the margin by which I am to 'uncomplicate' my revision?" His eyes were boiling with a rage that was only overshadowed by the deliberate pacing in his speech.

"If it serves your revision well, you may think of it in that way," Uncle replied. "I suspect others will more readily grasp the gist of your revision as well."

Nicosta forced a smile. "You will have it by dawn."

The meeting ended and everyone started for the door. Everyone except Faron and Nicosta. I pursed my lips tightly as the corners of my mouth fought to curl. This wasn't the time for gloating, especially with the two of them watching so intensely. But the corners of my eyes were tightening as bubbles of laughter tried to force their way up my throat. In the struggle for poise, I held my breath and pretended to occupy my attention with Nicosta's document. Unfortunately, Nicosta and Faron were not the only ones who had remained.

Svari Yadin approached Uncle and me with perfect poise and a masterfully manufactured smile. "Charlee," she began, tone nauseatingly upbeat. "How is my baby brother?"

"As well as can be expected Va. How's Arcturus and Katarina?" Uncle was considerably better at being cordial than I was.

"Art is busy with work as usual but Kata is doing quite well. She finishes university this anum and is on track to graduate number one in her class." Svari bragged. "Speaking of bright young ladies," her eyes shifted to me. "That was quite a show you put on up there. More displays like that and Nicosta may finally resign."

"I simply wanted to prevent incidents caused by misinterpretation." I managed. Talking to Svari was always taxing because she scrutinized each word for weaknesses she could exploit later. It reinforced my aversion to the throne as in this position, even family couldn't be fully trusted.

"I'm proud of you nonetheless. As a ruler, you must do everything in your power to avoid appearing weak in front of the other houses. You never know who may be plotting your downfall." The words held for an uncomfortably long time, until.

"You always were paranoid Va." Uncle's voice shattered the awkward energy.

"This coming from the survivor of four assassination attempts," she retorted.

"I'm too good-looking to kill, which is why El has preserved me."

Svari's sinister smile broke and a genuine laugh took its place—one that infected Uncle and me. Despite how much I feared this woman, a part of me wanted to love her even more.

"I'd best be on my way. El preserve you my 'good-looking' brother. Sa'Sha, do keep him out of trouble my dear." Svari said with a hug before slinking away.

With the palace empty, Uncle and I made our way through the *Tempus Court*. He was probably anxious to retire to his bed chambers, and I would be satisfied with a bit of quiet time in my quarters.

"I can't recall one time I've ever seen you so insistent on legislative revision. Have your interests changed?"

"Hardly," I said. "The Royal Army answers to you, but the Primus essentially owns the DOP. That proposal potentially granted him more power than his position warranted. My apologies for the outbursts, but the implications in that document didn't sit well with me."

"I should be thanking you for reminding me that wisdom comes through courageously seeking after understanding. I've become too preoccupied with appearances amidst the fellow houses. So, thank you for voicing your opinion, where I failed to." I looked at Uncle, smiling as my chest tingled with a warm pride.

"That said," he continued, "you would do well, employing tact for sake of maintaining positive relationships with senior kingdom officials. As a ruler, your image is more important than you think."

"But I thought you said not to become too preoccupied with appearances. Shouldn't I care more about what the people think?"

"Image and reputation go a long way, especially with senior officials and nobility. If the people regard you as Aruria's sweetheart, but the elite have all but openly rebelled against you, everything will become an uphill battle or worse. Your aunt's intentions may have been dubious, but she had a point. There are those who wish us ill, waiting for an excuse to take action. The last thing you want is to feel and appear to be a flawed one-person team. Many rulers of times passed were ruined in this way." I fell silent, considering his words. Openly making enemies of kingdom officials would only put a target on my back. And that would not serve me or the people.

"As I've always said," he continued, "opportunity is inextricably linked to obligation. Your life is filled with opportunity, and you must be prepared to fulfill the obligation it demands. The Autumn Gala next dec could be employed as a forum to improve your image, you know."

The gong of the *Tempus Court's* oversized time board rang with an echo. "By El's name," Uncle thought aloud, "midnight already? Let us retire for the night. We can discuss matters in greater depth, at breakfast." His words were still heavy in my mind. But I forced a smile and nodded.

It wasn't until I began ascending the first flight of stairs that I realized how tired I really was. Thankfully, Alanda had my nightgown waiting on my bed— and it couldn't have looked comfier. I slipped it on and closed my eyes the moment my head touched the pillow. Even as I drifted off, my mind couldn't help focusing on the exact "matters" Uncle wanted to discuss at breakfast.

[7]

GALA

Breakfast was awkwardly quiet. Uncle sat at the table, eating like he was on a half-day lunch break, watching the news stream on his digipad. I wondered why he even wanted to eat breakfast together, when his attention was so focused on everything happening within Aruria. But then it occurred to me. *Why am I fretting over an otherwise enjoyable silence, when I could be savoring the rich flavors of palace cuisine?* Even the Guild's food couldn't compete, and there wasn't a day that I'd even come close to tiring of eating at the Guild.

"Sa'Sha, my dear," Uncle said, rolling up his digipad. "Tell me, where have you been as of late?"

I hesitated. "I've been...nearby. Out of the spotlight, if that's what concerns you."

"Not entirely. Though, I do find it rather disconcerting that I cannot pinpoint you at a moment's notice."

I paused. "You wish to restrict my time away from the palace."

"Not at all. I'm in favor of you exploring the world in your own way. The experience grants insight that cannot be taught within palace walls. But, I also would've hoped you might happen upon a potential suitor or two by now."

"I'm not looking for a suitor right now." Not a moment after the words left my mouth, Serec's face flashed through my mind, and my thoughts suddenly lost coherence.

"I could just as easily arrange for worthy suitors. Duke Draken of Imeraste thinks the world of you."

I scoffed at the thought. "I'd sooner marry Duchess Ventusili."

"You are your mother's daughter—El rest her soul. I know you prefer resolving issues your own way, but you needn't be so cold on the matter."

"I don't mean to be. I simply do not see it as an issue." Uncle took a deliberate breath and sighed as he watched me with the eyes of a placating father. "And what of you, Uncle?"

"What of me?"

"Considering the resources at your disposal, why have you not found someone? It's been nearly five anums since Aunt Margaline..."

His chest jumped with a bitter chuckle. "Losing Mar felt like losing a piece of myself. Five anums and I'm not certain I'll ever recover." He was quiet, almost reflective. He wasn't much for courting after Aunt Margaline had passed. But I wondered how long it took him to arrive at the conclusion that he'd lost his soulmate forever. Her illness came as suddenly as her passing and was one of the first documented cases of Plaga Viridi. She fell ill mere decs after the sky's transformation prompting a storm of studies into the issue. What began as minor motor control issues deteriorated into full paralysis and ultimately, death within the anum. It was a tumultuous time for our family; Uncle especially. The sudden sickness of the sky, the death of his wife, the murder of his sister, and the adoption of a niece whom the world would know as his daughter and heir. I always thought my life was difficult at that time. But it couldn't compare to what Uncle was experiencing. We shared a moment of silence for the two wonderful women, before the wistful look in Uncle's eyes faded. "I will table the discussion for now. But it is my sincere hope that at least one young man— worthy of your fancy — will be fated to cross paths with you soon, my dear." It was too early to be certain, but I wondered if his hope was already bearing fruit.

"Have you ever questioned your place in the world?" I asked Alanda looking up at the curving branches of the koa tree as I lay on my back. "It's not as if I am ungrateful. Being the princess of the most powerful nation in the world has its advantages. I just—wonder what life would have been like if I were never kidnapped—if my parents were still here."

Chartreuse specs of light peeked through the tapestry of wood and gray-green leaves. Koa trees were revered as some of the most beautiful and insightful trees in the world. Great thinkers throughout history would sit under them for days at a time pondering life's mysteries. For Alanda and me, it served as a great escape within Domus Regalia; especially considering it was seated atop one of the palaces highest towers.

"I have," Alanda admitted. "Specifically, why some rule while others serve."

"That was quite... direct."

She chuckled. "Don't worry Blissful, the issue is far more abstract than our relationship."

"Sounds questionable Highness," Sir Doriel said from one of the tree's branches.

"You would know questionable wouldn't you Mr. Lucel?" Alanda retorted.

"Comment withdrawn," Sir Doriel conceded flatly.

"Mr. Lucel?" I asked.

"It's a long story that I'm sure Sir Doriel would love to share." Alanda said raising her voice slightly.

"Can't. Busy keeping watch," he quickly deflected.

"Sir Doriel aside, what do you mean by more abstract than our relationship?" I asked.

"My clan has served House Martinel for literally all of recorded history. It's said that the Zoay clan allied with Aryus the Great during the *Fracturing*. What I find interesting about this is that according to histories, the Zoay clan held more power than House Martinel at the time of the alliance." Alanda explained.

"This is sounding less abstract and more direct by the beat." I said.

"I mention this because I can't overstate its significance. When Aryus established the Kingdom of Aruria, the Zoay matriarch, Aya again chose serving Aryus over challenging his power, becoming the first Fidelissima."

"What do you think drove her to do that?" I asked, sitting up and meeting Alanda's eyes. They were so youthful, yet so insightful; like a tiny universe danced within them. Alanda was many things to me. And despite her age, mentor was certainly among them.

"I believe that those with true power have a duty to serve and I think Aya knew that. Sometimes it's not the place of the most powerful to lead; not from a throne at least. You are in a unique situation. You are not only a leader, but one of great power. Surprisingly, I don't think you believe yourself to be either despite overwhelming evidence otherwise."

My eyes lost hers finding the swaying grass in front of her. Like Surket, Alanda seemed to know me better than I knew myself. I hated not being in control—being so vulnerable. Why then was I so drawn to the only two people who could make me feel just that?

"Like me, the decisions of others have shaped your life, but you are ultimately responsible for the direction it takes. You owe it to yourself and our kingdom to realize the potential we all see in you. And that can only come from accepting that which you cannot change and changing that which you can."

"Is it really that simple?" I asked, almost rhetorically.

"No, it never is. Every day is a struggle, whether you're a beggar on the street, or the princess of the nation. But that struggle tempers you, giving meaning to all that you do. You mustn't hide from it." I gave a tired smile, wondering if I had the strength to be the person she saw me as; the one they all saw me as.

"You're awfully wise for someone with only fifteen anums behind you," I said.

"My sole duty is to serve the princess. But when she spends most of her time in places I can't follow her, I find myself—with a considerable amount of free time. How better to spend it than reading?"

Much like Surket, Alanda had given me valuable advice to consider while placing weighty expectations on me. But there was something wholly different about the way Alanda approached issues that made our talks more relaxing than anything. Alanda and I had five afternoons under the koa tree before the Autumn

Gala was finally upon us. It was a nice break from the dangers of life in the Guild. But, as usual, my time with Alanda was too enjoyable, and therefore fleeting. Before I knew it, the night of the Autumn Gala was upon us. Within the segment, Aruria's elite would gather to see and be seen inside the palace walls. I'd assured Uncle that, this time around, I would take on a more active role in the festivities, which ultimately translated to my trying harder not to fall asleep on my feet, while the relentless babble of politicians, nobles, and other elites filled the room. It would be a task. That much was certain. But I couldn't have predicted how true that would be before making my appearance.

From the hallway, the *Imperial Great Hall* echoed with talk of liberal agendas, offshore investment opportunities, and other topics that couldn't stoke my disinterest more. But as I stepped into the great hall, silence descended as if someone had tapped the mute button. I basked in the bright golden light, taking in the elaborate decor. Thousands of leaves woven from light fell from the four-story ceiling, complements of the hologram engines stationed around the venue. Warm tones of red, brown, and gold cascaded across the regal great hall evoking the serenity of an autumn sunset. It was a majestic display, to say the least. A legion of eyes followed me, cameras flashing endlessly as I strode forward, working to suppress the anxiety building as the storm of murmurs brewed around me. But in accordance with Uncle's wishes, I had to remain approachable. Smiles, cordial greetings, and two short interviews consumed what was nearly twenty hashes toward reaching the far end of the room, where Uncle stood on an elevated platform, overlooking the crowd.

"Well now, aren't you a sight to behold?" Uncle remarked, bowing with impeccable poise.

I returned the gesture. "I'm simply following your lead."

Uncle smiled, then raised a hand to cue the musicians to stop playing. As they did, everyone turned their attention to us. "I, Charlemagne Martinel VII, along with my lovely daughter, Sa'Sha, are pleased to welcome you to the Twenty-ninth Annual Autumn Gala. We are honored that you have chosen to grace Domus Regalia with your presence, and by the grace of El, it is our prayer that this night finds you all in good health and pleasurable spirits. Let the festivities commence."

The crowd roared with applause, as the musicians resumed and Uncle and I sat in our thrones. *How awkward*, I thought, looking over the crowd. *I've been a princess for nearly six anums now, and sitting in a throne during events still feels like I'm being put on display.*

"Your Benevolence," a royal steward said, approaching hastily, "your special guest has arrived."

"Splendid." Uncle sprang to his feet. "Come Sa'Sha. There is an important man with whom you should make acquaintance."

Pretending to look far more enthused than I actually felt, I accompanied Uncle into the Reception Hall, where a man in a military coat was standing with his back to us.

"Hachinatus," Uncle called excitedly. "What a pleasure it is to see you again, old friend."

"Hachinat...?" I quickly trailed off. The familiarity in the name caught me off guard, but, thankfully, I wasn't loud enough for Uncle to hear. The man turned around, confirming my suspicion. The crisp military uniform. The wise eyes that held a glint of youthfulness. The bearing that commanded a room despite his average stature. I stood face to face with Hachinatus Arenyu—legendary Army general—head of the Bureau of National Peace. And unbeknownst to most, director of IGIS.

He bowed. "I assure you, Your Divine Highness, the honor is all mine."

Uncle sighed. "If I've told you once, I've told you a thousand times. Please do away with the formalities."

"My apologies—Charlee. I haven't found informality quite so easy to come by since our academy days. Of course, if you hadn't conveniently omitted the fact that you were heir to Aruria's throne, I might have called you Your Divine Highness back then as well."

Uncle laughed warmly.

"I missed you at the Monarch's day celebration. How have you been, old friend?" the Director asked, extending a hand.

"I feel as well as you look," Uncle responded, grasping the Director's wrist and pulling him into a hug. Uncle's jovial aspect lifted my spirits so much, I couldn't hold back a smile. "Speaking of looks, I believe it's been quite some time since you've last seen my daughter, Sa'Sha."

"She was barely above my waist, when you first introduced us," the Director said, looking to me. "But it seems she's blossomed into quite the lovely young lady."

"Hachi," Uncle said turning to me, "is one of my dearest friends, whose abilities and merits have only been overshadowed by the amount of trouble he's managed to talk himself out of, across two lifetimes."

"That is saying a lot, coming from you, Father," I said. "Up until now, I was certain that no one could happen upon more trouble than you."

Uncle frowned at the Director. "Unbelievable. One complement and she's already taken to your side."

The Director shrugged. "What can I say? I have that effect on people."

"Sa'Sha, you remember the stories I used to tell you about my Army days?" Uncle asked.

"Of course," I began, "Noble young officers, infiltrating enemy strongholds to capture strategic targets in defense of our kingdom." I said, feeling wistful. When I was young, Uncle would tell me stories of his youth. Courting Aunt Margaline, training to be the next monarch, and the trouble he would get into with Aunt Svari and my mom all served as an exciting escape for me during my first anums in the palace. But the most exciting accounts by far were the stories of him and the Director during their time as army officers. Tales of visiting exotic lands, meeting interesting people, and surviving several life-threatening situations together painted a picture of a lifelong friendship.

"I wouldn't use the term 'noble'," the Director chuckled. "But we did have quite a few adventures in our youth."

"Indeed. Those were the good old days. Now we're just good and old," Uncle remarked. "I took the throne, and Hachi traded his signature hatchet for a BNP badge."

"The BNP has received quite a few accolades recently. It would seem we have you to thank for the recent drop in crime," I said.

"Indeed, we do," Uncle said. "Which is why Aruria's crime rate is lower now than it has been in over an anum, despite the steady rise in cases of consumed."

"I can't take all the credit," the Director said. "After all, the Bureau simply followed the Peace Enforcement Department's lead in bolstering forces along the areas known for high criminal activity."

Uncle frowned slightly. "You never were one for accepting praise, were you?"

"Would that have affected your reasoning behind appointing me to head the Bureau?"

"Not in the slightest."

"Then, perhaps there's hope for me yet." Uncle glanced around the room and leaned closer to the Director. "Speaking of hope," he whispered, "you are aware of the building crisis involving monster attacks, are you not?" The question was as unexpected as my reaction, my eyes locking onto the Director eagerly.

"I am," the Director replied matching his tone.

"I approved an executive order authorizing the DOP to take as much action as is necessary to neutralize the matter for the sake of civil peace and safety. But, I've received no reports as of yet, I suspect an information blackout has been imposed, which does little to quell my concerns."

"I'll look into it and send word the moment I hear something."

Uncle nodded and started to say something else, but stopped in place and turned to me. "Sa'Sha, there are a few additional details I need to discuss alone with Hachi. This would be a perfect opportunity to mingle with some of our guests."

I bowed "As you wish, Father. General Arenyu, it was a pleasure."

The Director bowed, "The pleasure was all mine, Blissful."

Unfortunately, the pleasure would continue to be the Director's while I spent the next segment schmoozing with an endless horde of gawking politician's wives, all too eager to help their husbands compliment my gown. Whatever Uncle and the Director needed to talk about, it had to be more interesting than everything I was tuning out. But even tuning out was proving to be more arduous a task than I expected and I ended up excusing myself to the more secluded upper tiers of the great hall at the first sign of uncontrollable yawning. After all, I'd made a promise to Uncle and the least I could do was try to keep it.

I brushed past Sir Doriel who was being chatted up by a girl in an unapologetically revealing dress. She was likely the daughter of a marquis looking to elevate her house. Surprisingly, Sir Doriel seemed to be having a worse time than I was. *I'd best rescue him.* "Sir Doriel," I began. "May I have a word?"

"Of course, Highness," he said.

"Good evening Blissful!" The girl blurted, bowing so low I thought her face might touch the ground.

"Good evening," I began, smiling. "Please forgive me, but I must borrow Sir Doriel." We stepped into the lift and rode it to the third floor. "Hopefully I wasn't being too presumptuous but you looked as if you needed an excuse to end the conversation." I said.

"Not at all, Highness. Lucel is an... old friend." I sensed a hint of life in his flat tone... an invitation to dig deeper.

"So that was Lucel?" I began. "I suppose that makes sense considering how talkative she was. Some time must have gone by since you last met."

"You're correct... our time apart was... intentional however."

"So, you've been avoiding that poor girl this whole time? It could not have been that bad."

"It wasn't. I just needed to open myself to... other options."

"Sir Doriel!"

"I've said too much. Can we, pretend this never happened?" He ran his thumb over his Phoenix Knight ring, a signal of distress in his order. A subconscious action such as that indicated that this was a deeper issue than I'd suspected and likely the reason Alanda had been teasing him earlier. But it wasn't a time for prying.

"I have no idea what you're talking about," I said, strolling away.

As I walked around the mostly secluded upper level, I noticed a man quietly half-slouching in a chair by himself, his chin cradled between his right thumb and index finger. He was staring down at the crowd but his eyes didn't seem to focus anywhere in particular. I was only surprised to see him there for a moment. But once I realized it was Alex Locke, the insanely rich tech mogul and CEO of Locket Technologies, that feeling dissipated.

Of everyone in attendance, Alex Locke was the only person I'd ever known to look as bored as I felt. An enigma in the truest sense of the word, who—despite his antisocial inclinations—never missed a palace event according to Sir Doriel. It was indeed a curious thing, and I'd already come up with a number of theories as to why a man of his growing worldly influence and unapologetic political disinterest would even bother, when he could be doing anything else with his time. A longstanding theory was that he always secluded himself in order to watch the crowd for ideas of new technological advances he could develop to siphon more of their frivolously spent credits into his union account. But it wasn't like I was so different. Every event, he quietly watched others, while I quietly watched him. Truth be told, even in his silent stillness, watching him was far more interesting than the conversations and goings on within the great hall.

"It must be a stroke of fortune, finding you unattended amidst such a crowd," a deep voice said. I whirled around to find a large man in a charmingly fashionable suit, smiling down at me. "Apologies, Blissful. My intention was not to startle you."

A rather tall man with a broad build, I imagined his size alone regularly betrayed his intentions. But the first couple of beats allowed for surprise to fall away long enough to notice the oddly attractive polished ruggedness to his face. He was likely close to Northe's age, but there was an intriguing look to his eyes that struck me as timeless.

"What makes you so certain that you've struck fortune?" I asked.

"I have an eye for the invaluable. And a nose for it. I'm flattered that Her Divine Grace would so favor the fragrance of Jasmine Jewel perfume."

"You're familiar with Jasmine Jewel?"

"A good fragrance deserves a man's recognition as much as it does any woman's." He bowed, then extended his hand. "Iam Rhasatto. A pleasure to make your acquaintance, Blissful." As I returned the gesture, he turned my wrist and planted his lips to the back of my hand. A swirl of warmth clenched in my stomach. The feeling was foreign, but intriguing. Not knowing what to make of it, I offered a smile and waited for his next words.

"Perhaps I'm mistaken, but you don't seem to be enjoying yourself nearly as much as your guests."

"What makes you say that?" My tone was softer than I'd intended, almost weak.

"I don't rush to conclusions, Blissful. I came to this conclusion through careful observation."

I swallowed as he took a half-step closer, and as I inhaled, my senses drunk in his delicious fragrance.

"Is that so?" I asked. His cologne was like nothing I'd ever smelled, almost beckoning me to lick my lips. *Who is this man?*

"It is so. And had I additional time to observe, I would gladly make good use of it. Regrettably, my attention is required elsewhere. I will take my leave, most grateful for this night's turn of events." Another kiss to the back of my hand. "Until next time, Princess." I gave a bow and, with an unsettling sensation pinching at the back of my neck, I watched as Mr. Rhasatto took the lift downstairs. In the moment of silence, I realized how extremely shallow my breathing had become. I also remembered that my initial distraction had come from Alex Locke, who had conveniently disappeared.

For the next segment and a half, I avoided as much interaction as I could until the gala came to its well overdue close. I accompanied Uncle in seeing the crowd off, when the Director approached. He bowed gracefully and offered a charming smile. "It was a pleasure seeing you after all this time, Blissful. I should hope to see you again before long."

I stifled the laughter bubbling at my throat and managed a diplomatic smile. "As should I, General Arenyu."

Once everyone departed, I retired to my room, happy to extricate myself from my fetching but uncomfortable dress. I yawned and stared up at the chandelier, a myriad of thoughts floating through my mind and eventually stopping on Serec. I wondered what my chances were in seeing him again. There was so much I wanted to ask. So much that didn't make sense. But all I could do was wait to see if the Director agreed to bring him into the Guild. Either way, one thing was certain. I really needed to see him again.

"Good morning, Blissful," Alanda said, her voice soft and full of cheer. "His Divine Highness has requested your presence in the garden."

I scrunched into a seated position. "What time is it?"

"6.50," Alanda replied, waiting patiently until I started walking toward my bathroom. "Would you like to wear anything in particular?"

"I defer to you. As of late, my taste in attire has been hit or miss with Uncle."

I stepped into the shower, the warm water carrying the scent of my custom jasmine soap. It was an invigorating aroma that lingered throughout the bathroom, even as I toweled off.

I slipped on the clothes Alanda laid out for me, then sat in my grooming chair.

Alanda stepped behind me and started brushing my hair with long, gentle strokes. "So...?"

"'So'...what?"

"I've been waiting patiently all dec for additional details about this boy of yours?"

"It was during a mission, so I only saw him briefly, and from a distance."

"Was he at least cute?"

"If he wasn't cute, we wouldn't be having this conversation."

"Scale of one to ten."

"I don't know. Like I said, I only saw him from a distance."

"You can always change your answer later."

I sighed. "An eight, I guess."

"Sounds like we have a contender."

"A contender?"

"For your heart!" Her enthusiasm made it difficult to temper my expectations. Though I was hopeful about seeing Serec again, the likelihood of that actually happening was depressingly low.

I sucked my teeth. "I don't even know if I'll be able to see him again. At this point, I'm just happy to know that he is alive. Best we not jump to conclusions as rumors around here are infectious."

"Fine," Alanda sighed. "Just promise me you'll keep me completely up-to-date?"

"Only if you drop it, until *I* bring it up again."

"Deal."

Uncle was sitting in the garden in front of a pot of tea as Genly, our head food attendant, laid out a spread of pastries and fruit. "Good morning, Blissful Sa'Sha," Genly said as he pulled out my chair.

I gave a polite nod. "Morning, Genly. And you as well, Father." I placed a hand on Uncle's shoulder and kissed his cheek. He smiled as I sat, Genly placing a napkin across my lap. Sometimes the responsibilities of a princess felt like nothing short of a chore. But the support of wonderful people like Alanda and Genly often made the role considerably more enjoyable.

"Did you rest well?" Uncle asked, as Genly poured a cup of tea.

"I did."

"What did you think of last night's festivities? Did you enjoy yourself?"

The Director and Iam Rhasatto flashed through my mind. "It was...interesting," I said with a smile.

"Splendid. In my conversing with Premier Krenus of Imeraste last night, the suggestion that I hold an event for every season came up. The idea has been ruminating all morning. And if you're beginning to find my events more enjoyable, then perhaps I should pull together a committee to start planning something for winter."

I paused long enough to force a smile. "Well, I think it could be very beneficial to our relations with the elite." Even as the words left my mouth, my shoulders sank forward a little. I may have sounded encouraging, but my body struggled with the facade.

Uncle smiled breathily and took a slow sip from his teacup. "You say you've been careful to remain out of the public eye during your travels, yes?"

"Yes."

He paused. "And what precautions are you taking to ensure your safety?"

"What other precautions should I be taking?"

"So, that would be a 'no'. Concealing your identity would be utterly meaningless were one of those monsters to find you, or—El forbid—another rogue group of Rho—"

"*Gifted*, Father."

"Pardon?"

"The proper term is Gifted." I said it so quickly, I could hardly control the tension in my voice. Rho may have been a commonly used term when referring to Refractors, but there was a history of bigotry behind it that turned my stomach every time I heard it. Even when used by those of pure intentions, it was a word stained with ignorance.

"Yes, of course. But the point is that there are people out there—Gifted or otherwise—with ill intent. And the more I contemplate the matter, the more I think it wise to send a small party of guards to accompany you along—"

"No!" I blurted. Uncle looked at me curiously, as my brain raced for a valid argument. "I mean...sending a party would make it very difficult to maintain anonymity. It could ruin the experience if I were discovered by the people. Considering nothing has happened as of yet, wouldn't you agree that Sir Doriel has done an excellent job of discreetly maintaining my safety?" He started to speak, but stopped and pressed a finger to his mouth. "I've been very careful to mitigate risk to myself and Sir Doriel," I continued. "And I'm certain that adding guards would only stifle my ability to learn more about the world and our people."

He crossed his arms and tilted his head forward, looking up at me contemplatively. But I held his gaze, until he finally nodded. "Sir Doriel may be one of our best knights, but he's only one man, Sa'Sha. So, please do be careful." I would have been satisfied had the conversation ended there. But Uncle was intent on making this breakfast a trying experience.

"There was something else I wanted to discuss with you," Uncle began, a hint of discomfort in his voice. Uncharacteristic. "Sa'Sha I'm growing old and you're growing up. The crown is closer than you think and I need you to begin taking your preparation more seriously." I knew where this was going. Evidently, so did Genly as he had quietly slipped away.

"I'm a bit confused," I began. "I've completed every lesson and followed every instruction you have given me. I'm making progress in improving my relationship with the elite and—"

"There is more to it than that Sa'Sha. You have far exceeded my expectations both as a daughter and an heir. I am incredibly proud of you but our house requires more from its next leader. I know you have other priorities but it is critical that you give serious consideration to a betrothal and marriage within the next two anums."

"Marriage!? Within two anums!?" *He can't be serious.*

"The crowns hold on the kingdom is tenuous at best. A union with a strong house would ensure that when the time comes, we have the support we need to maintain order."

"So, am I to assume that you don't believe in my ability to maintain loyalty of the Great Houses without marrying into one?" I managed to maintain a respectful tone despite my building frustration.

"Aruria is far more progressive than when I was your age but the fact remains that you will still be the first woman to wear the crown."

"You're saying as a woman, I'm incapable of ruling on my own." Anger began to bubble within me as the thought arose. It was infuriating to think that what was between my legs held more power than what was between my ears.

"I'm saying that regardless of your ability, you shouldn't have to."

"I don't know what to say, you hush me at council meetings, encourage me to play nice with politicians, and won't even let me learn the traditional defensive arts that every ruler before me was taught as soon as they learned to walk."

"There is more to my actions that you know. I am preparing you—"

"For what? To be someone's wife? To hand our kingdom over to my more capable husband? Forgive me, but I thought you were preparing me to *be* a ruler, not *marry* one."

Uncle watched with stoic eyes as my words cast a painful silence over the garden. A part of me knew that I should be making the most of my time with Uncle. In a few short days, I would once again be away from Domus Regalia, where it was likely I wouldn't see him again for several decs. But I couldn't get past his assumptions, his implication that I was incapable of ruling without a man to guide my actions.

"May I be excused?"

"Of course, dear." His voice registered somewhere between disappointed and regretful. Perhaps I'd gone too far. That very thought frustrated me even more. I bowed and hurried back to my room. I closed the door behind me, dove onto my bed, and buried my face into a pillow, yelling into it as loud as I could.

A moment later a knock came at my door. "May I enter, Blissful?" Alanda called.

I rolled onto my back and tossed the pillow. "Come in."

She entered, closing the door behind her. "Either you've just set a record for fastest breakfast eaten or something happened." I sighed. "So, what did His Divine Highness say this time?"

"Oh, nothing too insulting," I said , tone chipper. "Just that I might as well be some fragile object in need of a man to look after me."

"So, the usual." I narrowed my eyes. "Well, he is your guardian. You should be glad he cares and wants to see you happy and in love."

"I *am* happy, and love can wait. As long as I've got you and Uncle and everyone at the Guild..." Phoebe buzzed, interrupting my thought. Surket's face appeared as a small hologram projection.

Bird, I have news, but you'll have to wait until you return to hear it.

[8]

RECRUIT

Politics in Aruria is a curious thing. Unsurprisingly, power is centralized with the wealthy and granted to those who show loyalty. Traditionally, wealth has resided with the ruling class; members of the Five Great Houses and their courts. However, I sense a shift in power dynamics. Mass adoption of advanced technology has enabled those with drive and business acumen to create wealth for themselves. And a small group of these individuals has accumulated enough wealth for the nobility to notice.
    -The Travler

Surket might as well have told me the skies would be raining with fire, sending me a cryptic burst like that. Unlike Northe, who all-too-regularly sent pedestrian bursts asking something like if I'd eaten the last sweet roll or something, a burst from Surket while I was in Regalia meant big news. Unfortunately, surprises were rarely something that I looked forward to. Ever since I was small, surprises usually ended badly. Losing my parents, becoming a princess overnight, and losing contact with my childhood best friend had all been the result of surprises. It was anything but an exaggeration to say that I disliked surprises; almost hated them. And that gave Surket's burst sufficient weight to slow the remainder of my time in Regalia to a crawl. At least it would have, were it not for Alanda. When we were together, days passed like segments. She knew me too well, not to keep me in high spirits.

In the blink of an eye, my dec at Domus Regalia had come and gone and I was back in Vaticia, walking into D7. I headed straight for the office, only to find it empty. I tried Surket's room, but she didn't answer. I walked back downstairs into the den. Northe sat nearly motionless, completely immersed in a vid game.

"Northe," I said.

"Hmm?" He didn't move.

"Is Surket around? I tried the office and her room, but I can't find her." A beat of silence passed before Northe offered a disinterested grunt. With a dejected sigh, I headed back toward my room, when my eyes caught something moving as I passed the training room. I stepped inside to find Surket aiming at two floating green hologram targets.

"Targets are positioned five meters apart at a range of fifteen meters." Anni began. "Your probability of hitting both targets is 0.345%."

Surket held the blue string of her bow taut behind the tails of two bioelectric bolts pinched between her thumb and forefinger. Ever so slightly, her chest expanded, then her lips parted and she fired. The targets exploded into red specs of light.

"That's twelve consecutive hits." Anni reported as two more targets appeared. "Your probability of success has dropped below 0.01%."

Surket immediately formed two more bolts and took aim. *Surket must've tuned out her other senses if she hasn't detected me by now.* It almost felt wrong to interrupt her focus, but when she was in a state of flow, it wasn't uncommon for her to train into the night, and there was no way I could wait that long.

"What's the big news?" I said, and Surket flinched an instant before the bolts fired. Both bolts completely missed their targets—one hitting the ground, and the other crackling against the far wall and fizzing out.

She slowly lowered her bow. "If you were anyone else, Bird—"

"I missed you too, Surket. And you know how much I hate surprises."

She watched me with a dangerous look that hollowed out my chest. I started to regret breaking her concentration, when a mischievous grin grew on her face. "Our team might be taking on a new member."

"The boy from Monument Park?"

Surket nodded and my heart filled with flutters. "'Might' being the key word."

"Right," I said, feeling my excitement cut in half. "Assuming he passes the assessment."

"You sound a little pessimistic. Worried he'll fail?"

"No! I was just—"

Surket's grin returned. "K was right. You do have a little crush."

My face flushed, as I suddenly felt like I was under a spotlight. "It's not lit—I mean, it's not a crush." Even if I hadn't flubbed my words, Surket's grin widening into a cheesy smile was confirmation that my tone was too forceful for credibility. "Anyway," I redirected, "I assume you'll be mentoring him."

Surket shook her head. "Since he's K's recruit, you and I will only play support roles this time around."

"You think he can handle this recruit better than the last two?"

"This is the most excited I've seen him since he mentored me. Something tells me a little optimism won't be misplaced." The wistful glint in Surket's eyes said that she was more than a little optimistic. Like some part of her was really hopeful for Northe, the same way I was really hopeful about Serec. She and Northe had a history that I never fully understood. Mostly because she'd only ever divulged bits of information at a time.

"Anyway," she said, "that's the news, Bird. I'll be back shortly. I need to meet with Kareen and discuss our next move on tracking the monsters." She walked toward the exit, stopping at the doorway, but not turning to look at me. "Although I can't speak for K, your secret's safe with me." She walked out and the door closed behind her. I watched her as she turned and disappeared behind the walls, her warm, melancholy voice lingering in my mind much stronger than her words.

I looked around the training room. *Perhaps now would be a good time to rehearse some Semovet processes.* A martial art known only to the monarch and the Phoenix Knights sworn to protect him, the Royal Sword Art of Semovet was a fighting style touted as the most lethal in the world. Consisting of five sub-styles known as processes, it was effective in both armed and unarmed combat, making it incredibly versatile. It was one of House Martinel's most closely guarded secrets making its unauthorized instruction an act of treason. Fortunately for me, Sir Doriel opted to be a traitor and secretly bestow the lessons of the art upon me.

"Anni," I called.

"Raven?" Anni replied.

"Run Jump Protocol 5," I said.

"Are you certain? Your last attempt at this protocol was unsuccessful. I place your probability of success at 3.4%"

"Those are better than Surket's odds and she still hit those targets. Run it." *I can't surpass her if I don't overcome similar challenges.*

"Confirmed."

The floor glowed and ten humanoid figures formed from the light. Without warning, they rushed me. I began to flow through the red process, stoking the embers of passion until a flame erupted. Seeing Serec, battling Nicosta, meeting Iam Rhasatto, fighting with Uncle all melded into a passion that fueled my fierce movements. I sent a fist through the face of one figure, shattering its head. The flame inside melted my confusion and replaced it with clarity, focus. A round-house kick sent the head of another figure flying. This was my escape. My respite. It was why I chose to join the Guild. In these fleeting moments, I was powerful. I was in control. Losing myself in the thrill of the fight, I dispatched the others with extreme prejudice. I ripped my hand from the chest of the last figure as it evaporated into light.

"Congratulations Raven. You have successfully completed Jump Protocol 5, and in record time. How do you feel?" Anni asked.

"This was my favorite shirt," I huffed, realizing sweat had drenched my clothing. As my passion receded, so did my energy, replaced by a mix of satisfaction and fatigue.

"Well, I can't run diagnostics on your shirt, but your vitals are still within an acceptable range though elevated. I recommend calling it a night." Anni said. I did just that, spending the rest of the night on my digipad, revising some of the wardrobe designs I'd been reviewing with Alanda. It served as a nice calm contrast to the aggression I'd felt in the training room. Red process always did that to me, which is why I never used it. I couldn't argue with the results though; both in my performance on Jump Protocol 5 and the sudden clarity I'd gained regarding the recent dec. My feelings were still all over the place, and I still had much to sort out, but for the moment, my mind was at ease. The scent of fresh baked bread, eggs, and sausage filled D7. I drifted down the stairs taking in an aroma that was reminiscent of home on Moreaux Farm. The home I used to know.

Surket and Northe ate quietly in the dining room. "Morning," I said, grabbing a plate.

"Morning," they both said.

"Thanks for breakfast," I said, to Surket.

"How do you know I didn't make breakfast?" Northe asked.

"I'm surprised you're even up this early."

Surket snickered, but Northe looked unamused. "What's on your agenda for today, Bird?" Surket asked.

"Well, I didn't plan to do much today...except excel at my evaluation."

"Extensive sleep must've granted you confidence." I stuck my tongue out at her and her lips curled into a grin. "I'll see you in the training area in two segments then."

"I wouldn't miss it."

"Must be nice, doing whatever your precious little hearts desire. I, on the other hand, have some real work to do."

"We know," I said.

"About time," Surket added.

Northe sucked his teeth. "Ingrates," he murmured.

By the time I made it to the training area, Surket was already warming up.

"Early as usual," I said.

"The best leaders are."

Surket positioned me a meter from one wall and walked to the opposite wall. "Let's see how much progress you've made with your psionic deflection," she said, her bowstring appearing as she tugged on it.

I cleared my mind and projected a translucent field of psionic energy in front of me. "Ready when you—"

A blue bolt crashed into the field nearly overwhelming my reflexes. "You said you were ready," she said sternly.

"I did but—"

"No excuses, Bird. Just results." The switch had been flipped, and everything that made Surket like a loving older sister was buried under the veil of intense focus. She was in training mode. She aimed again, pausing for a breath, before firing again. The second bolt was considerably easier to deflect, as it should've been. I'd been focusing my training on psionic projection for several decs, so the first few bolts required little concentration. It wasn't long however, before I felt my limit approaching. Each bolt she fired, grew larger; heavier. At first, I thought it was a lack of mental stamina on my part. Until a bolt the width of a tree trunk plowed into my psionic field, shattering it and throwing me into the padded wall. The floor teetered and lights flicked as I pressed myself onto all fours. I panted, sweat dripping from my nose.

"You lasted much longer this time, Bird."

"How close was I?" I asked.

"Thirty shots, increasing one percent per shot." Anni explained.

"Thirty percent? That's all I could handle after all this time?" I thought aloud.

"Frustration won't help," Surket said. "Besides, you barely managed twenty percent last time. Just because you can't afford to slack doesn't mean you should ignore a victory."

"Right," I said, trying to push away the discouragement. Developing my psionic abilities had been exceptionally difficult. I first discovered them at thirteen, and quickly came to realize that manipulating psionic energy was nothing like my other abilities. But it did offer unique advantages, the Alpha Psionic Wave being the most powerful. Through pooling alpha brain waves I could focus the potentiated energy into a devastating telekinetic projectile with deadly accuracy. But the attack wasn't without its drawbacks. It required intense focus, and the recoil was severe. So much so that I could easily end up unconscious from overuse. I'd been training for almost three anums and four was my limit. My sessions with Surket proved that psionic shielding needed work too as all I could handle was thirty percent of Surket's maximum output. Reinforcement that I still had a long way to go to reach her level. Just as we were finishing up, I got the call from Northe. He'd made it to the soho shop, where he was expecting Serec to arrive any hash.

"You and Surket decide who was going to test him?" he asked.

"I am," I said with a sigh.

"Luck not on your side, huh?"

"You could say that."

Each team employed different methods to gauge a new recruit. For KO teams, that usually involved assessing a number of field-related qualities—the first of which was maintaining composure under stress. Allowing negative emotions like pride to cloud one's judgement could undo the chain of command and result in several unwanted consequences. It went without saying that respect, loyalty, and resiliency went a long way in the Guild. Still, I felt guilty, knowing that I was about to start our long overdue reunion on the worst foot possible.

"He's walking in now." Northe severed the link and I focused until my mind pinpointed his.

Reading minds isn't all that difficult. But at great distances, it can be considerably more challenging. With this situation requiring me to use Northe's familiar mind as a relay to skim Serec's thoughts, I was thankful that I would only be filtering the surface thoughts to Northe. Anything more would prove a serious strain. Of all the questions Serec had, Northe answered the bare minimum. But Serec's desires to gain strength and protect the innocent were noble in their own right. And that proved reason enough to accept Northe's offer to join.

Their arrival at Vaticia was my cue that my first task was complete. And even though my next task wouldn't start until they made it to D7, I had something much more important to focus on: finding the right thing to wear. It had been seven anums and even if it was a little petty, some part of me wanted him to regret not keeping in contact for all that time. I rummaged through my closet, searching for something that didn't say I was trying, but didn't say I'd just gotten out of bed either. The best way I could pull that off was with something athletic.

Surket and I walked together to greet Serec and Northe as the door opened. The moment his chartreuse eyes looked my way, my stomach erupted with butterflies, and my eyes fell short of his gaze. As he focused on Surket and Northe, I waited anxiously for him to recognize me. I knew that any moment, something would click in his head, and then we could talk about how much we missed each other and how much we had been running through each other's minds. Any moment, he would try to explain what happened seven anums ago, apologizing for disappearing so suddenly, and allowing me to believe he'd been dead this whole time. That he'd agonized over our time apart, and that he would never let it happen again. Then, we could finally start fresh. Instead, his eyes held on Surket for far too long, before shifting blankly over to me. It was as if he hadn't the slightest clue who I was, a feeling that made my eyes tingle of heat. I tightened my jaw, and swallowed the lump in my throat. *At least I won't have any trouble testing him.*

"I'm excited to be a part of the team," he said.

"Except you're still a recruit. That means you aren't a part of the team yet," I corrected, moving in front of Surket.

He cocked his head. "I'm sorry, and you are...?"

"This is our technician, Raven," Northe stepped in. "Anyway, let's go have a look at—"

"I'm the person telling you that you must earn your place on this team," I said, the words practically flowing from my mouth. "Or did you assume that you could stroll in and be welcomed with open arms?"

"I assumed," Serec said. "That I was being recruited to fight monsters, not a teenage girl with an attitude problem." With every word that left that arrogant, goofy mouth of his, my blood boiled hotter, until goading him into a fight felt like a natural response to his poor attitude.

Once he'd accepted my challenge for a not-so-friendly sparring match, there was no arguing that Serec had failed the first test. So, I proceeded to the next part: assessing his combat prowess. I needed to make sure what we'd seen at Monument Park wasn't an isolated event. I rushed him without warning, forcing him on the defensive with a flurry of punches and kicks. To my surprise, he not only managed to dodge in way that was so fluid it almost seemed like art in motion, but he took advantage of every intentional opening in my defense without missing a beat. It was clear that he'd had some type of formal training. But it wouldn't be enough to bridge the gap in skill between us, once Surket gave me the signal to stop holding back.

After his third masterful face-plant, I followed Surket out of the training area, keeping my attention forward. Of course, he demanded a rematch, but there was no way I would give him one that soon. It would only embarrass him further, and I'd already done enough damage for one day. I turned the corner, finally obscured from Serec's field of view, when an image of the Serec I used to know flashed through my mind. Suddenly, another lump formed in my throat, and a wealth of heat pressed at the back of my eyes.

"You hungry?" Surket asked, veering toward to kitchen.

"No," I said, my voice almost breaking. "I'm going to lie down until dinner, okay?"

"Sure." I started up the stairs, the heat intensifying as it spread through my face. "And hey." I stopped as Surket looked at me from the kitchen. "Good job today."

I nodded and continued up the stairs, almost running to my room. I sat at the edge of my bed for some time, fighting back the tears pressing desperately for freedom. Serec may have failed the first tests, but I failed him as a friend. And no matter how much logic I tried to add to it, I couldn't convince myself that he deserved that.

[9]

LOST FRIEND

It makes sense, but it doesn't. The thought turned in my head as I got dressed. *How could the Director become Serec's guardian? He's one of the busiest people I know—definitely too busy to adopt a kid.* There was a lot I didn't know about the situation. But the revelation that the Director was Serec's uncle elucidated some issues while complicating others. *Why am I focusing on this when I need to get down to the training room?*

"Maybe I should just ask," I said to myself as I descended the stairs. But the last thing I wanted was to risk giving away my identity. I'd changed a lot over the anums but I couldn't have looked *that* different. *What's going on in his head anyway? I mean, how do you forget your best friend of five anums just like that?*

I stopped short of the training room and took a moment to calm the twisting pressure building in my chest. I had a job to do, and if I couldn't keep my personal feelings in check, I was bound to lash out at Serec. Then again, four rounds of dominating Serec in sparring matches could easily give the appearance that the line between my job and my personal feelings had been blurred, if not crossed. In all honesty, it probably had a little. Even if his speed and reflexes demonstrated a marked improvement from our first match, he hadn't improved nearly enough to act so cocky. As far as I'm concerned, I was doing him and everyone else a favor by putting things in proper perspective.

"You've lost four matches. What weaknesses have you noted?" Surket asked Serec after he flopped onto the mat for the twelfth consecutive time.

After a short pause, Serec sighed and peeled himself from the floor. "In her or me?"

"Both."

Another sigh. "I'm too slow. But speed probably wouldn't be enough to beat her anyway. She's just too good." His frustration was almost palpable, and it twisted my stomach in knots so sharp, I had to turn away. Their exchange went on, but I was too in my own head to catch what they were saying.

"He's all yours, Raven," Surket said, walking past me.

Out of the three of us, my session with Serec would be the hardest. My original task was to simply familiarize him with the basics of being an operator. But, based on Surket and Northe's assessment, Serec had only shown considerable improvement in power, stamina and coordination. In other words, six decs of training yielded little improvement in his refracting abilities, and it fell to me to change that. I wanted to say something. But the longer I stood there, immersed in awkward silence, the more obvious it was that I had nothing worth saying.

"Don't be late tomorrow," I blurted hurrying out the door. I don't know why those were the words my brain settled on, or even why I rushed off. Was I afraid of what he might say? Whatever the case, I was half out the door by the time I realized how weird that probably looked.

I rose early the next morning, consumed with nervous energy; perhaps even a bit of anxiety. I got dressed and started for the door, when a pesky thought crossed my mind. *I'm only wearing standard deodorant. What if I end up covered in sweat from today's session with Serec?* The last thing I needed was for body odor to create another wedge between us. Unfortunately, I'd only ever kept the essentials in D7. Then it hit me: *"Midnight Myrrh!"* I checked under my sink and there was my favorite handmade, Lazurian-imported body butter. With the trade embargo between Aruria and our rival nation Lazuria in full effect, it wasn't easy to come by. I normally reserved it for special occasions, which were so rare with the Guild, I often forgot I even had it. Don't misinterpret me here, though. I'm not saying seven segments of one-on-one training with Serec warranted a rich fragrance like Midnight Myrrh. It was simply an act of necessity. Working with what was on hand.

I started for the training room, nearly fifteen hashes early. I strode downstairs and into the kitchen where Northe was sitting at the island with a cup of tea. His head jerked toward me and he narrowed his eyes, nostrils flaring.

"What's wrong?" I asked.

"You goin' somewhere important?"

"Just grabbing water before hitting the training room."

"Today your first day with the kid?"

"Yes, why?"

He opened his mouth, but stopped, a large grin creeping over his face. "No reason." He rose and walked toward the stairs. "Have fun."

I started to ask why he was acting so strange, but remembered Northe always acted a bit strange. A quick warmup and stretching was all I could do to help ease my mind as I was expecting Serec to arrive any hash. More than thirty "any hashes" later, Serec stumbled into the training room looking like a burglar caught in the act.

"I specifically told you not to be late," I said, my tone deliberate.

"Sorry," he replied. "It took me a little longer to get dressed than I expected."

Sleep was clearly more important. *I can't believe I wasted my Midnight Myrrh on him!*

I reminded him of his obligation to himself and the team, but he only responded with excuses and sarcasm. Not even five hashes in first day of training, and I knew our time together would be a chore. First on the agenda was figuring out why he was having trouble using his powers.

"Perhaps I can help. But, I'll need your consent first." I offered, explaining I could perform a superficial probe of his mind. He was not enthused about the idea but I managed to convince him. I stared into his eyes, fighting to maintain my focus. He may have been arrogant, tactless, and mildly inconsiderate, but he was still the boy I grew up with. Still my friend; even if he didn't remember he was. As my mind latched onto his, the training room grew dark and the walls began to melt away. I stood alone in the darkness for an uncomfortably long moment. I hated this part. Suddenly, a light shone in the distance and countless walls shot up from the ground, surrounding me. I found myself in an endless hallway lined with doors, not unlike a hotel. My mind rattled as hundreds of whispers emanated from behind the doors, chipping away at my focus. One of the doors opened and someone stepped out. The person I'd been waiting for all this time.

"Liza?" Serec said. That was the one word I needed to hear. I ran to him, throwing myself into his embrace as tears streamed down my face.

"Serec, you remember," I said feeling weak and invigorated and sad and excited and anxious and peaceful all at the same time. He looked into my eyes and I thought I would melt.

"I can't do this alone Liza. I'm not sure I can do it at all," he began, face growing serious, apprehensive. "I need you."

"I know. That's why I'm here. I'll always be here for you," I said squeezing tightly. Gently, I broke away and pressed my hand on his chest, light radiating from my palm. Would I could stay in his mind forever, with the version of him who knew me. But knowing at least a part of him remembered me would have to suffice. Doubt oozed from his subconscious. It was the last thing I would've expected considering he'd single handedly defeated one of those monsters. I fought the urge to press deeper, instead impressing upon his subconscious to over-write his paradigm of self-doubt with bravery and confidence. When I did, the inner Serec walked back through the open door and light burst from it, illuminating the entire hallway.

I found myself back in the training room where mere beats had passed. My intervention wouldn't be enough to completely fix his issue, but it went a surprisingly long way to improve his results. With little concentration, his hand was emitting sparks and whirling wind. His face lit with excitement and child-like hope that warmed my heart. His round, dreamy eyes pulled up to mine. "Raven, you're amazing," he said. For a moment, it felt like I was floating, and if the time was right, I would've happily lost myself in those eyes. But as Surket would say, I had to keep my wits about me.

I cleared my throat. "You're welcome," I said as flatly as I could.

As far as his powers were concerned, my mission was a success. Before our seventh day, Serec could form small gusts of wind and concentrate electricity into his palm. By the tenth day, he could do both simultaneously. It was impressive. Almost as impressive as the effort he put into his training. He did struggle to grasp a few tactical and technical aspects I tried to cover with him, but still, I was beginning to see why the Director supported Northe's request to add him to Team Seven's roster. I was also beginning to see that he had much more charm than I originally gave him credit for. Enough that—by the end of the first dec—I was even feeling hopeful about spending time with him. The Serec I knew was still in there. And he was coming out little by little.

It honestly made our final day of training bittersweet. Sure, I'd regain seven segments of my day. But being this close to him had been nostalgic. Some of our moments together felt too reminiscent of our time together in Frilare to maintain my cold facade. I even showed him my divarma, Nightfall. The obsidian blade was more an extension of me than a weapon, and a symbol of my achievements within the Guild. The significance was probably lost to him, but I felt compelled to show in some small way that I wanted to trust him. Our session had come to a close, and—despite the gratifying improvement our communication had taken—I thought it best not to linger and started for the door.

"Raven," Serec called. I stopped and looked over my shoulder, finding his hand extended. "I just wanted to thank you for training me. And I'm sorry I got on your bad side when we first met." It really had been difficult, meeting his maturity with hostility. Especially when it seemed like his respect for me was growing. But we were at the tail end of his assessment. And I wanted to see if he was still as dense as I remembered.

"How did you get on my bad side?" I said.

He shrugged. "I don't know. I just—"

"I'd advise against, apologizing when you don't know what you're apologizing for." I turned away. "Lest you end up making the same mistake and giving another pointless apology." With each step toward the door, the heaviness in my chest intensified. I could only hope we'd be able to put the tension behind us once he had become an official member. Northe was standing at the doorway. The moment he said Surket wanted to see me in her office, my tension eased a little. It was finally time.

"The Director and the Colonel are ready for our assessment, Bird," Surket said as I stepped into her office. "Of course, Northe and I have already made our decision, so we can close things out with your assessment."

"Well, we got off to a rocky start, and Serec still found the strength to put his feelings aside and take direction when needed. After everything I've thrown at him, he still offered a thank you and tried to apologize for his behavior."

Surket nodded. "That's reassuring."

"And romantic," Northe said, stepping into the office with a smirk.

I rolled my eyes and turned back to Surket, she glared at Northe with enough tenacity to burn a hole. "Were you able to determine his class?" Surket asked.

"Not quite. His potential sets him apart from most Refractors. His mind has somehow compartmentalized his power, like he's trying to unlock his abilities in pieces that are already there. I helped him break through one of his mental locks, but it's anyone's guess how many remain. I suspect he may be in the first sphere."

"First sphere? You can't be serious," Northe said, incredulous.

"Perhaps, there's a reason he was assigned to the only KO team in the Guild comprised solely of first sphere Refractors." I said, a hint of pride in my voice.

"Indeed," Surket said. "His skills are still sorely lacking though. So, how do you vote, Bird?"

"I vote yes," I answered.

"Then, it's unanimous. Good work playing your role."

"You really put your heart into that performance," Northe added.

"I only did what I had to," I said. "But a clean slate between us would be nice, once he's officially inducted."

"If the goal is to improve the dynamic of your relationship, you would do better easing him into your nicer demeanor," Surket said.

"Why?"

"So far, Serec has only seen you as an aggressor. Suddenly, flipping a 'nice' switch could be taken as flighty, and places his view of your character at risk."

As usual, Surket's logic made perfect sense. There was little I wanted more than a quick resolution. But I'd already done enough to unsteady our relationship. If impatience would make matters worse, I'd have to tough my feelings out a bit longer. "I guess that makes sense."

"It'll work out," Northe said. "Give it some time."

"The last order of business is Serec's designation," Surket said. Unlike the other KO teams, Team Seven had a tradition started by the original commander. The junior member would choose the designation of its newest member upon official initiation. It was supposed to help build trust in each other's judgment, assuming the initiate accepted the designation. "Have you come up with anything, Bird?"

"Zero," I said. "I based the name on his ability." Surket and Northe both stood there quietly for a moment, contemplating my explanation.

"I like it," Northe said. "It's pretty clever actually."

"It is, isn't it?" Surket said.

I smiled, feeling a bit of my anxiety fade in place of hope. After all, Serec had every right to reject it. But he didn't. When I revealed the designation, he happily accepted it. I almost smiled at him. And by "almost" I mean "did." But I quickly forced it back as Surket's warning came to mind. After the ceremony, we returned to D7, officially a four-agent team. It felt different having a fourth member for the first time, but I couldn't quite figure out why. I didn't have time to contemplate it however, as Surket called Serec and me into her office and passed me a digipad.

"I trust you've picked up a few new skills, Zero." she asked Serec.

"Yeah. Thanks to Raven." My cheeks warmed and again I forced back the smile. But Surket caught it, and her smile matched mine, as her eyes shifted between the two of us.

"And how do you feel about your designation?"

"I like it. It explains my ability pretty well."

"Good. Raven spent much time mulling over that name." I pretended to be too immersed in the digipad to hear them. But I felt Serec's eyes on me, and it made so much blood rush to my face, it I thought my cheeks might ignite.

"Anyway," Surket continued, "I'm glad the two of you are finally getting along, since we've been tasked with compiling all the information we can on the creatures you saw at Monument Park." Surket explained what happened to Team Six and that Serec and I would be performing a three dec long surveillance on the creatures. I didn't have to read Serec's thoughts. The anxiety radiating from of him lapped against my conciousness. I could't blame him. But as commanding officer, I would do all I could to mitigate risk. We watched the vid of Team Six's encounter with the monsters. I wanted to believe I was better prepared, having already seen the vid and the monsters. But watching it put me back in the alley with that first creature. I folded my arms, trying to gain distance from the memory. It was anyone's guess how Serec and I would actually accomplish this mission.

[10]

CONNECTION

I've come across a ranking system used by the *Others* and the Guild to classify both weapons and combatants. There are nine classes that are each divided into three tiers known as spheres. The lower the number, the more powerful the weapon or individual. For instance, warriors in the first sphere are among the most powerful of either side, while Class IX weapons some of the weakest. I have some idea of my power but I should test myself to be certain where I fall.

-The Traveler

Under most circumstances, a three dec of surveillance mission sounded too easy not to expect a drawback. This mission came with two. First, the targets of surveillance were terrifying and unpredictable monsters. Second, my partner would be my childhood best friend, who'd come out of puberty as a nicely-built specimen with a glance that could turn my heart into the world's greatest gymnast. Add to that, the fact that this would be my first mission acting as commanding officer and I had a rather potent recipe for unsettled nerves. But Surket and Serec's confidence in me seemed unwavering. I had to at least pretend to feel the same certainty they did.

Serec and I met in the war room, where the MADS had been integrated into the gameboard. I pulled up a grid displaying the monsters' locations over a map of Verdallyne and explained our mission objectives. If I'd learned nothing else from Surket's briefings, it was the importance of preparing for the unexpected. And this mission was no exception. Once I was finished, I looked at Serec, who quietly stared back at me. We watched each other for a beat, my heart climbing into my throat.

I swallowed. "Do you have any questions?"

"I'll just...follow your lead." It sounded more like he was asking me than telling me. But it said everything. I pursed my lips and took in a deliberate breath. It was a stretch expecting to be as good as Surket on my first try.

The MADS was showing a bit of good and bad news. Most of the activity seemed to be localized within southern Verdallyn—specifically New Callastryne. That left Uncle, Alanda, and all of Regalia safe for the time being. But the fact that Regalia shared a border with Callastryne, meant that if we couldn't get the issue under control in a timely manner, it was only a matter of time before the threat moved north. The terrarail hummed under my feet with a light, oddly soothing rhythm. Still, the ride to the drop point was uncomfortably quiet. I thought to say something, but as much as I wanted to dissolve the awkward silence between us, I also wanted to keep my mind focused on the mission. Add to that the fact that I couldn't think of anything worth saying, and it was clear that talking would prove counterproductive.

"There's something I've been meaning to ask you, Raven," Serec finally said.

"Yes?"

"Why'd you vote in favor of me?"

"Why would you ask me something like that?" There was an unintended punch to my voice.

He shrugged. "I mean... never mind. Forget I asked." I watched him for a moment; the weight of a stone in my stomach.

"We don't have to be best friends to be on a team." I looked away as Serec tried to meet my gaze. "You showed promise," I continued. "That's all there is to it."

"Is something wrong?" Serec asked.

"No."

"Sorry, I just..." He paused. "Did it really take a long time to come up with Zero?"

I shrugged. "I wouldn't say it was a long time."

"How long isn't long, if all you could come up with was Zero?"

"I don't kn—" Serec's laughter filled the compartment. "What's so funny?"

"It's nothing... like Zero!" It was far from nothing if he needed to hold his sides to contain himself.

"Fine," I said, crossing my arms. "Don't tell me."

Behind my facade of irritation, something in me shifted. The tension in my stomach eased. Even if—for as long as I'd known him—he'd been the biggest fan of his boyish humor, I was thankful it was still a part of who he was. The Serec I knew was still in there.

"Why are you looking at me like that?"

"Huh?" I said, breaking from the trance I hadn't even felt myself slip into.

"You look like something's wrong."

Heat flushed into my face. "Stop exaggerating."

"Exaggerating? You were staring right at me and—oww!" Serec rubbed his arm. "What's up with you?"

"I said to stop exaggerating."

"Do you always resort to violence when people say something you don't like?"

"It's only a natural response with you." Serec gave a sidelong frown and turned away, completely missing the growing smile on my face.

Our drop point was Utairi Hills. A heavily populated area that presented an enticing target for the creatures. But if they kept to the behavior we'd seen so far, it was unlikely that they would make a move before the crowd thinned enough to give them the full advantage of numbers.

"So," Serec said, "how does this work?"

"We'll observe from here until we find a good vantage point. Are you hungry?" I purchased two pumil wraps and two grilled nibos skewers from a food booth. But Serec only took a pumil wrap.

"You don't like nibos?"

"I'm a vegetarian."

"Since when?" The words escaped before my brain could filter them.

"Since before you met me." I paused, thankful my little outburst didn't give me away. Thinking back to dinners with Serec, I couldn't recall him eating meat. Then again, I was more focused on stealing glances at him than watching what was on his plate. I took a bite from the skewer and gestured for Serec to follow me into the bustling marketplace. The sun crept over the horizon and, like a machine, merchant and food shops started packing up and locking down. No one noticed as we slipped through the crowd of last-hash hagglers to find a choice rooftop for our surveillance.

"It's like a crazy swirl of yellow, black, and blue down there," Serec said, looking down at the crowd.

"A testament to our people's nationalism. I should've noticed it sooner. You being a vegetarian."

"It's smooth. You probably had more important stuff to focus on than someone like me."

"What do you mean?"

He shrugged. "I'm just pointing out the obvious."

I folded my arms. "And what exactly is 'the obvious?'"

"That you hate me."

"H—," I choked on the word. "Hate you?"

"I saw how you looked at me when I first walked into D7. Like you were disappointed or something."

"I was," I said, looking away. "But it had nothing to do with hating you."

"Right. Either way, I appreciate you pushing your training aside to work with me. It helped a lot."

"Just because we had a rough start, doesn't mean—"

"Could we change the subject?" His forced smile intensified an already melancholy mood.

"Sure," I said with a pause. "When did you become a vegetarian?"

"What makes you think, I wasn't always one?"

"I...assume most people aren't born vegetarians."

"Probably not. Hachi—I mean—the Director, is vegetarian. When he adopted me, I became one too."

"So you're adopted?"

"It's been a little over seven anums now."

"Where are your biological parents?"

"They were murdered when I was ten."

"That's terrible."

He shook his head. "It's smooth. I try not to cling to the past. Ya know? If anything, losing them inspired me to protect the innocent instead of just being a bystander"

It was all starting to make sense. The murder of Serec's parents had been all over the Frilare news streams, with no leads on who might've been behind it. To make matters worse, the stream wasn't made until the day after the event, so there was no way to act on the details in a timely manner. My parents immediately sprung into action, arranging a search party for Serec. But before they could get both feet out the door, the next report came in, confirming Serec's death. I didn't talk to anyone that night. I barricaded myself in my room, scrunched into a ball under covers, and cried until I had nothing left. It was the first of a string of unfortunate events in my life. Even as a stretch, it was very possible—even probable that the Director could have gained custody of Serec, and covered his tracks by falsifying the report of his murder. It made me wonder what type of trouble his parents were in. My heart sank at the painful recollection. But Serec probably felt considerably worse.

"You're not alone," I said. "I lost my parents, not long after you did. My reasons for joining the Guild are mostly selfish but, a part of me would like to believe I'm honoring their memory."

"Raven, I'm sor—"

"Don't be sorry, I've heard that for far too long. Just tell me, did you hate me back?" I asked.

"Huh?"

"When you thought I hated you. Did you hate me back?"

He paused before answering. "No."

"Do you hate me now?"

"Why would I hate you now?"

"I don't know. I mean...forget it. I—" A scream reached into the sky. I scanned the area but Serec was already a step ahead of me.

"This way," he called hopping off the rooftop. I teleported, materializing beside him.

"You can—"

"Later," I huffed as we ran. We rounded a corner to find one of the worst outcomes possible. Two monsters were cornering a man and woman. Saliva dripped from their jagged teeth as they closed in.

"We have to help them," Serec said not bothering to wait for my orders. He leapt into the air, landing between the couple and the monsters. *So much for surveillance.* In a flash, he punched both monsters sending them crashing into a nearby wall. Without hesitation, he unleashed electricity from his palms, shocking the monsters until they lay limp on the ground. The intensity and efficiency with which he executed this was astonishing. He truly had improved. Serec turned to the couple who stared at him with wide eyes. "Are you two okay?" He asked, reaching out a hand.

"W—what are you?" The woman asked, holding the man in fear.

"I'm just trying to help."

"P-please. Just get out of here. We don't want any trouble from your kind." The man said struggling to muster the courage to even talk to Serec.

"But—"

"Please, just go before I call the PEDs."

"That won't be necessary," a voice called from behind me. A man in a trench coat, a PED lieutenant approached flanked by ten peace enforcers with stun batons. "Young man, you are in violation of Judicial Code 77130. As such, you are under arrest," the lieutenant said as they surrounded him.

"But I just saved these people," Serec argued.

"Be that as it may, I'm afraid the law is the law," the lieutenant said flatly.

My heart kicked into a gallop so rapid the blood pulsed in my shoulders. As the PEDs closed in, my anxiety grew. My telepathic abilities wouldn't work on so many people at once making the truth painfully clear. I couldn't stop them. Not without violence. And hurting citizens was unfathomable. It would be a violation of both my office in the Guild and my position as princess.

The air in my lungs held fast; my breathing becoming completely voluntary. Two PEDs grabbed Serec's arms as two more pointed stun batons at him. Serec clenched his teeth, his eyes finding mine. He was struggling, but not with the PEDs. He was fighting to keep his emotions under control despite the injustice unfolding around him. Guild protocol was to allow a compromised agent to be arrested. Our philosophy on the matter was clear: we operated outside the law, but we weren't above it. The resignation in Serec's eyes drove that point home as the PEDs applied handcuffs. It was my duty to follow protocol. But I'd already lost Serec once. I was *not* going to let someone take him again. I ducked behind a wall taking full advantage of the fact that everyone was too focused on Serec to notice me. I removed the tie holding my hair in place and it fell to my back. It gave off a subtle sheen as I willed it to lighten. I had one more option, but it came at great risk,

"Lieutenant." My voice echoed, giving everyone pause as they focused on me. I approached them with the poise and regal bearing befitting my station. It was all

I could do to steady my trembling hands. I knew how foolish this idea was. But I was committed. I *would* save him.

"Ma'am," the lieutenant began. "This is a crime scene, please step bac—"

"Do you know who you're addressing, lieutenant?" I began, stepping up to him. He was significantly taller than me, but in this moment, I towered over him. "I am Sa'Sha Martinel—Duchess of Regalia, Matriarch of House Martinel, and heir to the throne."

The man held my gaze—evaluating me—scrutinizing. But I stood my ground. Unwavering. The lieutenant took a step forward—and fell to his knees.

"Your Divine Grace," he said, bowing. The couple and PEDs all followed suit. Even the ones restraining Serec awkwardly kneeled, forcing him to the ground.

"Rise, all of you" I said, tone even—powerful.

"This young man serves on my security detail. He is talented if not a bit overzealous. I accept responsibility for his actions and request that you return him to my custody immediately."

"Of course, Blissful. But, what are we to report?"

"You have two dead monsters that have suffered electrical burns and a squad of men with stun batons. I think you can figure it out lieutenant."

"Yes, Blissful," he said, resigned.

"Bartram," I called to Serec. He just stared at me—dumbfounded. *Not the time.* "We'd best be on our way before a crowd forms." The PEDs released Serec as I grabbed his arm and led him away from the scene. I wondered what was happening in that head of his, but one of us had to focus on exfiltration. My first mission as CO and everything that could go wrong, did. I couldn't think about that. I had to get us back to Vaticia.

"W—what just happ—"

"We'll discuss it on the terrarail." I interrupted. I never thought the hum of the terrarail would bring such relief. I sank into my seat, preparing myself for a series of difficult conversations. The first still staring.

"You can change your hair and eye color?" He asked, noting my green eyes and white hair. *Such a way with words.*

Let's unpack this slowly," I sighed. "Yes, my powers allow me to change my hair and eye color. It's one of the ways I protect my true identity."

"Which is Blissful Martinel?"

"Glad you were paying attention."

"You don't have to have an attitude."

"I don't, I'm just a bit overwhelmed right now. You placed me in a really difficult position back there and I'm not sure I'll be able to mitigate all the consequences." Silence overcame the conversation as my frustration melded with anxiety.

"For what it's worth, I'm sorry. I know I put you in a tough spot. But I couldn't standby and let those things hurt innocent people. Saving people is the whole reason I joined the Guild."

"I understand, I just... need you to trust me. As your CO, as your partner." Our eyes met, and hope poured into my heart, washing away the anxiety.

"I do trust you, and I appreciate what you did for me back there. I know it wasn't easy." A smile crept onto his face. "I can't believe I didn't notice before. You look just like her."

"Well I *am* her so... yeah." I said, allowing my hair and eyes to darken.

"NaRyn would flip if she found out I knew the princess."

"NaRyn?"

"Oh, my cousin. You're like her idol. I always thought your whole sweetheart persona was an act—and—I guess it kind of is," he said.

I cut my eyes at him. "What are you saying?"

"That the real you is way more awesome than the you on the vid streams."

My heart leapt as I struggled to find the words. *He thinks I'm awesome!*

"I can't imagine the Monarch being too smooth with you risking your life out here," Serec said bringing me back to Orbis.

"Do you intend to tell him?"

"I didn't realize it was that easy to get an audience with him. But no. It'll be nice to fall into the charade with Surket and Northe. Plus, the Guild probably needs you around as much as I do."

Even at its rapid pace, my heart skipped a beat. Of course, I wasn't about to let Serec know his words were affecting me. "And why exactly would you need me?"

"Are you serious? Two decs with you and I'm using my powers better than ever. If you're ever up for another session, let me know."

"You...want to train with me again?"

Serec flashed a dreamy smile. "Gotta make sure I don't become dead weight, right?"

I smiled breathily. "I'm beginning to doubt that'll happen."

Despite the complications of our mission, Surket was still pleased with its outcome. The Guild deployed Clandestine Services teams to eliminate evidence of the encounter with the PEDs, though I was still convinced the problem had not completely been resolved. With each passing night, Serec and I made the most of our mission, learning more about one another. Our ability to track the monsters improved significantly and thanks to Serec's extraordinary hearing, we were always able to maintain a safe distance for observation. We really did work well together. So much so that we even spent time together, outside of our missions. Morning trainings, brunch, mission prep. It became habit, spending our days in much the same way we did our nights. And we both benefited from our time together. Seeing Serec's continued improvements as an agent, started to pull Surket's high expectations into perspective. Watching Serec, I realized I had some of the same confidence issues holding me back that he'd originally had. But I was proving Surket right. With each passing day, I was proving to myself that I could be like her.

The morning after our mission ended, Serec and I met with Surket and

Northe to go over our findings. "Good to see the two of you still in one piece after all this time," Surket said.

"You could say we've become adept at handling these monsters," I said.

"She wasn't too worried about the monsters," Northe commented.

"Good work on your report, Bird," Surket said gesturing toward her digipad. "'Highly intelligent. Hunt in packs. Night vision. You've got some solid data here."

"Thanks," I said. "We didn't gather all the information we'd hoped, but I'm glad we were at least able to uncover some key details."

"These *malefactors* are starting to sound like sociopathic mutants," Northe commented.

"Malerfas... say that again," Serec said.

"Malefactors," Surket said. "It's the name we've adopted for the monsters. Were the two of you able to find any leads on their place of origin?"

I shook my head. "Their movements were too erratic to determine any patterns."

"Well, at least we—" Surket's TAB dinged. She tapped her earpiece. "Go ahead, Minerva...I see...I'll send Raven and Zero over now." She severed the link. "We'll continue this later. Kareen has urgent news."

"You aren't coming with us?"

"If I didn't trust your judgment, I wouldn't have positioned you as CO in the field for the past three decs."

Warmth bubbled into my chest and pressed a smile into my lips. "Fair enough. Ready Zero?"

"When you are," he said.

"MADS just picked up an interesting reading," Kareen started, the moment we stepped into her lab.

"Interesting how?" I asked.

"The signature matches a malefactor. But it's considerably larger than normal."

"You need samples." Serec said. "Point us in the direction, and we'll be back in no time."

"Center of Downtown, New Callastryne."

"The center?"

"This one didn't bother concealing itself. Which means it's mindlessly attacking the city, like someone I know." Kareen gave a side-eyed glance at Serec.

"What'd I do?"

"Raven told me how you knocked a hole the size of a wine barrel into two buildings, during your mission."

"Those buildings were really close together."

"Opposite sides of the same street?"

Serec shrugged. "At least it was the same street."

Kareen's eyes narrowed and Serec fell silent. "Anni, pull up a wide-view city security feed."

Her gameboard projected a screen with a fuzzy vid feed, revealing a malefactor, more than twice the size of any we'd seen. Thankfully, most civilians were keeping clear of the creature. All, except for two. A young man and woman were in front of the malefactor, dipping and dodging as it attacked. Without warning, Serec grabbed my arm and broke into a sprint that nearly compromised my footing.

I tapped my HOOD and linked Northe. "MADS picked up serious activity in New Callastryne," I huffed. "We need an air drop."

"I'm already on standby. Meet me at the launchpad," K said.

"Got it." I severed the link. "Serec," I started. "K is waiting on the launchpad."

We reached the double doors and Serec veered right, heading toward the launchpad, where the *Nighthawk* Aircraft was powering up. We jumped into the cargo bay, and the ramp closed behind us; the aircraft quickly ascending.

"Your gear is in the go-bags," Northe called from the cockpit. Serec and I unzipped the bags and pulled out our gear.

Serec unfolded his uniform, his eyes intense enough to give me pause. Then, he threw off his shirt, and I paused even more. His entire front was taut and rippling. He looked up at me and froze.

"Aren't you gonna change?" he asked.

I nodded wildly, and cleared my throat. "Y-yeah! I'm about to change right now."

"Let me know when you're done," he said, turning an equally toned back to me. I closed my eyes and took a breath, before changing. I finished up as Northe gave the two-hash warning. Serec braced himself, focused on the cargo door.

"Everything okay?" I finally asked.

"I hope so."

Before I could make sense of his answer, the ramp started to open. The howling wind assaulted us, and I shielded my face against the pressure. "I'll be right behind you," I yelled to Serec. He activated his HOOD and gave me a salute. Northe slowed the Nighthawk over the drop zone, as we watched the fight unfold thirty meters below us.

"Hold here—" Serec leaped from the aircraft, before I could finish. Anxiety grew in my chest as I took aim at the monster. An Alpha Psionic Wave would buy us valuable time and tip the scales in our favor. But my attention kept drifting toward Serec. I could teleport to him the instant he hit the ground. And yet, it felt like we were a world apart. *What did he see on that feed?* Whatever it was, I had a nagging feeling that it was the catalyst to some change that I wasn't prepared for.

[ELEMENT 3]
THE BOOK OF NARYN

[1]

CHOICE

If I've gotten one thing in life down to a simple science, it's school. The path to rewards is clear, and your greatest investment is time. Navigating the maze of prep school life was a little complex at first. But I figured it out. So, things should've been pretty easy, right? Wrong. For whatever reason, it's never that simple. Not for me anyway. Not with so much at stake. Optimism wasn't always a stretch for me though. My tendencies toward realism were the result of dealing with bad people and worse events.

"Last question of the day," Mr. Jeriston said. "Can anyone explain the relationship between the Hiyama Square incident and *the Rho Code*?" The class pretended to scan their textbooks, but no hand went up. Not for *Jeriston the Judge*. "Perhaps Ms. Hayden would like to give it a try?" It was the fifth time he'd called on me that day. Not that it was out of the norm. But it was becoming harder to stifle my sighs.

"Judicial Code 7713Q—more commonly referred to as the 'Rho Code'—is the law created in response to the terrorist attack on Hiyama Square. Because the terrorists responsible were found to have supernatural abilities, the Rho Code established societal protection for all citizens without special abilities. This came in the form of legislation, stating that any unauthorized use of supernatural powers is considered illegal and punishable by fine, imprisonment, or death. It is also marked by the day that *rho* became the colloquial term for persons with supernatural abilities." I recited as the bell rang.

"Correct, correct, and correct," Jeriston cheered "Ms. Hayden, you never disappoint. Until tomorrow, class."

"Ya know," Shuran started, "I'm thinking we should bump our study sessions up to twice a dec. You're obviously holding out on us, Rynnie."

"I know, right?" Harra said. "Or maybe her rho power is ultra-accelerated learning."

Shuran and Harra had been my best friends since primary school. Shuran was tall and fit, like a model. As you might expect, she enjoyed bragging about herself whenever she could find someone willing to listen. That said, she was way more clever than most people expected from a pretty face—even at Royal Verdallyn Academy. Harra, on the other hand, was a cutesy, dolled up girly girl. Her features were soft, and she was so short that even I had some height on her. But academically, Harra's aptitude far exceeded Shuran's, rivaling mine at times. Still, she was the timid, soft spoken type and I often wondered if her condition had anything to do with it. She'd been living with Plaga Viridi for about five anums, and despite experiencing milder symptoms than most, she opted to live a more deliberate life. That meant strict diet, low stress, and a tight circle of friends —Shuran and me to be exact.

"If we're still playing with your theory that I'm a rho, you could at least come up with a less lame power, Harra," I said. "Plus, it'd be stellar if you actually used your theorizing time to help me brainstorm a way to deflect more attention in Jeriston's class."

"Nothing short of battery acid to the face is gonna keep all these guys from gawking at you," Shuran said.

"Or all the girls from jelling on you majorly," Harra added.

I sucked my teeth. "Whatever, frosties. I meant Jeriston anyway. I couldn't care less what everyone else thinks"

Shuran snorted. "You're the frosty. How does one of the most popular girls in school not even care about being popular?"

"The universe is a strange place," I sighed. "Guarantee if I wanted to be popular, no one would even look in my direction."

"Like Shuran?" Harra said.

"Can it frosty." Shuran snapped.

But Harra just chuckled. "Speaking of frosty," Harra added, "how about sohos after school? My treat." Shuran and I exchanged a cautious glance.

"I've been monitoring my diet all week. I have room for a small treat."

"Sounds yum," I said. "But I have practice today." Shuran and Harra shared their classic exaggerated sighs. "Seriously, I can't."

"Fine," they said in unison. Just then, the person I least wanted to see, walked by. Minari Geordan—better known as "Mean little Mina." Her impish face somehow always soured my mood. Especially at times like this, when she had a minion along to bear witness.

"Hey Nana," she said, slowing down enough to examine me. Then, with a quick glance at Shuran and Harra, she added, "And cronies." Her friend chuckled. I never bothered to learn her friend's name, since there was literally nothing less important.

Shuran scoffed. "We can never tell who you're looking at with that wide face.

It's like your eyes are on opposite sides of your head." Shuran may have been defending herself, but Mina lived for these moments.

"Nana, could you send word to your golem that lowering her head from the clouds would help her see us more clearly?"

"Do you guys smell that?" Harra said, making a performance of sniffing the air, before covering her nose. "Does she have diarrhea of the mouth?" Harra turned to Mina, "Do you have diarrhea of the mouth? We should leave, I hear its contagious." The three of us turned on our heels.

"You coulda drove a raeda through her stuporing mouth on that one." Shuran said as we walked down the hall.

"Yeah," I added. "You totally shut that little gremlin down. Awesomely crispy."

"All the more reason to celebrate over a soho, Rynnie," Shuran said, nudging me. "Come with us. It's just one practice."

"For life or limb, but not for a soho. We're too close to the Metro Championships." They both groaned. "How about I grab some for our study group this dec?"

"And...?" Shuran prompted.

I sighed. "And some sweet buns. Geez Shuran! Way to make me a fattie."

"If the *Gymnastics Goddess* can go lardo in a night, we're all doomed."

I rolled my eyes. "Bye, you two."

"There's my star," Mr. Frunde said as I stepped into the gym. "I hope you're ready for some serious work today. Tertuze Elite's new recruits might give us some trouble this anum." A neighboring province and long-time rival to Verdallyn's best gymnastics teams, Tertuze Elite Academy could never be taken lightly. For three anums, Tertuze had dominated nationals. But after my performance the previous anum. Royal Verdallyn Academy was hopeful that we would finally have a much-needed edge. No pressure.

"I won't let you down, Coach," I said.

"I'm certain you won't. But—"

"Certainty is only acquired through diligence," I finished. It was the motto he practically spoon fed us. And he held us to it at every practice, which is why I ended up heading home well after sunset that night. The caelrail crept to a stop, and the doors opened to a chilly fog that bit into my exposed face. I pulled my hood over my head and stuffed my hands in my pockets, before stepping out. It was already 18.70. Most people had the sense to be inside by now making the soft, hazy glow of street lumens my only companion. The walk wasn't long. But by the time I reached my block, the rhythm of crickets chirping had become the new silence. Then, something low and deep cut through the quiet. I slowed, looking to either side of me. Mostly dark houses, lining a quiet, empty neighborhood. But nothing out of the ordinary.

"Probably someone's pet," I told myself, regaining my pace. But a few more steps and I heard it again. This time, it was loud enough to make my stomach clench. Loud enough to send a surge of heat flooding up my arms and through my pores. I didn't know what it was, and I didn't need to know. I only needed to get to the dorm. I lengthened my strides. *Just over a block away. Keep it together.*

The echo of my heels hitting the pavement and the rapid thudding in my chest drowned out everything else. Then, a shriek. I froze in place. Another shriek. I started toward the sounds. *Dumb.* It was not my concern and the safest move would've been to keep it that way. But my legs had other plans. I stopped at the corner and crept toward grunting coming from just past the trees up ahead. A few more steps and I found myself squinting at the figure coming into view. It swayed from side to side, ambling toward what looked like a tall girl. The figure raised its arms and let out a snarl that had the girl pressing her back to the wall; her breathing loud and stuttered. Whatever it was, it didn't look human.

Just off to my left, I noticed a rock, about half the size of my hand. I grabbed it and tossed it at the creature. *Really Dumb.* "Hey!" I yelled. The rock thumped against the creature's back and it turned away from the girl long enough to train its eyes on me. *Ulti-dumb.* Large and tinted with an orange glow, the creature's eyes fixed on me, as it stepped out of the shadows and into the moonlight.

My arms tingled with fearbumps as the large, gray creature—and its claws— became fully visible. "If you can hear me," I yelled past the creature, "You should run, while this thing is distracted." The girl didn't respond. "Like, right now." The creature growled as it shifted onto all fours. It trotted closer and I started to back away. But I'd barely gotten anywhere before it picked up into a gallop. I stumbled backwards and fell flat on my butt. But there was no time to feel the pain. In fact, there was no time for anything. The creature was too close, and I was out of options.

It lunged at me, fangs bared. I countered the best way I could on such short notice, with my eyes closed and my hands thrust out to guard my face. I heard a choked wail. Then, a thud. I opened my eyes to find the monster's face pressed into the pavement under an invisible weight. I hurried to my feet and backed away. It took a bit more effort, but the creature eventually managed to wrench itself back onto its feet. An odd noise gurgled from the base of its throat as it tilted its head at me, its eyes unblinking. A quiver ran down the base of my neck as the creature hunkered low and lunged again. I threw my arms out again, this time, more in control as I removed gravity. The creature flew overhead and hit the ground with a heavy, tumbling crash.

I took a breath, finally starting to take hold of the situation. But the creature wasn't feeling quite so confident. It wobbled, leaning to one side as it rose again. Without another glance, it turned and scurried off. I watched quietly as it fled, my body trembling from the adrenaline high. Once the creature was out of sight, I turned to check on the tall girl. She stepped into the light, sniffling and wiping tears from her face, as she fixed her clothes and hair.

"You ok...?" The question barely made it out of my mouth, before I realized—. "Shuran?"

She looked at me like she'd just seen a ghost. "NaRyn? You...you're a rho?"

[2]

CONSEQUENCE

Do the ends justify them means? He asked me this during one of our more personal engagements. It is a question I ask myself every day. My hands are drenched in the blood of my allies and enemies alike. I have betrayed people; used them for my own goals, then discarded them. I take no pride in it. But this is war. And casualties are inevitable. One individual holds a peculiar place in my mind: Asset 33. She's a sprightly young thing full of hope and potential. She was not meant for this life but is exceptionally good at it. I can only hope she doesn't become another casualty in this conflict.

-The Child

It's not every day your best friend witnesses you using powers she's not supposed to know you have. Especially, when she's the kind of friend that would tell the world about it. *Thanks a lot, Shuran! You can be such a huge dose of rumor sometimes.*

Not even twenty segments since I'd saved Shuran from whatever that thing was, and half the school was already treating me like some kind of rho vigilante. Some applauding or smiling. Others acting like I had some kind of ultra-contagious form of Plaga Viridi. All day, random people came up to me and asked questions like, "Did you really explode a pack of ravenous desert bears with your mind?"

The rumors were quickly becoming so ridiculous that the whole thing started to seem like a big joke. And yet, the matter never imploded on itself like I'd hoped. By lunchtime, I was feeling particularly low on fuel. I did all I could, slipping past the gawkers lining the hall to the cafeteria.

"Rynnie!" Shuran called, waving from the middle of the line.

"Don't 'Rynnie' me. What's the deal, big mouth?" I whispered so loud, there was hardly any point in whispering.

"What's the deal with what?"

"Don't play dumb. Everyone in school is talking about special powers and fighting wild animals. Remember how I said I *didn't* like a bunch of attention?"

"But the only person I told was Harra."

"You weren't supposed to tell *anyone*. Having powers—and *using* them—is kind of illegal, remember?"

"Okay, okay. I'm sorry. But I couldn't leave Harra out of the loop on a secret like that. It would've been nice to know that our roommate could... make monsters fly or whatever you did last night."

Despite the chaos I'd been dealing with all day, Shuran had a point. The last thing I would've wanted was for Harra to feel alienated. And Shuran was just the kind of big-hearted friend to keep that from ever happening. If only her mouth weren't as big as her heart, my day might've gone a bit smoother.

"Any ideas on how it spread?" I asked.

Shuran shrugged. "Like I said, I only told Harra?"

"At what volume?"

"Uh, what's that supposed to mean?"

"It means you aren't exactly the soft-spoken type."

Shuran sucked her teeth. "I can so be soft spoken when I want. And I probably was when I told Harra, so cool it."

"Probably?"

"It's not like I remember every little detail of my life. All I know is that I was probably soft spoken enough, okay?"

I sighed. "Why do I even bother?"

Shuran wrapped an arm around me and squeezed as she leaned her head against mine. "Because you're the best, and you always will be."

"Speaking of Harra, where is she?"

Shuran pointed. "Saving us a table."

"Well well well," an annoyingly chipper voice called from behind us. Mina stood, propping her lunch tray against her hip. "If it isn't the girl that chased off a pack of desert bears with her face." The two cronies behind her cackled.

"Speaking of far-reaching merits, how's it feel being stuck in thirteenth rank all anum?"

"I'd imagine it's not too different from being stuck at twelfth."

"Too bad all you can do is imagine." My jaw tensed so much it made my throat tight. If I responded before recomposing myself, the fact that Mina had, yet again, struck a nerve, would be too obvious.

"Not for long, wolf-face," Shuran interjected. "Rynnie's on your mangy tail, and it's gonna be so crispy when she smashes past your rank."

Mina paused for a breath, her eyes hovering somewhere between Shuran and me. "Nana, would you send word to your golem that I am incapable of deciphering the language of anyone ranked below two-hundred?"

"Why's it always sound like you're eating marbles when you talk, troll?" Shuran was referring to Mina's accent. An exchange student from Lazuria, Mina was the only foreigner at RVA—a fact that made her both intriguing and suspicious to most students. I always thought it was strange that our nation's best diplomats managed to keep the foreign exchange program with Lazuria open but Lazurian netsites were completely blocked over here. Priorities people.

Mina sighed with a smile. "Well, I've had my fun for the day. Enjoy waiting in line, Nana." She started off. "Give the golem my regards."

Shuran huffed, her eyes burning a hole in the back of Mina's head. "That imp isn't worth it." The rest of the day was more of the same. Gawking, whispers, and other typical prep school crap annihilated any hope I had of a peaceful afternoon. When school finally came to an end, all I wanted was some time alone to collect my thoughts and recharge. *Monument park should work.*

As I waited on the eight-story caelrail platform, I watched the distant rails zip through New Callastryne. It was the birthplace of dreams, and the graveyard of innocence. Growing up in the largest city in Aruria made for an exciting childhood, if not a bit fast paced. I'd always appreciated that though. And in most recent anums, it was crucial in helping me forget. But for all the effort, I put into distracting myself, there were always people who felt the need to constantly help me remember. My timechain buzzed pulling me out of my head.

"We have an assignment for you," said the shadowy figure on the burst message. *Of course you do.*

"Details," I replied. A set of coordinates appeared on the tiny timechain screen. *Good thing I have a free afternoon.*

The most dangerous people aren't the ones with super high stakes. It's the ones with nothing to lose. They just don't care. I was pretty close to that, but there was still one thing I had to protect—family.

"If I hurry, I can still relax with Shuran and Harra," I said to myself as I stepped onto what should've been a half-empty caelrail. Instead, it was so crowded I could only spot three open seats. One was next to a pair of whiny children. *Nope.* The other was by a large, sweaty woman whose girth spilled over into what could be my seat. *Super Nope.* And the last one was next to a guy about my age, thoughtfully staring out the window. I should also mention the guy had strikingly cute grey eyes. *Winner winner.*

"Mind if I sit here?" I asked.

He looked at me for a beat longer than a casual glance and said, "Please do." He held out a hand as soon as I was seated. "My name is Shawin."

I felt a deep flutter as I grabbed his wrist. "NaRyn," I said, smile pressing into my face. *Where'd that come from.*

He smiled back. "Nice to meet you, NaRyn."

"Likewise."

"Are you heading home?"

I shook my head. "Just going for a stroll in the park." *Lie.*

"Sounds relaxing."

"Yeah. Just need to clear my head." I wanted nothing to do with anyone at the moment. And yet, I strangely found myself wishing I could tell this complete stranger with pretty eyes my life story. Maybe I just needed someone to talk to. A few short hashes of small talk and the caelrail drifted to a halt.

"This is my stop," he said.

"Oh, okay." I got up feeling a hint of disappointment.

"It was a pleasure speaking with you, NaRyn." Our eyes met and the apathy that had been building all day started to recede. "I hope this day brings you peace and you find what you are looking for." *What a strange thing to say.*

"Yeah... uh. You too." He started for the door.

"Hey," I said grabbing my timechain. "Let me give you my chainlink." He pulled out his timechain and I tapped it with mine. "Shoot me a burst," I said, giving the most enticing smile I could manage. *Hopefully he isn't creeped out.*

His smile grew. "Will do," he said.

The location on the coordinates was a bar in Saldarian Flats. Bars were some of the only establishments in the city where surveillance was prohibited, making them perfect for illegal activities. A girl with fifteen anums walking into a bar in mid-afternoon should have been a cause for suspicion. Or at least the setup for a terrible joke. But I'd been to Saldarian Flats several times before, and I'd gathered that no one really seemed to care how suspicious something looked. I sat at the bar like I had several times before and waited for the bartender.

"You look familiar," the tall bartender said leaning against the bar. He was pretty nondescript save for an extraordinary black mustache that nearly shielded most of his mouth. I'd have complimented him on it if I wasn't on business.

"You probably know my parents, the Glassfields."

"I think I do," he began. "Your dad works over on Charvie street. And doesn't your mom work for Tulva?"

"Yeah. She's a sales rep now."

"So, she sells, briefcases?" He said, feigning incredulity.

"Boring right? But it pays the bills. They bring in like 14000 credits a dec."

"Can't argue with that. Well it was good seeing you." He grabbed a bottle of sparkling water and placed it in front of me. "Have a drink, on the house."

I stood on the platform waiting for the next caelrail to arrive. My bar exchanges were always my favorite part of a job I otherwise hated. Piecing together the information on my target was always a nice distraction. I never understood why my employer was so in love with anagrams though. *Charvie— Archive. Tulva—Vault. Briefcase... briefcase. At least they agreed to pay 14000 for this job. Time to go to work.*

The Arurian Archive was famous for its collection of rare books and priceless artwork. This being the case, I imagined they spared no expense on security. The sun was retreating behind the horizon as I put the finishing touches on my plan. I wondered how someone got detailed layouts of the Archive on the Arnet but then

I remembered that's an Archive problem. A third-floor balcony served as the perfect infiltration point. They didn't even bother to lock the door. Not like most thieves could reach it from the outside.

I slid in and immediately inverted gravity around me. I fell for a beat, landing softly on the ceiling. After a moment of orienting myself to the inverted room and checking my location on my timechain, I was off. Bookshelves hanging over my head, guards patrolling "above" me, ancient dust falling upward as my steps dislodged it, all came together to form a surreal scene akin to a drug induced romp through the park. It was an effective way to remain out of sight. Shame my body didn't understand that the first few times. You really haven't lived until your vomit spills "up". Fatally ladylike. Luckily, my stomach knew the deal this time and I was able to easily make my way to the vault. The massive array of books filling the archive was staggering. I'd hoped my first visit to the Archive would have been as a scholar, not a thief. The universe has a sick sense of humor.

The vault was pretty easy to recognize considering it was the only massive metal door in the place. Guess there was no need in concealing it when most couldn't even get to it. A guard stood... guard with a multimag gun. The lightweight magnetic weapon could fill my chest with a hundred lethal metal darts in under a hash. *Yeah, some serious stuff is in there.* I slowly released the gravity and floated down, landing behind the guard. With enough gravity infused in my palm to knock the poor guy unconscious, I slapped him across the back of the head.

Now I just need to manipulate the mechanism in the lock and—. A metallic clank rang from the door echoing throughout the archive. The massive door slid open revealing a small room bathed in blue light. Fog crept out propelled by a mild chill. I was met by a rectangular silhouette sitting on the table in front of me. A metallic briefcase came into view as the fog dissipated. My target. The clang from the door opening had alerted someone as footsteps on the marble foreshadowed an impending conflict. I grabbed the briefcase, hopped out of the vault and inverted gravity again, as six guards turned the corner and sprinted to the vault.

My fingers tingled and my heart raced as I gently shut the balcony door and inhaled the crisp night air. I hated this—and loved it. I was a thief—a criminal. And a good one at that. But what other choice did I have? My parents' debts were astronomical. And my employer didn't care that they were blackmailing a girl of fifteen anums. The decs I spent grieving after their death were miserable. But that was the easy part. 17.00 arrived quicker than expected but I'd managed to complete the job and make the drop in record time. If only my next day had gone as smoothly.

[3]

OPEN WINDOWS

"Just the young woman I was looking for," Principal Matta said as I passed her in the hall. I'd managed to avoid her for the first few days of this mess but I knew that would only last for so long. "A moment of your time please, Ms. Hayden." I seriously doubted it would only be "a moment," but Principal Junera Matta was hardly the type to take no for an answer. I followed her into the office.

"Care to explain these rumors I'm hearing about your extraordinary exploits with feral boars and mountain ligorns?"

I shrugged. "I wish I could, but I'm as surprised to hear them as you are."

She gestured for me to sit as she plopped into the chair behind her desk and swiveled around. She methodically leaned onto her elbows, slid her fingers together, and nested her chin between her thumbs. All key signs that our moment might be the first of many to eat away at my precious time.

"Is there truth to any of them?" she asked.

"I can honestly say that I've never even seen a desert bear, feral boar, or a mountain ligorn in person. And I still haven't figured out who got the rumors started in the first place." *Lie.* Principal Matta studied me carefully. But if life taught me one thing, it was how to keep calm under pressure.

"I have two of the nation's King's Elite Youth Scholars under my watch—a circumstance that I can only take partial credit for. If, however, an investigation becomes warranted due to wild rumors circulating, all blame will fall squarely on the closest authoritative figure over the matter."

"Principal Matta I—"

"It is true that you are one of those aforementioned students and that your skill as a gymnast is unmatched. Yet despite these great accomplishments, you insist on—other activities." *Necessary activities.*

"I have managed—against my better judgement— o ignore those offenses. However, I cannot protect a Rho who uses her powers for violence. Where you were once an asset, you are now a significant liability and it is unfair of me to place your needs above that of the other 325 students at this school.

You better not.

"It pains me to do this at such a critical time in the anum but until this issue is satisfactorily resolved, I have no choice but to suspend you from Royal Verdallyn Academy. You are to leave the campus immediately."

I paused. Astonished. Aghast. Floored. And every other synonym for surprised as Hadal. She might as well have taken a gun and put three slugs in my skull. With one sentence, Junera Matta shattered my world and drove the pieces into my hollow chest. I just... sat there. No argument. No retort. Just—silence.

"Hopefully, this will provide sufficient motivation for you to start taking your academic career more seriously. That will be all Ms. Hayden." Matta yanked me back into reality. I didn't say anything. I just left. There was nothing to say. She was right. I messed up. In *their* eyes anyway. I ambled down the hall feeling— nothing. My racing thoughts drowned out my senses. *Ten anums of work, all at risk. What will I tell Uncle Hachi? How will I survive if I lose my scholarship? So much for meeting Blissful Martinel.* Suddenly, everything came into infuriating focus as Mina and one of her minions appeared in front of me. Poor minion. She didn't even get two words out before my fist was colliding with her jaw.

I couldn't remember the last time I'd been through such a crazy dec. Not that I wanted to. If I didn't already have a crappy backstory, this would have definitely been the worst dec of my life. I went back to the dorm immediately, craving soli- tude like a predator craves meat. Matta's words bounced around in my head as I entered my room. *Suspended.* Becoming the top ranked student in the nation was difficult enough without being persecuted as a Rho miscreant. Now, it seemed even holding on to my current rank was about as likely as seeing my parents again. My jacket remained on my back. My shoes on my feet. The clothes of the outside world stayed with me like the burdens they accompanied. I fell into my bed, and the tears finally came.

I lay awake in the bed staring at the sterile white ceiling. My eyes were puffy and sore from a night of sobbing into my pillow. It was the last day of the school dec, and I was in bed, wondering why the universe saw fit to send my life off course... again. A part of me wanted to curl in a ball and douse my pillow in tears again. Another part of me resented the fact that I had cried in the first place. Despite the appeal of wallowing in a bed of self-pity and despair, I opted to grab my timechain and contact the only person who might understand.

My excitement practically boiled over when I saw Serec standing in the door- way. His absence hadn't been so apparent to me until we were together again. Hugging him brought reassurance, though, it didn't fully feel like I was hugging the same person. Sharing the details of the past few days with Serec was the easy part. He'd always been a great listener, contrary to what everyone else seemed to think. Holding back the tears was another matter altogether. This vulnerability made me feel small... insignificant. But he helped me to find my strength. To keep fighting. Serec and I always encouraged each other. But this was different. Something had changed him. And in such a short time.

"Do you feel up for a walk? There's someone I'd like you to meet," he said.

"Meet?" I wasn't thrilled about interacting with anyone at the moment.

"I know what you're thinking, but I need you to trust me on this." He flashed his classic, "I've got this under control" smile, which would be reassuring if it always preceded positive results.

It wasn't often that I got the opportunity to see a fleeting tree up close. If I'd known there was one walking distance from my dorm, I would have visited it while it was in season. Of course, the person sitting under the tree would have provided even more incentive to visit. "Serec, it's been a while brother. How have you been?" Shawin said extending a fist to Serec. *Brother?* Maybe it was the serendipity of the situation or its simple irony. Or perhaps it was the way those profound pewter eyes lit up when he saw me. But suffocating melancholy air that had been struggling to maintain a hold on me finally receded.

"It would seem fate has brought us back together," I said, feeling my confidence returning.

"For that, I am thankful," Shawin said. His voice was so comforting; something I'd wouldn't expect from someone I barely knew.

Serec explained my situation to Shawin who seemed more interested in stealing glances at me. I couldn't blame him though, considering I was doing the same thing. It appeared Shawin was more than just an enticing pair of eyes. He was a martial artist—one who was responsible for the changes I'd seen in Serec. Perhaps things weren't falling apart in my life, but falling into place. Regardless, I was ready to move forward.

[4]

COMPACT

He's beginning to surface again. I'm seeing signs of his handywork every-where. I knew he would not remain idle forever, but this is almost reckless. I'm certain he knows what he's doing but I question his interests. And I will need to prepare for the possibility that they do not align with my own.
-The Child

"One of the most important factors in defending yourself," Shawin said, "is controlling your center of gravity." He threw a hand at my face. I dipped to one side, careful not to drop my guard. "Which means...?"

"When I'm attacking, I need to disrupt my opponent's center of gravity." I said.

"Exactly." He threw another attack, and I dipped to the other side.

"So, once I have the hang of defense, offense should be a breeze, right?"

Shawin smirked. "That's the idea." Shawin feinted and swept an arm at my front leg, but I shifted past him and threw a kick into the back of his right knee. His leg buckled for an instant, before he twisted to one side and recovered. "You're picking this up a lot faster than Serec. He thought offense was everything."

"Sounds like Serec. Always anxious to get the first hit in. You must've had a tough time with him."

"Let's just say it took some additional motivation to adjust his approach to fighting."

I'd been training for several decs with Shawin and—despite being on school holiday—balancing training sessions, holiday studies, and that other thing I did that Shawin knew nothing about, was pretty tough. But I couldn't argue with the results. If I could take down, thugs, monsters, or whatever else the universe threw at me without powers, maybe I could actually save someone without lighting my academic future on fire. Also, Shawin's gentle demeanor and good looks were a pretty good motivator to stick with it.

Fortune had been behind me as well regarding school. After just a dec on suspension, Matta called me in and apologized for everything—well more like begrudgingly admitted fault. Turned out that no witnesses had come forward to confirm that I was using my powers. After some serious pressure from her superiors, Matta was forced to reinstate me just when I was getting used to lazing around the dorm all day.

Everything fell into place from there. Shawin and I spent most of our free time together which was nice considering Serec had essentially disappeared. We usually avoided training late, since our schedules were kind of all over the place. But the one night we did end up finishing over a segment behind schedule, ended up being another girl's lucky day. We were roughly halfway to my dorm, when we saw what, at first, looked like two people locked in a tugging match next to a parked raeda. Turns out they were a young woman and a thief fighting over a timechain.

Shawin ran ahead of me yelling, "There he is, Peace Enforcers! Surround him!"

"What are you doing?" I whispered. "There's no way he'll fall for—."

Like a child engrossed in the confines of imagination, the thief's head darted left and right, before he released the timechain and dashed around the corner. "He actually fell for that. In a residential area, no less." But Shawin shrugged as if to say, "Don't overthink it."

"I can't thank you enough," the woman said, brushing the hair out of her face as she adjusted her clothes.

"It's fine," Shawin said. "I'm just glad we were in the area."

The woman presented her timechain. "Let me send some credits to your union account," she said. "It's the least I can do."

Shawin shook his head. "It was the right thing to do, which makes it the least we could do."

The woman smiled and got into her raeda. "You must be new here."

Shawin offered a smile. But as soon as she hovered away, his smile faded. I walked quietly, more hesitating than waiting to say what we were both probably thinking.

"This isn't the first time we've run into trouble where no one was around to stop it," I said.

"You're right."

"And I know it could be dangerous, but I'm starting to think maybe I should be using all the training you're giving me to help more people?" Shawin's mouth scrunched to one side, which usually wasn't a good sign. "Think about it. It would be good practice for me to better protect myself, and it's not like the problem will go away if we just ignore it, right?" Shawin turned to me; his face completely unreadable. "At least consider it. I mean, it makes sense, right?"

"Right," he said after a pause. "But we should have a plan and some guidelines to lower our risk of getting caught."

"Like what?"

"Like not using powers."

I froze. "Our powers?" I whispered so loud I might as well have just said it. That was becoming a bad habit. "Why didn't you tell me?"

"I didn't find it relevant."

"Yeah, but you've known about my powers this whole time."

"Does that change anything between us."

"Well, no but—"

"I felt like now was as good a time as any to get it out there, since you sound serious about us working together to help people."

"I guess that's fair."

"But we'll have to rely on our combative prowess. Not our gifts."

"Also fair."

"Good. And we should conceal our identities and coordinate maneuvers in case a situation becomes greater than we can handle."

"Fair fair fair. Now, when do we start?"

We started the very next day, at least with planning and prep. Shawin was serious about us having good teamwork. Very serious. So, I was more than a little surprised when—only a few days into our training—he suggested we try our luck out in the field. Shawin suggested the Central District as a place to practice scoping our surroundings. It was close enough to home and less crowded at night than some of the other districts. I don't think either of us expected much to happen within the first few days, which was probably why Shawin suggested it. We'd been ambling through Downtown for a while, before the lack of activity started gnawing at me.

"Can I ask you something?" I said.

"You just did."

I nudged him. "Anyway, why do you never talk about your family?"

"What's there to talk about?"

"You know? Who they are, where they are, what they do. That kinda stuff." Shawin paused. "Look, if it makes you uncomfortable, you don't have to—"

"No, it's not that."

"Then what? I mean, I'd like to meet them at some point. Unless...you don't want them to meet me."

"It's not that eith—" Something clanged in the distance.

"Did you just hear—"

It clanged louder, then crashed. I started toward the sound, when Shawin stopped me. "We're trying to blend. Remember?"

"So, we should ignore it? Someone could be in trouble."

"We won't ignore it, but we should maintain our current pace to avoid drawing attention."

When we were close enough to make out the grunting coming from around the corner, I grew tense; my mind already preparing for the worst. Shawin peeked around the corner, then looked back at me. He held up two fingers, then waved me closer. Cautiously, I peeked around the corner and saw two men in large jackets and black masks, trying to crowbar a window open.

My body eased a bit, but my mind was still whirling. The idea of thwarting burglars seemed dangerous, and exciting. More than anything, I experienced an almost comedic sense of irony. I'd assumed the role of burglar more times than I cared to admit. Now I was taking it upon myself to prevent others from playing the same part. I slipped on my mask as Shawin checked around the corner, waiting for the right moment to give the signal. As soon as he did, we stepped out into the open.

"You two lost?" Shawin said sharply, and the burglars jumped.

"Who are you supposed to be?" one burglar asked.

"We're the ones about to bring you to justice," I said. *That sounded a lot less juvenile in my head.*

The burglars shared a look of disbelief, before bursting into laughter. "Sure," the other burglar said, walking in our direction. "How about you start with this?"

He held the crowbar like a bat, preparing to take a swing at me. The burglar came at me with a glint in his eye. "You wanna be a hero, little girl?" he said, reaching for my arm as he raised the crowbar over his shoulder.

I swatted his arm away and jumped back. He offered a devious smile. "What happened to all that talk? What, you scared of big bad me and my little bitty bar?" I jumped back, twisting to either side as he jabbed the bar at my stomach a few times, like it was a sword.

He wasn't taking me seriously. And I could use that to my advantage. I slipped to one side, just as he thrusted the bar out and kicked his hand. He lost his grip on the crowbar, and I used that moment of surprise to throw another kick to the outside of his knee. His leg buckled, giving me time to follow up with a third kick to the inside of his other knee. He grunted as his knees jammed into the pavement. I thought the fight was over. At least until he twisted around and kicked my legs from under me. Now, I was on the ground; wincing from the throbbing heat moving across my back.

"Open your eyes," Shawin called.

But I heard him too late. Another sharp pain hit my legs when the burglar kicked the back of my right thigh with tremendous force. I screeched in pain and twisted to one side, trying to roll away enough to give me a chance to get up.

I was starting to panic, to feel like the walls were closing in on me. *If Shawin has time to watch me fight, why isn't he helping me? Is he testing me?* Not the best time for an evaluation, but it was enough to propel me back onto my feet, just before the burglar could take a second swing. I dipped under his arm, gritting my teeth as my right leg screamed. But I knew I could endure it, because he was about to feel something much worse. I lunged at him, grabbed him by the jacket, and pulled him in as I shoved my knee into his stomach. Something between a cough and a gasp fled his mouth as he collapsed to his knees. A swift kick to the head send him down like a dead tree.

"A little rough in execution," Shawin said, "but with practice, I'm certain you'll find easier ways to disable an attacker. How's your leg?"

I rubbed it gently. "Stings," I said. "But it should be fine. Did you call the PEDs?"

"I was watching to make sure you could handle yourself first."

"Would've been nice if you'd handled the guy with the crowbar, dontcha think?"

"And leave you with this one and his pocket knives?" he said, nodding at the other thief sprawled out behind him.

"I didn't even realize he had knives."

"Exactly."

Sloppy work Ryn Ryn. The operator answered and I reported the criminals. "Someone should be here in ten hashes."

"Then, we should head home." We headed to the caelrail platform. "Can I ask you a question?" Shawin asked.

"You just did." I smiled, but Shawin's expression remained unchanged.

"Were you having second thoughts just before we stepped out in front of those thieves."

"More like I was relieved it was only thieves."

"What were you expecting?"

I told him about my fight with the creature that tried to attack Shuran. Even he found it hard to believe what I fought was an actual monster. Still, we agreed that I could use more training, whether I was fighting monsters or criminals. One dec into it, we'd stopped three crimes—two of which would've probably landed people in the hospital. The more I felt like we were making a difference, the more I wished I'd encouraged Serec on it. Thinking about how he was so willing to fight for others, even when he was the only one who believed it was right, made me feel like I'd been closing my eyes to what was around me. Sticking with what was safe and comfortable. But between saving Shuran and spending time with Shawin, my perspective had shifted significantly.

The next day, Shawin asked me to lunch. He had something important he wanted to talk about. Shawin took me to a cute little restaurant called, "Pumil Wraps & Plant Greens." As the name suggested, that was all they served.

"If I'd known you were that hungry, I would've come earlier," I said observing Shawin tear into a pumil wrap.

"What do you mean?"

"I'm barely into my second wrap, and you've already devoured your whole plate."

He nodded blankly, like he was waiting for me to make my point. "Anyway, you had something important to tell me?" He cleared his throat and nodded again.

"I know you've been curious about me and my background for a while, and I'm sorry that I've been so closed off all this time."

"It's okay," I said. "I'm sure you have your reasons." But I wasn't sure. I was just glad he'd finally called attention to it.

"Well, I have something to ask you, and I don't know how I can do that if I don't tell you more about me."

Something about his words made me uneasy. "Okay."

"You've probably suspected it already, but I'm not from here."

"Like, not from Aruria?"

"No. Technically, I am a citizen of Aruria."

"But you aren't from here?"

"Correct. Are you familiar with the island of Vallah?"

"The uninhabited wildland to the far west?"

Shawin chuckled. "It is pretty wild, but it's far from uninhabited. It's actually my homeland; where my entire family lives."

"Seriously? Why keep that a secret?"

"You see. I'm a member of a secret clan. Wolfhounds, to be exact."

I paused. "Why does that sound familiar?"

"Serec may have mentioned it. He seemed to be quite interested in our way of life. We're one of several long-standing Gifted clans, that most people on the Mainland know little about. There are several reasons we allow people to think we don't exist, but the main one is security."

"Then why tell me?"

Shawin's eyes trailed down to his fidgeting thumbs. He inhaled deeply and looked back up at me. "Because I want to—" A booming crash outside ripped through the moment. Shawin jumped to his feet and rushed over to the window. He hurried back, the look in his eyes intense enough to make my stomach clinch.

"What is it?" I asked.

He waved his timechain over the table and a hologram that said "Paid, thank you" flashed over it. "Let's just say I believe you now."

We ran outside, and anxiety gripped me the moment I saw what had caused the crash. Another monster, nearly twice my height, stomped its way through the streets, roaring and knocking around benches, parked raedas and any other inanimate objects that upset it, as people scrambled in every direction.

"Is that the monster you fought?"

"Not unless it grew up. That thing looks like it could eat the one I fought."

"That's reassuring," Shawin sighed.

"And that was sarcasm," I pointed out with a smile.

"I suppose I'm teaching you to fight and you're teaching me how to act my age," his smile matched mine. But another roar shattered the moment and reacquainted us with the ugly truth that stood before us.

"Wonder what has him so upset," I said.

"We can ask him after he's been incapacitated."

We ran behind a building and slipped our masks on, then raced down the middle of the street. The creature already looked huge from a distance. But once we reached it, I gained a true understanding of the danger we were in. A woman and her son were trying to run away, but the beast threw a raeda into their path, narrowly missing them. The woman shrieked and hugged her son close. Shawin veered off and ran toward a nearby tree. He jumped and yanked a branch down, then ran closer and tossed it into the back of the monster's head. Wood splinters and leaves burst from the branch. But the monster barely reacted. It turned with a booming snarl, and its large orange eyes trained on Shawin and me.

[5]

SACRIFICE

A roar from the gargantuan beast set off scenarios in my mind of the many ways my life could end in the next few hashes. But Shawin's voice focused my attention and strengthened my resolve. "Remember our rule about not using our powers?"

"Yeah."

"Forget it." I nodded, my mind trying to overwrite the terror I felt. The kind of terror that drowned out all senses when you needed them most. "I'll distract it, while you find an opening." Shawin yelled.

"R-right"

He probably didn't notice the fear that was trying to take hold of me. Or maybe he was choosing to ignore it, hoping I would get myself together before it was too late. He ran toward the monster and it immediately started flailing its enormous arms at him. I watched as Shawin dodged every attack the monster threw at him, including a trash bin that would've taken my head off. Thankfully, the idea of nearly ending up in a full-body cast brought enough clarity for me to get angry. That stupid beast was determined to kill us. I intended to return the sentiment. The creature was surprisingly quick, but I managed to fluctuate the gravity around it enough to keep it off balance, while Shawin threw whatever debris was in his vicinity.

"This isn't working," Shawin yelled after some time. He was right. All we were doing was keeping the behemoth busy, as we wore ourselves down. But what else could we do until the BNP or PEDs arrived? "We need to take its legs out." Shawin said. It was a good starting point, but there was no guarantee the monster would stay down. We needed a more... permanent solution. That's when a flipped raeda caught my eye.

"Can you lure it over to that raeda?" I yelled. Shawin nodded, still dodging the monster's massive arms. Despite being roughly the size of my fist, raeda fuel cells, contained enough energy to power the floating vehicles for decs. *If I can crush the cell, it'll create an explosion great enough to send that monster straight to Hadal... hopefully.*

Slowly, methodically, Shawin led the creature to the flipped raeda. "When I give the signal, make him as light as you can." Shawin said.

"Got it!" I yelled.

Shawin ran in a wide arc to get the monster to turn its back to me, before sliding between its legs and vaulting over the raeda. "Now!"

Before the monster could react, I molded the gravity around it to what I imagined it would be like in space. The monster's movements became erratic and clumsy, as it struggled to maintain its balance. Shawin sprinted forward, leapt, and kicked the giant in the back of its right knee. Its lower half lurched forward as its upper half moved in the opposite direction. Resisting gravity over something so massive was like trying to press twice my weight overhead. But, if I could hold on a little longer, the monster was sure to lose its footing. Except, it didn't. With a booming grunt, the massive creature stopped in place and fought the momentum working against it, until it was lurching further forward and back into an upright position.

"Move!" I yelled to Shawin. "I'm losing my grip on it." Shawin leapt away, and I released my gravitational hold. To my surprise, the monster's body jerked forward and back wildly, and I immediately realized what was happening. *It can't regain its balance in that position under normal gravity.*

I had to time it just right. I refocused and waited. Patiently anticipating the monster's next move. The creature rocked itself backward, and I knew this was my opportunity. I threw up my hands and immediately shot them down. A wave of gravity bombarded the creature's face throwing its head backwards. With a quaking boom, that rattled my bones, the monster toppled onto its back, crushing the raeda and cracking the pavement. A much more timid boom followed. The raeda's fuel cell had exploded, muffled by the monster's girth. I expected it to be more... climactic. But it was definitely more exciting than a painful death. The monster laid motionless. Huffing, I watched the creature half-embedded in the street, astonishment accompanying my relief. I'd done more damage to it than I knew I was capable of.

"I'm starting to think you could've handled this on your own," Shawin said.

I wrapped my arms around him and squeezed. "I wouldn't have even known I was capable of this without you."

I was fatally exhausted yet somehow invigorated with pride. Shawin and I held each other, laughing between breaths. After a brief moment of quiet, people began to emerge, applause and cheers filling the street. In that moment, I was elated. It was as if I'd finally found a true purpose. Our actions made a difference. We'd saved countless lives because we weren't afraid to do what was right, even if it meant breaking some dumb law. Though my parents were law enforcement, I knew they would have been proud of me.

"It's still alive!" someone screamed. Everyone went into a panic as the creature's body began convulsing. I looked away for a beat at a screaming woman. I almost doubted my eyes when they returned to the creature. Its abdomen had swelled so much, I thought it may float away.

"Get out of here!" Shawin yelled, scattering the crowd.

The last thing I remember seeing were his clear eyes as he dove at me. A blinding flash—followed closely by a deafening boom rattled my entire being before everything turned fuzzy. My ears rang so loud I thought I'd gone deaf. My head throbbed like it'd been split open. A sharp pain radiated throughout my body. For an instant, the pain consumed me. I couldn't make sense of anything except that I hurt all over. Then, my eyes shot open, squeezed shut at the glare, and carefully peered open again. A massive plume of black smoke slowly came into focus. *Did it blow up?*

I cautiously wiggled my fingers and toes. *All still there...thankfully.* I gritted, pushing against the warm road until I was sitting upright with my knees folded under me. I called out for Shawin, but there was no answer. I called out to him again. No response. When my eyes could finally focus, I realized he was right behind me. I crawled over to him and gently shook him. "Shawin, are you okay?" Still, no response. "Shawin? Please say something." My eyes were on fire. My lips trembled. *You'd better not be—.*

I placed my head against his chest and listened. A faint heartbeat. I held the back of my hand over his mouth. Shallow breathing. Some relief. Little, but some. But even that was short lived. I rolled him onto his side, and discovered a huge hole burned into the back of his shirt. Where I should've seen skin, I only saw a large patch of red glittered with debris. I could hardly think straight, but I knew he needed immediate medical attention. Not that it even mattered, given my current situation.

Shawin tried to speak, but my ears were still ringing. "It's okay," I said. "I know it hurts, but try to stay calm."

But he wouldn't calm down, and I couldn't blame him. It probably hurt too much to put into words. Shawin's eyes widened, his body tensing, as two words strained from his mouth. "Look out."

I looked over my shoulder and saw a raeda about to flatten us. My hand went up, instinctively repelling enough gravity to shift its trajectory. It crunched over the pavement, hardly a meter away from us. I fell onto my hands, my arms on fire and spasming. My body was too ready to give out. Shawin rolled onto his hands and knees.

"You shouldn't be moving," I said.

"Can't you feel it?" he said.

Before I could ask, the ground shook under me. A slight pause, then another shake. Then another. It was almost as if I was feeling the planet's heartbeat.

"What is that?" Shawin said, looking off in the distance.

Something was heading toward us. Something nearly as tall as the two-story shops lining its path. Sunlight reflected off the metallic sheen of its rounded body.

A single red eye in the center of its head beamed like a beacon. And its massive arms swung just shy of the ground. It looked nothing like the first creature. But the one thing they had in common was the very reason we had to escape.

"Get out of here," Shawin said. "There's still time."

"What about you?" I asked.

"I'll slow it down."

Shawin tried wrenching himself to his feet, but he couldn't hold himself steady.

"Don't be stupid," I said. "I won't leave you behind."

The creature picked up speed, the ground cracking under its feet. Between the two of us, it would take a miracle to make it out alive.

"Its going to bowl us over," Shawin said, as his eyes turned clear.

"How do we stop it?"

"All we can do is stay out of its way. First attack is coming from its right."

It wasn't very reassuring, but it was better than nothing. In no time, the monster was about close enough to crush us, and we dove in either direction. The monster pivoted and I ducked, nearly toppling as a lethal swipe from its hand whooshed overhead with terrifying force. And before I could appreciate still having a head, the creature's arm came full circle.

"Jump," Shawin yelled, and the instant I did, something whirred past the space between my feet and the ground.

Shawin yelled again. But I didn't catch what he said. I did, however, catch something heavy enough against my shoulder to devastate my left side and send me flying sideways into Shawin. The fuzziness came back, and so did the ringing. But they were joined by a new friend: my screaming shoulder. Everything— including the monster—was spinning. I should've been afraid. In fact, I'm sure some part of me was terrified. But my senses were dull. *This is how it ends, huh? Some weird beast is about to smack me into roadkill, and I can't even focus enough to see it coming.* An ironic peace washed over me as my end approached. I knew I hadn't finished all I'd hoped to accomplish. But a part of me was just happy to be free of all my worries. That freedom would have to wait though.

A beam of light rained down from the sky, and the monster let out a howl so loud, I could hear it through the ringing. Something cracked into the asphalt with a jolt, and the monster howled more sharply than before. My eyes were slow to focus, but when they did, a man in black combat gear came into view. He stood facing us. The monster suddenly attacked him from behind, right arm swinging in a wide arc. But the man threw a hand up—and caught the creature's arm! He grabbed the arm with both hands and in a twisting motion, flung the beast down the road. The creature crashed into the ground skittering to a stop. *When did that thing lose an arm?*

"He's all yours," the man said, as a woman in similar dress appeared.

The woman placed two fingers to her temple. "Brace yourself," she said, and the temperature shot up an instant before a blinding light flashed in front of her and a boom erupted a moment later. When the light faded enough to open my eyes again, the monster was nothing more than black smoke swirling around burning flesh and shards of flaming metal.

"You okay?" the man asked, looking over his shoulder at me. Well, maybe at me. I wasn't certain, since a band of dark blue light covered the top half of his face.

"She's probably in shock," the woman said, walking over. I was so tired I could barely think straight. Sirens suddenly came into earshot. "That's our cue," the woman said. "You ready?" But the man didn't answer. He just sat there, quietly watching me. "Zero?"

The man flinched, and cleared his throat. "Yeah."

The woman touched the man's shoulder and they—evaporated into specs of golden light. *Delirium—awesome.* The next thing I knew, medics were lifting Shawin and me into an ambulance. "Don't worry," the medic said, placing a breathing mask over my face. "You two are going to be just fine."

[6]

RECOVERY

It had been almost a dec since Shawin and I nearly died fighting that giant monster. The thought was so outlandish, I could hardly believe it. But that didn't weigh nearly as heavy on my mind as the fact that I hadn't seen or heard from Shawin since the hospital released me. I kept asking myself if he was okay. But I couldn't let myself believe he wasn't. Especially since he wouldn't have been there if I hadn't suggested we become vigilantes in the first place.

"Orbis calling NaRyn," Harra said. "You've been in your head for like three hashes now."

"Oh," I said. "Sorry. What were you saying?"

"I was—" The door chime rang, and Harra responded with a sigh. "Hold on a beat." But her voice chippered right up after answering the door. "Looks like someone's got a secret admirer."

"What're you talking about?" I sighed.

"Aside from the fact that you're blushing? This." She held up a vase of flowers and a covered platter holding a breakfast that Blissful Martinel would envy. A warmth of hope spread through my chest. "Was someone attached to the food and flowers?"

Harra shook her head. "It was sitting in front of the door with this note." She handed it to me, and my fingers almost ripped it in half trying to open it. It read:

Sorry I haven't been around lately, but I'll see you soon.

"So...?" Harra said.

"So...?"

She frowned. "Who's it from?"

"It doesn't say."

"Guess."

"You know I'm not big on speculating." *After all, the last thing I need is more potential for deflated hopes.*

Harra rolled her eyes, then placed the food on my lap. "I'll get a vase for the flowers. Just promise me you'll give me the details before Shuran this time."

I held up a hand. "You have my word."

I kind of felt bad keeping Shawin a secret. But, if Harra and Shuran knew about Shawin, and it didn't work out, I'd keep hearing about him until bigger news came into our circle. The same time the next day, another ring came at my door chime. I started to race for the door, but settled for walking when I realized how much running aggravates a broken arm. I opened the door to find Serec holding a platter of food and another vase of flowers.

"What are you doing here?" I asked.

"Happy to see you too, Ryn," Serec replied.

"No, it was...I was..." I shook my head. "I'm glad you came by. Now come in."

"Is that Serec?" Shuran said, scurrying over with Harra hot on her shadow with wide grins and glinting eyes.

"Hey Shuran. Hey Harra," Serec said. "How've you two been?"

"Good," Harra answered. "And you?" Her cheeks couldn't have been redder if she'd sat in the sun all day.

"Not too bad."

Shuran stepped closer and brushed a lock of hair behind her ear. "What have you been up to?"

Serec shrugged. "Same as always. Are you ladies taking good care of my cousin?"

"Whenever she's not locked in her room," Harra answered.

"Like she's been since the hospital let her go," Shuran added.

"I'm supposed to be resting," I said.

"It's really sweet of you, bringing breakfast and flowers twice in a row," Harra said.

"Twice?" Serec asked.

Shuran stepped even closer. "You know, you don't have to be such a stranger, Serec. You should stop by whenever you like."

Serec smiled. "Thanks, I'll keep that in mind."

"Speaking of keeping things in mind," I interrupted, pulling Serec into my room. "I'm pretty sure he came to see me, and my food's getting cold."

Shuran sucked her teeth. "Could you be more frosty right now?" I closed the door behind him and gave him the tightest hug I could manage with one arm.

"How's my favorite cousin doing?" he asked.

"Your *only* cousin is okay, I guess."

"Except...?"

"Except I think I'm starting to see why you had so many issues with Uncle Hachi."

"Did he lecture you at the hospital?"

"Discreetly, but I know he's saving more for later."

"Did he say it was my fault for influencing you?"

"No, but I told him it was a choice I made on my own anyway."

"And he believed you?"

I shrugged. "Dunno."

Serec paused for a moment, then shrugged too. "Not like it'll make much difference anyway. Here. You should eat." He placed the food on my lap and removed the lid.

"So," I said between bites, "do you still go out and fight too?"

He shook his head. "Believe it or not, I took Hachi's ultimatum to heart. And the more I think about it, the more it makes sense. We shouldn't go looking for trouble if it means there's a good chance we'll end up using our powers."

"But what about helping people who need us?"

"We can't help anyone from detention."

"So, we should just ignore it?"

"Hardly. But there's gotta be another way, you know?"

"Like what?"

"I dunno."

I wanted to argue, but the image of Shawin's seared skin came to mind. "Yeah. Maybe you're right."

"Either way, you should do what feels right. You know I'll always stand by you."

His words were more therapeutic than any med. "Thanks, Rec Rec."

"No problem, Ryn Ryn. How's Shawin doing?"

My eyes evaded his. "I'm not sure, we haven't really. talked since that day."

"Need me to go talk to him?"

"I wish it were that simple, but it seems like he wants nothing to do with me."

"I highly doubt that. Just give him time." I hoped that was all it took. Though experience told me otherwise.

After another segments, Serec left, and I thought Shuran and Harra were going to get into a fist fight for the final flirtatious word on his way out. The morning had gotten off to a late start, but aside from the segment Shuran, Harra, and I spent going over homework, we didn't do anything except watch vid streams together. It sounds relaxing, but not when your best friends can't stop verbalizing how much they're fawning over your cousin the whole time. It seemed like the only real distraction was the back-to-back slew of ads about joining the Life Reciprocal. A humanitarian aid/ life coaching organization, it had exploded in popularity in recent anums. It was a testament to how much some people just wanted to belong somewhere. I wanted to criticize the members' terrible life choice in joining. But having gone through several life altering events in recent anums, a part of me understood their struggle.

That night, I couldn't stop thinking long enough for much sleep. Shawin and I hadn't spoken in a dec, and I was starting to think maybe he'd come to the same conclusion as Serec. Of course, for all I knew, he was at home wondering if I'd given up on our crusade. The one certain thing was that we needed to talk. I got ready the next morning to finally confront Shawin. But, as soon as I opened the door, I found an unexpected reason to put the excursion on hold.

"NaRyn Hayden." A tall man in an exquisitely subtle black suit watched me intently.

"W-who are you" I managed, anxiety already burrowing into my mind.

His tone remained flat...even "I am the one who will help determine if your dec will end with you in your home or a detention cell."

[7]

INSIDE

I probably looked like an idiot, just standing there, staring for so long. But the man didn't seem to mind.

"I will make this brief," he said, shattering the silence. I nearly jumped at the sudden sound. But he didn't notice. Or maybe he just didn't care.

"I am an official of the Kingdom of Aruria. You have been identified as an individual with supernatural abilities and as such, I have been instructed to bring you in for questioning."

"Questioning?" I said, a flood of anxiety finally breaking through. A government official was at my door threatening detention. And all I could do was stand there. No witty remarks, no carefully crafted retort, just silence. But with my mind drowning in all the possibilities of how my life could effectively end, there was no brain power to spare.

"You are not being detained if that is your concern, but I will need you to come with me immediately."

My thoughts began to pool into coherence and with them, an unsettling suspicion about the man standing before me. Though I knew nothing about my employers, they knew everything about me. And considering how easily they blackmailed me, I wouldn't be surprised if kidnapping was next on their agenda.

"Not trying to be difficult, but I don't know you. A girl my age can't just wander off with a stranger."

"A girl your age should probably avoid opening doors for us strangers as well," his tone remained as lifeless as his face. He held out an open palm, and his data ring projected a persona card. "Sir Doriel Silivas III, Phoenix Knight."

My resolve faltered at the revelation, and I almost wished he had been with some criminal organization. The Phoenix Knights were ten of the most skilled fighters in the world and worked directly for the Monarch. Their duties ranged from personal guard to law enforcement and I could count on one hand the number of people whose authority exceeded theirs. If a Phoenix Knight was at my door, this was fatally more serious than I thought. But I had to maintain composure, even after he took me to a secluded warehouse that seemed less questiony and more torturey.

"Please have a seat," he said gesturing to a nondescript metal table. Sitting while he continued to stand only heightened my unease. But what I saw next abruptly shifted the situation from tense to bizarre.

"What happens next?" I asked reaching for any information I could glean.

"That isn't for me to decide," Sir Doriel said, looking away into the darkness.

The tapping of heels announced the presence of another person as the sound filled the warehouse. From the shadows emerged a woman. One whose very presence made me question the validity of my current reality. *I must've taken one too many meds.* It was the only explanation for the obvious lie my eyes were telling me.

"Hello NaRyn. I am..."

"B-blissful Martinel?!" I blurted, fear warping into a nervous excitement. Not what I imagined myself saying, but when the princess of the nation—and one of your favorite people of all time—is standing in front of you, it beats going all crazy screaming fanatic. At least, that's what I told myself. It was strange. Standing before me, with flowing white hair that practically glowed and emerald eyes that I could get lost in, she seemed more like a dream than a real person. Yet despite everything I'd seen—everything I'd read about her, she seemed surprisingly... normal. That's when I remembered. *Hadal!* I scrambled to my feet and bowed, feeling like an idiot.

"I suspected you would know who I was." She gave a soft smile. One I would have paid to see again.

Wait, why would she suspect I knew who she was. How's she even know who I am?

"Apologies for our surroundings, but I had to endure discretion. How have you been?" She asked.

"Me?! Um, well, Blissful—um." I nodded, waiting for my brain to catch up. "I'm well."

"Please, let's do away with formalities. It makes for bland conversation. Treat me as you would anyone else."

"Uh, o-okay... Sa'Sha." *Did I just call the princess by her first name? Is the princess even here? Guess I'll entertain this imaginary princess until I come off this high?*

"So, how may I be of service?" I asked noticing how dry my throat was.

"I wanted to extend my personal thanks to you and your friend, for what you did last dec."

My chest went cold. "W-what did we do last dec?"

"You saved lives, despite the serious risks associated with using your powers in broad daylight."

Not only did the second most powerful person in the nation know I was one of the Gifted who used my powers publicly, she knew exactly when and where it happened. With the snap of her fingers, the enforcement entity of her choice could haul me away. But for some reason, she looked like she was...proud of me.

"Am I going to be detained?"

Sa'Sha laughed so hard, it almost looked like it hurt to recompose herself. *I made the princess laugh! Oh—my—. Quit gushing and get it together.* Logical me was back and serious as ever.

"As I stated, I'm thankful for what you did. I'm hoping you might provide clarity on what exactly happened."

"Okay," I said, trying not to sound as suspicious as I felt. And yet, the more I talked, the more comfortable I felt talking to her, despite Sir Doriel's lifeless stare. By the end of my recount, she knew just about everything that had happened with the monster Shawin and I fought, and the one that attacked Shuran.

"Do your parents know about your powers?" Sa'Sha asked.

"Actually—they were among the BNP agents who died during the attack on Hiyama Square."

"Forgive me." A shade of sorrow overcame her face. It wasn't sympathy or pity, but something more...grounded.

I shook my head. "It's fine. They're a big part of my reason for doing what I did. I guess you could say they've inspired me to take up a similar cause."

"Your parents' footsteps were definitely something to be admired. There's nothing wrong with wanting to continue their legacy." The wistful look in her eyes made it seem like she was saying that more for herself than for me. "So, have you figured out how I knew about you being Gifted yet?"

"Were you in the crowd?"

"Not exactly. But, I was there that day." Sa'Sha gave a subtle grin, as if she was waiting for me to piece together her clues.

"The woman in the uniform? With the thing over your eyes?"

Her grin widened. "That was me."

"No way?! You were amazing! You could've taken out that monster by yourself."

"I was fortunate. Someone recognized my potential a long time ago. Thanks to her, I grow a little each day. Now, I'm here to offer you the same opportunity."

"Like...to train me?"

"I wouldn't be the only one. But yes."

"Are you sure I'm good enough?"

She extended her hand. "Let's find out together."

The moment I took her hand, an unsettling energy began to pulse throughout my body. The pigment in Sa'Sha's green eyes swirled until they glowed a pale hazel and her lustrous white hair became a rosy brown as darkness engulfed us. "Focus on the sound of my voice," she said.

"On the count of three, your test will begin."

"Test?"

"You'll be fine as long as you remained relaxed and maintain focus."

"Okay."

Easier said than done when the room was suddenly shaking under my feet. I squeezed her hand tighter. "One...two...three."

The walls collapsed and we were suddenly on top of a skyscraper in the center of some foreign city. Fires burned across the scorched landscape, creating black clouds that reached into a scarlet sky. Sa'Sha was holding a long black sword and wearing an outfit similar to what I'd seen her in the dec before. But she wasn't the only one. I was also holding a sword.

"Where are we?" I yelled over the howling wind.

"The most turbulent battlefield anyone can face. The one inside your mind."

"My mind looks like this?"

"This is a projection of your inner conflict. A manifestation of the doubt and uncertainty swirling in your subconscious. You'll need to conquer it in order to move forward." Sa'Sha ran to the edge, leapt, and landed on the next rooftop.

"Trust in yourself," she yelled.

I nodded and took a deep breath. When it came down to it, my mind could go in a thousand directions—most of which were riddled with doubt. "Alright, recap. I'm currently inside my mind—which is a warzone—with Blissful Martinel—who is Gifted— nd knows I'm Gifted. If this is real, it will make a fatally good story. If its a dream, this should wake me up." I said to myself, as I burst into a sprint.

"Don't think, just jump. Don't think, just jump. Don't think, just jump!" I threw myself off the ledge, sailing through the air. I landed well past the edge of the building, rolling to disperse my momentum.

"You have more power and control than you give yourself credit for," Sa'Sha said with a hint of a smile. "Follow me." We jumped from rooftop to rooftop until we were near the center of the city. From our vantage point, various aircrafts, fighting vehicles, and soldiers were easy to see. And they were all engaged in a battle surrounding a tall, thin tower.

"Our objective is the base of that tower," Sa'Sha said.

"How do we get through?"

She drew her sword. "Not with our good looks," she smirked.

"Okay. I can do this."

"Of course you can." Sa'Sha and I dove into the sea of soldiers, wind whipping through my hair. We crashed into the ground, creating a shockwave that sent soldiers flying in every direction. Sa'Sha wasted no time cutting soldiers down. But for every soldier she dispatched, two more took their place until we were cut off in all directions.

"Create a path," Sa'Sha said.

Acting on instinct, I lifted my sword and leapt high into the air; higher than what should have been possible. With an intense field of gravity behind me, I jammed the tip of the blade into the ground. The terrain cracked in every direction, sending nearby enemies skyward. We sprinted until we'd reached the tower's base, where an energy field suddenly sprouted up behind us, and a hulking figure, standing at least three meters tall, appeared in front of us. The armor-clad giant glared at me, as his fingers twisted around a massive sword.

"This is as far as I can accompany you," Sa'Sha said, as her visage started to fade.

"What? Where are you going?"

"This test is the manifestation of *your* uncertainty. I'm afraid you must conquer it alone. I trust you have the ability to see this through. You must have the same confidence," she said as she faded away.

The giant's intense red eyes burned like hot coals. *No denying its determination to stop me.* But I was just as determined. The giant stepped closer, and the ground shook under my feet. Nothing had ever gotten easier with hesitation. And this situation was not different. I ran at the giant, focusing on the movement of its arms. It raised its sword, and I hunkered low in preparation. I dove into a roll as the monster took a heavy swing. I went for its neck the instant it missed me. But it was faster than it looked. With one swat from its free hand, I was separated from my sword and tumbling, before skidding to a painful stop. The ground shook again and I looked up. The giant was coming closer. But even as I tried to regain my footing, my body recoiled in pain.

How am I supposed to stop that thing?

"NaRyn," a voice, called out. "You are the master of your own mind. Trust in yourself. And conquer this fear."

I thought about all that had happened in my life; all those who'd supported me. My parents, Uncle Hachi, Shuran, Harra, Serec, Shawin, and now Sa'Sha. I refused to quit. Not when they'd placed their faith in me. I don't know why or how, but something in those words made my blood run hot. My arms and legs tensed as I found the strength to push away from the ground just in time for the giant to bring its sword down like a guillotine.

"It doesn't end here," I said slipping past its attack and running to grab my sword. I ran in a wide arc, then charged, manipulating the gravity around the sword as I swung. The giant brought its sword down again, but I was ready. I brought my sword up... and blocked the attack! I swung, knocking it off balance. It stumbled back, quickly regaining its footing. With a deafening war cry, the giant slashed at me. Big mistake! Infusing all the gravity I could manage within my blade I met the giant's sword, shattering it like an angry rock through a glass wall. The force threw the giant on its back and I leapt into the air.

Serenity engulfed me, suffusing my being as confidence displaced the doubt. With my sword positioned perfectly over its chest, I hammered down, plunging the blade deep. The fiend howled as a blinding light shot up from the wound and swirled around me. The light intensified flooding the scene in white. Suddenly, I found myself back in the warehouse, gasping for air.

"Welcome back," Sa'Sha said.

"What? What was that?"

"The first step in a long journey. Now that your mind is open to your potential, you'll need training. And I would be honored to oversee it." Sa'Sha seemed so confident. Like she could already see future me. And it was that confidence that reassured me there was only one answer.

"When do we start?"

[ELEMENT 4]
THE SECOND BOOK OF SEREC

[1]

FORBODE

"What have you done with the power I have bestowed upon you?" Anne's voice echoed through the enveloping darkness. Her icy eyes bit into my resolve. But her outstretched hand pointing off in the distance provided incentive for me to keep moving. Set on my path, I raced through the thickening fog. But my sprint abruptly ended when I tripped over a small object. I ran my hands along the ground until my fingers found the golden spherical obstacle. As soon as I took hold of it, the fog lifted, allowing me to identify it. Only, I couldn't identify it. It was too... foreign. Despite being small enough to fit in my hand, it was much heavier than it looked. Making it seem even more unfamiliar.

Another voice called out to me, and I dropped the object following the sound until it led me to Sa'Sha. She was trapped in some kind of muck, monsters surrounding her. A dark figure loomed over her holding some kind of flat-blade spear. She struggled against the muck as the figure lifted the spear high, ready to strike her down. I tried to run to her, but some invisible force held me in place. "Stay back," she warned, tears streaming down her face. "This is too much for you."

"What do you mean?" I said. "What about all the training?"

"It wasn't enough to prepare you. I'm sorry."

"What do you me—" The figure's malevolent, violet eyes locked onto me, and I lost my words.

"Have you lost sight of your objective so soon?" Anne called to me.

"Only one objective matters right now," I said through my teeth. "Sa'Sha needs me."

But my time focused on Anne was more than enough for me to lose sight of

Sa'Sha and everyone else. All that remained were tatters of Sa'Sha's clothes lying in a pool of blood.

"I'm too late?" I whispered, my voice suddenly as weak as my resolve. "No—no! What did you do?" I yelled, turning to Anne. But she was gone. Everyone was gone. And I was alone, smothered by failure's embrace. Tears were my only solution. Tears that stayed with me as I jolted upright, my heart racing. It was a few moments before I realized it was all just a dream. But the smothering feeling lingered. And with it, the unsettling impression that this was more than a simple nightmare. I wiped the tears from my face and twisted around to grab my timechain. "8.2. Might as well get up and shower off this fear," I said to myself noting the sweat drenching my clothes.

Hachi and Surket had approved my recommendation to recruit Shawin after our last mission. But due to my junior status, Sa'Sha had to accompany me to actually recruit him. It turned out to be a busy few segments for Sa'Sha however, as she'd recruited NaRyn earlier that day. I'd originally wanted to keep NaRyn's identity a secret. But I had no choice but to be honest once Sa'Sha expressed her interest in recruiting her; an idea I vehemently opposed. But when Surket and, to my surprise, Hachi supported her request, the matter was no longer up for discussion.

It would be Shawin and NaRyn's first full day with the Guild. And since the previous day was so busy, all we had time to do was walk them into Vaticia, issue their TABs, and show them their bedrooms. As soon as I was dressed, I walked to Shawin's room. But before my hand could reach his door, it slid open. "Hey brother," Shawin said. "Did you sleep well?" To wake up in a strange new place, he seemed surprisingly at ease.

"I slept fine. You like your room okay?"

"It's much larger than my current bedroom. These sheets are much softer too." He nodded as if agreeing with himself. "Definitely pleasant."

"Good. I'll take you to meet the team, then show you around D7." We started at the office, where Surket was typing away.

"Zero," Surket said. "Last to the party as usual." I frowned. "Try not to look so surprised after all this time." She walked over to Shawin. "You must be the new recruit."

"I am," Shawin said. Surket and Shawin held a quiet gaze for an oddly too long, before she extended her hand. *Is he...nervous?* I had to fight back a smile at seeing Shawin's apprehension. It was the last reaction I would have expected from him but Surket had that effect on people.

"Surket—designation Bolt," she finally said. "Commander of Team Seven."

Shawin grabbed her wrist. "Shawin. Nice to meet you. I don't believe I have a... designation."

Surket nodded at me. "Zero will cover that with you."

"Yes ma'am," I said. "By the way, have you seen K or Raven?"

"K's off doing whatever he does when he isn't needed, but Bird and the other recruit should be close."

"Morning, late riser," Sa'Sha said, stepping in.

"NaRyn?" Shawin began. "You're here too?"

NaRyn's looked at us with wide eyes. "Shawin... and Serec!? Why are you here?"

"It's good to see you Ryn." I said, forcing a smile. I was genuinely happy to see her. But I was still struggling with my reservations about her joining in the first place.

"This was the familiar face I mentioned last night," Sa'Sha explained to her.

"Does Uncle Hachi know about this?" NaRyn asked.

"Sooner or later, we'll have the Director's entire family in here," Surket said.

"Director?"

"It's a long story, Ryn," I said. "We'll explain everything later."

"So," Northe said, strolling in with impeccable timing, "why isn't there any breakfast laid out?"

"Uncle Kaz?!" Shawin exclaimed.

"Uncle Kaz?" Everyone's eyes shifted between Shawin and Northe.

"Shawin?!" Northe said. "Is that you?" He nearly knocked me down to get to Shawin and lift him into a hug. "Look how much you've grown." I hadn't seen that kind of excitement on Northe's face since... ever.

"That's the Uncle Kaz we were looking for?" I asked.

"Yeah," Shawin strained. "Thanks for finding him."

After a moment, Northe glanced at NaRyn and immediately lowered Shawin. "Sorry about that. I know this kid personally. Anyway, welcome." Northe extended his hand. "I'm Northe."

NaRyn grabbed his wrist. "NaRyn. It's a pleasure to meet you."

"What an enchanting young lady you are." He glanced at Sa'Sha. "And if I didn't know any better, I'd say she's already gravitating toward Zero here."

"Actually," I interjected, "this is my cousin."

"Oh!" Northe laughed and looked at Sa'Sha again. "Got lucky this time." Surket flicked a spark at Northe's arm. "Ah! Geez! Where's breakfast?"

Surket flicked another spark. "If you're hungry, plug your mouth with your foot Peipei. I'm certain we would all benefit." Northe feigned a sour laugh. "In the meantime, you can supervise Raven and Zero, training the new recruits. The sooner they're assessed and initiated, the sooner our full attention can go back to the malefactors."

Over the next dec, Sa'Sha and I trained NaRyn and Shawin as much as we could, considering their injuries. Northe occasionally dropped in to check on Shawin, but he never lingered long. Dinner was our only time together as a team. But for the first couple days, the atmosphere felt a lot more like boys versus girls for some reason. Every time NaRyn looked at Shawin, his eyes fell to his plate, like he was embarrassed about something. But Sa'Sha and I weren't much better. Neither of us could hold the other's glance, which didn't take long to start feeling awkward. Especially after all the time we'd spent together on recon. Of all of us, Surket and Northe were probably the most comfortable being antisocial, since it was pretty in-the-norm for them. That night, I had the same unsettling dream. I jolted out of sleep, feeling more anxious than before. It was hardly a surprise that my clothes were covered in sweat yet again. After a quick shower, I started for the office.

"Team Seven's nearly doubled and you're still the last to rise," Sa'Sha said from the bottom of the stairs. Shawin and NaRyn were with her.

"I've never known him to go to bed before early morning," NaRyn said. "Serec's probably part nighthawk." The sight of everyone in good spirits put a smile on my face. Whatever had happened, at least they seemed to finally be on speaking terms.

"Surket and Northe are in the office looking over some device that Clan extracted from that giant malefactor," Sa'Sha said. "Now that you're up, we can see what Surket wants to do with it."

"And the sooner that's done, the sooner we can have breakfast," Shawin added.

"Why is food always the only thing on your mind?" I said.

"Yeah," NaRyn said. "Why is that?" She poked the back of Shawin's neck and smiled when he twitched. "It's not," Shawin said, poking her stomach.

"Yeah. Could you guys save that for when I'm not around?" I said.

"Glad you two are here. I need you to take this to Minerva?" Surket said, gesturing to an object in Northe's hand. "We suspect this could hold a few clues about the malefactors."

"Careful, Kid," Northe said as he handed me the spherical object. "This thing is—"

"Heavier than it looks," I interrupted almost in a whisper; astonishment looming. *That's impossible.* There was no denying it. I was holding the very same object I'd seen in my dreams.

"Serec?" Sa'Sha said, breaking my trance.

"We should go. Staring at that thing won't provide any answers."

"Oh. Uh, right." The walk to Kareen's lab was a blur. My mind was preoccupied with deciphering what my recurring dream was trying to tell me.

"Raven, what a pleasant surprise," Kareen said. Her eyes went to me. "And Zero," she said with less enthusiasm.

"Good to see you too," I said as I placed the object on her table.

"Surket thought you might want to examine this device that Clan extracted from the giant malefactor," Sa'Sha said.

Flame sparked in Kareen's eyes. "If Clan extracted it, then why does Team Seven have it?"

I took a step back. "Don't ask me?"

"I swear everything has to irritate me today."

"What's that supposed to mean?"

Kareen ran her hands over her face. "Time of the cycle,"

"Whoa!"

"She's talking about her cyclic inventory reports," Sa'Sha clarified. "Kareen hates inventories."

"Damn right I do! What's it matter to STRATCOM where all my equipment is every five decs? Whenever something goes missing, I make certain my voice is heard. So, when I'm quiet, that means there's nothing to talk about. Period."

I slowly turned to Sa'Sha. "I said it's not that, despite her word choice" she said. I immediately understood why Surket and Northe waited for me to wake up and take the object to Kareen.

"Sure enough, this is occult tech," Kareen said, studying the object. "Nothing too fancy, but we'll need some time with it. Gimme a day, and I'll have some answers," she said dismissively.

"Thanks," Sa'Sha said. Right now, this device is our best lead."

"Anything else you can tell me about this thing?"

"Well," I said, "this may sound crazy, but I saw it in a dream."

"You're right, that does sound crazy?" Kareen said matter-of-factly. "What'd it do?"

"I dunno." I turned it over to reveal a thumb-sized indentation on the bottom. "But this part kinda seems...significant." I tapped the indentation twice, and the device flashed on with a low, whirring sound.

"What did you do?" Sa'Sha asked.

"I dunno. I just..." Almost without thinking, I ran my finger from the indentation to the top of the object where I found another indentation. I tapped it three times and a low beep began to ring from the object. On the third beep... the device shot out of my hands and began rotating in midair. Golden light emanated from it, painting a detailed map of Aruria.

"You sure you didn't know how to operate that thing?" Sa'Sha asked.

"There you have it," Kareen said. "It's a positioning device."

"With a built-in hologram engine," Anni added.

Sa'Sha pointed at the blinking dot. "This looks like the same area where that giant malefactor attacked."

"Hmm" Kareen began. "Perhaps we can use this device to determine the monster's point of origin."

Kareen grabbed the floating orb and tinkered with it. When she finally let it go, the device was displaying a blue line tracing a path from an island, west of Aruria, leading into Downtown Callastryne.

"Is that Kunai?" I thought aloud.

"Someone payed attention in geography class," Kareen said. "Well, it looks like your team has its next lead."

[2]

SIREN

My anxiety had an unexpectedly strong hold on me. Sa'Sha warned me that she'd felt the same way on her first infiltration mission. But the seed of doubt my dreams had nurtured had taken root inside my mind; making me dwell on the dangers that awaited us.

"This is an infiltration mission," Surket said as a holographic map sprouted from her TAB. "Our primary objective is locating the facility suspected of producing the malefactors and collecting as much intel as possible. Our secondary objective is effectively halting production. If detected, you are to abort immediately. K will be on standby to provide emergency support."

"You two will be the first unit. Synchronization is far more vital now than in your recon missions. I'll be operating as the second unit."

"We won't let you down," I said. As the Nighthawk neared the northern shore of Kunai, my mind quieted. Sa'Sha and I shared a glance before activating our HOODs.

"I've been meaning to ask," she said, "are you mad at me?"

"For what?"

"Recruiting your cousin. I know you were against it."

"I was, but knowing her, she would have just gotten into more trouble. You had her best interest in mind," I shrugged. "So, I don't get to be mad."

"Why haven't we talked then?"

"Because you've been avoiding me."

"Not true."

"Very true. You've been so distant, I didn't know what to say when I saw you."

"Anything would've been better than nothing."

"Maybe but—"

"I'm serious. Don't shut me out. Just say something next time. I don't care how unapproachable I may seem." A chuckle bubbled up from my chest. "What's so funny?"

"You finally admitted you're unapproachable."

"No, I didn't."

"Yeah, you did."

She looked away; not hiding the smirk pressing into her cheeks. "You make some pretty illogical assumptions," she said, smile growing. "But I won't hold that against you."

In school, I'd learned that the island territories were uninhabited; a fact I'd only recently learned was complete nibos crap. Though I wasn't exactly expecting the coast of Kunai to be crowded with locals. I definitely wasn't expecting it to be so empty. There'd been so many malefactor attacks over the past semi-anum that more people were starting to doubt it was just some urban legend. But everything looked quiet—peaceful even. And that unsettled me more than anything.

"Call if you need me," Northe said.

"Try to stay awake this time," Sa'Sha replied.

Northe scoffed. "One time and you act like it's every time."

The sloping terrain and dense greenery was sprawling with life. The plant and animal life existing together in perfect harmony elicited a sense of oneness with nature. Unfortunately, that oneness didn't extend to my feet, and I found myself tripping or stumbling every few hashes.

"I still don't get why Northe isn't coming with us," I whispered.

"You'll have to ask Northe about that story," Sa'Sha said. "Even I don't know all the details."

"So, it's always been like this?"

"Depends on how dangerous the mission is. He's our pilot first, and provides backup in emergencies. Surket and I can handle most of it on our own."

Northe didn't strike me as an unreliable person, so much as emotionally distant. Whatever happened must've been pretty serious for him to regularly sit out field missions. We walked through a seemingly endless thicket of trees, before Surket came to an abrupt stop. She surveyed some trees a few meters away, stopping on one in particular. Then carefully drew her bow. The leaves rustled, revealing a well-blended figure between two branches.

"Hold," the figure said. His voice was deep enough to tell it was a man. "I mean you no harm." He leapt down and approached us. "We defend man."

"That man may someday defend himself," Surket finished. *Some kind of passphrase?* The man pulled back his hood, revealing a head of dirty golden hair. He looked a bit older than me, and his tan skin was similar to Surket's.

Surket deactivated her HOOD and the man's eyes widened. "You're—"

"I mean you no harm," Surket said, tone even. I wanted to believe that the man's reaction was simple suspicion. But his suspicion seemed much more akin to fear. The man nodded and tried to compose himself, but he couldn't completely mask the tension in his face.

"We discovered the facility three seasons ago. Because they have yet to trespass on our villages or impede our lines of trade, we've held our distance."

"How do we find it?"

"Continue south and you'll reach a large clearing."

"Call off your scouts. I doubt they'll want to get pulled into the fray."

"Understood. We shall withdraw immediately." He lingered for a moment, examining Surket. "Oe?" He asked. At least, I think it was a question. Surket replied in an unfamiliar language that seemed to match her accent. The man nodded and hurried back into the trees, quickly disappearing.

"Stay sharp and keep your wits about you," Surket said to Sa'Sha and me, then reactivated her HOOD.

"What was that about?" I asked Sa'Sha.

"There's a story behind that too."

I sighed. "Does everyone in the Guild have a story?" Surket and Sa'Sha both held a finger to their lips. A little further south, the trees began thinning out. In the distance we spotted a large yet nondescript building. Surket suddenly stopped.

"What's wrong?" I asked.

"This is where we split up." She placed two fingers against the tree to her left. Her hand fizzled with electricity, and burned an 'x' into it. Then, she marked the tree to her right. "Learn what you can, and stick to the shadows. Don't engage the enemy unless absolutely necessary. We'll regroup just behind the cover of these trees."

Sa'Sha and I nodded and continued forward. I looked back to check which way Surket was heading, but she was already gone. "Man, she's quick," I noted.

"You should see her in familiar terrain. She can slip into hiding almost anywhere inside D7," Sa'Sha replied.

We crept along the side of the building and came upon a door with a fingerprint scanner. As we were examining the door, the rhythmic tap of hard-soled shoes on metal pinged my ear. I signaled to Sa'Sha and we scurried back around the corner. Beats later, the door squeaked open and I heard voices. Two guys in lab coats, had emerged.

"These new test subjects are the worst batch yet," one of them said, taking a puff of his smoker. The orange light on the long thin smoker cast a gentle glow against the man's gaunt face as a small cloud of vapor poured from his nose.

"You aren't lying," the other man said. "Why were they so anxious to rush the process anyway? Do they want more of these abominations on their hands? Even a Rho can only handle so much radiation at once before the brain starts to deteriorate."

"Yeah. I doubt they care though. It's no surprise considering how they treat us. I haven't seen my family in almost an anum." The man scoffed.

"You have a point. Speaking of point, we'd best get back before *Mistress Siren* makes her rounds." They stashed their smokers in their lab coats, and went back inside.

Sa'Sha's eyes met mine. "'Test subjects?'" she whispered.

"Let's see for ourselves," I said, moving back to the door.

Sa'Sha grabbed my arm. "Discreetly. Don't get reckless in there."

"Yeah, I know." I said, ignoring her glare. "You got this?"

"Give me a moment." Sa'Sha placed a hand to the door and her eyes became an eerie—almost inhuman gray. "There's an empty walkway that leads to a closed door. Just to the right of it is another open walkway. Stick to the shadows and we should avoid their surveillance system." The door lock clicked open and we hurried inside.

We crept through the dimly lit corridor until we came to another locked door. Sa'Sha unlocked it, revealing another long, dark walkway. I couldn't help wondering what the point of all the locked doors was if the facility was nothing more than a bunch of lengthy walkways. As soon as the door closed, we were swallowed by darkness. After a moment, lights flickered on, guiding us to metal bars lining the corridor.

"It's a detention facility," I said.

"Stryker? Willow?" Sa'Sha said. *Did her voice just crack?* She cupped her hands over her mouth.

Behind the first set of bars sat two frail looking prisoners. Dirty and disheveled, the pair slowly, meekly raised their heads providing confirmation. Major Olan "Stryker" Miles and Captain Teresa "Willow" Althea were the only two faces I recognized from the vid Sa'Sha showed me. And now, a hollow version of those faces stared back at me.

"Olan," Sa'Sha called. "Teresa."

"Another experiment? You can double my dosage if you leave her out of this one."

Sa'Sha knelt down and deactivated her HOOD. "Major, it's me. It's Raven. We're here to rescue you." The major leaned closer; a glimmer of hope finally reaching his eyes.

"Team Seven?" Miles said, incredulous. "How'd you find us?"

"I'll explain later. Where are the others?"

Miles lowered his head. "They...they didn't make it."

"I-I'm sorry," she said, eyes dropping for a beat before refocusing. "Can you guys walk?"

"We can. If you can get us out, we can manage."

Sa'Sha held a hand up to the cell and the electronic lock beeped twice, before the cell bars retracted into the ground. Miles tapped Teresa and she finally snapped to; her eyes widening when they reached Sa'Sha.

"Raven? Is that you?"

"It's me. The path should..."

Teresa lunged forward, almost falling into Sa'Sha. "I was starting to think... no one was coming," Teresa said.

Sa'Sha wrapped her arms around Teresa and squeezed. "Thanks for holding on until we did. You have no idea how happy I am to see you." The two held each other's gaze for a beat. "Are you strong enough to escape?"

Teresa let out a deep breath and nodded. "Yeah. Don't worry about us. We'll be fine."

"Good. Stick to the shadows and you should be alright." She handed Miles her backup communicator.

"Thanks Raven," Miles said as they started for the door. "We'll see you two on the other side."

Sa'Sha remained still, watching as they disappeared into the darkness. She held her hand over her face for a beat, before reactivating her HOOD.

I placed a hand on her shoulder. "Are you—"

"I'm fine," she said. Let's keep moving."

Sa'Sha's ability allowed her to adjust her vision for heat signatures. A ridiculously useful ability that helped us find the main laboratory, below an otherwise inconspicuous grated steel walkway. We climbed up to the walkway to get an overhead view of at least a dozen scientists, mixing chemicals in a rainbow of colors. The chill of the room mixed with the mild anxiety swirling in my head put fearbumps over my forearms. Guards clad in dark green armor patrolled the area, monitoring the scientists closely. Their firearms caught my eye as they bore a striking resemblance to the ones I'd seen those burglars carrying the night I met Green-eyes. A set of double-doors sat at the far wall. The two guards stationed there made it clear that something important was on the other side. But before Sa'Sha and I could determine what it was, a woman in a hooded green cloak burst through the doors.

"Were any of you idiots aware that we have visitors?" the woman screeched. There was something both incredibly annoying and unmistakably frightening about her voice. As everyone froze and lowered their head, I got the impression that they agreed.

"See that flat-blade spear she's carrying?" Sa'Sha's voice rang in my head. *"That's a class V divarma."*

I tensed. *"How did she get such a powerful divarma?"* I thought back. I hadn't fully gotten used to having Sa'Sha in my head. But it proved invaluable in situations like this.

"You're guess is as good as mine."

"M-Mistress Siren that's impossible," one guard stammered. "My men have been sweeping the entire facility, and no one has seen or—"

She threw a sharp hook to the guard's jaw, knocking him to the ground. "Are you arguing with me?"

"N-no Mistress. Please forgive my arrogance."

"I'm disgusted by your incompetence. Three silent alarms triggered, and two prisoners are missing. Beg forgiveness once you've gotten results that amount to something. Now, go." She turned to the scientists.

"There was only one way they could've gotten in here undetected. So, which one of you *geniuses* went on a smoke break?" The scientists cowered at their workstations, maintaining a delicate balance of avoiding eye contact while showing deference. Though the culprits were clearly among them, neither were dumb enough to say anything. "I swear if Lord Astaroth didn't require your *expertise*, I'd slaughter the lot of you. Lucky for you, good help is difficult to come by." She threw the doors open and stormed out. "Get back to work!"

Slowly, the scientists resumed their work, a mix of tension and dread looming over them. In the momentary silence, my heart was all I could hear. It pounded like I was on my last breath. Which made sense, considering I hadn't been breathing since Mistress Siren walked in. Sa'Sha and I shared an intense glance, as I tried to take hold of my racing mind. I wondered if she was as rattled as I was. We continued forward until we reached a small hatch at the other end of the lab. It dropped us into a large open area that resembled a hangar. At the far end, light peeked in from a door left ajar. A sight that immediately unsettled me.

"This feels wrong," Sa'Sha's thought flowed through my mind. I wasn't alone in my angst. And before I could give form to that very thought a fiery voice halted our advance.

"And just where do you think you're going?" We whirled around to find the warrior woman staring us down; malice filling her vicious violet eyes. "This assignment has been far too much of a bore to pass up an opportunity for some fun."

The ground shook, a low rumbling building around us, as a horde of malefactors spilled out of the shadows. Everything suddenly fell into place in my mind, as Anne's question rose to the surface: *"What have you done with the power I've given you?"* My eyes went to Sa'Sha and my blood ran cold as hopelessness attempted to work its way into my mind.

"Timing will be critical," Sa'Sha whispered. She slid her hand over Nightfall. "I can create an opening for us to escape. When I give the signal, run as fast as you can."

"No," I said.

"What?"

"I'm not running."

"What do you mean you're not running? We're surrounded."

"I have a feeling we'll be taking a huge risk if we run."

"We're taking an even bigger risk if we stay! That woman has a divarma and this could be our only chance to escape." Her eyes contained equal parts fear and confusion. She didn't understand my rationale. I didn't fully understand it to be honest. But I knew running wasn't an option.

"Back me up."

"What? No! Our main objective was—"

I grabbed her shoulders and looked into Sa'Sha's eyes. "Please."

Her eyes darted away. It was like she couldn't find the resolve. I held her gaze. Waiting for the tenacity to return. The fighting spirit that—more than anything—commanded my respect. When her eyes finally did meet mine, I found in them the confidence I needed to see this decision through.

"Well," she said, getting into a fighting stance. "I suppose we did have a secondary objective."

[3]

DEPARTURE

Annihilation; the process of matter and antimatter coming into contact and ending one another's existence. It's poetic in its morbid efficiency and reminds me too well of wars fought to the extinction of both sides. The *Others* have found a way to harness this process using a device called an *annihilation engine*. The scale at which this tiny device operates would be unfathomable to worlds of my past. But incorporating these devices into weapons they employ in their wars brings the poetry of annihilation full circle.

-The Traveler

The first malefactor lunged, and Sa'Sha threw out a kick that sent it careening into its feral comrades.

"You can hold back a little you know," I said. "There are plenty for both of us."

"If we must take this path—" Sa'Sha buried her fist in a malefactor's chest. "The least you can do is let me enjoy it," she smirked.

One after another, malefactors assaulted our defenses like waves crashing against the shore. Everything became a blur, as we were swallowed by a sea of adrenaline. Previous experience with the monsters offered confidence that we'd emerge victorious. However, my inexperience with Mistress Siren quickly eroded that confidence. And the fact that she was content with being a spectator created a well of anxiety in my gut. I needed to hold back for the moment she decided she was done watching. But a seemingly endless barrage of claws and teeth made holding back against the malefactors a less viable option by the beat.

Before long, my hands were starting to sting from all the punches against their hardened, bony faces. This coupled with the fatigue building in my arms made me wonder if they were getting faster, or I was getting slower. But just as I began to question how much longer we could last, a malefactor leapt high into the air, ready to pounce on us like a ligorn pouncing on dinner. At that moment, an almost primal rage sparked within me. These creatures. These monsters, had to be eradicated. I no longer cared how much force it took. I would pour it all into ending this fight. With a war cry that echoed throughout the hangar, I slammed my knuckles into the malefactor's body. Something cracked inside of it, and it thwacked into what turned out to be the last two behind it.

I stepped closer as the remaining two recovered. One of them charged, trying to swipe my head off. But that just amplified my anger. I dipped to my left and drove my fist up into its unguarded chin, lifting the malefactor high enough to kick me in the face. I caught it by the ankle, and swung it into the one behind it, before flinging it at Mistress Siren like a spoiled child throwing a toy. She leapt into a high somersault, effortlessly cleaved the malefactor in two, and landed with an aloof ease.

"Just so you know," she began, "I would have eliminated those peons you two struggled with in half the time."

"Next time I'll bring a spear," I spat, blood still boiling.

"Your little girlfriend probably understands better than you that a weapon is an extension of its user." Sa'Sha scowled gripping the hilt of Nightfall. "That said, disputing matters with ignorant children bores me. You seem to be more eloquent with your fists. So, come, let's see what you can do."

I couldn't afford to take her lightly. Thankfully, she hadn't seen the full extent of my power. So, maybe I could catch her off guard. I focused my breathing, drowning everything out but the rhythmic drums of my heart. Suddenly, a well of warm energy surged throughout my body until my vision sharpened and extremities coursed with power. Taking the offensive, I shot toward Siren like a mag round leaving a gun.

"Zero, no!" Sa'Sha called. But I was already committed.

I feinted a kick at her face, and swung at her head. I barely saw her move before her spear slashed at the back of my neck. Siren twirled the spear into a second attack at my back, but I'd already shielded my back with stone. Her blade clanged, and she shuffled back before I could make another move.

"Maybe you're not as stupid as you look," she said.

"Too bad you're as ugly as you look," I replied.

"You've got some mouth on you." The head of the spear began glowing red.

"Zero," Sa'Sha yelled, "She's ignited the annihilation engine! Watch out!"

In a flash, the woman was in my face; her spear a bevy of red flashes. I could barely harden my skin in time to block it. But it wasn't enough. With every slash of her blade, a searing pain bit into me as the stone literally melted off. When her barrage finally subsided, something plowed into my stomach, and I went crashing through the wall behind me. Bright heat caressed my eyelids. I was finally back outside the facility. With daylight and more room to maneuver, I finally had the advantage. I couldn't let it go to waste. I rolled over, ignoring the stinging traversing my arms, and pressed back onto my feet.

"Strength isn't everything," Siren called from behind me, twirling her spear overhead as she ran at me. "Not unless you know how to wield it."

I didn't have time to ready my body for the next round with her. Even worse, my eyes were barely keeping up with her angry twirling blade. I could only stumble around. Desperate to avoid a lethal blow. I was in serious trouble. She feinted a stab at my leg. I tried to react when a blur flashed in front of my face and my head jerked back so suddenly it threw me to the ground. I stumbled to my feet. But something slammed into the back of my legs, sweeping my feet from under me again. My shoulder screamed as it collided with the ground, the burning throb intensifying. The back of my head smacked the ground, dulling my senses until it sounded like everything was whooshing.

"Zero," a voice called over the ringing. My eyes popped opened and I was met with a smoldering blade preparing to cleave my face in two. A bright light flashed, forcing my eyes shut again. And just like that... I was done. For all my talk, I couldn't even survive two hashes with Siren. And now Sa'Sha would be left to the whims of that screeching psychopath. For an instant, there was only silence. I lay still, waiting for everything to fade away. But it didn't. In contrast, everything began getting louder, until... The stench of burning metal singed my nostrils, forcing my eyelids open as I went into a coughing fit. I rolled over; the ground still blurring as the realization hit me. *I'm not dead?*

"You okay, Zero?" I looked up and saw Sa'Sha standing over me. The soft orange glow of Nightfall's ignited blade cast a sinister light on her soft face.

"Heartwarming," Siren said. "Throwing yourself into my blade's path to save your useless little boyfriend. Our order may have a use for someone like you."

Sa'Sha answered with a glare that was, unfortunately, obscured by her hood. "Back me up," She whispered. "We can't beat her, but if we wear her down a bit, that may create an opportunity to escape."

I gritted, a sharp ache shooting through my shoulder and down my back as I attempted to peel myself from the ground. "You sure this will work? I couldn't land a single hit."

A thick haze still swirled in my head, but it wouldn't take long for my accelerated healing to dispel it. I just needed a little time. Not that we had any to spare. I filled my lungs and exhaled slowly, willing what little energy I could muster into my ears and legs. My hearing returned just in time for a crackle followed by a pluck to resound deep in my ear. Without a second thought, I wrapped my arms around Sa'Sha's waist and dove to one side. A beat later, an explosive bang erupted where Siren was standing. I looked over my shoulder and there was Surket, approaching us with chilling intensity.

"This thing is dangerous, you know," Sa'Sha said, glaring at me as she reached for Nightfall. The entire blade was buried in the ground leaving only the hilt exposed.

How did she drive it in the ground so quickly?

"This divarma could've seriously injured us both had I not taken precautions. How about a warning the next time you want to pull a crazy stunt like that?"

"Backup has finally come out of hiding," Siren said, shaking one of her wrists. "So, it's three versus one then?" Surket's bowstring glowed, as she pulled back on it; another bolt crackling as it formed.

Sa'Sha's apprehension showed through her HOOD. "Stay with Zero," Surket said, her eyes trained on Siren as she planted her feet and lined up her shot. "What name should I have chiseled on your tomb?"

Siren gave a fiendish smirk. "Such arrogance from someone who relies on ambushes to—"

Another bolt slammed into Siren. At least, I thought it did at first. The distance should've been too short to react, and yet, Siren managed to bring her blade up in time to catch the bolt. Sparks flew in every direction as the bolt exploded against Siren's blade with enough force to knock her off her feet. But she was back up a moment after her butt brushed the ground.

"Sarani is the name my parents gave me," she said. "But Siren is the name my master blessed me with. You?"

"I've no need for a tomb, since my plans don't include an untimely death."

Siren sucked her teeth and charged at Surket. But Surket's next shot was ready for her. Fire filled my eyes and I blinked just long enough to release the visual speed enhancement. By the time I had, Siren was tumbling back to the dirt. With a shriek high enough to shatter glass, Siren released a deluge of sound that was too massive for Surket to avoid. She guarded her face just before Siren's sound wave crashed into her with enough force to lift her off the ground. Surket struggled to regain her footing as Siren astonishingly managed to maintain her note.

"I'll be back in a beat," I said.

"What are you talking about?" Sa'Sha asked. "Surket told us to stay here."

"She told *you* to stay here. And that was before any of us knew about Siren's powers."

"Don't be rash. We can't just—"

"Rush in? No, we can't. But just sitting here isn't the best option either."

With a choked breath, Sa'Sha stopped herself short of words. She sighed. "Her ability extends to a superhuman lung capacity."

"I guessed that much. But if I catch her when she pauses for air, I'll have a chance."

It was easier said than done. I didn't know exactly how I was going to determine the limit of her lung capacity, but I looked on anyway, as if I'd already figured out my next move. Then it happened. Surket dug her heels into the dirt and hunched forward, resisting Siren's push. It shouldn't have surprised me that someone as strong as Surket would eventually find a way to resist Siren's attack. And with that resistance came the sign I was waiting for. I started at Siren with every bit of speed I could muster, tackling her with such unexpected force that a high-pitched honking escaped her mouth. We tumbled, but she pulled away and recovered first.

"Wretched brat," Siren spat, clenching her side. She grunted and torqued her body to one side. Then, my head followed.

Pain flashed along the side of my face, and my legs buckled under me. So much so that I didn't notice as Siren took in more air. But a spark pinged deep in my chest, compelling me to move away. I followed my gut and narrowly avoided the high-pitched shrill that erupted from her throat. The ground rumbled beneath, dust and dirt flying in all directions. I wanted to shield my eyes, but a second ping had my senses going haywire. I scrambled to my feet and scurried away as fast as my legs could manage. I'd hoped to lose her by the time I was in the clear. But Siren was also on the move, and only a few steps behind me. I would've assumed her goal was reaching clean air before her next sound wave, but the moment we were both clear of the dust cloud, her blade appeared over-head glinting with the promise of death.

My eyes squeezed shut a moment before the blade connected. So, I could only guess what I thought I'd heard. But when my eyes finally opened, Surket was standing nearby, her bow at her side as she waited for me to recompose myself. Siren lay face-down in the dirt, the back of her cloak singed but surprisingly intact.

Surket turned and walked to Sa'Sha, whose attention was focused in a completely different direction. I limped over as Surket asked, "What do you see, Bird?"

"More guards," Sa'Sha replied. "Closing in fast."

"Then, it's time we left."

"I think Siren has the same idea," I said. We all turned to Siren who was staggering away. "How much did you hit her with?"

"Not enough," Surket said, taking aim for another shot.

"Contact left!" Sa'Sha yelled just before a group of guards emerged from the trees and opened fire. But the rounds stopped just short of us, colliding with a translucent blue wall. Before I could process what had happened, Sa'Sha grabbed my arm.

"Let's go Zero! That psionic field won't hold long," she said. We took cover behind the building. Surket checked around the corner, then gave Sa'Sha a weird hand signal. She fired an array of bolts from her fingers, that I could only assume hit their marks, as we received pained cries from the guards in return. Then, Surket rushed around the corner, trailed by Sa'Sha.

I started after them, but Sa'Sha held a hand up. Screams erupted from the guards, one after the other. About a hash later, Sa'Sha and Surket reappeared.

"We're done here," Surket said. "Let's exfil before more reinforcements arrive."

"What about Siren?" I asked.

"No longer our concern. Our mission objectives were—"

"There she is!" Even as I pointed, Siren disappeared into the building as quickly as her battered body would allow. Sa'Sha called after me, but I wasn't about to let Siren get away. Capturing her could help us put an end to the male-factors permanently. And it'd be stupid to let her get away, when she was so worn down—despite the fact that I wasn't feeling so great myself.

She stumbled into a room that extended to a thin walkway. The flashing lights silhouetted her in a way that made her seem larger than life. But she wasn't. She'd been defeated. And it was time to bring her to justice. At the top of a short flight of metal stairs, Siren continued to stumble until she fell through a doorway. The burning in my legs was intensifying as I stepped through the doorway. It was anyone's guess how much longer the chase would continue if I didn't end it. I gathered the little energy I could spare and shot out a spark that crackled against Siren's back, dropping her to the ground. Unable to stand, she rolled over, settling for a final burning glare at her pursuer.

"There will be blood for this," she spat. Her voice was weak and raspy.

"No, it's over Siren," I said, authority infusing my words. "You're gonna help us stop these creatures whether you like it or not."

"My comrades will see to it that our plans continue."

"We'll stop them just like we stopped you."

Siren gave a menacing smirk. "Talk big when you can handle your own battle. Anyway, you're too late. I've initiated the self-destruct sequence, so you and your friends are good as dead."

"Nice try. But shouldn't there be warning alarms going off?"

She rolled her eyes. "This isn't a vid. Why else would I tell you how I'm going to end you when it could provide a means of escape?"

"But you just told me."

Her eyes glowed. "Exactly."

Before I could make sense of her words, Siren was back on her feet, her spear arching down at me. As I tried to cover my face, I realized the blade was aimed at my torso. And there was no time to stop it. She'd bested me again. And I was stupid enough to step right into her trap. All I could do was wait for her blade. When the blade finally made contact, it felt less like a slice and more like a tremendous force striking me. Breath fled my lungs as the impact threw me to the floor. A scream rang out, accompanied by loud buzzing.

My eyes opened to what I almost thought to be a dream. Surket was lying on top of me, her arm around my unharmed waist. Siren was nearby, a trail of blood above her head as she slid down the wall and crumpled into a heap with empty eyes. I blinked hard at the gaping hole where Siren's heart should've been. But Siren wasn't the only one to suffer from the exchange. Surket looked like she would pass out any moment. And if Siren's warning wasn't a bluff, the timing couldn't have been worse.

"We have to get out of here," I said. "There are bombs all over and—"

I paused, suddenly overcome with terror as the pieces slowly fell into place. A warm liquid was seeping into my pants, exactly where Surket was positioned. I looked down at the expanding crimson pool. And everything froze as my eyes traced back to the source.

"That's no longer an option," Surket said weakly. "You and Raven... need to get out of here. I couldn't disable every bomb before..." Surket's body grew heavy as she trailed off. Numbness invaded my body. Flames engulfed my eyes. My vision began to blur.

"I... I can't leave you," I said. Three thunderous booms outside interrupted our conversation, rattling the building. I wanted to say I'd find a way. That I'd carry her back to Northe and we'd all get off Kunai no matter what. But the words wouldn't come.

"My time has passed. I go into the *Tashi* with no regrets. It all falls to you and Sa'Sha now. You two... I'm so proud of you two. Go now. Protect Sa'Sha. Trust her. I know you can." With a weak smile, Surket closed her eyes and she was gone.

Tears welled at the corners of my eyes. There was no way to thank Surket for saving me yet again. No way to apologize for being incapable of fighting my own battle. All I could do was see her final request through. Even if the cost was my own life—the very life Surket died saving—I would protect Sa'Sha with all I had. I owed her that much. "I promise, I will protect her," I whispered to Surket.

I rose, heart heavy and looked to the doorway. In it, stood the last person I wanted to see there. She trembled, eyes wide through the HOOD. Time slowed. Everything went silent. Until one sound rang through that pierced my very core.

"Surket!" Sa'Sha wailed running toward us. We had to go. If we didn't escape, we'd join her. But Sa'Sha was determined to reach her. Determined to save her. Fate had other plans however. Other horrible plans. One beat, I was watching Sa'Sha running toward me. The next, I saw a bright light escorted by a deafening boom. When the darkness receded, I was still in the facility, ears ringing and vision fuzzy. But when I looked to my side, anxiety sobered me up like a shot of adrenaline. Sa'Sha lay motionless beside me.

No. No. No. No. No. No. No.

I wrenched myself to my feet—fighting the pain and fatigue—and stumbled over to her. She was face down, dark blood pooled near her lower body. Cautiously, I rolled her over praying she still had a pulse. Relief washed over me as the steady rise and fall of her chest gave substance to my hopes. My eyes trailed to her thigh and I confirmed the source of the blood. Shrapnel protruded from her leg, blood drenching her pants. Explosions rumbled in the distance reminding me how dire the situation was. Carefully, I took her into my arms. I looked around but Surket was gone. Leaving felt so—wrong. But what choice did I have? With a heavy heart, and heat pressing at the back of my eyes, I ran outside.

The exterior was a war zone. Debris littered the landscape, explosions kicking up a veil of dust, as smoke and fires sprouted in every direction. As I ran into the surrounding woods, I started to feel faint. Like the burden of my actions would crush me under its intensifying weight. But the explosives weren't going off any slower on my account, and I had a promise to keep. It was a battle of will, ignoring the cramps building in my legs; the stitch in my sides. But even as the malefactors appeared in droves, I didn't slow down. Thankfully, they were just as anxious to get away from the explosions as I was. Unfortunately, they proved as much an obstacle as every other large rock or uprooted tree trunk in my path.

Suddenly, like a riptide pulling algae out to sea, my stamina left without warning. I all but fell to my knees, my lungs practically cooking in my chest. *Did I push too hard again?* I dismissed the thought as soon as it surfaced. The feeling was akin to exhaustion, but I'd been careful not to overextend myself this time. Still, I couldn't begin to guess why my knees were trying so desperately to buckle. Before any ideas came to mind, an immense force threw me off my feet. I squeezed Sa'Sha tight in an attempt to shield her from the fall. But as we hit the ground, she slid out of my grasp. I scrambled over to her to make sure she was okay, when a voice echoed from behind me.

"Where is it?" My blood ran cold. *That voice. That dead voice.* I turned around, facing the nightmare. Green Eyes stalked toward us, unphased by the explosions behind him.

"Where's what?" I said quietly—timidly.

"Don't toy with me. I know you're not leaving empty-handed."

"Then you've been misinformed. Because we are leaving *more* than empty-handed."

He scrutinized me with a petrifying gaze that shone from beneath the ragged tattered hood obscuring his face. Then, he stepped closer. "Perhaps, I was unclear. Give me the key, or I'll incinerate you where you stand." A ball of fire sparked in his palm. He held his hand out at me, and the flame doubled in size. I needed to stall until I could think of some way to get us out alive. Almost on instinct, I reached my hand up at him and said, "You think that's enough to stop my next move?"

"I'm willing to find out," he said. "Are you?"

My situation wasn't looking too good. Whether I kept up my bluff or admitted I had no way to stop him, it still didn't change the fact that I didn't have whatever key he was talking about. And that meant there was no way to stop him from burning Sa'Sha and me to a crisp. The heat of his flame intensified pressing against me. I was out of time. Even if we both died in that moment, there was no way I'd let it happen without putting up a fight to protect her.

With everything I had, I blasted a gust of wind at Green Eyes, hoping to extinguish his flame and show him that I wasn't just some pushover. The flame in his hand danced apathetically, and I wondered if the subtle twitch in his in eyes signaled irritation or disgust. But that didn't matter nearly as much as the fact that the flame doubled in size yet again. I squeezed my hands to control the trembling, as I stared into the brilliant flame. It was hard to fathom the thought that after everything, this would be where it all ended. I was out of time. And all I could think was that if Surket and I had switched places, at least Sa'Sha would've been safe. But it was something in that thought that motivated me to try one more time.

I fired another gust. Miraculously, a vortex sprang forth, swallowing Green Eyes like a serpent. It pulled him into the air and planted him waist-height into the dirt. *Did I just...?*

"Let's go children!" Northe called from behind, before my mind could latch onto the possibility that I didn't know my own strength. "That won't hold him long."

I scooped Sa'Sha up, and powered through the final dash up into the Nighthawk's cargo bay. The bay door closed behind me, and Northe wasted no time in pulling away. Through the side windows, I could see Green Eyes watching us from the shore. Even as his image grew smaller, the glow in his eyes was all too clear. As was his expression. The next time we met, he'd be out for blood.

[4]

REVERSAL

I could say I felt numb. But I honestly don't remember how I felt. Empty, maybe. Anxious, probably. Angry and helpless, definitely. Some swirling jumble of emotions that came and went and came again. I was caught in a nightmare, that was descending further into Hadal by the beat. My only solace was the girl laying on the bench across from me. Her brown hair rested over her face in a way that made her look peaceful—and beautiful. But I knew it wouldn't last. Once she was awake and aware of the fact that I'd left Surket behind, we'd probably go back to day one at D7. And that would be a best-case scenario. The weight of my decisions loomed over me; my shoulders slumping as my eyelids fought gravity. My mind was so busy racing through the terrible things that were in store, I hadn't realized how tired I was. I leaned against the wall of the aircraft and, within beats, everything went dark.

"Three hashes out, you two," Northe called, and my eyes started to peel open.

I turned toward the sound of his voice, when a sharp pressure stretched from my shoulder halfway up my neck. The pain was so intense, it was a wonder I hadn't noticed it sooner. At least, until Sa'Sha stirred from her sleep and slowly looked up at me; pulling my entire focus to the well of anxiety bubbling in my chest. I knew what she was about to ask. And every beat of silence between us might as well have been a knife dangling over my throat. Her gaze broke just long enough to scan the aircraft before returning to me.

"Where's Surket?" she finally said.

My eyes didn't pull away from Sa'Sha's. They fell away. As if gravity had concentrated on that part of my face. There was no right way to answer that question. But I had to say something. I cleared my throat the best I could. But the lump there had doubled in size taking most of the power out of my words before I could speak them away.

"Umm," I started, trying to clear my throat again, but to no avail. "Surket—"

"Did what she had to so you two could escape," Northe finished. "That's how I knew to come for you." His voice was uncharacteristically gruff.

The hum of the Nighthawk engine filled the silence following Northe's words. The heat of Sa'Sha's eyes demanded my attention. But I couldn't find the courage to meet them.

"Surket is...gone?" Sa'Sha asked. Her voice was shaky, like she was on the verge of tears. A prickling heat filled my eyes as I nodded. "How could...why did we leave her? We have to go back for her."

Northe didn't answer.

"We can't leave her. Northe, we have to—"

"She gave specific instructions to leave if things went south and that's what I did. Alright?"

"Maybe you heard wrong. Did you ever consider that? She couldn't have said that." Sa'Sha was growing more and more erratic. But from the sound of it, Northe wasn't having the easiest time coming to terms with the situation either. Still, he opted for silence in lieu of acknowledging anything else Sa'Sha said on the matter. Sa'Sha looked at me with wild confusion. "What did you do? How could you let..." Her eyes fell to her feet, and my heart began pounding just as wildly in my throat.

"I just wanted to get you back safe," I said. "Surket asked me to."

"She asked you to leave her behind? Did she also ask you to run after Siren and jeopardize her life along with the mission?"

"No." The engine's hum filled my head as Sa'Sha's glare burned into me like hot steel. "I'm...sorry," was all I could manage. I reached for her hand. But she pulled away without a moment's hesitation.

"Leave me alone," she said. "Team Seven was fine without you."

Her words were like a punch to the throat; intensifying the ache that had been building ever since we departed Kunai.

"So, what's our story?" Northe said. "What are we telling the Colonel when we touch down?"

I could only take the fact that Sa'Sha kept her head down as a terrible sign where I was concerned. This would probably be my last mission. But that was the least of my worries.

"Everything that went wrong with this mission was my fault," I said. "I'll make sure my explanation keeps you guys out of the fire." In the silence that immediately followed, I could only imagine how bad that fire would burn me.

"We were caught off guard by the sheer number of malefactors," Sa'Sha said. "Siren ambushed us with abilities and fighting prowess that proved overwhelming. It was only through Surket's sacrifice that we managed to escape Kunai." She looked up at Northe who seemed to be more focused on flying than participating in the conversation.

"Surket always took pride in Team Seven's loyalty," he replied after a pause. "Don't say anything when we land, Kid."

"But what if—?"

"Just follow our lead," Sa'Sha barked. "Or are you still determined to do everything your way?"

"Sorry," I said, focus returning to the floor.

I'd single handedly ruined the mission, but Northe and Sa'Sha were still helping me. If I'd accomplished nothing else as an IGIS agent, I promised myself I would find a way to repay them. As the Nighthawk prepared for landing, my pulse quickened, and I immediately noticed the contrast in moisture between my clammy hands and dry throat. Even if I wasn't supposed to speak, I doubted it would be that simple. The cargo door opened to two medics pushing a medical table. It took more effort than I expected to push to my feet.

"Meet me inside after the medics take Sa'Sha," Northe said and stepped out of the Nighthawk before I could respond.

"What happened to her?" one of the medics asked me, looking over her wound.

"She—" Sa'Sha's scowl made my words catch in my throat.

"A bomb went off and shrapnel caught me in the leg," Sa'Sha said.

"I see," the male medic said. He looked to his partner and after a nod they lifted her onto the medical table and started rolling her down the ramp.

"You don't look so good yourself," the female medic said. "Come to the Med-Fac so one of the docs can look you over." I nodded. "We'll notify you when Raven is all patched up, so you can visit her."

"That won't be necessary," Sa'Sha said without pause. The medics shared an awkward look, then continued down the ramp and toward the MedFac.

What will become of Team Seven? It was the first thought to cross my mind as I stepped off the aircraft. We'd lost our commander, half of our team was still in training, and I couldn't imagine Sa'Sha or Northe feeling up to the task of taking command. Team Seven would likely end up disbanding before the end of the dec. I hurried to catch up with Northe in Stratcom. But the sharp rhythmic voice, assaulting my ears the moment I entered the building, told me exactly where to go. I followed the sound to find Northe with the Colonel, who looked about as livid as I would've expected.

"Zero," he yelled. "Explain to me why your team has returned one agent short." I looked to Northe. But his eyes remained squarely on the Colonel.

"Well?" the Colonel said.

The blood drained from my face as I searched for words. "I uhh...she was hurt and uhh...the building...umm."

"Spit it out, dammit."

I shook my head. "I don't know, sir."

His eyes went so wide, I thought they'd jump out and attack me. "You don't know? Raven's leg is full of shrapnel, and Surket—the best of all of you—was killed in action, and of you two gentlemen, one is unscathed and the other looks like he fell into a paper shredder. But you don't know. So, what am I missing here?" The Colonel's eyes shifted between Northe and me with burning intensity. I'd never known of anyone to give a more threatening glare than Hachi until that moment.

"Get over to MedFac, and see if they can't fix whatever memories were knocked loose on Kunai, Lieutenant. And I expect a full report on whatever happened out there within the next twenty segments, you two. Dismissed." Northe and I saluted and the Colonel stomped off so loudly, everyone within a few meters of him cleared a path.

Northe turned and started for the door. "I contacted the MedFac while you were passed out. I'll see you tomorrow."

"But, what about the report?"

"Raven can handle it. The Colonel knows I wasn't in the thick of it, but I'll co-sign whatever I can from what you two say."

"But—"

With a hop, Northe lifted into the air and disappeared into the sunlight. I turned and ambled toward the MedFac, trying to wrap my head around how everything could go so wrong in just one day. None of the animosity Sa'Sha or the Colonel had toward me was unexpected. And I wouldn't be surprised if Hachi, NaRyn, and Shawin had similar reactions. I mean, it was Surket after all. But Northe's reaction was what puzzled me. With him it almost seemed as if nothing happened. And yet, somehow, it seemed like he was in another world, even when I was standing right next to him. As I approached Vaticia's three-story medical facility, I noticed a woman sitting on a small bench next to the automatic entry doors. She wore a lab coat with wireframe glasses, and her skin was a pale bronze that could only be overshadowed by her flowing red hair.

"Anne?"

She rose. "Hello, Zero. Glad you finally made it."

"What are you—?"

"I work here." She rested a hand on my shoulder, pressing against the scrapes and bruises. But I didn't cringe. Her touch was unexpectedly gentle. "Now, let's make sure you're okay."

She guided me through the lobby and down a long hall, until we reached a cozy room with polished hardwood flooring, leading to grayish-blue walls that somehow drew my attention toward a cream-colored sign. It was a quirky painting of two small arrows pointing from a seed to a sapling to a full-grown tree with the words: "Things get better with time," directly under it.

The familiar scent of serenity blooms wafted from her hair.

"You should feel special," Anne said, patting the bed for me to sit. "I was saving this room for you."

"I didn't know you worked for IGIS," I said.

"You didn't ask." She pulled a device from her coat pocket that resembled a tiny flashlight and began carefully running it over the cuts on my face. The sensation was like small fires igniting all over my face, as the tiny green light knitted my skin back together. But I tried not to make it too obvious that I was in pain.

"I'm sorry hun," she said. "I'm sure it's not comfortable."

"No, I'm fine," I said.

She stopped and looked into my eyes with a smile. "Then why are you scowling at me?"

"Just...caught off guard."

"Well, the pain won't last too long."

She leaned close and gently blew over my face. It would've been awkward if it didn't make me feel so much more at ease. Then, she kissed my forehead in the way only a mother could. The way my mother used to.

"Let's check your vitals before I clear you to leave," she said as she pulled out and unrolled her digipad. But I didn't want to leave. It had been a long time since anyone made me feel so certain everything would be okay. Even in the midst of turmoil.

"Do you have a designation too?" I asked.

"Of course. They call me, *'The Mother.'*" She tapped the screen and a green light shone from the digipad, traversing my body.

"As the Guild's Chief Medical Officer, I'm ultimately responsible for the wellbeing of every person within IGIS."

"Not too daunting."

"Not always, though I rarely have free time. I'm trying to increase our pool of medical staff to get off double duties. The number grows a bit each anum, but the decrease in workload remains marginal at best."

"I think I'm beginning to understand the feeling of being forced into extra work. The Colonel can be pretty harsh at times."

"Would you like me to have a talk with him?"

"Thanks, but no. I don't need anyone else getting yelled at behind me."

Anne chuckled. "I doubt AJ would be so quick to yell at one of his peers."

"Peers? Like *of equal rank?*"

She nodded. "Lie down please."

It was hard to believe the very same woman I'd saved from an overweight criminal held a rank equal to the Colonel's. And decs after joining IGIS, I discovered she'd been here the whole time. She pressed two fingers over seemingly random parts of my chest and stomach.

"You're dehydrated," Anne said as she prepped a needle. "I'll give you an IV to help speed up your recovery. Now, onto the real issue. What happened during your mission?"

"A lot," I said with a heavy sigh.

"I gathered that much." She pulled her chair in front of me and sat down. "But why does your face look like your world is coming to an end?"

I almost didn't want to answer. But if she was at the Colonel's rank, there's no way she wouldn't eventually find out.

"I really don't wanna burden you with my stupid problems."

"My designation is 'The Mother' for a reason. In this field, a large part of the job has nothing to do with my medical abilities."

I wanted to believe her. But how many agents messed up a mission as fatally as I had? How many were responsible for the death of their team commander? Telling her the truth might make it impossible for her to look at me the same. But even as fear flashed through my mind, her large, autumn eyes watched me patiently. I told Anne about my time with Sa'Sha and how after what happened with Surket on Kunai, Sa'Sha probably hated me more than when I first met her. Anne's eyes remained on me as she rose to her feet. I didn't know how to interpret her solemn expression, but I was almost certain it wasn't good. She wrapped her arms around me, and squeezed.

"I know you meant well, dear. You're probably feeling like things are at their worst right now, but remember that everything has a purpose. Don't let your missteps be the end of your journey. Trust that they'll forgive you in time."

My chest was still tight with anxiety. But Anne's advice was starting to put me at ease. The road to earning their forgiveness may be long, but having faith in Sa'Sha and Northe was a great place to start.

"Thanks Anne," I said.

Just then, her timechain buzzed in her coat pocket. She fished it out and opened it. "Dr. Kartnia speaking... How are you? I'm well, thanks for asking... Yes, he's right here." She looked at me with a smile. "He'll be fine... No, no trouble at all... Of course. You as well... Bye now." She put the timechain back in her pocket. "Seems your uncle is rather concerned about you."

"Right," I said, eyes falling to the ground. But Anne's smile didn't waver.

"That goes for him too."

"Huh?"

"Trust in him too."

Easier said than done. It was practically a hobby for Hachi to point out my shortcomings. And after showing enough trust to let me join IGIS, I'd probably let him down the most.

"And I'm serious about you resting. I'll give you some vitamins to help with your recovery, but without rest it's no good, okay?"

"Yes ma'am." She frowned and removed the IV. "Is everything alright?"

"To be completely honest, I hate when people call me ma'am."

"So, *Mother* then?"

"It honestly doesn't feel too great having everyone calling me mother either. It makes me feel old. But for some reason, it sounds right when you say it," her smile widened.

Anne was one of a kind. I couldn't remember the last time anyone made me feel so comfortable and... well, special. And it didn't seem to take any more effort than applying bandages. I followed Anne back through the lobby, taking notice of the closed doors lining the hallways on either side of me. "Is Sa'Sha doing okay?"

"She's out of surgery and doing well." Anne noted after checking her digipad. "Would you like to see her?"

Her eyes were encouraging. Like she wanted me to say yes. But I wasn't so sure I could face her just yet.

I shook my head. "That's okay."

The sun was on the horizon and Aio was peeking out by the time I was standing in front of D7. I'd spent more time talking to Anne than I realized. And now that I was alone again, it was all too easy to feel the fatigue returning. I didn't have an appetite for much of anything but sleep. I stepped in and started for the stairs when NaRyn's voice echoed behind me.

"Serec, where is everybody? Uncle Hachi said you guys got back segments ago. But it sounded like something happened."

"Sa'Sha and I had to go to the MedFac, but we're okay."

"The Director only mentioned you and Sa'Sha in the medical facility," Shawin said, walking up to NaRyn. "He never told us where Uncle Kaz or Surket went."

I shouldn't have been surprised that they would be short on details. Hachi probably wanted NaRyn and Shawin to hear it from a member of Team Seven. Unfortunately, I was the only member around to tell the story that Sa'Sha hadn't completely worked out.

"Yeah, about that. Northe...took off."

"Took off? Where?" Shawin asked.

"Don't know. He was upset about Surket. She didn't make it out of the mission." Before I realized it, my eyes were fixed on the floor. And, no matter how much I wanted, I couldn't bring them any higher.

"But, Surket's supposed to be like the strongest person here," NaRyn said, incredulous.

"The woman Surket fought was almost as strong as she was. Surket defeated her, but the woman had one last trick that took us all by surprise, and Surket got the worst of it. We couldn't go back since she blew up half the island, and one of the bombs exploded near Sa'Sha. That's why she's in the MedFac now."

The visible disappointment they shared turned out to be harder to endure than I'd imagined. I started toward the stairs.

"What's going to happen now?" NaRyn called.

I paused to consider the possibilities. None of them seemed particularly favorable. "I don't know," I said and kept moving until I reached my room. I buried my head in the pillow just as my brain fluttered with nothing but panic. No matter what explanation I gave at the debriefing, the higher ups would scrutinize it, picking it apart, right down to the tiniest detail. And that's when everyone was sure to turn on me. A knock came at my door.

"Yeah?" I called.

"It's me," Shawin said. "Can I talk to you for a hash?"

I took a deep breath and sat up. "It's open."

The door slid open and Shawin stepped in. "Hey."

"Hey."

"Your mission sounds like it took a turn for the worst. Will you be alright?"

"Sure. I just—need to figure some things out."

"The best way to tell everyone what you told us?"

"Yeah. I doubt they'll take it as quietly as you guys."

"Not if you omit the same details you did with us."

My face went flush, before I could think to hide it. Not that it mattered. Shawin had that look in his eyes again. Like he was peering into my soul. "What gave it away?"

"Your hesitation said a lot."

"So, you know what happened?" I asked, somewhat hopeful.

"Unfortunately, I can't say that I do. But I think something is happening with my powers. Probably because of my time here. It's not uncommon for Wolfhounds to experience an evolution in their abilities during their Journey of Intention. It might have something to do with discovering our purpose. And so, it becomes both easier and harder to see what's coming."

I frowned. "What's that supposed to mean?"

"Most precogs can only see the immediate future. But recently, I've been having visions that are days or decs in the future. With every action I take, the outcome changes slightly."

"What do you mean?"

"Two days ago, I already knew you would have a mission. But starting yesterday, something about it made me uneasy. So, I tried to visualize how it would turn out."

Trepidation surged through me. "And?"

"I saw Sa'Sha. She was lying in a pool of blood. And a woman with a spear was looming over her."

My body went rigid. *How can Shawin's vision be so similar to my nightmares?*

"Are you saying that Sa'Sha was supposed to die?"

"Possibly. But if she's still alive, it could mean that the events leading to that outcome were altered somehow. I think that change may have led to Surket's death in place of Sa'Sha's."

"But what could've made the outcome change?"

"It's hard to say, since I wasn't there to see exactly what happened."

That should've made me feel better. On some minute level, it should have. But it didn't. Even if my actions are what saved Sa'Sha, they still caused Surket's death in her place.

"Are you alright?" Shawin asked, and I realized how tense the muscles in my face were.

"Yeah," I lied. "I'm smooth." Shawin still had the look in his eyes. But I couldn't bring myself to say any more—even though I wanted to.

"Part of why I joined the Guild is because I trust the people here as much as I trust in what they fight for. Trust that I'll always be there when you need a friend. NaRyn too. I know she means a lot to you. So, don't be afraid to let her see how human you are."

"She's seen plenty. Especially, the mistakes."

"And she respects you because of your determination despite the mistakes. Same goes for me."

Shawin's eyes had changed again. They'd become warm and endearing, almost like Anne's. He was speaking from the heart. And it made me smile, the same way Anne would.

"What?" Shawin asked.

I shook my head. "Thanks."

He smiled and offered a fist bump.

The encouragement from Shawin and Anne lingered in my mind, pressing against my earlier, more panicked thoughts. Still, the question remained unanswered. Could I really trust everyone with the whole truth about the mission? My talk with Shawin made one thing clear. What I *didn't* say during the debriefing would have the greatest magnitude.

[5]

OMISSION

I didn't think my stomach could ever be in enough knots to skip breakfast. But the perfect blend of jitters and anxiety I was experiencing made eating seem like an unrealistic prospect. The debriefing was a couple short segments away, and still no sign of Northe. Maybe he wasn't coming back. Maybe he'd given up on IGIS altogether. Surket's death must've hit him harder than I thought. Despite Sa'Sha's plan, I couldn't keep my mind from skimming through the mission like scenes in a vid. I had to be prepared for any question. I couldn't expect things to go too smoothly. But thinking about the mission only worked to make me more restless. I left my room and found Shawin and NaRyn in the training room, going through Yenta Gin drills.

"How's the new student been working out?" I said.

"She's much more disciplined than my old student. Better looking too," Shawin said with a grin. His sense of humor had improved a lot since I first met him.

NaRyn giggled and poked him behind the ear. A smile wiped across his face before he went for her stomach. *Why can't things be this simple with me and Sa'Sha?* The sight of NaRyn and Shawin simultaneously warmed my heart and hurt my spirit. I wasn't jealous or anything. But a part of me still wished we could have what they had.

"Wanna join us?" NaRyn managed through laughter.

"Actually, I wanted to talk to you guys for a hash."

"About what?" Shawin asked.

"My mission report is in a couple segments. As members of Team Seven, I think you guys should be there to hear the details for yourselves."

"Sure. Sa'Sha told us about it this morning. We'll be there."

"Sa'Sha is here?"

"Not anymore. She changed and said she would be in Stratcom until it was time for your mission report."

"She looked irritated when your name came up," NaRyn added. "Did something happen between you two?"

It was hard enough explaining what happened with Surket. As bad as it felt knowing Sa'Sha hated me, I knew talking about it wouldn't make me feel any better.

I shrugged. "Probably just taking the whole Surket thing the hardest. Sa'Sha was her apprentice."

"Yeah. I guess she would be most upset."

"Either way, we'll be there," Shawin repeated.

Their first meeting as members of Team Seven could also be their last. And Shawin was still as optimistic as he could be. The thought settled into the back of my mind, and knowing I was the cause of it all was more than a little discouraging.

"See you guys there," I said, and walked back to my room with the most hollow feeling imaginable in my chest.

I probably could have blamed it on the severity of the situation. But the beat I stepped into the conference room, I was wrapped in cold suffocation. Everything from the harsh overhead lumens lining the center of the ceiling to the piercing echo of my heels clacking against the taupe marble floors felt larger than life. Kareen and everyone from Team Seven sat at one end of the long, narrow table positioned perfectly center. But to reach them, I had to pass a small group of older faces I didn't recognize. Hachi and the Colonel sat dead center with an empty seat between them.

Not the best scenario by a long shot. But it's not like the veterans of Team Seven were doing much better. The only thing that stood out more than the contemptuous look in Sa'Sha's eyes was the pair of crutches leaning on her chair. And Northe looked like he hadn't slept at all since I'd last seen him. I started toward the empty seat between Hachi and the Colonel, when the door swung open and the last person I would've expected hurried in.

"Thank you all for waiting," she said as she walked up to me. She placed a hand on my shoulder and smiled. "You're looking better."

"Anne?"

"That's my name." Her eyes directed me toward the seat I'd somehow failed to notice before.

"Oh," I said. Anne gave my back a small rub as I moved past her and into the seat next to Shawin.

The Colonel rose. "Ladies and gentlemen, please take your seats so we can begin with today's proceedings." He was speaking to a small row of old faces seated in a balcony above the door.

"I asked you all here because an incident occurred during an infiltration mission by Team Seven of Kinetic Operations on the island of Kunai. The circumstances of said mission are currently under investigation. Due to the sensitive nature of the investigation, I will take this opportunity to remind everyone that under no circumstances will any discussion of this be permitted outside this room. As it stands, Captain Kazimus and Acting Commander, Captain Martinel have been privately questioned about the chain of events ultimately leading to the death of Major Surket Akerallos. We will now take record of Lieutenant Arenyu's statement."

Northe and Sa'Sha already told their story?! How do I go along with what they said if I don't know what they said? The thought unsettled me enough to send my heart into a gallop. My safest option would be to stick to the story Sa'Sha worked out earlier and hope to El that would be enough.

The Colonel nodded at me, "Lieutenant Arenyu, take your place at the podium."

I rose and walked toward a small podium at the center of the room. I unconsciously scanned the room which proved more than enough to feel the weight of everyone's eyes on me.

"Our mission was—" My voice cracked. I cleared my throat and tried to swallow back the rock stubbornly blocking it. The mission was to gather information about a facility in Kunai, where we believed the malefactors were being created. We had authorization to reduce enemy numbers as long as it didn't compromise the mission's primary objective."

Without even looking at them, I could sense the pain and disappointment emanating from Sa'Sha and Northe. It jarred my train of thought to the point of stupefying silence.

"Something wrong, Lieutenant?" the Colonel asked.

I shook my head and cleared my throat again. I inhaled a deep, shaky breath desperate to stop my lips from trembling. My eyes scanned the room a second time, stopping once they found Anne's. They blinked slowly as if to remind me to remain calm. As if to remind me this wasn't the end of the world and that I had friends who wouldn't abandon me as easily as I'd feared. Friends like Shawin and NaRyn. And maybe even Northe and Sa'Sha. After all, the only reason we were even having this debriefing was because they refused to throw me onto the rail when things were at their worst. It wasn't fair of me to forget their loyalty.

"I made a call I shouldn't have. Sa'Sha and I were ambushed by an enemy we couldn't defeat. Instead of taking advantage of our first chance to escape, I chose to stand my ground against her. The only reason I'm alive to tell what happened is because Surket saved us. Then, when I thought Surket weakened the enemy enough, I ignored her orders and tried to pursue her. I thought if I could capture her, we could get some answers that could put a stop to the malefactors before the problem got worse. More importantly, I was too focused on proving myself to Team Seven. I didn't see it coming until it was too late, but it was Surket who shielded me from the enemy's lethal surprise attack. It's my fault Team Seven lost its commander."

The room watched me in cold silence, as I watched my shaking hands. Low murmurs swirled around the room, before a chair screeched against the floor.

"Arenyu," the Colonel said dangerously, forward as his knuckles pressed into the table. "Can you tell us what in El's name could've possibly compelled you—?"

Hachi held up a hand. The Colonel's eyes held on Hachi's just long enough for him to recompose himself. The Colonel closed his eyes and inhaled deeply, then sat back down. "Lieutenant," Hachi said, looking to me with a calm, sharp glance as he interlaced his fingers and leaned onto his elbows. "What prompted your choice to engage the enemy in the first place?"

"A dream," I answered. More murmurs erupted.

"Silence please," Hachi commanded. "Elaborate, Lieutenant."

"It was more of a nightmare than anything. But I kept having the dream, even before I knew we were going to Kunai. So, I figured it might be a premonition. A woman with violet eyes and a divarma killed Raven, and I was powerless to stop her. So, when I found myself in the very same situation on our mission, I felt compelled to alter the outcome. I believed that I might lose Sa'Sha if we tried to escape, so my only option was to fight. But she was too strong. That's where Surket came in."

Everyone was silent, their eyes carrying a wealth of emotions that swirled around me like a rainbow, ranging from sorrowful to enraged. But Hachi's reaction was most surprising. He looked sad. But, for some reason, it looked like his sadness was directed at me.

The silence lingered for what fseemed like an eternity, but Anne was the first to speak. "Is there anything else you would like to say, Lieutenant Arenyu?"

"I don't know if I'll ever be able to make it right. Training under someone as amazing as Surket was an honor." I looked at Sa'Sha. "But for what it's worth, I'm sorry. I really am. And I'll accept whatever punishment I'm given."

The senior officers whispered amongst themselves momentarily. Then, Hachi stood and addressed me. "Lieutenant Serec Arenyu, your actions could easily be considered as insubordination. And despite your conviction, your unwillingness to follow protocol repeatedly placed the lives of your team at risk, resulting in the death of your commander. As such, termination of your agent status and expulsion from the Guild is an appropriate punishment for your infractions."

Termination? Expulsion? After all the struggle; all the hardship I'd experienced to reach this point, my time in IGIS would come to a devastatingly abrupt end. I fought with all I had to maintain my composure. Because as much as I hated to admit it, I agreed with Hachi.

"However, ensuring Captain Martinel's safe return and playing a role in saving the lives of the remaining members of Team Six warrants consideration. These facts coupled with her explicit request to offer you leniency, has led us to a decision. In light of what has transpired, you are hereby suspended from all Team Seven field missions indefinitely. Until a verdict has been made at the conclusion of our investigation, you are to remain within the confines of Dorm 7."

With that, I was, yet again, under house arrest. The Arurian Army chewed me up and spit me out. Now, IGIS was essentially doing the same thing. But one thing was different. I actually cared this time. I cared so much it took everything I had to hold back tears pressing at the corners of my eyes.

"Furthermore," the Colonel added, "while it pains me to do this, I must point out that the loss of a commander, coupled with the current investigation of a team member and injury of a technician, places Team Seven in an unstable position for field missions. Therefore, I am hereby removing Team Seven from active status until further notice."

The Colonel's words hit me like a raeda. With one choice, I'd essentially condemned my entire team to involuntary confinement with me. I bit down on my lip so hard I thought I would draw blood. But I needed to feel something other than disappointment in myself before my composure broke in front of everyone.

[6]

TRINITY

After the debriefing or trial or whatever that was, I was thankful to at least be allowed to escort myself back to D7. As soon as I stepped into my room, I plopped onto my squoosh bag and sighed. It would take some time to mentally readjust to caged life. But I wouldn't be remotely short on time for a long... time. I sunk deeper and stared up at the ceiling, wondering if there was any action I could've taken that might've changed the outcome. But the answer was simple. Surket died because I was too weak to fight my own battles. If I was stronger, I would've sent Siren on a one-way trip to Hadal the moment she threatened Sa'Sha. And if Green Eyes wanted to act tough, I would have been happy to make it a two for one deal.

I would have to become stronger, no matter the cost. Otherwise, everything would just keep repeating itself. The decision couldn't have come at a better time, as far as I was concerned. My pre-mission anxiety might've passed, but the post-mission stress was quick to replace it. Whatever final verdict Stratcom gave, I was certain I wouldn't like it.

A sudden sense of calm engulfed me as my resolve began to solidify within my mind. But the moment I slid my door open, that calm immediately drained away. Sa'Sha was standing in the doorway; her expression falling somewhere between uneasy and contemplative. Her unexpected countenance robbed me of words. So, I just stood there...awkwardly.

"Hey," she eventually said.

"Hey," I replied.

"May I speak with you for a moment?"

"Uh, yeah. In my room, or...?"

"Yes. If it's not too much trouble." I backed up and she limped along on her crutches. "Is it alright if I sit on your bed?"

"Y-yeah, sure." Watching as she carefully lowered herself onto my bed had my heart thumping hard enough to feel my pulse in my head. I swallowed hard. "What'd you wanna talk about?"

"How are you?" Her voice was soft, calm.

"I... shouldn't I be asking you that? What'd the doctors say about your leg?"

"They've repaired all superficial damage. As long as I'm careful, I'll be back to normal in a few decs."

"That's good."

"Yeah," she nearly whispered.

Not the smoothest response. But it's not like I was expecting a visitor in the first place. And having Sa'Sha in my room made me more anxious than when she was probing my mind. I mean, your room says a lot about you. And I couldn't help unconsciously, then consciously, scanning the area for anything potentially incriminating.

"How long are you going to keep guard over there?"

My eyes drew back to her patting a spot next to her.

"Oh, sorry." I never thought I'd have a girl—especially one this pretty—sitting on my bed with me. The very idea of it had my heart doing flips. And now it was actually happening. It was so nerve-wracking that a part of me would probably be more comfortable sitting next to Green Eyes than Sa'Sha.

"About the debriefing..." she began. "Why did you tell everything that happened? If you'd stuck to our plan—"

"It wouldn't have been fair to everyone else on the team. Even though you all hate me now, you deserve to know the full truth."

The softness in Sa'Sha's face faded. "What's your problem?"

I was so caught off guard by her first reaction I didn't notice the fire in her eyes. "What?"

"Don't what me! Why do you keep suggesting I hate you? I'm here to compliment you for doing something I probably wouldn't have had the courage to. But how can I say anything nice when you constantly insinuate that I hate you?"

"I never thought of it that way," I said after a pause. "Sorry. But the way you were looking at me back in the conference room... I'm just saying, I'd understand if you were thinking it should've been me instead of Surket."

It was a painful thought for sure. But it seemed like the right thing to say. Even if I'd lost the nerve to look Sa'Sha in the eyes as I said it. Even if I still couldn't find the strength to meet her gaze as she stood and faced me. Without warning, a jarring flash of pain stung the side of my face as it forced my head toward my right shoulder. For a beat, my brain was processing everything in slow motion. I was so caught off guard I could only look up at her in confusion. But there was another surprise I couldn't possibly have anticipated. The tears welling in Sa'Sha's eyes.

"Stop making this all about you," she said. "I was there too, and I couldn't do any more than you could. It's hard enough dealing with that without you saying such hurtful things."

She lowered her head, sniffling. Struggling to recompose herself. I hunched over, feeling the weight of our combined sorrow would crush me any moment. "Sorry. Just ignore me when I say something stupid."

"Why do you say things like that?"

"Because I'm holding Team Seven back."

"I don't think anyone would agree with you."

"Even after what happened?"

Sa'Sha shook her head. "Surket knew better than anyone that no matter how unpredictable life can be, there's a purpose to everything. Fate placed her in an impossible situation. And she did what she believed was right. We must all be prepared to face such dilemmas."

"My mom used to say life is filled with the few choices you get to make and a bunch you don't. So, it's important to choose wisely."

"Yeah, she was..." Sa'Sha froze.

"She was...?"

"She was...quite wise...to say that."

"Yeah. Sorry for what I said. I'll work harder to consider your feelings next time."

"That's the issue. I don't want it to be hard work."

"What do you mean?"

"I'm not some special case. You shouldn't feel like you have to work hard to avoid upsetting me."

"But... you're special to me," I said. Sa'Sha frowned. "I'm serious. I consider you to be a very special person."

"Because I'm a princess?"

"Because you're my teammate... and my friend. And because I care about you." Sa'Sha's eyes widened, drawing more awkward energy into the room. *Did I go too far?*

"You think I'm special?"

"Yeah. That's what I said, right?" I didn't mean to sound so defensive. But it was already out there.

"Then you shouldn't have to work hard, right?" Her eyes held mine, until I broke; no longer able to contain the chuckle building in my throat. "What's so funny?"

"Now you sound defensive."

"Excuse me?"

"If you don't want me to work hard then stop being so difficult with me."

She rolled her eyes. "You don't have to be so mean about it."

"Deal. Then... can we just start over? Please?" I stood and held out my hand. "Hi. My name is Serec Arenyu."

I would've thought she was hesitating, the way she just watched me. But the corners of her mouth started to curl, betraying her impassive face. "Sa'Sha Martinel," she said, gripping my wrist.

"I've never considered myself good at making new friends, but I'm thinking this might be different."

"That's interesting, considering NaRyn told me you were pretty popular in prep school."

I shrugged. Popularity doesn't bring real friends."

"I'm guessing there's a story behind that."

"My time in the Army is the story. A couple prep school buddies got into Military Academy with me, and were part of the reason I moved forward with it. We'd been friends since our first anum at RVA. In all those anums, they didn't seem like the type to abandon a buddy during a difficult time. But my court-martial disproved that theory. Thinking back, I realized they were benefiting from my popularity a lot more than I was. So, Shawin was my first real friend in a long time."

"Well, I'm not the type to abandon friends. So, know you can depend on me through the good times and bad."

"Yeah. You've already proven that," I smiled. "When Hachi mentioned that you asked for leniency with me, I almost couldn't believe it. That has to be one of the nicest things anyone's ever done for me."

"I believe everyone deserves a second chance. Plus, I was getting used to having you around." Her smile matched mine. "That does bring up another question though, if you'll indulge me. Aside from NaRyn, when was the last time you had a real friend?"

"Back when I was a kid, living in Frilare."

"You didn't keep in touch after you moved?"

"Couldn't. The night I lost my parents, Hachi and I relocated to Olde Callastryne. So, I never got the chance to say goodbye. I didn't have any way to contact her, since my parents kept up with things like chainlinks. I tried using the Arnet to find her, but after three anums with no success, I started thinking I'd never find her."

"Three anums? You searched for all that time?"

I nodded. "I started assuming the worst. Still, I might've kept up the search if not for Hachi telling me to let it go and move on."

"What was her name?" Sa'Sha asked quietly.

"Eliza. Eliza Moreaux."

Sa'Sha pulled me into a hug. It was unexpected. Yet it was exactly what I needed in that moment. "Is she important to you?"

"More than I express with words."

"I'm sure she feels the same about you. So, don't give up, okay? I'm sure you'll find her."

"Thanks," I said, brining my arms around her. Her words offered a hope I hadn't experienced in a long time. And she was so warm and strong and stable and soft. I inhaled the fruity scent of her hair and squeezed a little tighter. Her heart thumped against my chest, almost perfectly in sync with my own.

"Can you tell me something?" she asked in a whisper. My eyes closed at the soft vibration of her words.

"Yeah," I whispered back.

"What did Surket tell you before...?"

I paused for a breath and swallowed. "She told me to trust you... and protect you."

"Trust me? Protect me?"

"She said she knew I could. And the more I think about it, the more I'm starting to believe it myself."

Sa'Sha's arms tightened around me, her body pressing against mine.

"You have a long way to go," she said, and let out a sweet, breathy chuckle. It was both contagious and intoxicating.

"We both do. But it's not impossible if we put in the work."

"Together," she added.

"Yeah. I'll watch your back if you watch mine. Just promise you won't do anything reckless." She pinched my back and laughed when I contorted to one side.

"Take your own advice, E. You still can't even exercise enough restraint to win a sparring match."

"E?"

"It's the nickname I've chosen for you."

"I think I like Zero better."

"Nope. I'm calling you E now."

"But Zero was your idea."

"That was for everyone else."

"Do I get to choose a nickname for you?"

"Do you have one in mind?"

Unfortunately, nothing came to mind. "You must've known Entropi is my second name to call me E. So how about I do the same?" She froze. "Something wrong?"

"I don't tell anyone my second name."

"Not even me?" She started to reply, but stopped and shook her head. We both paused awkwardly. But I couldn't let the mood take on the same tone. Sa'Sha and I had never been so comfortable with each other. "Don't worry about it."

"It's not you, it's just—"

"No, really. It's smooth. I'll come up with a nickname."

She nodded. We shared another quiet moment; our glances moving between one another and the floor. I didn't know if I was ignoring my nerves or responding to them, but all the same I closed the gap between Sa'Sha and me and reached for her hand. She wove her fingers between mine; my heart pounding in my head as she looked at me.

"Maybe I should tell him," a familiar voice echoed in my head. *"He hasn't forgotten me. He just doesn't recognize me after all this time."*

Are these—Sa'Sha's thoughts?

"Why is he looking at me like that?" the voice continued.

As the realization imprinted onto my mind, the face of that little girl I once called my friend, flashed before my eyes. I witnessed in awe as she matured from nine to twelve to sixteen, the changes in her features were more pronounced. But one thing remained the same. Those sparkling, honey-brown eyes were as watchful as they'd always been. And I could've kicked myself for missing it for so long.

"Eliza?"

Sa'Sha's eyes lit up as she cupped her hand over her mouth. Tears welled as she nodded excitedly.

Turns out her tears were just as infectious as her laughter. Heat prickled over my eyes, and I was too deep in shock to fight it. "It *is* you. Why didn't you tell me?"

She drove her face into my chest, squeezing tighter than anyone ever had. "I'm sorry, but I needed you to remember me, remember us."

"Always. I could never forget you."

It was as if my words held some unknown power the way she looked up at me. But her gaze held the same power. I was entranced. Uncontrollably captivated.

BZZZ! We both jumped so hard from the vibration, I nearly dropped her. It was coming from Sa'Sha's pants, but she took longer to figure it out than I did.

"Sorry," she said, fumbling her timechain out of her pocket and clearing her throat. "H-hello Alanda...I'm needed now?" She looked up at me, her face becoming an open book of disappointment. "...Okay. I'll be there soon." She closed it.

I forced what turned out to be an awkward laugh. "Bad timing, huh?"

She nodded. "The worst. I'm needed at the palace."

"I understand Blissful. The nation needs their princess." I placed a hand on her shoulder. "Just don't stay away for too long, Eliza."

She smiled. "I'll try not to." I helped her to the door. "Train hard while I'm gone, E. I'm looking forward to our next rematch."

An almost hysterical joy swept over me as I closed the door. All I could do was smile like a kid in a sweets shop. Two days later, my sentence was finalized. Ten decs restricted to Vaticia with an additional ten dec suspension from all field missions. In the meantime, I would spend every waking work hash steeped in data entry for the Intel department. I couldn't remember the last time I'd looked forward to ending a workday. But data entry changed that. Every night while Sa'Sha was away, I lay in bed staring up at the ceiling. Wondering what she was thinking. Wondering what would happen between us when she returned. I could almost feel her in my arms again.

The following dec, IGIS held a memorial for Surket. Sa'Sha had only made it back from Regalia late the night before, but she was insistent on giving the eulogy alongside Hachi. He was quick to agree. Probably just as much for himself as for her. They were both pretty emotional the entire time. But so was everyone else in attendance. Well, almost everyone. Northe might've been the only person with an unreadable face during Surket's memorial, though it shouldn't have been surprising. In the dec and a half following the mission, Northe seemed completely emotionless. But I was still willing to bet that the whole situation was just as difficult for him as it was for Sa'Sha. And when the memorial ended, I had reason to believe my bet was a solid one.

"It's me," I said, knocking at Northe's door.

"It's open," he called.

I stepped into the room and found Northe lying on his bed, staring at the ceiling. His room was bare and, aside from a small plant positioned near his corner desk, the room was filled with bland tones of white and gray.

"Hey," I said. "You wanted to talk?"

Northe pushed himself into a cross-legged position. Then, quietly looked down at his hands. "Was there ever something you wanted so bad you thought you'd do just about anything for it? And when you finally get it, you don't even know what to do with it?"

"I'm not sure that's happened to me, actually."

"The gifts of youth," he said, smiling. "Ever since that day, the numbness hasn't gone away. Not even a little."

"What do you mean?"

"When Surket told me to leave without her, I started to argue. But I knew I didn't have the right."

"Because she was our commander?"

"Because I'd wasted the past seven anums sitting on my hands. Letting stupid ideologies get in the way of what really mattered. She sounded so weak and helpless, I..." He rubbed a hand over his heart. Like every word was painful.

"Are you mad at me for what happened?" I asked.

He shook his head. "I can't blame you without blaming myself first, Kid."

"But you didn't do anything."

"Exactly. I just sat on that aircraft, closed off from the world—away from the fight. When I heard her voice, I wanted to go to her so bad it hurt. So much left unspoken. So much regret." He took a slow, deliberate breath and sighed. "Too little, too late."

I wasn't sure how he'd react. But if there was ever a time to ask, this was it. "Why do you sit out on missions?"

He looked at me and offered a half-hearted smile. "We're more alike than you know."

I reflexively frowned. His words were more than a little unsettling, considering the state he was in. "What do you mean by that?"

"When I was your age, I was just as quick to fight as you were. Always up for a challenge. Then, I experienced war firsthand, and it nearly knocked the wind out of me. I wouldn't wish that on anyone."

"You fought in a war?"

"We're still at war."

"With who?"

His face hardened. "The Soldiers of Liberty. The only enemy that could pose an unchecked threat of this magnitude for this long. They took my brother from me. And a part of me with him. Shortly after Shawin was born, I felt my resolve to fight returning. So, I traveled to the mainland where I met the Director. He convinced me to join IGIS, claiming that we would eventually bring peace and end the fighting between all refractors. But the opportunity to fight SOL was probably my biggest motivator."

"Why have I never heard of SOL?"

"We have a habit around here of not explicitly naming them. Brings too much dignity to their hateful existence." There was an uncharacteristic intensity in his voice that stoked my curiosity while raising my concern.

"So, when did you meet Surket?"

"Not for another two anums. There were only six teams back then, and with my arrival the two-member requirement was met to create a seventh."

"So, who was the other member?"

"A genius named Kaiden. If Shawin reignited my resolve to fight, Kaiden reignited my love for the sport of it. He was the more grounded version of my older brother, and skilled enough to carry the weight of Team Seven, successfully operating as the only two-man team for over two anums. Then, when IGIS recruited a remarkable electricity-wielding archer, it was my job to train her as Team Seven's third member."

"Surket," I said.

"Yup. And like you and Sa'Sha, it wasn't long before we got close. Really close."

"Wait. You don't mean you and Surket were—"

"Engaged to be married?" He nodded. "Didn't last long though. The day I proposed to her, I promised I would protect her from this unforgiving world. And that was the same day we were sent on a mission that was far beyond what we could handle. Like you, I made a foolish decision. And SOL claimed our leader, Kaiden. I never forgave myself for that. What's worse, I let my fear of losing Surket get the best of me and tried to convince her to run off with me and leave IGIS behind."

"Did she?"

"Let's just say she and Sa'Sha think alike. Either way, I felt betrayed when she refused and there's been a wall between us ever since. But before I settled into my current role, I did leave."

"Where'd you go?"

"The southern shores of Imeraste, where I could spend my days as a vagabond and try to forget why I didn't want to fight anymore. By the time, Surket and the Director found me, I was a completely different person, and Surket lost every bit of respect she'd ever had for me. Over time, she grew into the legend that the Guild knows her to be, and I allowed myself to forget my promise to protect her. Our last conversation made that painfully clear. But, like I said, it was already too late."

I was slow to respond at first. But the uneasy silence eventually ate away at my apprehension. "What are you gonna do now?"

"What else is there? Get back into the swing of things. If I let Team Seven flounder and disband, I'd be dishonoring Surket and Kaiden's memory. The Soldiers of Liberty have already taken three of the people that matter to me. And I'm not about to let their crimes go unpunished." He took a slow breath. "Besides, you all need a lot more training. So, I'll be pulling my weight from here on out."

Northe's renewed determination, brought a smile to my face. It was inspiring to see someone who'd been hurt so many times still finding the strength to do what he felt mattered. "Does that mean you'll be our new team commander?"

Northe burst into laughter. "I didn't say all that, Kid. Plus, I'd rather see Surket's legacy live on through her apprentice. She's a better fit for the job than I'll ever be."

Team Seven remained inactive for fifteen decs. Longer than I'd have expected, considering the situation had only gotten worse with the malefactors. But it created a wealth of time for Sa'Sha and Northe to train Shawin and NaRyn. Despite being fatally busy at Intel, I was allowed to help with training occasionally. But between data entry and running tedious errands for Ari, one of Intel's team leads, my ability to contribute to new recruit training was minimal. And aside from Sa'Sha's sporadic visits—which Ari was quick to openly label a productivity nightmare—I rarely received updates on Team Seven's mission-related activities.

When Shawin and NaRyn were officially inducted into the Guild, I was allowed to attend, since it was tradition for the junior member to choose designations for new agents. I had more than enough time to juggle around codenames for both of them. But during the actual ceremony, I immediately understood how anxious Sa'Sha must've been coming up with mine. But NaRyn seemed surprisingly happy with the designation, Lift. And Shawin said he knew and accepted that I would choose Prophet before I did.

Calling it a relief when my twenty dec suspension finally ended was an understatement. Team Seven had a special dinner to celebrate its return to full operational capability. I was beyond ready to return to the field. And when Sa'Sha called me to the war room for my first mission briefing, I almost couldn't hide my excitement. We'd been tasked to hunt a courier suspected of having a connection to the organization responsible for the malefactors. The Colonel made certain to inform me that Ari had been asking about me and if something went wrong, he'd be more than happy to reassign me to data entry permanently. I reassured him that I wouldn't have any problems handling the mission professionally. So, I was more than a little surprised when Sa'Sha walked up to me in a cute dress and looped her arm around mine.

"No uniforms on this one," she began. "I want you to look your best for our first date."

I froze, certain she hadn't just said what I thought she did. "Did you say 'first date?!'"

PART TWO | CONSPIRITORS

[ELEMENT 1]
THE BOOK OF LOCKE AND KEYES

[1]

COURIER

SEREC

"You sure I'm not underdressed?" I asked, looking at the menu printed over linen paper. "I feel like I need a tie. Or maybe a monocle."

"You're fine, E" Sa'Sha replied without pulling her attention from her menu.

"I guess the Duchess of Regalia wouldn't be phased by a place like this."

Sa'Sha shrugged. "You'd be surprised. I know a lot has changed, but I'm still the farm girl you knew in Frilare. I've simply—matured. A beam of sunlight fell perfectly over Sa'Sha as she tilted her head at me. "Besides, it's only Vista Grove."

"Right. Only the priciest districts in Verdallyn."

"Being overly self-conscious won't help you blend in, you know."

"Guess I could take a page from Shawin, huh?"

"Please don't."

"That bad?"

She let out a defeated sigh. "A triple-A dining hotel, and he dresses like he's at a beach lounge." An image of an upscale-trendy Sa'Sha paired with a vacation-casual Shawin came to mind. I could only bite my lip to stifle what would've been a toothy smile.

"Hearing your opinion of Shawin's taste in clothing doesn't exactly make me feel any better."

"I said you look fine."

"To my face, maybe."

"You know I don't talk behind people's backs. Shawin is well aware of my opinion on his attire. I can't say that I envy NaRyn."

"I see why you missed me so much."

"Make no mistake. My recon missions with Shawin and NaRyn were just as successful as my missions with you. And I didn't have to save either of them from detention. I'm simply more accustomed to the synchronicity that we normally experience." Her attention snapped back to the menu. But it didn't last. "May I help you?" She said, noting my smile.

"It's okay to admit you missed me."

"Our target has evaded two Kinetic Ops teams already. After twenty decs of degraded capabilities, Team Seven needs to take advantage of every mission as an opportunity to re-establish ourselves within the division. I've chosen you because our skill sets will prove more compatible in this type of mission. But my confidence in each member of the team is equally unwavering."

"No need to defend yourself. There's nothing wrong with missing me."

Her eyes narrowed, before looking at her menu once more. "Perhaps," she murmured.

"Good." I could tell she was about to frown, when her eyes detoured to my hand reaching for hers. "I missed you too, Liza." Her face softened. Our eyes held for a beat before her menu became a wall between us. But, just as I thought to pull back, her fingers laced between mine.

"It's been a long time since anyone called me that. Not the most appropriate, but I like the way you say it." She shifted in her seat, moving her right leg enough to reach my periphery. It was a perfectly toned, beautifully bronzed leg with a flawless shine wherever sunlight touched it. "What's wrong?" she asked.

"N-nothing," I said a little too quickly. "I mean...what?"

Sa'Sha watched me awkwardly. "Is something on your mind?"

"It was...I was just thinking it's been so long since our last recon together. And I haven't been on a hunt since my first mission with Northe" She leaned close enough for the gentle aroma of lenio flowers to fill my nose.

"Too long. But good things come to those who wait, right?" Her voice was as sweet as her scent. I'd never known her gaze to be so entrancing.

"They have free bread here, right?" I blurted, swiftly executing the moment.

Sa'Sha laughed; her face contorting in confusion. "Excuse me?" I cringed at the thought of repeating myself. Thankfully, Shawin linked before my mouth could embarrass me further.

"Yeah?" I said, opening my timechain.

"ETA on target is one hash."

"Got it," I said, and severed the link. "It's time."

Sa'Sha nodded with that classic spark of focus in her eyes. The focus that accompanied her mental shift to Raven.

"You ready?" she asked.

"As I'll ever be."

The hard clopping against the pavement drew our attention to the target: a scrawny man in baggy yet inconspicuous clothes. He wore a calm face. But his darting eyes betrayed his anxiety so masterfully, I noticed it from my position. Without a word Sa'Sha and I rose, took each other's hand, and started in the courier's direction. We kept in sync, until we were close enough to attract the target's attention. Instinctively, Sa'Sha wrapped her arms around my neck as I pulled her closer by the waist.

"If only you were this nice outside of our missions," I whispered.

"Stop finding ways to agitate me, and I might be," she whispered with a smile. A few more beats of idle banter allowed the courier to disappear around the corner without any visible suspicion. We hurried after him, but we failed to realize how fast he could move. By the time our heads peeked around the first corner, he was halfway to the next.

"Talk about speed walking," I thought aloud.

"I'll put the team on alert to cut off egress routes," Sa'Sha said. "We can't lose him."

"We won't." I activated my HOOD and sprinted off. "I'll update you when I have him cornered."

"*Zero,*" Sa'Sha's voice touched my mind.

"*Yeah?*"

"*Be careful.*"

I grinned. "*Will do.*"

By the time I'd turned the next corner, the courier was long gone. I needed to find him before his trail went cold. A short burst of energy was enough to hop onto the rooftop of the building next to me. From there, I had an overhead view as I bounded from building to building, until I spotted the courier turning into an alleyway. He stopped, looked around, then ran off again. He stopped at the next corner and looked around again. Then, the next. Then, again. I started to wonder if he was lost. But two or twelve stops later, everything started to look familiar.

He was running in circles. He started to round the next corner, only to stop and look up in my direction. It was so unexpected, I nearly slipped to avoid being spotted. By the time I peeked my head out to look for him, he was gone. I bounded a few rooftops before I found him again. He'd increased his pace. As careful as I was, he still must've realized I was following him. I needed to stay on him without giving away my location. Not like he was making it easy though.

And just my luck that one of his random stops would happen when I was on a slanted clay shingle roof. He scanned the area more deliberately this time adding to the challenge of remaining inconspicuous while remaining on the roof. I did my best to keep it together, leaning and twisting for balance like a drunkard. Gravity nearly got the best of me, but I managed to keep from tipping over the edge. Unfortunately, I couldn't say the same for one of the shingles I kicked loose in the process.

Time slowed as the clay informant sailed toward the pavement. Before I could react, it shattered, revealing my exact position to the courier, whose eyes reflexively found mine. For a moment, he held there, staring at me. *Maybe he's willing to tal—nope he's running.* He dashed away and I followed; a part of me relieved stealth was no longer an option. I could focus my full attention on closing the gap between us. The courier's focus, however, was too divided on losing me to notice he'd run himself into a corner. He stopped at the side of a three-story apartment complex; his eyes shifting.

I smirked. "Nowhere to go now—" I hardly got the words out before the courier ran two steps up the side of the apartment and leapt past me. The building to my right became his springboard into an open window on the third floor. "—is what I would like to say," I finished. I followed the courier's path to reach the same window just in time to see him scrambling down the hallway.

"Compatible skillset," I thought aloud. "Right."

[2]

RAILS AND RAEDAS
SEREC

I sprinted through the under-construction apartment, where the courier was busy knocking over everything within arm's reach, to block my path. The constant hurtling, dipping, and dodging was more irritating than anything. But I negotiated most obstacles quickly enough to stay with him as he barreled through the front door and lunged out an open window. He landed on the rooftop of a lower building and I leapt after him, a mix of determination and exasperation fueling me. A beat after I did, a furious flame suddenly burst from the window. Heat pressed into my back and hurled me forward as my mind spun in confusion.

I twisted uncontrollably, my trajectory now too short to land on the next rooftop. I reached out and pain stretched along my arms as my fingers narrowly caught the edge of the roof. Carefully, painfully, I hoisted myself high enough to brace my weight on my elbows and climb up. By that time though, the target was at the opposite end of the building.

The courier jumped before I could get close. A few beats later, a crash resounded in the distance. I caught sight of him as I reached the edge of the rooftop. He was hunched over a dented raeda roof as it swerved to a stop at the entrance of a five-lane raedabaun. Stretching throughout Aruria, this high-speed network of roads enabled raedas to travel in autonomous mode, allowing speeds up to twice as fast as on regular roads. The courier leaned over the driver's side window, and a beat later, the raeda entered the raedabaun and started picking up speed.

It would've been difficult to keep up if not for the large cargo raeda approaching. I took a few steps back, then ran and jumped. Careful as I was, the thud of my landing created a booming echo. Thankfully, the driver didn't seem to notice.

But even if he didn't, the courier did. He hopped onto another raeda. Then another.

I hesitated on following. Then, I remembered what Sa'Sha said about Team Seven re-establishing itself. I couldn't let her down. Not to mention all the collateral damage the courier could cause, even if I let him go. "It has to be done," I told myself, leaping onto another raeda.

A handful of panicked swerving raedas later, I finally had him cornered. He'd made the mistake of jumping onto a cargo raeda with a serious gap between it and any other vehicles. And there was nowhere else to go as I crept closer.

He crouched low, his round violet eyes trained on me as he vigorously rubbed at rough patches over his face. Gritting as skin flaked off, he resembled a tiny wild animal that had wandered into the city. But animals don't carry daggers. He pulled the small blade and snarled as he lunged at me.

I sidestepped, and his momentum threw him forward and nearly over the edge of the raeda. He arched his back, and swung his arms wildly to keep from falling. The thought crossed my mind to nudge him just enough to help the pavement kiss his patchy face. But I had a mission. I grabbed him by the collar and he stiffened dropping the dagger.

"You know, if you're that anxious to get away, I could drop you. I'm curious to see how far you can roll at this speed."

"Iga de ramu edes po!" He screeched.

"Should I assume that means you surrender?"

"Agramanuuuu!!" He snapped. He looked over his shoulder at me with a creepy, dark expression. "Boom!"

"I caught 'boom,'" I said after a light pause. "I think we're finally making progress on—"

BOOM!

Blinding light and searing heat blossomed from the back of the raeda as a sudden overpressure flung us into the air. I hadn't even noticed the caelrail running parallel to the raedabaun, until we fell on top of it.

I was still trying to steady the rattling in my head as the courier scrambled toward the front of the caelrail. The wind howled in my ears as I stumbled after him. The high speed rail system tracks curved up above the raedabaun as I fought to press forward on shaky footing. In no time, we were level with Vista Grove's bevy of eight-story buildings. I closed in on the courier cornering him once again.

His eyes darted in every direction as I backed him toward the edge of the caelrail. But then, we both saw it. The stretch of buildings quickly approaching on either side. A grin etched into his face. I lunged at him, but it was already too late. He jumped and hit the rooftops running.

"Now, I'm officially angry," I said to myself and leapt from the train.

Despite the distance, I never lost sight of him or his direction of travel. Just up ahead, another caelrail ran perpendicular to our path. If he made it onto that caelrail without me, there was no catching him. A concentrated surge of energy filled my legs and lungs and I powered forward, quickly eating away at the gap between us. The caelrail honked signaling its approach. The courier glanced over his shoulder at me, then picked up speed until I was only creeping closer with time completely against me.

The courier jumped at the caelrail as it crossed our path. Frustration squeezed into my jaw, then spread throughout my chest as I swallowed back the dry burning in my throat and watched helplessly as my target sailed toward his escape. But, just before he could reach the caelrail, a figure shot out of nowhere and collided with him, sending his body tumbling along the rooftop. He was slow to recover, and by the time he did, Sa'Sha was already pressing her heel into his chest with Nightfall drawn at his neck.

"Keep your hands where I can see them." She said, and the courier complied. I stopped a few steps short of Sa'Sha, taking advantage of the chance to catch my breath. "I don't think I've ever seen you move that fast before, Zero."

"Me neither," I said. I wiped at the sweat pouring down my forehead, as if more wouldn't replace it within beats. "How'd you get here so fast?"

"I've been waiting here for a bit." Sa'Sha pulled a data stick from his pocket

"Wait, how'd you—"

"I realized some time ago that these creeps cling to surprisingly predictable patterns. I had Anni run a few projections and once we settled on his most likely egress route, I simply waited."

A Nighthawk hummed as it zoomed in and hovered above us. Ropes dropped from it and four hooded agents rappelled down. In no time at all, they bound, gagged, and latched the courier to one of the ropes. Sa'Sha nodded at the hooded agents. Two of them nodded back and lifted the courier to her eye level.

"Today was a tiring day," she said. "So, tiring that when I snap my fingers, you'll fall into a deep sleep and won't wake up until you hear another snap. Understand?" The man nodded.

"He speaks Auric?" I said, but Sa'Sha held a finger to my lips. She turned her attention back to the courier and snapped. His eyes fell shut and his body went limp. Three of the hoods grabbed their ropes and tugged. The ropes holding the courier and the agents retracted into the aircraft, leaving the smallest hooded agent behind. She removed her hood and pulled down the cloth obscuring half her face. An exotic-looking teenage girl with tawny skin, piercing amber eyes, and umber braided hair smiled up at Sa'Sha.

"Ay Raven," she said in a thick Lazurian accent. "Been a while."

Surprise flickered in Sa'Sha's eyes. "Ambi! I didn't know you were our support for this op." Sa'Sha hugged the girl. "It certainly has been a while."

"Five anums since Clan Team two," the girl replied. "I just finished a two-anum undercover op at Royal Verdallyn Academy. Longest it's ever taken me to ID and apprehend a target. Thanks for today's catch, by the way. It's been a while since I've gotten an interesting toy to play with."

"He put up a fight. But he turned out to be an easy catch." I frowned, but

Sa'Sha, didn't notice. "Can you get this to SciTech?" Sa'Sha handed Ambi the data stick.

"Done and done." Ambi shot a quick glance in my direction. "This mute your boyfriend or something?"

Sa'Sha's rosy cheeks where visible through her HOOD and I just hoped mine didn't match hers. "Actually, he's my partner," she said quickly.

"And I'm not a mute," I added.

"Coulda fooled me," Ambi replied. "Anyway, where's Bolt? Can't imagine her retiring anytime soon with K still...bein' K."

Sa'Sha lowered her head. "She uhh...she didn't retire. We lost her during an intense mission almost an anum ago."

"Oh," she said, her mood instantly deflating. "That's the issue with under-cover work. You're always out of the know."

"It's alright." They shared a moment of awkward silence.

I reached out my hand. "Serec," I said. "Designation, Zero." Ambi looked me over before grabbing my wrist.

"Mia—designation, *Ambidex*. Call me Ambi." A subtle tingling crawled up my forearm as I grabbed Ambi's wrist."Well, this guy isn't gonna interrogate himself." She grabbed her rope. "Good seein' you, Raven."

"Likewise," Sa'Sha replied. "Stay out of trouble."

Ambi smiled mischievously. "You know me."

Sa'Sha watched quietly as the aircraft flew off.

"Something on your mind?" I asked.

"I just...wanted to thank you. And apologize."

"About the courier?" I shrugged. "Technically, you did catch him. I just ran him to you."

"No, not that. For Surket. She was like a big sister to me. And I really appre-ciate you stepping up when things got tough."

"Of course. I'm with you all the way."

"I know. That's why I appreciate you. It's also why I need to apologize."

"What do you mean?"

"The decs we've spent off active status have helped me to realize how selfish I was. I hadn't considered how difficult it must've been for you, leaving Surket behind. You saved my life, and I just cast judgement on you. I wasn't being very sensible."

"I hate to break it to you, but I have an even longer path to sensibility than you." A bubble of laughter escaped her, but she quickly covered her mouth. "Do me a favor, okay?"

"Hmm?"

"Don't hide who you are from me. Not your laughs or your mistakes or any other part of the real you."

"Are you certain? You might not like everything you see."

"If I've learned nothing else these past decs, its that what you are doesn't define you, but who you are. You don't define yourself by your rank or your station. You're just, Liza. I've always loved that about you."

Sa'Sha's honey eyes sparkled in the sunlight as they met mine. "Love?" She whispered.

Panic and longing paced around me like two hungry predators. "Um—I mean."

She closed her eyes and shook her head, her smile widening. "What will I do with you?"

"I love things about you too E," she said more casually. But her smile never faded.

"Know what else I love? Watching the sunset. How about it? Like back in Frilare?" She said, staring out into the city.

"Do we actually have time to watch a sunset? I mean, shouldn't we be—"

She placed a finger over my lips yet again. We'll have plenty of time to get bogged down when we're back at D7."

"But I—"

Sa'Sha pulled at my shoulders until I relented and leaned back against the side of the roof access door structure. "Hurry up and sit, E."

She sat next to me and leaned her head on my shoulder. I was at a loss for words. So, I placed an arm around her and she let out a small sigh as she hugged it close and relaxed into me. I inhaled the fruity scent of her hair and felt my muscles give in a little. The scent was addictive. Of course, I could say the same about her. No matter how busy we'd be once we got back to Vaticia, only a complete idiot would cut a moment like that short.

[3]

TASKFORCE 224

SEREC

I wasn't ready to get up yet. Not even a little. But I knew it could only be one person sending a burst so early in the morning. I rolled into a lazy stretch to grab my timechain, and pulled up the message from Sa'Sha:

Where are you? Our meeting with the Colonel is in ten.

Bitter Hadal. The urge to leave my bed was so unexpectedly overwhelming, I nearly fell onto my face trying. A splash of water to the face, a fresh uniform, and I was out the door only stopping long enough to take a breath and straighten my tie.

"I can't begin to imagine," the Colonel started as I entered the briefing room, "what might've been important enough to make you six hashes and twenty-seven beats late, Zero." He didn't have to check his timechain for accuracy. His brain could keep time as efficiently as any processor. Sa'Sha, Northe, Kareen, Ari, Mia, and a large guy I'd never seen before were seated around one side of the game-board. Hachi, Anne, an older woman, and four elderly men were on the opposite end. And everyone's eyes held on me as I took a seat in the last open chair, next to Sa'Sha.

"Sorry sir," I said. "I was…not feeling so well this morning." The Colonel only watched me, like he was expecting some other element to my excuse. I cleared my throat. "Also, I—"

"Zero, leave the lying to Clan. Your making K's lackluster excuses sound mildly reasonable by comparison." I looked to Northe. He gave a shrug that could only mean, "What'd you expect?"

"Now that everyone's arrived," the Colonel continued, "we can begin."

"You'd think this was the first time I've ever been late," I whispered to Sa'Sha.

"This *is* the first time you've kept seven senior officers waiting," she replied.

The Colonel waved his hand over the gameboard, which immediately synced with his data ring. Light emanated from the board weaving together to form an image floating in front of us. "What you are seeing is classified: PRIVY HIGH." A blurred photo of a man with glowing violet eyes and a dark hooded cloak sat before us. "Our sources have identified this man as *Astaroth*: the leader of the refractor supremacy faction known as *The Soldiers of Liberty*. It's unclear exactly how long this organization has managed to operate in shadow, but they've got ties to several supernatural criminal organizations—many of which, we have encountered in our operations. Arms smuggling, person trafficking, assassinations, terrorism, and even petty crimes are all part of their portfolio. But their greatest crime to date is the Hiyama Square Incident, which not only cost good people their lives but has drastically altered the politics in Aruria. Whoever they are, we can't afford to take them lightly."

It might've just been me, but the air in the room had grown particularly tense.

"So, we just take out this Astaroth guy and everything's smooth, right?" I asked. Sa'Sha's elbow to my ribs pre-empted the Colonel's glare. The Colonel waved his hand to change the image. "This," he said with a lingering glare, "is a malefactor. Thanks to Astaroth, these abominations have been wreaking havoc all over Verdallyn province. Despite their appearance, they are about as intelligent as they are numerous, with a count projecting well over a thousand. To counter this growing threat, Strategic Command has opted to assemble a specialized task force, comprised of our best agents." The Colonel turned his attention to me and the rest of the captains. "That's where the six of you come in. You have been hand-picked by your branch chiefs to tackle this threat to our way of life. Effective immediately, you will lead the new operative group we've codenamed, Task Force 224." Considering the additional responsibilities, it was a bit of a relief to know that our respective duties wouldn't change much.

Mia Kalantu—designation: Ambidex, was assigned the position of Task Force's Clandestine Services Lead. Ari Luki—designation: Sentinel, was Intel Lead. Dr. Kareen Ventus—designation: Minerva, would head up Science and Technology. Northe Kazimus—designation: K, would be our Air Officer. Jin Hiro —designation: Quake—was the only new face to me. But he was put in charge of Kinetic Operations. And that left Sa'Sha and me.

"Arenyu! Get up here," the Colonel grunted and I hurried to the front of the room.

"Captain Serec Arenyu—designation: Zero. You are the junior-most officer here. But you've had the most firsthand experience with the malefactors. And your skillset, potential, and resolve, are more than sufficient to warrant your place on this team as Operations Officer."

"Thank you, sir," I said.

"Martinel, front and center." Hachi and the other senior officers rose to their feet so abruptly that Sa'Sha couldn't help hesitating before walking over. Hachi walked up and stood next to the Colonel and gave Sa'Sha a reassuring smile that helped to offset the creepier smile the Colonel was forcing.

"Captain Sa'Sha Martinel—designation: Raven, has been with the Guild for over six anums now—during which time she's shown exemplary adaptive skill, serving within every branch." The Colonel carefully unrolled an expensive-looking document. "Her dedication to excellence prompted my request, which was immediately endorsed by Director Hachinatus Arenyu. Effective immediately, Captain Sa'Sha Martinel is promoted to the rank of Major. Task Force 224, I present to you your commanding officer." Everyone applauded, as Sa'Sha's eyes lit up like a little girl at a surprise party. "Care to say anything, Major?"

"Um...no. I—I mean...thank you, sir," she stammered.

The Colonel turned to Hachi. "Sir?"

Hachi stepped forward. "Let's close out this meeting with a simple notion. The Guild exists because people like you believed you could make a difference. Your contribution ensures the betterment of society and the safety of all its people. To expect great things of this task force, means that I expect great things from each of you, because both your destinies and the destinies of countless others are affected by your actions."

The higher-ups lined up beside Hachi to shake each of our hands. But they spent the longest time congratulating Sa'Sha. Wanting to make my words of encouragement stand out, I opted to hang back until most everyone else had filtered out.

"Congratulations, Major," I said. "I'm really proud of you."

She cocked her head to one side. "And...?"

"And if anyone deserved this promotion, it was you. The Colonel was right about your hard work being long overdue for recognition."

"You're full of surprises, when you want to be. You know that?"

I shrugged. "I had my suspicions." I held my elbow out for her. "May I escort you to the new operations center, Major?"

"Please do."

"Hold on you two," the Colonel called after us. He looked more concerned than usual.

"This can't be good," I thought aloud.

"Potential aside, Zero, you have an uncanny knack for pissing me off."

"I'll work on that, sir."

"You'd better. Because if you *ever* embarrass me like that in front of the Director again, I'll bust you down to a rank lower than recruit and ensure you stay there for the remainder of your natural life. Is that clear?"

I cleared my throat. "As quartz, sir."

"That said, my expectations of you two will be undoubtedly higher than the rest of Stratcom. Especially you, Raven."

"I won't disappoint you sir," Sa'Sha said.

"Zero, reliability aside, your uptake on tactical combat and covert operations is so remarkable it's almost freakish." *Did he have to say it like that?* "That's why we've assigned you the secondary role as Lead Operator.

"If I'm hearing right, it sounds like Sa'Sha and I are still partners, sir."

"Because that's how I want you two to operate. Of course, as your direct superior, Sa'Sha still gets final say. Don't forget that."

"Could be worse."

Sa'Sha jabbed an elbow into my side. "Thank you again, sir," she said.

"You can thank me by being careful," the Colonel said. "My gut is telling me we could be stepping into something we're not fully equipped to handle with this Astaroth character."

I snorted. "With our new task force, Astaroth's gonna have the real disadvantage."

"Just be careful; for your uncle's sake. He worries about you."

"Too much I'd argue."

The Colonel's face turned serious—almost grave. "I'm serious."

"Okay," I said with a nervous laugh. But his eyes held like stone, until my smile faded. "Okay."

He paused for a moment longer, then patted my shoulder and started for the door. "Good. Now, head over to your new Operations Center. Your team is waiting for you"

Sa'Sha and I shared an uncomfortable look, before she followed the Colonel out. My stomach tightened a little, as I followed the two of them out the door, trying to tell myself the Colonel was just being paranoid. But honestly, it was Sa'Sha's lack of a response that bothered me the most.

[4]

DRIVING FORCE

SA'SHA

"The Director's paranoia is infecting the Colonel," Serec whispered.

"Possibly," I replied. "I sensed something strange in him though. It felt like... fear."

Serec eyed me suspiciously. "You didn't read his mind, did you?"

"Not exactly. It was more of a passive experience. His emotions reached out to me and I interpreted them."

"That doesn't mean he wasn't exaggerating." Serec probably didn't realize how anxious he sounded. But I couldn't blame him. The Colonel's warning sounded too much like a plea to disregard as an exaggeration.

"You might be right," I said. "All the same, a bit of caution won't hurt."

"Yeah. Guess you're right."

I was overcome with awe when we entered the expansive operations center. From the wall-to-wall vid screens to the neatly arranged workstations to the rainbow of tiny blue, yellow, and green lights reflecting across two stories of clear glass and polished chrome. At the center of the semicircular facility sat a massive gameboard painting the area above it with a three-dimensional map of Verdallyn. I'd never seen so many electronics in one place. I followed Serec up one row of stairs and stopped at the second floor. Each captain had an office and mine sat in the center.

"How big is this task force supposed to be?" Serec asked.

"Quite large if it takes seven captains from different branches to lead it."

"Actually, it's six captains and one major."

I smirked. "Which is why I have the largest office." Serec frowned, and walked off. "Where are you going?"

"To see how much smaller my office is than yours."

If Serec's office was anything like mine, it was more spacious inside than it seemed. There was room for a desk, a few chairs, and a gameboard, with space to spare. The only downside was how sterile the space felt. Alanda would love a place like this; simply because she would view it as a blank slate for her design impulses.

"Raven, you have an urgent notification from Stratcom," a voice emanated from the gameboard, startling me despite its familiarity.

"Anni?" I said, trying to control my racing heart.

"Yes. I have been integrated into the systems here so that I may continue to assist you."

"I suppose that makes sense. Welcome to the team. Now what was that urgent notification?"

Anni explained the details of the mission as well as Stratcom's expectations of Task Force 224 and me. Serec entered, just as Anni and I finished crafting a reply.

"Your office is waaaay bigger than mine," he said.

"Shouldn't it be?"

"Only if we can use it to throw parties."

"Only if by 'parties' you mean mission planning."

"Not even a little." Serec pulled out his timechain. "Any chance we could head back to D7 and run training drills. I'm feeling a little restless."

"That sounds good to me. We'll need to incorporate our new team members."

"Smooth. I'm ready when you are."

"Okay." I raised my TAB. "Attention, Task Force. There will be a mission briefing on the floor in five hashes. Thank you."

"Interesting how you interpreted 'training drills' to mean another boring meeting."

"A good leader keeps her agents well-informed."

"Spoken like a true commander," Serec said.

"Here's an idea. Be a good agent and accompany your commander downstairs."

"Oh sure. Because by 'another boring meeting,' I really meant—"

I poked at Serec's rib cage and he flinched. "Less talking, more walking."

By the time Serec and I were on the floor, over a hundred agents were already standing by to greet us. The captains joined us at the gameboard.

"Good afternoon, and congratulations on being selected to join Task Force 224. You have distinguished yourselves as the top agents in your respective fields, and I'm honored to have you on our team. I am Raven, and I will be your commanding officer. Standing with me are each of your branch leads. Because this task force functions independently of the Guild, you are not to discuss your work outside of this room. However, your leaders and I are more than willing to address any and all of your concerns. So, please don't hesitate to utilize us to your advantage."

I activated the gameboard and light painted three grotesque forms. The gameboard was so large, the models of the beasts towered over us. The creatures before you are called malefactors. Because they're both feral and intelligent, stopping them is top priority for us. Currently, however, our highest priority lies with preventing the organization behind them from taking further action, which includes the continued production of these creatures. This group calls itself the Soldiers of Liberty, and we know that they have been involved in several criminal and terrorist activities. But there's a lot we still don't know, and that's where you all come in. My expectation is that each of you will do everything in your power to ensure that Task Force 224 remains ahead of SOL at every turn. Spend the rest of today getting acquainted with the rest of your team. Come tomorrow morning, we hit the ground running. Dismissed." Everyone snapped to attention and saluted.

"Good speech," Serec said, following me back into my office.

"You think it was well-received?"

"Well enough. Though, some of them didn't look too excited when they saw the malefactors."

"Neither was I. But I want them to have reasonable expectations."

Serec shrugged. "That's probably a good call."

"'Probably?'"

"Yeah, 'probably.' As in: I don't know why you're asking me like I have half the experience you do in this."

I forced a smile. "I'm probably overthinking it." I didn't feel that way though. If I couldn't inspire a hundred people who were on my side, how could I inspire millions who had mixed feelings toward me? Especially considering some of the people closest to me would be expecting me to fail miserably. Uncle and Surket had both placed their faith in me. And despite my apprehensions, I couldn't let them down. Task Force 224 would succeed, and I would lead them there.

Sparring with Serec turned out to be helpful for more than simply brainstorming maneuvers. It also took my mind off my doubts about leading such a large IGIS unit long enough to come up with some good ideas. Of course, the added benefit of a little one-on-one time with Serec was gratifying for its own reasons.

"Still trying for that win, Kid?" Northe said as he, Shawin, and NaRyn entered the training room.

"You come to cheer me on?" Serec replied.

"Actually, these younglings think they can win a two-on-one match against me. Thought it'd be a good chance to show 'em a few things."

"Then, why not join us?" I said.

"Four-on-one?"

"I was thinking two-on-three."

"Sounds a bit uneven," Mia called, sauntering in. "Maybe I can help?"

"Mina?" NaRyn exclaimed. "How'd you get in here?"

"Mia, actually. But call me Ambi."

"Ambi?"

"Short for Ambidex. And I got in because my time with the Guild far exceeds yours, Lift."

"Seriously?! Wait, who told you my designation?"

"It's called research, Lift. Great for all kinds of things. Like infiltrating that snobby school of yours."

"*Infiltrated?* Is that what we call walking through the door with false credentials? Was annoying me that important to you?"

"You don't matter enough to be on our radar. I was collecting intel on a shadow organization we suspected of recruiting prep schoolers. Messing with you was just a bonus, NaNa. You know, Nana really rolls off the tongue better than Lift. Why don't I help you appeal for a designation change?"

NaRyn's face had turned so red I thought steam would start coming out of NaRyn's ears. She started toward Mia, but Shawin held her back.

"Ambi," I said. "Was antagonizing my apprentice your only purpose in coming here?"

Mia chuckled. "You sound just like Surket." I held back my smile for NaRyn's sake. "But like I said," Mia continued. "I wanna join your match."

"This is a team exercise," NaRyn chimed. "And last time I checked you aren't a part of Team Seven."

"Ambi outranks you, Lift. Please show her due respect." NaRyn gave a sour nod. "Ambi, I'm curious to see how much you've improved in all this time. Anni, will you add one more?" For cooperation sake, Mia and Shawin were on my team.

"Ten to win?" Serec suggested.

"Sounds appropriate," I said.

It'd been some time since Mia and I fought together. But for a time, our synchronization was unmatched, giving us the projected advantage according to Anni. But, Northe could change all that. Surket and the Colonel had always given Northe massive amounts of grief about not performing anywhere near his potential. In all my time at the Guild, I could count on one hand the number of times he actually did. But I could just as easily remember that when he got serious, even Surket didn't take him lightly.

"Ten to win. Raven, Ambidex, and Prophet versus K, Zero, and Lift," Anni announced as we took our positions. "Match begins in 3...2...1."

Shawin held back while Mia and I rushed forward. I launched a flurry of attacks at Serec, that should've placed him on the defensive. But the Serec in front of me was far from the hothead I trounced on his first day. Mia and I had to double team him before Northe could jump in, just to get his back on the floor. Without a beat wasted, I charged at NaRyn, only a half-step behind Mia. But a wall of howling wind swept in to block my advance. Mia went for Northe. She rained a bevy of blue sparks down at Northe, forcing him to focus on defending himself long enough for me to continue towards NaRyn. But before I could reach her, a hand grabbed hold of my arm.

I twisted around into a kick that somehow ended with my back on the ground and Serec standing over me. "Point, team K," Anni said. Mia hit the ground next to me.

"Make that two," Northe said.

Mia sprang to her feet, narrowly avoiding a kick from NaRyn. She tried again, but Mia dipped low, and—in one fluid motion—rammed her shoulder into NaRyn's hip and stood straight up. NaRyn flipped completely over and flopped her onto the mat. The pacing kept up for some time, with everyone dashing around to score before someone from the other team got the best of them. But by the time we were tied at eight points, both sides had regrouped into a standoff; waiting for the person opposite them to make a move.

As luck would have it, Mia was opposite NaRyn. I didn't catch what—if anything—goaded NaRyn into the offensive, but the moment she charged at Mia, everyone sprang into action. I was confident Mia could handle NaRyn. And with Serec as my opponent, we had the advantage again. Or so I thought. Just before we reached each other, Serec changed direction, and I nearly rolled my ankle trying to keep up with him. Otherwise, I might've noticed the sparks fizzling at his fingertips before it was too late. A stutter step was all it took to put him within leaping range of Shawin. And just as Shawin dodged a kick from Northe, Serec swatted his leg.

Shawin stiffened, and Northe spun into a sidekick that knocked the wind out of him. Serec's victory was all but assured. But they were so focused on scoring against Shawin that they weren't prepared for my next move. I slid under NaRyn and clipped her ankles with a sweeping kick before she could regain her footing.

"Game point," I said.

A cheeky grin etched over Serec's face. "Only one way to end this match."

"Which would be?"

"One on one. No powers."

The look on his face was infectious. "Been waiting for that rematch for some time now."

"Had to be sure I was ready."

I snorted. "You think you're ready?" We assumed our stances, and the room fell silent.

"Final point?" Northe called.

"Final point," Serec answered.

Serec's eyes glinted with excitement. "Ladies first," he said. But I held fast. "I said ladies—"

I lunged forward with a kick. He dodged. But I stayed with him. We locked into a flow of movements that were too fast for my eyes to follow. So, I relied on instinct and experience. But it did little to help how heavy my arms were starting to feel. I pressed on, just missing as I'd broken through his guard. He shuffled out of fighting range.

"You finally get your precious rematch and you dodge instead of attack?" I said between breaths.

"You think I have to?"

Of all the times for him to be reserved. He was likely attempting to tire me out. He was succeeding. I lowered my guard, inhaling deeply. Before the air could penetrate my lungs, he rushed in with an aggressive barrage of punches and kicks. He could probably see on my face how much he had me on the defensive. I needed to make a move that counted, or my team's defeat would be certain.

Amidst his storm of punches, I grabbed hold of my frantic thoughts and surrendered to the void. Time slowed as my mind drifted to Sir Doriel and Alanda.

"Stop thinking Highness," Sir Doriel instructed as he dealt a swarm of furious punches. One connected with my chest sending me crashing into the koa tree. Alanda helped me to my feet, likely sensing my frustration. Blue process had been the most difficult to grasp; primarily because Sir Doriel insisted that mastering it meant separating my consciousness — in the middle of a fight.

"One of the guiding principles of Semovet is detachment. This is especially true for Blue process," he explained.

"I know you fear the void Blissful," Alanda began, squeezing my hand. "Letting go can be difficult." She opened my hand and placed a small flower in. "But when we let go, we open ourselves to countless possibilities. You mustn't fear the loss from opening yourself, but anticipate the gain." Her azure eyes were like a vast ocean. One I could lose myself in. A place where my being could melt into the endless nothingness. And find true peace.

Serec's fist closed in. But instead of blocking, I welcomed the attack; serenity overtaking me as Blue process flowed through my consciousness. I twisted slightly as his fist pressed into my abdomen. The subtle movement was all I needed to diffuse the energy of his punch and disrupt his momentum. I grabbed his wrist, and shifted my leg between his to anchor myself for a hip throw. To my surprise, he twisted his arm and I lost my grip, only to have him grab hold of mine. His knee pressed into the back of mine and it started to buckle.

But I stuck my left foot out for balance and twisted under him until I was in the perfect position to spin into a leg lock around his neck. A torque from the waist was plenty to send him toppling like an uprooted tree. We hit the ground... hard. But the match was over. "Score limit reached. Team Raven wins,' Anni announced. I laid there for a moment, the detachment of Blue process still swirling around in my head. I almost missed Serec's choked words.

"Hard to breathe."

"Oh. Sorry." I released the hold and he rolled over and hopped to his feet. He sighed and reached out to me. I took his hand, not expecting him to pull me up with such force. I arched and started to flail for counterbalance. But he caught me in his arms. Those wonderfully powerful arms.

"Sorry," he said.

"No," I blurted, averting my gaze. "I umm...It's okay. That was...you were...good."

Serec gave a breathy smile. "Glad you noticed."

"Nice moves, Raven." The voice snapped me out of my trance, and I noticed Mia approaching.

"Uh, yeah...thanks. You too."

Mia's eyes shifted from me to Serec, then back to me. "You sure he's not your boyfriend?"

"No," I said through a nervous laugh, as Serec and I immediately put more than enough distance between us.

She shrugged. "Maybe someday then." Before I could come up with a response, Mia started for the door. I turned to find Serec watching me. But his expression had changed. He almost looked disappointed. "That last move was pretty smooth," he said. "You'll have to teach me that one sometime."

"That may require a bit more flexibility than your body would like."

"Good point," he said almost sounding relieved.

I spent the rest of the day in the operations center scouring the Guild's database for any other info I could find on Astaroth. It was no surprise that all searches came up empty. But it wasn't as if my mind was fully focused anyway. I couldn't stop thinking about the look on Serec's face after what Mia said.

Maybe I shouldn't have moved away so quickly. After all, we're friends. Friends hug each other all the time. Right?

I sighed and pushed away from my desk; questioning what I was really even doing there. If it was bothering me so much, I needed to talk to Serec about it. I ambled out with the sun, ready to attain clarity. Unfortunately, the wind behind my sails of determination immediately died as I approached D7.

I walked in, stopped and looked up the stairway. *Talk to him now, or wait until dinner?* I started pacing down the hallway. "Calm down," I told myself. "It's not like we're a couple or anything. He doesn't get to be upset."

As I passed the training room, I caught movement in the corner of my vision. Serec was embroiled in the chaos of Jump Protocol 4. This protocol was unique in that it attempted to overwhelm the user with sheer numbers. A continuous flood of hologram enemies mounted a relentless assault. But Serec had every intention of remaining in control of the situation. Sweat flew in every direction as he executed each enemy with near primal fury. The chiseled muscles in his arms glistened. I began to understand why he watched me train when he first joined. It made me start second-guessing my attire and if it was actually the best time to force in a conversation. *I'm tired anyway. Plus, I don't want to interrupt his training. Perhaps after dinner.* A poor excuse, but I wasn't ready to confront him about the tension building between us. Especially since I didn't fully understand my feelings. But I didn't realize how tired I was. And by the time I rolled over, Phoebe informed me that the time was 5.34. Morning.

Intel and Clan had been working practically nonstop to compile information on SOL and Astaroth. So, when we gathered for our first intel brief, Ari and Mia were beaming with pride. Ari waved a hand over the gameboard and an image of Alex Locke appeared. "Getting right to the matter," he began, "this is Alex Locke. The eccentric and sometimes outspoken CEO of Locket Technologies—currently the largest tech corporation on Orbis. Recent findings have revealed the existence of a long-standing development contract between Locke and an 'anonymous client' of great interest. Protecting buyer identity is common practice, even among small businesses. And Locket Tech prides itself on maintaining customer anonymity. This contract, however, managed to catch our eye due to records of a sizable fee being paid in advance for 'undisclosed services' to be rendered."

"Definitely suspicious," I said. "But, how exactly does that implicate Locke?"

"The amount paid, the source, and the timing, were all indicators that warranted further investigation. Most notably because the few transactions we've been able to tie to the Soldiers of Liberty have had a similar style of encryption in their funds transfer data obfuscation."

"Say again," Serec said.

"Their way of digitally scrambling any information associated with their use of credits," Ari replied, adjusting his stylish thick-framed glasses. "Anyway, Locke has the technological means, influence, and financial backing necessary to ensure their success. And whoever's paying such a hefty price for his services also seemingly went to a lot of trouble to hide their activity. We'll keep digging, but I'd say it's a lead worth looking into."

"Please do," I said. "And have any of our people managed to make contact with him?"

"No one can get close to him, thanks in no small part to these two." Ari waved his hand and the image switched to a man and woman in business dress and sunglasses. "I'll let Ambidex take over from here."

Mia started to center herself behind the podium. But, seeing only half of her head was visible behind it, she stepped in front of it instead.

"Because Locke's personal assistants double as his bodyguards, they rarely leave his side. Our intel says they're highly proficient in hand-to-hand combat and considered extremely dangerous."

Serec sucked his teeth. "I could take 'em."

"Our sources say Locke spends a fair amount of time at his nightclub, Keyes. You'll find him in his upper level VIP lounge. He always keeps heavy security, including his personal bodyguards, and the only way to reach his lounge is by a lift secured by facial recognition software."

"Any chance we could intercept him in transit." I asked.

"Unlikely. His security team is on another plane. Somehow, they manage to move him without anyone taking notice. It's your call, Commander, but if you want to get close to Locke, Keyes is your best option."

[5]

ALEX LOCKE

SA'SHA

"Do you always drive this fast?" I asked.

"I've never driven a raeda with this much power."

"Try easing off the accelerator."

I could've said it twenty times and my words still wouldn't have reached him. Beneath his childlike excitement, I could sense a tangle of fear and doubt. I had to do something if there was any hope of making it to Keyes Nightclub alive. I pried my hand from the bottom of my seat and placed it on the back of Serec's neck. "We'll be fine." I said, attempting to sound calmer than I felt. "We're in this together and I won't leave your side. Trust me." The engine's roar waned to a hum as the tension in his shoulders eased. As soon as we were off the raedabaun, traffic started picking up. For one of the smallest districts in New Callastryne, Alyrian Heights was not only a social hotspot, but the very epicenter of Arurian nightlife. It was the kind of place where money opened just about every door.

"I've never seen so many hologram ads and vid screens in one place," Serec noted. His wide-eyed look reminded me of a kid seeing a festival for the first time.

"It's called the Night District for a reason, E. This place makes people lose inhibitions and cast themselves into a rapturous torrent of every pleasure and poison imaginable."

Serec glanced at me out of the corner of his eye, before choosing, "...Uh huh" as his response.

"Too regal?" I asked.

"I think I got all of it this time."

That said, Keyes Nightclub and Entertainment Lounge, was the exception. Social status preceded the number of credits in your union account. But that only made everyone fight harder to gain admittance, because Keyes never failed to deliver on class and style. We pulled through the circular driveway and two valets hurried to open our doors. "Do you guys have self-parking?" Serec asked one of the valets.

"No," he replied. "Only valet."

"How convenient." Serec surrendered the keychip. "Bring this back in exactly the same condition."

"The keychip or the raeda?" the valet asked, and his co-worker burst into laughter.

"Let's go, E," I said through my teeth.

"I signed this raeda out," Serec argued. "If it gets wrecked, Hachi will make sure I never drive again."

"Remember that the next time you start driving like a maniac. Now, give the man some credits and walk me inside." Serec sighed and pulled out his timechain. He held it near the vallet's and the two made a clicking sound, indicating a funds transfer. I held Serec's arm close with both hands, and led him toward the entrance.

"Can you at least try to be pleasant? I will mind-write a smile on your face if I have to."

"Not too invasive," Serec retorted, only to break into a smirk as I gave him a sour look.

"Is your name on the list?" one of the guards asked.

"There's a list?" Serec replied.

I patted Serec's hand and he watched me quietly as I gestured for the guard to lean closer. "Is that any way to address your princess?" I whispered. "I'm certain my father would be rather irritated to hear that I was denied entry into this establishment. Or perhaps I should make a call to have you both promptly replaced with the kind of staff who show the proper courtesies?" I responded to their flushed faces with a rather smug smile.

"Our apologies, Blissful," the first guard said.

"Please, come in," the other said. "We can call in a special bottle service for you, if it pleases you."

"You are aware that I'm nearly two anums shy of twenty, are you not?"

"Oh, uh, h-he...," the first bouncer stuttered. "Please forgive his ignorance, Blissful." The other guard nodded apologetically.

I nodded and pulled Serec through the front doors.

"I think I understand why Northe always sits back and watches," Serec said.

"Watches what?"

"When you drill into people. Like my first day on the team. It's entertaining when you're not the target." I pinched his arm. "You told me to have fun, didn't you?"

The lowest level of Keyes was a gentlemen's club and casino. Women in black and red outfits that I'd be embarrassed to even shower in, trotted amidst an overwhelming sea of smoker vapors and spicy colognes, serving drinks to the patrons gathered around gambling tables and machines. At the far end of the room, there was a door marked *Gentleman's Paradise*, which I interpreted as a haven for disgusting old politicians and business executives, eager to throw credits at women half their age as incentive for dancing provocatively.

We stepped into the lift, and I could feel the bass of the nightclub's speakers vibrating through my feet. Two floors up and the doors opened to a wave of bombarding sound. The dance floor was a small stadium, teeming with so many people we had to push our way through. A rainbow of laser lights flashed from every direction as the crowd bounced and gyrated to the music boosting from four towering speakers positioned near a fan favorite conductor at each wall. My plan was to take on the role of observer, until I understood the layout and an idea of where exactly Locke might be. But then I heard it. The melody my body couldn't ignore. I pulled Serec by the hand.

"Did you see something?" he asked.

"This is my favorite song," I yelled.

He nodded. "Smooth." His attention started to drift, but I yanked him again.

"Dance with me."

"Now? Shouldn't we be—"

I pulled him close and made my move before he could argue. I turned, reached one hand behind his head and leaned into him as I guided his hand to my hips. "We should make the most of the moment. Shouldn't we?"

Serec cleared his throat. "Yeah, okay."

Serec moved with surprising rhythm.

"Do all princesses dance so well?" he asked.

"A friend keeps me up to date on popular culture. But who taught you to dance?"

"You did."

"How?"

"My power."

Using your powers to dance? The idea was so cute, I couldn't contain my smile. "Clever. Your mimicry seems rather versatile."

"Think so?" Serec flashed a smile that probably could've melted me in his arms if I didn't have him on the dance floor. It had been a long time since I'd felt so alive. My heart was racing—my skin tingling under the warmth of his fingers. He wrapped his powerful arms around me, and in that moment, I felt safe. Another feeling that had often eluded me. Everything about that moment felt like we were in perfect sync. I turned around and as our eyes met, I almost forgot about the mission. I just wanted to live in that moment for the rest of the night. The song came to a booming end and the crowd let out a euphoric roar. Evidently, I wasn't the only one who appreciated the song. As the music transitioned into the next song, someone bumped into Serec, throwing us both off balance. Only, I didn't look nearly as awkward.

"What's so funny?" he said with cutely furrowed brows.

I wrapped my arms around him and squeezed. His face softened as my gaze tilted up to his. "Thanks for the dance, E."

"Anytime, Liza."

"We should get back to it," I said, still in his eyes. We held a moment longer.

"Guess so."

Two songs worth of pushing our way through the crowd put us in front of an inconspicuous spiral stairway at the far corner of the club. I dipped into the shadows and altered my appearance to Raven before ascending the stairs. We ended up in a long-extending bar where not surprisingly, two large men in suits served as our next obstacle.

"This area is members only," the first man said.

I almost didn't catch Serec's jaw tense as his chin lowered. I stepped between Serec and the men to prevent him from doing something that might draw more attention.

"Tiason, don't tell me you don't remember me," I said in a pouty voice. "Laici...one of Yasmin's friends. She promised me you'd let me into the bar when I asked back at the salon."

The man looked confused; almost nervous. "Oh! Yeah, of course. I remember you. Go on in." He nodded at the other guard, who reluctantly stepped out of our way. "Have a good time, Laici."

"Did you mind-write that one?" Serec asked.

"Didn't have to. He was so focused on how many credits his wife spent at the salon, his mind practically screamed it."

The bar was completely cut off from the dancefloor; its thick, glass walls dampening the booming music to a low rumble. The decor had an Old Empire style that likely appealed to the older patrons socializing over drinks. Throughout the room, wood-toned seating surrounded tinted glass tables; a perfect accent to the charcoal flooring. The only contrast was the red-orange wall behind the two bartenders, who were laughing and schmoozing with their patrons. And despite the powerful scent of liquor, everything about the atmosphere felt sophisticated.

Serec nudged me and nodded toward a lift across the room, where two more suits stood guard. "That's our way to the top floor. Got anything you can use against them?"

I took a moment to scan their thoughts. "Nothing I can work with. Their orders are to let no one through, so we can't talk our way in. And I can't mind-write at this distance."

"I might be able to work a little magic here," Serec said, taking my hand.

"What do you—"

"When I release your hand, open the lift as fast as you can, okay?"

"Sure, but how are you—"

Serec closed his eyes and inhaled. The moment he exhaled, everything fell silent. The patrons, the bartenders, even the security guards had frozen in place. We might as well have been standing inside of a three-dimensional photograph.

"And why didn't you stop time earlier?"

"Because it doesn't always...work the way I want it to," his voice wavered.

"And it takes a fatal amount of energy." His face had become a troubling red and a trickle of blood had begun reaching from his nose.

"Are you okay?"

"Please hurry." The strain in his voice almost kept me by his side. But I couldn't let his toil be for naught. I ran to the lift, placed my hand on the biometric scanner, and linked into the system. The door opened and Serec staggered inside behind.

"Are you sure you're okay?"

"Yeah, just gimme a hash." The doors closed and muffled music replaced the silence. Serec leaned against the wall, panting; a sheen of sweat covering his forhead.

My heart was in my stomach. "We're secure in here. Just take your time."

Watching him catch his breath and struggle to his feet was torture. It'd been quite some time since I'd felt that helpless. But thankfully, Serec was looking like his normal self before too long.

"I'll take my breakfast in bed tomorrow," he said, hoping to his feet.

A giggle of relief escaped, and I placed my hand over the lift keypad. "We'll see." Serec and I activated our HOODs as the lift began its ascent. Just before we reached our floor, Serec gave a very visible shudder.

"What's wrong?" I asked.

"Dunno. I felt a... strange energy or something." The door opened. "It's probably noth-"

BAM!

Serec slammed against the back of the lift. The culprit was a fist attached to a tall well-dressed man with sandy curls and features as sharp as his glare. I moved to defend Serec, but a tall woman appeared holding up her hand at me. Within her palm a furious flame sparked, immediately halting my advance.

"I bet there's a beautiful face under there," the woman began. "I'd hate to scorch it before finding out." This was what Serec was feeling. The woman took a step closer, and I shifted into a guarded stance.

"Ariel. Axel," another man called from behind them. "Is this how we treat guests?" They lowered their guard, and I followed their lead. "Bring them here." Axel started toward Serec, but I held my arm in his path.

"I'll bring him," I said, hoping my tone sounded more assertive than panicked. Axel shrugged and stepped aside. "Can you stand?" I asked Serec.

"Yeah," he replied. "I'm not that hurt." He stood and casually adjusted his clothes. But his clenched jaw betrayed his exasperation. Ariel and Axel waved us after them.

It took a moment to realize that no one was in the lounge. The scent of smoker vapors wafted from the back of the room where an antique table and a leather chair were perfectly centered on a large tinted window that overlooked the dance floor. But the chair was empty.

Then, something clicked from behind a small corner wall a few steps ahead. Serec and I froze as a familiar face emerged.

"Serec Arenyu and Blissful Sa'Sha Martinel," the man said with a heavy, mirthful timbre. The first thing the dim light revealed was the small glass of liquor in his hand. A moment later, the full form was illuminated.

"Alex Locke," I said.

He seemed taller from afar. Up close, however, he was somewhere between Serec's height and mine. Still, his face was flawless to the point that it was obvious how highly he valued his appearance.

He gave the glass a swirl, inhaled the aroma and smirked fiendishly. "Please, have a seat. I am certain your arrival will prove to be of great interest to me."

KNIGHTS

SEREC

The look in Locke's too green eyes was unsettling. Like he knew something about us most people weren't supposed to.

"Please, have a seat," he said. He gestured to a couch his bodyguards were posted behind. Sa'Sha and I shared a glance before sitting. "You'll have to excuse me, but I harbor strong aversion toward conversing with someone when I can't see their eyes."

"Of course," Sa'Sha said deactivating her HOOD. Rather than reveal my confusion, I followed her lead. "You two certainly looked like a pair of star-crossed lovers out on that dance floor. Dare I say, you stood out in the crowd." He chuckled to himself before taking a sip from his glass. "I must admit Blissful, whatever methods you use to alter your appearance is quite impressive. A shame it could not deceive my recognition software."

"Mr. Locke, I'm certain you understand that we didn't come here to make small talk," Sa'Sha finally said.

"I suppose not. Why would any sensible person travel all the way to Alyrri-an Heights, work the guards, and hack into my highly sophisticated security system, simply to gain access to my private lounge for small talk?"

"We have a few—"

"Questions, I know. But etiquette should demand that introductions precede interrogations, should they not, Blissful?"

Sa'Sha offered a forced smile. "But of course."

Locke gestured to himself. "Alex Locke. And you two are...?"

"Sa'Sha," Sa'Sha said.

"Serec," I said.

"It is a pleasure to make your acquaintances." He lowered himself into the armchair across from us, crossed one leg over the other, and smiled breathily. "Now, to what circumstance do I owe the honor of your presence?"

"We would like to ask you a few simple questions," Sa'Sha said.

"Then, I will be certain to provide you with equally simple answers."

"An organization known as the Soldiers of Liberty recently came onto the BNP's radar. Have you heard of them?"

"You said you weren't here for small talk, and yet we start with roundabout questions about who's heard of whom."

"Are you working with the Soldiers Of Liberty?" I interrupted.

"Better." Locke didn't seem the least bit affected by the question. "My company manufactures technology for consumers across Orbis."

"Are they one of them?"

"Despite Blissful Martinel's assurance of simple questions," Locke said, "it's clear you're assuming my mind is akin to an electronic ledger. Tallying every transaction procured and fulfilled. If, however, you're even remotely aware of the size of our pool of clientele, you would perish expectations of a definitive answer to that question."

"Now whose speech is roundabout?"

Locke chuckled breathily, then took another sip.

"This is getting us nowhere," Sa'Sha said telepathically. *"I'll have to dig deeper."*

"I'm certain you two have more pressing inquiries so let us not delay this any further." Locke said after a pause.

Sa'Sha leaned into me, looking like she was about to fall asleep.

"You okay?" I said.

She snapped out of her daze and rubbed at the back of her neck. "Huh? Uh...Yeah, I'm fine."

"Splendid," Locke interrupted. "Now I have a question for the two of you. Why am I a target for interrogation by our nation's princess and the nephew of the Director of the Bureau of National Peace in the first place?" My face went flush with surprise, which Locke immediately noticed. "It seems you hadn't considered the possibility that your target was also targeting you. How strange it must feel to be the hunter, suddenly in the sights of another predator."

"What are you talking about?"

"Such blatant meddling from someone who understands so little about the matters in which they deal. Let us hope that the risk does not outweigh the reward." A distant boom rumbled, rattling the building so much the hanging overhead lumens clinked against one another.

"What was that?" I asked.

Locke rose and looked through the large tinted glass. "A threat to my patrons." Locke nodded to his bodyguards.

"Secure cam: Street level — quadrant three," Axel said.

"Acknowledged," an artificial voice responded. A security camera fed the holographic image of a hooded man into the center of the room. His hands were raised overhead as he approached the building. The moment he shot his hands down another boom cried out, the building shaking sympathetically.

"The outer security ring has been compromised, Master," Ariel said in a surprisingly calm tone. "We should take our leave."

Locke sighed before one final sip. "Agreed."

On his word, Axel tapped a button on the hologram and a progress bar popped up beneath the word "downloading." Ariel gathered and placed a few electronic devices in a small cylinder-shaped aluminum case.

As they were executing their exit plan, so was Sa'Sha. She rose, her HOOD already reactivated. "ETA on evac is fifteen hashes," she said.

"Axel," Locke began casually. "has the building been evacuated?"

"Much of it has, master. Emergency Protocol Seven is in effect, and with all emergency exits opened, evacuation should be complete in under two hashes."

"Excellent. Ariel, is everything secured?"

"Right here, Master," she replied.

Another explosion. This one felt like it was right under us.

"Master, the main level has sustained catastrophic damage," Axel said.

"Then we'd best take our leave," Locke said. "Serec, Sa'Sha, this is where we part ways. Though, it was a pleasure." Locke offered a diplomatic smirk and followed his bodyguards into the lift. "In case you couldn't tell, this building won't last fifteen hashes." The door closed as if to stamp his final words with an epic period.

"I finally understand why no one ever talks to him at the events," Sa'Sha muttered to herself.

"What are you talking about?" I asked.

"Nothing important. Let's hit the stairs."

"I thought the lift was the only way up here."

"How would he get out during a power outage?"

"Good point. Any ideas on where the stairs are?"

"Yeah. I scanned the area while they were packing up. Follow me."

We blew through what looked like a solid wall at first, to a narrow stairwell. We made it down to the third floor just as the next explosion claimed a huge chunk of wall and the stairway to the first floor. The damage was too severe to a jump. So, our only option was the door to the third floor. Thanks to the explosions, the dust raining from the ceiling had joined the smoke from a legion of flames to create a blinding veil that blanketed the floor. Thankfully, Sa'Sha's vision couldn't be defeated so easily.

"Window, straight ahead!" she yelled pulling me forward.

The floor shook and cracked, massive pieces caving in around us. We sprinted over and around debris and paraphernalia littering our path, the noxious smoke taking its toll on my lungs. Without warning, a violent quake threw us to the ground. A loud crack followed and I spotted a massive marble pillar lumbering toward us. I shot forward, racing against the pillar as Sa'Sha struggled to regain solid footing. In one somewhat-fluid move I caught her by the waist and twisted into a feet-first dive. Air whooshed over as our heads just cleared the pillar, before the crash demolished the floor. My feet stuttered out of the clumsy tumble and I pulled Sa'Sha close as I raced toward the window.

Pointing my left shoulder toward the window, I encased my body in stone just before crashing through. But, in that moment before gravity could take hold, I realized a very important detail. I was two-stories up, holding Sa'Sha like luggage. *How am I supposed to land while preventing her spine from shattering on impact?* My grip on Sa'Sha gave way to hesitation when I thought I heard her voice. She shifted her knees under her and, as I started to pull her closer, she arched back and spring boarded away from me. My body smacked into the pavement with a loud crackle that stung across the back of my neck.

"Are you alright?" she said kneeling next to me as I waited for the blurring edges of my vision to clear.

"Yeah," I said through a cough. I let my stone skin fall away and Sa'Sha helped me to my feet. "Where are the explosions coming from?"

She pointed at a man in a hooded green cloak, approaching from the corner of the building. Behind him, malefactors were ravaging the area, attacking fleeing patrons and arriving emergency response personnel. "Can you keep him entertained while I handle the malefactors?" she asked.

"I'll figure something out," I said and she sprinted off.

"What's your problem," I yelled at the man in the cloak. "Couldn't get into the club?"

"Huh?" he said.

"I mean, why else would you go all gloom and boom on the biggest club in the Night District? Not the best way to make friends."

The man snickered. "My problem," he began, pulling back his hood. "Is the decadence poisoning this sick land." Pallid indigo eyes stared at me accompanied by a smile that made me wonder if he was short a few lumens.

"Name's Renes," he said sharply. "Sixth Knight of Just Death."

"Just death, huh? So, destruction and terror are a bonus? Or...?"

"You people deserve punishment for your frivolous nature. I shall enjoy burning your face into dust."

"And I'm going to enjoy watching you try."

I charged, and Renes reached a hand at me. It suddenly felt like I was in a furnace, and a stinging sensation coursed through my stomach. Acting purely on reflex, I vaulted high. I had only just cleared his head when an explosion resounded where I was. By the time I'd landed and turned, Renes' hand was reaching out at me again. I knocked his arm away and clipped his jaw. He stumbled back, but immediately threw another hand up. I dipped and ducked to either side of the explosions aimed at my face until I recovered enough balance to throw him off his. As soon as I had an opening, I sent a fist into his side and shuffled back before he could retaliate.

Dodging explosions was about as unpredictable as it sounded. My best hope at leveling the playing field was moving faster than he could aim. A quick surge of energy into my eyes and legs was all I had time for before his eyes widened in sync with the rise of his arms. I darted forward. But flashes of hot air engulfed me with every step. I strafed right, narrowly avoiding a flash that would've torched my face. My soles skidded as I shifted and shifted again to get behind him. His headed darted left and right, unable to keep up. He held his arms out at his sides and the air grew hot around his hands. A desperate move. And exactly what I was waiting for.

I yanked his arm and slugged him, hard. The way he tumbled to the ground, I figured he was more stunned than he looked. But by the time I went in for the next hit, his hands were already palm-up. Another bright flash. Another save by my reflex. I dipped, narrowly evading the boom and took off in a wide circle. Explosions roared all around me as I tried to close in. But it was worth it when I finally got within attack range. I slammed my forearm into his stomach, knocking the wind out of him.

Renes dropped to his knees, coughing wildly. His hands went up and I shifted to stay out of his path. "Su-surrender. I surrender."

I hesitated. I wasn't exactly sure how to handle a surrender. Especially considering another couple hits would've put him down. It seemed a safer bet. And after all the damage he caused, anything short of knocking him out felt like he was getting out easy.

"Just to be clear," I said. "Surrendering means I take you in. That smooth with you?"

He nodded and kept his head low. I watched him for a couple beats before moving to close the gap. His focus remained on the ground; his face a bright red. He looked unsteady, like he was having trouble breathing.

"You gonna be okay?"

He nodded. "Can't say the same about you though." His eyes snapped to mine as he closed his fists. A blazing heat encircled me. Then, a blinding light. Explosions thundered, surrounding me and knocking me around like a gang bullying a kid. My knees joined my feet. As the thought swam to the surface. *He got me.* Or, at least, he would've if I hadn't encased myself in stone the moment he looked up at me. Not that I made it out unscathed though. A chilling sting ran along my arms and back, in the areas the blasts had disintegrated my stone shielding. I picked my head up and found Renes lunging at me with a curved dagger in each hand. The blade edges glowed a fierce orange as he slashed. Throwing myself back, I rolled out of his path. But he twisted to stay on me; swinging like he'd lost his mind. His relentless assault eventually led to success as one of his daggers caught my right shin. I swung my arm and cast a gust heavy enough to knock him back. The gash pulsated with a searing heat. It didn't take a genius to determine that he wasn't using ordinary daggers.

"How'd you get that weapon?" I asked.

"Let's just say I work for the right crowd." He held out one of the daggers. "Looks like your leg has already had a meet and greet with Burn, but I think Slash is getting jealous."

I could've kicked myself for almost accepting his surrender. But that wasn't the worst of it. The fact that he had a Divarma escalated the danger of the situation to a critical level. I stood face to face with a refractor wearing a green cloak and carrying a Divarma. He had to be connected to Siren; which meant I couldn't afford to hold back if I wanted to leave in one piece. I poured energy into my arms and legs then immediately broke into a high-speed sprint. I was too fast for Renes to keep up with; even as he desperately tried to detonate everything around me. I circled inward until I was right on him. Renes swiped at my head. But he was already too late. In one sharp movement, I jammed my fist into his wide-open chin, launching him into the air. He landed with a hard crash and crumpled like a puppet.

Whirling wind accompanied the hum of what turned out to be the Nighthawk's engine. Sa'Sha was already aboard, waving and yelling as I ran toward her. I figured she was relieved to see I was okay after all the explosions. But then, she hoped out and started running toward me. And by the time I realized she was pointing and yelling, "Look out behind you!" it was too late.

Something slammed into my back, throwing me into a fierce tumble along the road. The last thing I remember seeing before everything went dark was Sa'Sha yelling frantically from the Nighthawk as it grew smaller and smaller. I blinked, and the aircraft was gone. The sky was still spinning, when I realized I was outside. The burning remains of Locke's nightclub slowly coming into focus. A phantom silhouette stood over me, glaring down with chilling green eyes. All at once, I was too weak to react. Too weak to even feel afraid. I could only watch as Green Eyes yanked me off the ground by the collar.

"You again. Was I unclear the last time?"

The air was too thin to inhale, like it had been purged of all its oxygen. He threw me to the ground and jammed a foot into my chest. My ribs screamed and my mind accompanied them, certain one or three had been cracked. Not that I could tell either way. Numbness had already seized my body. In no time at all, everything was dark.

All I could sense was Green Eyes' muffled voice. "Next time, I'll end you," he said. A moment later, the pressure over my chest faded and my lungs found air. But the darkness remained.

"He looks pretty messed up," a female voice said.

"And?" a male voice replied.

"And we should take him back."

"Those weren't our instructions."

"We can't leave him here."

"Master won't appreciate this."

"Master wouldn't appreciate us leaving him either."

The man sighed. "Grab him and let's go."

[7]

BRANCHES

SEREC

"**H**e's waking up."

The excitement in the familiar voice forced my eyes open. But a bright light made the figure overhead too dark and blurred to identify.

"Sa...Sha?" I uttered instinctively.

"Is that how you say thanks? Calling out for the girl who left you behind?"

Her crystal blue eyes slowly came into focus. I squinted out of impatience. "Ariel?"

She brushed back a handful of short locks that cast a golden glow as the light shone through them, giving her an almost divine aspect. "Oh, you do remember!" She smirked.

The lighting in Alex Locke's personal lounge was especially dim. So it wasn't particularly easy to make out many facial features. Maybe that was why I was so surprised to see how attractive Ariel was. No mistaking it now though. I pushed myself upright and realized I'd been lying on a medical table. "Where am I?"

"Oh you're welcome. Jumping back into the fray to save you was just *so* enjoyable."

"Sorry, I uh..." I cleared my throat. "Thanks."

"I'll forgive you this time, cutie."

My brain was more sluggish than I realized. But when it finally hit me that I was watching Ariel watch me, I reflexively looked away. "Feeling okay?" she asked after a pause.

"My chest is a bit sore and my head is throbbing, but I'll be fine."

She placed a hand to my forehead. Her skin was soft and carried a sweet scent. "Temperature feels normal. But you woke up earlier than anticipated, so no surprises that you're not fully healed."

"Earlier than anticipated?" I repeated. "How long was I asleep?"

"Just shy of fifteen decs." My eyes widened and, not two beats later, she broke into a fit of hysterical laughter. She sighed wiping the tears from her eyes. "I really couldn't help myself."

"It's not that funny." I said turning away. I was more irritated at myself for being so gullible.

"Aww, come on. Don't make that face. I wasn't sulking when you called me Sa'Sha, was I?"

"Fine."

"You've been out for about five segments. But it would've taken six for your *regen factor* to fully work its magic."

"Regen factor?"

"As in *regeneration factor*?"

"You mean my healing ability?"

"Yup. Honestly though, all that deep breathing...?" She crossed her eyes and exaggerated a huge breath. "Waste of time."

"Ariel," a voice called from the shadows. "The Master will want to explain things to the kid himself." Axel emerged, disdain in his eyes.

"Yeah, about that." I said hopping off the table and moving toward the exit. "I don't mean to sound unappreciative but I really do need to get back home."

A sharp chill suddenly engulfed me like I was caught in a raging blizzard. Flurries of snow and ice whipped around the dim room turning it into a frigid Hadal in mere beats. Axel appeared in front of me, predation shining in his glowing blue eyes. A whirling wind crystallized into a white ball in Axel's hand. The ball flattened and expanded as he ran his free hand over it, forming it into what looked like a blade of ice.

"Let me be clear, kid. You're not here by choice. Your presence is the will of our master. So you can either get back on that table. Or I can place your frozen body there."

It would've been stupid to challenge him. Especially, when my head still felt like it had been stuffed into a metal box. Even more especially, when my opponent wasn't the type of person I could underestimate on my best day. But I hadn't forgotten about that little surprise attack back at the nightclub. I formed a solid layer of stone skin over my knuckles and got into a fighting stance.

We both moved to close the gap when a flare bit at the back of my neck. "I like your spirit, so quick to get physical," Ariel's voice was as frightening as it was enticing. Her once divine blue eyes were glowing a Hadal-like red. The intensity in her eyes rivaled Surket's, except hers had a predatory twist that matched Axel's. I might as well have been standing between a mountain ligorn and an angry nibos. And something told me my greatest threat wasn't the ligorn in front of me. The moment I looked back at Axel, his features blurred. At first, I thought he was using his power to affect my vision, but everything else still looked normal as his gaseous form flowed around the room.

"Too frightened to make a move?" Axel said. "Fine by me."

Just as quickly as Axel disappeared, he reappeared in mid-air; a breath from my face. I twisted back to dodge, then shifted into a sidekick. But he vanished again. Just as I turned, I caught him out of the corner of my eye and spun backward into a high elbow strike. Before I could finish the movement, Axel's fist jammed into my lower back. My body seized from the pain, giving Axel more than enough time to get in front of me again. I took a step back, when an even sharper pain radiated through my stomach. My legs buckled, and before I could make sense of what happened I was doubled over and wheezing.

"Done already? The other one at lease offered some resistance." Axel said. A wave of frigid air brushed my neck, pulling my attention to the icy sword raised high overhead. "No matter. I'll make it quick."

My pulse throbbed all over as time slowed. Despite seeing the blade moving at a crawl, I was powerless to affect anything because my body was moving just as slow. Fear began to take hold of me, as fate closed in.

"I've given you power," a voice shattered the walls of my consciousness. *"The time has come for you to use it."*

A flash of intense heat collected in my right palm as the blade crept forward. My palm tingled as I instinctively pressed into the heat—and drew a blade. The ethereal weapon glinted as it solidified. On reflex alone, I tightened my grip and swung my arm upward. With an ear-splitting crash, my blade edge bit into Axel's —and shattered it. Icy shards scattered in every direction, throwing Axel off balance and opening him up for my final attack. I rushed forward, blade in hand but before I could swing.... "Enough," a voice called, throwing me off balance and into Axel's fist. I crashed into the ground dropping the weapon. I quickly recovered and grabbed the weapon to make a follow up attack, but to my surprise, I found Axel kneeling.

Bright lumens came to life overhead illuminating the large room. From the concrete floors to the smooth walls to the abnormally high ceiling, everything looked like it'd been buffed and polished. Aside from some neatly stacked crates against one wall, the room was completely bare. I wanted to ask what the room was normally used for. But I had enough unanswered questions already.

"That weapon. Where did you acquire it?" The same voice asked. I turned to find Locke approaching, gait casual yet deliberate.

"Why do you care?" I said, keeping my distance.

"I am a scientist. I seek to demystify that which I do not understand."

"Something tells me you know more about this thing than I do. And since you haven't bothered to answer any of my questions, I don't see a reason to answer any of yours."

Locke smirked. "Very well, you may ask one question."

"Why are you holding me here?"

Locke shook his head. "And just like that we've arrived at a monumental flaw. You're singular focus has led you to a question you were bound to get an answer to, had you exercised a modicum of patience."

It was clear as quartz why Locke and Axel got along so well. This colossus of a man who stood a half a head shorter than me was more interested in making me feel stupid than providing answers. "Fine then. Are you—?"

"Apologies, but that would be two questions."

"You didn't answer the first one."

"Again. Patience." I pressed my mouth into something just short of a frown to keep from giving him something else to complain about. "There comes a time for everyone, when a ray of clarity shines down. For you, young Serec, that time has arrived."

"If you're only answering one question, can you at least do it in plain Auric?"

"You know very little of your nature. And your lack of knowledge is a significant hindrance to your own progress. So, along with your answer, I'm offering you the opportunity to rectify that shortfall."

"What's the cost?"

The corners of Locke's mouth curled. "What makes you so certain there is one?"

"You're a businessman. Everything comes at a price for people like you."

"And I won't deny the half-truth in your conclusion."

"Half-truth?"

"Everything comes at a price for everyone. Successful businessmen have come to adopt that axiom in order to maintain their success. But first and foremost, that is a widely-recognized principle of life, extending far beyond any occupation."

Again, my mouth stopped short of a frown. "So, what's your price?"

Locke pointed at the faintly glowing sword in my hand. It was so light, I'd almost forgotten I was holding it. "I'd like to hold that for just a moment." I pulled the weapon closer. "Have no fear. You'll get it right back."

I observed Locke's stoic face. His too green eyes had become an inquisitive brown. *Is he a refractor too?* I would've been surprised if he wasn't, all things considered.

"And then I get answers?"

"More than you were expecting."

I held out the blade and Locke took it carefully. He examined it briefly, then smiled and started for the door. "Follow me."

"You said you'd give it right back."

"And I meant it," Locke said. "But I'll need it to provide an answer to your first question."

I looked to Ariel, who only offered an encouraging smile and nod. She'd returned to her original form, eyes serene and demeanor calm yet alluring. The same had happened with Axel and it made me wonder if I'd seen those fiendish forms at all.

"This is an interesting weapon you have here, Serec. The craftsmanship is exquisite," Locke said after a few wild swings. I was sure he'd hit something if he kept that up. Not that it concerned me. Rich as he was, he could probably replace the entire building and everything inside if he wanted.

"Uh...Thanks," I said, making certain to remain half a step behind him.

"How long have you been able to draw it?"

"Um...I'm not sure. This is the first time I've actually seen it as a solid object."

"Understandable. A weapon that both feeds and siphons energy requires considerable mental focus."

"Feeds and siphons?"

"Of course." He stopped and held the weapon out to me. "Here you are."

I grabbed the handle, and the sword immediately became a flurry of tiny light specks, before disappearing.

"How..."

"This way," he said, as I tried to piece together the cause of the blade's dismissal.

The hallway we traveled was a long, thin stretch of floor lumens lining either side. "I must admit, I rather enjoyed observing your capabilities" Locke said.

"Am I really that interesting or is everything around here that boring?"

"Full of questions, aren't we?"

"Maybe I wouldn't be if you actually gave me some solid answers."

Two flights of spiraling stairs later, we were standing in front of a set of large, recessed double doors. "Welcome to my study," Locke said as soon as I stepped through the massive doors that opened to an even more massive room.

It was several times larger than his lounge at Keyes, and twice as extravagant. Ambient rays of morning sunlight poured in through curved floor to ceiling glass panels that served as the back wall. The stunning view that reached across Callastryne provided definitive evidence of our location: Vista. The wealthiest city in Aruria outside of Regalia, most people couldn't even afford to look in Vista's direction. It was common knowledge that Locke lived here but a part of me was surprised he brought me to his home. The flagrant scent of meteor leaf wafted in the air filling me with a mix of nostalgia and sorrow. The oil of the meteor leaf was a favorite fragrance among men for its light yet assertive aroma. My dad was one of those men. Everything he wore held that smell. And the fragrance wafting in Locke's study was a sad reminder that it was one of the few things I had left of him.

Locke walked over to a dark leather chair and sat. "Please...have a seat," he said, motioning to a large, plush chair positioned across from him. The chair cradled me as I sunk into it, tasting the luxury Locke experienced every waking moment.

"Thirsty?" Locke asked.

Before I could answer, Ariel was ready with a bottle of lightly chilled water. "Thanks," I said, and took a sip. The flavor was clean—almost sweet. So much so that I wanted to keep drinking it, even after my thirst was gone. It was honestly the best water I'd ever tasted.

"Now, onto why you're here," Locke said. "I'll start with Kurai. I imagine you're wondering why there's an altercation every time you two meet."

"Kurai?"

"The hooded young man with the green eyes. He attacked you in front of my nightclub, did he not?"

"Yeah," I said, pushing back the growing chills. "What's his problem?"

"His *problem* is that he is a key player in the developing situation your people are investigating. I have yet to determine his current motive, but it considerably outweighs his interest in you."

"Is that why he's been trying so hard to kill me?"

Locke smirked. "I assure you, if Kurai wanted you dead, we wouldn't be having this conversation."

"That's pretty pessimistic."

"The truth tends to be. Serec, do you believe in fate?"

I thought about it, then shrugged. "Kind of. I guess."

"A simple 'yes' or 'no' will suffice. I will ask a slightly different question. Have you ever had an instance, a defining moment where you believe the course of your life would drastically change, had you made a different decision?" I thought back to the alley where I saved Anne—to Kunai and Surket. I nodded, wondering if he could sense the pride and regret swirling inside me.

"What if I told you that you have made the opposing decision? That you have, in fact, made every possible decision—experienced every outcome."

"I'd wonder if you'd been drinking." I said.

Locke paused for a moment. "Our reality does not exist in a vacuum, but is instead a stream, branching in an infinite river of time."

I nodded slowly. "And what does this have to do with me?"

"Our meeting and your repeated encounters with Kurai—all are the culmination of an infinite number of possibilities aligning precisely to bring us to this moment."

"And what would the purpose of all that be?"

"Your development."

"My...?"

"One million, two hundred forty-seven thousand, eight hundred fifty-two individuals with supernatural abilities currently roam Orbis. Out of a population of roughly four billion, that averages three out of every ten-thousand people. And out of that, two people currently possess a potential greater than any gifted individual who has ever lived. You are one of them."

"Me?"

"Your unique ability, likens you to the number zero. Alone, you're no different from any regular human being. But when others gather around you a limitless potential can be tapped into." *Guess Sa'Sha nailed my designation.*

"You mean my mimicry?"

"A rather pedestrian way of referring to it, but yes. Despite your recent strides, you have a long journey to unlocking your full potential. But that can only happen once you have a better grasp of how your ability actually works."

"So, you're gonna help me understand my ability?"

"Not me." Locke looked to his bodyguards. "Ariel. Axel. Take him to the grounds."

"Right away, Master," they said in unison, and started toward me.

"But I still have questions about the Soldiers of Liberty and—"

Locke raised two fingers and the bodyguards stopped. "Though your singular focus does limit you at times, it would serve you well in this instance to concentrate on the matter at hand."

I was starting to feel like I was talking to Hachi. "There are monsters out there ripping people to shreds," I argued. "Now's not the time to worry about my powers if you can help me stop whatever's causing this."

"Despite what you may think, I do have the best interest of the majority in mind. And though I admire your zeal, I honestly find your ignorance exasperating."

He snapped his fingers and the last thing I saw was his eyes, glowing a faint red as the room faded into darkness.

[8]

EVOKE

SEREC

Nothingness surrounded me. A blackness so intense, I couldn't even see my hand waving in front of me. In the depths of the void, it wasn't fear or anxiety, but a hopeless loneliness that clawed its way to the top of my mind. Thankfully, a warmth pulled my shoulder; reminding me that this void was a only a pathway, not a destination. The heat intensified with the force of the pull until...

"Snap out of it, Serec," a voice called.

My eyes jolted open. A bare and rocky terrain came into focus all around me.

"You plan to lie there all day?" Ariel said, leaning over me. "We have work to do."

I sat up, transparently confused. "Where've you taken me now?"

"Khost Desert, South Lazuria," Axel answered, his back to me. "Let's get moving."

"Khost Desert?! That's on the other side of Orbis across closed international borders."

"That's irrelevant," he began. "You should be more concerned about those things"

I stood and peered out into the distance to see exactly what *things* Axel was talking about. "Malefactors," I thought aloud.

"Is that what you call them?" Ariel asked. "That's cute."

"I still don't understand why you guys brought me here."

"It's the perfect place to teach you to *evoke*."

"To what?"

"Evoke. It's the process of calling forth your *Aetharma*."

"You mean Divarma?"

"No. I don't."

"What's an Aetharma?"

"A living organism—far more powerful than those toys you call Divarma. Aetharma are exceptionally rare—inextricably linked to their users which allows them to evolve as their user does. They exist as energy in etheric space, only given form when evoked by their predestined user."

"So, you're saying that weapon I summoned was an Aetharma and you want me to fight the malefactors using it?"

"That's the idea," Ariel began. "And I recommend doing so quickly."

They were closing in fast; close enough for plain sight. At least fifty of them approached, ranging from the smaller ones, to the towering monsters that stood at about three times the average man's height. The feral horde raced toward us like a violent storm of claws and fangs. Despite their numbers, it didn't sound like Axel or Ariel had any intention of helping me. I steadied my breathing as the distance between me and them grew smaller by the beat. One of the larger ones had a lead on the others. And judging by the tremors its feet created with each heavy stride, it would take every bit of strength to kill its momentum.

Just as I was about to charge in, Axel stepped in front of me, completely ignoring the beast bounding from behind. "Pay close attention," he said. "I'm only going to show you once. Your Aetharma responds to your will, instantaneously coming to your aid. So, your intention must be clear."

Axel reached a hand out to one side and a bright light flashed in his palm. With a booming roar, the massive malefactor sprung up behind him.

"Behind you," I yelled.

With his arm extended, Axel whirled into a tight spin as he leapt high into the air. A streak of light was all I could see in that moment. He landed; his eyes trained on me confidently. A beat later, I saw it. The thin, long blade glowed white-hot, smoldering the air around it.

The monsters that took his blade head-on more than suffered for it. With a lumbered groan, it teetered forward and collapsed onto its side.

Oily sludge glopped out onto the sandy dirt from the beast's wound.

As the next wave of malefactors made it within striking range, Axel effortlessly cut them down, almost bored.

"Time for some reinforcement cutie," Ariel said. "Pay close attention. The last wave is yours."

Ariel held out her hand. And, just like with Axel, a light sparked from her palm. The light grew five long tails that danced around her arm like a skirt of grass. She squeezed her fist and the weapon solidified into what looked like a flimsy, sparkling sword. As she drew in her arm, each tail of the sword coiled simultaneously. Then, with one lunging strike, the tails whipped out at the closest malefactor, slicing through its body from all angles. The malefactor squealed as its skin burst into flames, before it plopped into a charred, bubbling heap. They made it look like child's play. In less than one hash, Axel and Ariel decimated most of the monsters. And at least a couple were bigger than anything I'd ever fought. It might've inspired a feeling of safety with them if not for the dark predatory smiles painted over their faces.

"Your turn," Axel said as he and Ariel's Aetharma evaporated into light.

"Ok," I said after a breath.

Talking the malefactors out of attacking seemed a more possible feat than evoking my Aetharma. Even as I could almost feel a well of warm energy flowing into my hand, nothing changed. The malefactors were nearly on us. Not that it mattered in the least to Ariel or Axel. One of the creatures roared in anticipation, shaking me out of whatever I thought I was starting to feel. I was out of time. I'd have to rely on my other powers. I started by encasing my fists in stone.

"I forgot to mention," Ariel said, "Our master has given us the order to kill you if you fight without your Aetharma."

Her expression was even more haunting than before. And next to her, Axel stood ready with his ice sword again. I almost thought they were joking. But that predatory look from before pressed into my mind, and made me decide against testing that theory. My blood ran cold. To Hadal with the malefactors. The real threat was standing right behind me. The monster's thunderous roar forced my attention forward just in time to find it already in mid-swing. But I was too paralyzed to stop the wrecking ball of an arm about to break every bone in my body. I shut my eyes, hoping it could at least end quickly.

Just then, my arm jolted as a bright flash of heat sparked in my palm. Acting on instinct alone, my hand clenched the light; my eyes opening as my Aetharma sliced through the malefactor's hand with no resistance. The beast howled; its fingers split like carved wood. In that moment, something clicked, my fear losing its foothold. I leapt and ran the length of its arm until I reached the middle of its back, and plunged my blade deep. A flailing screech was all the malefactor could muster before crashing to the ground.

I yanked my weapon free and whipped the blade around just in time to cleave through a smaller malefactor that lunged from behind. As I did, something became clear. Fighting malefactors, regardless of size, was like fighting any beast. The thought was frightening because *they* were frightening. But their movements were becoming familiar— predictable even. And thanks to the training I received from Shawin and Team Seven, defending against them was almost too easy. That realization empowered me to cut down every malefactor within range without hesitation. Before I knew it, there was one left. It eyed me cautiously until I gestured for it to come closer. It charged, snarling viciously as I lunged into a wide spin. A beat later, I was behind it, my blade sizzling with black blood as it dripped from it. I turn to face the creature, just as its head rolled off its neck. It slumped to the ground and oozed the same dark sludge puddles as each of its comrades. I stood there, scanning the field of corpses. My body still trembling from the flood of adrenaline. My attention turned to my Aetharma. I stared at the reflection of my eyes in the azure blade, wondering if I was seeing the real me for the first time.

The hand on my shoulder startled me so much I spun into a defensive stance. "Don't be so jumpy," Ariel said with a smile. "The threat's been eliminated."

I clutched my blade tighter. "Has it?"

Her sudden laughter nearly startled me a second time. "You're too cute." Her aspect had returned to that of a carefree girl. And I found myself wanting to just relax and trust her. But as Surket would say, I had to keep my wits about me. I took a step back.

"Awww come on. Don't be like that," she pouted. "I promise we aren't a threat to you," she said, placing a hand over her heart.

"Didn't you just say you were going to kill me if I couldn't evoke my Aetharma?"

"The more important question is 'did you actually believe us?'"

If she was trying to reassure me, she wasn't doing a great job, despite the alluring twinkle in her eyes. Golden specks of light started floating between us, and I realized my Aetharma was disintegrating. I squeezed the hilt tighter, trying to maintain focus. But it wasn't working. "No! Why's it disappearing?"

"For the same reason Axel made a show of nearly killing you. And the same reason I threatened your life. Aetharma respond to the greatest emotion or intention a person has."

"Meaning what exactly?"

"Your fear of death activates your intention to survive. This intention summons and sustains your Aetharma. No immediate threat, no Aetharma."

"So, fear is the only way to use an Aetharma?"

"For now. But, in time you should be able to draw on a stronger emotion than fear."

"What's stronger than fear?"

"If you have to ask, there's no point in telling you."

I frowned. "Why not?"

"Evoking is different for everyone so it's something you'll have to discover for yourself."

"How long does that take?"

Ariel shrugged. "That depends entirely on you."

"But here's the deal, kid," Axel interjected, stepping forward. "Our master has instructed us to train you under the condition that you hold no outside allegiances."

"What do you mean?"

"We'll only train you if you agree to leave your organization."

"Why? They don't pose a threat to you."

"It's you we're concerned about," Ariel said.

"I pose a threat to you?"

"They're holding you back."

"How?" I said louder than intended. "I'd never have gotten this strong without them."

Axel snorted. "Strong? If your little band is stupid enough to place faith in your 'strength' then one of you is bound to suffer for it."

"You think a few lucky hits makes you so much better than me? How much longer than me have you been training? The way I see it, I'm well on my way to wiping the floor with you."

Axel shook his head. "No surprise there. Most kids are too stupid to know a good offer when they hear one." He shrugged. "Fine. Stay with IGIS and see where it gets you."

"I *will* stay with..." I paused. "How'd you know the name of my organization?"

A smug look crept over Axel's face. "We're heading back," he said and turned away. "Our master has something for you."

"Answer my question. How'd you learn about IGIS?"

Axel continued to ignore me, so I started after him. But Ariel pressed a hand to my chest and shook her head. The situation had quickly become frustrating. They were demanding my full cooperation, all while collectively dodging every question they didn't like. Still, I wasn't really in a position to make demands myself.

"Fine," I said with a heavy breath. Ariel moved her hand from my chest to my shoulder and—like before—everything went dark.

[9]

RETURN

SEREC

"How was he?" Locke asked, as we entered his study.

"Better than expected," Axel answered. "He shows potential."

I didn't know how to react to Axel paying me a compliment. Somehow, that translated into my avoiding eye contact with anyone.

"Excellent." Locke said. "And what say you of my proposition, Serec?"

"Proposition?"

"Did my assistants not offer to train you?"

"Oh, that. Yeah, I'm not leaving IGIS."

Locke sighed. "I can't say that I'm particularly surprised to hear that. But here." He placed a small vial of orange liquid at the edge of his desk. "It should provide a few answers."

I tilted the vial up to allow light to pass through it. Not that I could make more sense of what I was holding. "What is this?"

"Something I have no further use for. Your people, however, will find it... enlightening."

I wondered if Kareen would feel the same when I brought it to her. If not, I'd be better off leaving empty-handed.

"Thanks," I said.

Locke gave a small nod. "My assistants will see you out. Until we next meet, Serec."

"What makes you so certain we'll meet again? And why is it so important that I leave IGIS?" Darkness swallowed me before the words could reach Locke's ears. When the light returned, an awe-inspiring view of New Callastryne stared back at me. As I took in the scenery, I spotted a massive pile of charred wood and rubble filling the sky with a veil of dark smoke.

"Why are we on top of the Arurian Credit Union Plaza?"

"Afraid of heights?" Ariel asked. "It's only a few hundred meters."

"Yeah, like four-hundred."

Ariel shrugged. "Too bad about the nightclub. Guess I should've danced with you before it all went to ash."

"So, Keyes is gone for good?"

"Master will have the place rebuilt and structurally reinforced before the anum is out."

"What are we doing at the edge of the Central District?"

Axel nodded in the direction of the caelrail station. "The caelrail takes you back to your organization, doesn't it?"

I hesitated. *How much did they know?* "Yeah. Thanks"

"You should reconsider our offer."

I shook my head. "I can't leave IGIS."

"Can't or won't?"

"Both."

Ariel shrugged. "Then, I guess we'll see you around."

"By the way, the lift's broken here, so you'll have to take the stairs."

"What?! Wait, no. We're over a hundred stories..."

And just like that, they were gone. Even if they had dropped me close to the caelrail, the walk down would make up for what could've been a convenience.

The whole way back, all I could think about was what Locke said. How was IGIS holding me back?

"Am I missing something?" I thought aloud. "Northe might not have saved me from Kurai back at the nightclub, but he did back on Kunai. Or maybe, I wasn't the one he was saving. Both times, Sa'Sha was there. And both times, Northe made sure she got away safely, even if it meant leaving a team member behind."

I shook the thought away. It was a little early to jump to conclusions. Locke was fatally intelligent and cunning. I couldn't overlook the possibility that he was just trying to get into my head. Trying to turn me against the team, so that I would join his side. But why? How did he benefit from teaching me to evoke my aetharma?

A shrinking tail of light stretched from the horizon by the time I'd finally made it back to D7. Not two beats after I came through the front door, the floor thumped in increasing succession and intensity.

"Serec!" NaRyn yelled, as she jumped from behind the wall and tackled me with enough force to nearly knock me over. She pressed her face into my shirt, squeezing me harder than she ever had. "I'm so glad you're okay." She whimpered until my shirt was spotted with tears. "Where were you? We were so worried."

I wanted to calm her down; to tell her not to assume the worst. I understood her concern. She'd already experienced so much loss in her life. I couldn't expect her to blindly believe everything was alright. I could only smile quietly; pressing my tongue against the roof of my mouth to slow the growing heat in my eyes before my own tears could come. "It's alright Ryn, I'm here now," I managed.

The quick clomping of footsteps drew my attention. By the time they came to a halt, Sa'Sha appeared clad in combat gear. For a moment, she was frozen in place; her eyes fixed on me. I offered a smile. But her expression hardly changed.

"Hey Liza," I said, exercising all the restraint I had to approach her slowly. I wanted to run to her—to hold her. Just being in the same room with her brought reassurance that I'd made the right decision in staying with IGIS. But there was something different about her. She was more... guarded.

"Hey E," she said, almost sounding out of breath. "Where were you? Your timechain and HOOD were both dead and—"

"I know, and I'm sorry I just—"

"Thought it would be okay to let us worry. To allow us to fear the worst?"

"It wasn't that simple!" I snapped. My voice echoed, a reminder that I could never take that outburst back.

Sa'Sha locked eyes with me. And what I saw made me regret my words even more. Dark puffy circles were perched under her eyes which were a tinge of red. *Has she been awake this whole time?*

She let out a long sigh and turned away from me. "Welcome back," she said, almost sounding defeated. She pressed the communicator on her HOOD. "Call off the search Northe. He's here." Sa'Sha started toward the stairs without a second glance.

I started after her. "Liza wait—." But a hand on my shoulder drained my resolve. "Let her go," NaRyn nearly whispered reminding me she was in the room. "It's been a really long day. She needs some time."

"You guys had a search party?" I asked NaRyn trying to forget about our exchange.

NaRyn nodded. "Teams Three, Five and Seven have been rotating personnel, since you disappeared. Northe and Shawin are out with half of Team Five right now." A lump formed in my throat. *They'd actually been searching for me the whole time.* And all the while, I'd been hoping their reason for leaving me would be good enough. NaRyn looked up at me. "What's wrong?"

I shook my head. "Just tired," I said. "I could use a shower and a nap."

NaRyn pulled back with a smile. "Yeah, you smell like you've been rolling around in dirt and sweat."

A knock startled me out of my sleep, and it took a beat to realize where I was. "E?" Sa'Sha called softly from behind the door.

I blinked hard and cleared my throat. "Yeah?"

"Can I come in?"

I sat up and the room slowly illuminated. "It's open." The door slid open and Sa'Sha stepped in. "Hey Liza?"

"Hey, may I sit?"

"Yeah, sure."

She sat down next to me, looking like she was searching for words. "You missed dinner."

"I did? How long was I asleep?"

"Only a few segments." She paused, eyes meeting mine. "I wanted to apologize."

"Apologize? If anything, I should be apologizing to you for not keeping it together."

"I appreciate that. But you still deserve an explanation for my behavior earlier. Since last night, all I could think about was finding you. The fact that we couldn't find any leads was starting to wear on me. Then, you appeared out of nowhere. And all I felt was guilt and frustration for not being able to find you."

"What happened back there? It was kind of a blur, before I saw the aircraft pulling off."

"The co-pilot said the situation was too dangerous to remain. And rather than stopping him from taking off, Northe stopped me. I tried to teleport to you, but for some reason, my powers wouldn't work. Northe told me to have faith, as we left you behind."

I nodded. "Hm. Makes sense."

"No, it doesn't," Sa'Sha argued. "It was just like what happened with Surket."

"In what way?"

"For the second time Team Seven exfiltrated a mission, one member short."

"I came back, didn't I?"

"What if you didn't? Doesn't it bother you, being left behind?"

"Honestly, it kinda did at first. But what happened on Kunai was different. I'm glad Northe did what I would've wanted him to do."

"What do you mean?"

"If Northe had waited for me and you ended up getting hurt, it would've been my fault. I think Northe understands how much it means to me that you're safe."

"And what about me, Serec? You think I'm okay with everyone sacrificing themselves for me? All because..." She looked away.

"Because what?"

"Because I'm the princess. I didn't come here expecting special treatment. I don't want it."

"Then, it's a good thing we both know that IGIS isn't giving you special treatment."

Sa'Sha examined me, as if waiting for me to take back what I'd just said. But I held her gaze patiently, until her eyes returned to the floor.

"Humor me," she said. "What I'm saying may sound crazy, but considering what's happened, it doesn't feel quite so farfetched." Her voice was so soft and heavy that it almost weighed me down. I took hold of her hand and looked her in the eyes.

"I can't speak for everyone in IGIS. But, princess or not, me and everyone else on Team Seven would risk our lives for you, because you're important to us."

"More important than Surket or you?"

"I'm not saying that. I think we all do what we believe is right in that moment. We don't always have time to figure things out. We just have to act, ya know?"

Sa'Sha nodded and laced her fingers between mine. "E, I need you to make me a promise. If you really want to protect me, don't be so reckless. I can't lose you too."

The look in her eyes made it hard to say no. Even as my heart pounded at the sensation of her hand in mine. I wasn't sure if I could keep the promise. Because I knew that there was so much we didn't understand. Locke, Kurai, and Astaroth could just be the beginning. But I nodded anyway, an affirmation of my intention to remain by her side. "Yeah."

"Thanks E." The corners of her mouth creased. "Are you certain my being a princess has no bearing?"

"Well, I was kinda hoping to be knighted...Hey!" Sa'Sha's smirk contorted as she pinched the skin on my arm and twisted, until I reflexively pulled away. "Seriously though, it would be a big deal if Aruria lost its next in line to the monarchy. But I don't feel like I'm saving the princess. I'm just protecting Liza— the beautiful girl I've known since childhood. Saving the princess is just a bonus."

"You think I'm beautiful?"

I cleared my throat. "I mean, ya know. I'm pretty sure I told you already."

Her eyes stayed on me, and she tilted her head as a smile etched softly across her face. "Nope. I don't believe you have."

It suddenly felt impossible to hold her gaze. I tried to hide it by forcing a laugh through a wall of nerves. "Why are you staring like that?"

"Like what?" she leaned in, looking for my eyes again.

I looked at her, my focus drawing to her bottom lip as her teeth softly pressed against it. She leaned even closer, and I froze. Not sure of what to do next. What I was supposed to do next. But I didn't have to do anything. Her lips were already planted onto my left cheek. A cool tingle spread from my cheek down my throat and deep into my chest. And in one cooling breath, my smile overtook hers. She watched me, watching her, wishing that kiss could've held just a little longer.

She leaned her head against my chest and pulled my arm around her. I inhaled the sweet, flowery scent of her hair, and tightened my grip around her waist. I felt light. Like I was inhaling a warm cloud. I closed my eyes and inhaled again, deeper than before. The feeling was intoxicating.

"Your heartbeat is so strong," she said. "And fast."

"Oh," I said, "Sorry."

Sa'Sha giggled. "Don't be sorry. It's just an observation."

"Oh. Can I ask you something?"

"Mmhmm."

"What happened, when you tried to read Locke's mind?"

"It was strange."

"Strange how?"

"His mind felt empty. And when I tried digging deeper, I felt this creepy sensation. Like a warning not to push any harder. It was unsettling. He was unsettling." I couldn't exactly blame her for feeling that way. He was fatally mysterious, and it seemed like he, Ariel and Axel wanted to keep it that way.

Sa'Sha lifted her head. "I'm keeping you awake, aren't I?"

"No, you're fine," I said too quickly. "I mean, you don't have to go anywhere if you don't want to."

Sa'Sha giggled again. "Lie down." I did. She crawled over to the other side of my bed and nestled her head back on my chest. "I'm glad you're back."

"Yeah. Me too."

I don't know how long we laid there, before her breathing turned to a soft purring. But it all felt so...right. If anything, it made it harder not to think about how soft her lips felt against my cheek. The thought circled in my mind until I started drifting, only to hear her purr turn into a goofy snore.

I tried to stifle my laughter. But my chest shook so much, it startled Sa'Sha out of sleep. She sprang up with a confused look on her face.

"E?" she said.

"Yeah?"

"I fell asleep."

"Yeah."

"Sorry."

"Don't be."

She rubbed a hand over her face, before pushing to her feet. "I should head back to my room."

I watched her until her door slid shut, then turned out the lights and got back under my covers. But I wasn't sleepy. I only stared up at the ceiling through the darkness, inhaling what was left of Sa'Sha's scent. Somewhere in that mix, my mind went to Kurai. Then, to what Ariel said about my Aetharma. I couldn't imagine a way to defeat Kurai without the Aetharma. But what was supposed to be a stronger motivation than survival? Whatever the answer, I needed to figure it out soon. Otherwise, there was no way I could keep my promise to Sa'Sha.

[ELEMENT 2]
THE BOOK OF FACES

[1]

EXOL

SEREC

Fifteen unaccounted segments was plenty of time to raise questions. And that's exactly how my day started the moment I entered the Operations Center. Hachi broke from the Colonel, almost running to pull me into a tight hug.

"Sometimes, I swear you're working to give me a heart attack," he said.

"Is a heart attack even possible for someone like you?" I replied.

"When Raven told us you'd returned, a weight was lifted from all of us," the Colonel said. "Your old man was about to suit up to join the search himself." He patted my shoulder. "Luckily, the good news came before sundown."

"I appreciate the vote of confidence."

"K gave us a heads up on the guy you were tangling with. Nearly stopping Team Seven from exfiltrating Kunai isn't easily overlooked."

"Unfortunately, that wasn't my first encounter with him either."

"Which is why this conversation will continue upstairs with the other captains," Hachi said. "We should all have an understanding of what we're dealing with."

Within hashes, the Colonel and the other captains were gathered in Sa'Sha's office. Before I got into what happened with Kurai and Locke, I remembered I still had the vial Locke gave me. I pulled it out of my pocket and handed it to Kareen. "Locke said we'll find some answers after running some tests on whatever's in here."

"Then, it would've been nice to have the moment you returned," Kareen said, not bothering to hide her displeasure.

"Leave the kid alone," Northe said. "Nestled in the safety of your experimental tavern, you've clearly forgotten what it means to barely escape with your life."

Kareen glared at Northe, then started for the door. "Time is against us. So, I refuse to waste any more on you, when I could be acquiring answers." She shifted her attention to Hachi and the Colonel. "Back in a segment, gentlemen."

With everyone waiting for Kareen's results, I had ample time to explain what happened with Locke and his bodyguards after my encounter with Kurai.

"It seems it would be in our best interest to consider larger teams," Hachi said.

"I'm not so sure," I began. "Bigger teams would slow us down."

"We don't have enough information to determine the best way to counter Kurai's abilities. Consolidating task force operators ensures team safety."

"Perhaps," Sa'Sha said. "But wouldn't that solution prove temporary at best?"

"Exactly," I added. "We'll be at greater risk of being compromised, which defeats the whole purpose."

The look on Hachi's face was unlike any I'd ever seen from him; like he was examining me. But this felt different from his usual scrutiny. Unfortunately, Kareen returned before I could find out what it actually meant.

"Hope you're ready for some answers because we've got some juicy ones," Kareen announced strolling back in. The game board illuminated projecting a floating model of a molecule. "That chemical from Locke turned out to be Exolvunturine, better known as Exol." We all looked on patiently, waiting for Kareen to connect the dots. Kareen let out a disappointed sigh. "Exol is a theoretical chemical compound that, up until a few hashes ago, I believed to be impossible to synthesize. The fact that it exists means someone has developed some incredibly sophisticated machinery—and pumped a small fortune into research."

"I believe I've read about this," Sa'Sha began. "The wonder serum that could cure all disease."

"That would be it. Exol's effectiveness in fighting illness lies in its ability to alter genes. Doctors were hopeful it could be used to counter the effects of Plaga Viridi and Malachite's Consumption. Unfortunately, it looks like whoever Locke is dealing with has more nefarious applications in mind."

"Are you implying what I think you are?" Hachi asked.

"Anni and I will need to run some more tests but I think we finally have a solid hypothesis."

"And what would that be?" I asked.

"Exol is a key component in creating malefactors."

"So, whoever's buying Exol and using it to create malefactors has a lot of credits to throw around."

"Yup. Emphasis on *a lot*. More interesting is that only a select few companies have the necessary equipment to make use of Exol. So, this person is most likely using one of those companies—directly or indirectly—to accomplish this."

"Then, there must be a paper trail leading back to the company in question," Sa'Sha chimed. "Sentinel, I'll need you to look into it and develop a list of all possible companies." Ari nodded. "As for everyone else, make the most of your downtime. As Minerva and Sentinel uncover more details, I'm certain we'll have our hands full."

After a disappointingly short few segments of downtime—which I mostly spent in the training room trying to conquer Jump Protocol 6—Sa'Sha called us back to her office.

Since Northe and I were the last to arrive, Kareen wasted no time getting started the moment we stepped through the door.

"The malefactor blood and tissue samples all tested positive for Exol. I believe this provides sufficient evidence to support my theory. With a few additional tests, I can start separating conjecture from fact."

Sa'Sha turned to Ari. "Were we able to determine which companies require our attention on this matter?"

"My team and I have scoured the Arnet and Lazuria's Lanet for possible leads. Thus far however, no company seems to manufacture Exol as a complete compound."

"Does that suggest that there are companies currently producing incomplete compounds?" Sa'Sha asked.

"That it does. Our narrowed search has revealed two companies that each specialize in different components needed to produce Exol. Norsen Pharmaceuticals—based in Tertuze Province, Aruria—and Gerin Pharmaceuticals—based in Geringrad, Lazuria. Despite what should be an open and shut matter, I should mention that we failed to find any connection between the two companies. They don't seem to share interests or even serve a shared consumer base. In my humble opinion, we've arrived at a point where field investigations are more likely to fill the information gaps that digital exploitation cannot."

"It would seem the field is finally calling me back," Jin said, stepping forward. It was the most I'd ever heard him say. And his subtle enthusiasm seemed to shine through his normally solemn demeanor.

"You and me both," Mia said. "I haven't seen the homeland in a while, and I can speak *Lazy Tongue* better than anyone here."

Ari smirked and said what I could only assume was something in Lazurian. Mia gave him a devious look and answered in the same fashion, turning Ari's pale face as red as a PED siren.

Mia looked to Sa'Sha, her smile even wider. "Don't ask."

"Trust that with you, I know better," Sa'Sha said, then looked to Jin. "Quake, assemble a team of your choosing for Norsen."

"That suits me," Jin said.

"Ambi, you have Gerin."

"Already on it," Mia said, with a hint of excitement.

We all saluted and made our way out. "Serec," she called just before I reached the door.

"Yeah?"

"May I speak with you for a moment?"

I held until everyone was gone.

"What's going on?"

Her eyes trailed to her feet momentarily, but she seemed to force them to meet mine. "This is rather sudden, but I have a very important favor to ask of you."

[2]

NORSEN

NARYN

L eading up to my time in IGIS, I'd infiltrated over twenty facilities and relieved them of their valuable items. But I never believed I'd be asked to employ this desirable skill set by a legitimate organization. Especially considering no one in the organization knew I had said skill set. The idea of working with Jin and Shawin on an infiltration mission in Norsen Pharmaceuticals had me a bit on edge. Mostly because I worked alone. But also because the stakes were way higher this time around.

Fortunately— and I mean that in the most sarcastic way possible—my role was the temptress decoy to some fogey old security guard who really just wanted someone to listen to him yammer on about his stupid speed raeda. He probably hadn't attracted anyone with that hunk of metal since I was in diapers. What's worse, he actually had pictures of the antique rust bucket lining his desk! *Welcome to the past. Population: you!*

I don't know how I managed to hold out for Shawin's signal. But phase two was long overdue. Old man Rent-A-Ped was asking for my chainlink, to seal the deal. And there was only one way to handle that: excuse myself to the ladies' room, and never look back.

I found Shawin waiting for me just behind the 'Authorized Personnel Only' door.

"Here," he said, holding out a pale gray jumpsuit.

"A janitor's uniform?" I asked.

"Good guess."

As I slipped on the jumpsuit, I noticed Shawin ogling me like a nighthawk. "What?"

"I was taking note of how attractive you are, regardless of what you wear."

Heat flushed to my cheeks. "Great intention, terrible timing," I said, planting a kiss on his cheek.

"Ample motivation for me to finish this quickly."

My grin bloomed into a smile. "If you like it that much, maybe I'll wear it on our next date," I said, rubbing the lip gloss off his face with my thumb.

"For now, let's hope this mission gets a little more interesting. Where's Quake?"

"Close. Follow me."

We snuck along the labyrinth of faded gray hallways, until we came to an open area where two men in dark green uniforms were patrolling with multimag guns.

"Stay close," Shawin whispered as we crept through the shadows. At some point, Shawin stopped directly under a ceiling lumen and pressed his back up against the wall. His hand gently pressed my stomach, guiding me to follow his example. I flattened as much as possible, and held my breath. Voices and footsteps grew louder from one side of the intersecting hallway up ahead, and it sounded like they would reach us any moment.

Shawin kept his attention on what was coming, and I kept my attention on him. *Is he using his powers?* I could never tell in situations like these. And it always made me anxious. The footsteps echoed louder, and I pressed my back even harder against the wall.

The pressure of Shawin's hand eased, and he lightly patted my stomach. For whatever reason, it was enough to remind me to breathe. An instant later, the footsteps stuttered to a halt, and my breath caught again.

"You okay?" one voice asked.

"Yeah," another voice replied. "These clunky boots trip me up all the time. The Wardens said there'd be challenges to this calling. But I never thought footwear would be among them."

The footsteps started back up, and two men moved past the hallway—both too preoccupied to waste a glance in our direction. The tension in my stomach started to ease enough for oxygen to reach my lungs, when Shawin grabbed my arm and ran toward the end of the hallway.

As we ducked around the corner and planted ourselves in a dark spot, I heard voices coming from where we just were. And right after I noticed those voices another person, I hadn't even noticed was heading from the direction we were heading only to turn into the hallway we'd just hurried out of. In hardly any time at all, The mission had become far more dangerous than I'd expected.

"Interesting enough?" Shawin asked.

"A bit more than I'd like actually. Think you could have a few guards take a break?"

After a few rounds of hiding and sprinting past mystery doors and security guards, we reached a ladder that led into the ventilation system. We crawled through two rooms of cramped winding darkness before finally reaching Jin. He was lying stomach-down, opposite a steel grate. The faded blue light that filtered up through the slants seemed to accent the hardness in his stony features.

"Good work with the security guard," he said softly.

Aside from our mission orders, this was the second time Jin—the man of few words—had ever spoken to me. Maybe that's why such a large smile overtook my face. "No worries."

He pointed down at the console in front of several large black towers.

"That console is our way into their network. Guards are posted outside and the floor is pressure sensitive. After Prophet and I lower you down, plug this device into the console data port." My mind went to work, trying to determine a better way to execute the plan but I was at a loss. I couldn't use my powers because fluctuations in gravity could set off the pressure sensitive flooring—even if I was on the ceiling. He presented a small data stick the size of my thumbnail and everything came into focus.

"I'd go down but I doubt you can support my weight." He placed the data stick in my hand. "When the red light on it flashes, remove it and we'll pull you up."

My heart was pounding so hard as I slipped into the harness, I almost couldn't hear my thoughts. Not that I really wanted to hear, *"No pressure. This is crazy. But no pressure"* on repeat anyway. Just saying.

Jin carefully tore the metal grate from its hinges, in much the same way I tear a sheet of paper. I activated my HOOD and carefully lowered myself through the opening. I froze halfway down, but Shawin placed a hand on my head to pull my attention. I looked up at him and followed as his free hand joined the hand that was holding my rope. And opposite him, Jin had a vice grip on the slack. I took a deep breath and lifted my arms straight up, only to realize that I wasn't even holding myself up. Shawin nodded, and they lowered me until I dangled in front of the console. The harness dug into my stomach, restricting my breathing. I plugged the device into the console, then shifted my attention back and forth between the connector device and the guards for what felt like an eternity. Five or so of the slowest hashes of my life later, the small red light was finally flashing. A small wave of relief lapped against my consciousness as I removed the device and glanced at the guards one more time.

I gave a light tug at the rope and it dug into my waist as I slowly ascended. *This actually worked.* Famous last words. Suddenly, the door to the room blew open and guards rushed in. Too bad for them that I'd already been pulled into the ventilation shaft. As I watched them clear the room, an eerie sense of nostalgia crept into my mind. I always, told myself I hated performing those "jobs". But maybe I just hated my anonymous employers. Feelings aside, this was something I was good at — something that felt natural. I just hoped the allure of this special brand of thievery wasn't starting to get the better of me.

[3]

DRIVE

SEREC

"I'm not sure how to ask you this so I'm just going to do it," Sa'Sha said bringing her eyes to mine. "Will you be my date for the Winter Jubilee?"

Her words hit like a speeding cargo raeda sparking a myriad of thoughts and emotions in a single beat. Sa'Sha must have noticed, because the apprehension on her face gave way to giddy laughter. A laughter that accompanied me into the next morning as I tried to dissect her intentions.

"Even with Shawin's powers, I couldn't have seen something like that coming," I said staring into my mirror as if it had all the answers. "I mean, I've wanted to ask Sa'Sha on a date for probably like an anum now. Our recons have been fun. But missions and pretend-dates don't exactly require a mutual attraction or anything. Plus, having a childhood friend—whom I already had feelings for—blossom into one of the prettiest girls on Orbis super complicates things. If we cross that friend barrier and things don't work out, where would that leave us?

"But she's more calculated about things like this than me. So, maybe she believes we'll find a way to work things out if we do become more than friends. Or maybe I'm overthinking this whole thing. I mean, she's never shown any strong interest before. So, why now? Ahh, this is too much!" My mirror self remained silent, which was probably for the best.

A knock at my door jolted me out of my thoughts. "Are you okay in there, E?" Sa'Sha called through the door.

"Y-yeah, I'm fine," I replied, starting to panic at the realization, that she might've been able to hear what I was saying.

"Are you coming to breakfast?"

"No. I'll just meet you at the briefing." In all honesty, I was hungry. But I couldn't face her immediately after my minor meltdown; especially when she may have heard some of it.

"Oh," she said with a short pause. "Okay. See you at the briefing then."

As usual, Northe and I were the last to walk into Sa'Sha's office. Sa'Sha was sitting on the edge of her desk and discussing something with NaRyn and Kareen. But she noticed as soon as I entered and offered a polite smile. I nodded, but was still a little too embarrassed to maintain eye contact.

"Getting right to it," Ari said, "The data we extracted from both companies shows supply ledgers consistent with your average pharmaceutical company. But when we turned our focus to their suppliers, we stumbled upon an interesting commonality that only these two companies seem to share."

"Which is?" Sa'Sha asked.

"Transaction records connecting each to a pharmaceutical depot centralized in Oltresulle."

"Theall Medical Corp," Mia said. "I worked it out of one of the guards at Gerin."

"But how would a simple guard know?" Sa'Sha asked.

"He wasn't a simple guard. Apparently, Theall plants guards from their own personal unit among the ranks of both Norsen and Gerin's normal security. It's their way of ensuring no incriminating information leaks out from under their noses," Mia said.

"Now that we're clear on that," Kareen interrupted, "let's refocus on the fact that Exol should not exist considering the tech required to produce it. We've gone through it a few times now, but Anni and I can't seem to form a connection between the mundane equipment Norsen and Gerin possess and the synthesis of Exol."

In the silence that followed, a fuzziness welled in my throat, snowballing into an embarrassingly loud cough. "Sorry," I said. "Had trouble sleeping, so my throat's a little fuzzy today. Gonna have to grab some cough chews after this."

"MedFac has plenty of it," Kareen said, waving a hand dismissively.

I shook my head. "*Coughs Away* is the only brand that works for me and doesn't taste like rotten sweet chews."

Kareen groaned. "You sound like some stupid ad. There's no difference between that trash and any other..." she paused, eyes widening. "That's it! Zero, you're a genius."

"I am?"

"Figuratively speaking. The point is, *Coughs Away* is produced by Theall Medical Corp." I nodded blankly, which I can only assume didn't sit well with Kareen, since she turned her focus to the half of the room that didn't include me. "Theall lists the exact same ingredients as the other companies, but their products are widely speculated to be more effective. This is one of the reasons, Theall is on the very short list of companies that can sell their products internationally. At one point, they were even investigated for either intentionally omitting ingredients or falsely listing what was in some of their products. But the courts ruled in their favor, agreeing that companies had the right to maintain secrecy of their proprietary blending process."

Most everyone else took on the same blank look that I had.

"A company's ingredient cultivation process is considered a trade secret. As it stands, corporate law within the Three Great Nations generally favors protecting trade secrets. And Theall has no shortage of them after having bought out countless smaller companies to integrate new proprietary processes, until they could come up with a means of increasing medicinal potency far better than anyone else in their market."

"Assuming your theory is correct," Sa'Sha said, "would you be able to emulate their process and reproduce Exol?" Sa'Sha asked.

"The greatest obstacle to producing Exol is creating a solution potent and stable enough for practical application," Anni chimed.

"Precisely. The vial Locke gave us was plenty stable. But Anni and I still have the mystery of potency. Give us a couple days with this. Even great genius requires time."

"Take all the time you need. I don't expect we'll need it too soon, since we'll have our hands full with our new target. Right, Sentinel?" Sa'Sha asked.

Ari smirked; his thumbs already tapping his digipad like little lightning bolts. "My team will have a thorough report of Theall Medical Corporation in no time."

"I'd expect nothing less. Dismissed. Zero, may I have a word?"

The morning's embarrassment—that had almost faded from memory—came rushing back. "Uh, yeah," I said. "Sure."

Once everyone left the room, she closed the distance between us.

"You look tired. Ever since your time with Locke, your mind has been elsewhere."

"I could say the same about you."

She sighed. "To be honest, the Winter Jubilee has me a little frazzled. But it's nothing I can't handle."

"Worried I'll cause an international incident by using the wrong spoon?"

She chuckled, not realizing I was half serious.

"Nothing like that. I just—have too much going on to worry about you right now."

"Then don't. I'm smooth."

She watched me like she was expecting to catch me in a lie. And I began to feel the need to raise my defenses. I knew she meant well, but with Kurai, Locke, Astaroth, and who knows how many SOL minions roaming around, there wasn't much Sa'Sha could say to turn me from my path. "Would you tell me if you weren't?"

"Yep."

"I'm serious, E. Rank aside, we're still partners. Or have you forgotten that?"

"Actually, I haven't forgotten. Maybe that's why I trust you when you say you can handle it. I mean, partners are supposed to trust each other, right?"

The fire in Sa'Sha's eyes told me she was about to make me regret those words. But surprisingly, she abruptly extinguished the flame, her eyes falling to the floor as she brushed past me.

"Whatever you're afraid of. Whoever you're afraid of you need to get that fear under control. You promised Surket you would trust me. It's time you started honoring your word."

Before I could respond, she was gone. Leaving me with the shame her words uncovered. "Didn't you already train earlier, Rec Rec?" NaRyn said.

"Yeah," I said. "Got a couple moves I need to work on."

"You train more than you sleep. You're gonna wear yourself out."

"Don't worry, Ryn Ryn. I'm smooth."

"You said you were tired at the briefing, right? Why not rest for the day?"

"Seriously, I'm good."

"Shawin and I were thinking about watching a vid. Right, Shawin?"

"We were," Shawin said, approaching from the other end of the hallway. "Would you like to join us, Serec?"

"Maybe after I'm done training."

"Shawin," NaRyn said, "tell Serec he's pushing himself too hard. He thinks I'm just worrying for nothing."

"Actually," Shawin said, "Didn't you mention having a cough due to lack of sleep?"

"Does everyone pay this much attention to everything that happens in a briefing?"

"Bear in mind that overtraining can be counterproductive. Potentially, even more so than not training at all."

"You're right. I'll keep it short, okay? Really. And then I'll either come join you guys for the vid, or I'll take a nap. Smooth?" I hurried into the training room, before the uncertainty on their faces could fuel them into a longer debate.

Even if they were making a valid point, Axel, Ariel, and Kurai had all made their counterpoints painfully clear. Taking a break from training was a luxury I couldn't afford.

My stamina couldn't hold out for long using multiple abilities at once. I may as well have been sprinting at full speed or swimming against a riptide. Then, there was the matter of evoking my aetharma at will. I needed to get a better handle on it all if I wanted a chance at closing the gap between me and the stronger refractors I'd come across in recent decs.

Okay. Start slow.

I extended my arm and — with a sharp exhale — I willed the air from my breath into a small, swirling force centered over my palm. Once my breathing steadied, I focused the electrical currents flowing around me, until they condensed into small sparks encircling my other hand.

My breathing was already starting to feel more labored. But, as long as my breath remained deep and steady, I could handle it. I hardened the skin along my back and the outside of my arms until it became a thin layer of stone. The air in my lungs felt like it was under triple gravity. But I couldn't let that stop me just yet. I had to push for a fourth.

A small boost of energy flowed deep into my ears, and within a few beats, I could hear the electricity flowing through the building as clearly as I could hear my accelerated pulse.

The air was simultaneously growing thinner and heavier by the beat. But I had to push a little more — if only for a few more beats. I took a deeper breath and kicked into a slow, steady jog. A few dips and side steps were all I could manage to work into my movements. And even then, I nearly lost my footing every few steps. Sweat was starting to bead all over and my body began to feel like an oven on preheat.

Not twenty hashes in, my body was drenched in sweat, and dizziness started to overtake me. With a sudden exhale, I let my stone skin fall away as everything suddenly sounded muffled. I hunkered into place, my knees slightly bent, as I willed my lungs to fill with oxygen. By the time my mind was alert enough to properly move my body, I realized the elements in my hands had all but faded from existence.

I released my hold and plopped onto the floor, exhausted and feeling like my entire head was still tingling.

"Your vital signs are creeping out of your acceptable range. I recommend temporarily suspending training," Anni suddenly chimed.

"Not you too Anni," I huffed softly, more discouraged than angry.

With my energy fading fast, and the pool of sweat expanding under me, I could've called it on any more training for the day. But just as the thought crossed my mind, so did Ariel's words about my Aetharma.

"Evoke with an emotion other than fear," I thought aloud. "But what's a stronger emotion than fear?" I paused to consider the options. "Maybe she meant anger. Or even..."

"Here you are," Sa'Sha said, walking in with a plate in her hands. "Kareen has some new information for us. Meeting is in a segment."

"Okay," I said, pushing to my feet.

"Are you hungry? I brought food."

"Oh, you didn't have to do that."

"It's fine. If you like, we can eat in your room before the meeting?"

I shook my head. "It's smooth. Don't let me slow you down. I'm just going to clean up and grab a nap. Thanks though."

"Of course," she said, voice soft, almost...nervous. Her voice projected a subtle pain I couldn't understand but knew I was responsible for. The thought drained what remained of my energy. "See you at the meeting," she said.

"Liza wait." But she was already gone. Another opportunity to make things right with her, gone in an instant.

The sun was on its last leg, when I stepped outside, offering little respite from the chill of the wind. A chill that matched the coldness plaguing my heart and mind. I attempted to sleep after training, but my exchanges with Sa'Sha weighed on my conscience, robbing me of the peace needed for a restful sleep.

I could tell I was — yet again — the final person to arrive, as Kareen started the beat my face made it past Sa'Sha's office door.

"It's unstable," she said, referring to the small sealed vial in her hand. "But the molecular structure is comparable to that of the solution Alex Locke provided."

"Can it be stabilized without the same pharmaceutical equipment?" Sa'Sha asked.

"Unlikely. And the machinery — as you can imagine — is costly; even for most large companies."

"In other words, we finally have sufficient reason to investigate Theall Medical Corporation."

[4]

THEALL

SEREC

"How many agents do we have in 224 now?" I asked.

"Are you asking for sake of small talk?" Sa'Sha said.

"Not exactly."

She cocked her head to one side. "Then why are you asking?"

"Curiosity."

"Just shy of two hundred," Sa'Sha said. "Anything else?"

"Any idea how many of them are trained for recon missions?"

"No."

I nodded. "Has the Director ever gone on field missions?"

Sa'Sha shrugged. "I wouldn't know."

"Were you aware that I don't like recon missions?"

"You're point being?"

I crossed my arms and mirrored her expression. "Guess I am just making small talk."

I could feel Sa'Sha's eyes on me, even as I lowered my gaze. But I couldn't think of anything else to say, so I held my focus on my shoes as if I'd found something interesting there.

"I don't believe I've told you the story of my great grandfather," she said.

"Charlemagne Martinel V?"

A wry smile crept across her face. "He's referred to in the histories as Charlemagne the Timid. But this is a gross understatement. My great great grandfather, Charlemagne the Bold, passed away during the Third Great War, and his son took the throne. Divinus Martinel IV was known for his tenacity and fearlessness on the battlefield—often placing himself on the front lines to fight alongside his men. He was idolized for both his bravery and his innate ability to bolster morale.

His battle prowess was of such caliber that it seemed Lazuria couldn't produce a force great enough to contend with his indomitable will. And when he passed, Aruria's Great Houses expected to witness a similar performance from the new monarch. But, my great grandfather was nothing like his father." Sa'Sha's eyes intensified. "He was the kind of man who hid in his palace and threw lavish parties; drinking himself into a stupor, while men fought and died in his name. Would you believe he never once attended a war council meeting?"

"But, didn't he end the war?"

Sa'Sha's eyes narrowed. "By no merit of his own. We lost every bit of ground we'd fought countless battles to gain. Lazurian forces were within days of reaching Callastryne, and with the walls closing in on him, Divinus Martinel V went behind the backs of the other houses, petitioning his ambassadors to negotiate a peace treaty with Geringrad. The fruits of that treaty remain to this very day. Closed international borders, geopolitical tension, and a cold war that's lasted nearly sixty anums. Selfishness and poor leadership ultimately led to our defeat. Tens of thousands of soldiers bled and died defending a coward who couldn't have been more eager to surrender."

Sa'Sha's fists clenched as blood rushed to her face. I hesitated, searching for an appropriate response. I didn't know if it was one of those moments where I was supposed to hug her or say something to show I understood how she felt. In the end, I settled on something neutral. "Can't imagine that making it into history books."

"History is shaped by those in power. And those in power have a responsibility to everyone under them. Rulers, commanders, even team leaders. We must always be ready to fight for and alongside our subordinates." Sa'Sha's eyes found mine, and her expression softened a little. "Sometimes that means going on *boring* recon missions."

It was enough to pull my lips into a smirk. "And here I thought the mission would be what bored me to sleep."

She rolled her eyes and turned away from me. But not so much that I couldn't see the smile that followed. "You seem to be feeling better. I'll take that as proof that you followed our advice on getting to bed at a decent time. I wish it wouldn't have been such a struggle though." Her subtle smile thinly veiled the pain behind her eyes. A pain that put knots in my stomach.

"Look Liza, I know I've been pretty focused since I got back. It's just, Locke made it painfully clear that we're not prepared for the storm to come. I intend to change that."

Sa'Sha raised an eyebrow. "Alone?"

"No. I know you and the others were just concerned about me. And I'm sorry for... you know."

"It's alright E. I understand your concerns. Just remember that there are other people on this team."

The lift opened and we stepped out into an underground parking garage. "*I've never been to this drop point,*" I thought to Sa'Sha.

"I wouldn't expect otherwise. We don't exactly frequent Oltresulle."

My eyes widened. *"We're in Oltresulle? Seriously?!"*

"Why else would we have spent two segments on the terrarail?"

"How would I know? I mean, I knew the ride was taking longer than usual, but I didn't realize it was that long. On that note, why are you always so sarcastic when you're in my head?" Sa'Sha didn't reply, but the twitch at the corner of her mouth said plenty.

Sa'Sha whistled, and a double-beep drew my eyes to the sleek, white luxury raeda up ahead. Sa'Sha went for the passenger door, while I found myself gawking longer than I care to admit. Like most of the Guild's vehicles, the raeda had a mix of luxurious and practical features: cream-colored leather interior, multi-media surround system, heads up display, and ballistic glass for those unpredictable scenarios.

I hopped into the driver's seat and pressed the start button. The engines gave a low hum as we began to hover and I couldn't help feeling like a kid with a new toy. I eased out onto the road, and then, floored the accelerator. Sa'Sha didn't say a word. She was too preoccupied with scouring the audio streams for the perfect channel. And when she found it, I knew I was in for the kind of long ride no raeda was fast enough to outrun.

"What is this?" I asked, noting the upbeat song.

"The fact that you have to ask makes me feel you should lose about ten smooth points," she replied.

"If you're in charge of awarding smooth points, you can take 'em all."

Sa'Sha jabbed a finger into my side. "Quiet you."

"May not want to mess with me while I'm driving. Especially since I'm pushing eighty."

"Good point. I'll save it for when we hit our next checkpoint. Oltresulle is riddled with them."

I'd hoped her last statement was part of her joke. Turns out it wasn't. We seemed to stop every ten hashes for another checkpoint. But Mia and Kareen had thought ahead, providing us with two valuable tools. The fake persona cards Mia made us were so indistinguishable from the real thing, I worried we would get detained for them being *too* good. Kareen's contribution was even more astounding. I looked over to Sa'Sha after the sixth checkpoint. Except it wasn't her. Kareen had pushed an experimental update to our hoods that projected a thin mask over our faces. The Facial Alteration Intelligence Construct or FAIC allowed us to conceal our identities without looking too suspicious. As far as anyone in Oltresulle knew, we were reps for an Arurian investor — looking to throw an astronomical amount of credits behind Theall Medical Corporation. It was enough to get us past a lot of doors, right through the front door of Theall Medical HQ.

The vice president Athan Karles met us in the lobby. A balding man in his late 40s, with thick eyebrows and an even thicker mustache, Karles looked like age was exacting a hefty tax on him. That didn't seem to stop him from going right to work bombarding us with everything there was to know about how Theall was the best and only real choice for everyone's medical and pharmaceutical needs. He even threw in a history lesson on how the first pharmaceutical company got started. Between Sa'Sha's taste in music and Karles' encyclopedic sales pitches, I could feel my brain turning to low-grade mush.

But the tour did allow me the chance to find patterns in the building's huge layout.

When Karles finally stopped talking long enough for questions, Sa'Sha jumped at the opportunity. "When do you expect the president to return?" she asked.

"Unfortunately, Mr. Rhasatto's busy schedule is extremely difficult to predict."

"Are we to assume that you would have no inclination whatsoever as to where the head of your company is at this time?"

Karles smiled uncomfortably. "Our president has done an impeccable job of coordinating things in a way that enables us to function nearly as flawlessly in his absence as we can in his company. But if memory serves me, there was mention of charity work at one of the orphanages in Araman."

"That's rather philanthropic of him." *More like convenient.* "When will he be returning? Our employer would love to meet him to personally close this transaction."

"He should return some time in the next few days. But again, under my close watch, things have progressed smoothly. So, please inform your employer that I would be more than happy to meet with him in Mr. Rhasatto's stead."

"I'm sure he'd be thrilled to hear all the same stories you told us today," I said, actually trying to hide my sarcasm. But that still earned me an elbow to the ribs while Karles wasn't looking.

"Thank you," Sa'Sha said, gripping his wrist. "We will be in touch."

Once we were back in the raeda, I let out the yawn I'd been holding for the last segment. "How can he live with himself, knowing that he's the most boring man in Oltresulle?"

"You didn't have to be so obvious about the fact that you didn't care."

I shrugged. "Sorry for trying to get on with the mission, before the sun goes down. Which it did."

"Our mission can't even start until the sun goes down." I yawned again and she chopped me in the stomach. "Hurry up so we can get changed."

I pulled out of the nearly empty lot and parked in a quiet, secluded area. We slipped on our stealth gear which was a modified version of our combat uniforms. As the name implied, they were better suited for sneaking missions like this.

"There are still a few employees left in the building. They have quite a few security personnel patrolling as well." Sa'Sha reported as her ash gray eyes scanned the building.

"And the security system?"

She blinked slowly and her eyelids fluttered a bit before revealing deep ruby red eyes. "It's far more sophisticated than I expected. I might have to—got it. The detection system is down but the window of time is small, so we'll need to move quickly."

"You're getting pretty good at this," I noted, remembering our issues with the security system on Kunai.

"You're not the only one who has been honing their skills," she said, moving toward the building.

We snuck through the loading dock and up to the seventh floor, where Sa'Sha picked the lock to the restricted access area and technopathed us past two more high-security doors. When we made it to Theall's central processor room, we spotted two guards, roaming around inside. *"Body armor and multimag guns? Seems like overkill dontcha think?"* I commented.

"Agreed. Whatever is on that network clearly points to something more than just drugs and medical supplies"

We waited for just the right moment, then Sa'Sha deactivated the electronic lock and we scrambled inside.

The guards hardly realized what was happening before two knife hand chops convinced them it was time for a nap. The two processor technicians, hunching over their large workstations were even slower to act. Sa'Sha ran a finger across the back of their neck and whispered "goodnight" before they fell back in their chairs. Sa'Sha plugged in the device Kareen had given us and connected her mind to the corporate mainframe. She began typing furiously while I watched the door. We should've been in and out in a hash or two, but she seemed to be taking longer than usual to break into the system.

"What's taking so long?" She didn't respond. I started to ask again, when her voice popped in my head.

"I've never seen this cyber defense suite before. It's custom, far more security than I was anticipating."

"How long will that take?"

"Longer than I'd like. I'm not sure who built this system, but it's making the entry process slow going even with my powers. Just, give me another hash."

But we didn't have another hash. Another guard was on the other side of the door and heading our way. I ducked down and put my back to the wall, finally realizing I hadn't moved the guards or the technicians that were in plain sight. Sa'Sha looked over at me, and I motioned for her to keep working.

The guard must've seen the bodies, because he rushed in, gun drawn. I waited for him to enter, and slipped my arm around his neck. I tightened, and after a few beats, he stopped fighting. I lowered him softly, and moved him and everyone else over against the wall.

"I'm in!" Sa'Sha thought.

"Bout time."

Her lips pressed tightly together and for a moment, I thought I saw her eyes roll under her HOOD. *"This is weird. Some corporation, calling itself the*

Humanity Omega Foundation, had a recent transaction with Theall Medical Corporation for an unspecified item. But it looks like—"

"Alpha team, what's your status?" a half-muffled voice called through static. It was coming from one of the guard's communicator. "Alpha team, do you read me? Come in Alpha team."

I looked over at Sa'Sha. "I need two hashes," she said, leaning closer toward the screen. I wanted to tell her we didn't have two hashes. But it was too late. We couldn't leave empty-handed and arguing would only take up more valuable time.

I peeked down the hallway, through the door window. More guards were coming, and I could take them all out without being seen. I'd need to disable them as quickly and quietly as possible. And I needed to do it away from Sa'Sha.

The muscles in my legs tensed and I paused, focusing intently on the clamor of footsteps. Ready to jump out the instant they were close. But all of a sudden, the steps went quiet. I couldn't make out anything over the hum of the processors and my heartbeat. I swallowed at the dryness forming in my throat, my mind racing to anticipate what would happen.

Suddenly, the footsteps started back up and I crouched behind the door, ready to make whichever guard was in front regret it. But the sound of footsteps quickly faded into the background. I peeked around the door to see that all the guards were gone.

What's going on? Why would they all just up and turn back? I had all of two beats to think about it before an ominous feeling sparked so strongly in my mind, it made me jump. A vision of large dark eyes flashed in front of me, and fear-bumps prickled all along my arms. Something was coming for us.

I looked around the room, blinking with wild eyes. I turned and peeked out the door again. *What am I sensing?*

"What's wrong, E?" Sa'Sha asked.

I looked at Sa'Sha. *"We need to go. Now."*

She looked up for all of a beat, before panic formed on her face too. "Some-thing's coming?" I nodded. *"I need fifteen more beats."*

Sa'Sha glued herself to the screen, focusing more intensely on what she was doing.

I peeked out the door again, hoping we could afford another fifteen beats.

My heart was beating so heavy and fast, I could literally feel the sound pulsing through my eardrums as my eyes shifted quickly between Sa'Sha and the hallway.

"Come on Liza!"

"Done!"

She finally stopped typing and pulled out the device. Then, as if I hadn't just warned of the impending danger, she placed a hand over the processor and bowed her head. *"What are you doing?!"*

"Erasing traces of tampering," her thought was forceful. "They'll know we were here, but they can't know why."

There was no point in arguing with her. Mostly, because she was right. Evidence of a break-in was inevitable at this point. But the least we could do was cover our tracks. Still, every beat felt like time was taking its sweet time. And it's was giving my fearbumps fearbumps.

"Okay," Sa'Sha finally said, jumping to her feet.

I double-checked the hallway, then we hurried down the stairwell. Four flights down, our chances of escape were looking a lot less chancy, and hope welled in place of the anxiety. At least, until we reached the door to the second floor.

Just as I went for the handle, a sense of danger tightened in my chest, and I froze.

"What's wrong?" Sa'Sha asked.

"We should go back."

"What?"

"The third floor," I said, grabbing her arm and starting back up the stairs. She tried to ask why, but I pulled her arm harder, forcing her to stay close behind me. Just as I opened the door to the third floor, the second-floor door swung open with a clang and a clatter of footsteps.

I raced down the hallway, peering to the point up ahead where the path cut into a sharp curve. I stopped at the center hallway and looked back down the way we'd just come. "Where is it?" I thought out loud.

"Where's what?"

"The emergency exit. Every floor should have one between the stairs and the center hallway, but it's not here."

"If you had been paying attention, you would have heard when Mr. Karles told us that due to an accident a few decs back, they had to seal off the doorway to the third floor emergency exit." *Just my luck.* The door at the stairwell squeaked open and we ran down the center hallway.

"So, where's the new door?" I said as low as I could.

"I didn't ask."

"*You* didn't ask? The only other person I know who plans for everything?"

If they found out we were here, it would defeat the whole purpose. The guards and technicians would wake up soon, with little to go on. But we couldn't afford anyone finding out what we were looking for.

"Not to unsettle you, but the intruder detection system should be coming back online any moment now" Sa'Sha added.

We hurried down the hallway, until it split in two directions. We turned and ran until the hallway opened into a large lobby. I didn't know where I was going. But I ran anyway. At the other end of the lobby was another hallway that forked left. I stopped for a beat, feeling indecisive at the worst possible time.

"They're coming," Sa'Sha whispered forcefully. Footsteps clamored quickly through the lobby. There wasn't any more time to second-guess.

I took the left pathway and ran until it ended and bent right. At the far end of the pathway was another emergency exit. "There it is," I said, picking up the pace.

I jammed the door open and let Sa'Sha run past me. The moment she did, a large man appeared from around the last corner we'd sprinted down. I froze, not knowing what to do. The man didn't move. He just stood there watching me, looking too calm. I forfeited the staring contest and powered down the stairs like an obstacle course, only a few steps behind Sa'Sha. Just as we made it to the ground floor, an alarm sounded. We sprinted to the raeda and sped off into the darkness.

"How did you know someone was after us?" Sa'Sha asked, between breaths.

"Don't know," I said. "But I can count the number of people who gave me that feeling on one hand."

"Who gave you that feeling?"

I hesitated. "Locke for one."

"And...?"

"It doesn't matter. What's important is that we were spotted. At least, I was."

"How do you know?"

"When you ran past me, I saw someone standing at the end of the hallway, watching."

"What did they look like?"

"A tall guy. I couldn't see his face all that well. But he had this resigned look, almost like he'd given up on trying to catch us."

Sa'Sha got quiet for a beat. "Why would he give up so quickly?"

"I'm just saying that's the feeling I got from him. Maybe he didn't know if we'd taken anything. Just because you see someone running away doesn't mean they took something."

"Somehow I doubt most people would remain so optimistic if they were the potential victim. What was he wearing?"

"I don't know. A suit I guess."

"What kind of suit?"

"I don't know," I said a little louder. "What does that have to do with anything?"

I could feel Sa'Sha's eyes scrutinizing me, but I pretended to be too focused on driving to notice.

Sa'Sha plugged the device into a small port in front of her. She pulled out her timechain and called Kareen to make sure she was ready to extract the information as it was uploading into the Guild database.

It wasn't long before I felt Sa'Sha watching me again.

"Can I help you?"

"It's nothing," she said.

It wasn't nothing. We both knew that. But something told me if she wasn't in the mood to share, the last thing I should be doing was probing further. I went for the audio stream.

Sa'Sha stopped me. "I'm a little tired," she said. "Do you mind if we just enjoy the quiet for now?"

I expected segments of quiet to fall somewhere between boring and awkward. Especially, since I could feel her staring at me every few hashes. But I spent half the time in my own head about what was giving me such a bad feeling back at Theall. I wondered if there was someone else out there like Kurai. Someone else who could make me look like a joke in a fight. I sure hoped not, because I absolutely hated that feeling, and I could only get stronger so much faster.

The terrarail arrived at HQ, and my mind was already in the training area waiting for my body to catch up. But before I could even make it back to D7, an alert hit our TABs. Sa'Sha read it. "Malefactors in the shopping district," she said. "Let's get to the launchpad,"

"Right," I assented, already in the mood for a good warm-up.

By the time we reached the pad, Northe, Shawin, and NaRyn were already waiting for us, clad in combat gear. "And here I thought you two were gonna miss all the fun." Northe remarked, handing Sa'Sha Nightfall. "You know us, we like to keep the suspense high." I said as we boarded the Nighthawk. The engines screamed and before long, we were dropping into the shopping district.

I ran past people screaming and running in every direction. Seeing the victims—lying helplessly in pools of their own blood—didn't give me the urge to run. It gave me the urge to vomit, to cry, to send every last one of those abominations screaming to Hadal. The cold determination on Sa'Sha's face told me she felt the same way. She was trembling on the outside about as much as I was on the inside. The stench of blood mingled with the aromas from the food and perfume shops producing something nauseating. It was the first time we'd seen malefactors attack victims up close, and it felt like a warzone. The kind that made something as simple as walking hard to remember. Bile pushed up the back of my throat and I struggled to swallow it back before it reached my mouth.

"Lift, Prophet, you're with me. We need to clear the monsters out of this area and treat casualties. Zero, you and K try to find where they are coming from," Sa'Sha said, sounding like she was working to find her courage. I nodded and hurried toward the center of the shopping district, still trying to find mine.

If medics were on the way, they would need the area cleared of danger, which meant I had to work fast. Just as importantly, I couldn't just leave those monsters to act as they pleased or it would only be a matter of time before the number of casualties rose. The squeamish feeling in my gut turned to fire and my jaw clenched tight as the heat spread to my face. The first one I saw was biting into the arm of one of the mannequins from a clothing store. The muscles in my face went tight and I charged over and punched the creature so hard it squealed and tried to run. But I wasn't about to let it continue its bloodbath. I chased it down, kicking and punching it until there was no air left in its vicious body.

More appeared, and one after another, I tackled, punched, and blasted them with extreme prejudice. There couldn't have been any more than twenty or so, so the fight was over pretty quick—a testament to how hard I'd been training. But, the threat was far from handled. Two guys in familiar green hooded jackets approached, looking completely unfazed by the chaos around them.

"Who are you and what do you want?" I asked.

"I'm sure you remember me," one of them said. He pulled back his hood and I immediately recognized him. Renes. "I brought my buddy, Xaster along this time." The other guy removed his hood. "I think he wants to say hey."

I took a step, and Xaster disappeared before my heel could reach the ground. I stopped in surprise, and half a beat later, he was right in front of me. My head jerked violently, and I stumbled back, almost falling.

I found my balance and took a swing at where Xaster should've been, but he was already back standing next to Renes. "Greetings," Xaster said with a cheeky smile.

I'd been anxious to test myself against an actual person anyway. I figured Xaster and Renes would be a great place to start. I enhanced my eyes, legs, and arms. "Let's see who's faster," I called back.

Xaster looked like he was ready to take me up on the offer, but Renes wasn't quite as anxious to let me get close. I started at them, and a wave of explosions suddenly fired off in front of me. If I were any slower, I would've gotten caught in the blasts. But my eyes were as fast as my feet. I changed direction, and started into a wide circle. But another flash of light exploded in front of me. I twisted my body low and changed direction again, but everywhere I ran, another explosion erupted, until a ring of bright light, hot gas, and heavy wind surrounded me.

Maybe if I jump high enough, I can clear the area. I bent low and swung my arms back for momentum, when something plowed into me from the side, and I tumbled uncontrollably. Clutching my ribs, I looked up to find Xaster standing just out of arm's reach. *He's really asking for it.* I sprang to my feet and lunged at him. But he was too quick. He literally ran circles around me and my eyes were the only thing that could keep up—barely.

A one-on-one would be different. But facing them together was more than I could handle by myself. And that irritated me enough to try anyway. I charged at Renes as fast as I could, keeping Xaster in my peripheral. Renes had his guard up, expecting a head-on attack. But I didn't give him one. I cut left, keeping my head turned to him, then cut right for an attack from the side. I glanced out of the corner of my eye, and saw Xaster starting to move. He figured out what I was going for, and was moving to stop me. But he was wrong.

As my foot hit the ground, I twisted around and took a heavy swing where Xaster should've been. But my attack was too early, and I only grazed his chin. He stumbled back as I stumbled forward, fighting to regain the footing to follow up before he could move. He tried to twist away, when a devious spark flashed behind him. He seized up and fell to his knees.

Mia emerged from behind him. "And here I thought we were friends. All this excitement and no one bothers to invite me," a creepy smile covered her face.

"No need. We knew you'd crash the party anyway," I smiled back.

Xaster struggled to his feet, and I moved to stop him, when a light flashed between Mia and me, and I dove into her before it could hit us. A small explosion popped just over head with a boom. I looked over my shoulder at Renes, who had his arms extended at us. His face was straining as his arms lowered to his sides.

"Not so easy, when gravity hits. Is it?" NaRyn called out, walking up behind Renes.

Renes looked over his shoulder at her, and smirked. I knew what that look meant, and it wasn't good. A spark of light formed behind NaRyn's head. "Behind you!" I yelled, lunging toward her. The heat was so intense, I felt it throughout my entire body. I wasn't going to make it in time.

But before the ball of fire could take form, Shawin appeared and knocked Renes to the ground. The light vanished, leaving Renes at the mercy of NaRyn and Shawin. His eyes almost glowed hot as he glared down at Renes. And just as Renes tried to move, Shawin kicked his chest. Renes' violet eyes went so wide as he reeled in pain, and a warmth grew in my throat. *I knew there was a reason I liked Shawin.*

I turned to look for Xaster, but he was gone. "Where'd speedy go?" I asked Mia.

"Bathroom?" she shrugged. "Your guess is as good as mine."

I scanned the area, but even with the street lumens, it was too dark to see everything. A multimag gun pattering of footsteps was suddenly coming from my right.

I turned in time to see the blur of green shooting toward me. By the time I saw it, it was too late to dodge. But he collided with an invisible wall, that turned out to be a massive vortex. It wrapped around Xaster, lifted him off his feet, then sent him crashing to the ground.

"Sorry Kid," Northe said, descending behind us. "No sneak attacks."

Xaster gave a bitter laugh. "We've stalled long enough anyway."

"Stalled? Stalled for...?" I couldn't even finish the question before the tense feeling came back.

"I've grown immensely tired of your interference," the voice was as dark as Hadal and twice as frightening—Kurai. "I should put an end to these encounters, before I regret it."

"Touch him, and you'll have something else to regret," Sa'Sha warned.

Kurai glanced at Sa'Sha, then at all of us. He didn't move for a few beats, and I wondered if that meant he was considering retreat. But instead of running, he casually waved a hand out and a hateful wave of energy rippled through the air at us. I barely covered myself in stone in time to stand my ground, while everyone else went flying behind me. I didn't even see where they fell before Kurai started toward me. His emerald green eyes glowed as intensely as ever, and I boosted my speed in anticipation. But he still disappeared, too fast for my eyes to catch. Following the earlier example from Renes, I held my hands out and focused on the small circle of space just out of arm's reach. I concentrated on rapidly heating the air. *I hope I've got this one down by now!*

A flash of light and heat exploded in a circle around me. But it didn't faze

Kurai. He reappeared and ran right through it so unexpectedly fast, my brain couldn't even register a reaction before he had a vice grip on my throat. And with a sweep at my legs, Kurai planted me into the pavement with enough force to feel like someone took a sledgehammer to the back of my head.

My eyes squeezed shut, as the sting tingled hotly down my back. I fought the urge to lie there, instead forcing my eyes open. The impact must've numbed out a couple nerves, because I didn't even realize his hand was still clenching my throat. "Let him go!" A voice rang in my ear. *Sa'Sha?* He held his free hand in the air and a blinding light flashed over him. A metallic clang echoed through the streets; vibrating deep in my ears. The light dimmed, and I forced my eyes open again. He was holding a sword; using it to effortlessly deny Sa'Sha's attack with Nightfall. The blade glowed deep blue, smoldering the air around it. The strain on Sa'Sha's face was a strong contrast to the mix of disinterest and exasperation that colored Kurai's. "Admirable. And foolish." The glow in his eyes grew more intense and, in an instant,, a wind howled past, grabbing Sa'Sha and launching her toward the others.

Before I could react, the tip of the blade was hovering over my face. "You're like an annoying little fly. Too small to matter, too pesky to ignore, and too stupid to know when you're in over your head."

He rose the blade high, and I immediately knew it was about to end for me. Frantic to fight death back, I punched left then right, hitting his ribcage as hard as I could. He didn't even flinch. I tried to swing again, but he squeezed harder, pulling my head off the ground and slamming it back down. I tensed and my body wouldn't respond anymore. I felt so...weak. So helpless. My eyes slowly squinted open to see the blade coming down, and I flinched. I held for a beat, never feeling the plunge of hot metal. A grunt brushed my ear and the grip on my throat loosened. I heard the ringing of metal clanging against pavement. And I immediately wondered why I still didn't feel anything. Reluctantly, I opened my eyes and realized Kurai was gone again. Another grunt, and this time I followed the sound. Kurai was kneeling on the ground, reaching for his blade, when a roaring blast of fire pelted him.

I turned and realized the fire had come from Ariel. Axel was walking alongside her. "What are you doing here?" I asked, feeling the strain in my voice thanks to Kurai.

"It's nice to see you again too, cutie" Ariel said, flashing a wild smile.

"You've lost. Take advantage of the opportunity to escape with your team while you can," Axel warned. Even when he was helping me, he was obnoxious.

Kurai went for his weapon again, and Ariel and Axel both shot a blast at him, keeping him in place.

"What are you waiting for?" Ariel asked.

"Right. Thanks." I jumped to my feet and hurried toward the rest of my team. They were back on their feet too, looking irritated and confused.

"Raven, are you okay?" I asked placing a hand on Sa'Sha's shoulder.

"I'm alright, but what are Locke's people doing here?" She asked.

"What's up with my powers?" NaRyn panicked. "They're not working!"

"Kurai can block powers," I explained. "But if we put some distance between us, they'll work and we'll all live to see tomorrow. Now, let's go."

We raced to a clearing where the Nighthawk was waiting for us. We loaded up and it sped back to base.

The ride was quiet. Too quiet. The worry on Sa'Sha's face made me carefully consider my words. "You okay?" I managed.

"Yes," she answered weakly. "You?"

"Yeah."

"Thanks, for coming to my rescue back there."

The corners of her mouth curled just slightly. "I'll make sure I get the rescuing part right next time." she said weakly.

Her breathing was quiet, but still faster than normal. I rubbed her leg, hoping to calm her. She grabbed my hand and held it tightly between both of hers. I shut my eyes and tried to clear my mind. But I couldn't keep some part of it from replaying Kurai's comment about me being a stupid fly. I told myself it was only a matter of time before I would make Kurai eat those words. And then, we'd see who the stupid fly really was.

[5]

JUBILEE

SEREC

We gathered in Sa'Sha's office to try and piece together what happened back at the shopping district. But for everything we knew, there was something we couldn't figure out. Like, who the guys in the green hoods were and how the malefactors knew to attack everyone but them. Judging from their attire and malevolent violet eyes, we knew they were connected to Siren, which would also explain why the malefactors didn't attack them. There was also the question of why everyone except me lost their powers during my fight with Kurai. And all we could do was speculate on whether me keeping my powers was intentional or beyond his control for some reason.

"That Divarma Kurai was using." Sa'Sha said. "I've never seen one that could produce such a dark energy."

"Were you able to determine any of its properties?" Kareen chimed in, homing in on the one thing she seemed to care about. "It was hot," Sa'Sha replied flatly.

I hesitated to speak. The last thing I wanted was to lead the discussion toward more questions I didn't have the answers to. But I couldn't just ignore the fact that Sa'Sha was looking directly at me for my thoughts on the situation.

"It wasn't a Divarma," I sighed.

"But what else could it have been?" Sa'Sha asked.

"Most likely an Aetharma." Everyone looked even more confused.

"You just make that one up?" Northe asked with a stoic look.

"Locke's assistants told me about it. They said it's stronger than a Divarma, and it's something only a few people have the ability to use."

"But how did Kurai get one?" Sa'Sha asked.

"Remember how I beat that malefactor holding the little boy, back at the park last anum?"

"That was an Aetharma?"

I nodded. "I finally found out after talking to Ariel and Axel about it."

The room went quiet.

"But you still don't have control of yours, do you?" Northe asked.

I shook my head. "I just need a little more time."

"So then, how can we stop Kurai if he's that strong *and* he has an Aetharma?" NaRyn asked.

"Don't worry about Kurai," I said. "I'm his target. He could have easily killed Sa'Sha but chose not to. He's after me, and I'll find a way to stop him."

"But he's crazy strong."

"And you're just plain crazy if you think we will sit back and let you fight him alone," Sa'Sha added.

Sa'Sha's TAB beeping narrowly conquered the tension building in our conversation. Sa'Sha's eyes stayed on me as she took a deep breath. "Go ahead Sentinel."

"Apologies for the late call," Ari said over the TAB, "but I've made an interesting discovery concerning the Humanity Omega Foundation."

"Interesting in what way?" Sa'Sha asked.

"Bottom line, they don't exist. Not in a physical sense, at least. Only on paper, through Oltresulle's national business registry. And since their inception more than eight anums ago, they've never actually provided any kind of service to anyone. The short of it is that this name is a front for The Life Reciprocal."

"You mean that cult that has been advertising on the vid streams?"

"The very same."

"Do you have a location on Life Reciprocal?"

"Not at the moment, but my people are on it as we speak."

"Good. Keep us updated."

The room went quiet. The strain on Sa'Sha's face made me decide to say what everyone else was probably already thinking. "You think a group like Life Reciprocal is really sending monsters out to attack innocent people?" I asked.

"I certainly hope not. Despite, their painted image of a loving society that embraces the world with open arms, they're as shrouded in mystery as a government intelligence organization. And considering their elite member pool, I imagine they also have the financial backing of one."

"That would explain a lot," Northe added. "Those green jackets Serec fought are probably elite soldiers. You don't find too many non-aengel walking around with Divarma, considering the cost and connections it takes to get one. Everything, from the Divarma to the malefactors, to the matching wardrobe all point to deep pockets and organized institution. And I can't think of many institutions more organized than religion."

Sa'Sha nodded thoughtfully. "They put up a good fight today, and we need to prepare ourselves for whatever else their deep pockets can throw at us. For now, let's all get some rest."

Everyone headed to their rooms. Everyone except me. "Please don't tell me you're going back to the training room Serec," Sa'Sha complained.

"Why are you so worried about my trainings?"

"Because I can tell you're overdoing it."

"There's no such thing as overdoing it when someone like Kurai is waiting for his next chance at me."

"At least give your body one more night of rest. We can start fresh tomorrow with team training."

"I have to plan for times when I won't have a team around to help me. Or have you already forgotten how everything played out today?" I was speaking more forcefully than I meant to, but it wasn't like I didn't mean what I was saying. And everyone nagging me about over training—yet again was really starting to bother me.

"So, now it's our fault?"

"That's not what I said—"

"You didn't have to," Sa'Sha interrupted. "I thought we were past this but evidently, I was mistaken. Just...do as you please." She stormed out of the room.

Normally, I knew better than to chase after someone as determined as Sa'Sha when she was upset. But for whatever reason, I couldn't just let the conversation end the way it was about to. I hurried after her.

I called her name, but she ignored me and kept moving. I called again.

"What do you want, Serec?" she snapped.

"I want you to understand where I'm coming from."

"The feeling is mutual"

"What do you mean?"

"I harp on this overtraining issue for a reason. But, it's not like you care."

"Believe it or not, I care a lot."

"Then, why does it feel like you couldn't care less what I think?"

The question caught me by surprise. And my face was quick to broadcast that fact which she didn't take very well with my next question. "What are you talking about?"

She rolled her eyes and turned away. "Wait, wait," I said, grabbing her arm. She spun with a fiery glare.

"What?"

"Do you really want me to rest that bad?" I asked.

"Do you really have to ask?"

"Fine," I said. "If it's that important to you, I'll skip my training for tonight and go to bed. But only on one condition."

The sour look on her face softened a bit. "Which is?"

"You have three beats to stop being mad at me and hug me like you're glad I care what you think." The look on her face went blank, like I'd just told her to float in mid-air. "Three...two..."

She wrapped her arms around me and squeezed tight. "I swear I don't know why I put up with you sometimes," she said.

"I'm glad you do."

"You have a team, you know. You really need to act like it."

"I know. I'm sorry. You really came through for me today. It's just, sometimes I feel like I have such a long way to go."

"We all do but you can't just keep pushing until your body gives out."

I wanted to believe her. "I just want to be strong enough to protect you. Whether it's Renes or Xaster or Kurai or even Ariel and Axel, I just want to have the strength to keep you out of harm's way."

"I feel the same way. When Kurai attacked you, all I could think about was that night at Keyes. I brought Nightfall down on Kurai with all my might but it didn't even phase him. I felt so powerless. I just—don't know what I would do if I lost you again." Her voice softened. And it made my entire rib cage tingle.

I wrapped my arms around her. "I'm not going anywhere Liza—not without you." Even in the hallway's dim light, the soft brown in her eyes was clear as she looked at me. Pressed up so close, I could feel her heart beating even faster than mine.

"We should head on to bed," she said abruptly.

"Yeah, I guess so."

"Sleep tight."

"Yeah, you too." My voice was probably noticeably deflated. Sa'Sha brushed her fingers along my forearm and walked past me. Tingly sensations sparked everywhere she touched, and I turned to watch her disappear into her room. I immediately regretted promising to skip my workout since — thanks to her — sleep wasn't about to come easy.

The next few days of training with our task force field agents turned out to be a little tougher than I'd expected. But considering our intensity on day one, it didn't seem too unlikely that a few decs might actually be enough time to whip everyone into pretty great shape. Unfortunately, the rhythm that started over the first three days grinded to a halt on day four. The day of Regalia's Winter Jubilee.

Sa'Sha had to return to Regalia the night before, and I asked Jin and Northe to run training without me, while I got ready for the big night. As soon as I was ready, I headed over to Stratcom. Since nothing short of losing a limb could keep Hachi away from one of the Monarch's events, I was hoping I could ride with him. He knew the ins and outs of elegant parties, and I knew I could really use a few pointers on how to avoid looking like a total idiot in front of the Monarch. Plus, I hadn't seen much of him in the past few decs, and honestly, I was really starting to miss him.

"Look who's been taking fashion tips from agent K," Juli complimented, looking me over with a smile.

"I don't think I've ever seen you quite so spiffed, Zero."

"Thanks, Juli. Is the Director busy?"

"And then some. He just started a meeting that in his own words 'could take anywhere from a few hashes to a few segments.'"

"Can you send him a burst?"

"I'd loved to help, but he explicitly requested that I avoid any interruptions during the meeting. Perhaps you could. I'm not certain if he'll be free to respond, but it's worth a try."

I figured Juli had a point, and I decided I could at least try, before letting my spirits drop. I chatted with Juli for a few hashes to pass the time. And as expected she asked how Northe was doing. I mentioned that he was currently training the task force field agents, and that lately he'd been a lot busier than usual. Thankfully, most of what I was saying was true. But I still felt bad for not leveling with Juli about Northe's commitment issues.

When Hachi finally responded, telling me to take a raeda, since he's meeting didn't even look close to ending, I figured it was probably the universe getting back at me for not being honest with Juli and telling her to give up on Northe and move on.

The closest drop point to Regalia was still a thirty-hash drive so I had plenty of time to mull over everything. The whole drive, a swirling anxiety occupied my chest. Probably because even if I didn't do anything particularly embarrassing, there was still Sa'Sha's motive to consider. As close friends, was it possible she had another reason for asking me, of all people, to pretend to be in a relationship with her? *What if she's testing to see if I'm real boyfriend material?* The second the thought passed through my mind, a flutter of hope grew in the pit of my stomach. But, before I could relish in it, my brain went into overdrive with enough doubt to twist the hopefulness into more anxiety.

After crossing multiple checkpoints between Callastryne and Regalia proper, I was finally within view of the royal palace. Domus Regalia was easily the largest structure in the nation, towering over even some of the skyscrapers in New Callastryne. The stone colossus was situated on a mountain that backed up to the sea, a narrow strait of land connecting it to the rest of civilization. The palace began to slowly eclipse Aio as I approached, until the moon was completely obscured, along with the rest of the sky.

I pulled up to an elegant silver gate standing between two enormous stone walls. The gate had a shiny gold phoenix in the middle, symbolizing house Martinel. *Not too intimidating.*

"State your business, please," a voice said through the speaker attached to the left wall.

I cleared my throat. "I was invited to your Winter Jubilee by the princess." No response. "I'm her date." For whatever reason, my attempt at clarifying made me feel like a total fool, and I almost wanted to ask for a retry.

"You're a segment early," the speaker said.

"The princess asked me to come a bit early." A few more beats of silence. "Uh...hello?"

The gate clicked and began to slowly swing open. "Please pull through and park your vehicle in the west lot, sir."

"Which way is the west lot?" Another pause.

"West, sir. Just follow the path and take a right where it forks." *Why didn't he just say that to begin with?*

Two young women wearing simple beige robes were waiting as I stepped out of the raeda. "Welcome, Mr. Arenyu," one said with a bow. "Please follow us."

We walked through a long-winding garden. The bushes were just tall enough to block my view of the bottom half of the palace, but even still I could see the gold and white cube with its rounded sides and pointed spires that pierced the sky.

The garden path ended at a long, burgundy carpet extending all the way to a pair of tall double-doors. The first woman led me through a larger-than-life lobby, where everything from the row of pillars to the floors were cream-colored marble. A faint scent of lenio flowers mixed with the aroma of pastries baking.

"Your waiting quarters are this way," the other woman said. Two rounding flights of stairs brought us to yet another massive room. It took a conscious effort not to gawk like a child staring at the moons for the first time. I sat in one of two large plush chairs, and studied the space, imagining how many posters, games and other cool electronics I could fit into my room if it were the same size. "It is my honor to present Fidelissima Alanda Zoay."

It took me a moment to realize the woman was talking to me. "Huh? Fideli—."

"Fidelissima. It means most loyal," A young woman said stepping through the door. Her stylish burgundy garb distinguished her from the other women dressed in beige. Something about her clear blue eyes immediately struck me as wise almost sage-like. But soft features and a bright aspect told the story of a girl who had to be closer to NaRyn's age. Another woman with trays of silverware trailed behind. "On behalf of his Royal Highness, Divinus Charlemagne Martinel VII and her grace Blissful Sa'Sha Martinel, it is my honor to welcome you to Domus Regalia."

"So, you're Alanda?"

Alanda's courteous smile grew into a more playful one. "I am. It's a pleasure to finally make your acquaintance. The princess is nearly ready, but there is still time to cover a few rules of proper etiquette with you, before she arrives."

We went through the names and uses of each of the ten utensils on the tray, a few times. Then, Alanda showed me the proper way to walk while leading a lady to and from a chair or dinner table, and a bunch of other interesting stuff that I had no hope of retaining, despite my effort. It was a fatal amount of information to absorb and just a fraction of everything Sa'Sha knew. It made me wonder how she managed to balance her life as a princess with her responsibilities as a commander.

"This is all a bit overwhelming. Is there some kind of a cheat sheet I could hang onto?" I asked, once we'd finished.

"Perhaps on your next visit," she smirked.

"Assuming I don't mess things up tonight."

"You will do fine."

"At least you have faith in me."

"She's not the only one," Sa'Sha called from the door.

I turned, and awe smacked me so hard, I forgot how to speak.

"I almost failed to mention that it is not polite to gawk," Alanda whispered, and I realized I was staring, mouth open.

"Hello there," Sa'Sha said with a warm smile.

"Hi," I managed. I expected to come up with something more appropriate but my brain wasn't giving me much to work with at that point. It was busy etching the image of Sa'Sha in her flowing blue gown into my memory. Her make-up was subtle, but very effective at making everything from her vibrant green eyes to her full lips stand out. Her powder white hair flowed down her back, a small but striking silver crown resting atop her head. The straps on her gown wrapped around her neck, and masterfully highlighted her curves. She was stunning, art in motion. I could only hope she hadn't noticed how much of a fight it was, pulling my eyes where they were supposed to be. But considering how long she stood there watching me watch her, I had my doubts.

"You look nice," Sa'Sha finally said with a growing smile.

"You too! I mean... you as well Blissful," I recovered.

She forced back a chuckle, and it made her chest jump. *Man, oh man! This was gonna be a challenge.* I'd always considered both Sa'Sha and Blissful Martinel to be fatally attractive, but seeing them as the same person, without the barrier of a vid screen brought gravity to it all. She wasn't just Raven or Sa'Sha or Liza or Blissful Martinel, but all of them. And from that understanding came an immense respect for the little farm girl I grew up with, the agent I fought along-side, and the future ruler I vowed to protect.

Sa'Sha took a few steps closer and held out a hand. I looped my arm around hers and placed it over my bicep.

She squeezed it gently and whispered, "Don't be nervous," her voice as sweet as her perfume. It was beyond me how she hadn't realized that hearing that from her had the opposite effect.

"So, I'm just doing the pretend boyfriend thing, right?"

"Yes, something like that," Sa'Sha answered getting into character.

"I don't know how I feel about being seen as the princess' highly desirable prize."

She pinched my arm and I twitched in confusion.

"Let's try and keep the hallucinations to a minimum tonight, E," the corners of her mouth creased upward.

"The time has arrived Blissful," Alanda informed. "Do try to remember everything I showed you Serec."

I looked at her blankly and nodded, then back at Sa'Sha. "Where do we go from here?"

"I'll guide you," she said, leading me over to the edge of the staircase. We walked downstairs as people filtered in. She nodded toward the Monarch, standing at the door. *"Uncle wants to meet you, before we head into the Imperial Great Hall,"* her voice rang in my head.

No pressure...

Remembering what little I could of Alanda's hasty instruction, I led Sa'Sha down the winding staircase and approached Divinus Charlemagne Martinel VII, Monarch of Aruria. My hands suddenly felt clammy. And my heart beat three times between each step. I couldn't determine which was more daunting: meeting the ruler of the nation, or the guardian of the girl I was very much in love with. A few steps from reaching him, a barrage of flashing lights assaulted us from outside.

Live music was playing in the great hall, one room over. But the clamor of voices easily drowned them out.

"What's going on out front?" I asked Sa'Sha.

"Royal events are like a credit union for journalists. Most news organizations stream live as their reporters interview the politicians, nobility, and high-power business executives on their way in."

"Do we have to go out there too?"

"Uncle thinks I should work to increase my public presence, but I'm not fond of the idea of playing the socialite role for camera's sake."

"This coming from the girl who models her own fashion line."

"And those cameras are nowhere near as nosey as these are," she retorted. "Letting them watch as I introduce you to Uncle should be more than enough to appease all parties. Just, don't be surprised if your face appears all over the Arnet tomorrow."

Despite having an understanding of everything, my nerves still insisted on stealing my smooth.

"Divinus," Sa'Sha called, as we stepped within view of the media. The Monarch turned with bright eyes and a wide smile. Over the anums, I'd seen the streams of the Monarch giving speeches and attending all kinds of ceremonies. But it was nothing like seeing him up close. He was a tall man with a thick, well-kept beard lining his prominent but rounded jaw. He and Hachi were supposed to be the same age, but the wrinkles littering his face made it clear who'd aged better. Still, he was trimmer than most men his age.

"I have someone I would like you to meet." Sa'Sha gestured at me and the Monarch excitedly reached for my hand.

"What a pleasure it is to finally meet you, young man," he said gripping my wrist firmly and shaking vigorously. "Charlemagne Martinel VII. And you are?"

"He is the nephew I've been speaking to you about, Your Highness," a familiar voice called over the cacophony.

We all turned in surprise as Hachi stepped forward in his formal military uniform.

"Hachinatus! It's always a pleasure!" The Monarch grabbed Hachi's wrist and pulled him into a hug. "So, this is the nephew you've told me so much about?"

"My name is Serec Arenyu, Divinus. I'm very honored to meet you as well." I bowed.

The Monarch laughed and I wondered if I'd done something wrong. "I can tell you're worth your weight in spices," he said. "It's no wonder the strapping nephew of one of my most highly-esteemed friends would catch my little girl's eye so sharply."

For a moment, I thought I saw Sa'Sha's face take on a red hue. But when I looked more closely, the redness was gone.

"You praise me too much," Hachi said.

"I praise you just as you deserve, and you, my friend, must learn to accept it." They shared a laugh. "Now, if you will excuse me, I mustn't neglect my duties as a host. Please enjoy yourselves and I will expect the four of us to reconvene for tea and laughs, before the night comes to an end."

The Monarch walked off to greet another guest and Hachi walked with Sa'Sha and me back into the lobby.

"I thought your meeting wouldn't be over for a couple segments."

"Thankfully, it ended sooner than expected. Speaking of expectations, I don't think anyone expected the two of you to look so perfect together." I glanced around, noticing the numerous eyes on Sa'Sha and me, and tension filled my jaw spreading down the sides of my throat. "No need to be shy you two." But the more Hachi spoke, the harder it was not to be shy. In fact, my eyes couldn't focus on anything except the marble floor.

Hachi placed a hand on our shoulders. "Relax, I'm just making you sweat a bit."

"Mission accomplished." I remarked.

He chuckled. "It's alright. Go, mingle, and make the most of your time together. I'm sure you two will run into a few interesting people here."

Hachi couldn't have been more right. Not a hash after he walked off, I noticed an eerily familiar face.

"Serec," Sa'Sha said, snapping my attention away.

"Yeah?"

"I said the banquet should be starting any hash now, so we should head into the next hall."

"Okay."

"What were you looking at?"

I leaned closer. "Remember when I said I saw someone watching as we escaped, back at Theall?"

"He's here?"

"Maybe. I thought I saw him over there." I nodded toward the entrance to the great hall. Of course, the crowd was filling in quickly, and whoever I thought I saw had disappeared.

"If he's one of the guests, then we should have the perfect opportunity to locate him during dinner."

I led Sa'Sha into the great hall, searching the crowd as I absentmindedly started toward Hachi's table. There were at least two-hundred people filling up most of the tables. A faint, sharp aroma filled the room.

"We're eating at the head table with Uncle," Sa'Sha's voice echoed in my head. I abruptly turned and headed for the back wall, where the Monarch was stepping up to his seat. As soon as Sa'Sha and I took a seat, he raised his glass and clinked it, signaling the musicians to stop playing.

"I, Charlemagne Martinel VII, am honored to welcome you all, my esteemed guests," he began. "It delights me to find so many familiar faces at our kingdom's first Winter Jubilee. My wish this anum is undoubtedly the same as it shall be every anum. May each and every one of you eat, drink, and make the most of this night, that El has seen fit to bestow upon us. Create lasting memories with those dearest to you, and never forget the unity that we share, not as several great houses, but one mighty nation."

The Monarch bowed and took his seat as the crowd applauded and the music resumed. A line of wait staff emerged from the kitchen and set out the first course of the meal: a steaming bowl of creamy otamo stew with a sprinkle of cheese. I was anxious to dig into it. But I stalled trying to remember which spoon was the soup spoon, when the Monarch called over to me. "Are you enjoying the stew, Serec?"

"I was just about to try it, Divinus," I said, looking back at my silverware like time was slipping away on a million-credit question.

"The smallest spoon, closest to the bowl," Sa'Sha thought, just in time.

I dipped the spoon, blew it a couple times, and tasted it.

"This is the most flavorful stew I've ever tasted."

The Monarch nodded proudly. "Each of the palace chefs focus on their specialties and nothing more. The chef responsible for this stew is a genius with creating robust flavors using most any ingredient. Task delegation is a skill in and of itself, my boy. Your uncle's abilities within the Bureau are a testament to that."

"I couldn't agree more, Your Highness. It's probably why I idolized him as a kid."

"Why stop there? You're never too old to idolize someone," the Monarch said with a smile, before going back to his food.

"Why does that sound so strange coming from you?" Sa'Sha whispered.

"Maybe, you've heard so many strange things, you can't tell what's normal anymore." She held her handkerchief up, as the corners of her mouth curled.

"Speaking of strange, why haven't you figured out how smiles work for guys yet?"

"What do you mean?"

"Men work pretty hard to make a beautiful girl smile. So, I can't understand how it's so easy for you to hide what keeps me going. Unless you're a sloppy eater."

She started to turn her face away, but I watched expectantly as her smile grew. She turned for all of a beat, and lowered her handkerchief, flashing her teeth at me. But one beat was plenty to make the heat rise from my chest, up into my face.

When dinner, had finally ended, the music shifted to more energetic selections that people could dance to. Sa'Sha suggested we use dancing as a cover to move around the room and look for the guy from Theall. But I didn't make it halfway through the first song before it stopped feeling like just a cover.

Holding her and swaying around the dancefloor was like holding an exotic flower. Firm enough to resist a strong touch, and so soft I didn't want to let go. She leaned in, wrapping her arms tighter around my neck, and as the sweet flowery scent on her skin filled my nose, I pulled her closer. Everything but the music hazed out, as we moved together like a single body. Lost in each other's warmth.

"Pardon the interruption, you two," Hachi said, and my head turned with a start. "We would appreciate it if the two of you would join us for tea." Hachi gestured to a lift in the corner of the room.

Sa'Sha cleared her throat. "But of course. We'll be right there."

We exchanged a nervous glance and followed Hachi. The conversation started off simple enough, with an emphasis on *started*. But somewhere along the way, it shifted into the worse possible topic.

"Tell me Serec, the Monarch started, "how is the Army treating you these days?"

The tea nearly jumped out of my mouth. "A-uh...Army?"

"Yes. Last I heard from Hachi here, you were a cadet at the academy. If my memory serves, we should be nearing the two anum mark, shouldn't we?"

"Uh...we should," I glanced at Hachi, not sure if giving any additional details would be the best way to handle the question.

"Should I take that to mean you are no longer active?"

"Actually, I was discharged."

His look turned dangerously curious. "On what grounds?"

"Striking a superior officer, Divinus."

"And what reason seemed powerful enough to drive that course of action?" I was starting to feel like El pressed replay on the conversation Hachi and I had the day the Army booted me back home.

"Well...uh, you see Your Highness...there was this, um, there was this...this guy—"

"Do you recall the military council's pushback on inducting the Bureau of National Peace into the Department of Peace, despite your avid endorsement Charlee?" Hachi interjected.

"Do I?" the Monarch scoffed. "I started to question how much power a monarch really had after the uproar they produced."

"Thank Lieutenant General Jibbs for that one."

"Jibbs made Lieutenant General?" the Monarch threw his hands up and shook his head in disgust. "Probably Nicosta's doing. But when you reach positions like ours, it's vital to pick your battles, isn't it?"

Hachi nodded. "You would know better than I would."

"I swear to El almighty I shouldn't have let up on the fight to push him into some flowery position where he was barely more than an employee number and silver name plate in some stuffy corner office with a view."

"Serec was discharged for striking Junior Lieutenant, Jibbs, the General's grandson. Whatever the reason, Serec seemed to catch his eye as a prime target for hazing."

"And you're suggesting nepotism was a factor?" the Monarch asked flatly.

"Charlee, after six anums in the same unit, do you really have to ask?"

They shared a sly smile. "A rhetorical question for that very reason."

"I won't argue that Serec should've handled the situation more maturely. But my chastisement remains relatively minor in this case."

"Lest hypocrisy take an unshakable hold over you." The Monarch smirked. "You were no different at his age."

"How else would I have earned the nickname 'Hatchet?'"

"The stories I could tell to answer that particular question," the Monarch said, lifting his eyebrows almost like he was asking indirectly.

"I wouldn't, unless you've figured out a way to incriminate me without incriminating yourself."

"The crux of my dilemma," the Monarch said thoughtfully. "So then, Serec, if you can no longer call yourself a man of the Army, is there any other particular line of employment worthy of your devotion?"

"Actually, I work in the Bureau now."

"An avid seeker of excitement, are we?"

"There's not much excitement in data entry."

"A lofty position?" The Monarch eyed Hachi. "Where's the fun in that? Kids need action. It builds character."

"The day you enlist Sa'Sha into the Bureau to build character, is the day I throw Serec headlong into battle against the nation's greatest threats."

"Fair enough," the Monarch said with a breathy chuckle. "Then, the least we can do is regale them with an Army tale or two. How about the time we were in that crossfire with Lazurian soldiers and you promised to give up drinking if we made it out alive?"

Hachi smirked wistfully, as if the idea brought back some long-forgotten feelings. "Why not," he said after a pause.

Hachi may have seemed a little reluctant at first, but as the story recounted bar fights and partnered pranks on their superior officers, the Monarch soon had Hachi as engrossed in the story as Sa'Sha and me. Even with his eloquent way of speaking, there was a lighthearted—almost cynical—tone to half of what he said. Not at all what I expected from a monarch. I wondered if he was always that way, or if it became a part of him after he'd taken the throne.

Before I could get to asking him, or even hearing the rest of the story, a large man in an expensive suit interrupted.

"Please excuse the intrusion, Your Highness," the tall man said, bowing before he approached our table. He had a strange heavy sounding accent that was as interesting as it was unsettling. "I had hoped for the opportunity to meet the illustrious General Hatchet some time ago, but time was not in my favor during the Autumn Gala last anum. I simply couldn't allow myself to miss the opportunity this time."

"It's been quite some time since anyone has referred to me by that moniker," Hachi said with a smile. "I'm especially surprised to hear it from a citizen of Oltresulle."

"The only legacies worth creating are those that transcend the simple barriers of time and locale. Wouldn't you not agree, Divinus?"

"I would," the Monarch replied very matter-of-factly. "Well said."

"Hachinatus Arenyu," Hachi said, gripping the man's wrist.

"Iam Rhasatto."

"President of Theall Medical Corporation. You're working on quite the legacy yourself, running an international company, while maintaining such an active role in politics and philanthropy."

Iam smiled. "It seems I'm not the only one to keep up with people of interest outside of my country." Iam suddenly noticed Sa'Sha and me. "Speaking of people of interest, I see a familiar face." My jaw tensed as his eyes shifted between us. I could feel Iam getting ready to drop the bomb that he'd somehow figured out it was Sa'Sha and me in Theall's security footage. Instead, "It's a pleasure to see you again, Blissful," were the only words I heard.

"Likewise," Sa'Sha replied, her voice soft, almost...enticing. I bit back the urge to look at her in front of him.

"And who might this strapping young man be?" Iam asked looking at me again.

"That is Serec Arenyu, General Arenyu's nephew and Sa'Sha's date for the evening," the Monarch announced proudly.

"Date, you say?" he began, extending his hand. "Winning the favor of such a lovely young woman surely makes you a target of envy among men." His too perfect smile widened.

I cleared my throat, smiling uncomfortably as I gripped his wrist. "Thank you, sir."

"Are you planning to follow in your uncle's footsteps?"

"Not exactly."

Iam smirked and nodded, but he didn't say anything. His large dark eyes fixed on me. Two black holes that devoured any sense of calm I previously held. They seemed out of place on an otherwise perfectly polished face. I felt the need to fill the silence, but my mind supplied me with a lot of nothing.

"No harm in forging your own path," he finally said. "I didn't follow in my father's footsteps either." Another awkward silence came and went before he asked, "Have you ever been to Oltresulle?"

I hesitated. For such a simple question, something about his tone felt strangely interrogative. "How could I when the border's closed?"

"My apologies. I assumed someone of your uncle's status would have secured an international travel pass for you by now." He looked at Hachi expectantly.

Hachi raised his eyebrows in place of a shrug. "I guess I've neglected to make it a priority for some time now. Perhaps I should look into starting the paperwork." I could tell by Hachi's tone, he was just being polite. There were a lot of things everyone *should* be doing. But should and would are two very different things.

"Why not?" Iam said. "A boy his age, would really appreciate the landscape's rugged charm. Despite our country's fiscal struggles in recent anums, our situation is steadily improving. From the looks of things, it won't be long before things are as they should be."

I nodded uncomfortably.

"Mr. Rhasatto speaks truth," the Monarch chimed. "After spending many Summers in Creize, I can attest to its wholesome serenity."

Iam bowed slightly. "You are too kind, Divinus. And as you have so graciously opened your home to me, nothing would please me more than returning the favor by taking on the role of host to each of you in the near future. For now, I had best take my leave."

"So soon?" the Monarch said.

"I do have quite a long trip ahead of me, and I would prefer to preempt the traffic a clamor of guests will bring."

Iam bowed and turned for the lift. I tried to refocus on the conversation as Hachi and the Monarch resumed. But I couldn't shake the weird feeling I got from the way Iam looked at me. I glanced down into the great hall at the sea of guests, and for all of a moment, I could've sworn I saw Iam watching me. Everything about that moment reminded me of the man standing in the hallway, back at Theall, watching as Sa'Sha and I escaped.

"Serec," the Monarch said, pulling my attention. "If I absolved the discharge and gave you a clean record, would you return to the Army? I could have you reassigned if you believe that would help." *Is he serious?* The thought made my heart skip a few beats, and I tried to think up the politest way to say, "not even if someone planted explosives in my brain and threatened to detonate them." But the Monarch's laughter punched through my anxiety. "You should have warned him, Hachi."

"Of your dark humor?" Hachi said. "Where's the fun in that?"

They both laughed, and I was a little surprised when Sa'Sha joined in. But not as surprised as when I felt the corners of my mouth pressing into a smile.

"I think I see why Sa'Sha chose him," the Monarch said watching me proudly. He turned to Sa'Sha and nodded approvingly. Sa'Sha looked at him with wide eyes, before glancing at me as blood flooded her cheeks.

The embarrassment on Sa'Sha's face made it a fight not to laugh. But the Monarch and Hachi were clearly losing the fight, laughing even harder. Watching them, reminded me of how hard Sa'Sha and I used to laugh together back in primary school. Even though I wasn't a fan of being the target of a joke, it was the first time I'd seen Hachi having so much fun in a long time, and it created a warmth in my chest.

"I do hope this won't be the only time I'll see you at a royal event, Serec," the Monarch said, gripping my wrist.

"I hope the same, Your Highness," I replied.

"Good man." He patted my shoulder. "Take care of your old man. And my little girl."

I smiled and bowed, then caught up with Hachi at the door.

"If you're interested in riding back together, I can have your raeda retrieved first thing tomorrow," Hachi offered.

"Sure, but I wanted to say goodbye to Sa'Sha first."

"Here comes your chance now."

Sa'Sha hurried over to me, careful to maintain her poise.

"Hey," I said.

"Hey yourself," she said.

"I'll meet you in the raeda, Serec." Hachi turned to Sa'Sha. "A pleasure seeing you again, Blissful."

"The pleasure was mine," Sa'Sha said with a smile. "Until we next meet."

Hachi smiled and walked off.

"You guys do that every time?" I whispered.

"More or less." Her hand moved toward her mouth, just as the smile on her face grew, and I took her hand in mine.

"Your smiles are wasted when you hide them." Her smile widened and she looked away shyly. "That goes for your eyes too." Her eyes slowly moved up to mine.

"Then, you should meet me tomorrow for breakfast? You will have plenty of opportunities to see me smile then."

"Back here?" I asked.

"A cafe not far from you. I'll send you the location."

"How's 9.00?"

"Perfect."

She gave me a big hug, and I wrapped my arms around her waist. "Thank you for helping me out tonight," she said.

"Thanks for the invite. It was, a lot more enjoyable than I expected."

"It was, wasn't it?"

The longer her body was pressed against mine, the faster my heart thumped. Her body was firm, but also soft in all the right places. I closed my eyes and inhaled the scent of lenio flowers in her hair. I exhaled louder than I meant to, but she only pressed tighter against me.

"Can I stay here like this forever?" I muttered.

"What?" she laughed softly.

"N-nothing," I stuttered nervously. "I'm just...kidding."

When she started to pull away, I took a step back, feeling even more self-conscious. She brushed back one side of her hair and removed a small flower that she had tucked behind her ear. She took my hand and placed the flower in it.

"Lenio flowers have a scent that helps you sleep easier. I hope it helps you sleep soundly until tomorrow."

"I'll keep it by my pillow." She smiled again. which should have made it easier. But I still felt the tremor in my hand as I reached for hers and kissed the back of it. "See you tomorrow, Blissful."

She placed her hand over her chest, watching me with warmth in her eyes. "Goodnight."

The fluttery feeling spread up to my neck and shoulders as I turned and walked to the raeda. I waited until I was nearly out of sight before glancing over my shoulder one more time to see if she was watching me leave. And my heart flipped when I saw that she was.

"Did you enjoy yourself tonight?" Hachi asked as I got into the passenger seat.

"Yeah," I said, thinking of Sa'Sha. "It was nice."

"It looked like you and Sa'Sha really connected tonight."

"It was just for appearances. The Monarch's been pressuring her about finding a suitor, so I agreed to come."

"If I had known that was all it took for you to attend a royal event, I should have said old Charlee was pressuring me to bring my nephew along a few anums ago. He would have known you about as well as he knows me by now."

"Actually, Sa'Sha asked me to be her date. But, like I said—"

"It was just for appearances," he finished. "I get it." But the smile etching into his face told me he was getting something else too.

"What?" I asked.

"Oh nothing." His smile grew bigger.

"What?" I asked louder.

"Nothing," he replied, matching my volume and ignoring the suspicious look I gave. "I'm proud of how you handled yourself tonight. You made quite an impression with everyone, especially the Monarch."

"Thanks Uncle Hachi." Having a chance to talk after so long felt therapeutic, and it was the perfect opportunity to ask something else that was bothering me. But I hesitated.

"Is something on your mind?" Hachi asked, quickly picking up on it.

"Remember what you said to the Monarch? You know, about what happened with the Army and all?" Hachi nodded. "Was it true?"

"When I first took on the role of director for the Bureau, Major General Jibbs from the finance directorate of all places was the one voicing the heaviest protest. An old classmate from the academy, Charlee and I hated Jibbs for his elitist views and sense of superiority. Despite this, he made his way through the ranks and has just picked up his first phoenix, to everyone's surprise. And because he had a few sympathizers in the war council, he was able to throw his weight around. All he did was fight against everything I was in favor of, including founding the Bureau. But he couldn't establish a majority vote, and when the BNP was officially founded, I was offered the position of director. Since then, he climbed to the rank of Major General. And whether it was planned or simply bad coincidence, his grandson, Junior Lieutenant Jibbs, saw fit to target you amongst a few others for hazing."

I scoffed at the idea. "How fair is that?"

"It's not unfair, if that's what you're asking. Hazing has always been common practice with junior cadets. And it's completely at the discretion of a superior officer."

"So, how'd you know I was being targeted?"

"I personally groomed Captain Raines,"

"You mean the guy who put me in a chokehold when I tried to defend myself against Jibbs?"

"Believe it or not, he went easy on you. And yes. Raines was gracious enough to confirm my suspicions, the day after you were detained for assaulting a superior officer."

I never even got to use the military discount that he promised me on day one. But hearing Hachi's end of the story, I kinda felt bad for calling Captain Raines a traitor all that time, even if it was only in my head. And if Hachi knew the real story from the start, it explains why he'd gone out of his way to knock my sentence down to house arrest. It was probably harder to accomplish than he was willing to admit. Even with his government connections.

"Would you have let me rot in military detention for five anums if you didn't suspect Jibbs or the General was behind it?"

"You're my nephew, the closest thing to a son I'll ever have. And I'll always fight for you, even when you don't like it. That's what it means to be a parent. That's what it means to love someone."

Hachi always tried to teach me that fair was fair. But I couldn't help wondering if somehow it was all relative when it came to the people you cared about.

"The Monarch said you were like me when you were my age. What did he mean by that?"

"It's not something I'm particularly proud to admit. But let's just say I was not the calmest person in my younger days, and I had to learn a few things the hard way. Which is why I didn't want you to have to. But when Northe came to me about recruiting you, I realized I'd been wrong for trying to shelter you from mistakes. You have to make mistakes."

I sighed. "I haven't stopped making them. Or did you forget what happened to Surket?"

"Life requires mistakes. It's the only way we learn and grow. Surket did what she believed was right. Whether she sacrificed herself for you or someone else, it's a part of who she was. That's why so many people admired her. And had you not joined, it might have only been a matter of time before your vigilantism put you in a situation you couldn't handle. What then?" I thought about Kurai, and my mind blanked on arguments.

"I've never been a fan of what-if situations that don't aid you in some way," he continued. "But, what if everything works out just as it's supposed to when it's all said and done?

I couldn't think of anything to say to that. Even if I could, what was the point? It was the kind of moment I hadn't had with Hachi in a long time, and I wasn't interested in spoiling it. "There's the smile I wanted," he said, glancing at me. My smile grew. I probably smiled the rest of the way home.

The next morning, I met Sa'Sha at the cafe. She wore a long, flowing green dress, that hit her curves as the wind blew. It was the blue gown all over again.

We shared a light breakfast of fresh bread with cream cheese, and a tall glass of juice. She must've been about as hungry as I was, because we spent the first few hashes eating, and watching each other eat, a lot more than we talked. Even though we'd eaten together plenty of times — both inside and outside of the Guild — something about our quiet meal felt a bit different. After the night before, it felt like there was more to our meal than a meal, even if we barely spoke. And the more I thought about it, the more I tried to pile more food over the wild tingling in my stomach.

"Did you sleep well?" she asked, when we were down to our last few bites.

"After about a segment of staring up at the ceiling," I complained.

"Aww, I'm sorry," she said.

"But, that lenio flower really helped me relax. It's probably the only reason I'm not half asleep right now."

"And the first time in a while you don't look like it." I frowned and Sa'Sha chuckled.

"Thank you for yesterday. Uncle went on all morning about how pleased he was about the Jubilee. And he wouldn't stop talking about you."

"Maybe I should pretend to be your boyfriend more often." Sa'Sha froze and her eyes stayed on me for all of a beat before cutting away. "I'm just kidding," I said, immediately losing my nerve. "It was...it was a dumb joke."

"It wasn't that—"

"Has everything been to your liking?" the waiter asked, stepping in at the worst possible moment.

Sa'Sha smiled and nodded. "Yes, thank you. Everything was great."

I tapped my timechain against the small payment device he was holding and it made a small beep.

"Thank you both. Please do enjoy your day." He gave us a polite smile and walked off.

I looked at Sa'Sha, who was already watching me.

"Did you..." She looked down for a beat, then forced her eyes back up to mine. "Did you like pretending to be my boyfriend?"

My heart was suddenly pounding so heavy my whole body jumped with each beat. "I mean, I know it was all for show," I said. "I just...it was nice," I said, trying to sound as smooth as possible, before I lost my nerve and looked away. "But, you know..." I cleared my throat, searching for the words and only finding emptiness. Stupid emptiness. "Sorry, I'm not making any sense."

"No!" Sa'Sha blurted. "I mean, that's fine. It's not like it was all for show the whole time. You...being with you made me feel—"

Sa'Sha's timechain buzzed. She looked at the screen, then at me. "I should probably take this." I nodded. She cleared her throat. "Good Morning," she said into the timechain. She listened for a few beats before her eyes widened and she looked at me. "I'll be there in thirty hashes." She severed the link.

"What's up?" I asked.

"The Life Reciprocal."

"What about it?"

"Ari found it."

[6]

THE LIFE RECIPROCAL

NARYN

"We've found our entry point to The Life Reciprocal's compound in Oltresulle," Sa'Sha announced to the task force. "As a means of recruiting new blood into their ranks, Life Reciprocal holds retreats for prep school and university-aged candidates. Considering Ambi's success in posing as a prep school student during one of her previous missions, she and one agent of her choosing, will go undercover and glean information from the Life Reciprocal's retreat, two days from today."

Mia stepped up, looking about as full of herself, as usual. Clearly starving for attention, she paused for dramatics and looked around the room, as if she hadn't already made her decision. It was one of many things that so easily bothered me about her. But Mia wasn't the type for spontaneity. So, I knew there was no way she would've come to the meeting without knowing exactly who she wanted to work under her. And that bothered me even more.

I'll never get these ten beats back. Her eyes scanned the pool of agents for the longest ten beats of my life, and my heart decided to run sprints in the anticipation. Her eyes found me and held there for an instant, even though we both already knew she would pick me. But her eyes continued on as if she'd immediately lost interest. A flutter of hope sprung up in my chest. But hope and anxiety have the kind of love-hate relationship you often see in old couples. Her eyes moved all the way across the room, and she still looked indecisive about her options. Her eyes scanned back, and as they did I could almost feel my head shaking from the rush of adrenaline, hoping someone else—anyone else seemed like a better choice than me.

"Lift," Mia said cheerfully, as if her eyes had just finally located me. *Thanks for the unnecessary suspense.* I wondered if smacking the smarm off her troll face in front of everyone, would be enough to get me out of the mission without facing too serious a punishment. But for some stupid reason, I just stepped forward instead.

We ended up in some quiet little town called Curran. A humid dust bucket in Tertuze province that served as one of the few still open ports between Aruria and Oltresulle. For all the credits in the world, I couldn't guess why any country would build a national maritime checkpoint in such a small town. A town so small that any resident could probably recite the name and relatives of every other resident with ease. It was the perfect recipe for a boring nosey town. No one spoke as Mia and I moved through the checkpoint line, even though I could feel them all watching. It was starting to creep me out. But one man made a show of it, pointing out people and waving. His confident, charismatic persona was equal parts annoying and entertaining. That man introduced himself as Tarver Vemeri, heir to the Vemeri Foods conglomerate, which made up about a third of every teen's diet with a variety of fatally good sweet, salty, or spicy pre-packaged snacks.

Tarver was tall, tanned, and pretty with light eyes, lighter hair, and a million-credit smile. He livened up the crowd for nearly the entire segment it took us to get through, even passing out some of the crispy treats I grew up with. *At least the mission isn't all bad.* When we finally made it to the other side, Mia and I stepped onto a ferry packed with people for the retreat. Thankfully, the ride was short, because Mia even found a way to make it grossly annoying sitting next to her as she opened package after package of snacks, shoveling them down her throat like it was her last meal. Between our full ferry and the one behind us, we nearly filled the wide auditorium to capacity. Despite low-lighting and the crowd's general lack of movement, the pitiful breeze coming through the vents was like a drop in the pond against the building body heat of so many people. Just one more fault my brain tallied against this mission.

"Have you ever felt like you were different?" Tarver's voice boomed over the speakers. "Special in a way you couldn't understand? Has it made you feel out of place, like you didn't belong? Your environment does all it can to either embrace or condemn you for what makes you different. And knowing that, wouldn't you think it makes more sense to put yourself in the kind of environment that embraces that difference? Whether or not, you know it, each and every one of you has the potential to be a true asset to this world. And if you let me, I'd be glad to show you how."

Tarver had the crowd practically eating out of his hand within the first five hashes of his impassioned speech. He ended with a vid highlighting the sick and impoverished families across Orbis. An ongoing side effect of the green sky and economic downturn that resulted from Oltresulle and Lazuria's open conflict. Considering the number of trade cities within both countries, relying so heavily on international trade, all three of the Great Nations took a sizeable financial blow when war sparked. But Oltresulle suffered worst of all. "You know what I've learned?" Tarver continued. "You never have it quite as bad as you think you do. There's always someone who has it worse. We have a responsibility to help those in need and reshape this world into one we can all be proud of. I hate to sound bleak—but it's the only way things are going to get better."

The vid took an upturn to the smiling faces of the less fortunate receiving clothes, food, and even small shelters from people donning robes and plain clothing with the Life Reciprocal's sigil on them.

"The Life Reciprocal was founded to provide guidance and assistance to people just like you. People who were swallowed up by the same negative environmental circumstances that we will happily show you how to overcome. Delivering food, water, medical supplies, creating shelters — whatever it takes to create the kind of world we want to live in. The kind of world we should all want to live in."

The crowd boomed in applause as TLR representatives slipped between the mass of people, gathering information like it was their life's ambition. Tarver popped out of some part of the crowd with a flock of desperate women hanging close at his feet.

"Alias," Mia suddenly whispered.

"What?" I asked. But Tarver had already reached us.

"Welcome ladies," he said with that charming smile. "I assume some part of my presentation spoke to you?"

"You could say that," Mia said, tone enticing.

"Who might you be?"

"She's Nana," Mia said quickly, placing a hand on my shoulder.

"Cute name," Tarver said. "And what's your name?"

"Mimi!" I interrupted, just as quickly. Tarver's eyes shifted to me, then back to Mia.

"A beautiful name for a beautiful girl." He winked and Mia made a noise that was probably meant to be a giggle. It took all I had to keep from gagging. You see, I have a condition. The kind where the more time I'm forced to spend around Mia, the more my stomach turns. And per usual, her infatuation with the spotlight served only to prolong our time together.

"We're having an elite mixer in about a segment at the *Drifter's Inn* and I would love for you two to join us."

"Where will everyone else be during this mixer?" Mia asked.

"All new members will be transported to our main campus shortly." Tarver leaned closer. "But I'm offering you access to an exclusive celebration before that happens. Don't you want to celebrate with me?"

Mia gave Tarver a coy smile. "How can I say no to an invite like that?"

It was about as easy as it sounded. But we still ended up boarding the passenger raeda with twelve other exclusive female invites. At least the hotel was nice. Eight stories tall, painted a rich white with shiny gold trim. Drifter's Inn looked almost as upscale on the outside as it did on the inside. The tiled floors were the first thing I noticed when we followed Tarver inside. They were so clean I could nearly make out my frown in the fuzzy reflection.

My guess was that Tarver was a regular at Drifter's Inn, seeing that he'd hardly said anything before one of the front desk clerks handed him the keycard to his room. "Follow me to the master suite, ladies," he said, and a few of the girls in our group cheered.

There was barely enough room for us to squeeze inside the lift, but Tarver didn't seem to mind. Instead, he insisted that we try, assuring us that girl's our size wouldn't come close to the lift's weight limit. But I wasn't an idiot. He and his raeda driver were obviously looking to take perverted advantage of the chance to squeeze themselves between a pool of women, so I made certain to be one of the last ones in the lift. Once the door closed, giggles erupted from the girls closest to Tarver and his driver. I could only thank El I wasn't close enough for them to try anything on me, since I would've likely forgot about the mission and brought the lift—and everyone in it—crashing down.

Inside the suite, Tarver was leaning against the minibar with a smile, as he watched us find a comfortable place to sit. And in a room that large, believe that there were plenty comfortable places. Two massive beds, chandeliers, plush carpeting, a large vid screen and a beautiful view of whatever city we were in. Even though I didn't care much for the situation I was in, I could at least appreciate the aroma of citrus wafting in the air.

"Make yourselves at home ladies," the driver said smugly.

"Time to mingle," Mia whispered.

"Mingle?"

"Yeah. Ask the other girls a few questions about how they ended up here. Hopefully, we'll find a pattern."

She turned and started for the closest girl, before I could ask what kind of pattern she was looking for. After talking to the first couple of girls, who only seemed interested in partying and spending a wild night with Tarver, my guess was that the pattern either involved loose tendencies or a lack of activity in the brain. At least, until I found the only girl in the room looking more out of place than I felt.

"Hi there," I said holding out my hand. "I'm Nina."

"Nice to meet you, Nina," the girl said gripping my wrist. "I'm Baneira."

"So, what brings you here? Aside from a chance with Tarver?"

"A chance with Tarver?"

"You know, to have some fun later," I clarified.

Baneira looked uncomfortable. "That's not why I'm here. But I'm not judging you, if that was your intention," she said quickly. *Thank the universe, there's at least one other girl in the room who isn't just trying to party.*

"Far from it actually."

"That's reassuring. My principal suggested coming here after he found out about my..." she trailed off.

"About your what?"

She looked away. "Nothing." I knew that look. It was the same look I had when half the school found out about my powers.

"Are you a rho?" I whispered.

Her brow furled tight as she looked up at me. "I hate that word," she huffed quietly.

"Sorry," I said, holding my hands up. "I just figured you might have special powers."

Her face softened. "How'd you know that?"

"Because I have powers too. Did they know you had powers before you came here?"

"I'm not sure. I never told anyone."

"Hold on a beat, okay? I'll be right back."

I rushed over and pulled Mia away from her conversation with two other girls. "Yup?" she asked.

"One of the girls here is a refractor. Maybe all the girls."

"Of course," Mia replied plainly. "Tarver selected us because he sensed our abilities. Now, if you'll excuse me." She hurried back to her conversation, as I stood there, wondering if she really understood just how easy she made it to hate her.

I don't doubt that everyone at the first event is a refractor but how would he know this?

Just then, Tarver reappeared with a familiar looking man in a green, hooded jacket. "Breakthrough," Mia said quietly.

"Breakthrough?"

"Have a look."

I stared at the wiry-framed man's sunken cheeks and frizzy hair and it all came back to me. The speedy guy Serec fought back at the shopping district. He looked directly at me and I stupidly froze like I was caught in a lie. I jumped when Mia placed a hand on my shoulder and suddenly started chuckling.

"What's so funny?" I whispered with irritation.

"Laugh like an idiot, before they discover us, idiot," Mia warned forcing the chuckles.

"You are such a troll," I chuckled through my teeth.

The man's eyes moved off of me, and continued scanning the room.

"I'll let you all in on a little secret," Tarver said. "The Life Reciprocal is a tiered organization. That means there's more than one level of service that you can provide for the cause." I didn't like where this was going. "I've chosen each of you because I believe you have what it takes to join the upper tier of our movement. And just to be clear, joining the upper tier makes life unlike anything you've ever dreamed. Everything you could ever want will be practically laid at your feet. And the cost is simple." *Here it comes.* "Swear an oath of full commitment to The Life Reciprocal. If you're not interested, you are more than welcome to go to our main campus. But this offer only comes once in a lifetime."

Silence descended upon the room. And I couldn't blame anyone for hesitating. As far as I was concerned, only an idiot would accept a vague no-turning-back deal like that.

"I'm in!" one girl said, raising the wine bottle in her hand. "I'm ready to be pampered anyway!" Two girls cheered in agreement and stepped up behind her.

"Anyone else ready for the good life?" Tarver asked the rest of us. Two more girls stepped up. "Sorry, but I don't think I'm upper tier material," one of them said, and the other girl nodded in agreement.

"If that's how you feel, you will always have a place with the lower tier members," Tarver said, voice reassuring. He gestured for the man in the hooded jacket to escort the two girls out. "Does anyone else want to make good on this opportunity before it's gone forever?"

Three more girls joined Tarver, and one more joined the man in the hooded jacket. That only left me, Mia, and Baneira. Baneira looked around timidly, and her eyes stopped on me. I could tell she was a sweet girl, which had me hoping she'd decline Tarver's offer, just like I'd planned to.

"We're with you all the way," Mia said, pulling me over to Tarver's side with her.

"That's what I like to hear," Tarver said.

My eyes went wide with shock as I stumbled behind Mia. I nearly smacked Mia's hand away. But I couldn't risk blowing our cover. I fought hard to keep the scowl hidden from view. But I definitely felt the same muscles in my face going tense. I looked at Baneira, who was studying me like I had the answer she needed. And I did. I just couldn't say it out loud.

"What's it going to be?" Tarver prompted. Everyone looked on, watching to see what decision Baneira would make.

Don't choose Tarver, don't choose Tarver.

Baneira stepped in with the rest of us, and my heart sank. The man in the hood led the other girls out of the room, as Tarver's driver brought out a tray of glasses and passed one to each of us for a toast.

"Let's celebrate with a glass of sparkling juice—just in case any of you lovely ladies are below legal drinking age," Tarver teased. But considering the mess Baneira and I were in, I'd almost wished for something a little stronger than juice. Tarver raised his glass high. "To your future—and the future of the world." We raised our glasses and drank.

A hash later, everything began to tilt, going fuzzy as my legs became weak and wobbly. The room started spinning and before I knew it, I was on the floor. My body suddenly grew heavy. Really heavy. The last thing I remember thinking about was how surprisingly soft the carpet was.

[7]

INITIATE

NARYN

I woke up to darkness. The floor's arrhythmia jostled me around too much for it to be a dream. My body was heavy, and it felt like someone had packed my brain up with cotton balls.

I tried to move, but no such luck. *My hands must've been tied behind me.* It was a little extreme, considering whatever was in that juice did a fabulous job of knocking everyone out and making me fatally drowsy. Then again, if every girl in the raeda was a refractor, it was arguably a smarter move on Tarver's part.

I tried to move again, but the resistance felt stronger. My body refused to respond to my commands and my senses were so dulled, I hadn't noticed the cloth pressing over my eyes. *A blindfold? They aren't sparing any precautions, are they?* And if that wasn't bad enough, I wasn't in the most comfortable position. But with my body very aggressively ignoring brain signals I was stuck playing the role of a sack of rice.

I stopped resisting, even if that resistance was completely localized in my mind. They'd gone to all the trouble getting me thoroughly drowsed up, and I wasn't keen on wasting energy fighting a losing battle.

Fine. Guess I'll just see where this goes for now. It was my final thought before unconsciousness reclaimed me.

Bright light drilled deep into my eyes the moment they opened. The cool air mirrored the chill of whatever I found myself strapped to.

Every few beats, something jerked my body to a stop. A few more beats passed and it jerked back in motion. Well, not my body exactly. Whatever was under it. I was still groggy, and it hurt to open my eyes. But I'd never like surprises. And these last couple surprises were downright nasty. I needed to see what was happening. Where I was going.

I forced my eyes back open, squinting hard through the light at the conveyor belt under me. A meter or so ahead of me was a girl from the hotel. I forced my head up to find more girls ahead of her, but I couldn't tell who. The conveyor stopped again, and a robotic arm moved over one of the girls. Once it pulled back, the conveyor started back up. The same thing happened with the next girl in line, and it wasn't until I was one girl away that I realized what was happening.

The conveyor belt stopped, the robot arm lowering and inserting a small needle into her chest. It buzzed as the syringe drained, injecting a pale orange liquid into her. The arm pulled back and the conveyor belt started up again, with me next in line.

Whatever that thing was injecting, I wasn't interested in sampling. The belt jumped to a stop leaving the arm directly over me. The syringe reappeared it's stock of orange goo replenished. My heart was pounding so fast, the grogginess all but evaporated from me. I focused as much as anyone could while violently trembling with panic.

The robotic arm started at me, and I pushed hard against the gravity around it. It kept lowering, the syringe resembling a razor-sharp fang up close. Trying to suck in my chest, I realized I hadn't been breathing. Not that it mattered though. I could breathe once the crisis was averted. My body became lighter, lifting slightly off the conveyor belt as my hair fluttered in front of my face. But lifting closer to the arm was the last thing I needed, and removing gravity wasn't making a difference to the machine. I released the flow of gravity and fell back against the belt.

The syringe was about three beats from biting into my chest. My brain tried to freeze up on me, as my lungs pulled at my throat for air. *Why does gravity only move...?* I didn't need to finish the thought to find my answer. I intensified gravity. But rather than pulling everything down, I pulled everything up, much like when I walked on ceilings.

"C'mon!" I strained. "Move!" The syringe shuddered for a beat. A dangerous beat. But just as the arm was about to make contact with my chest, the shudder became a violent shake. I jolted back, and I jerked forward, stuck under the new, conflicting pull of gravity. The straps gave, but only by a bit. Without them, I would've thrown myself into the needle. The drugs were seriously messing with my powers.

My face felt like someone was squeezing it, and my eyes were bulging too much to close. I concentrated on making the syringe the center point of my gravitational push. The robot arm shook harder. I gritted as my temples pounded so hard, I thought my head would burst. Finally, the machine buzzed as the orange liquid spurted out from the syringe and spilled upward into the robotic arm. The machine buzzed again and started moving away with a shrill strain.

I released gravity and plopped back onto the conveyor belt. A wave of dizziness washed over me as red and blue sparkles swirled around. But I'd beaten the machine. I squeezed my eyes shut, but the sparkles were still there. *Just breathe. Slow and steady.*

Once everything stopped spinning, Mia popped in my head and I wondered if she was okay. I hadn't seen her anywhere, and — annoying as she was — I hoped she was alright.

The conveyor belt came to a complete stop, and I could hear two men talking. "Another fresh batch of stupid girls," one of them said.

"You might want to keep it down," the other one warned. "One of them ends up the next knight, and they'll make you wish your thoughts stayed that way."

The first one scoffed. "These dumb test subjects are out like a lumen. Probably too drugged to remember me anyway."

I peeked an eye open and made a mental note. I'd definitely remember him alright. One by one, they put us in a large room. It wasn't until after they locked the door behind us that I realized only half of us were there. And Mia wasn't among us. There was a tall girl with blond hair, a girl with short dark hair, and Baneira. For whatever reason, they'd split us up.

The room looked like a cross between a gym and a detention cell. Bare walls surrounded us and a thin layer of what felt like rubber, padded the floor. It did little for comfort, but it was better than the smooth, hard concrete just outside our cell. Two doors sat on either end of the cell. The top third of the main door—better known as the only exit—was a think glass pane big enough to crawl through if it weren't there. My mind immediately went to work trying to calculate how much force would be required to break it. But I arrived at the conclusion that it was probably designed to withstand far more punishment than I could issue.

A little after everyone stirred, I pretended to wake up with them.

"Where are we?" one of the girls asked.

"I don't know," another girl moaned, rubbing her head.

They didn't seem to care about being in a locked cell, but maybe they just didn't have the energy for it yet. A bright light flickered on from a vid screen sitting high in one corner of the cell.

"In exchange for your commitment to our cause, you'll soon notice an improvement in your abilities. But that's just the beginning. Your devotion will be further tested, and depending on your performance, you may find the opportunity to gain more power."

The vid screen died as abruptly as it had come to life. We all sat there, waiting to see who would speak first. "What was that supposed to mean?" the blond girl asked.

I wanted to tell them about the forced injection. But that could expose the fact that I was able to avoid it. "I don't know," the girl with dark hair replied. "Whatever it means, they drugged us to do it."

The echo of a lock clinking and a door sliding on its track pulled everyone's attention. Footsteps clapped along the concrete. Two faces appeared in the doorway and looked us over for a moment, before the front door unlocked and slid open. They walked in with two trays of food.

"Why are we trapped in here?" the blond girl huffed.

"We're just the cooks," one of them replied almost apologetically.

"Well, did you cook drugs into this like you did with the juice?"

The cooks shared a baffled look. "Juice?"

"Don't play dumb!" A translucent blue something formed around her arms. "Just let me out, before I force my way out." The cooks paled and started backing away carefully.

"No need for that," Tarver called, stepping through the door with two people in green hooded jackets close behind. "I promised you power, and I'll need to keep you here until I've fulfilled that promise."

"Why does it have to be here?" the dark-haired girl asked. "Why are we closed off like this?"

"Because the second part of your treatment works best in this kind of environment."

"Second part?" I blurted. Tarver looked at me for a moment.

"Yes, Nana," he said plainly. "There are two parts to the process." Even without showing much emotion, his words felt like a smug slap to the face. "Don't worry though. You'll be monitored closely for as long as you're here." *Even better.*

The blond girl stepped closer to Tarver, her eyes threateningly defiant. "Then, the least you could do is not put us in cages like—"

A loud, sharp snap interrupted her, and she awkwardly fell flat on her face. Then again, there really is no non-awkward way to fall on your face.

The girl stumbled to her feet, swaying as if the room was shifting. That was when I noticed one of the green hoods behind Tarver had a hand extended. Her manicured nails betrayed her gender. After a beat, she relaxed her fingers and lowered her arm. The blond girl collapsed again, this time with a little more control. We all watched quietly as she took a moment before cautiously bringing herself back to her feet.

"I should apologize for failing to provide advanced warning," Tarver finally said, "but my friends here don't respond particularly well when my authority is challenged. That said, I strongly suggest you all eat your food, since my cooks went to the trouble of preparing it for you. The food isn't drugged, and things will be better for you if you eat now." He turned for the door. "I'll be back once we've finished prepping your rooms."

He walked out with the cooks and the hoods, and the lock on the door clicked behind them, solidifying our reality. We were detainees. And test subjects.

We exchanged quiet, glances, then sat at the table and looked at the food on our trays. Baneira was the first to start eating.

"How is it?" I asked.

"Pretty good," she said softly. "But it could be that I'm just very hungry."

It was the first thing she'd said since waking. But I didn't doubt her for a beat. The food's aroma was doing a great job of making my mouth water and I was plenty hungry myself.

It had been two days since Tarver had us paired off two to a room. Thankfully, Baneira was paired with me. The room was roughly the same as the holding cell they had us in earlier, just smaller, and there was a bunk bed pushed off to one corner. I took the bottom bunk.

Unfortunately, the first meal was the biggest meal they'd given us. Since then, it was just enough to stave off starvation. It honestly made keeping up with their force-fed propaganda vids harder than it should've been. But their message of radical change was clear. The only other thing I did manage to commit to memory was the two ways to identify other TLR members. One way was creating two fists with the thumbs extended and pressing them together. But reciting their secret phrase, "Life without freedom ensures death without cause," was even more common.

Near the end of the third day, one of the green hoods led us into a massive open room surrounded by large gray walls. It was the first time I'd seen Mia since the Drifter's Inn. I never thought I'd be so happy to see her. But I guess happiness is relative when you're trapped in a secret experimental detention facility.

A raised platform supporting a small skybox sat on one end of the room. Tarver was already inside, watching us. "It's time for us to test your abilities," Tarver announced. "Whether or not, you've experienced significant changes in your powers, this will serve as a benchmark, before the second part of your treatment.

"You okay, Nana?" Mia asked.

"Maybe if you stop calling me Nana," I said. I leaned closer to whisper. "Did they inject you with anything?"

"They tried. But controlling water has its advantages. You?"

"I reversed the push of gravity to keep it away."

"You mean pull."

"No, I don't."

She smirked. "Whatever you say, Nana."

"To determine your potential, you'll be paired off against one another in a sparring match. The fight will go on until one of you either yields or is knocked unconscious. And the winner will earn double portions on all meals for the rest of the dec."

As luck would have it, I was paired up against Mia. And as much as I would've relished the opportunity to send a gravity fueled fist into her jaw, fighting was the last thing I was in the mood for. Especially, when I'd be needing her help to escape soon.

The first two up were the dark-haired girl and a girl that had been separated into the same group as Mia. Tarver introduced them as Dara and Fileece. Fileece also had dark hair. But her hair was much longer, running down her back. She was also taller and stockier, and she looked like she'd been in a fight or two before. Of course, as she and Dara stood in the center of the arena, watching each other uncomfortably for what seemed like an eternity, I realized how deceiving looks could be.

"Let's go, ladies. Douuuble Portiooons," Tarver said, his upbeat tone churning the bile in my stomach. The lack of fighting experience was painfully obvious, judging by their pathetically amateur stances. Fileece charged forward, and threw a punch, aimed at Dara's face. But Dara disappeared in a blur, and reappeared behind Fileece, knocking her to the ground with surprising force. Dara grabbed a handful of Fileece's hair and pulled viciously.

"I yield!" Fileece cried.

"Dara, the speedster wins," Tarver announced excitedly. Dara released Fileece's hair and helped her up. They returned to the sidelines with the rest of us, Dara beaming and Fileece rubbing a spot in her scalp. The next match was between the blond girl and a lanky girl with a power I didn't get a chance to identify, since the match was only about half as long as the first one. The blonde wrapped herself in a translucent shield of energy and plowed right into the lanky girl, before she could make a move. The hit was nearly enough to knock the lanky girl unconscious.

Mia and I were up next, and I couldn't have been more disinterested. I'd always imagined I would settle things with Mia in the last dec of school, maybe in front of the entire student body. I hadn't figured out exactly how I would do it, but whatever the method, it would be big enough to wipe the smarm off her troll face for good. But after seeing the previous matches, I just wanted our match to end as quickly and painlessly as possible for both of us. And I was pretty certain, Mia wanted the same.

The word "fight," left Tarver's mouth, and an instant later, I was narrowly dodging a wave of blue electricity. She dipped around too much to trap with any significant gravitational force and leapt at me the moment she was close enough. Out of reflex, I swung at her ribs, hoping to stun her. But I was too focused on landing my attack to notice Mia had the same idea.

As I connected with her ribcage, a sharp pain stung just under my right arm, and I leaned into it. A sudden and powerful surge of electricity ravaged my body, and I convulsed so hard, breathing seemed impossible.

Determined to leave a mark of my own on the way to the ground, I thrusted my hands out at Mia and pushed with all I had. I caught Mia flying back, just as I hit the ground. Judging by her speed, I figured she had a good chance of hitting the opposite wall, if there was such a thing as justice in the universe. I laid there until the involuntary jitters stopped, which must have taken a while, since a couple of medics were helping me to my feet when my eyes finally opened again. I looked for Mia, but she was already back on the sidelines, with what looked like a grimace hidden behind a fake smile. It was the best I could hope for, after losing.

Baneira and the last girl were already in the middle of the room, by the time I was back at the sidelines. Baneira was watching patiently, as the other girl concentrated for a moment, then held a hand out in her direction. *What's Baneira waiting for? Maybe she's too scared to move.* The look on Baneira's face was unexpectedly calm when the beam of light shot out from the girl's hand. But I knew something bad was about to happen, and it made my stomach tighten.

Just as the beam made contact, there was another blinding flash followed by a shrill scream. Then, another sound echoed across the room but; but not one I expected. I tried to open my eyes, but it took a few beats for them to adjust through the strain. What sounded like repeated slapping accompanied by wailing echoed throughout the cavernous room.

"I yield! I yiel—" Something cracked loud enough to rattle my bones.

"The match is over!" Tarver yelled. "Guards!" When everything was finally in focus, I was almost certain I was hallucinating. Baneira was being pulled away from the other girl. The girl lay on the edge of death, her face a bloody mess.

Baneira, on the other hand, was trying violently to wrestle her hands away from the guards. Hands that were also covered in blood.

Medics rushed over to the girl as the rest of us watched on in silent horror.

Tarver cleared his throat. "Though your enthusiasm is appreciated, killing fellow initiates is strictly forbidden. Congratulations to those of you who've earned double portions. Rest assured, there will be additional opportunities for each of you."

Half of the girls looked pretty excited. And I was willing to wager it was mostly due to their abilities improving. The double portions were just a bonus. It seemed like they'd all already forgotten what had just happened. But there was no way I could forget. Especially after seeing Baneira's transformation.

"Nana," Mia whispered, jolting me back to reality. "We're running out of time. Part two of the treatment is three days away. Four at best. And we can't handle part two."

"Why not?"

"My guess is without the first part of the treatment in our blood, the second part will either kill us or turn us into something like a malefactor. Then kill us."

That put my brain on pause.

"Hurry up," one of the girls called from behind me. "I want my double portion."

"I should have a way for us to get out of here soon," Mia whispered. "Be ready." They split us up again.

I stared at my single portion with disappointment. A part of me expected Mia to win. But it didn't make the loss any easier. "You want some of mine?" Baneira asked, offering some of her meal.

"It's okay," I said.

"I can't eat this much. Maybe you could take a little, so the food doesn't go to waste?" I knew she was lying. Just a day earlier, she'd commented that the servings were so small they were practically teasing her stomach. But she was as sweet as I was hungry. Too sweet to nearly kill someone with her bare hands. Did the injection cause her wild mood swing earlier?

"Thanks," I said, taking a couple spoons of food from her plate. "You feeling okay?"

"I feel great," she said cheerfully. "I was a little uneasy at first. But after my performance today, I realize I should want to develop my power. The more I do, the better I can serve TLR."

I forced a smile. "That's...great."

"The best part is, now that bitch won't bother us anymore," A dark smile crept over her face, beckoning fearbumps across my arms.

She put a hand to her head, grimacing as she rubbed at her temple.

"Are you sure you're feeling alright?"

"I'm fine. The weird pressure in my head feels like it's spreading throughout the rest of my body."

"Does it hurt?"

"Not really. It's just pressure. Don't worry about it."

But I was worried. So much I could hardly sleep that night. *What's happening with Baneira and her sudden aggression? Is it a result of whatever was causing the pressure in her body?*

All I knew was that something very wrong was happening to her, and the longer she stayed, the worse it would get. I told myself I'd try and convince Mia to let Baneira break out with us first thing in the morning, when I heard groans coming from her bunk.

"Baneira?" I said cautiously. "You okay?" She moaned again. I hopped out of bed to check on her. She was curled up in a ball, trembling. "Baneira?" I touched her shoulder, and sweat covered my hand.

Nina," Baneira groaned. She opened her eyes, and a shriek pushed from my throat as two sickly pools of orange stared back at me.

[8]

NIGHTMARE

NARYN

"**Y**our eyes!"

"What about them?" Baneira asked, still clutching at her stomach.

"They're orange!"

I tried to help her to the bathroom. But before I could even get a good grasp on her arm, she lost consciousness. Fighting back just enough panic to focus on solutions, I rushed into the bathroom, ran cold water over a folded towel, and placed it over her forehead. I used a second towel to wipe the sweat from her neck and face.

Is everyone else experiencing the same transformation? If so, calling for help would raise suspicion. And it wasn't like I could anyway. They made sure communication was one-way in our rooms. We were isolated, just like Tarver said we'd be. *Slime ball!*

My heart was galloping, sweat beading on my forehead. I turned on the bathroom faucet and splashed water over my face. *Get it together, Ryn. You'll have to be ready if she turns into a malefactor.* I couldn't afford to be pessimistic at such a crucial time. *No, she won't turn. She's too sweet to turn into a savage malefactor. She just needs me to keep an eye on her for now.*

She'd been asleep for about a segment, without so much as a peep. A good sign. But staying awake was getting harder by the hash. And I couldn't assume she wouldn't have another episode, just because she was so placid at the time.

I lied back down, telling myself a good friend would find a way to push through the next few segments. But it couldn't have been more than a few beats, before my eyelids started getting heavier.

The next thing I knew, something was growling over me. I jerked up, wide-eyed and my arms tensed to guard my face. But nothing was there. *Is Baneira turning again?* I scrambled up to check on her. She was still sleeping quietly. I wanted to tell myself it was nothing, but I couldn't risk it any longer. I was no good to her, tired as I was. And if I fell asleep again, I'd be the one with the problem.

I grabbed my pillow and blanket and locked myself in the bathroom. The floor was cold and hard, so I wrapped the blanket around tight, like a cocoon, and passed out much quicker than I thought possible.

Something knocked against the bathroom door, and I screamed as my head popped up. "Are you alright, Nina?" a voice called from the other side. It was Baneira.

"Uh, yeah," I answered reflexively.

"Are you asleep in there?"

"I uhh...I guess I dozed off," I lied.

"You were snoring pretty loud."

"Sorry. I... felt a little sick."

"Are you...with child?"

"What?!"

"It's okay if you are. I know you mentioned coming here for Tarver."

"Actually, I said I wasn't interested in Tarver."

"I didn't know if that meant you'd already been with him and maybe now you—"

"No, no," I interrupted almost yelling. "I never have and never will be interested in Tarver."

"Well, even if you were, I wouldn't think any different of you." I could only wonder what she thought of me before.

"By the way, they just made an announcement that they're going to have doctors examine us in about a segment, so we'll need to get ready soon."

Just my luck!

A guard walked Baneira and me into a large testing room with triangular tables and bolted chairs. All the girls were already there when we entered. Mia was keeping to herself in a corner. Despite the circumstances, I was almost surprised to see her not trying to be the center of attention for once. She nodded her head for me to come talk to her, when she saw me.

"Did anything weird happen with your roommate last night?" Mia whispered. I told her about Baneira, and she confirmed the same thing happened with her roommate. Her eyes were a little red, but otherwise, she looked like she'd decided on the bathroom option a lot sooner.

"What do you think about all this?" she asked.

"They probably want to turn us into malefactors. But I don't see why they wouldn't have brought more people, if that was their goal."

"You're forgetting the pattern here."

I thought for a moment. "Our abilities."

"Exactly. Why create pawns when you could create knights? The serum they're using is different from the Exol we analyzed at HQ."

"Meaning?"

"I think Exol may be the second part of the treatment. This definitely complicates matters. If they're testing us today, and part two of the treatment is two days out, we're about out of time."

"For the mission?"

Mia nodded. "Fact is, we can't keep up the charade for much longer. Bottom line, I'm terminating the mission. We exfil tomorrow, before our roommates go full-feral and try to kill us. Until then, get all the rest you can. You look terrible, Nana."

I was about to tell her how she always looks terrible, when Tarver entered the testing room with his hooded bodyguards, two doctors, and four assistants rolling in equipment. They set up quickly and called us over one at a time. Most of the girls looked concerned. But since Mia and I were the only ones whose eyes weren't speckled with orange, I'd argue that we had the most to worry about.

By the time they got to me, my hands were trembling slightly. I had to give the right answers if I wanted to avoid suspicion. Hopefully, they wouldn't think to test my blood for that serum.

"How are you feeling?" the doctor asked as I sat in front of her.

"Okay, I guess," I answered.

"Your eyes are a little bloodshot and puffy. Are you getting sleep?"

"A little. I've been feeling a lot of pressure in my head since yesterday. In fact, it feels like the pressure's been spreading throughout my whole body." Maybe if I have similar symptoms to Baneira, they won't get suspicious. Even if it was a little behind their schedule.

The doctor flashed a light inside my mouth and ears, and took my pulse. "Your pulse is a bit rapid," she said, writing something in her notes. I tried to peek over, but she kept the notes angled toward her, which probably didn't help my pulse.

"Okay, we're done for now," she said, getting up and moving to the next girl.

Baneira walked over. "What did they say?" she asked.

"That I looked terrible and my pulse was elevated. What about you?"

"That I looked well-rested and my heart rate was a little slower than normal. But according to them it's perfectly normal at this point."

As much sense as that almost made it mostly didn't.

"Well, as long as you're feeling better."

Baneira looked at me like I'd just told her a riddle. "What do you mean?"

"Last night."

She thought for a moment. "Do you mean with the double portions for dinner? Like I said, I wasn't that hungry anyway. You can have some of my food today too, if you want."

"Hey there," Mia interrupted from behind me. "My name's Mimi. And you are?"

"I'm Baneira. It's nice to meet you, Mimi."

"Likewise. You mind if I borrow Nana for a moment?"

"Who?" Mia nodded at me. "Oh, you mean Nina? Sure, go ahead."

"Thanks," Mia said, pulling me off to a corner. "Nana was a better fit for you," she said.

"Is that all you wanted?"

"I hope you haven't gotten too attached to your little friend there." Mia nodded at Baneira.

"What's that supposed to mean?"

"It means we're out of here tomorrow night, before the docs catch on. I dunno if you've noticed, but they don't seem very impressed with us right about now."

I glanced over Mia's shoulder at the doctors. They were eyeing us suspiciously, and saying something to Tarver and the guards as he reviewed their notes.

Tarver approached us wearing a diplomatic smile. "How are my favorite ladies feeling this morning?"

"A little tired," Mia said instantly changing her tone to something more alluring. "But now that you're here I'm sure we'll manage."

For the first time since...ever, I was too nervous for Mia's flirting to turn my stomach. But Tarver seemed to like it.

"Exactly why you two are my favorites. Now I don't mean to alarm you. But it would seem my medical staff experienced a few minor issues with some of our testing equipment. So, I'm going to have some fresh new equipment sent over and we'll need to re-examine the two of you first thing tomorrow morning. Sound good?"

If it means seeing that handsome smile again," Mia said. Tarver stroked a finger along Mia's chin playfully and headed for the door. As soon as he and his guards walked out Mia's smile faded and she turned to me with a deathly serious look in her eyes. "As I was saying," she continued in a whisper. "Be prepared, cause we're leaving tonight."

[9]

BREAK

NARYN

"Escape tonight? But you just said—"

"Be ready to exfiltrate just after lights out." Mia interjected.

"I wanted to ask you about that," I whispered. "Do you think there's a chance we could bring any of the girls with us?"

"Sorry, but your little girlfriend is on her own, Nana."

A rush of heat raced across my face. "Why do you have to be such a b—?"

"It's not up for debate. Your safety is my only concern. Besides, she seems pretty happy here."

I wanted to argue, but Mia was right. Baneira seemed more excited than upset about what they were doing to her. And it wasn't like I could challenge Mia's orders anyway.

I was low on sleep that night, mostly out of anticipation. Baneira however, had no issue filling the cell with her thunderous snoring. I waited for what felt like segments, before I heard bumping coming from the hallway.

I peered into the dark hallway through the door window's obscured view. Nothing. I blinked a few times to ease my eyes and when I looked again, I nearly screamed. Someone was watching me from the other side of the glass. Still feeling tingles, I took a cautious step closer.

The eyes dropped out of sight and after a few scratching sounds, the door unlocked with a clank and swung open to reveal Mia smiling smugly. I squeezed my eyes shut and pursed my lips tight before the irritation in my soul could leap out of my mouth in a verbal attack.

"You ready?" Mia whispered. I looked back at Baneira one last time, and walked past Mia without saying a word. She grabbed my arm. "Wrong way."

"What about the guards?"

"Make sure you don't trip over them." Mia closed the door, and my throat tightened.

I stared at Mia with wide eyes once I noticed the unconscious guards lining the hall floor ahead of us. She smirked, flashing a keycard, then turned and jogged toward the door.

We turned a corner and eventually came to a fork. Mia turned right, and I followed her down the long-curving stretch of hallway. But I was running on borrowed fuel, and the gap between us began to grow.

"Keep up gymnast," Mia whispered over her shoulder.

"We couldn't all earn double portions or restful sleep," I snapped.

"No time for tears, Nana," She said, picking up her stride.

My throat and lungs burned as much as my thighs. But I forced myself to keep up. It was anyone's guess how her troll legs could move like lightning for that long. My hands fell to my knees the moment we stopped at another intersection. My lungs were nearly spazzing with hot intensity.

"We're heading right," Mia said.

I shook my head, panting. "Can't run anymore."

"Hope you can walk fast," she replied.

Even in a life or death, hating her felt right.

I started behind Mia, when I realized there was a door at the end of the hallway. An exit. Seeing our escape made running seem much more possible. But the relief that had begun to wash through my being was instantly contaminated. Standing in front of the exit, our only means of escape was the hooded woman.

She pulled her hood back, revealing menacing violet eyes that overtook her fair complexion. Her sharp features and athletic build denoted a woman who was as dangerous as she was beautiful. Her dark brown hair was a noticeable contrast to her milky skin that indicated an age close to mine. Mia slowed—probably waiting for me. But I slowed too. I wasn't about to rush into a fight with a hood when my body was still trying to make the most of the air I could give it.

"Why are you out of your cells?" She asked in a soothing voice that contrasted just as sharply with her glare, as her skin did with her hair.

Mia and I looked at each other, then back at her. Without saying anything we both rushed at her. She snapped both fingers, and We suddenly split up. I attacked the floor with my face, while Mia battled against the wall, before fiercely tumbling in front of me.

"Admirable effort, unimpressive results," the woman said as she approached.

I tried to slow her advance, but my powers weren't working. At least not like they were supposed to. Mia seemed to have the same problem. She fired out a wave of electric sparks that completely missed their mark.

I kept trying, but I couldn't sense any signs of gravitational shift. The closer she got, the more furiously I tried, until frustration polluted my mind and I began altering gravity at random.

"Not me," Mia yelped, and I stopped. I tried to focus my gravitational shift on Mia again, but nothing happened. More deliberately, I selected areas to alter gravitational fields. After a few tries, I started lifting off the ground, and it was so unexpected, I almost dropped myself back on my face.

The woman would be on Mia any beat, and using my powers was burning a bunch of energy that I didn't have. I had to figure out why my powers were behaving like I'd never used them before. Quickly, carefully, I tried removing more gravity from the space that lifted me off the ground. Instead of rising, my body was weighted back to the floor. I added gravity there again and started floating. Everything was beginning to make sense.

Through pure luck I found the area necessary to affect Mia, and lifted her just as the woman kicked at her. She barely grazed Mia and nearly lost her balance.

The woman trained her eyes on me and I knew I was in trouble. The cold intensity of her gaze provided excellent reason to be frightened as she darted forward and lunged at me. Unfortunately for her, the only way to me was through ia. I increased gravity in the space I'd identified as Mia's, and despite her efforts, she couldn't keep from stumbling through my gravitational field.

The gravitational field ensnared the woman, slowly lifting her off the ground. She soon joined Mia, who was pressed against the ceiling overhead. She looked over her shoulder at Mia, probably planning to make the most of the chance to at least subdue one of us. But I wasn't about to make it so easy for her.

I reversed gravity, before she could attack and Mia flopped on top of her, both falling to the ground with a thump. Neither of them moved for a few beats— stunned by the fall.

But with Mia's coordination and motor control still glitching as much as mine, the woman was the first to make her move, putting her hands around Mia's neck. Mia desperately squirmed, until tiny sparks began racing around her body, an electric crackle echoing throughout the corridor. The woman convulsed violently, gritting her teeth as stray sparks scared the walls. When Mia finally ceased, the woman went limp, and my body stopped acting so foreign.

Mia was back on her feet right after me. And as soon as she was, she dashed toward the exit. I rushed after her, and the burning in my legs returned with a vengeance. But I didn't care. I stayed at Mia's heels the whole stretch, leaping outside just after Mia slammed through the door at full speed.

A rush of chilled night air breezed over me, providing some consolation to the aching that my mind was struggling to suppress as I kept up a steady jogging pace.

"You can fly, right?" Mia asked.

"Kind of."

"Better than a 'no.'"

Electricity sizzled and whirled around Mia, just before she leapt. Once her feet left the ground, her body quickly ascended.

Reversing gravitational waves on a moving target is about as difficult as it sounds. And it wouldn't be any easier considering how exhausted I was. I altered gravity as I jumped, and nearly lost my balance when I fell back to my feet.

Perimeter sirens roared, and lumens flashed, searching for us. The best I could manage was hovering slowly. Far from enough to escape.

"Anytime Nana," Mia called.

"I'm trying," I yelled.

The lumens locked onto us and I spotted another hooded guard running our way.

"Nana, it's fight or flight. If you can't make this work, we'll have to fight our way out. Your call."

If it were my call, I never would've come in the first place, and I sure as Hadal wouldn't be struggling to fly when I could be flying. But flight was nothing like my normal walking on the ceiling.

Wait. That's it! I was proficient at ceiling walking, which required me to invert gravity around me and "fall" up. I just had to pretend the sky was a huge ceiling. As I concentrated, my hair and clothing began to float around me, answering gravity's gentle call.

"They're getting closer, Nana," Mia warned.

"Shut up!" I yelled as I unbound the full gravitational force, and shot into the sky.

Wind whipped past as I fought to gain control of my ascent. When I finally managed to stop myself, Aio and Karon greeted me in the sky.

"Bout time," Mia yelled, catching up with me. But I wasn't in the clear yet. I'd pulled myself into the air, but I was still positioned over the compound. I repositioned gravity again and started losing altitude fatally fast, when a heavy force suddenly pulled me forward. I released it and pulled up again. Watching me move was probably like watching a vintage vid game character traverse the screen in choppy four-directional movements. I didn't care. I was flying. And choppy or no, flying felt good.

"Our extraction point is just beyond Oltresullean airspace," Mia called, trying to keep up with my erratic movements.

"You coordinated an extraction?" I yelled behind me.

"Not like we can fly all the way back to Vaticia."

When we finally made it back to base, Mia released me until the next morning's debriefing. "Well done, Nana."

"NaRyn," I corrected.

Mia held my gaze for a moment, then smiled. "NaRyn," she finally said with a nod. "Get some rest. You've earned it."

I wasn't going to argue there. And neither was my body. I must've been really tired, because the next morning even Serec was already up and dressed when I was just stepping out of my room.

At the debriefing, Mia listed out all the information she'd collected, which had me wondering how she found the time. I had to admit, sitting in on the debriefing gave me a whole new respect for her abilities.

"This is where we were taken for the TLR retreat," Mia said, pointing to an area on the gameboard map.

"That's Neran province," Ari chimed. "A sizeable portion of that area is unsettled. The Life Reciprocal might have easily jumped at the opportunity to purchase it from the Oltresullean federal government."

"If so, do you suspect the area could be housing their main base?" Sa'Sha asked.

"It's not impossible, but I have my doubts. Still, with more time we can probably confirm this."

"Not knowing is unfortunate. But I trust your judgment Sentinel." Sa'Sha said. "Did you manage to learn anything else useful Ambi?"

"Sure did. On our way out, we got into a skirmish with one of the hooded guards, like the green jackets we fought before at the shopping district. Lift provided the perfect opportunity to place a tracker on her. As soon as it's activated, we can let her lead us back to their main base."

"Go for it Anni," Kareen said and the tracker activated, synchronizing with the gameboard. "If the guard is still wearing the tracker, we'll have her location in few beats."

"How did you sneak in a tracking device? They confiscated everything, as soon as we got there." I said.

"I kept it some place no one would look." Mia said casually with a wink, and I immediately regretted asking.

Kareen manipulated the hologram on the gameboard, until a red dot appeared over the three-dimensional map. "Is this where you two were?" she asked.

"Close," Mia answered. "About fifty kilometers southeast of that point."

"I'd say we've found our point of interest," Sa'Sha noted.

"Sentinel sir!" A man yelled, bursting through the door. "Sorry to interrupt," he said with a quick bow.

"What is it, Pit?" Ari asked.

"It's the news stream, sir."

Kareen manipulated the gameboard pulling up a hologram of the news stream. "...philanthropist has indeed been kidnaped. We've received confirmation that Iam Rhasatto, President of Theall Medical Corporation has been abducted by two Rho wearing green hoods," the reporter announced.

Serec and Sa'Sha exchanged a look that I couldn't quite read.

"It finally comes together," Mia's voice cut into the silence.

"What comes together?" Serec asked.

"One of the notes I found, mentioned a key. My guess is whatever their master plan, it'll require a key to work. Maybe Mr. Theall knows where that key is."

"Our most recent intel made mention of a key as well," Ari chimed. "I assumed it was code for something else, but perhaps it's just as simple as it sounds."

Serec had a troubled look that Sa'Sha picked up on right after I did.

"What's on your mind Zero?" Sa'Sha asked.

"It's hard to explain, but something about this feels off."

"Off how?"

"Not sure. Maybe it's just...maybe it's nothing."

Sa'Sha studied Serec for a moment, then turned to the rest of us. "For now, we'll need to focus on extracting Iam Rhasatto before they can siphon information about this key from him. It appears our infiltration mission just became a hostage rescue."

[10]

MR. RHASATTO

SA'SHA

"This the place?" Serec asked.

"According to Mia's tracking device," I replied.

The massive dome was covered in vegetation, with no visible entrance. For an organization with such vast resources, TLR's location was undoubtedly strategic. I doubted anyone would've thought to look for their main base in such a remote area.

"We'll need to find a way in, before the Kinetic Ops teams fall asleep, waiting for our move," Serec said.

"Says the guy who falls asleep right in front of the Colonel, during a meeting."

"That was one time! Besides, when a meeting drags on like that, I'm surprised anyone can keep their eyes open."

"Still terrible, but your excuses are improving. Northe trained you well."

"Ha ha," he mocked.

An agent from Clandestine Services approached. "Commander, we've located a point of entry."

We followed the agent nearly one-third of the way around the large dome, and stopped at a shaded area between two large trees.

"Here we are," the agent said.

I scanned the area. "I don't follow."

"Because they've chosen such an effective spot for hiding. This entire area is blanketed in some sort of magnetic field." *That explains why I can't see into the dome.* The agent knelt down to a thick patch of grass, just off-center between the trees. He moved it back to reveal a large metal trap door. It was extremely easy to miss; especially without my powers. Two nearby camouflaged Clan agents walked over and lifted both ends for us, revealing a small row of stairs leading into a long passageway.

I looked at Serec. "Ready?"

"I'll lead the way."

Serec stepped in first and reached out a hand to help me down. He was a real gentleman when he wanted to be. At a glance, we had stepped into a long, dark cavern. It was surprisingly clean, despite the pungent odor of moldy dirt wafting up from beneath us. A row of lumens was embedded into the walls, illuminating the length of the narrow passageway. At the end of the path stood a large, solid-looking metal door with a small slot at eye level.

Serec turned to me as he pulled his brown cloak hood over his head. He waited for me to pull mine over too, then turned and knocked on the door. The eye slot slid open, and eyes peered through at us. "Life without freedom..." the voice prompted.

"...ensures death without cause," Serec recited. The pair of eyes shifted between Serec and me once more before the slot closed, and the door opened.

The area was larger than expected and filled with a mass of people moving about, like ants in a terrarium. And the way the enormous domed ceiling enclosed us, I almost felt like an ant. Nearly everyone wore hoodless robes in a dark shade of brown or gray. But surprisingly, no one was wearing green. The scent of grain wafted across my nose, drawing my eye to a large group of hoods, filling bags with grain and loading them into a container. That led me to make other observations. Clothing production, water purification, even construction of components for modular dwellings. This place was exactly what it claimed to be. *Could we be wrong?* I shook the thought away. I knew as well as anyone that a benevolent facade could hide an overwhelming darkness. Everyone went about their work, too preoccupied to even send so much as a glance in our direction, which I had no qualms with. A few meters above us, a second floor extended around the dome. But in the center of the floor was a large opening. Gray cloaks moved around this upper area but still no green.

The cloaks' color probably denotes hierarchy.

"Probably," Serec's voice echoed in my head. I stifled a yelp, trying to mask my surprise.

"Did you just read my mind?"

"I wasn't trying to if that's what you're asking. Maybe, think quieter?"

Having to watch the audible volume of my thoughts with Serec unsettled me for obvious reasons. The idea of him possibly hearing what went on in my head, made me consider running as far from him as my legs could carry me.

"Speaking of mind reading, it would be a huge help if you could skim a few people for info, before we get started. I know you try to avoid that but—"

"If I don't we may inadvertently reveal we don't belong. I understand," I replied.

I stepped into the crowd and positioned myself shoulder to shoulder with a member wearing a brown robe.

"Perhaps, you can help me," I said, pulling his attention. He froze as I scanned his mind. Five beats was all I was willing to risk, in order to avoid drawing attention from others. It only took three to see he had no particularly useful information.

"Back to work, initiate," a man in a gray robe ordered the man I had just probed. "You don't have time to be standing around talking, when there's work to be done."

Piece one of the hierarchy solved. I walked up to the man in the gray robe and looked into his eyes. "Hold still for a moment, would you?" I said, freezing him in place. There was more to sift through, which turned a moment into several. But the information I gleaned was much more useful.

"What'd you find out?" Serec whispered.

"A couple of things. For one, the people in green hoods function as elite enforcers. So, we'll only see them around if there's trouble. Secondly, there's apparently a very important private meeting happening one floor above us."

"Sounds interesting. Think it may have to do with Iam Rhasatto."

"I think we'd best find out."

We negotiated our way through the sea of brown and gray robes until we found the stairway leading up to the second floor, and discreetly hurried up the stairs. There was a row of doors at the top of the stairway. I attuned my eyes to detect heat signatures and scanned through the doors for any movement.

"Any guards?" Serec asked.

"There doesn't appear to be any. But I do see three heat signatures further ahead."

We crept over to the door in question and found a biometric lock. I quickly disabled it and slid the door slightly ajar. It was dark, but faint murmurs emanated from somewhere further inside.

"There's another room at the back of this room," Serec said, peeking in. "I see light coming from under a closed door inside."

He carefully pushed the door open and I crept in behind him. I tried to ease the door shut, but an unexpected suction pulled it out of my hands and it closed with a loud thump. I tensed in surprise, and the murmurs stopped. They had to have heard us. I scrambled through the darkness and into the corner directly across from the inside door. We crouched, watching the other door for movement. Another moment passed and I reattuned my eyes to infrared. No one was moving, and everything was still silent on the other side of the door. My heart sounded like it had switched place with my brain, pulsing heavily in my ears and filling the deafening silence. After what seemed like an eternity, the voices resumed. I told myself that they probably did hear something, and that the sensible thing to do would've been to wait it out, as a precaution. Finally taking a bigger breath, I looked over at Serec, who was watching me patiently. I nodded, and we moved to either side of the doorway to listen closer. I looked through the wall at two heat signatures as I eavesdropped.

"I don't have a problem with waiting," one voice began, "but the *Noctus Drive* has been operational for decs now. Why the delay?"

"Calm down, Tarver," another voice said. "We will fire the Drive as soon as Lord Astaroth decides the time is right, and no sooner." The voice sounded familiar, but I couldn't quite place it.

"Easy for you to say," The first voice argued. "You're sitting comfortably at Theall, playing President for so long it's all gone to your head. Selling your boss to the Soldiers was too easy, wasn't it?"

Athan Karles, vice president of Theall Medical Corporation is a part of TLR? The more I thought about it, the more it made sense. He could provide the perfect opportunity to get to Rhasatto, his boss trusted him enough to regularly let him run the company in his absence. But perhaps, it still wasn't quite regularly enough.

"This coming from the man who allowed himself to be outsmarted by a couple of prep school girls?" Karles challenged.

"Shut your mouth, Karles!" Tarver snapped.

"Peace, you two," a third voice warned.

"Yes, Lord Astaroth," Karles and Tarver said, almost in perfect unison as they bowed.

Three figures entered, from what looked like an adjoining room. One of the figures was almost a head taller than the one next to him making him the tallest person in the room. It was difficult to be certain, but I could detect a fourth figure, still in the other room. The figure was also larger in size and hunching over awkwardly. I could tell the men that stepped in were all wearing cloaks, and I wouldn't have been the least bit surprised if they turned out to be green. The center figure sat down in front of Tarver and Karles with a heavy thud. "The night of the full moons approaches, and our final segment nears," he said. "All that's left is the key."

Key?

"Lord Astaroth, if I may," Tarver began. "How are we to control so many creatures once the people have turned. Five percent of the population is quite significant."

"You should know as well as anyone that the *maculosus* are a mere byproduct of this process. They will serve their purpose, then our true goal will come to fruition," he was so... calm, so sickeningly casual about such an atrocious act. "Speaking of which, Tarver, what are our current numbers?"

"Roughly fifteen thousand and counting, sir," Tarver answered.

"And our catalyst?"

"We definitely have enough to proceed with the plan, my Lord," Athan replied.

"Very good. Tarver, have you managed to find a replacement for Sarani yet?"

"I believe so, my Liege. We are currently working between five girls from the Disciples Program. One has shown great potential and has been brought here for further service. You may have your next knight."

"Let us hope so. Considering your blunder with the two that escaped, the least you could do is produce admirable results before our plan is put into action."

"Yes sir. Please forgive me."

"Harine informed me that they were skilled enough to surprise and overwhelm her. All the more reason to bolster our forces quickly. Place the girl with 'great potential' in our ranks for a test run today, so I can personally judge her merit as a capable vessel. As you can imagine, I'm disinterested in any further tarnishing on the reputation of my Knights of Just Death."

"Yes, Lord Astaroth," Tarver said, lowering his head.

"On to our final order of business," Astaroth said with the snap of his fingers. One of the hooded figures yanked another figure into the room. Judging by the way the figure stumbled in, my guess was that he was bound at the wrists and ankles.

"Mr. Iam Rhasatto," Astaroth said playfully, "why the grimace?"

"Do you expect smiles and laughter from everyone you kidnap, or are you simply of a foolhardy disposition?" Iam said defiantly.

"You can't speak to Lord Astaroth that way," Karles erupted.

"How dare you speak so callously to me, you traitor! I took you in and helped you transform your failing business into one of the largest companies on Orbis. I should've seen the signs sooner."

"Mr. Rhasatto, you have quite the strong will," Astaroth noted. "But will is a capricious thing under the right circumstances. I intend to see just how capricious your will is. And what circumstances are required for you to share with me the location of the key."

"Find someone else to torture. I don't have any key."

"I'm not asking if you have it," Astaroth corrected. "I'm asking where it is."

"I wouldn't tell you if I knew." Iam spat.

"So be it." The hoods grabbed Iam by the collar. Iam tried to resist, but the guard punched him in the stomach, and when he doubled over, the guard struck him over the head. He collapsed and the guards dragged him out. To see such a proud and confident man reduced to a detainee ignited a zealous desire for justice within me. We were going to escape with Iam. And Astaroth was going to answer for his transgressions. We made our way back down the stairs.

"What's happening in there?" Serec asked.

"They're teaching Mr. Rhasatto the price of resistance. And I'm certain, that was only a taste. We have to save him."

"Any ideas?"

"Not at the moment." I narrowed my focus, and scanned around the building. "But hopefully, accessing their main database will shed a little light on whatever this key is supposed to be. "There's a massive collection of electronics with a heavy power output two floors below us."

We stepped inside a large processor room and found a single woman in a lab coat, hunched over her workstation with eyes glued to the screen. If Kareen and

Ari had a daughter, I imagined she wouldn't be too different from her. I snuck up behind her, placed a hand on the top of her head, and implanted the thought that she was way past due for a nap.

"I don't think I'll ever get tired of that." Serec said with a smile.

"You're next if you don't slow down on the training."

Serec gave an unamused side glance, as he moved the woman to the floor. "Can't stop until I at least beat you."

I took a seat in her work station. "At least?" I inserted Kareen's Portable Hacker's Assault Kit, or *PHAK* drive into the data port.

"This isn't gonna take forever, like last time?"

"The PHAK drive is a significant upgrade to the last model, but it will still take a while to sift for pertinent data."

"So, what you're telling me is: Yes, it will take forever."

"Some hero you are."

"Please. There's a fine line between a hero and a martyr."

"Can you keep it down, please. I need to concentrate, so we can get out of here, before someone scary comes in here and makes my poor hero break a nail."

I could feel him scowling, and I had to fight back the smile as I pretended not to notice. The PHAK drive sifted through their network almost as fast as I'd expected. But fast wasn't fast enough, and I sensed at least a few of the ominous energies roaming the compound. The fact of the matter was that Serec and I were both struggling to ignore the disquiet creeping up. Perhaps if the moment weren't so tense, I could have better appreciated how cutely his eyebrows knit together when he was worried.

"Done," I said, snatching the PHAK drive from the data port. "Iam is in a detention cell on the west side of the first floor's outer ring."

"Did you cover your tracks?" Serec asked.

"I left a log bomb in the system to do it for me."

"Log bomb?"

"Logic bomb," I clarified. "It's a nasty bit of code that will not only erase all traces of my activity, but delete vital files and cause a system reboot. It's time triggered and we only have approximately ten hashes to recover Iam and exfiltrate before it detonates. Which means we have to hurry"

The cells were just like the ones on Kunai. Dark, dank, and depressing. I hurried along the winding hallway, until Serec stopped and turned toward one of the cells.

"Mr. Rhasatto?" Serec called. "Are you okay?"

Iam sat hunched on a small stool with his head hanging low.

"Try as much as you like," he said without bothering to lift his head, "I won't help any of you."

"You misunderstand," I said. "We're here to help you." I placed a hand over the electronic pad and the cell door unlocked, sliding open.

"Who are you?" Iam asked warily.

"Friends."

"You'll have to forgive me. But at the moment, I'm rather doubtful of who I can actually consider a friend."

"Please, Mr. Rhasatto, we—"

"For all I know, this is just some plot by that Astaroth character. He's clearly running out of time. It would be naive to assume that he wouldn't resort to such a measure to gain my cooperation."

"Will you at least come with us?"

"You hide your identities, and yet you expect me to blindly trust you?" Iam scoffed. "For all I know, he sent you himself."

"Quite the contrary, I can promise you. At least allow us to break you out of here first. You can do whatever you want once we get you outside."

"Or perhaps you two are looking to acquire the same information for your own ambition. If so, following you could be akin to jumping out of the pot and straight into the fire."

"I promise you Iam," I began, pulling my hood back and altering my eye color. "We've reserved the fire for Astaroth."

The defiant reservation evaded his face, replaced by utter disbelief.

"What are you—"

"I know what I'm doing. This scenario is far from ideal. But if he knows anything about the key to the Noctus Drive, then getting him out of here could save millions of lives. Leaving him is not an option."

"Blissful?! Is it really you? I must be going mad."

Serec removed his hood. "You're not going mad," he said. "But if we don't hurry, we'll see firsthand what happens when everyone here does." Lumens flickered a few times, then cut out completely.

"Will you come?" I asked Iam.

"Yes, of course," he said. "Please, forgive my doubt, Your Grace."

I severed Iam's restraints, and we raced down the hallway behind Serec. The signal I was picking up from the security system, told me our chance of escape was narrowing quickly.

"The system is already rebooted and it's using me to lock onto our position."

"How much time do we have?" Serec asked.

"Not sure. But I know we're nearly out."

A few of the members looked at us in startled confusion, as we pushed past them and toward the door. The same guy was standing guard.

Without slowing, Serec punched the guy in the face so hard his head banged against the door and he fell unconscious. He pushed him out of the way, and yanked the door open.

"Stop!" a voice called from behind us. I looked back to find five hoods in pursuit.

Iam and I ran through the doorway, and Serec pulled the door closed behind us. We sprinted the entire length of the tunnel, as a cacophony of voices boomed behind us. Reaching the light at the end of the tunnel, I threw the door open and scurried out with Iam and Serec right behind me.

"The enemy is on our tail," I warned the team guarding the door. They collected into a battle formation, anticipating an explosion of guards. But no one emerged.

"If you guys are looking for peons to pop up, you're wasting your time," a voice called. I spun around to find two men in green hoods, smiling as they approached. One of them was thin and wiry. The other, dangerously large and imposing. "I'll only say it once," the larger one said. "Return Rhasatto, and your deaths will be quick."

[11]

I AM ASTAROTH

SA'SHA

They pulled back their hoods, and I instantly recognized the thinner man from our last fight. Xaster, the speedster. But the second guy was a new face. A face that had likely seen its fair share of battles. Tanned leathery skin covered sharply chiseled features, a scar running from his forehead to his left cheek.

Serec started in their direction. "You should get Rhasatto to safety," he said.

"What are you talking about? I'm not leav—" Serec thrusted his palms down and a devastating wall of wind sprouted from the ground, blowing my hood back and nearly knocking Iam off his feet. "What in Hadal do you think you're doing?!" I yelled through the invisible wall separating us.

"Keeping you safe," Serec yelled over his shoulder, as he threw off his brown cloak. "Just guard Iam." Anger melded with anxiety sending a pulsing heat to my face as I watched the back of Serec's infuriatingly thick head. "Correct me if I'm wrong, but you guys are part of the elite guard, right? The Knights for Death?"

"*Knights of Just Death*," the larger one corrected. "You've got some real stones taking us on alone."

"Stones for brains, maybe," Xaster corrected. "Or did you forget how much help you needed last time?"

Xaster smiled and became a blur. I looked back at Serec, surprised to see him standing there, looking unimpressed. Suddenly, Serec shuffled back, and extended his leg in front of him. An instant later, Xaster reappeared, crashing to the ground and tumbling clumsily into the wall of circulating air. The wind flipped him back in the opposite direction; a sight so comical, I would have laughed if I wasn't furious.

I expected a swift retaliation from the larger knight. But he cackled instead.

"At least, you weren't wiped out on the first move. What's your name, kid?" he asked.

"Zero," Serec replied. "You?"

"Hypersol."

"Hyper? Soul?" Serec repeated.

"It's one name! Don't break it up!" he corrected.

"Your partner seems to have the situation under control," Iam noted. "Perhaps it would prove prudent to take our leave?"

Perhaps Iam is right. Serec seemed to be handling himself well enough. And despite Serec's blatant abandon, Iam was considered precious cargo. It would be imprudent to place him at risk.

I waved one of the agents over. "Keep a close eye on Mr. Rhasatto," I ordered. "If anything happens, get him somewhere safe." I knew it would have been wiser to take him myself. But I didn't care how Serec felt. I wasn't about to leave him on his own again.

"I would feel a lot better if you came with me," Iam said.

"I'm afraid I can't do that Mr. Rhasatto. We don't abandon our own." I threw off my cloak, my eyes still following Serec like a nighthawk. He and Hypersol were locked in a stalemate—neither of them budging. It wouldn't have been a problem if Xaster hadn't just gotten back to his feet. He zipped around the two of them, building speed for his next attack.

Serec's footing was starting to falter. His left knee lowered closer to the ground. Hypersol's size, strength, and stamina were about to get the best of him, and I unsheathed Nightfall, preparing to teleport past Serec's barrier. Serec's knee came dangerously close to the ground and I caught sight of the green blur zipping through the air at him.

I started to warn him, but he dipped both knees and rolled back in time for Xaster to dropkick Hypersol square in the face. An instant later, their bodies jerked up into the sky, and Serec's heels were the catapult. One backflip later, they both slammed back to the ground. "Commander," a familiar voice called from behind. Jin rushed over with a dozen Kinetic Ops agents behind him.

"The EVAC craft is waiting at the landing zone, and reinforcements are on ground. We're all standing by for your orders," Jin informed.

"I'm afraid I cannot make use of you all. Zero is deliberately blocking us from stepping in on this fight."

"What in Hadal is he thinking?" Jin blurted.

"My sentiments exactly," I said. "But Zero's fought Astaroth's elite guards on multiple occasions now, so he knows what they are capable of better than anyone. And my guess is that he's trying to avoid unnecessary casualties."

But even as I explained the most logical rationale, a heaviness pressed against my throat. *Why doesn't he trust me to help in the fight? Is he doubting me?*

The longer the fight raged, the more anxious I became. I didn't expect Serec to maintain the advantage if the fight went on for too long. And Hypersol did everything he could to ensure that it did. Hypersol may not have had the array of abilities Serec did, but his combat prowess and stamina were right on par. Even worse, he'd proven himself immensely resilient. No matter how many times Serec hit him or knocked him to the ground, he continued to get back up. And the more Serec threw at Hypersol, the harder it was getting to put him back on the ground.

Maintaining the barrier of wind was taking its toll on Serec much faster than he could handle. And after two hashes of dominating the two-man battle, Serec was panting like he had been on the receiving end of the fight.

Serec's barrier suddenly collapsed, and I started to rush in, when one of the agents yelled, "Malefactors!" from behind me. I spun around to find malefactors teeming by the thousands.

"Quake, concentrate your forces on penetrating the enemy line," I ordered. "We have to get Mr. Rhasatto to safety."

"Yes, Comman—" Something sent Jin flying, and he crashed into a tree with a burst of dust and wood splinters.

"I'm afraid that won't be necessary, Blissful," a familiar voice boomed. I turned to match the voice with a face, and didn't make it halfway before an intense force overwhelmed me and sent the world spinning. I collapsed and tumbled along the ground, the crackle of leaves popping in my ears like tiny explosions. Then, there was nothing but the sound of wind whooshing overhead, chilling me as something burned hot within. My head throbbed with intense pressure, as I fought to regain my wits.

"Are you okay?" The voice sounded like it was a world away.

I slowly picked myself up, my head screaming. I grabbed it reflexively, as the pain radiated down to my neck. A hand grabbed hold of my arm and wrapped it over a shoulder, helping me to my feet.

"Zero?"

"It's okay. I'm here." Serec's voice became clear.

Everything slowly steadied until Serec's soft green eyes came into focus. He watched intently, his mind screaming his concern.

"I must confess, I've enjoyed playing my part in this game," the voice said. "But as the saying goes, all good things must come to an end." Finally, with my vision clear, the ominous voice had a face to match.

"No...this...this can't be. You can't be..."

Heat licked the back of my eyes, as I trembled at the utterly impossible nightmare, turned too real to deny. Iam was standing over me and smiling like a ligorn looming over wounded prey.

"Oh, but it's true my dear princess," Iam said darkly. "I am ASTAROTH."

[12]

DEVASTATION

SA'SHA

Why didn't Serec let me fight with him? Why did he have to shut me out? Why did he have to act like such a self-absorbed fool at such a critical moment? I had a million questions shuffling through my mind. And not one of them could have done anyone a bit of good at that moment. El! How could I have been so blind? Waves of anger swept over me with each passing beat, and I wanted to kick myself for failing to recognize the obvious.

"I should applaud you two," Astaroth said, his voice booming as it echoed through the woods. "Infiltrating our stronghold was no small feat. And single-handedly defeating two of my knights—truly remarkable." The sea of malefactors parted, as four more knights walked up and stood behind their master. "Still, you've taken the better of my patience," he said coldly. "Capture the princess. Do as you please with the rest."

Malefactors, Knights of Just Death—the whole of Astaroth's forces rushed into the fray. We were severely outnumbered. And with Astaroth's knights on the battlefield, there was no certainty that our skill advantage over the malefactors would make the difference. But it was what we'd been training for. We were the most skilled fighting force in the world. And I refused to believe otherwise. I steadied myself and Serec released my arm, allowing me to retrieve Nightfall. I lifted the blade high. "Task force!" I yelled. "Defensive positions!" With a resounding war cry, everyone rushed forward into battle.

"Are you okay?" Serec asked.

"Fine," I said trying to hide the pain of my throbbing head.

"You're in no condition to fight right now. You should sit this battle out."

I looked at Serec, not caring to hide my irritation. "So should you. I'm sure you're out of steam after treating me like your second-class apprentice."

"One of us had to watch Iam," he defended.

"So, why not me, right?" Serec gave a blank stare that set my jaw tight. "Nothing to say? Were you expecting a thank you for that brazen disregard for orders or logic? You compromised us," I said coldly. "Our advantage was time, and you just wasted it."

"But Astaroth—"

"Could have been handled if he was isolated," I interjected.

Heat surged through my veins, and I couldn't look at him anymore. I turned on my heel and ran into the battle. He called after me, but it wasn't the time for conversing. We were well past that point. The task force was performing admirably against the malefactors, but Astaroth's knights kept forcing holes into our defenses. Agents were dropping left and right, the more the knights intervened, and only those closest to the captains were keeping up the fight. But they weren't the only ones who could exploit openings.

A horde of malefactors advanced as Renes emerged from the crowd, combusting pockets of air in front of him. A small group of malefactors congregated. Easy prey for Nightfall. I ran in an arcing path, ignoring the pain stabbing in my head with each step, each breath, each passing beat. The hungry blade screamed through the air, rending flesh without the slightest resistance. I lunged at Renes and twisted—my head screaming in agony as I jammed my elbow into the middle of his back. He groaned and fell to the ground. For a moment, we both laid sprawled in the dirt, trying to press away the pain that consumed us. Suddenly, he flipped himself over and extended a hand at me. I narrowly rolled away from the splash of heat that followed. I sprang at him again, and he extracted two daggers, slashing once I was close. But close-range combat clearly wasn't his strength. In less than a hash, I'd knocked both daggers out of his hands and booted him back to the ground. I stood over him, hovering Nightfall just above his throat.

"You can't hold me here forever," he said. "Not unless you don't care about the rest of your team getting torn to shreds."

"You're right," I smirked. "Sleep." His violet eyes rolled back and he immediately began snoring. The tranquility on his puffy face reminded me of a resting baby.

A glint from the side made my synapses fire and I reflexively jumped back. A nearby tree burst into splinters as an object embedded itself. A cool mist mingled with the dust as it cleared revealing a jagged chunk of—. *Ice?* I searched for the source, only to find another knight projecting a fusillade of ice shards at me. I leapt back again and spun around, sprinting between trees for cover as the shards ripped through the air and lodged into tree trunks. I needed to find a good vantage point to launch a counterattack. But it wouldn't be easy facing someone who so easily could rip a hole in me from so far away.

But also, not impossible, I reminded myself. *Surket taught me how to handle myself in similar situations. If I account for his abilities and adjust my approach, this will be far from impossible.*

I started to turn, my confidence building, when I saw three more of Astaroth's knights approaching fast, with no one from my side within range to help. They stopped in front of me and pulled back their hoods. Two girls I'd never seen before and the big bruiser, Hypersol.

"Lord Astaroth wants her alive, right?" the taller female knight asked.

"Correct," the taller male knight answered, walking over. He was the one responsible for the ice. "And we'll need to do it quickly."

My eyes darted between them, as the list of options flooding my brain narrowed to two: defeat these miscreants or go down fighting.

The taller man looked at the other girl—the smallest one there. "Initiate, time to prove yourself."

In my state, I shouldn't have used it. I should have found another way. But in that moment, I wanted nothing more than to end the fight. Blood rushed to my head, and heat swirled around me as a mass of energy pooled in front of me. A sudden calm enveloped me as the girl gritted her teeth and charged. With a will strong enough to burn the surrounding forest, I unleashed an Alpha Psionic Wave large enough to envelop her and her comrades. But something strange happened. She threw her hands in front of her face and with a blinding flash, a monstrous wave slammed into me, propelling me through the air, before I crashed and tumbled across the ground. Everything throbbed the way my head did. I forced my eyes opened to a blurry, slowly spinning world. My vision kept fluttering as the ringing in my ears grew louder, until it was all I could hear. I tried to move, but my body only trembled. And even as I gripped at the ground beneath me, I couldn't feel a thing.

The next thing I knew, all five knights were looming over me, violet eyes trained on me like predators. Warm liquid ran from my nose, down my cheek. It had to be blood. Paralyzed and planted in the dirt, surrounded by enemies, I closed my eyes in resignation. Suddenly, a war cry roared out loud enough to overpower the ringing in my ears. My eyes shot open to a massive squall yanking two knights right off their feet. The others turned and were met with a blast of lightning, that sent another flying with an ear-splitting crackle. The taller man and woman were the only ones left. And they did a much better job of dodging the next wave of projectile attacks. But doing so, left me unattended. I lifted my head and there was Serec.

He charged at the last two knights, swinging and kicking furiously at the taller man. But unlike Serec, the man fought with an undeniable finesse, effortlessly dodging Serec's attacks. All the while, he kept firing off shards of ice that Serec was struggling to avoid. Fortunately, the few attacks that did connect weren't strong enough to break Serec's stone skin. But once the other knight joined the fight, Serec's disadvantage became glaringly obvious. The dark-haired, fair-skinned woman reached a hand out at Serec. I tried to yell. To warn him. But my words jumbled into something incomprehensible. I still hadn't recovered. The woman snapped her fingers, and Serec's knees buckled and he tripped over himself clumsily.

The man stood over Serec and pressed his hands together forming a long hunk of jagged ice between them. "That thick skin of yours is a problem," he said. "We'll have to chisel it away."

Serec tried to pick himself up, but for some reason he just squirmed on the ground. As he struggled, the other knights reappeared. And they didn't look too happy. The taller knight lifted the ice and just before he could bring it down over Serec's head it shattered in his hands. "Hardly seems fair, fighting two against one and hitting a man while he's down," Northe said, landing nearby.

The knights all turned to attack, but fell short, catching themselves on their hands and knees, before they collapsed into the dirt. I scanned the area and found NaRyn taking cover behind a tree, as she held the knights down. Mia, Shawin, and Jin ran to Northe's side, and Serec pressed back onto his feet. "Bout time you guys joined the party," he said.

"Take a break, Lift," Northe called. He pointed to the taller woman. "Keep this one down a little longer though." After a moment, each of the knights pushed back onto their feet. They tried to spread out—probably to look for NaRyn. But the rest of my team blocked them. "How about a little one-on-one?" Northe said. "I much prefer to play by the rules after all."

They clashed in a mad flurry of attacks my eyes strained to follow. Hypersol eventually solved that issue, when he broke into a mad dash like a wild nibos, slamming into trees and anything else in his path. Everyone—even the other knights took care to stay out of his way, which eventually gave him the opening needed to locate NaRyn. She shrieked in terror as he barreled headlong at her. But he didn't even get close. The moment Shawin recognized her danger, he rushed at him and delivered a barrage of attacks that even he couldn't shake off. And like a raeda with flawed steering, Hypersol veered off to one side and crashed so thunderously, his legs collapsed over his head. My eyes found Serec, in mid-air and descending quickly toward a now awake Renes. In one fluid motion, he palmed the back of Renes' head and thrusted him face-first into the ground. Without a moment wasted, Serec spun and fired a surge of electricity at Xaster, who for all his speed, was unable to move away, before the blast knocked him off his feet. Serec's anger was almost palpable. And for some reason, seeing that relentless determination gave me hope.

"Enough!" Astaroth roared. "Your enemy should've been crushed under your heel long before now. The fact that you struggle so ceaselessly—and all for naught —disgraces your order. I suppose, I shall have to get my hands dirty."

He rocketed toward Northe, who blasted a gale in defense. He sliced through the wall and Northe sprang high into the air. But Astaroth stayed with him like a shadow, grabbing his ankle and hurling him into a tree. Shawin positioned himself to break Northe's fall, but there was too much velocity on Northe. He plowed into Shawin, and together they collided against the tree and collapsed to the ground—Northe, writhing in pain, and Shawin unconscious. Astaroth fixed his sights on Mia, and methodically stalked toward her. Her hardened determination formed a mask that failed to hide the terror in her eyes. Mia quickly backed away, firing off salvos of lightning. The bolts bounced off his thick skin, like crumpled paper. He continued closer. She tried to prepare a stronger attack, when Astaroth zipped forward and clutched her throat.

I had to do something before my entire team fell. I leaned forward, laboring to move my limbs. But my body only trembled, before the dirt reclaimed it. *I should have expected as much. That girl's power allowed her to reflect my Alpha Psionic Wave back at me.* The delayed and severely jumbled communication between my brain and my nervous system must have been an aftereffect.   A desperate cry rang out. I twisted my face in the dirt to confirm what I had already expected, and cringed at the sight of an unconscious Mia. Her face, a deeper red than I had ever seen on her. I surveyed the area for Astaroth, but he was nowhere in sight.

I heard another shriek that could only be NaRyn. But from my position, she and Astaroth were completely out of my line of sight. I wriggled and twisted desperately to find them, but the resounding of Serec's voice pulled my attention. My eyes barely held his image, before he blurred out of sight, in the direction of the shriek. I pressed harder and with one sharp movement, I torqued my body around to find Serec, completely stopped in his tracks, as his shoulders pressed at the back of Astaroth's knees. He was putting every bit of strength he had into it, and Astaroth didn't even budge.

Astaroth regarded Serec like a parent watching an insolent child. And in the blink of an eye, he hammered his fist directly into the middle of Serec's back. Serec collapsed, thudding against the ground. NaRyn yelled, straining as she pressed her arms against invisible resistance. Astaroth turned his head to watched her in fiendish amusement. He took a step closer, and my heart dipped into my stomach as I watched NaRyn's determination erode into panic. With each step she retreated, Astaroth advanced. And with her gravitational manipulation doing nothing to help the situation, NaRyn could only scan her immediate surroundings for ideas.

Suddenly, something shifted in her. The fear, and anxiety morphed. *"I won't let them take her!"* NaRyn's mind screamed. *No! Don't!* She dipped low, serenity blanketing her face. *You have to run! You have to—*But it was too late. NaRyn shot toward Astaroth leaving a crater in the ground. She spun into a kick that could've dropped a tree, committing to her path. But Astaroth casually brought up a hand —and caught her leg.

He grabbed her by the wrist, and she squealed in agony as his grip clenched tighter. Without the faintest sign of effort, he lifted her to eye level, and she dangled stiffly in his massive hand. "I will not prove nearly as incapable as Tarver, when it comes to getting what I want," he said. "And since you and your team of gnats don't seem to understand when you've lost, I think I want them to see what happens to those who repeatedly defy me."

He lifted his other hand to her face, certain to make whatever he'd done to Mia look like a mercy. I pressed for control again, finally finding my legs and arms. "Stop Iam!" I pleaded, wrenching myself away from the ground. "I'll do whatever you want. Just let them go." I staggered toward them, heat enveloping my eyes, as our victory slowly slipped away with each step. Astaroth stopped, eyes finding mine as NaRyn quaked in silent terror. He dropped her to the ground, and turned to me. A prickle stabbed into the pit of my stomach, as we drew close. But I held firm.

"My sweet Princess," he said, smiling darkly as he gripped my shoulders and lifted me like a trophy. "The ever-precious key to my dreams. After six anums, you have finally returned home." *Returned home?* Hypersol and the tall knights, were the only ones still standing. But not nearly as easily as when the battle had begun. Astaroth looked over his shoulder at them. "We're done here," he announced. "Grab the others."

Agents and malefactors were strewn across the field. Most were incapacitated, unconscious, or worse. And that included three of Astaroth's Knights of Just Death. But NaRyn's pain was more psychological than physical. She reminded me of a hurt child, as she pressed her wrist close to her chest, and watched Astaroth carry me away. But there was no room for tears where I was going. And the sight of her sitting there, defeated and powerless took every bit of resolve I could muster, not to succumb to the burning in my nostrils or the prickling heat circulating around my eyes.

"Let go of her!" Serec yelled, running after me in angry desperation. A desperation that left him completely off guard as Hypersol blindsided him, sending him tumbling along the dirt. Hypersol walked over and pressed his heel to Serec's face. And before I could protest, the situation shifted from terrible to calamitous.

Kurai appeared in all his malevolence. There was a brief exchange between him and Hypersol, before Hypersol nodded and hoisted Renes, Xaster, and the smaller female knight over his shoulders, and followed behind us. We'd failed. I'd failed. And I had all but lost hope. Even worse, Serec's greatest threat was looming over him. A part of me felt oddly relieved to be forcefully removed from the battlefield, before everything could finish playing out. And it was difficult not to loathe that part of myself.

[13]

DETERMINATION

NARYN

I've never considered myself a weak person. Not in school, at home, not even at my "job." But my encounter with Astaroth made me redefine weakness. Despite the searing throb in my wrist, I was arguably the most capable agent on the field when Astaroth carried Sa'Sha away. And yet, I'd resigned myself to cowering in the dirt and nursing my wounds. I cringed as the heavy breeze ignited my wrist where Astaroth had squeezed, nearly crushing the bones. *We almost had them. If not for Astaroth this could've been our victory.* Frustration weighed against my shoulders like a wet coat, my stomach sour with disappointment. A pained wail pulled me out of my head, and reminded me that some remnant of a fight was raging. Serec and Kurai were locked in combat, and Serec was hanging by a thread to keep up.

"When did Kurai get here?" I thought aloud, rushing to help. Serec roared at Kurai with the ferocity of a feral beast. But anyone watching could see it was all bark. Serec was running on reserves, and even without Kurai there, I didn't expect him to last another hash. I pressed out a wave of gravity to slow Kurai. But he danced around Serec as if I hadn't done anything. I wondered if he even knew I was there, or if maybe he'd put up a precautionary field to block anyone's powers if they got too close.

Serec collapsed, coughing globs of blood, and my face went so hot, it could've exploded. Inundated with adrenaline, I raced toward Kurai. No plan. No powers. Just rage. My goal was simple: inflict pain. See to it that—whatever it took—Kurai regretted showing when he did. And I was determined to see that goal through. But a ball of angry fire burst across Kurai's chest an instant before a ball of ice pounded his right arm, freezing it over. To my left, Locke's assistants were closing in looking... amused?

Kurai wasted no time darting into the trees and making his escape. I waited for them to pursue, but they stopped at Serec's unconscious body instead. I started back running, anxious to make sure he was okay, but I didn't make it half the distance, before Locke's bodyguards both placed a hand over Serec and disappeared with him in a thin plume of smoke. I slowed to a stop, searching the area, more confused than I wanted to admit. Sa'Sha was gone. Serec was gone. All that remained was a field of injured and dead; the aftermath of a battle we clearly weren't prepared for. My nerves were more than shaken. But nerves or no, I couldn't stand the idea of wallowing in self-pity when people needed me. Especially people I cared about. I took a breath or five and hurried over to check on Shawin and Northe.

"He's unconscious, but he'll live," Northe said, voice raspy, like he was trying to keep his breathing shallow. "He's got Kazimus blood in his veins. He'll make it."

He was probably saying it more for himself than for me, but Northe's words helped to ease my anxiety all the same. In fact, seeing everyone up close was honestly a breath of relief. No one looked quite as critical as I'd imagined.

Northe strained, reaching a hand to his HOOD. I reached for it and pressed the button for him to speak. "Dropships one through five, this is K," he said. "Proceed from LZ to my position for immediate EVAC of all forces. Medical teams, standby for casualty evacuation." He nodded and I released the button and turned my attention back to Shawin until transport arrived with the medics, who quickly had their hands full with injured agents. Thankfully, there weren't any serious casualties, and aside from a very select few, the vast majority was predicted to make a full recovery within a few days.

I sat alone in the Medical Facility waiting room, with too much time to think. I was too tired to move around or think straight, and yet too restless to shut my brain off long enough for sleep. But my few coherent thoughts drifted between Serec, Sa'Sha, and Baneira. If I'd pushed a little more, maybe I could've acted as Baneira's voice of reason. Maybe I could've kept her from becoming one of Astaroth's puppets. And one less knight, might've been all the advantage we needed to get out with everyone, before Astaroth showed up. The longer I thought about it, the more I felt like I'd let everyone down. How fatally crappy.

"And how are you holding up?" a soft voice asked, as a hand gently touched my shoulder.

Dr. Anne Kartnia's soft amber eyes watched me with the kind of tenderness only a mother could produce. I guess her designation was appropriate. The longer she stood there, the more she reminded me of my mom. Authoritative and poised, but soft-spoken and gentle.

"I'm good ma'am," I answered.

Her smile faded a little. "I'd like to believe you, dear. But your eyes aren't sending nearly the same message as your mouth. And we both know which messenger never lies." Her eyebrows raised expectantly.

"Really, Doctor. I—" Before my brain could relay the complete thought to the rest of me, the doctor's arms wrapped around me and squeezed.

"Call me Anne," she said warmly. "And I would appreciate it if you were honest with the both of us."

"B-Both of us?"

"As in both me and yourself," she clarified. "Hiding your feelings from yourself won't make anything better. And an important part of my job has nothing to do with bandaging physical wounds."

Everything about her was warm and comforting. Yet tears suddenly began streaming down my face, as if I was right back in the midst of it all. I didn't say anything for a while, and neither did she. I pressed my face against her shoulder as the stream continued, and she squeezed a bit harder.

"Astaroth may have won today's battle, and abducted one of our own. But the war isn't over, and the only way to win it is with resolve."

"That sounds nice," I said, pulling back and wiping my face with my sleeve. "But resolve can't create miracles. Serec and Sa'Sha are both gone, so no one's left to lead the task force. Plus, the odds are fatally stacked against us right about now."

Anne cupped her hands to my face and wiped at the tears with her thumbs. "Then, stack your resolve higher than the odds," Anne replied matter-of-factly. "Miracles only happen when your faith is nothing short of unshakable."

Anne didn't strike me as the "hopeless blind faith" type, even if her words said otherwise. And even though I knew the situation wasn't nearly as simple as she made it out to be, the simplicity in her answer was still fatally encouraging.

Anne hugged me again, which made it a lot less awkward when I wrapped my arms around her and squeezed back. "I see why Serec thinks so highly of you," I said.

"Does he now?"

"Yeah," I said smiling. "He told me you were kind of amazing."

"Funny. He said the same thing about you." Her tone was peaceful, but she was smiling almost as wide as I was.

"Forgive the interruption, ma'am," a man in a lab coat said, bustling through the door. "There's an important stream that I think you'll want to see."

Anne unrolled her digipad and pulled up the news stream. My gut almost wrenched as Astaroth appeared in one corner of the screen, under the visage of Iam Rhasatto, interviewing one-on-one with none other than Nel Laurelli, Aruria's most despised journalist. Half of the screen was devoted to an image of Sa'Sha, Serec, and a few the task force agents standing guard around Iam, who was too conveniently kneeling behind them.

"I have reason to believe that this was not an isolated incident, which leads me to consider this an act of terrorism by corrupt parties within the Arurian government," Iam said.

"But why the government? And why now?" Laurelli asked.

"Unfortunately, I've yet to ascertain that information, Nel. But after Aruria's very own princess took me hostage, I have little room for doubt that some Arurian organization—or perhaps, their government itself—is involved."

Laurelli pointed at the image of Sa'Sha. Thankfully, her HOOD obscured her eyes and nose. "So, you believe that this young woman with the dark hair is in fact Blissful Martinel?"

"I do."

I grimaced. *Serpent.* I caught the word before it forced its way out of my mouth.

"Would you happen to have any evidence to support this accusation?" Laurelli pressed.

"I would actually. The testimony of an Arurian Peace Enforcement Department lieutenant who says the princess used her authority to cover up the illegal activities of a Rho last anum. He stated that Blissful Martinel ordered him to release the Rho and falsify the report. That very same Rho can be seen here with the woman I know to be the princess."

"A rather compelling argument Mr. Rhasatto. So, how do you intend to respond to this act of terrorism."

"Serpent," Anne muttered, before remembering I was there. "Apologies."

"Although it pains me to do so, I am fully prepared to devote the entirety of my resources toward bolstering and promoting Oltresullean retaliatory capabilities, should the responsible party refuse my generous offer to provide adequate restitution. I'm formally requesting a private audience with Blissful Sa'Sha Martinel within the time frame spanning no longer than one dec from today. Refusal of this offer will be considered a refusal of diplomatic resolution and I will be forced to press for retaliatory measures against the Arurian government."

"There you have it citizens. A gracious compromise to forego a potentially devastating outcome. If Aruria's monarch is worth his weight in salt, I expect a swift and diplomatic response is already underway."

The stream cut to an ad, and Anne rolled up her digipad.

"Correct me if I'm wrong," I said slowly, "But that sounded a lot like a declaration of war."

Anne looked at me and nodded, her expression almost brooding. "That's because it was."

PART THREE | VISIONAIRIES

[ELEMENT 1]
THE BOOK OF TURBULENCE

[1]

RESOLVE

NARYN

Quiet, peaceful dinners were never my thing. For me, peaceful was just another word for lonely. I sat at the dinner table, alone and very aware of it, as I pushed the food back and forth over my plate, until a knock at the door broke the monotony.

"Sir?" I pulled the door open for the Colonel, snapping to attention as he stepped in.

"Relax Lift. This visit's informal."

I let out a sigh and loosened up. "I came to send word about the mission debriefing tomorrow."

"In person?"

"Personal touch is better in this case."

"Northe's still at the medical center, sir. Would you like me to pass the info to him?"

"K knows. You're my last stop for the night." I paused. "We need an account of what happened from at least one person who got eyes on Astaroth up close, without suffering head trauma in the process."

I watched him for a moment, then nodded. "What time?"

"8.50."

"I take it the Director will be overseeing the proceedings sir?"

"Afraid not."

"More meetings?"

"He's on his way to meet with the Chief of Peace Enforcement. Likely, to turn himself in."

"Turn himself in?" I repeated, with a frown.

"He's going to reveal the existence of the Guild and take full responsibility for what happened in Oltresulle and led to the disappearance of Raven and Zero."

"No!" I protested. "That's insane!" The idea of Uncle Hachi tossing everything he'd worked for into the wind just didn't make sense. "We have to stop him!"

"That time's past. He thinks facing this now is the best option, and I agree."

"But shouldn't we be using this time to go further into hiding?"

"I'm expecting a thorough investigation of both IGIS and the Bureau. Our move against Astaroth has to come before that happens. The Director's talk with the Chief should buy us a little time."

"But he should be here to help us plan our next move. We need him," I argued.

"You all did just fine before with him in the background. He's got faith in us. Don't squander it." His tone was so self-assured—so matter-of-fact, it always made me think twice about questioning him. But this was different.

"And what'll happen to him—while he's buying us time?"

"I suppose they'll throw the book at him. They've got their pick of charges. Embezzlement, misappropriation of specialized government funding, high-treason, you name it."

The bitter taste of bile rose up my throat, as I thought about the kinds of things they did to people guilty of high-treason. "Permission to speak freely, sir?"

"Granted."

"You seem calmer about this than I'd expect from someone so close to my uncle."

The look in his eyes was sincere and sobering. "Hachi's one of my dearest and most respected friends," he said softly. "He bought us time, and put his faith in us to see this through. As a loyal friend, what would you have me do?" I paused to fully consider what he was saying. The longer I did, the more I realized I didn't have an answer. "8.50," he said. "Don't be late." He walked out, leaving me alone with my dinner and even less of an appetite. The debriefing started promptly, and ended just as promptly. I gave my account of what happened after Northe, Shawin, Jin, and Mia were incapacitated, which—according to the Colonel—only further validated their accounts and added potentially useful information about how Astaroth functioned. In a little over forty hashes, the debrief was adjourned and I went to MedFac to visit Shawin.

"He asked about you this morning," Northe said, doing his best to catch up. I slowed down for him.

"How's Shawin doing?"

"He's stable. His ribs got a little bruised from the impact, but it's nothing major. We have some tech that can accelerate his healing and have him back to normal in a few days."

I made a mental note not to hug too hard when I saw him. And after everything that had happened, I could really use a good hug. "So, how are you doing?"

"My wrist hurts here and there, but It seems like I'm doing much better than everyone else."

"I'm not asking about your wrist," Northe said flatly.

I fought back a frown.

"You look defeated," he elaborated.

"We *were* defeated."

"Yeah, *we* were. So, why are you placing the weight of that loss all on yourself?"

My throat tightened so suddenly that it became difficult to speak. "You do read faces pretty well, don't you?"

"It may be an ongoing joke I've played on more Guild newbies than I can count, but I'm still legitimately decent at it. Besides, I've experienced the same feelings enough to recognize it from kilometers away."

I stopped, my eyes trailing to my feet. "Any tips?"

"Nothing that'd do a bit of good for people like you and me. Or Sa'Sha, Serec —even Surket—for that matter."

"What about Shawin?"

"Shawin doesn't wear his heart on his sleeve like the rest of Team Seven. That gives him a slight emotional edge, needed to be a good soldier."

"But we're not soldiers," I argued. "We're agents."

"Take it from someone with twelve anums in the game: the difference is marginal at best. And being driven by your heart isn't a long-sought-after trait."

"So then, what drives Shawin?"

"Loyalty. It's kind of ironic, since even loyalty requires heart. My injuries versus his are a perfect example."

"What about his injuries?"

"I could tell from my body's trajectory hat when Astaroth hit me, I shouldn't have come close to hitting anyone. Managing to break my fall must mean that Shawin's powers allowed him to see what was about to happen—where my body would fall. His powers have evolved. And that evolution allowed him the opportunity to throw himself in harm's way out of loyalty to the only uncle he's ever known."

"Maybe he already knew he'd be okay if he tried to save you."

"Maybe," Northe said thinking. "In his own words, the problem with his powers was that if he tried to change the outcome of one of his visions, it created a change in almost every other part of the vision."

"So, you don't think he knew he would end up in the MedFac?"

"Don't know for sure. I just know I love that kid like my own. And right now, the fact that he's on bed rest because he tried to save me, is something I can't ignore."

I understood Northe's logic. But part of what he said needed to be addressed. "Sometimes, you're all Shawin ever talks about. And it hardly seems fair that Shawin's only uncle gets to throw himself in harm's way for his nephew's sake, but not the other way around."

"Being fair is the last thing I'm concerned about, if it means losing the next generation, just so I can avoid Hadal a bit longer. Losing the chance at laughing together and sharing unforgettable memories with you guys—it's a small price to pay if it means you all get the same chance we had to learn, make mistakes, and get the next generation started."

There was no doubt in my mind that Uncle Hachi felt the same way. And his actions made even more sense after talking to Northe. But accepting the situation didn't feel any easier. I pursed my lips and turned away from Northe, as the back of my eyes stung so much my vision started to blur.

"What good are memories and mistakes when you make them alone?" I asked.

Northe wrapped his arm around my shoulder and gave a light squeeze. "I could write a book on the loneliness I've felt as a result of my mistakes. Not sure if anyone would care to read it though," he thought aloud. "But I could tell you from personal experience, loss is no reason to avoid conflict. Especially, when you've been given the kind of gift that can make a difference. So, you can either play a role in creating the kind of world you want, or you can stay out of it and leave it to everyone else—accepting that you don't get to complain when a few people you care about are lost in the process."

I stood there for a bit, pondering Northe's words. Northe only pulled me closer, turning me into him, as I fought to keep tears from escaping. "It's okay," he said. "They can change my bandages if they get too wet, but holding back won't help. And I'm sure Shawin would feel a lot better starting his morning off with your smile."

"Yeah," I said, pulling my arms in tight and leaning my forehead down against Northe's chest, as tears slipped through my defenses.

"Team Seven is all about heart. That means, no matter what we feel, we feel it together. So, feel what you need to for a hash. Then, we'll go see Shawin together."

[2]

RECEPTION

SA'SHA

I jolted up, wincing at the bright light assaulting my eyes. Waiting for everything to come into focus provided ample time to notice the beads of sweat covering my forehead. I surveyed the windowless room for clues, but the minimalist furnishing provided little information. Aside from the bed I was sitting on, the room was almost completely bare. I wiped the sweat from my face and took a deep breath to calm myself. Staying sharp and keeping my wits about me was the only way I would have any chance of escaping. Ceiling to floor, the room was polished and empty, as if I was its first visitor. It was simple in design, to the point of dull, and completely uninspired. For all I knew, I had fallen into a drab, lifeless white-on-white purgatory. I scanned the walls and my eyes stopped at the outline across from me. It looked like a door, though it lacked any identifiable way to open it.

I sat up to tuck my legs under me, when a sharp pain shot through my right leg. As my body reflexively leaned forward, everything came flooding back. The battle, Kurai standing over Serec, the helplessness on NaRyn's face as... A chill slivered down my sides. "Astaroth...abducted me," I remembered aloud. "Iam Rhasatto is Astaroth!"

My stomach turned sickly knots, as his final words on the battlefield replayed in my mind. *Key to his dreams? Back where I belong?* I had a strong inclination that I would be better off not knowing what he meant by that.

"Welcome back, Blissful," a soft, stern voice called. The sickening tightness in my stomach spread to my chest when I recognized the woman standing by the door. *The tall knight.* Her dark forest green cloak draped over her shoulders, starkly contrasting with her luminescent violet eyes.

"What do you mean by 'welcome back?'" *And why does this scene suddenly feel so... familiar?*

She took a step closer, and I tensed. "I didn't come here to harm you," she said, stopping in place. "I only wish to talk."

"I can hear you just fine from there," I said unapologetically. Her uncanny eyes remained placid as she nodded. "Did Astaroth send you to negotiate my ransom?"

"I assure you that you are of far greater value to us than any amount of money your kingdom could hope to produce," she answered, almost reverently.

"Then, treat me with the respect due someone of value, and release me."

"That I will not. I have orders that I intend to see through, no matter what."

"We shall see."

I bolted from the bed and swung at her face, hoping to catch her by surprise. Instead, my arm went right through her. I recovered and spun into a kick that should have sent her tumbling to the ground. But the only thing I connected with was air.

"You've probably gathered that, I'm not physically with you. I suspected your initial response would be hostile, despite my equanimity."

"Says the guard to the detainee," I scoffed.

"I hope you've at least extinguished some portion of your aggressions. It would make dinner considerably more civil."

"Dinner?"

"Yes, my master wishes to employ that particular time as opportunity to explain his actions. You'll find access to a shower, clean towels, and a fresh change of clothes in the bathroom just behind you. Please make use of it to prepare. Dinner will be ready shortly."

Something beeped and a doorway opened out of the wall behind me.

"I refuse. Show me to your master," I ordered.

She examined me, a smirk occupying her face. "I thought you more refined, Blissful."

I looked down at my clothes—or rather—what was left of them. There were a ripped and tattered mess, revealing more of me than any man should see before exchanging vows with me.

"Fine," I said, ambling indignantly to the bathroom. I was honestly a bit surprised at how perfectly everything fit. The material was comfortably soft, with a sturdy thickness that resembled a thin layer of armor. If the knights' clothing was made of the same material, it helped explain why they seemed so resilient.

When I stepped out of the bathroom, I saw the girl leaned against the wall by the door.

The thought to attack again crossed my mind. But the clarity I'd gained from my short time in the bathroom held me in place. Speaking with Astaroth, would be my best chance at acquiring answers. So, I could afford to wait a bit longer before attempting an escape.

"Those clothes suit you well," she noted.

"Let's just get this over with," I sighed.

Her sigh matched mine. "Right this way."

Off the battlefield, I would have never believed she was a soldier or a killer. She might have been a few anums older than me, and everything about her fair skin, shoulder-length black hair, and gentle smile painted a deceptively dainty picture.

She stepped in front of the door. Something beeped and the door opened to a long, white hallway that turned out to be about as plain as the room I was just in. "My name is Harine, by the way," the girl said.

"I'm Sa'Sha," I replied. "But you already knew that, didn't you?"

She half-turned her head and smiled. "Right you are."

Her kindness seemed so out of place, I had to remind myself not to let it disarm me, even if I wanted to believe there might be a nice person somewhere deep inside.

We came to a large, elaborately decorated dining room, where a small feast had been laid out on the large table. Waitstaff were quickly moving around the room, applying the finishing touches.

I stepped in and everyone suddenly stopped and lowered to one knee, with their heads bowed. Turning to Harine, I realized she was also bowing.

"I trust your new attire meets your fashion standards," a deep, familiar voice pressed from behind. I spun around to find Iam Rhasatto towering over me with a hand extended.

"It is an absolute pleasure to have you as my guest Blissful. You will soon find that we have much to discuss."

[3]

PRECURSOR

SA'SHA

I am's chilling violet eyes held on me with an almost predatory starkness, as he pushed my chair under me, then took his seat. "I am very pleased you could join us, Blissful," he said with a wry smile.

"I imagine the excitement must have been incomprehensible, if it led you to orchestrate my kidnapping in lieu of a more civilized approach, such as a simple invitation."

The smile became a smirk. "Considering dinner was not my only objective, I'm afraid 'an invitation' would not have sufficed." He lifted a forkful of plant greens to his mouth, watching me as he chewed deliberately. "Please," he said after a pause, "eat to your heart's content. I imagine you must be famished, after today's events."

The muscles in my face tightened, into a hard glare. But Iam didn't seem to mind. Within the first three bites of his food, Iam seemed to have completely forgotten I was there.

"Forgive my impatience, but what are your intentions Mr. Rhasatto?" I asked bluntly.

A lump of food slid down his throat, barely grazing his teeth. "Please. Let us enjoy our meal first. Then we will discuss the matter."

I started to open my mouth in protest, but the fresh, subtly spicy aroma reminded me too well of palace cuisine. Delectably fragrant spices and flavors danced around my senses, making my mouth water. I tried to swallow it back, and my stomach grumbled in response. I was starving.

"Your food will get cold," Iam warned. But I didn't budge. Even if it meant using the meager strength I had left to clench my teeth, for fear I might inhale the food in my next breath.

With eyes of stone, Iam sipped his wine. "As you wish, Your Highness.

Despite your apprehension, I can assure you that my intention is to restore trust between us."

"You've gotten off to a poor start," I scoffed.

"The end result is what matters most, Princess."

"Then, you should understand well that you will find the end result of my abduction most displeasing."

"My means will either achieve each end I've sought, or I will leave you at a loss as to why not accomplishing *every* goal is still a perfectly acceptable course of action."

"Do you intend to speak in vagaries throughout our conversation?"

"Please take no offense, Blissful. But you—of all people—should understand that detail are reserved for those who have earned my trust."

I wanted to smack the methodical, smug right of his face. Instead, I gave myself a moment for composure. El knows I needed that, and a lot of willpower to remain in my seat. "Am I simply here to help you fill a personal void with your exasperating repartee?"

His smirk widened. "No need for such a tone, Your Highness."

"No need for procrastination, when one can be direct."

Iam tilted his head, his eyes softening with his voice. "Would it really be too great a request to ask that you at least eat as I speak? I assure you the food is exceptionally palatable, and I would hate for it to go to waste."

It was like talking to a fusion of Shawin and Locke turned criminally insane. I almost wished he would just start laughing maniacally like the villains in Serec's comic books. At least then, I would have some idea how of how to approach him.

I looked down at my plate, wondering if I could trust it. My stomach wanted to. "You'll find no poison in your food, if that is your concern."

The more I thought about it, the more I realized how little sense, poisoning my food would make. I was already a captive in his lair, and he had ample time to poison me, as I slept.

I picked up my fork and took a bite. I nearly shuddered at the explosion of rich flavors, rejuvenation flowing through my body.

"I've taken you into custody to address a problem that, up until now, no one else has been able to remedy."

"Theall Medical Corporation has always endeavored to develop medicines that improve peoples' quality of life. But medicine, like anything in life, has its limitations. From disease and illness, to war and conflict, to alienation and loneliness, limitations are the cause of people's suffering. The desire to stop this suffering can lead to absolutism and conformity. We're seemingly left with two choices: Embrace uniqueness and the suffering that accompanies diversity, or accept conformity, coercing principles of unity through homogeneity upon the populace. In doing so, everyone can live on equal terms, for peace and prosperity sake."

"You're describing an autocracy; one in which there is room for only one set of beliefs and values. You achieve peace at the cost of freedom."

"On that, we can both agree, my dear princess. Which is why I've chosen to leave the messiness of politics to my compatriots and contribute to our cause as a scientist." He waved Harine over, who had been sitting at the opposite end of the table, with the tall knight that controlled ice. In the calmness of the room, it was easy to see that they were related. He nodded at me as I glanced at him. But remembering how he nearly decapitated me during my fight with Renes, I casually looked past him.

"Perhaps you've already gathered this, but the young man at the other end of the table is Kaleb, Harine's older brother."

I glanced back at the fair-skinned man, who worked harder to make his presence known the second time around, by smiling and holding up a hand in greeting. I gave him half a nod, out of obligation, and quickly turned back to Harine, as she stood next to Iam.

"When I adopted Harine and Kaleb ten anums ago, her condition was much worse than it is now."

"Condition?"

"*Sol Mortem.* A condition with which I'm certain you're all too familiar."

I hesitated. "How is that possible? Even in mild cases, Sol Mortem creates the distinct symptom of scarred skin. And the scarring can greatly intensify based on the severity."

"As I stated, her condition has improved."

"But how? There's no cure," I argued. "And she hasn't a scar on her."

"After conducting my own research, I learned that the chemical *protoporphyrin* accumulates in the skin cells of Sol Mortem sufferers. The sun's UV radiation, triggers a phototoxic reaction. And without a viable treatment, the condition gradually worsens."

"Then why is Harine improving? For that matter, why doesn't she have any visible symptoms?"

Iam looked to Harine and nodded. Harine unbuttoned her top and peeled away her cloak. The sight almost turned my stomach. Dark red splotches and brown scabs covered Harine's stomach. Then she turned to reveal a mass of crusting scars and patches along her back. A sickening flood of bile pressed at the bottom of my throat.

"A few hashes of direct exposure to sunlight elicits severe skin reactions in Harine — a marked improvement compared to her condition the day I found her and Kaleb in that horrid orphanage." Iam's face darkened. "A collection of unfathomable ignorant and detestably intolerant women and children. Without a devoted brother like Kaleb, I can only imagine what might have..." Iam trailed into a pause, took a breath, and quietly recomposed himself before looking up at me again. "I made them two promises that day: First, that I would do everything in my power to give them the same kind of freedom the rest of humanity enjoyed with reckless abandon. Second: That I would remake the world into one that our kind can live in without fear of persecution."

My heart softened as I watched Iam, listening to his story. His motive was undeniably noble. But there was no way I could find justification in his means. "Speaking of reckless abandon, how do you explain all the trouble your malefactors have caused, viciously ravaging the nation in steadily increasing numbers?" I asked. "Were they an intentional component of your promise? Or are they simply a convenient byproduct of your experiments?"

"Malefactors?" Iam repeated. "Is that what you call them?" He paused in consideration, and the corner of his mouth slowly curled. "I'd previously designated them as 'maculosus', but I must admit 'malefactor' seems a bit more appropriate."

"You're dodging the question."

"Not my intention," he said quickly. "Initially, they were an unintended consequence of my work. But, with their creation, they too have gained a purpose."

"Which would be?"

A small chuckle hummed in his throat. "That question, I *will* dodge. And rightfully so, considering we've gotten off topic. I'm certain by now, you have discovered that these beings are product of Exolvunturine exposure. What I will share with you is that Exol is one of the threads that binds us together as players in this grand drama."

I started to press him for more information. But as I opened my mouth, a flurry of images flashed through my mind so suddenly, I lost all focus. I blinked away the barrage. But the flood of images quickly returned. *What is this? What am I seeing?* The thoughts echoed along some distant space within my mind. And I sat frozen, unable to move.

A hand grasped my shoulder and, with a gasp of air, I returned to the dining room.

"Are you alright, Princess?"

"Yeah," I said, rubbing my eyes. "I'm fine."

"As I'm sure you can imagine, I have quite a number of medicines on hand, should you need anything..."

"I don't. But thank you." In truth, I didn't know what I needed. All I knew was that my mind felt foggy, like I'd been startled from a deep sleep. But considering I still had questions, with no promise of another chance for answers, I would have to push through the feeling.

"Harine's symptoms..." I started slowly. "How did you improve Harine's condition? Did you successfully employ Exol to cure her."

"Actually, that's where you come in, Blissful."

"Me?"

"Harine's protoporphyrin levels were one hundred times higher than what had been previously recorded. Her condition was quickly becoming life-threatening, and once she started exhibiting serious symptoms like anaphylaxis and immunodeficiency, I began to lose hope. But just when things were at their worst, a colleague of mine informed me about another young girl, diagnosed with Sol Mortem and measuring astronomically high protoporphyrin levels.

And yet, she experienced no symptoms whatsoever. Looking into the matter personally, I told myself not to expect a miracle before I saw ample proof. And despite my inclination to skepticism, there you were. A miracle. The cure I'd been seeking for almost two anums." Iam smiled excitedly, and an uneasy chill hit my stomach all over again. "Somehow, your body was filtering out the effects of the sun's ultraviolet rays, shielding you from your own congenital debilitation. Once I understood how your ability was protecting you, I could replicate that filtration process for Harine, her life could be as unhindered as yours was."

Suddenly, everything clicked perfectly into place. "You're the one who visited my father, asking about my condition."

"I was."

"He stormed into the house that day, telling me over and over that I wasn't some test subject. That I was just as human as everyone else."

"He clearly misunderstood my inten—"

With every bit of strength I could summon forth, I slapped the words from his foul lips.

"It was you! All of it!" I said, suddenly trembling. As the overwhelming truth devoured me. "You had them killed so you could abduct me. Just like you would've killed my friends if I didn't surrender today."

"I needed time to study your abilities, if there was to be any hope of replicating the process. And despite what you may believe, I never intended for any harm to come to your parents."

"I don't care what your intentions were. Whether it was your hands, your words, or just your twisted, conniving mind. Their blood is on your hands. And I'll never forgive you." Tears welled in my eyes as the anger, sorrow, loneliness, and hatred coalesced into an overwhelming pain. The heavy throb in my head had returned with a vengeance. I inhaled deep knowing if I didn't regain my composure, I'd miss the opportunity to acquire the answer I'd been wanting for nearly seven anums. My head pounded as I etched the suggestion through my subconscious mind to quell the pain, both physical and emotional.

"You Grace?" Iam said. "You don't look well. Perhaps we should end here and—"

"What did I do?" I forced through gritted teeth.

"I beg your pardon?"

"What did you make me do? What was the purpose of all this?" Iam watched me contemplatively for a moment.

"You used your power to alter the magnetosphere—a truly marvelous feat I might add."

"To what end?" I asked.

"The liberation of our kind. We are the chosen of this world, yet those in power would label us miscreants, oppressing us through laws that justify their brutality. Instead of embracing our talents, we are forced to hide them for fear of persecution. Your government—with their 'Rho Code'—is the greatest of offenders. By remaking the sky, you have shaped the radiation from the sun into an energy source for our kind. One that has caused an evolution in our abilities."

"So, you used me to make all refractors more powerful? Then why did you kidnap me again?"

"The process was arduous. So, it needed to be conducted in phases. And just as we approached the final phase, you were abducted by another party, leaving the process barely more than half-complete. Conditions such as Plaga Viridi and Malachite's Consumption are a result of this incomplete process."

"So, you're saying if I don't help you, more will die from the Plague? More will be consumed?" I thought about Shora — about Aunt Margaline — about the millions that have been killed by Consumed or died from the Plague. I hated the idea of helping him play El. And I had no assurance that helping him would yield the results he claimed. More troubling was his desire to strengthen the abilities of refractors worldwide. *What is his endgame?*

"You and I both know the answer to that. You may argue against my intentions or my means. But you cannot argue with results." Iam asserted. "Had my mission seen its completion, the sky would not have become the sickly green mess the world has been forced to accept. And no one would be suffering its ill effects. That is why you are here. To help me make the world right."

I watched him. Knowing I couldn't trust him, struggling to find an alternative. If everything he said was true, then finishing what he'd started might be the only chance I would have to make things right. To help the millions of lives my powers had worsened.

It was a lot to consider. And, as luck would have it, my mind chose that moment to incite a revolt against me. My vision blurred and I felt a dizzying swirl of light-headedness. "I need to be excused," I said, almost in a whisper.

"Of course. Think on the matter. Harine, please show the princess back to her room and see to her needs." She helped me to my feet, and Iam bowed slightly as she helped me back into the hallway. "It has been a pleasure, Blissful."

The dizziness intensified with each step, and my body started to feel like jelly. Just as I began to realize I didn't have the strength to make it back to my room, everything flipped upside down and faded to black.

When my eyes opened, Harine was sitting in front of my bed with a small tray in her lap, holding a cup of water and a pill.

"Take this," she said. "It will make you feel much better." I teas too disoriented to argue, and too disinterested in feeling terrible anymore. I took the pill and water, as instructed and laid my head back on the pillow, not tired enough to sleep anymore, but not wanting to keep my eyes open either.

Once the room stopped spinning and I felt my strength returning, I focused my mind on scanning for electromagnetic signals around the room, which proved a lot more difficult than I had expected. The more I pushed to use my technopathy, the more I could feel a resistance, dampening my power within the walls. I was admittedly impressed Astaroth actually thought far enough ahead to Sa'Sha-proof the place. I detected three small microphones, positioned around the room.

I concentrated on weakening the sensitivity of each microphones' sensor, which took time. But I managed to distort them until they could only pick up an explosion. After a breath, I slowly sat up and turned to Harine, still feeling a linger of grogginess.

"I assume you want to speak in private?" Harine asked.

"What makes you say that?"

"You destroyed the listening devices." Surprise froze over my face, and my mind couldn't begin to develop an excuse. "It's fine," she said, smiling patiently. "What's your concern?"

[4]

HOMECOMING

SA'SHA

"Why are you following someone like Astaroth?" I asked softly. "Even if he's trying to help you, doesn't it bother you that he's done horrible things to people?"

Harine's lip curled faintly as her eyes trailed to the floor. "Kaleb and I had been living in an orphanage when Lord Astaroth found us. Before that, we were hiding in an abandoned slaughterhouse in Araman, during the war. Because of my condition, we could only move at night, and luxuries like food, shelter, and security were in short supply. But Kaleb never complained. He said all he wanted was to see me smile. But it was difficult, knowing how much he was sacrificing for me. Knowing that if it weren't for my condition, he would never have lived in an orphanage in the first place."

"They didn't turn us down, but they never accepted us. We were alienated and avoided as much as possible. Even the women running the orphanage and professing the love of their gods—a love they claimed was meant for everyone—treated us like some deplorable plague. I told myself as soon as the war ended, we could leave."

"Astaroth came along before the war ended?"

Harine nodded. "But that shouldn't have mattered. Early into our second anum at the orphanage, our province had become stable enough for us to leave, without the fear of being caught in a crossfire or attacked by enemy soldiers."

Harine paused, her posture slowly collapsing into a slump. I hesitated, not certain if I should ask the next burning question.

"Kaleb wouldn't even entertain the idea," she finally said. "He'd been trapped in that orphanage for so long, he couldn't even pretend he didn't hate it there anymore. But he wouldn't agree to leave. I only pressed the matter once. And when I saw the fear in his eyes, I never brought it up again."

"Fear?"

"Of seeing me in pain again. After so much time in the orphanage, we had no idea how much things might've changed in the outside world. For all he knew shelter was more difficult to find. And because of how everyone treated me, he refused to go scouting around, because he would have to leave me there to do it. We'd become trapped in our way of living."

Sorrow veiled her eyes, turning her into a completely different person. Vulnerable and desperately lonely.

"But Kaleb was willing to live that life with you," I said. "You were blessed, having such a compassionate older brother."

"Too compassionate to deserve that kind of burden. Having him by my side meant the world to me. But there was no forgetting the fact that, because of me, Kaleb could never live a normal life." She paused to look up at me. "Have you ever really wanted something that you knew you could never have, all because of circumstances beyond your control? Because you were a detainee of your own life?"

It was like she was looking into the piece of my soul that I had been hiding from the rest of the world. And as I saw the resignation coloring her eyes, I saw the same helpless girl that I once was. The circumstances may have been different, but Harine and I had more in common than I cared to acknowledge.

"Yes," I said quietly. "Yes, I have."

Harine nodded, offering a faint smile. "Kaleb and I had essentially given up hope by the time Lord Astaroth appeared at the orphanage. But Lord Astaroth told us we didn't belong there, and he offered us a place to call home that same day. He signed the adoption papers, and as he walked us out of the nightmare that we'd known for so long, an enormous weight lifted from my shoulders. Thanks to Lord Astaroth, Kaleb stepped foot outside of the orphanage for the first time in over two anums."

Perhaps I hadn't given Iam his full credit as anything other than a monster. As far as I was concerned, he ruined my life. But he'd also saved two lives. Whether or not Harine agreed with his methods, I could understand why she didn't question them. "When did he start working on a cure for you?"

"Immediately."

"He admitted me to the best hospital in Oltresulle, where I received constant care. With my protoporphyrin levels so high, improvement was slow, but I felt like it was okay to dream again. And my first big dream was to stand outside long enough to see the sunrise," Harine said wistfully. "I spent the next two anums in the hospital, working with a trainer and being closely monitored. Kaleb and Lord Astaroth came to visit me nearly every day, and sometimes Kaleb was allowed to spend the night, to keep me in good spirits. Even if I never did get to stand outside and watch a sunset, things were better than they had ever been and I told myself that was enough. Then, early one morning, Lord Astaroth and Kaleb walked into the hospital and with the doctor's approval they led me outside. I remember being nervous, almost shaking. But Kaleb gripped my hand firmly and told me to close my eyes and not to be afraid. When we finally made it to the hospital entrance and I could open my eyes, I thought I was in a dream. The harsh orange light of dawn I was expecting had been replaced with a beautiful shade of emerald. To be safe they only kept me outside for a few hashes, still more time than I'd ever spent outside in daylight. And I relished every beat of it. I was one step closer to living the normal life Lord Astaroth promised me. And with you here, he finally has a chance to make good on his promise."

I wanted to tell Harine not to get her hopes up. That there was no way I would help a monster like Astaroth continue such a dangerous plan, that might very well make the world even worse than it already was.

I started to question whether or not I really had the right to condemn Astaroth. After all, his sacrifices weren't all that different from the kinds of sacrifices Team Seven had always been willing to make for each other. The same kind of sacrifice that Surket was willing to make for Serec and me.

But then, a flash of heat rose up inside my chest. *No. What Astaroth was doing was nothing like Surket. Surket would never place innocent lives at risk, regardless* of the outcome.

"Forgive me, Harine," I said firmly. "I truly wish things could have been different. But considering the number of people impacted by Astaroth's first attempt at altering El's design, I have my reservations about blindly helping him. Even if it's the only way to cure you. The only way to help the plagued and consumed. There's no guarantee that countless lives won't be negatively impacted all over again."

Harine's eyes grew as somber as they were on the battlefield. "There are no guarantees in life. There is only action or inaction. Concern or complacency."

If there was one thing I couldn't fault in Harine, it was her indomitable sense of loyalty. For that reason alone, I presumed her words were driven more by a desperation to see Astaroth's goals realized, than they were her own personal gain.

"Are you prepared to risk countless lives just so your master can chase his ambitions?"

"I believe in my Lord. More importantly, I understand that sacrifices and mistakes bring us closer to a solution that benefits the masses. Any lives lost in this process, would serve as prerequisite martyrs for a better world." There was an unshakable certainty in her words that intrigued as much as it disturbed me.

"Are you implying that one life can be valued over another?"

"A rather inapt question for a princess to ask, don't you think?"

"What is that supposed to mean?"

"Your life is of higher appraisal than the lives of everyone you know, save for the Monarch himself, is it not?"

"No one life holds greater value than another. I am no exception."

Harine tilted her head at me. "Do you truly believe that?"

"I do. Though I know those around me likely do not." If her goal was to sow doubt, she was succeeding.

"Obviously you've found yourself in a situation where lives were in danger. Are you honestly saying that your life has never been given priority over someone else's?"

More than anything, I wanted her to understand just how wrong she was. But without even trying, I could only think up the countless situations where Surket, Northe, or Serec risked their lives to save me.

"The selfish and irresponsible nature plaguing humanity, has created a world of conflict and bloodshed," she continued. "You yourself descend from a proud line of warlords who eradicated entire populations for their own ambitions. And if placed in the same situation, you would do the same. The only thing that separates patriots from war criminals is victory."

Before I could respond, a faint buzzing interjected. Harine pulled out her timechain. "Please excuse me," she said, turning away. "Harine...Yes, I am...Right now?...I'll be there shortly." She severed the link. "My apologies, but it seems our conversation must be postponed."

"Of course," I said.

She studied me momentarily, before stepping closer. I reflexively raised my guard.

"Kaleb and I weren't the first."

"The first?"

"People Lord Astaroth cared about," Harine clarified. "There were others before us, also a brother and sister, I believe. He doesn't speak of them openly, but he's mentioned them at times when he didn't realize I was listening. There was something he couldn't save them from, and he's never forgiven himself for it." Her eyes trailed, as if she hurt just as deeply from the loss. "He's not heartless." Her eyes moved back up to mine. "A man without a heart wouldn't go to such great lengths for anyone but himself."

Harine walked out and the door closed behind her, leaving me to stare at the spot on the wall where she had been.

I don't remember how long I stared, while a gamut of thoughts swirled in my mind. *Is there some vital component to Astaroth that I'm missing?* Whether I was wrongly condemning a man with good—albeit misguided—intentions, or playing a role similar to Harine's, where other lives were being valued below my own—all because of my birthright—the thought cultivated the apprehension within me.

I didn't want my ties to royalty to make my survival more important than everyone else's. More importantly, I hated the possibility that the notion might have been the unspoken consensus throughout my career in IGIS. Being next in line to rule Aruria, was something I had to accept, because there was no other way to ensure stability and prosperity. But I couldn't accept my friends throwing themselves in harm's way for me if I couldn't do the same for them.

"But Surket was different," I thought aloud. "Surket sacrificed herself because Serec would've..." A cold shiver washed through my entire body, as the image of Kurai standing over Serec flashed through my mind. It was the last thing I'd seen as Astaroth carried me away. The last thing I remember before waking up in the strange room.

He found a way out. He had too. It might have been foolish to believe he was okay, but that hope was all I had. If Kurai had taken Serec away from me, I couldn't begin to imagine what I would do—how far I might go to bring him to justice.

In better conditions, locating Serec telepathically might not have been out of the question. We'd spent plenty of time communicating mind-to-mind, so I was familiar with his cerebral signature. But, far away in some secluded part of Oltre-sulle, I had no idea where to start my search.

Frustration bubbled inside me. *None of this would have happened if Serec had treated me like a partner, instead of a liability.* The more I thought about it, the more it infuriated me. Thanks to Serec's undying need to be the hero, I could only hope he wasn't in the afterlife, explaining to Surket how he'd single hand-edly derailed another mission. But, whether or not that was the case, I had no way to find him confined within these lifeless walls.

"Liza," a familiar voice called. "Wake up. You're going to be late."

My eyes shot. Mama was standing over me, her hands on her hips. Her soft emerald green eyes perfectly matching her dress.

"Up we go little lady. Your father is almost ready to go and here you are, still in the bed."

I groaned. "Okay, okay. I'm getting up."

I rolled over and surveyed the room, my room. Not Domus Regalia. Not D7. *My room.* I squinted across the room at the Frilare Prep School calendar posi-tioned at perfect eye level next to the door. *Frilare Prep School? But I never went to—.*

"What happened to good morning, little lady? Or are you just that excited to graduate today?"

I sprang up and wrapped my arms around her. "Who needs to graduate?" I exclaimed. "I could stay like this forever!"

Mama laughed. "Sa'Sha Eliza Moreaux, I swear you are one of a kind. Number one in your class and number five in the KEYS 100 and you don't want to graduate? Divina Martinel herself will be there to congratulate you. Now hurry up and get dressed, little lady. I don't want you to be late today."

"Aunt Margaline is coming?! I'll be done in no time."

Her voice was so vibrant, so full of life it energized me. For some reason, it felt like an eternity since the last time I'd heard it.

"I had the craziest dream, Mama."

"Tell me while you get dressed. You can handle that can't you?"

I smiled and ran into the bathroom. "I was the princess living with Uncle Charlee, but I was also a secret agent. I couldn't tell him, but I had a team who were Gifted like me. And we fought against other Gifted and monsters and some guy named—" A dark face abruptly flashed in front of me. I blinked, trying to make sense of the image.

"Sounds like quite a wild dream. I'm sure your father will enjoy hearing about it."

The door closed and there was silence.

I looked at myself in the mirror, but for some reason the image was out of focus. I rubbed my eyes and looked again, and the image shifted strangely. It was me, but not the me I was expecting.

My hair was in the same braids mama always put them in, but it was a snowy white. My eyes had also become a bright green. I focused on the image, wondering who was staring back at me.

It was just a wild dream. I opened my closet door. The only thing inside was my school uniform. But it had a different emblem over the left side of the chest. I reached for it, and a barrage of images bombarded me the moment my fingers made contact. I saw myself back when I joined the Guild, angry at Serec for forgetting my name, talking to Surket. *Who's Surket? And what's the Guild?* I pulled back, and the images ceased. My heart pummeled my ribcage. *What is all this? Is something wrong with my powers?*

"Hurry up, little lady," another familiar voice called. *Daddy?* "Your mother has breakfast ready. Throw on some clothes and come give me my morning hug."

"Okay," I yelled back. I looked at the uniform emblem again, and shuddered expectedly. *I've seen this before somewhere. But where?*

"Hurry up Liza!" mom called. "Your daddy's walking out the door in five hashes."

My eyes widened. I couldn't afford to waste any more time. I grabbed the uniform, and my mind rushed with so many images my body trembled. Everything flashed through my mind—every memory, every sensation, every promise—from my last normal day in Frilare, through the day I was eating with Astaroth, Harine, and Kaleb. Then they all turned to me, smiling warmly.

"Welcome back," Harine said as darkness consumed me. "We've missed you."

I was awakened by the thrum of... *Medical equipment?* I tried to open my eyes, but my lids wouldn't respond. A bright light flashed and held steady over me, penetrating my eyelids with a faded red, as muffled voices faded in and out.

"We've administered the Exol. She should be ready for radiation therapy in a few segments," a voice said.

My head jolted up. I was in my dad's old cargo raeda. "You say something, Daddy?"

"I'm really proud of you. It's been a struggle these past anums. But you've always done what's right. And I know you will continue to."

I rubbed my eyes to clear the fog.

"What if I don't know what's right?"

The corners of his mouth curled slightly. "We all find ourselves in situations where we must choose between two bad choices. In these instances, we must strive to do what we believe will be most right for the most people. It's never easy, but in times like those, El reveals to us who we really are."

As I watched the open fields zipping by, a serenity grew over me, until it turned into a lightheadedness. But rather than fighting it, I eased into it and leaned against Daddy's arm. The spicy-sweet aroma of his favorite cologne enveloping me. He knew how much both Mama and I liked the cologne, and he always saved it for special occasions.

"Her progress is astounding," Daddy said in a weird voice.

"What progress?" I asked.

"Almost there, kiddo. I believe we're going in the direction you need." I opened one eye to peer out the window. But the bright landscape had morphed into a foggy wasteland. More than a little confused, I looked at Daddy again. His dress pants and plaid shirt had become a hunter green cloak.

"Daddy, where...?"

He pointed out the front window. "That girl up there, on the mountain," he said.

I followed his finger, wondering how he or I could see someone so clearly way up on a mountaintop. But I could see her too. A woman stood in a matching green cloak.

When she pulled her hood back, I saw... me. *What am I doing up there? And how am I down here?* The me in the cloak, locked eyes with me. The dead violet glow frightened me as much as it stoked my curiosity. A thick, bright ruby aura encased her as she reached a hand up to the sky.

I wanted to stop, her. To tell her she didn't have to do it. But I couldn't move. The malevolent radiance of the aura seemed to swallow the entire mountain, as sparks crackled around her hand, and a light shot from her palm. I reflexively shielded my eyes. And when I looked again, a tiny, bright red ball of light, hung high in the sky. It disappeared after a few beats, before exploding into a brilliant wave. The blast grew, sweeping across the sky in a massive sheet of violet.

As my double and I stood silent, watching the sky, a twinkle on her face caught my eye. A tear rolled down her cheek. A tear that matched the one brushing my cheek. It was over. We'd finally remade the sky.

Remembering my parents, I surveyed the area, and my eyes stopped at an empty, broken down raeda. "Corruption took them away," my double said. "No one acted when there was time, but now that can change. You can act. You have the power to remake the world. We can do it together."

My double vanished, and I found myself standing on the mountaintop. My new family surrounded me, a proud glow in their violet eyes. "Well done sister," Harine smiled. "Thanks to you, the final phase of our operation can begin." She opened her hand, revealing a small ring. "This is for you." I took it, and slid it onto my finger. Together we marveled at the new sky together. The first step toward a brighter future.

"You are one of us now. You are a Knight of Just Death."

[5]

EX NIHILO

SEREC

"*Unfathomable potential, stifled by ignorance,*" a familiar voice echoed in my head. I forced my eyes open, to nothingness.

"Where am I?" I asked gruffly. But no one responded. "Hello...?"

A pair of icy sapphire eyes pierced the darkness. "Have you forgotten your objective?" a woman's flat voice asked. It took a moment to recognize the owner of the eyes.

"Anne," I said. "I haven't forgotten. I need to get stronger."

Bright light neutralized the darkness and I found myself standing with Anne.

"The strength you require is not achieved through physical means," she said. "You value power too highly."

"That's not true."

"Progress is attained through self-awareness. Reflect on the causality between your desires and the actions they've inspired."

I was about to ask exactly what she meant by that, when more bright light assaulted my eyes, forcing them shut.

"Looks like he's finally awake," a familiar voice said, as I twisted onto my stomach.

"Who are you?" I asked. "And where am I?"

She chuckled. "Too late for the tough guy act, cutie. The fight's long over."

"Ariel?"

"So, you do recognize my voice. I'm touched."

"What happened?"

"You were as good as dead after that beating you took back there," a deeper voice said plainly. "So, once again we had to step in and save you." It had to be Axel.

"Anyway," Ariel took over, "give your eyes some time to adjust. Sunlight is a lot harsher in the Khost Desert, and—"

"What happened to everybody else?!" I interrupted, as everything came flooding back to me. "Did they...?"

"Once your little girlfriend surrendered herself to Astaroth, he let the rest of your people go," Axel answered. "Everyone's probably gone back where they came from by now."

"Why didn't you stop him? Why'd you help the others"

"You're the only one we're interested in," Ariel said. "And you're welcome."

Enduring the ache of the harsh light, I opened my eyes to a squint, and rose to my feet. "Take me back."

"Seriously?" Axel's voice jumped in pitch. "You're not the sharpest knife in the kitchen, are you? And we're still waiting on that thank you."

"Thank you," I said darkly. "Now, take me back." Neither of them said anything. I sighed. "...Please?"

"We're not taking you back," Ariel said.

"I need to rescue Sa'Sha."

"Why do you want to save her so badly, hero?" Axel asked.

"What do you mean 'why?'"

"I mean why."

"That's a stupid question."

"Then it shouldn't take too long for your brain to muster up a sufficiently stupid answer. Now, why do you want to save her?"

I thought I had the answer. But when I opened my mouth, nothing came out.

"You're actually thinking before you speak for once," Ariel teased.

"I'm not surprised you want to save her considering it's your fault she got captured in the first place," Axel added. "You're reckless, and you live in a dream world where being a superhero is as simple as being gifted. But being one doesn't necessarily mean being the other. You need to wake up and realize that, before you start creating the kinds of problems no one can fix."

My head felt heavy. My eyes warmed. My nostrils burned, and it didn't have anything to do with the desert heat. There was nothing I could say to something like that. Maybe there was nothing to say. Either way, Sa'Sha was gone, and I could only hope everyone on my team was alright. Either way, I could only blame myself for how things turned out.

"What were you hoping to achieve?" Ariel asked.

"Hoping to achieve?"

"Charging headfirst into every battle, until IGIS asks you to join. And then, acting like you could hold the combat power of the entire guild on your shoulders?"

I thought about it for a beat, wanting to say I just wanted everyone to be safe. But I wanted more than that. "I wanted to be recognized as a hero. To be the strongest in and outside of IGIS. I wanted my strength to be what created peace in the world."

"This may come as a surprise to you, but putting people in danger first, negates the whole hero thing." Axel said, sounding annoyed. I kept my head down, my fists clenching in quiet frustration. "For all the leaps you take, the least you could do is know why."

The more his words sunk in, the heavier the weight grew over me. I thought about Sa'Sha. Then NaRyn, trying to stand up to Astaroth and being thrown aside. I should've learned after what happened to Surket. But I was so focused on individual power that I was actually making my team weaker. Even after all my time in IGIS, I was still the anchor. Still putting them at risk.

"I shouldn't have been given this power," I said, voice shaking. Tears welled in my eyes, and I opened them wider to keep tears from forming. "It's as simple as that. I don't know how to be a hero."

Axel sighed. "Is this pity session going to take long? Because Astaroth still has the princess, and your tears won't bring anyone back."

"Why are you always so obnoxious?!" I scowled, as tears started pressing out.

He shook his head. "Unfathomable potential, stifled by ignorance," he said to himself. I froze at his words. *How did he—?* "It isn't too late to make things right, hero."

I looked Axel in the eye, not caring if he saw my tears. "I said I'm not a hero."

"Then, you won't save the princess?"

"I will save Sa'Sha. Just like I'm going to stop Astaroth. But not as a hero. I'll bring her back, because I'm her friend. Because she means to me than you care understand. Because I owe it to her."

As I spoke, a peculiar energy subtly overtook me. Like my body was vibrating. The feeling intensified, until a surge of heat swept over me. My right hand grew heavy, the familiar heat coalescing in my palm. Even in the stark sunlight of the desert, my palm flashed so brightly I squinted as I instinctively reached forward and grasped at a pool of energy that reshaped into my aetharma.

"Great job cutie," Ariel said. "It looks like you've finally earned your aetharma."

"It took you long enough to figure it out, kid," Axel said. "Denying your true self only delays your progress."

I examined the blade. It looked a little different. The blade was longer and the glow was more concentrated. And even though the handle felt thicker than before, the weapon felt lighter as a whole. I looked at Ariel. "This what you meant by—"

"Focusing on what matters most." she finished. "Yes. When it happens, your weapon instinctively resonates with your heart. It's the only true way to evoke your aetharma."

I paused. "So, what now?"

"Now," Axel said, stepping forward, "we have a little fun."

He rushed me, and I reflexively blocked his first attack and parried the next two. It was a lot easier than I'd remembered. "You're looking better already," Ariel said. "I think I'll join in on the excitement."

"Already?"

"We're short on time. And if you aren't confident you can handle what we throw at you, you won't stand a chance against Astaroth."

Axel rushed me again, and I parried and jumped back. "Fine," I said, surprised at how much the challenge excited me. "Let's see what you guys can do."

Later that afternoon, Ariel and Axel led me to a small hut not far from where we were training. It was barely darker than the pale dirt around it, and by myself I would've easily missed it.

The whole place looked rustic and barely lived in. Not surprising, considering how rarely Ariel and Axel left Locke's side. As I stepped inside, the strong soothing scent of burning wood wafted into my nose. And despite the lack of pictures, windows, or furniture, I felt oddly at home.

Ariel went to the sink, rinsed her hands off, and filled three glasses with water. She handed me and Axel a glass. "There isn't much here, so don't expect to do anything except eat, shower and sleep, when you're not training."

"How long do I have to train anyway?" I said, taking the glass from Ariel.

I studied the glass before taking a drink. "And how do you have running water out here?"

"What does it matter?" Axel interrupted.

I opened my mouth to answer, but Axel had already turned away. I had to give him credit though. There weren't many people who could maintain the balance between helpful and unpleasant like he could.

I took a gulp of water.

"Drink another glass before bed. It's not hard to dehydrate out here."

"I can imagine." I scanned the room for a beat. "Where am I supposed to sleep, by the way?"

"There's only one bed here," Ariel replied.

The expectant look in Ariel's eyes made me double take. "...Okay," I said cautiously.

"And Axel always takes the couch."

"...Okay," I repeated.

She stood there, waiting for my answer. I turned to Axel, who looked completely immersed in the act of sipping his water. Then I turned back to Ariel, whose eyes sparkled in a way that had my heart jumping around in my chest. I cleared my throat and swallowed, before a nervous breath. "I—"

"You'll have to sleep on the floor," she said. "Hopefully the blankets will be enough for you."

"Y-yeah. That umm...that's fine," I recovered, not sure why I felt a little disappointed.

For the next four days and nights, we trained. Each day was harder than the last. But even compared to day one, everything I'd done up until that point felt like a vacation. And thinking of Sa'Sha was more than enough motivation to give everything I had. In the little downtime I had each day, I wondered if she was okay, and hoped she hadn't given up hope on me coming to save her.

By my last night, my body was starting to get used to the training. And by bedtime, I actually had the energy to pay attention to what was pressing on my mind.

"Axel?" I said. "You awake?"

"What do you want?" he said, rolling over.

"Remember how Ariel said when the right thing resonates with my heart, I can evoke my aetharma?"

"What about it?" I would've guessed judging by his tone meant he wasn't in the mood to talk. But if that were the case, I doubt he would have responded in the first place.

"She said that was the only way I could draw it out, right?"

He sighed. "Yup."

"Then why did it work before, when I was in danger?"

"Because fear was in your heart. With fear driving you, your weapon was able to resonate with that fear to achieve your heart's desire."

"My desire to be afraid?"

"Your desire to survive. But fear and anger are weak, fleeting emotions and can't endure over time like love. So, focusing on protecting people you love, makes your weapon stronger."

I thought I'd been focusing on protecting people before. But it could've been more about the fear of losing them.

"Goodnight," he said abruptly, rolling the other way.

"Hey Axel?"

He didn't respond.

"Axel," I said louder.

"What do you want?"

"I just wanted to say thanks. For everything. You guys saved my life a bunch of times now, and you trained me, even though I never left IGIS. I just wanted you to know I really appreciate it."

A few beats passed and Axel hadn't said anything. *Guess he really didn't want to talk anymore.*

"You're welcome."

The aroma of wasn't a bad way to start my morning. I lifted my head to Ariel in the kitchen, pouring juice.

"If you're hungry, come take a seat," she said. "There's plenty of food here."

"What's the occasion?"

"Completing your training."

"So, that's it? I'm done?"

"As soon as you eat and leave," Axel said.

I took a seat and looked at my plate. Buttered toast and sausage. "I probably should've said something earlier, but I'm a vegetarian."

As soon as the words left my mouth, Axel stabbed his fork into the sausage on my plate. "More for me."

"Interesting," Ariel said smiling thoughtfully.

"What? Axel's manners?"

"No, kid," Axel said. "Our master doesn't eat meat either." He took a huge bite of sausage.

"Why do you always refer to Locke as 'master?'" I asked. "Isn't he more like your boss?"

"It's complicated," Axel said.

"Our master is more than our employer. We've served and studied under him for as long as I can remember," Ariel added.

"Like...since university?" I asked. They exchanged a glance. "What? Prep school then?"

"I always have trouble remembering who the king was when master took us in. You remember?"

"Come on?" I interrupted. "Charlemagne VII has more than thirty anums in the monarchy. Unless you guys are way older than you look, there's no way that..." I trailed off at the head-tilting look of interest they gave in perfect unison. "How old are you guys?"

Ariel pushed a finger to her chin.

"It's not so easy to remember after the first couple, but we have somewhere near 250 anums."

"Plus or minus ten anums," Axel added.

"Guys, seriously..." I said. But they didn't budge.

"I don't look a day over twenty, do I?" Ariel asked, her boastful manner making me wonder if she was actually telling the truth.

"But how—?"

"Alright kid," Axel snapped. "Questions over."

"Don't mind him, cutie," Ariel said. "Axel is terrible with goodbyes. The grumpier he gets, the more he cares."

He shot her a fiery stare. But she pretended not to notice.

"So, what's your next move?"

I took a beat to think. "I hadn't actually given it much thought," I admitted. "But I'd appreciate it if you guys took me back to Oltresulle."

Axel swallowed. "I didn't think you'd be so eager to die, after claiming you'd protect everyone."

"Believe it or not, the message got through this time," I said. "I can't do it alone. I know that. And since Astaroth's Noctus Drive will fire soon, I'm pretty much out of time for training. But if there's any chance of winning this battle, I'll need Sa'Sha's help."

"I'll take you back," Ariel offered. "But with your training complete, we're no longer authorized to help you. You'll be on your own from here on out."

"And getting your girlfriend back might be harder than you think," Axel added.

"What makes you say that?"

"Astaroth needed Sa'Sha for her powers," Ariel explained.

"So? It's not like she'd help someone like him."

"Unless he's done something to make her cooperate," Axel said.

I shook my head. "Her mind's too strong, and her will is even stronger. She won't give in."

"She already has," Ariel said.

Ariel's face turned somber. "What do you mean?"

"Finish your breakfast first and I'll show you."

I tried to force a couple bites, but my appetite had vanished.

"I'm not that hungry. Can you just show me now?"

She looked at Axel, whose complete focus remained on his plate. She sighed and walked to the front door. "Might as well take you back while I'm at it," she said. I waited for Axel to get up, but he didn't budge.

"You're not coming?" I asked.

"Why would I waste good food?" he asked in a way that told me he wasn't looking for an answer.

"Fine," I said with a shrug, and followed Ariel.

"Good luck, kid," he said from his seat. "No more room for doubt, alright?" He shoved a forkful of sausage in his mouth.

A small grin pressed at the corner of my mouth. "Yeah," I said, and stepped outside.

"The sky's changing," Ariel said, pointing off in the distance

"Why's it so—purple?"

"Sa'Sha's powers are an important part of Astaroth's plans with the Noctus Drive. The change in sky color was something only she could've done. I'm guessing it'll reach where we are by the end of the day."

Nausea hit the pit of my stomach. "You mean Sa'Sha...?"

"You'll see soon enough."

But I didn't need to see. The chill in my veins was already warming into a boil. I tried to bite back the trembling in my jaw, as the heat reached my eyes. I was going to crack Astaroth's skull, first chance I got. But the time wasn't right. And I would have to keep my emotions in order until it was.

"I doubt it'll be any more than a deck, before we storm Astaroth's compound, in case you were wondering."

"I wasn't," Ariel said flatly. "'No longer authorized to assist,' remember?"

"Right," I said, feeling more than a little disappointed.

"Of course, if chance puts us around the same place, at the same time, defending ourselves would be a given." She flashed a mischievous grin and winked. The tension in my jaw loosened, and I let myself hope that chance would be on my side when the time came.

I took a deep breath and looked back at the sky with a sigh. "I'm ready."

Ariel threw her arms around my neck and squeezed. "Take care of yourself, cutie," she said softly.

"I will." Her body was firm, and soothingly warm. And there was just a little give, as I squeezed her waist. Until that moment, I hadn't realized how similar her body type was to Surket's. And being reminded of her, in that moment, provided a subtle comfort. "Thanks again...for everything."

Leaving a hand on my shoulder, Ariel turned to the violet sky, and my body instantly felt lighter. Then, everything went dark, and the next thing I knew, I was back in the same spot where Ariel and Axel had rescued me. Ariel took a step back and winked again, before vanishing into a thin plume of smoke.

The area was so quiet and peaceful, difficult to imagine the chaos that had occurred just a few days earlier. I spotted someone in a dark green cloak, standing alone in a clearing. *One of Astaroth's knights.*

"Hey!" I called out. "I'm here for the princess. And I don't feel like wasting my time beating an answer out of you." The knight turned around. "So, I'm only asking once. Where is sh—?"

I trailed off into a speechless stupor, as the knight drew back her hood. *This must be a dream. It can't be—* But the pain of my heart plummeting into my stomach felt pretty real.

"Liza?" I said, hoping my eyes were somehow failing me. Without a word, she unsheathed Nightfall, and charged.

[6]

LAST KNIGHT

SEREC

"**L**iza!" I said quickly. "It's me!" I wasn't expecting an overjoyed reception. But Sa'Sha's, burning violet eyes that followed my movements perfectly was low on my list of things I would have expected. Swinging furiously and far too accurately, her blade stayed within a hair's width of my face, as I strafed and jumped around as fast as my feet hit the dirt.

"What happened to you?" I yelled. She responded with another swing of her divarma. "Liza!"

"Lord Astaroth set me free," she said, voice callous as she continued swinging. "Now I can act based on what I want. I can live for myself."

"Acting selfishly might make you feel better at first, but it won't make your problems go away."

"Don't lecture me on selfishness," she hissed. "It's your selfish fault I was captured in the first place."

"By Astaroth! So, why are you helping him?"

"Because helping him means hurting you!"

She slashed again, and her blade nicked my forearm. The cut was clean and superficial, but it still screamed. The downside of fighting against a divarma wielder. And even though the pain was all too real, I felt like I was dreaming. If hurting me mattered more to Sa'Sha than stopping Astaroth, I had to question my sanity. Or hers.

"You're like a child," she continued. "Your self-indulgent thoughtlessness always creates messes for others to clean up. But no more."

She came at me again. Swinging so fast, I was certain every move I made would be my last.

"You're right, Liza," I forced between panting breaths, when I finally got enough distance between us. "I'm sorry. I never meant to hurt you."

"Save your apologies and at least learn to finish what you start."

"I'm here, aren't I?"

"Then, stop running."

"I'm not running. I'm trying to save you."

Sa'Sha's eyes narrowed, and she lunged at me without warning. I barely covered my arm in stone in time to block. "You always want to be the hero, saving the helpless princess. Did it ever occur to you that I was fully capable of protecting myself?" she snarled.

Whatever Astaroth had done, it had unleashed a dormant rage; one that couldn't be quelled by words alone.

"I know you can protect yourself. We all do. But it's not about that. We need you."

Sa'Sha looked up at my eyes, and hers softened slightly. She started to ease up on her Divarma, and I followed. Suddenly, she leaned back and her heel stabbed into my chest as she booted me away.

I rolled back and pushed to my feet in one fluid motion. Her malicious violet eyes glowed hot as she took a step closer. The unforgiving look in her eyes was ten times worse than any pain the heel of her boot could ever cause.

"What do I have to do for you to forgive me?"

"Give up," she said, a little too quickly.

"I'm not giving up." She just stood there, unblinking. "Fine," I said. "If you want me to throw our friendship away, then beat me. But if I win, you have to agree to come back to the Guild with me."

"You won't win."

"Do we have a deal or not?"

She studied me for a beat. "Fine," she said. "Deal."

Before the words reached my ears, she was on me, swinging Nightfall like I was a fly that needed swatting. I took full advantage of the sturdy skin covering my arm, blocking her half-crazed assault. I shouldn't have taken much to hold her at bay, but I'd either forgotten how strong Sa'Sha was or newfound strength was another gift that came from Astaroth.

I dug my feet into the dirt for stability and gave one hard shove forward. But when I pushed, she leaned back and I stumbled forward as she spun around me. Something flashed out of the corner of my eye, and acting on pure instinct, I covered my head and neck in stone. Sa'Sha's blade thudded against the back of my neck with a shrill clang a beat later. I twisted and flung a knife hand chop at her waist, but she slipped under it and used my momentum against me, with a sweep to the back of my legs.

I fell back, wincing as I smacked into the dirt. My eyes opened to Sa'Sha falling toward me with the tip of her blade aimed at my chest. I rolled over and jumped back, before her follow-up slash could catch me.

"You're still running," she said eerily. Adrenaline flooded every muscle in my body so vigorously, the jitters mildly disrupted my senses. "You're finally taking this seriously," she observed almost robotically. "So shall I."

Her eyes glinted and my senses went haywire as the air tensed. The mass of energy building somewhere in front of me, made the hair on my arms stand on end. I strafed right, just as the energy condensed into a visible flash of light. A loud whizzing boom echoed, as the force of the explosion hurled me to the ground. I twisted around and shot out a blast of wind. But a wall of psionic energy rose in front of Sa'Sha to block it.

Note to self: Watch out for new, dangerously enhanced abilities, courtesy of Astaroth. My body tingled as another mass built up behind me, and I rushed out of the way, before it exploded. I kept running, circling around Sa'Sha at a safe distance. She stood there, making no visible effort to keep me in her sights.

As far as I understood, Sa'Sha's alpha psionic waves were only a good option when she had eyes on her target. If she wasn't trying to keep sight of me, it must have meant she had other plans. It also meant she understood the difference in our objectives. She may have been trying to harm me, but I only wanted to neutralize her until I could get her back to HQ where Kareen and Ari could hopefully figure out how to get her back to normal.

It was probably safe to assume she already knew that much. What I couldn't assume, was that more knights wouldn't show up soon to outnumber me. I darted at her from behind, shortening my stride at the last second. I kicked out and she spun around just in time to catch my foot with hers.

"I can predict your intent to attack," she said. I pushed away and raced around her, attacking a few more times from different directions. But somehow, she blocked each attack without even looking. "You've never learned to accept fact as fact."

Maybe it wasn't simple luck, but I wasn't ready to believe that a few well-timed blocks made her idea of being untouchable anything close to a fact. I zipped around in random, confusing patterns—only slowing enough to attack from unpredictable angles. But her repeated masterful reactions made me wonder why it seemed so much like she *was* predicting my attacks. For that matter, I still didn't understand how she was holding ground against me without breaking a sweat, when I had to be moving somewhere around the speed of sound.

As the fight progressed, it was looking more and more like Sa'Sha was—and always had been—the one with the real advantage. Defending against high-velocity attacks should've required a massive amount of strength and stamina. But even after all my attacks, she held steady. And from the start of the fight, Sa'Sha had displayed a power that seemed to be in the same realm as Ariel and Axel. It wasn't a stretch to assume she'd figured out how to boost her physical capacity with telekinetic energy too. All the while, my effort to hold back had my legs burning out, and my lungs working overtime.

I wasn't fighting smart enough. If I was going to win, I needed time to think. I pulled back and zipped between trees, until I found one thick enough to hide behind.

"Back to running already?" Sa'Sha called.

A whizzing boom echoed a meter away, forcing my attention toward a tree as it burst into splinters. I stiffened, watching what was left of the tree as it fluttered to the ground. Another tree burst into splinters from my other side. *She's taunting me.* Sa'Sha could easily find my heat signature among the trees. She wanted me to face her. But psionic waves were the worst way to convince me.

Out of all Sa'Sha's abilities, condensing and detonating psionic energy was by far the toughest and most dangerous ability to both her and her target. In the past anum, I could count on both hands, the number of times Sa'Sha went through dizzy spells, trying to push for a third or fourth consecutive psionic blast during her solo training. Suddenly, she was blasting the whole forest with as much ease as walking.

Another tree exploded, pelting me with splinters. Ironically, the one time I actually wanted to think first, it wasn't an option. I'd just have to come up with a way to save Sa'Sha during our fight or risk sitting and getting my face blown off. I stepped out from behind the tree.

"You're pretty set on killing me," I said. "That much is obvious. But you're about to see that I'm even more serious about getting you back. The real you."

"This is the real me," she said casually.

My jaw tensed. But I wasn't about to waste time arguing with her. "How about we stop dragging this about?"

"You're the one holding back."

"Not anymore." I took a deep breath and focused my mind on my singular goal: saving Sa'Sha. How good it would feel to have her back, safe and sound. To hug her again, and laugh with her. And how if I couldn't give her back her freedom, I would never get the chance to have the future with her I'd wanted more than anything. My heart felt like it was shaking. Then, the vibration spread throughout my body, and my palm glowed hot. I reached out and grasped the energy, and it took form as my Aetharma.

Sa'Sha readied herself to strike with Nightfall, and disappeared in a flash of psionic energy. She blurred left and right across the field, trying to circle around me. But my eyes kept up. She appeared right in front of me, lunging. I went for the block, and she dipped lower. Her blade slit sharply at the side of my arm.

I swung down at her, but she zipped away again. Before I could give any attention to the blood trickling down my forearm, she appeared from my left and I spun to stop her attack with my Aetharma.

The pace only picked up as the fight went on, our weapons clanging and clashing repeatedly. She was moving so quickly, attacking so fiercely, I had to keep my abilities heightened the whole time. But it was longer than I'd ever fought with my powers maxed out. And even with the boost of my Aetharma, my sight eventually started burning.

Next came the aching burn in every muscle—another sign that I needed a breather ASAP. I shot out small gales of wind and burst of electricity to try and back her up. But she stopped everything with her psionic fields, staying on me.

Our powers were clashing at a violent stalemate. And when my vision started blurring more, I was sure she would take the fight. But she was beginning to feel the effects too; her movements becoming less precise and blood starting to drip from her nose. She had to be at her limit on her psionic abilities. But the tingle across my skin told me that she wasn't through trying. I threw out a large burst of electricity, just in time and the energy exploded between us in a shock wave that sent me tumbling backward and into a tree. Stunned by the excruciating impact, my back throbbed with a fiery pain that spread throughout my whole body. My head was throbbing, as the world around me slowed.

I couldn't make it to my feet, so my hands and knees would have to do. Salty red fluid dripped down my nose and mouth, offering sacrifice to the ground below. Sa'Sha wrenched herself to her feet, looking ready to pass out as she slowly propped herself up with Nightfall. With shaky legs, I pressed to my feet and grabbed my Aetharma.

She rushed me, a few steps away and closing in fast. She blinked, and for a fraction of a beat, my eyes focused on hers. A single sparkling tear fell from her face, confirmation that the real Sa'Sha was in there—somewhere. Half a beat later, she vanished and before I could make another move... Nightfall, Sa'Sha's trusted companion—a blade that had saved me countless times—was pressing against my neck.

It was too late to block. Too late to dodge. She had won. And the hatred that consumed her, would be the true instrument of my demise. I closed my eyes, reigned to my fate. And drew my final breath.

[7]

WHY WE FIGHT

SEREC

I stood there, frozen in nothingness. No pain. No sound. Nothing. But when I opened my eyes, there was Sa'Sha, still ready to relieve my body of my head. Nightfall, remained against my throat; a subtle reminder that these were my last moments. Only, my last moments should have already passed. Surprised, I stumbled back, briefly scanning the area. A couple of a leaves hung in the air; their intention to fall, but their objective hindered. They were frozen in place—like our environment—like Sa'Sha. *I froze time*, I realized. The pressure rapidly increasing in my lungs, cued me to act quickly before time resumed.

I moved behind Sa'Sha, trying to come up with the best way to stop her. There were any number of ways I could have ended the fight. But I didn't know if her body was still being enhanced with psionic energy. If it was, and my attack was too weak, she'd likely counterattack. My only other option would be to hit her hard enough to break through her barrier. But that was assuming her body was still clad in psionic energy. If she'd already released the barrier, a hit like that would do serious—most likely irreparable damage. My lungs felt like they were about to burst, as lightheadedness set in. I was out of time. Unwilling to take the risk, I let go of my aetharma, and as it evaporated into light, I released the air from my lungs and reflexively inhaled.

Time resumed with a thunderous howl, and Sa'Sha stumbled forward. My knees buckled and I kneeled to catch myself. Sa'Sha whirled around, frantic to find me and glaring when she finally did.

"You... used it, again didn't you?" she asked. I was too focused on keeping my knees from buckling to answer. "Why?"

"How else could I avoid your attack—"

"Don't play dumb," she spat. "I was frozen in place... completely open... why?" A second tear ran down her cheek.

"Some battles aren't fought for sake of winning." Surket's words had never been truer. "I'm not here to win. I'm here for you... because I care about you. Because I need you."

"Don't say you care about me! You need me to validate yourself as a hero. You need me because if another major dies on account of your selfishness, even The Director won't be able to save you from the punishment you deserve."

"Now who's playing dumb?" I sighed. "Or are you finally ready to admit you hate me?" Sa'Sha quietly stared back for a moment, then looked away. "Yeah," I continued. "I haven't forgotten how it feels, saying such hurtful things."

"All this time I've been trying to prove myself as something other than an anchor to Team Seven. I've been trying to prove I could be as strong as you." The sorrow in her watery eyes was all I could focus on as my body started shaking. "I've done a terrible job of being a team player. But I needed you to acknowledge me. I needed us both to feel like I was the kind of man that was worthy of being your friend—of being more."

"Stop," she said, her lips quivering.

"Somewhere along the way, that became most important. And the more you or anyone tried to stop me from reaching that goal, the harder I wanted to push to overcome it."

"Stop," she repeated.

"I fear what would happen if I lost you. Because despite any promises or what anyone else says or thinks, I can't imagine life without the woman I love. And I won't let anyone separate us this time, even if it costs me my life. So, don't you dare tell me how I feel about you." I swallowed against the burning in my throat. My vocal chords felt like they were withering. "I can't do this without you, Liza."

"Do what?" she asked weakly.

"Live." Fire brushed against the back of my eyes, triggering a well of tears. I accessed the last of my reserves, and stumbled to my feet. As Our eyes met, the violet hue infecting her's began to fade; returning to the serene honey tone I'd fallen in love with.

My legs began to waver, but she grabbed me, pulling me into an embrace. "I won't fail you again," I continued. "Not as a partner, or a friend."

"I know. We're in this together."

Before I could say anything else, a subtle glow caught my eye. Panic struck, as the glow rocketed toward us.

"Liza! Watch out!" I yelled, voice weak.

The glowing object smashed into an invisible wall behind us. When the dust cleared, I saw two of Astaroth's knights in the distance.

"We have two knights behind us." I said, struggling to get the words out.

"They've been watching the whole time." Sa'Sha sighed. "Their belief that I would kill you kept them out of the fight. Now they know they were mistaken."

She slung my arm over her shoulder and helped me walk toward a nearby clearing. "We can teleport out of here if we can just reach that clearing," she explained. But El was determined to add difficulty to our objective. Standing in front of the clearing, were Ariel and Axel. Their predatory eyes trained on us.

"You guys picked a great time to help," I called to them as we approached. But they just held there, silent, like a pair of ligorns waiting to devour their wounded prey. Wounded was a great way to describe us. I couldn't walk without Sa'Sha's assistance. And each labored breath she drew was a not so subtle indicator that she was operating on reserves. A myriad of negative thoughts tore through my consciousness. *Was it all just a lie? An elaborate plan to weaken us, so they could finish the job?* I didn't want to believe it? But the longer they watched us with a primal intensity—a base hunger—the more dread seeped in, poisoning the faith I had in them.

"What are Locke's people doing here?" Sa'Sha thought to me.

"I don't know. I'm as surprised to see them as you are." Another explosion crackled behind us, as we continued forward. When we finally reached the point of no return, I found myself fighting to maintain consciousness. Ten steps separate us from Ariel and Axel, whose eyes continued to silently follow us.

"E," Sa'Sha began. Nine steps. "I don't know what will happen in the next few moments." Eight steps. "But know that despite our difficulties." Seven steps. "Despite the turbulence we've faced together." Six steps. "I'm glad we found you." Five steps. "Happy to have you back in my life." Four steps. "And proud to call you my friend."

I was too tired to respond. Too worn out to let her know how fortunate I was to have her as my friend. How honored I was to have her as my partner. My senses faded, until my wild heart beat was all I could feel.

[8]

DEFEND THE DIRECTOR

SEREC

When my eyes finally opened, they were greeted by a myriad of sparkling lights against a regal white backdrop. *How'd I get here?* I wondered. *And where is here?* The large bed plush I found myself in was a clear indicator that 'here' was someone's bedroom. And the perfect arrangement of orange, pink, and silver throughout the room, suggested it belonged to a girl, probably one my age, and clearly used to the finer things. *Sa'Sha!* I sprang up.

"Would you mind remaining in bed?" a familiar voice called, and my eyes darted over to Alanda, sitting in a chair on the other side of the room. "Her Grace should be out shortly."

"So, she's okay?" I asked, feeling the walls of my stomach pinch as I remembered how Ariel and Axel stood between us and escape. "How did we?"

"Her Grace wishes to answer all your questions personally."

"Can you at least tell me where I am?"

"Her Grace's private dwelling. Aside from myself and Sir Doriel, you are the only person who knows about it." She looked over at a tall man standing in the corner whom I'd somehow missed during my initial survey of the room. His clothes reminded me of something Locke would where, while the apathy covering his face made me wonder if he and Axel were somehow related.

"Why does she need a 'private dwelling' when she already has what I assume is a massive room in the palace?"

"To serve as a home away from her home away from home."

The answer flowed out of Alanda as if she answered the question on a regular basis. I paused and replayed her response in my head. "You've lost me."

"Sometimes her Grace requires solace from her obligatory stressors. This home functions as a realm between her lives; offering respite from both the pressures of Domus Regalia and her responsibilities at the Guild. Her schedule hasn't allowed for ample time nor opportunity to come here lately, especially since her promotion. So, I keep things fresh and lively here in her stead."

Sa'Sha had a secret home that she'd kept hidden from me all this time, and Alanda, was completely in the know about IGIS and what Sa'Sha did there. The longer I thought about it, the more questions joined the already long list in my head. "Speaking of the Guild, why didn't we go there?"

"The Princess requested we come here, now that IGIS has disbanded."

"But we—" I froze, hoping I'd heard her wrong. "Did you just say IGIS disbanded?"

"Director Arenyu turned himself over to the authorities after Astaroth's interview with Nel Laurelli. He claimed grievance against the Guild and declared a conditional war on Aruria. The images of Her Grace holding Iam Rhasatto hostage were especially disconcerting to His Royal Highness."

"Uncle Hachi turned himself in?" Even as I asked, I didn't know if I was ready for her answer.

"Nearly a dec ago. Unfortunately, I can't imagine it gaining him much leniency, considering the sky has become violet and the fact that the three of us are the only people currently aware of the Princess' whereabouts."

I buried my face in my hands and sighed at how right I was. I was nowhere near ready for Alanda's answer. The pinch in my stomach intensified all over again, spreading up the base of my neck.

"I have to fix this," I said.

"How?"

"I don't know, but I have to do something. It's my fault this happened."

"I was hoping you would have learned by now," a voice called.

I looked up and my heart skipped a beat. "Liza!" I said, jumping to my feet and wrapping my arms around her, relieved to see her unharmed.

"Not so tight please," she moaned. "Not all of us can heal in a few segments like you can."

I loosened my hold. "Sorry. But what was I supposed to learn?"

"That this isn't all about you. In victory, we share glory, and in defeat we share blame."

"I cost us valuable time in my fight with Hypersol and Xaster."

"And Astaroth was only able to use my image because I made the choice to reveal my identity, in order to save him. I'd say that we both could have made better decisions."

I nodded. "Still, I'm sorry for being such a selfish partner. I should've—"

Sa'Sha cupped my face in her hands. "Hey—" She looked into my eyes for a moment, then smiled. "I heard you the first time."

My eyes started to lower when Sa'Sha lifted my face and dipped her head, maintaining my gaze. She smiled playfully.

"Maybe you don't understand how hard some of us girls have to work," she said, "trying to get a guy to smile at them."

My mouth pressed into a small smile that grew until it erupted into a breathy laugh. "Better. You okay?" she asked softly.

I took a beat to admire the sparkle in her eyes. "Yeah."

"Good. We have important work to do, and we're short on time. So, I need you to get dressed."

Within a few hashes, I'd cleaned up and donned the new uniform Sa'Sha had laid out for me.

"Admit it. My fashion sense is unrivaled," Sa'Sha said as I stepped out of the bathroom.

"It beats the standard issue IGIS and task force uniforms," I admitted. "But I'm not so sure if this color—"

"It looks great and you love it," Sa'Sha said, quickly as she took my hand and pulled me behind her toward a lift. "I'll meet you at the rally point in six segments, Alanda," she called behind her.

"Affirmative Blissful," Alanda called back.

"Where are we going?" I asked.

"Where else? The Director's trial."

"He's on trial right now?!"

"I said we were short on time."

We got off at the top floor, and walked up a flight of stairs and through the roof access door, *where an aircraft was waiting. The tall man from the room was standing by the aircraft. How'd he get up here so fast?*

"Welcome aboard, Highness," he said. "There's tea already prepared for you and your guest."

"Thank you, Sir Doriel," Sa'Sha said, reaching out her hand for assistance.

I moved to help her, but Sir Doriel put a hand up. "Allow me, sir."

I shrugged and he took Sa'Sha's hand and helped her into the aircraft. Then he turned and reached his hand out to me.

"Thanks, but I got it," I said.

"Just let him help you." Sa'Sha thought to me. *"It's his duty."*

"But I don't need any help." I thought back.

"Sir Doriel takes his job very seriously. You'll upset him."

Is she serious? I sighed, and let Sir Doriel support my arm as I stepped into the aircraft. Sir Doriel smirked, looking more amused than polite. He probably understood exactly how stupid I felt, and was not-so-privately enjoying every beat of it. I looked up at Sa'Sha, whose lips were also curling slightly, and I fought back a scowl. I forgot that getting Sa'Sha back to normal, meant I had to watch out for her unpredictable sense of humor.

The passenger cabin of the aircraft was fatally luxurious. The carpeted cream and gold interior was complete with a plush lounge chair stretching along one side, and two pairs of cushy cream-colored leather seats with gold trim and a phoenix embossed on the back. I sat at the gold-trimmed, glossy wood table across from Sa'Sha trying not to look too surprised at how clear my reflection was in it.

The zips of white in my peripheral pulled my attention to the windows. I paused, marveling at how incredibly fast we were moving. But Sa'Sha casually sipped her tea, like it was an everyday thing. It amazed me how someone who could be so excited, dancing in a nightclub, could also be so unimpressed riding in her very own flying piece of luxury. I would've laughed at the irony if her eyes hadn't suddenly locked onto me and made my throat tighten.

"Sir Doriel," Sa'Sha said. "Would you excuse us for a moment, please?"

"But of course, Highness," he said with a bow, before moving into the cockpit. I waited, not sure what I was expecting her to say. But she didn't say anything. She just sat there, watching me quietly, making my stomach knot up.

"So," we said in unison, then laughed nervously in unison.

"What were you going to say?"

My mind blanked, and my eyes darted around for the answer. Nothing came. "I... honestly don't remember." *Awkward!* "But what were you going to say?" I recovered.

"I umm...I just wanted to apologize for attacking you before," she said. "I allowed Ashtaroth to exploit the doubt and anger I harbored and make me into one of his puppets."

"It's not like you could help it. I mean you were brainwashed."

"Not quite. Exol's primary application is genetic alteration. But Astaroth has found other uses for it. While his version can turn regular people into malefactors. It also has the ability to alter the thought patterns of refractors. Because of you, I realized I could've fought it, if I really wanted to. But, also because of you, I chose not to."

"Why not?"

"Exol works almost like alcohol, peeling away inhibitions. Once it was in my system, it was like I had become an observer in my own body. And the detachment I felt was so liberating. But then you showed up, and I realized I wasn't an observer at all. I was still in control. Unfortunately, you were the last person I wanted to see. You shut me out when I wanted to fight alongside you, ultimately costing me my freedom and our victory. I wanted you to feel my pain—my failure. It was an inexcusable, unforgivable thing to do. And it nearly cost you your life." Sa'Sha's look was stern, determined. I didn't realize someone could reprimand me while offering an apology.

I placed my hand over hers, and her eyes dipped to it for a beat. "It's alright Liza," I said softly, and the tension in her face softened, especially around her eyes. "We both could've made better choices."

One side of her mouth curled, and as she brushed the tops of her fingers under my hand, a deep shiver went down my legs.

"Deepest pardons, Highness," Sir Doriel said through the intercom on the table, and we both jumped. "I've just received word from REAP that they are currently standing by and awaiting our landing, we will be on the ground in five hashes."

Sa'Sha pressed a button on the intercom. "Thank you, Sir Doriel."

Yeah, thanks a lot. "Who's *Reap?*"

"The Royal Entourage to the Arurian Princess. Alanda thought to organize a small group of my most loyal attendants and personal guards to work in secret on special matters such as these."

"The palace, the Guild, and REAP? No wonder you needed freedom."

"Actually, REAP is solely Alanda's responsibility. She established it to make my life easier, which is exactly what REAP has done."

"What else have they done?"

"They found my private dwelling."

I frowned. "But I thought Alanda said no one else—"

"Knows of it?" Sa'Sha nodded. "That's true. Using REAP as a resource, Alanda singlehandedly procured the space to prevent the possibility of word reaching the palace. Believe it or not, there are many enemies and false friends lurking among the elite. I needed a neutral space to ensure my lives remained separate."

"I didn't realize Alanda was responsible for so much."

"I don't know what I would do without her."

The aircraft landed, and the door opened to reveal a line of royal guards on either side, weapons drawn. "Who goes there?" one of the guards yelled, and I started to suggest another way in, when Sa'Sha casually stepped out, and everyone froze in disbelief.

"The Princess?" a few of them gasped. After a few beats of shared awe, the captain quickly stepped forward. "Group," he yelled. "Present arms!" They snapped to attention and saluted as Sa'Sha passed, and I hurried behind her. We took the rooftop stairway down to the lift, and got off on the main floor. Four doors and about ten guards later, we pushed through the last set of doors and into the main tribunal hall. The Monarch was in the middle of a heartfelt rant directed at Hachi, when Sa'Sha and I stepped in. Unlike me, she didn't stop halfway across the room. A deathly silence descended upon the room, and Sa'Sha to take full advantage. Her heels clacked on the marble floor as she walked up to the podium to address the Executive Council—the most powerful group of men and women in Aruria. The Monarch was the first to challenge the silence.

"S-Sa'Sha? Do my eyes deceive me?" He said, the cracks in his composure strikingly apparent.

"No Divinus. It is I. And I'm here to bring to light the deception you've all been subjected to." The confidence she projected brought hope to a situation that seemed fatally bleak. And to my surprise, the Council remained quiet, likely influenced by curiosity. "Iam Rhasatto has purported that I hold ties to a terrorist organization. I assure you, this claim is outright false. Mr. Rhasatto was never in any danger. He, in fact, was—and still is—the danger, to both Aruria and the rest of the free world."

"Your Grace," a chubby man next to the Monarch interjected. He was wider than I remembered, so it took a beat to recognize him as Primus Nicosta. I wondered if the uncertainty surrounding Sa'Sha's whereabouts had gotten the best of him. "I must say it is a relief to see you safe and back among friends. But, with all due respect, I must voice my skepticism regarding our claim. We are in the midst of a diplomatic nightmare and baseless accusations will only serve to weaken our position. On what grounds are you basing your accusation?"

"My words are based on my experience as Mr. Rhasatto's prisoner." Low murmurs erupted. "During my time in his custody, I came to learn that his identity as Iam Rhasatto was a facade, fashioned to hide his true identity as Astaroth—a being arguably more daemon than man."

"And how do you explain your escape?" Nicosta asked with a hint of suspicion.

She pointed at me and my blood ran cold. "Director Arenyu's nephew, risked his life to save me." The Council, behind the Monarch shifted glances between Sa'Sha and me, and whispers reclaimed the room, until the Monarch put up a hand, quieting everyone. Everyone, that is, except Hachi. With his back to me, Hachi sat quietly in tethered chains, never glancing in my direction.

"Combining the resources of Theall Medical Corporation and the Life Reciprocal organization, Astaroth is solely responsible for creating the monsters that have been terrorizing the streets of Aruria this past anum," Sa'Sha continued. "Furthermore, Astaroth now possesses a device that will instantly turn millions of people into these beasts, and he is mere days from using it."

The murmurs returned and quickly grew into fearful clamors.

"Order," the Monarch yelled. "Princess, please understand that the gravity of your claims has the potential to spark another international conflict, and will require a thorough investigation, before I sanction any reactive actions."

"We have no time for a thorough investigation, Your Highness. Astaroth will be ready to act in days."

"I will not storm into another country, demanding their compliance. You should understand as well as anyone, the tact required in foreign affairs."

"Tact and diplomacy require time." She looked to the Council, appealing to the leaders of each great house. "What will you do, when your streets are filled with millions of bloodthirsty monsters—when your citizens become those creatures?"

All eyes went to the Monarch, as he contemplated Sa'Sha's argument. "What are you proposing, Sa'Sha?"

"With Director Arenyu's assistance, an assault on Astaroth's compound would prevent the device from firing, saving millions worldwide."

"Out of the question," the Monarch bellowed. "Director Arenyu has already confessed to establishing a paramilitary organization and recruiting you into said organization. And despite his reasons, he recklessly placed you—heir to the throne—into harm's path."

Sa'Sha spun on her heel. "I was not placed in harm's path. Any actions taken on the battlefield ere of my choosing, and mine alone."

"Are you mad!?" he erupted. "The battlefield is the last place for a princess. You belong at Domus Regalia under the protection of your sworn knights!"

Sa'Sha's eyes narrowed, but she took a breath before her irritation got the best of her. "Aryus the Great, spent thirty anums fighting on the frontlines, alongside his men. The valor and bravery he exhibited in leading campaigns against our enemies are what earned him his place on the throne. You regaled me with stories of his battles day and night as a child, and I held those stories close to my heart—wanting to protect all that he fought for. Wanting to continue the legacy that his descendants maintained. Why then, should I cower when our nation's safety is threatened? Why now—when an enemy presents himself before that very throne —should I disgrace myself, sitting idly by, under the protection of my knights, when my actions can make a difference?"

"What power would you use against the dangers that threaten this country?" Even from the back of the room, the vein in the center of the Monarch's forehead was visible.

"This power," Sa'Sha said, closing her eyes and creating a luminous gold aura around herself. Their faces were a tapestry of awe, amusement, reverence, and disgust. But the serenity that surrounded Sa'Sha, evoked a confidence that seemed almost supernatural. "I—am gifted." The room boomed with gasps and murmurs. "I didn't want you to discover my abilities in this manner, but I've been using my abilities to fight alongside Serec and many other Gifted within the Director's organization. And we need Director Arenyu, now more than ever, if there is to be any hope of protecting the people of Aruria."

The room became so loud with exclamations and hysteria, I couldn't hear everything the Council said. But none of it was good. The Monarch's lost stupor only lasted for a few beats, before he recomposed himself and yell. "Order! Order, I say, I will have order!"

Sa'Sha's aura faded, and she turned to the Monarch, her eyes still glowing a rich gold. "If you choose not to release the Director, Serec and I will simply face Astaroth and his army of monsters alone," she said sternly. "We are both prepared to die for our country's safety, if necessary."

The Monarch's eyes shifted over to me sharply, and I straightened up holding his gaze. My jaw twitched, as his eyes trained on me with an uncomfortably long silence. But if there were ever a time I needed to prove my determination, this was it. Finally, the Monarch nodded, and motioned the Primus and the Council over. As they whispered back and forth for what felt like a segment, Nicosta and a couple other faces darkened, before they all moved back to their seats.

"All rise for the verdict," one man ordered, and everyone in the room stood.

"General Hachinatus Jahn Arenyu, your guilty pleas for embezzlement and treason are more than enough to sentence you to death. Add to the list, recruiting the heir to the throne and repeatedly placing her in mortal danger. These crimes come together to make you one of the worst offenders in our kingdom's history. My heart pounded in my throat, as my eyes went to Hachi. He held his poise, still unmoving. But I could read the misery in his face like an open book.

"However," the Monarch continued, "I trust in Blissful Martinel's warning, and will therefore grant the opportunity to prove her words true. General Arenyu, I placed you in charge of the Bureau of National Peace because I believed you were the most capable. Clearly, I'm not the only one who feels that way." The Monarch looked at Sa'Sha then at me. "I am ordering the temporary release of Director Arenyu for the sake of absolving Aruria of this issue. This release is temporary and will be revoked once national security has been restored. Do not disappoint us." The room went wild with a mix of reactions, as Hachi's restraints were removed and he was escorted out of the room.

"You did it," I said, hugging Sa'Sha.

"Because I wasn't alone," she said, squeezing just as excitedly.

"I swear, you become more like your mother with each passing anum," The Monarch said, approaching. "But, it's my fault you're as stubborn as I am." He brushed a hand across Sa'Sha's cheek, and she smiled. He smiled back and turned to me. "Glad to see you're taking that promise as seriously as I had hoped, Serec."

I looked at Sa'Sha, then back at the Monarch. "Very seriously, Divinus."

The Monarch placed a hand on my shoulder. "I'm in your debt," he said with warmth in his eyes.

"No, Your Highness," I said, shaking my head. "You've placed your faith in us and freed my uncle when you had every reason not to."

His face became a somber mask. "He's not in the clear yet."

"None of us are, Divinus," Hachi said, walking over. "I know your decision will be unpopular with the people and the other houses. But Astaroth is still preparing for war, and although I know it's a lot to ask, I'll need Sa'Sha's help on this one." The Monarch eyed Hachi suspiciously. "Charlee, I'm sending mine in to make sure yours comes back. But I'll need yours for the very same reason." The Monarch frowned, and nodded. "Hachi, you are my dearest friend and a treasure to our nation. But had circumstances aligned any differently, you would be in a *Waking Grave* instead of walking free. I'm placing the fate of the nation and my little girl in your hands. See to it that my faith is not misplaced.

[9]

NOSTALGIA

SA'SHA

Our fate was uncertain, but our resolve was unshakable. We raced back to Vaticia; ready to alter the path Astaroth had set Orbis on. REAP had already alerted Task Force 224 and they were standing by when Serec and I arrived at the Operations Center. The moment we stepped in with the Director, the entire task force boomed with applause.

"Zero!" NaRyn squealed, nearly tackling Serec.

"Where were you? I thought—" Her composure wavered. "I thought you were—"

"I know Ryn," Serec said softly, hugging her close. "We're all back together. I'm gonna make sure it stays that way."

NaRyn nodded and squeezed him tighter.

"Hate to ruin the moment," the Colonel said, stepping forward, "but time isn't exactly on our side. I've got a team working on your new accommodations as we speak. Now that y'all are back, I can resume overseeing it."

"New accommodations?" Serec asked.

"A handful of Nighthawks won't be enough to stop Astaroth. Your commander will provide details, and in two days, you'll see for yourself." the Colonel answered, before walking off.

"What did he mean by new accommodations?" Serec asked.

I looked at him and winked. "You'll see. But, first things first."

I took my place at the front of the Operations Center, the room falling silent. "Before I begin, I'd like to thank you all for your hard work and dedication." I began, "The last dec has been one of the most difficult many of us have ever experienced and I'm thankful that you all have found the resolve to see our mission to its completion. We suffered a significant defeat at the hands of Astaroth and his forces. But if we've learned one thing, its that strategy and preparation win the day. We have reached a critical point in our journey. One in which we stand as the determining factor between a peaceful world and the chaos Astaroth promises. As I speak, our technicians and engineers are working on our new base of operations — a massive airship — code named: Ophanim. Astaroth will fire his Noctus Drive in three days. We won't allow this. Task force 224 will deploy the Ophanim and take the fight to him. With the firepower it wields as well as the skill and determination of everyone in this room, Astaroth will realize that provoking us was the mistake of a lifetime."

The room burst into a cacophony of wild cheers and inspired roars. After the devastation we faced during our first battle, they deserved an opportunity to allow hope into their hearts again. "Take these days to recharge and prepare for the battle to come. For better or worse, this will be our final mission. Task force dismissed."

Everyone saluted in unison and another uproar started that penetrated my office door even after I closed it.

"Let's get down to business," I said to the captains, approaching the gameboard. The holographic display sprouted to life with almost no mental effort. I paused for a moment, not sure how or why my technopathy was suddenly working on its own. It had to be a side effect of whatever Astaroth had done to boost my powers — an action I would make certain he regretted.

"This, is a raid. And I plan to employ all of our resources to destroy this threat." Astaroth had taken so much; destroyed so many lives. It had to end. I wasn't driven by vengeance or anger, but conviction. A conviction that offered a striking clarity.

"The bulk of Astaroth's forces are most likely positioned near the Noctus Drive. Since we'll be knocking down his front door, the majority of our forces will be tasked with cutting away at his defenses."

I pulled up a display of a device that looked like a cross between a short-barrel cannon and a telescope. "This is the Noctus Drive. We lost much of the data on it during our last mission, so I'll need you and your team to analyze the data and search for any weak points, Minerva."

"My team is more than capable of handling that task, Commander," Ari said.

"I know. But your team is the only one that can uncover information on Astaroth's defenses. Find every weakness within and around his compound."

Ari adjusted his glasses, and smirked almost devilishly at the challenge.

"Quake and Ambi," I began. "You two will command the strike force, and I'll need your agents prepped for heavy combat."

"Lastly, while Zero and I focus on infiltration and deactivating the Noctus Drive, K will be responsible for gaining air superiority. Questions?" Silence. Only their faces spoke, anxiety being the primary topic of discussion. "Then, I'll see you all in two days."

Everyone saluted and hurried out. But Kareen remained.

"Was that Anni helping or were you doing that?" she asked.

I hesitated. "That was...me," I said, certain of why she thought to ask.

"Your powers are developing more rapidly than expected."

I hesitated again and nodded. "Yes."

"Perhaps it would be a good idea to check and see what tinkering Astaroth might've done inside your head. I could run a few tests, and—"

"That's okay. I'm—"

"Analyzing this data won't take long," she added quickly. "In fact, we could even—"

"It's alright." I interjected. "I've had enough tests for now."

Kareen examined me with a mischief in her eyes. "If you change your mind, you know where to find me."

Serec and I spent the next few segments in front of the gameboard, running battle projections with Anni. I glanced up at him from across the gameboard. It was the first time we had occupied space so quietly for so long, and the first time I had seen Serec giving his undivided attention to something other than training. I was too busy admiring his soft green eyes as they sparkled against the luminescent blue glow of the gameboard. A good explanation for my simple glance becoming an undeniable stare.

"Everything alright?" he asked, looking up at me.

"Oh! Yes. Of course," I managed. "Why would you think otherwise?"

"I can feel you staring at me."

My face flushed with heat. "I was...umm...daydreaming."

"About what it's like to stare at me?"

"More like...thinking. That we haven't eaten in a while."

"I know," he agreed flatly, before his eyes went back to the game board.

I moved in front of him. "So, why don't you join me for a bite? I could use a break, and I was thinking maybe we could spend some time together."

He raised an eyebrow. "Got a place in mind?"

"Actually, I know the perfect spot."

Alanda was waiting when we returned to Domus Regalia.

"Welcome, Blissful and Serec," Alanda said, more cheer accompanying her words than usual as she led us through one of my secret entrances.

"Is sneaking around the palace a normal thing for you?" Serec whispered.

"I'm suspecting it will be for a while," I whispered back. "Reporters, journalists, and even nobles looking for information have been swarming Domus Regalia for the past dec."

"Speaking of which," Alanda added. "The media is still in a frenzy over the footage from Director Arenyu's trial. Everyone has an opinion about the revelation that you are a Gifted."

I frowned. In retrospect, making a public display of my powers probably wasn't the best direction to take, despite its effectiveness.

"Don't worry. REAP is working to contain the rumors and focus the public eye on more positive matters."

"You're a lifesaver Alanda. Please do what you can and keep me updated."

I led Serec down the hall and into Uncle's art gallery. Some of the best paintings and small sculptures in Orbis lined the length of the hallway.

"I should have known you would have a museum in your house." Serec said. "Say, remember when we had field trips to the museum and you always rushed to partner up with me?"

"Most of the other kids thought it was boring."

"What about Chelsi Grumun?"

"The quiet girl with the rainbow braces?"

"I thought you were gonna claw her eyes out that time she partnered up with me."

Despite how insignificant it was, I found my temperature subtly rising. "She whined about her original partner until Ms. Dumas forced us to switch, and I had to pair up with that obnoxious kid who bragged about how many kids he'd beat up."

Serec erupted into a fit of laughter that only made me more irritated at the memory. "It's not that funny," I said.

But to him it obviously was. He clutched at his sides as tears pressed through his eyelids. I rolled my eyes and started off in a huff. "Wait, wait." His chest was still shaking and his face was red from trying to stifle his laughter.

"What?" He took a moment, breathing deep to work himself down from it. "What?" I repeated.

"I just..." he took another breath. "I just wanted you to see my smile. I know how hard you girls work to—"

I sighed and grabbed his hand. "Come on," I said. "There's something else I want to show you."

The elaborately adorned set of double doors stood out, even amongst the already regal design of the hall. A relief of a great phoenix occupied each door, standing guard over the secrets they protected. Pale golden sunlight rained down into the dark pebble gray room, highlighting the treasures within.

"What is this place?" Serec asked.

"The Martinel Observatory," I said. "A private family hall, built to honor the teachings of El and his Divined. Each generation must maintain the oral tradition, passing the *Story of Divinity* to the next generation."

"His Divined?"

"The beings that serve El directly."

"What's the story about?"

"I'm not at liberty to share it with anyone outside the Martinel bloodline. Not even Alanda. But refractors aren't seen as the fearsome anomalies some make us out to be. We have a purpose. And the Guild comes closer to fulfilling that purpose than any organization in recorded history."

"You think that had anything to do with your uncle's decision to let Hachi go?"

The idea had never crossed my mind. "I suppose we'll never know," I said, heading for the door.

"Where are you going now?" he asked, trailing behind me.

"You'll see."

Vibrant purple and orange light filtered through the gray leaves of the Koa tree painting Serec's face with a gentle glow as he lounged beside me. The crisp air brushed against my face, carrying with it calm reassurance.

"Colorful," Serec said, taking in the pastel cascade of the sunset over the cityscape. "I never would have guessed that a koa tree — of all things — would be hiding up here.

"Sometimes, I come up here with Alanda and Sir Doriel to get away from the disenchanting humdrum of some of Uncle's events."

"I can understand why. You can see most of Callastryne from here." After a moment the energy in his face faded and he sighed.

"Is something bothering you, E?" I asked.

"I was...just wondering..." He paused and shook his head. "Nothing."

"You know," I said nudging him, "you only make me more curious when you do that."

Serec looked at me, apprehension shading his face. "I hate to ask. But how did Eliza Moreaux, end up as Blissful Martinel? I remember you saying you lost your parents but I was just wondering how you got here."

My time with my parents suddenly came to mind. Not the real time we spent together, but the vision I experienced as Astaroth's prisoner. It was all so vivid, so close to reality, I still questioned if it was really just a dream. "If it makes you uncomfortable," he started, "you don't have to—"

"It's okay," I said, steeling my nerves as I leaned back against the tree trunk. "It all came back to me while I was captured. Not long after you disappeared, someone approached my father about studying the way my body was miraculously coping with my condition."

"What condition?"

"It's called Sol Mortem." As I said the words, Serec's nose crinkled as if his mind was trying to decipher the term. "It's a congenital condition that causes severe sensitivity to the ultraviolet radiation found in sunlight. But I don't experience the symptoms, because my ability to manipulate light makes me immune to it."

"So, even though you have it, it's like you don't have it?"

I nodded. "Somehow, Astaroth learned of my ability, and after my father declined Astaroth's request to make me into his personal test subject, Astaroth had my parents killed and kidnapped me in order to alter the magnetosphere and filter ultraviolet radiation out of natural sunlight."

"So, Astaroth used you to turn the sky green, then?" Serec asked. My eyes lowered as I nodded once more. "So, why'd he kidnap you twice? Turning the sky green didn't fix the problem or something?"

"Astaroth meant to turn the sky violet from the beginning, for his knight, Harine's sake. She also has my condition, but unlike me, her powers don't protect her. And before Astaroth could finish what he'd started, Surket rescued me. That was how I first met Surket. A couple of days later, Surket discovered my uncle was the Monarch, and my closest relative. So, she brought me here, expecting the palace to keep me safe from outside threats like Astaroth."

"Surket rescued you from Astaroth, by herself?"

I turned. "We are talking about Surket, remember."

Serec's eyes lowered. "Yeah," he said wistfully.

"Plus, I don't believe she got into a direct confrontation with Astaroth. I can't imagine even she would have made it through that completely unscathed."

Serec sat up and watched the horizon, quietly tense. "Did you know this whole time? That Astaroth used your powers to change the sky?" His tone was soft, brooding, like a brewing storm.

"No. It wasn't until Astaroth tried to convince me to join him, that I came to remember everything."

The muscles in his jaw started to bulge. "It's hard not to hate someone like that," he finally said. "Manipulating people to his own ends. No matter what his reasons, he didn't have the right to make you into his tool and try to play El. And I intend to make him pay for that."

"*We* will, but for now," I said, looping my arm under his elbow, "do you think you could pretend like you're enjoying the view with me? This is my peaceful spot after all."

The muscles in his face eased as he looked at me. "Sorry," he said softly.

"Don't be sorry," I said, watching the sunset's warm reflection in his eyes. "Just be E."

The corner of his mouth expanded until a faint dimple appeared. "Will do."

I leaned my head against Serec's shoulder, and he tickled the top of my forehead as he brushed the side of his face back and forth over it.

"My apologies for interrupting," Alanda said, appearing behind us. "But your food has been ready for a few hashes now."

"A few hashes?" I asked.

"You sounded like you were in the midst of a serious conversation. I didn't want to ruin the moment." In other words, she didn't want to miss any juicy eavesdropping. Serec and I sat in the grass while Alanda and her assistants placed a large tray of food in front of us. "Will Serec be staying the night?"

"I should probably get back to D7 and—"

"Stay here tonight," I interjected a little too quickly. Except when Serec's eyes twitched, I immediately realized how awkward I'd just made everything.

"I'd be happy to arrange for suitable accommodations." Alanda chimed, with a bit too much enthusiasm.

"Thank you, Alanda!" I said, enthusiasm awkwardly matching hers.

Alanda bowed and turned away, the impression at the corners of her mouth sealed high into her cheekbones.

"If it's not too much trouble," Serec said. "I think I will stay tonight."

As we ate and watched the last few hashes of the sunset, I stole a glance or two from Serec. He ate quietly — much quieter than usual. I wouldn't have thought much of it, but his silent brooding had returned as he watched the sky. A part of me wondered what he was thinking, but another part of me could easily sense it, and the thought made me uneasy, as the malice in his words swam in my mind.

"It's hard not to hate someone like that... I intend to make him pay for that."

[ELEMENT 2]
THE BOOK OF INVAISION

[1]

PARTING GIFT

SEREC

The bed in the palace guest room was probably the cushiest, most comfortable bed I'd ever slept in. I sat up noticing a note sitting on the nightstand.

Serec,

Due to pressing business, Her Grace is regretfully unable to join you for breakfast. Please use the chainlink below, if you would like breakfast before your departure. Sir Doriel will come to your room at 8.50 to escort you to the location of your choosing. Your clothing has been cleaned and pressed.

Thank you and Sincerest Regards,

Alanda Zoay

Fidelissima

I wondered how someone so young could be so capable. But considering the competency of Sa'Sha, NaRyn, and even Shawin, Alanda's abilities shouldn't have surprised me. I checked my timechain, and a wave of disappointment sighed right out of me when I realized it was already 8.40. Too late for breakfast. Just as I slid on my shoes, Sir Doriel appeared at the door. 8.50 exact. Once back at Vaticia, I took a detour to STRATCOM to check on Hachi. I entered the reception area, finding Juli notably absent. But I knew my way around, so I showed myself to Hachi's office.

A bright smile hit Hachi's face as I walked in. "Hello Serec!"

"Serec?" I repeated. "No designations today?"

"We won't be officially up and running until the end of the day."

I nodded. "Good to know...Uncle Hachi"

He stretched his arms out. "So, what can I do for you?"

For a moment, I didn't know how to respond. It was the first time I'd been in his office in a while without him having something important to do or already in progress.

I shrugged. "I guess I just wanted to ask you why you turned yourself in so quickly."

Hachi looked at me with thoughtful warmth. "When you truly believe in something, you're willing to risk losing everything for the sake of it."

"You sound surer about that, now that you're free." The words fell out of my mouth before my brain could do any filtering. Surprisingly, Hachi's smile remained. "Without Charlee, the Bureau would never have happened. Which means IGIS couldn't have existed as it is. Appreciating my circumstances for what they were, it's difficult not feeling guilty for keeping such an important secret from one of my closest friends."

"But if you'd said anything before he would've stopped you."

"I can't know that since I didn't give him the opportunity. I was too afraid I wouldn't find another way to see my convictions through. And when everything else falls through, your convictions are all you have."

"How did you know that the Guild was your conviction?"

"Who said it was?."

"But I thought—"

"I didn't hesitate to shut IGIS down, when Astaroth was calling for blood. Why keep the organization active when it can't serve its main purpose?"

"I thought creating a peaceful world for all people *was* the Guild's main purpose."

"If that were the case, what purpose would the Bureau serve?"

I thought I had an answer, but considering the Guild's purpose, it wouldn't have made sense having two organizations with the exact same function. "Why did you create IGIS?"

Hachi sighed. "Hiyama Square." He ran a hand through his hair. "Up until that day, I believed there might have been some validity to the Army's claim that the Bureau was a power threat. But witnessing that massacre first hand..." He took a deliberate breath and sighed again. "It was then that I realized how grossly everyone had overestimated the Bureau's capabilities. Three hundred seventy-three people died that day, and we couldn't so much as identify a single assailant. I can't imagine the number of families that were destroyed that day. But the one I was certain of was one too many."

"You mean NaRyn?" Even as the words came out, my chest constricted. I remembered that night like it'd just happened. NaRyn and I, were in my room, watching some silly vid she liked. Hachi stepping into the room, looking like he'd nearly suffered a heart attack. And the heavy blow when he gave us the news. NaRyn looked like her entire world had collapsed in on itself, and I'd never seen anyone cry so hard for so long. Every day, for the following few decs, it seemed like every little thing triggered more tears. Remembering made a flash of heat burn against my eyes, as my stomach panged with the kind of emptiness you feel when you haven't eaten in days.

"Your Aunt Mara was one of the most dedicated and persevering people I've ever known. She felt guilty about not spending more time with NaRyn, but—like me—Mara couldn't relax until she knew she had done all she could to create a safer environment for her. And Vyctor was far too competitive to let his wife outdo him in anything, even if it meant being more selfless for selfish reasons." Hachi shook his head and chuckled bitterly. "Those two were meant for each other."

"Did you ever find out who was responsible?"

"They had the common sense to hide their faces behind masks. My only clue was their leader — a man in a blue cloak. I pushed on with that one detail for all I could, until I managed to trace what still seems like a loose but undeniable connection to the Soldiers of Liberty."

"The group we thought was behind the malefactors?"

"I had reason to suspect that they were targeting members of a group I belonged to in my younger anums."

"What did your group do?"

"Nothing that we thought would put us on SOL's assassination agenda. Despite their ambitions, the attack was far more brazen than I would have anticipated. I can't even begin to imagine what we could've done to gain their attention."

Deep creases pressed just above Hachi's eyebrows and his gaze became distant. Like our conversation had thrown a part of him into the past he normally avoided. "So," I said, changing to a less depressing subject. "You created IGIS once you realized there were bigger threats the Bureau couldn't handle."

"The Guild existed long before the attack. But it has evolved significantly since the attack. I had to take drastic action if I was going to keep my promise to your parents."

"Promise to my parents?"

"Amani asked me to take care of you if anything happened to him and your mother."

"It seemed a little odd that he would ask me to make a promise like that just after you were born, but I assumed it was a simple paternal desire to set up every assurance he could for his son. But I could never have imagined that I would have to make good on that promise." Hachi paused again, his eyes squinting as his nostrils flared with each breath. "Whomever executed the foul act were professionals, leaving no evidence. It was anyone's guess if or when they might strike again. I moved you to Olde Callastryne, to cover our tracks, and did everything I could to continue building IGIS into what it is today. Or rather, what it will be again by the end of the day."

I nodded. "You think Astaroth might be as strong as SOL was back at Hiyama Square?"

Hachi looked at me, and a spark of the same hope from when I'd walked into his office reappeared. "I don't think it matters."

"Why not?"

"IGIS is much stronger than the Bureau ever was. And you're strong enough to handle Astaroth. You just have to believe in yourself like you did before you got here."

I paused. "No," I said. "I'm not strong enough to handle Astaroth. But the task force is. And together, we will put a stop to Astaroth's plans."

With a breathy smile, Hachi placed a hand on my shoulder and gave a light squeeze. "You finally get it."

I got up and headed for the door. "Serec?" Hachi called. "You already have what it takes right now. You just have to believe you do. Like all three of your parents do."

With everything that was about to happen, I wanted one more chance to think at my favorite place in all of Aruria. I sat in the thick grass and leaned back against Brain's trunk. It's gritty bark was something my skin had become used to over the anums. I'd sat in the same spot so much my back had worn the bark smooth. Despite the awesome view at Sa'Sha's koa tree, there was something liberating about being under my tree. Hachi's words circled in my head as I watched the sky, glowing warm like a painting in shades of orange, purple, and faded red.

A violet sky wasn't nearly as creepy as a green one, but it still seemed unnatural. Maybe Astaroth did mean well, on some level. But if he really planned to use the Noctus Drive to turn millions of people into malefactors, I couldn't see any supposed benefit that could overshadow such a deplorable action.

A gust of wind raced across my face, tipping me over and snapping me back to reality in time to hear something brushing over the grass.

"Didn't this happen already?" I called over my shoulder.

"Circumstances were different back then, Kid," Northe said.

"At least back then there wasn't the looming threat of millions instantly getting turned into monsters. And my mistakes were only big enough to affect me."

Northe took another few steps and stopped parallel to me. "At your age, I'd say you're still entitled to a few."

"Maybe. And the grander the scale, the less I probably get to make."

"Probably. But expecting to avoid mistakes altogether is mistake in itself, you know."

I brushed my fingers through the blades of grass next to my knees. *It must be nice not having to worry about making stupid mistakes. Having the luxury of sitting around and waiting for rain or sunshine to give you all the energy you need until the next time they come around.*

"Between the two of us, there's probably enough mistakes to write a book on how *not* to do the whole hero thing."

"Think it'd be any good?"

"A story about our kind of tragedy? People eat that stuff up."

I looked over at Northe, wishing I could feel as carefree as he looked.

"Remember when you said your reason for fighting is the only thing you can lean on when nothing else makes any sense?"

"What about it?"

"How do you know if your reason for fighting is even good enough? What if your reasons lead to people getting hurt?"

Northe's eyes softened. "Because your reason for fighting is *your* reason. Nothing more, nothing less. Just keep your actions in line with that reason. At the very least, you'll find it easier to save lives when you can, and to accept that sometimes you can't."

My eyes trailed back to the grass. It didn't take much reflection to know that my actions weren't always in line with my reason.

"When I first saw you in action, against that malefactor in the park, it reminded me of myself. I've been meaning to thank you for that ever since."

"Thank me?"

"You reminded me of my reason for fighting; the conviction that drives me."

"I wasn't actually trying to get you involved in that fight. I just wasn't expecting it to try and run."

Northe shrugged and looked down at me. "You're human. And that means you're never too strong to accept help." He turned around and started back.

"Thanks," I called after him. "For everything."

"You make it sound like we'll never see each other again. See you back at D7." He leapt into the air and floated off, until he was out of sight.

I got back into a comfortable position and watched the city lumens turning on, one after another, as the sun lowered over the horizon. I could've sat there all night if the wind hadn't started picking up, bringing with it an intense chill. *Isn't it supposed to be warm in Spring?* As soon as the thought crossed my mind, a wave of heat flushed over me, and I turned to find that I wasn't alone.

"I must be preparing for the final battle because everyone wants to talk to me today," I said as Ariel and Axel approached.

"Still making this all about you, cutie?" Ariel said, sounding as upbeat as ever.

Axel however, was the expected opposite. "We're not here for some emotional send-off," Axel said. "We're here to collect."

"Collect wha—"

Ariel's hand touched my shoulder, and suddenly I was back in Locke's study.

The room was eerily dim, Aio's faded red light filtering through the windows. Locke was standing in the center of the room, looking as coldly casual as ever.

"You have had quite the eventful time since our last encounter," he said. I wasn't sure if the moonlight had anything to do with the blood red glow in his eyes, but they added an element of darkness to his words that almost made me shudder.

"You have no idea," I said, unable to maintain eye contact.

"You would be surprised at the ideas I have." As usual, his words were too cryptic to even begin to make sense of.

"Not to sound ungrateful or anything, but you really could've picked a better time to kidnap me."

"Tell me. What have you learned about yourself? About your strengths and weaknesses?"

"Well," I said, taking a moment to think, "my friends are my strength. There are probably some weaknesses I'll never get past. But as long as I have them, I have a reason to fight, and a strength that makes up for some of those weaknesses." I looked at Ariel and Axel. "That includes you guys. As far as I'm concerned, you're friends as well, even if you never save me again."

Locke smirked. "There may be hope for you yet."

Is that supposed to be a compliment? "Uhh...thanks?"

He pulled something from his pocket and held it out to me. "Here."

"What's that?"

"A parting gift."

Once it was in my hand, I could see it was a data stick. "Why do you keep helping me?"

"I have my reasons."

I extended a hand. "Well, whatever they are, I wouldn't feel right if I didn't thank you too."

He examined my hand. "Your thanks aren't necessary," he said matter-of-factly. But as I started to lower my hand, he grabbed my wrist firmly. "But they don't go unappreciated."

A flick of a grin came over both our faces simultaneously. "Until next time," he said, looking past me and releasing my wrist.

A hand touched both my shoulders, and a beat later everything went dark. The next thing I knew, I was back at Olde Hill Park.

"End of the line, Kid," Axel said.

"Good luck, cutie," Ariel said, as they walked off.

"I meant what I said, you know," I called after them, and they stopped. "You guys are friends too."

Only Ariel looked over her shoulder at me. She flashed a smile and winked.

"Keep those wild fantasies to yourself." Axel said, a beat later, as they vanished.

I turned and looked out at the city. Karon had joined Aio, the two looking like accomplices in a bloody murder. I couldn't remember the last time they had been that clear. And behind the backdrop of the dark violet sky, that was probably as bad an omen as any.

DROP

SEREC

"The Ophanim is ready," Sa'Sha said over my timechain. "so, I'll need you at the docks immediately."

"Be there in a segment."

"Don't get lost on the way."

"I'd find my way back to you, even if I did."

She chuckled. "You'd better. See you soon, E."

I hurried back to prep for departure on the Ophanim, an airship so massive you could see it from the opposite end of Vaticia. But seeing it up close was a completely different experience. It was unlike anything I'd ever seen, a floating triangular city with enormous engines sprouting from its edges.

I walked up the long ramp and found Northe waiting for me just a few steps from the boarding deck.

"Are we the first ones here?" I asked.

"When have we ever been the first to anything?" Northe replied. He led the way to the main briefing room. "Raven and the others are already inside. You ready?"

"We'll find out together."

Northe opened the door, revealing Sa'Sha and the other captains all gathered around a game board. It had been created especially for the Ophanim and was larger than the one in the Operation's Center.

"Now that we're all here, let's go over the details," Sa'Sha said. "Ari, we'll start with what you've found."

Ari nodded and adjusted his glasses, as Anni pulled up a holographic display of Astaroth's base. "Getting right to it, we know that Astaroth's main base is situated in Neran provinces neighbor Creize. This province is known for its dense forests, making the base difficult to access — or even locate. What's troubling is the array of well-arranged ground and anti-air defenses, positioned just outside the main base of the compound. We can't be certain, but it would seem they've been there since the base's construction."

"You're saying Astaroth had the firepower to gun us down last time, but didn't," Sa'Sha clarified.

"It would seem that way. Overhead thermal imaging led us to this conclusion. And unless they weren't fully functional, the only explanation we can surmise is that Taskforce 224 made it to Astaroth, because he allowed it." I didn't have to guess why Astaroth would allow something like that. And I imagined Sa'Sha had come to the same conclusion. He needed to finish what he'd started with her.

"We can't afford to assume he'll grant passage a second time, now that war has been all but officially declared," Sa'Sha said.

"Agreed. Another factor to note is the array of four substations supplying power to the main base. From what we've gathered, these substations work together to create a massive kinetic barrier over the central structure."

"So we can't get in?" I asked.

"Doubtful. A kinetic barrier with this kind of power should have no issues buffering indirect attacks. The only way to do any damage from the outside would be to deactivate the barrier from inside the compound first."

"Which requires us to knock out the power first, right?" Northe asked.

"Exactly." Kareen answered. "Based on the information from Locke's data stick, the substations outside the barrier only supplement the power that the barrier draws. The kinetic barrier is composed of two layers, and both are generated by dense electromagnetic fields. The outer layer prevents all energy and matter from passing through, while the inner layer only repels metal. And because the outer layer requires astronomical amounts of energy, taking out the substations, should be our first priority."

"Is there a specific method to deactivating the inner layer of the barrier?" Sa'Sha asked.

"Locke's data stick contains some sort of viral algorithm. Once it comes in contact with the software controlling the Noctus Drive, it can infect the system and shut down the barrier. According to the schematics, the Noctus Drive's data port is directly under the main display panel."

"Sounds easy enough," I said.

"Except for the fair assumption that we'll be up against an army of anywhere between ten and twelve thousand malefactors, most likely positioned near the substations," Ari said.

"Quake and I will handle that part," Mia said with childlike pep. "We've reorganized our teams to ensure each area has sufficient combat power to take out their anti-air defenses, and then their substations."

"Perfect," Sa'Sha said, turning to Kareen and Northe. "I'll need you two on air support, assisting Quake's team with the power stations, until Zero and I can get the barriers down. As soon as we do, go for the Noctus Drive."

"I can handle myself up there," Northe said casually. "But don't expect too much from Minerva. After anums of sleepless mad sciencing, she's probably lost her edge as a pilot." Kareen glowered at Northe. "Keep talking and my edge will cut your lazy ass in half."

"On that note," Sa'Sha interrupted, "Astaroth's Knights of Just Death will be expecting us this time. If the situation deteriorates, we may need you providing ground support, K. Especially considering the small window of opportunity to destroy the Noctus Drive we'll likely have."

"Knights or no," I began, "once the Noctus Drive is destroyed, I'm throwing everything I've got at Astaroth."

Sa'Sha's mouth opened and I prepared for a verbal bout. But she paused once her eyes met mine. And with a sigh that was just barely audible in the intense quiet of the room, the ferocity in her eyes quickly softened, and she nodded.

Sa'Sha's TAB dinged and Juli's voice rang from it.

"All preparations have been completed, and we are ready for launch, Commander."

"Thank you, Juli," Sa'Sha replied. "Set a course for Oltresulle and let's get this ship airborne."

"Confirmed."

An automated voice echoed throughout the ship, warning all passengers to fasten in and prepare for take-off. We hurried to the seats on either side of the game board and fastened in as the Ophanim's engines rumbled to a whirring start that slowly propelled the ship straight up. The ship turned and held for a few beats, before Juli announced, "Launching," over the intercom and the ship thrusted forward.

Once we reached cruising altitude, Juli gave the signal that it was okay to move around the ship, and each of the captains moved to their stations with the rest of their teams. Sa'Sha and I made our way over to an elevated platform at the back of the bridge, where it would be easier to see the numerous agents manning the control stations. It was like watching a cluster of Processor Technicians working overtime to fix a software bug.

"I almost don't want to admit how nice it looks from this angle," Sa'Sha said, nodding toward the massive window to my right. I looked out at the sea of purple-tinted clouds swimming by. I could understand why Sa'Sha felt that way. But the angle wasn't enough for me to overlook the anger that boiled over when I viewed Astaroth's unnatural creation. All I could think about was how he exploited Sa'Sha to do it, and how much I wanted him to suffer for it.

A moment of silence passed between us, before Sa'Sha looked up at me. "Since arrival into Creize is estimated to happen roughly two segments from now, it might be a good idea to take advantage of our last opportunity to rest a little and mentally prepare for what awaits us." *If anyone had better be prepared, it's Astaroth.* Sa'Sha rested her hand over mine. "You want me to show you where your quarters are?"

She probably knew as well as I did that I wasn't in much of a mood for rest. But it wouldn't hurt to get my mind in a better place. "Yeah," I said.

I didn't realize I'd passed out until the announcement that we were a segment out from Creize came over the intercom. I changed into my combat uniform, and headed for the ship's hangar.

"These new suits aren't half bad," Northe called from his gunship on the far end of the hangar. "Of course, they could be a little less rigid around the chest."

Using Sa'Sha's KOJD uniform, Kareen reverse engineered the entire combat team's uniforms to house a sturdy skin-like armor to protect the torso. It was a little restricting for certain movements, but if it would stop a malefactor's claws and dampen enemy attacks I doubted anyone would complain.

"You're free to switch back to your standard issue," Kareen yelled at the back of Northe's head as he jumped into the cockpit.

"Let's go kid," Northe said, completely ignoring her.

The gunship rumbled to a start.

"Can you hear me kid?" Northe said over HOOD.

"Yeah," I said wondering what compelled Northe to ignore Kareen for once.

"All air units," Juli called. "We are now crossing into Oltresullean airspace, and you are clear for departure."

"You heard the pretty lady," Northe said. The engines roared and we shot forward with enough force for me to hit the rear door if I wasn't secured. "You okay back there kid?" Northe asked.

"Never better."

"We're about fifteen hashes out from the drop zone. I'll give you a warning when we're close."

My nerves started building up and I took a few deep breaths to relax. I tried to focus my mind on what was happening around the battlefield in preparation for the jump. But unlike Sa'Sha, my mind struggled to make sense of the faint cacophony of voices, especially with the roaring of the gunship's engine.

"It's time," Northe said, and the aircraft started to dip.

"Hey," Sa'Sha said, with surprising clarity. It almost sounded like she was right in front of me.

Where are you?

"Right here."

"Where's here?"

She sighed.

My eyes opened to Sa'Sha sitting in front of me, arms folded and smiling. "What are you doing here?"

Her smile matched mine, though I got the feeling it was meant to be ironic. "It's nice to see you too, E."

"Sorry," I said. "I mean, thanks."

"I just wanted to see you one last time before chaos ensues. Be careful out there, okay?"

"You too."

"I'm not the one taking a 10,000-meter plunge into hostile territory."

"Are you trying to make me nervous?"

Sa'Sha pursed her lips. "Perhaps just a bit."

"Three hashes out, kid," Northe announced.

"I'd best go," Sa'Sha said, looping her arms under mine for a hug.

The fruity scent lingered as she pulled back to look into my eyes. Everything tingled as we held there, and I almost forgot about the mission. Even in combat dress she was gorgeous. Her honey eyes sang a sweet song of life—and love. If for no other reason than to look into those eyes again, I intended to see the mission to completion.

"Two hashes," Northe said, breaking the moment.

"No goodbye kiss?" I asked, wondering how she'd react.

Sa'Sha's eyebrows lifted, in a way that intensified the flutter in my stomach. "This isn't goodbye."

"You don't know that."

Her eyes narrowed as the corners of her mouth pressed into a grin. "Come back with a pulse and we'll see."

"What if I lose an arm?"

"Then, the deal is off."

She winked and vanished with a ring of pale pink light.

"One hash," Northe said.

I adjusted my HOOD, trembling through each attempt at deep, steady breathing.

"Initiate countdown to mission start," Sa'Sha commanded over the HOOD. Northe opened the rear ramp, as Juli counted down from ten. Glaring light and howling wind filled the cargo hold, as my heart thundered through every part of my ribcage. The yellow standby light illuminated next to the open ramp, as I stood at the edge of the ramp.

"Three," Juli counted. "Two...one...initiate."

I closed my eyes, held my breath and leaned over the ramp. The chilled wind hit with so much force, I had to gulp the air down to my lungs. The voices over the HOOD grew dimmer until everything went to static. My eyes opened to the expanse of green, and I wished I had time to appreciate the view, but my focus stayed on adjusting my trajectory as the bullying currents tried to knock me off course.

Just as the static became words again, the forest lit up with shots firing from every direction, tearing into the landscape with small explosions. Malefactors raced out of the buildings like ants evacuating a freshly stomped anthill, and the ground units cut them off at several points. I started to wonder if everything was going too smoothly, when something flashed in my periphery.

Two projectiles raced toward me, and in a reflexive twist, I planted a hand past the head of the first one. I pressed into a spin, maneuvering along the length of the large missile and narrowly cleared the second. Relief started to wash over me, when I realized I wasn't the target. The projectiles forked into separate paths ending at Northe and Kareen's gunships.

"Missiles incoming!" I yelled into my HOOD. Kareen's gunship banked, just in time. But Northe was too preoccupied with evading fire from the anti-air guns to react to the missile.

Northe's gunship took a sudden nosedive toward the anti-air guns, followed by a hard loop and a heavy spin. The ship dipped between enemy fire like a pugilist toying with his opponent. It was a spectacular show, until the anti-air fire hit the missile, catching Northe's tail in a violent explosion.

"I'm hit!" Northe said.

Beats later, his gunship bulleted past me and I watched in horror as it plowed into the ground, erupting into a plume of bright flames and acrid smoke.

"Northe!" I yelled into the expanse.

"K," Juli called over the radio. "K, come in."

I waited in silence, my stomach clenching with chills, as the ground grew wider. "K? Come in, K," Juli said again. I held my breath, anxiously awaiting a sign. Any sign.

"I have eyes on K," Jin finally said. "He took down the final power station."

There was heavy static, before Northe's voice came through. "Had some trouble guiding my ship into that last power station. Bet they regret shooting me down now." He said it like he was in some vid game. Leave it to Northe to lighten the mood.

I let my eyes close as a huge breath of relief entered my lungs.

"Melodramatic imbecile!" Kareen yelled through the com.

"You always know just what to say, don't you? Glad you missed me." Northe teased.

Just as I was starting to let myself enjoy the moment, the wind started whistling louder in my ears and the roof of Astaroth's compound approached fatally fast. I forced all the air I could into my lungs. Small pillars of stone began to grow from my body as I formed a stone wall around me, leaving only a small opening to see through. Sparks crackled around me as I encased my stone pod in electricity to penetrate the second barrier.

"Ambi's infiltration force is in position, and we've got eyes on you, Zero." Sa'Sha said.

I picked up speed, and passed effortlessly through the blue barrier. *Uneventful. But welcome.* I punched through the roof with a thunderous crash, before plowing through several floors.

Finally, a floor mustered the courage to stand against my self-made meteor, and bringing me to a sudden stop. I held there for a beat, as the stone cocoon began to fall away in large slabs. My eyes took a moment to adjust as electricity danced beneath me. Surveying my entry point brought assurance that I'd done significant damage. Sunlight trickled down the vertical tunnel, alerting me to the fact that I was several floors underground. No surprise considering Astaroth was hiding a world altering weapon.

I found myself in the center of a large empty area that was faintly lit by hundreds of tiny lumens. I started to move, when I felt an eerie presence behind me. I whirled around to find five of Astaroth's Knights of Just Death.

"I take it you've been expecting me?"

[3]

PENULTIMATE

SEREC

"I hope you guys have been practicing," I said. No response. "I said I hope you—"

"We heard you," one of them snapped, flat tone matching the apathy he wore.

"Well a response would be—"

"Get him," he commanded before they all rushed me.

I shrugged. "Guess I'll take what I can get." Energy pulsed through my body as I stood ready.

Xaster and Hypersol sprinted ahead of the rest. But my eyes caught everything they threw at me, making dodging and countering effortless. Xaster and Hypersol tried to go for the high-low approach. But a hard-enough kick to Xaster's shins and a well-timed uppercut against Hypersol's jaw put them both on the defensive.

Footsteps from my right turned my attention to Renes. I shifted Yenta-Gin stances, in preparation to use his own momentum against him. Suddenly, my legs buckled, and my body stopped responding to my commands. Lifting my left arm, turned my neck, and pulling my knees under me, shrugged my shoulders forward.

Harine. NaRyn warned me of her abilities. But she also told me how to counter them. I focused my mind on where she was standing, and increased the gravity around her. It was still a power I couldn't use well. But it was all I could think of. I imagined the gravitational waves pulling down on Harine and intensified their force. As I did, my head and shoulders started sinking under an immense weight that felt like it meant to break me, until I relaxed and it eased away.

The small vibrations my fingertips felt could only mean the knights were back on their feet and coming after me. I squirmed and struggled, desperate to get my brain and body back in sync. But time was obviously against me. In a desperate attempt, I inhaled deep, blew all the air out of my lungs, and molded it into a raging squall. The wind sucked them closer, and I pressed a wave of bioelectric energy out through my pores.

Strained grunts announced my success. And the moment my body was working together with my brain again, I got back to my feet. But one knight was still standing, watching from a safe distance.

"Not gonna help your team?" I asked.

"You believe I should?" His tone was eerily calm.

I shrugged and knocked the dirt off my uniform. "Doesn't seem like you're much of a team player. Maybe you enjoy watching them get knocked around."

"Not particularly. But all achievements require *some* sacrifice." He said, raising a hand. A flash of light beamed, and I dodged in time to get away with a nick across my cheek. A cold burning tingled over my cheek, and I wiped at the liquid running down the side of my face, before it reached my jaw.

Blood. I looked back over my shoulder and spotted a chunk of jagged ice staked into the ground. I turned in time to see the next beam fire, and waved out a wall of wind to block it.

He strafed to one side, firing beams of ice, one after another. I pushed out wave after wave to block it, moving after him. But he kept backing up and darting around, firing like a madman.

"Are we fighting, or playing?" I yelled in frustration.

"Neither," he said smiling. "It's called stalling."

"Stalling?" My eyes widened and I spun around to find his entire team, back on their feet and charging toward me.

Annoyed at how long holding back was taking, I spun furiously, throwing out a huge wave of wind. None of them could resist the force of it, not even jumpy old ice boy. But as I relished in the action of putting them all on their backs, I caught something moving on the ceiling. That "something" was a horde of malefactors crawling down through the hole I'd made like angry ants. And like ants, a tingling anxiety began to crawl through my veins.

Fighting a horde that large, I wouldn't reach the Noctus Drive for segments, if at all.

A snap penetrated my senses, and my legs buckled on me again. I tried lifting my left arm, which turned my head enough to get eyes on everyone behind me. Hypersol was charging at full speed. A surge of electricity might slow him down if I could concentrate enough. A tall order considering. But I had to try.

Tensing every muscle involuntarily, I pushed until I felt like electricity sizzled around me. Then, I repelled it in every direction, hopeful that some part of the energy would connect. And it almost did, until the smallest knight, Baneira, jumped in the way and deflected it right back at me.

My body jerked and stiffened as the electricity hit my back, and my eyes squeezed shut in reflex. Just as well. I wasn't keen on watching Hypersol trample over my face anyway.

Two monstrous booms echoed deep in my ears, and the ground shook. I forced my eyes open, realizing my body was working normally again. Harine was trembling on her hands and knees, fighting away from the ground.

"Don't worry about this one," NaRyn said, walking up behind her. "She's mine."

"Consider him neutralized as well," Sa'Sha said, standing over Hypersol.

My body still had a mild twitch, as I pushed back to my feet and looked in time to catch the glint of white rocketing toward the side of NaRyn's head. Before I could act, something knocked it off course, and it cracked as it hit the ground.

My eyes traced back to Northe, Shawin, Mia, and Jin, rushing over.

"Attacking a defenseless young lady like that," Northe lectured. "Not very honorable."

Baneira rushed at NaRyn next, and Northe tripped her up with a small gust, followed by a larger one that knocked her away like a fly. "But who am I to talk?"

"We can handle this," Jin called. "Get inside."

"But if we fight together we—"

"You were just fighting them single-handedly," Sa'Sha argued. "The rest of us can manage here."

There wasn't much room to argue when she put it like that. "See you inside," I said, racing off.

The rapidly pattering feet told me Xaster didn't like the idea of me getting away. I turned, preparing to attack, when he suddenly seized up and collapsed. Mia was standing behind him with her arm extended.

"Don't you have somewhere to be? Off you go." she said.

I reached a large room nearly identical to the last. Two rows of spaced pillars cut the room into thirds, and large boxes were neatly stacked in threes in various places. A few thick pipes hugged the walls, rarely extending out into the open walk space, but still close enough to give off an odd smell of wet fabric steaming over metal.

A large cylindrical device was nestled against the far corner. The Noctus Drive. It reminded me of a telescope and was so tall, it extended through a hole in the ceiling. Considering all the trouble it could cause, I wasn't expecting to find it sitting unguarded. *No need questioning favorable luck for a change.* I thought, jogging over.

There was a blank screen with five buttons positioned around it, and not one of them were labeled in a way that made any sense to me.

I pressed what looked like a display button. Nothing happened. I pressed it again. Still nothing. I tried another button, and when nothing changed, I held the button down for a three-count.

A jingle played as a small display powered on, beeping in sync with a timer that was counting down.

My fingers scrambled through my pocket for Locke's data stick, and just as I fished it out, a deep voice boomed.

"Back to pilfer more information, I see." I jumped and twisted around to find Astaroth moving toward me with an ominous intensity behind his pearl black glare.

"Actually," I said, ignoring the stabbing chill in the pit of my stomach, "I'm here to give *you* something this time."

"Serec Arenyu," His mouth morphed into a daemonic grin. "I had my suspicions about you."

"Funny. I had mine about you."

"That is funny. You know, you would have made an exceptional knight. Such a shame I can't let you leave here alive."

[4]

TWILIGHT

Thirteen hashes were all that separated Orbis from an abysmal new age of violence and terror. I intended to prevent that. Astaroth intended to stop me. He shot forward, and I dove to avoid him. We moved in a circle, watching each other, like two predators waiting to see who would strike first. He bared his teeth and lunged again. I dodged, twisted around, and sprang forward with a hard swing at the back of his head. But he landed and spun in time to catch my fist with his open palm.

I swung again, and he countered with an uppercut that my eyes barely recognized in time for me to stagger back. He was quicker than I expected, and I knew I needed some distance between us, if I wanted to find a hole in his defense.

I took another step back, but the space between us didn't change. I took two more steps, quicker this time. But he stayed with me, as he threw his hands together, trying to smash my head in with the clap of his hands. I got my arms up in time to block, but the sheer force behind his attack jammed the side of my hands against either side of my head, and I lost my footing.

The sting in my forearms intensified on the fall. But I couldn't afford to give any thought to the pain as Astaroth moved over me. I rolled with the fall and pushed back to my feet, then sprang up with all I had. He might've had time to dodge or block, but since he was so determined to maintain his momentum, it worked against him, and I managed to knock his arms up with mine, and jam my left knee into his chin. He stumbled back a couple steps, before he caught himself.

His head lowered slowly, and he stared at me with curled lips. "Better than I anticipated," he said. "But still underwhelming."

He disappeared, and by the time my brain had realized he did, he was right in front of me. I tried to brace myself, but he rammed into me and I stumbled back, barely catching myself when he disappeared again.

His laughter echoed around the room and no matter where I looked I couldn't find him. Not two beats passed before a faint whoosh from behind, made me spin around with my arms up. Something large and heavy, jammed into my right forearm like a brick. It turned out to be Astaroth's massive fist, priming for another attack.

He punched again, and I ducked under it, throwing a couple punches of my own at his torso. But he didn't budge. His body was almost as solid as stone. But I could do better. I drew back my right arm, covered my knuckles in stone and launched a cross punch. It connected with a devastating crack that made Astaroth howl and dip to one side. *One more time!* I aimed the next punch at his jaw. But he leaned away and grabbed me by the shoulders. In one motion — too quick to counter — he tossed me clear across the room, and I tumbled across the stone ground before finally catching myself and rolling back to my feet.

The ground rumbled beneath me as he thumped closer. "You've really become the exasperating little obstacle boy," he spat.

"You have no idea. I won't let you destroy millions of lives for your own selfish gain," I said.

"Ignorant child," he said, going into a full charge. I shielded myself in stone and threw out a fist to meet him halfway. He slammed his fist into mine with a heavy, hollow thud. He pushed and I pushed back harder, determined to show him what I could do. But the last thing I was expecting him to do was lean back. I stumbled forward clumsily, unable to do anything to stop myself from crashing into him. But a boot to my chest assisted with that. I fell to my knees, nearly convulsing as the pain radiated to my extremities.

"Who are you to pass judgment?" he spat. "You think because you weren't cursed with the same disadvantages as the minorities of society, that you and your overlords have the right to oppress them?"

"Not sure if you've noticed," I wheezed, "but I am the minority." Just as I nearly had my feet under me, Astaroth's foot slammed into my chest like a speeding raeda, and I flew into the air, crashing onto my back.

"You rho are no different than the rest. Most of you are worse. You feel entitled because of a power you didn't earn. You don't understand what it's like to truly suffer; to truly toil. You're no better than the humans you claim to protect." *Didn't you kidnap a princess just to get what you wanted, Mr. Completely-Entitled-Psychopathic-Villain?* It sounded so good in my head, I really wanted him to hear it too. But the pain was too intense to speak.

"At least your princess had the sense to consider reason. Even if her juvenile emotions severed the link to reason I'd created."

Hearing his words flooded my veins with enough adrenaline to forget how much pain I was supposed to be feeling. My muscles tightened and heat pulsated throughout my entire body, as I pressed to my feet, suddenly feeling like my weight had been cut in half. I ran at Astaroth, preparing for another attack. But when he put his guard up, I slipped past him. He reacted quickly, twisting to follow. But I was too quick. The next thing he knew, I was back where I'd started. And this time, my intention to attack was real.

I unleashed a barrage of punches, pounding fiercely into his torso. His body lifted a little, curling in more with each hit. Despite his weight, I could feel my attacks wearing deeper into his body, softening him up like a meat tenderizer. But fighting at that level took a lot of energy. And mine was slowly fading.

Astaroth started pulling away, resisting each punch more effectively as my arms started to burn. His stamina for taking punishment was beginning to outlast my stamina for issuing it. Still, I had to push harder. I clenched my fist even tighter and torqued into an uppercut that nearly threw him off his feet.

His head was finally in perfect range and I wasn't about to pass up the chance to knock some sense into him. My knuckles knocked against each side of Astaroth's thick jaw with an oddly satisfying rhythm. But the last hit had him keeling to the left. I swung my left arm out, creating a wave of air that I expanded and shifted around to hit Astaroth from the side he was falling on. The force crashed into him, but he was heavier than I expected.

I recirculated the air, pushing again with every bit of force I could generate. Slowly, his body tilted back toward me, and I leapt just as he was nearly standing up straight. With a heavy grunt, I twisted and slammed my shin across the side of Astaroth's face, sending him toppling over.

I landed clumsily, huffing as sweat beaded over my face, dripping like a leaky faucet. But, assuming the best, I maybe had ten hashes left to upload Locke's virus. I tried willing myself to stand, but my muscles resisted me the whole way, and I fell onto my hands and knees. I tried again, grunting steadily through gritted teeth. My legs were like mush. But I maintained the fight against gravity until my wobbly legs completely straightened.

One step at a time, I pressed closer to the Noctus Drive. I dug into my pocket for the data stick and studied the front of the large machine. I pressed the same button as before, and the beeping started back up in unison with the remaining time on the front panel. I had nine hashes.

The counter ticked as the beats slipped away, and a flicker of surprise pulsed tight in my throat. I had less time than I thought, but hopefully it would be enough for the virus to do its job.

I pressed the button that looked the most like an eject button, and an upbeat tune played accompanied by the word '*Initializing...*' blinking across the screen, just above the countdown, which was already down to eight hashes and thirty-two beats, as if I needed the additional pressure in my life.

The ground shook and I looked around cautiously, wondering what kind of device takes that long to initialize. But I froze with wide eyes once I'd realized the change in the room. Namely, that the area was one-person emptier. My eyes darted around, scanning for

Astaroth.

The ground rumbled again, and the sound of quick footsteps echoed from somewhere off to my right. I studied the area, my eyes holding on every pillar, box, and pipe momentarily, before moving on to the next.

If it hadn't been so quiet, I might have lost my head in the situation. Literally. But the whistling behind me caught my attention just in time for instinct to make me leaned to my right as my head turned left. With claws in place of fingernails, Astaroth slashed where my head had just been. I stepped right and backed up as fast as humanly possible, dodging Astaroth's mad swipes at my face.

With a vicious snarl, Astaroth lunged at me, swinging down with both claws. I almost didn't get the layer of stone over my arms in time, not that it mattered much. His razor-sharp claws came down with more than enough force to sink right through the stone covering the outside of my shoulders. A wail escaped me as the stone cracked away, leaving his talons to dig freely. With one quick push, he drove his claws through my shoulders and pinned me to the ground. Blood ran down where his claws had penetrated, creating a small pool of crimson where my back met the floor.

"I won't let you sabotage my Noctus Drive. Too much is at stake."

"That just makes me want to break it more." I strained an ironic smile.

"And your insolence makes me want to break *you* more." he said, sinking his claws deeper as he squeezed.

A cold, sharp sensation shot through my fingers and my teeth parted, uncaging a violent scream. He lifted me and pulled my arms in opposite directions. The pressure intensifying in my shoulders, forced my eyes shut. Like old rubber bands, the tendons and ligaments in my shoulder stretched to their limit, and were ready to snap at any moment.

Suddenly, a blinding light penetrated my eyelids and a devastating crack reverberated through the stone walls. I fell to the ground, relieved to be free of Astaroth's claws.

"I hate to disappoint," a voice called. "But we need his arms attached." Sa'Sha called. When I opened my eyes, she and Team Seven were approaching. Northe shot out a stream of wind against Astaroth, pounding him into the ground.

"You okay Brother?" Shawin asked.

"I'm smooth," I answered. "Just need a beat to gather some energy."

"Then, we will cover you."

"What can you tell us about big ugly over there?" Northe called over his shoulder.

"Way strong, fatally quick," I said, huffing a little. "If you can put him on his back, it'll slow him down."

"That I can do." Northe said and continued in Astaroth's direction.

"Lift, help K distract Astaroth until Zero can recover." Sa'SHa began. "We'll need our entire team if we are going to finish this."

NaRyn nodded and raced toward Northe. "Take your time," Sa'Sha said.

I closed my eyes and took a few breaths, focusing enough healing energy throughout my body to drain away the fatigue and help the wounds close. It would take longer to fully heal the tissue damage my shoulders had taken. But closing the wounds would at least stop the bleeding.

"What about the Noctus Drive?" Sa'Sha asked.

"We've only got a few hashes before it fires. And Astaroth's doing everything in his power to keep it guarded."

Sa'Sha's eyes grew determined. "Hashes? Lovely."

Before I could answer, Astaroth roared and the ground shook as if he willed it.

"Incoming!" Northe called, just before Astaroth knocked him away and came charging at us.

"Welcome home Blissful. I shall make your demise quick."

Instead of doing the sensible thing, Sa'Sha followed my logic and shot forward toward Astaroth. But before he could pounce on her, she jumped, tucked into a ball, and with a sound not too different from a blade slicing through air, she disappeared. A beat later, the same sound came from my left, followed immediately by a hollow thunk that sent Astaroth crashing sideways into the wall.

Sa'Sha landed, in a low crouch. "I believe you are mistaken." she said. "I intend to make your demise quick."

Astaroth tried to come at us again, and Northe blasted a whirling ball of wind at him. But Astaroth powered through it, picking up speed with each step. I encased my hands in stone, bracing myself to attack.

"Need a Lift," Sa'Sha called and a few short steps from reaching us, Astaroth's feet left the ground.

"On it!" NaRyn called. Her eyes were focused on Astaroth, and her fingers outstretched.

I leapt in front of Astaroth and struck him hard enough to jerk his head back. My shoulder screamed, but I'd hit my mark. Unfortunately with the gravity so light around us, his body slowly floated in a backward spin. Though just out of reach, he furiously clawed at me, drawing closer with each swipe. But I had a plan.

"Drop us, on my signal, Lift."

"Confirmed," she said.

I gathered a mass of energy into my upper body, focusing it into my right arm. From my fist, all the way up my back, a well of heat circulated like ants in a frenzy.

I waited as an upside down Astaroth clawed around, anxious to get himself back right side up. And just as the back of his head crowned from under his feet. I squeezed my fist into a tight ball, lifted it past my head, and yelled, "Now!"

Gravity tugged us down as I swung at Astaroth's head. Astaroth caught himself, landing perfectly on all fours, and a beat later, he caught four stone-encased knuckles to the back of his skull. His face crunched into the ground with a forced breath that sounded like he was snoring and sucking his teeth at the same time.

"We'll keep him busy, Zero," Sa'Sha called. "Get back to the Noctus Drive.

Prophet, cover him."

Shawin nodded at me, and we sprinted to the Drive. I almost cursed when I saw the blank screen. It was probably an auto shutoff function. And the timing couldn't have been worse.

I held the button down, and the jingle played as the screen turned on again to reveal the timer at five hashes and counting. I pressed the button for the data port to open and a small red light blinked next to it as the screen read: *preparing.* I didn't know what kind of preparation a data port needed to open, but I was seriously considering using my bare hands to avoid finding out.

The battle raged on so intensely behind me, I thought the whole building would come down. I turned to make sure everything was okay.

"We can handle it," Shawin said with a stern assurance, his eyes still on the battle. "Just trust us and focus on your task."

Waiting had never been so difficult. Especially with the rumbling growing louder

"Watch out!" Sa'Sha's voice suddenly rang in my ears, and I whirled around.

"The machine, Zero," Shawin said. "We'll handle this, remember?"

I turned back around. The message had gone from 'preparing' to 'opening.' But the port was still closed.

I would've screamed, but I didn't want to risk distracting Shawin or the rest of the team at such a crucial moment. With a painful groan, the ground trembled beneath my feet, and I peeked over my shoulder. Astaroth lay face down.

"Prophet, you—?"

"Handled it," he interrupted quickly. "The machine." A hint of irritation colored his words.

"Right. Sorry."

According to the display, the port was still 'opening,' which looked remarkably similar to 'preparing.' Even worse, we were down to four hashes.

"What in Hadal is going on down there?" Kareen screeched over the com. "My sensors are showing the Noctus Drive's barrier is still active."

"Because it is," I said. "This dumb machine won't—"

"Zero!" Shawin coughed. "Look out!"

I turned to find Shawin on the ground and Astaroth about to take my head off. I lifted my arms, and his claws hammered down. My shoulders shook under the weight, unable to hold him back.

One after another, everyone hit Astaroth, careful to avoid injuring me in the process. But Astaroth didn't flinch. "I will see my work to completion. And your pesky little friends, pinching and nipping at my heels, like the ants they are, can do nothing to stop me." My arms trembled, lowering until his claws were hovering over my face.

"I'm low on ammo, and these anti-air defenses aren't giving up," Kareen said. "The Ophanim and I have the munitions required to kill that machine. But I can't dodge all day here."

"Give us a bit more time," Sa'Sha replied. "We'll end this one way or another."

The air grew dense as subtle sparks cracked, a sensation I was all too familiar with.

"Your little princess is wasting her time," he said. "You're too late to stop the Noctus Drive."

"You sure about that?" I asked confidently. A beat later, the air shifted, and Sa'Sha's psionic wave exploded against Astaroth's back with a thunderous boom.

A daemonic smile etched over Astaroth's face, as if nothing had happened. "Yes, I am." His grip on my arms tightened, and he hurled me over his shoulder. A bed of wind blew against my back, howling as it slowed my momentum a half-step before I reached Sa'Sha. If Astaroth hadn't earned my full attention, I would've thanked Northe.

"I'm rather low on patience at the moment," Astaroth said with a malicious glint in his eyes, then vanished.

A jackhammer of footsteps bombarded my ears from every direction, and a swirl of panic tensed deep in my throat, as I struggled to track any of it.

"Open your senses," Northe shouted over the sound.

I shifted into a relaxed stance and pulled my attention inward. *Just breathe. Relax and let the sound come to me.* Once my body relaxed, the sound grew clearer. The random footsteps suddenly had a pattern. I looked left, ready to cut Astaroth off at his next move. But everything went quiet.

The air shifted again, growing thick like suffocating fog. Something dark flashed from the corner of my eye. I turned, finding Astaroth looming behind Shawin. He swiped at Shawin, and I stiffened. Shawin jumped to his hands and thrusted his legs behind him, crunching his heels into Astaroth's jaw. Astaroth stumbled back, but quickly recovered and spun into another attack.

Shawin dodged perfectly. "Was he always this slow?" Shawin said.

"Don't make him angrier!" I yelled.

"His anger is of little consequence," Shawin said, dipping under the swing of Astaroth's claws.

Astaroth turned feral, clawing and swiping wildly as Shawin danced around him. "You little bug!" he roared. It took a beat to realize how distracted Astaroth was. But once I did, I understood what Shawin was doing.

"*Liza,*" I called telepathically. "*Can you fire another psionic wave?*"

"*Of course,*" she replied. "*Do you have a plan?*"

"*Something like that.*" I linked my mind with Northe and NaRyn. "*I'm using Sa'Sha's telepathy to keep Astaroth from hearing us.*" Northe and NaRyn's eyes found mine. "*I think Shawin is—*"

"*Creating a distraction,*" Northe interjected.

"*Yeah. And now's a great time to take advantage of the situation.*"

They both nodded, and refocused on Shawin's skirmish. We'd probably only get one chance to catch Astaroth off guard, and we had to do it without hitting Shawin. I tried to swallow back the hesitation and pressed my hands together. A pool of bioelectrical energy gathered so slow it shallowed my breathing, the air trembling as it passed my windpipe. But, thankfully, Astaroth didn't seem to notice.

Astaroth kicked and slashed, nearly tearing into Shawin's face. But Shawin slipped between the attacks and glanced over his shoulder at me so unexpectedly, I almost didn't hear the word 'now' leave his mouth, before he rolled out of the way.

I pushed a tangle of electricity that combined with Sa'Sha's psionic blast and Northe's typhoon. Astaroth noticed a beat too late. He yelled as the energy exploded against him with a loud crackle. But it was obvious that he could endure it.

"Hit him harder," Shawin called out.

"Easier said than done," I called back, pulling all the bioelectricity I could into another attack. Time wasn't on our side, and I wasn't exactly brimming with energy to throw around. I had to hit him harder somehow. Suddenly, I thought about the way Surket used her powers, and something clicked. She condensed it into a concentrated bolt. If I could hurl a condensed bolt at Astaroth, it might make all the difference.

"Prophet can't hold Astaroth much longer," NaRyn said. "Victory won't pull itself out of thin air."

Another click. "Lift, you're a genius," I said.

As I focused bioelectrical energy into my left hand, I condensed a coil of wind in the other. I formed the electricity into a bolt and held the swirling wind up like a bow, taking aim.

"Raven, K. This bolt might not hit its mark."

"We've got you," Northe said.

Sa'Sha smiled. "A novel solution," she said. "Surket would be proud."

I pressed out, and the air uncoiled with a sharp whistle, propelling the bolt clumsily forward. Not missing a beat, Northe stabilized it with a jet of wind, just as Sa'Sha sent forward a beam of light that enveloped it.

That bolt held the hopes of everyone in IGIS. Maybe all of Orbis. So, when Harine and Kaleb jumped into its path to shield their leader, my heart plummeted.

Astaroth was strong and fatally durable. Even with that much power, I could only hope we would've wounded him enough to buy us the time needed to capture him. But against a human, that arrow was unquestionably lethal. I had never, in any moment, wished so hard that my shot would miss its mark.

But, just as quickly as the they had jumped into the arrow's path, Harine and Kaleb's bodies were flung into opposing directions. And between them emerged Astaroth with a short, but powerful roar that preempted the arrow finding its mark.

With a deafening crack, the arrow exploded against Astaroth's chest, and his feet slipped from under him.

"Down!" NaRyn yelled as the speed of his fall increased, and he slammed on his back.

Sa'Sha and I rushed to the Noctus Drive, and when I saw the remaining time at forty beats, my heart pulsed in my throat.

"Ready to fire Minerva?" I asked.

"Not without targeting data and clearance to fire," Kareen replied.

"Transmitting targeting data now," Sa'Sha said. "Fire on my mark."

"Data received, working technical solution now," Kareen said. "What's our count?"

I looked at the display and my throat constricted at the back of my mouth. "Thirty beats," I said.

"What are you waiting for?!" Kareen screamed so loud I thought my eardrum would burst. "This data port to open!"

I banged and punched the machine, and the slot finally slid open. I inserted the data stick and in no more than five beats, the onscreen message read: *Upload complete. Magnetic barrier offline.*

"FIRE!" Sa'Sha and I yelled in unison.

"Firing!" Kareen replied.

I stiffened as the countdown ticked down its final three beats. But it never made it past one. "Come on, Zero!" Sa'Sha yelled, pulling me behind her, as she ran toward the rest of the team. I tried to keep my balance, but a wave of booms shook the entire building, and I lost my footing.

"Target destroyed! Target destroyed!" Kareen exclaimed.

Cheers flooded the com, and let my shoulders slump as I sighed in exhausted relief. I wanted to yell along with everyone else, but since I was out of air, catching my breath would have to take priority. The odor of dirt and sweat seeped into my nose as I closed my eyes and inhaled deep. A smell I was looking forward to washing off as soon as I got home.

BOOOM!

A secondary explosion sounded from behind the machine, and a large chunk of ceiling caved in, separating me from Sa'Sha. The sound of muffled voices drowned under the ringing in my ears, as thick dust enveloped me. I coughed and squinted as I felt my way through the rubble, climbing anxiously to get above the smoke.

The higher I climbed, the thinner the dust became, until I was high enough to get a better look at everything. I wiped my eyes on the inside of my shirt and looked around. My eyes followed the movement in my peripheral and I found Sa'Sha and the rest of the team waving excitedly.

The tension in my throat eased, and I waved back. But, for whatever reason, they kept on waving. In fact, they were waving even harder, as I waved back. NaRyn and Sa'Sha cupped their hands around their mouths, yelling something I still couldn't quite understand.

I stepped closer careful not to fall down the other side of the crumbled roof.

"What?" I said, looking for the next place to step. NaRyn pointed behind me frantically. Frowning, I started to look over my shoulder, when something crashed into me, hurling my body into the stone wall.

[5]

NECESSITY

SEREC

The world spun, and ringing dominated my hearing as I pushed to my knees. A thick haze lingered as I lifted my head, blinking to refocus. But the moment I saw what was standing over me, every last bit of haze sobered right out of me. A monstrous dark creature, covered with spiny horns stared down at me with massive, orange eyes. It bared a mouth full of jagged fangs, each probably as long as my arm. A tail the length of its monstrous body trained on me like a serpent — a giant barb protruding from it.

The creature spewed a violent roar, shaking the entire structure.

"Your blood shall be restitution, boy," it bellowed. The polished arrogance of its odious words brought the horrible truth to light.

This massive beast is Astaroth.

It gave a breathy hiss as it stalked closer. The wave of bloodlust reached me before he could and I leapt back, scarcely avoiding his pounce. He swiped repeatedly, and my reflexes became autonomous. I went on the offensive, throwing wind into Astaroth's eyes and slamming a fistful of bioelectricity over his head. But it had no effect. Astaroth snapped his head to one side, throwing me to the ground. My leg smacked the concrete, and I winced at the sting of shooting pain. Astaroth swatted at me again, and I moved away as fast as I could. But at his size, my speed was only good for evasive maneuvers. He was still too quick for me to find an opening.

He zipped out of sight, and the vibration between my feet pulled my attention behind me. His tail shot forth nearly skewering my head. I rolled forward and scrambled between his legs. Before he could find me, I encased my hands in stone and jammed both fists into his underbelly. He backed away, roaring in pain. I chased after him, my fist ready to take out one of his knees. But his paw came out of nowhere, knocking me away with so much force I skidded sideways and plowed into the wall like a skipping stone. Every part of me was throbbing; broken for all I knew.

I wouldn't survive another hit like that. I needed to fight carefully, which was extremely difficult considering his size and speed, and the fact that I'd been fighting alone the entire time. At that moment, I realized I hadn't seen the rest of my team since Astaroth had taken this form. I surveyed the area, ignoring the pinpricks as I turned my neck. My eyes caught something moving at the far end of the room. A blurred version of Sa'Sha and NaRyn waving frantically and pressing against a violet-tinted translucent veil. *Another barrier?*

"Your friends won't be able to save you this time," Astaroth hissed. "Once I've squeezed every bit of life from your fragile body, I'll pick them apart, one by one."

His jagged grin widened, and my blood became lava. I stood, every muscle from head to toe tensing, as I reached a hand out. "One problem with your plan," I said. "You have to make it through me first." My Aetharma solidified, and the moment I grabbed it, a well of energy circulated between me and the blade.

He laughed maniacally. "I would've preferred to savor your demise. But if you're that determined to end your life, I'll take my time with your friends instead."

I knew he was baiting me. But I didn't care. One way or another, I needed to end this. I exploded forward and slashed with more speed and power than I thought possible. He yelped and hollered in agony as his tail flayed open cleanly down the middle. Astaroth lunged with fangs bared. Probably intending to snap me between his jaws, if his teeth didn't impale me first. But I jumped and swung the blade again, forming a deep cut on the inside of his left front leg. He hollered wildly, crumpling forward as he landed.

Astaroth curled into a ball, and I half-assumed it was a sign that Astaroth recognized his disadvantage. But when the spikes lining his back angled up, I started to think maybe I'd overestimated my advantage. His hind legs pushed off and the ball of spikes rolled at me with devastating speed. I dove to the side, but Astaroth changed direction, and one of his horns cut the outside of my right thigh. I skipped away to create distance, my right leg throbbing with prickly heat each time I put weight on it. The thundering of his feet pulled my attention over my shoulder, as Astaroth pushed off his hind legs again. I raced out of his path, and my leg tried to buckle. I leapt and twisted, narrowly escaping another serious injury. As soon as I landed, I scrambled away, paying more attention to where Astaroth was than where I was going.

As he turned around and prepared for another roll, I finally realized the peril I'd placed myself in. Between the barrier and the rubble from the roof, I'd wedged myself into a corner—wide enough for Astaroth to reach, but too small to avoid getting run through and squished all at once. This was it. This was how it would end. As far as I'd come — as we'd come—I couldn't let it end with me being flattened by Astaroth's abominable mass. My friends were depending on me. And I refused to fail them.

The titanic death ball careened toward me and — with hardened resolve — I squeezed both hands around my Aetharma and sprinted forward. As the gap between us shrank, the weapon glowed hotter with an unfamiliar sensation. Like it was repelling my hands. I tightened my grip, resisting the force as I pressed on. I lifted the blade to shoulder level, and the hilt suddenly repelled so intensely my arms were thrown to my sides. Though I had no time to process it, the sight of the blades glowing on either side of me was undeniable. My one Aetharma—had become two! A deluge of energy roared through my body. I wasn't sure if it was the adrenaline or how right holding two Aetharma suddenly felt, but the only option in my mind was to press forward. With both blades extended, I leapt at Astaroth and twisted into a mid air spin. I was met with no resistance as my blades sliced through flesh and bone. Astaroth's agonizing screams filled the room, as I landed not so gracefully behind him. Limping twice as hard as before, I picked up my Aetharma, and the wealth of energy flooding through me dulled the pain. I braced myself over the weapons and wrenched myself toward Astaroth. He'd reverted back to his human form and finishing him in his current condition would be too easy.

"I saved them," he whispered between heavy breaths. "My greatest work may have been ruined by a misguided group of self-righteous children, but this sky is permanent. Harine, Kaleb and all your kind will have a fighting chance to live without fear." A tear trickled down his cheek. And for a moment, I forgot that he'd just tried to kill me. "It's true what they say: helping others brings meaning to life."

"At least we agree on one thing." I said as I approached. "My parents always said that we thrive as a species because of our ability to cooperate."

He offered a bitter laugh. "Wise words. A shame this ability has also been your undoing. As it will be in times to come. My kind will make certain of that. He coughed up a glob of blood, his eyes becoming glassy. "You'd best put an end to me. My work is complete and I've nothing else to say to you."

Despite his calmer aspect, a part of me wanted to accept his offer—badly. But the decision wasn't mine to make. "No one has the right to decide whether or not someone else lives," I said.

Astaroth laughed bitterly. "You're quite the pious simpleton, aren't you?" The look in his eyes was hauntingly familiar. Just like I'd felt when Surket sacrificed herself to protect me, and when Sa'Sha was kidnapped. It was almost like he wanted it. As if death was all that was left for him. He'd come so far, only to fail.

It was hard not to sympathize with Astaroth. Twisted as his thinking could be, I wondered if maybe there was a chance he could learn from his mistakes too. He deserved the same opportunity as everyone else to at least try. My grip relaxed, as peace etched into his face. I started toward Sa'Sha and the others, when lightheadedness suddenly washed over me, and the air grew thin. I fell to my knees, and my Aetharma clanged against the ground, a beat ahead of me. My Aetharma evaporated into light and I instantly knew why. I scanned the room, my eyes landing on the green specs glowing through the shaded doorway.

No. Why now? It hadn't occurred until that moment that Kurai had been conveniently absent the entire fight. And after confirming his affiliation with Astaroth, it would've been safe to assume he'd eventually appear. He stepped out of the shadows, his cold eyes fixed on me. Astaroth groaned, rolling to sit upright as he clenched his side. Kurai passed him without so much as a glance, but stopped in front of me.

"It's about time you arrived," Astaroth hissed. Kurai turned his palms up and light coalesced into two wicked blades. The faint glow and heat emanating from them were a clear sign they were Aetharma.

He stood over me, his chilling darkness devouring my resolve. He was at least as powerful as Astaroth. And I'd already exhausted all my reserves. Plus, with no powers I had no hope of replenishing them.

"What are you waiting for?" Astaroth snapped. "End this debacle."

"With pleasure," Kurai replied.

I needed to get away. But my legs wouldn't move. Kurai raised his arm high, and his blade came down in a flash. I flinched, hearing only the distinct sound of cleaving flesh. I didn't want to open my eyes. Seeing where he'd cut me, would make it all real. Terribly real. And if I was going to die, I could at least do it peacefully.

But after a few beats of still drawing breath, I grew curious. Kurai had his back to me, his Aetharma buried—deep in the base of Astaroth's neck and stomach. Blood ran the length of the blades, as Astaroth wheezed with disbelief. Kurai yanked the blades out and spun, elegantly separating Astaroth's head from his body. Blood spayed where Astaroth's head had been, and his body collapsed in a heap. Horror seized me as I watched the red pool expand along the floor. The thought to move away finally came a beat before it could reach me.

"What's wrong with you?!" The words exploded forth before I could stop them. The point of his bloody blade appeared in front of my nose, draining what little resolve I had. Kurai stared with a cold intensity that said more than words ever could.

"Wasn't he your boss?" I asked, my voice shaking.

"I answer to no one." He opened his hands and his Aetharma vanished with a flicker.

"But why kill him?" I honestly didn't know why I cared to ask, especially when there was little stopping him from turning on me for interrogating him. But his actions were too vicious to say nothing.

Kurai's glare intensified, and the air caught in my throat. "He had become a liability." My vision started to blur. "Sacrifices are always a necessity to achieve one's end. You will learn in time the necessity of pruning the dead leaves."

Heat spread up my neck and face, burning with a pressure that made my eyes roll back. The next thing I knew I was floating in darkness; my thoughts a cloud of nebulous impulses. Suddenly, something grabbed me.

"Serec, wake up!"

My eyes fluttered open, and two faces blurred into view.

"Liza?" I said weakly. "Ryn?"

Somehow, I'd made it outside.

Sa'Sha and NaRyn were kneeled over me, tears in their eyes. "Thank El, you're okay!" NaRyn said in a whisper. Together they squeezed most of the air out of me.

"Don't scare us like that," Sa'Sha said just as weakly.

"I hope you're happy, Kid," Northe said, walking over to Shawin's side. "You really had us worried."

"What did I do?" I asked, struggling to push myself up while Sa'Sha and NaRyn clung onto me like they were pulling me back from the hands of death.

"Kurai said something to you and you collapsed a moment later," Shawin said. "By the time we reached you, you were —."

"I was?"

"Dead E." Sa'Sha said wiping her eyes. "You were dead. It's anyone's guess how you managed to wake up. But I'm glad you did."

"Where's Kurai now? Did he really kill Astaroth?" I asked.

"Yep," Northe said. "Astaroth took a one-way trip to Hadal. And the remaining malefactors are getting cleaned up as we speak."

"What about the knights and the Noctus Drive?"

"Intel and SciTech are collecting its remains. Ari and Kareen'll have a blast analyzing Locke's work."

"So, that's it?"

"That's it," Sa'Sha said with a smile.

Sa'Sha and NaRyn helped me to my feet, and into a Team Seven group hug that Northe and Shawin quickly joined.

"You kids really pulled it together on this one," Northe said. "Whatever happens from this point, Team Seven will always be the best team the Guild has ever seen."

"Couldn't have done it without you, old man," I said.

"Senior member," Northe corrected with a flat look that made me realize how much it hurt to laugh.

My mind couldn't rest as we flew back to Vaticia. Even with Astaroth defeated, there was still so much to worry about. The future of IGIS was the biggest issue on my mind. Would IGIS actually have a future? We'd operated in secret for as long as we could, but after Hachi's trial everything was brought to light with the Monarch and the rest of the world. And with the whole Astaroth thing over, it was hard to imagine a positive outcome for the Guild or anyone in it — including Sa'Sha.

"It's you," Anne said, as the medics rolled me out of the Ophanim.

"It's me," I replied.

[6]

STABILITY

SEREC

ccording to the timeboard above the door, I'd been in the medical facility for two segments. Fighting the bandages covering my body, I forced myself to sit up. A dull ache was all that remained of my pain.

"How are you feeling?" Anne asked as she stepped in.

"Better than I expected."

"Accelerated healing is a wonderful thing, isn't it?" I grinned and nodded. "Considering you were sent straight to me, I may be the first one to tell you how proud I am of what you and your team did out there."

"You are," I said. "And thanks. It means a lot, coming from you."

A knock at the door interrupted us, and before I could ask who it was, Team Seven strolled in. Everyone was back in casual attire. "Hey Rec Rec," NaRyn said, hugging me. "You feeling okay?"

"It was nothing a couple segments of rest couldn't fix," I said proudly.

"E, you've been asleep for over two days," Sa'Sha said.

"Seriously?" I began. "But the timeboard said..." I trailed off, realizing how dumb my argument would've been. Most wall timeboards didn't display the day.

"Don't worry, Kid. The way you performed out there, you deserve every hash. You had me worried at first, but you really pulled through."

"I wasn't the only one," I said, reaching a fist out to Shawin. "We all did our part." Shawin smiled and bumped his fist to mine.

"Speaking of," Anne interrupted, "the Director would like to see all of you in his office. The Colonel and a special guest are waiting to speak with you." Anne said, tapping her digipad. "You are hereby discharged."

We stepped into Hachi's office, where he, the other captains, and the Colonel greeted us with applause. But the final guest was the one who gave me pause. Standing next to Hachi in all his royal splendor was Divinus Martinel.

"Our guests of honor have finally arrived." the Monarch said, stepping forward. "Hachi tells me that you five were responsible for stopping Astaroth and his device."

"Actually, Your Highness, Minerva's the one who destroyed it," I said nodding at Kareen.

The Monarch examined Kareen with a frown. "Do I know you from somewhere?" he asked.

Kareen's eyes trailed. "Of that I am not certain, Divinus."

The Monarch's eyes narrowed. My guess was his suspicion was bothering him too much to let the issue rest. But everyone else in the room eyed her suspiciously for a different reason.

"I know you all value your privacy, but I must ask, what is your family name?" the Monarch asked.

"Ventus," she said reluctantly.

"Would that be short for Ventusili—Duchess of Marset and sixteenth in line for the royal throne?"

"There's no way she of all people—" Sa'Sha nudged Northe and he went quiet.

But his sentiments were clear and inarguably shared with the rest of us.

Kareen cut her eyes at Northe, then smiled politely at the Monarch. "You are correct, Divinus. I am Duchess Illiana Kareen Ventusili, Matriarch of House Ventusili."

The Monarch turned to Hachi. "Exactly how many children of nobility have you poached? You're uniting the great houses better than I ever could."

"I promise you, it's not intentional," Hachi chuckled.

"That said," the Monarch continued, "I would like to officially congratulate you all on your victory. You also have my sincerest gratitude for Sa'Sha's safe return. As for the future of IGIS..." The Monarch paused, his eyes scanning past each of us. Nervous tension colored my face so bright, the Monarch's eyes stopped on me longer than everyone else, and I could've sworn the corners of his mouth lifted slightly. "You have proven your worth to me and the Arurian people. Astaroth's actions have brought your existence to light and opened you to scrutiny. But I believe you all have the potential to make Orbis a safe place for all of us. It is for that reason, that I would like IGIS to merge with the BNP."

I sighed inwardly. Relieved that IGIS would remain but also a bit hopeful that we would do more good as a public organization.

The Guild held a brief award ceremony, where the Monarch awarded each of the task force captains and each member of Team Seven with the *Cross of Sophia* — Aruria's highest military honor. For some reason, my mind went to Lieutenant Jibbs during the ceremony. One part of me wished he could've been there to see how in less than two anums, I'd accomplished something he could never hope to in his lifetime.

Once the ceremony came to a close, everyone went their separate ways. NaRyn and Sa'Sha wanted to plan out a celebratory dinner for the following night, which Shawin, Northe, and I weren't opposed to, as long as we didn't end up with a massive list of things to do in the process. But just as we started toward D7, Ari asked if he could meet with all the captains, and we sent Shawin and NaRyn ahead.

"Nel Laurelli interviewed Alex Locke this morning," Ari said.

"You mean the serpent who interviewed Astaroth?" Kareen asked.

"The very same. It appears Locke has plans to acquire Theall Medical Corp. If this deal goes through, Locket will be the largest company in the world and his net worth will reach Monarch-status."

"Why would a tech mogul expand his empire into the pharmaceutical world?" Kareen asked.

Ari rubbed his chin. "For all we know, it could be nothing more than a credit grab. But, the idea of one man amassing that much wealth and power, something about it unsettles me."

I wanted to believe it was nothing more than a credit grab. But Locke, was too unpredictable to do anything other than hope for the best and see how things turned out.

I waited until everyone retreated to their rooms to talk to Sa'Sha that night. It was time I said what I'd held back for too long. Astaroth hadn't managed to kill me. So a simple conversation with Sa'Sha wouldn't—I hoped.

I stood in front of Sa'Sha's door for at least a hash before knocking—the first few beats trying to control my breathing—the next trying to figure out what I would say when her door opened.

I finally stopped thinking and knocked. "It's me," I said.

The door slid open. "Hey," Sa'Sha said. She wore a loose pink nightshirt with matching shorts. Like most of her personal clothes, the shirt had a monogrammed 's' over the left side of the chest. Her look was print model cute, like she belonged on a fashion netsite for teenage girls.

"Hey," I said. "Can we talk?"

"Sure. Come in."

I swallowed and entered. "You look really pretty," I said nervously.

"You too. I mean, you look handsome," she corrected.

"I'm glad you think so," I said, sharing a nervous laugh.

But then our laugh fell into a flat silence that only made my nerves worse as she watched with expectant eyes.

"What did you want to talk about?" she asked, breaking the silence.

I took a breath and stepped closer. *Now or never.* I opened my mouth, not certain what I would say. So, I wasn't too surprised when I didn't say anything. My eyes darted around as if I could find the words in her room.

"I," we said in unison.

"I'm sorry," I said. "Go ahead."

"It's okay. You first."

I took another breath. "I hope this doesn't come out weird or anything. But I...I think..." *Why can't I find the words?*

"You think...?" she prompted.

"I think you're special," I blurted. "Like...special to me. Not like princess special — I mean, you *are* a princess, but that's not..." I sighed. "You're amazing, Liza. And I don't know why I can't stop thinking about you. But I can't."

I blanked, as if everything inside my brain had exploded out through my mouth and there was nothing left but silence. An intense quiet followed, and my heart retreated so far up my throat I could almost taste it. "Did I just make everything awkward?" I blurted again, not sure where the words were even coming from.

"Do you want to stop thinking about me?" Sa'Sha asked.

"No. No, that's not what I meant."

"Good. Because I love you too, E." I stared in disbelief, my mind blanking. "Sorry, it that was too sudden."

"No," I said quickly. "I mean, it was sudden, but—" I shook my head. "I love you Liza. Or, I love you too. Wait...why'd you say 'you love me too?'"

"I already told you. Your emotions speak to me. And they've been betraying that secret for quite some time," she smirked. As she looked up at me with her enchanting brown eyes, I felt as if every part of me was being stripped away, and breathing didn't seem quite as easy.

She leaned in close, and I could almost taste her breath. She licked her lips, and I just couldn't ignore it any longer. I swallowed back my nerves, pulled her close, and kissed her soft, full lips so hard, I knew she'd push me away. But she didn't. She kissed back just as hard. Wrapped her arms around my neck and pulled just as tight.

Everything drowned out, and my body felt like it was sinking into a pool of bliss. The warmth of her breath, the sweet smell of her skin, the feel of her body pressing against me. I wanted to hold on to that moment for as long as she would let me. And whatever it took to be with her, I would do it. Because she was my strength. My reason to be a hero.

EPILOGUE

For all the chaos Astaroth created, no one could've predicted half the good that would come from stopping him. But even indirectly, Astaroth set the world on course for a peace and prosperity that no one had seen in over a hundred anums.

Alex Locke's hostile takeover of Theall Medical Corporation propelled him to the forefront of political and economic influence. And just as Ari predicted, Locke used it to his advantage. After Locket Technologies rebranded itself as Locket Industries, Alex Locke held sole ownership of the largest corporation in the world. And with a net worth that outranked even the Monarch's, his voice was heard loud and clear when he requested the Three Great National leaders gather to discuss the terms of dissolving the international mandate restricting non-citizens from crossing national borders. His actions wouldn't end the conflicts between the nations, but it was a step in the right direction, and an indicator of his mindset. In his words, "As you squabble over inconsequential grievances, the true enemy sits on the edge of reality, waiting for you to destroy one another."

Agreeing that, under the guise of Iam Rhasatto, Astaroth acted without governmental sanction, Lazuria and Oltresulle signed a treaty, ending their longstanding armed conflict. With this treaty enacted, each nation's borders opened to all peoples, permitting a boom in trade that infused the global economy with new life and created a sense of unity the people of Orbis haven't felt for many generations.

Locke profited as much as anyone, if not more so. With all barriers to international trade abolished, he was free to expand his company's reach and influence to every part of Orbis. But Locke also maintained Iam Rhaasatto's philanthropic organizations; providing increased funding and technological upgrades to each orphanage and facility. In under a semianum, Locke had built an empire that benefited the poor and wealthy alike.

Astaroth held true to his word about the sky. It remained violet, and there was nothing any scientist or engineer could do to change it. After a while though, it seemed no one wanted to. The number of people suffering from Plaga Viridi and Malachite's Consumption plummeted. Sun-related illness from the once blue or green skies was also eradicated creating a world where the sky was no longer a tool of oppression and malice.

As for IGIS, everything returned to the way it was — mostly. Task Force 224 was officially disbanded, and the Guild refocused the majority of its efforts on policing aengel and refractors, and hunting down what was left of the malefactors. The Arurian Great Houses jumped at the opportunity to integrate IGIS into the Department of Peace, though the details had been tabled for more pressing matters. In Sa'Sha's case, that was a long overdue vacation with this guy.

"I don't think I've ever seen water this clear," Sa'Sha said.

"Or sand this white," I added, letting the warmth of the silty sand massage its way between my toes.

"I should let you plan our vacations more often."

"Let's not pile on the pressure yet. We just got here."

"Can you believe a semianum ago, we were in this country fighting for our lives?" She noted. "Unable to appreciate something like this. Guess Astaroth was right about the beauty of this place."

Sa'Sha stopped, her face becoming pensive.

"Everything alright, Liza?"

"Considering all the malefactors still appearing, I wonder if he really was the mastermind behind it all. We know the Soldiers of Liberty are still active. And I question if Astaroth really was at its head."

"Well, you can wonder some other time. We're not here to talk about work."

"You brought it up."

Sa'Sha unlaced her fingers from mine and took a swing at me. I leaned away and caught her by the elbow. And with a tug, she fell into my arms and cupped my face. The wind and ocean roared as powerfully as my blood when she pressed her lips to mine, and held there.

"Aww, I'm jealous," a familiar voice called and I immediately tensed. Ariel and Axel approached casually.

"You know the drill, kid," Axel said.

"Please inform your boss that we aren't required to follow his orders," Sa'Sha said. "He may have purchased half of Orbis, but we aren't his property."

"Why the hostility, Blissful," Ariel started, "We're only here for a friendly conversation. By the way, you're welcome for those tools we provided that allowed you to take down Astaroth's barrier."

"Refresh my memory, if you would. Who was it that built the device that required a barrier in the first place?"

"We're in top form today, aren't we?" Ariel teased.

Sa'Sha started at Ariel and I slipped between them before things got ugly. "What does Locke want?" I asked.

"Our master has some information you might find useful," Axel said, extending a hand to me.

"If I go, she goes," I demanded. Ariel rolled her eyes and huffed, extending her hand to Sa'Sha.

"Can we trust them?" Sa'Sha's thought pressed into my mind.

Probably.

We took their hands, and everything went dark, before my body jumped into a cold desolate desert. I didn't last two beats, before my stomach felt like it would push my lunch back the way it came.

"E, what's wrong?" Sa'Sha asked, her voice heavy with concern.

"Keep it together kid," Axel yelled over the howling wind.

"What's...happening to me?" I strained.

"This area is dense with radiation," Ariel said casually. "Concentrate on your healing ability and it'll pass."

I took a deep breath and closed my eyes. After a few beats, the heat in my gut subsided enough to stand again. I wondered how Sa'Sha wasn't having a worse time than I was, but another strange feeling hit me, before I could ask.

"What is that massive energy signature I'm seeing?" Sa'Sha said.

Sa'Sha pointed to a colossal structure, sitting in the distance.

"You should be focused on why those two are about to walk into it," Axel said, nodding at two figures walking toward the structure. I enhanced my sight and hearing.

"Kurai?" I said, an intense chill overcoming me. "What's he—?"

"Don't talk," Axel said. "Just listen."

Kurai and a figure in a blue hooded cloak strolled through the rocky desert, as violent flashes of lightning and roaring winds swirled directly above the structure.

"Are you certain killing Astaroth was prudent?" the figure asked with heavy distortion in his voice.

"He was becoming too much of a liability," Kurai replied. "It was foolish using the Noctus Drive as a method of controlling the Gifted. He exposed too much."

The figure paused. "And what of the boy?"

"He lives, for now. He may prove useful. At the very least, he can lead us to the Aeons."

"Agreed. Just, do not grow too attached to him. Should he learn your true nature, it will... complicate things."

They stopped in front of the ancient structure, adorned with intricate alien markings.

"So, this is the Yottalith—the prize of Terra Morrum?" Kurai asked.

"It is. Let us waste no more time. Everything must be in order for *his* arrival."

REFRACTORS VOLUME II
THE FIRST CHAPTER

NOTE: THIS IS AN EXCERPT FROM A WORK IN DEVELOPMENT AND MAY BE DIFFERENT FROM THE FINAL VERSION.

Defending the people ensured our downfall. It was a fact I'd refused to accept. But as a shadow loomed over our great kingdom of Aruria, I could no longer ignore the devastating truth. We rushed to the Cadelux, our supernatural portal into battle. Anxiety and anticipation intertwined in my mind, giving life to my fears.

"Zero!" Sa'Sha called, shaking my mind free. "Lift and Prophet are already on the ground. They confirmed the reports we've been receiving from Team Six and Five. Malefactors are attacking en masse at the Politico!"

Perfect timing in its own twisted way. The Politico was the site were the Senate held sessions to vote on new legislation. And they just happened to be in session. Worse, they were voting on finally repealing the Rho Code, a set of discriminatory laws against Refractors. It would be a huge step in quelling the tension between Refractors like us and ordinary humans. The timing of the attack couldn't be a coincidence. Which meant we had to move.

"I'll drop in and help secure the area. We can't let them harm the Senate," I said.

"Agreed! I'll be right behind you."

As her words touched my ears, a hand grabbed my arm. I turned, meeting Sa'Sha's serene eyes. I fought because the people needed me — because the world needed me. But above all, I fought for her. Our nation's princess. Our team's commander. The woman I loved. I leaned in as she pulled me close and pressed her sweet lips against mine. For those few beats, none of it mattered. We were in a world all our own. Not two agents of a paramilitary charged with defending the world from supernatural threats. But two people in love's embrace. I would give anything to stay in that moment forever. But we had work to do. The serenity in Sa'Sha's eyes gave way to determination.

"Be careful down there E," she whispered.

"I love you Liza," the words were as natural as taking a breath.

"I love you more," She began softly. "Which is why I won't have you being reckless." Her tone shifted, authority infusing her words. I offered a carefree smile and stepped onto the Cadelux with Kinetic Operations Team Three. A recent discovery of our Science and Technology division, the Cadelux could teleport us from our flying airship to the battlefield in an instant. I preferred to get a bird's eye view before dropping in. The intricate weaving patterns on the floor illuminated, birthing a rainbow of light. I activated my HOOD and, in a flash, I was a hundred meters over the Politico and falling fast. Hundreds of black specs moved about through the jumble of buildings roads and parks. I enhanced my sight as I fell targeting a specific cluster of black. A storm of malefactors had cornered a group of over a hundred evacuating citizens. I adjusted my trajectory, hoping desperately that I could reach them in time. Suddenly, a thin beam of light shot down into the hoard, and a tiny explosion erupted, vaporizing the malefactors caught in the blast. When the dust cleared, a glowing form emerged — Sa'Sha. *So much for being right behind me.* A smile wiped across my face. Sa'Sha seemed to have that situation under control, so I scanned the area again, finally close enough to the ground to make out the individual forms. Malefactors had formed a perimeter around the Politico blocking all egress routes. There were four major openings, and each one was blocked by malefactors that appeared to be trying to press inward to attack the Politico building. But between Teams Three, Five, Six, and Seven, we were holding them back. At least until an explosion roared out to the north, and a massive dark form appeared. I'd found my target.

"You guys seeing this?" A young female voice called over the comm. It was terrifyingly familiar — the voice of Team Seven's technician — NaRyn. Like Sa'Sha, NaRyn was incredibly important to me.

"Lift, Prophet, K, that's a titan class malefactor." Sa'Sha's voice was calm, but noticeably anxious. "I'm heading your way now, but we need a plan to stop that thing without endangering the citizens."

"Raven," a grizzled voice called over the comm. "This is Stryker. We're down south and if we can just break this line of enemies, we can use this road to evacuate civilians."

"What will that take?" Sa'Sha asked.

"We'll never get through at this rate. We need support."

"This is Quake," a man chimed in, voice calm — Jin. We hadn't talked since Task Force 224 disbanded. "We can assist but we are blocking the main avenue of approach for the Politico building. If we pull off to help, the Senate will be left unguarded." His words hung in the air for a moment before another voice chimed.

"This is Morrigan," a woman began , voice unexpectedly smooth. "There is an alternative. We can help secure and evacuate the Senate. Unfortunately, there are several hundred people in the area trying to make their way south. If we cease our attack on the malefactors to help the Senate, these people will get slaughtered."

The options waged war in my head as I knew they did in everyone else's. We didn't have time to deliberate. We needed a decision — an impossible decision. Save the several hundred average citizens. Or protect fifty of the most important people in the kingdom who were working to end the oppression of our people.

"Protect —"

"We can save them all!" I chimed. "I'm heading toward the big boy now. I'll take it down and secure the north for evac while Team Seven helps the Senate."

Silence. "I'm not sure about this," Stryker said.

"Neither am I," Sa'Sha agreed. "But I don't see any other way to save everyone. It's a gamble, but we have to try."

"We're with you," Quake said.

"Ready to execute," Morrigan added.

"Alright, let's get these people to safety," Sa'Sha said before cutting out.

As I closed in on the colossal beast, my stomach tightened. *It's all on me. Time to take this thing down.* It was a task as daunting as the beast in front of me. Standing at roughly twenty meters, the monster towered over most buildings in the area and could demolish the Politico in one swipe. I inhaled deep and a well of energy overflowed, flooding my body. My vision narrowed as I threw back a fist and shot it right into the beast's reptilian face. The monster stumbled back, as I landed in front of it. "Alright ugly, time for a bit of one on one."

I charged as it dropped a massive hand on me. I rolled to the side and jumped onto its scaly hand, sprinting up its arm. Claws from the other hand dug into its arm as it tried to scratch me off like I was some annoying bug. But I leapt onto the other hand and kept sprinting toward my target. As I closed on its head, I shot out a hand and golden light coalesced into a long pole in my hand. At the end of the pole, a wicked axe head. My Aetharma had evolved. I'd given it the name Ex Nihilo, a fitting title to complement my designation. It had changed drastically over the past two anums, able to become whatever weapon I could imagine. And this weapon had a devious purpose.

I leapt at the monster's head and spun, driving my axe into the side of its neck with a satisfying crack. The creature wailed and I left my axe lodged in its neck as I fell to the ground in satisfaction. But it was a short-lived victory as a hand bore down on me and drove me into the ground. Encasing myself in stone at the last moment prevented me from getting squished. Unfortunately for the monster, being lodged into the ground only managed to fuel my burning rage. That rage manifested as a scorching jet that burned a hole through my foe's hand as I shot up to meet it. Black blood spurted from the monster's neck, as I dismissed my

Aetharma. Ascending into the air, above the monster, I called Ex Nihilo again, this time as a blade, and pressed down toward the monster's head. But it wasn't ready to go down yet. It opened its mouth and a blinding light flashed, followed by intense heat and pressure sending me flying. My reflexes had become insane, and I shielded myself in stone again without even realizing it. When the heat subsided and it no longer felt like I was tumbling in the air, I released my stone skin. I was high. Really high. Too bad for ugly.

I condensed the air behind me and combusted it, causing an explosion that sent me plummeting to Orbis like a meteor. The creature had turned its back on me. Big mistake. I summoned Ex Nihilo and with the force of a mag round, I drove it and my entire body through the back of the monster's head and out one of its eyes. I landed, making a tiny crater in the ground as black blood rained on me. It was as satisfying as it was disgusting. The beast teetered forward, then fell just short of a group of fleeing citizens with a terrible crash. They looked on, a mixture of awe and relief covering their faces. I walked up to them, trying to look as heroic as possible.

"Guys, the titan is down," I said in my comm. "We can start evacuating."

"Sounds good. Great work Zero," Sa'Sha said. As I started moving toward the Politico to rejoin the team, I felt a small hand in mine. A little girl, maybe seven, was walking along side me. "You saved us. Thank you," she said. Her voice was so soft. So delicate. I picked her up and smiled.

"It was nothing," I said taking up a jog.

"You really are a hero," she said.

"I try," It felt amazing. Helping people. Keeping them safe. Relief swept over me as Team Seven came into view — my team. They were assisting senators, nobility, and their assistants in getting to safety. We'd done it. We'd saved them. Disaster *averted.*

PBROING! The other worldly vibration reverberated through my bones. *What in hadal?* I whirled around. A light glowed inside the monster's abdomen, a pulse emanating from it. Suddenly, my senses went crazy, and I reflexively dodged in time to narrowly miss a beam of concentrated energy.

"You okay," I asked the girl, clutching her in my arms as I surveyed the horror. The beam had left a trail of charred bodies in its path. "I'm okay, but who are they?"

Terror gripped me as I looked up and spotted an old man in a blue cloak. The same man I'd seen with Kurai on Terra Morrum nearly two anums ago. Flanked by two masked guards on each side, he wore a satisfied smirk. I put the girl down and guided her behind me. Whatever they intended, I didn't want her to end up like those people.

"Impressive young Serec," the Man in Blue said. "I should have known that pragmatism would fall to your idealism."

"Who are you?" My voice was commanding as the rage began to burn again. "Me? I'm no one of consequence. Just someone who wanted to see where your loyalty lies." He lifted a withered hand and pointed. And where hers did. He leveled his finger at Sa'Sha. "But alas. You two are dreadfully indecisive. So, it appears I must teach you both a painful lesson." He raised his hand and snapped. In an instant, the creature's corpse birthed a blinding light, and an unnatural force began to pull on me. I grabbed the girl and became stone, protecting us from the debris flying toward the monster. I looked into the light and saw a tiny core, *antimatter*.

"Zero!" Sa'Sha's voice rang in the comm. "She was meters away, obscured by a translucent shield. We had to get there. I pressed against the pull of the core. One step at a time, until we finally reached the shield. Others had realized what I was doing and made a run for the shield. Some made it, most didn't. As I handed the girl to Northe, I felt a hand on my shoulder. I turned to help, thinking it was a citizen, but hateful red eye greeted me instead — the Man in Blue. Before I could react, he leaned in close and whispered simple words that would profoundly change me. "You can't save them all." He pushed me into the safety of the shield and in a violent flash, the antimatter core exploded.

When I finally regained my sight. I surveyed the area. The shield had held. But outside of it, there was nothing. People, plants, buildings, nothing remained. Even the ground beneath our spherical shield had been eaten. We looked in horror and disbelief as we sat suspended in a gargantuan crater. It was gone — all of it. The entire Politico district had been annihilated.

ABOUT THE AUTHORS

The Brothers Epps are two brothers on a journey to entertain and enrich through their writing.

Brandon Epps is a writer of Action Adventure, Fantasy and Science Fiction and an avid philosopher. When he's not questioning the nature of reality, he spends his time reading, writing, practicing photography, playing video games, researching big social problems, traveling, hiking and hanging out with his wife and two daughters.

A U.S. Army veteran of 13 years, his travels have taken him from the icy mountaintops of Afghanistan to the sunny beaches of Hawaii (where he failed miserably at surfing). He's been described as both amiable and cynical, and his experiences in the military have shaped how he approaches storytelling and life. He is a huge fan of fantasy and sci-fi, and his influences include: Pierce Brown, Brandon Sanderson, George R.R.Martin, Neal Shusterman, Hajime Isayama, and Hideo Kojima. Brandon is an introvert who really likes people and loves connecting with other authors and readers.

Milan's background is as diverse as his interests. He'd like to think that contributes in some profound way to his abilities as a writer. He started his creative writing journey back in elementary school. But it wasn't until middle school that he started to wonder if it could be anything more than a hobby. Roughly ten years later, in his final year of college, he started believing it actually could be. His journey toward becoming a writer placed him on a ten-year path of learning, researching, writing, revising, and editing until he could produce something he felt was polished enough to share with the world. That something is Refractors Volume I: Evoke. When he's not writing, he's exercising, animating, watching anime, reading, learning something new, or doing any number of other things that seem fun in the moment.

Connect with the Brothers at: www.thebrothersepps.com